# THE
# *American*
# DREAM
## ROMANCE COLLECTION

Nine Historical Romances Grow Alongside a New Country

# THE
# *American*
# DREAM
## ROMANCE COLLECTION

### DiAnn Mills
### Jane Kirkpatrick

Kristy Dykes, Laurie Alice Eakes, Carla Olson Gade
Lisa Karon Richardson, Ann E. Schrock
Amber Stockton, Jennifer Hudson Taylor

## BARBOUR BOOKS
An Imprint of Barbour Publishing, Inc.

*Carving a Future* ©2012 by Carla Olson Gade
*Trading Hearts* ©2012 by Amber Stockton
*Over a Barrel* ©2012 by Laurie Alice Eakes
*Impressed by Love* ©2012 by Lisa Karon Richardson
*When the Shadow Falls* ©2006 by DiAnn Mills
*New Garden's Hope* ©2012 by Jennifer Hudson Taylor
*New Garden's Crossroads* ©2012 by Ann E. Schrock
*Free Indeed* ©2002 by Kristy Dykes
*A Mother's Cry* ©2012 by Jane Kirkpatrick

Print ISBN 978-1-63409-332-3

eBook Editions:
Adobe Digital Edition (.epub) 978-1-63409-579-2
Kindle and MobiPocket Edition (.prc) 978-1-63409-580-8

All scripture quotations are taken from the King James Version of the Bible.

This book is a work of fiction. Names, characters, places, and incidents are either products of the author's imagination or used fictitiously. Any similarity to actual people, organizations, and/or events is purely coincidental.

Published by Barbour Books, an imprint of Barbour Publishing, Inc., P.O. Box 719, Uhrichsville, OH 44683, www.barbourbooks.com

*Our mission is to publish and distribute inspirational products offering exceptional value and biblical encouragement to the masses.*

Member of the
Evangelical Christian
Publishers Association

Printed in Canada.

# Contents

# CARVING A FUTURE

by Carla Olson Gade

# Dedication

To Joyce Buckley—my "first editor," research companion, and amazing mother! Thank you for our big birthday road trip and all our excursions for the research of this book including Colonial Williamsburg; Glastonbury, Connecticut; and Mystic Seaport.

With special thanks to the Glastonbury, Connecticut Historical Society for their assistance; and for so faithfully preserving the history of this charming New England town on the Great River. To the curators of the ship carving shop at Mystic Seaport; and for the spectacular display of historic figureheads. And to world-renowned figurehead carver and historian, Martin Jeffery, whose expertise was essential to my writing about this legendary craft. Fair winds to all!

*And whatsoever ye do, do it heartily, as to the Lord,*
*and not unto men. . .for ye serve the Lord Christ.*
COLOSSIANS 3:23–24

# *Chapter 1*

Constance Starling stood on the quay, the chain around her waist secured to a granite post. She cast her eyes toward the ship moored behind her—prison for the past six weeks. Or had it been seven? Mounted on the prow of the elaborately decorated merchant vessel, a figurehead of a mythological creature with the proud front of a horse, mane blowing wild, and the coiled tail of a seahorse, hugged the bowsprit. Bold and free, it mocked her. She had likely wearied the Almighty with her petitions for freedom, as she, too, was weary from uttering them. Yet she managed once more, "Lord, save me."

The heat of the sun beat down, moistening Constance's brow with perspiration, or perhaps it was fever. Her hat might have proffered some protection, but it had disappeared in the struggle that landed her in this frightful predicament. Then a cool breeze drifted off the river, providing a trickle of relief, and a subtle reminder that God was still with her.

Her stomach cramped from the meager portions of food on the long voyage from England, biscuits and water having been her only sustenance. Enough of neither. The slapping of the water against the hull of the docked merchant ship did nothing to squelch her queasiness. Her legs wobbled in rhythm and her knees buckled beneath her, throwing her into a filthy and rumpled heap on the rough, planked wharf.

Her captor yanked Constance up by the elbow, nearly pulling her arm from its socket. "Stand up, lass. You'll be good to no one, not even yerself, if ye can't even stay on yer feet. If I don't sell yer indenture, there'll be no hope for ye—you'll never survive another long journey."

The stench of liquor on Captain Smout's breath made Constance retch. Her eyes stung as she glared at him in defiance. She tried to swallow the lump forming in her throat, but it was far too parched to allow her to do so without pain.

The gruff man lifted a tarnished flask to her mouth and poured a bit of rum between her chapped lips. As it dribbled down her chin and neck, his ire rose. "For pity's sake. Drink up. You're worth little enough to me now, and you'll be no good to me dead." The liquid burned her throat and she spat it into his face, like water spraying from a whale's spout into the angry sea.

The captain hoisted his punishing hand in the air but another, far stronger, intercepted it.

"That is enough!" A brawny man twisted the captain's arm behind his back. "You will do as I say and leave her be." His stormy eyes sailed toward hers through the raging sea of his anger. For a fleeting moment the tempest abated, and she found safe harbor there.

"All right, mate. Easy now. I meant no harm." Smout tried to shake loose, but the man kept a firm hold. "Truce," Smout pleaded.

Her protector turned the captain around and relaxed his grip. He stepped back and took a protective stance near Constance. All she could see was the hale form of this gallant man in brown breeches and a long, tan waistcoat. A queue of dark hair tied with a leather cord hung down upon his broad shoulders. "Release this poor woman," he demanded.

Her gaze darted back to Captain Smout as he began to speak again, a sly grin appearing through his burly gray whiskers. "I'm willin' to consider it. Let's say we negotiate the terms of her indenture."

Constance tried to keep her wits about her, to see what fate would come—though murky voices and blurred images swirled around her like a raging whirlpool pulling her into a deep abyss.

☙

Nathaniel turned at the sound of a faint whimper at his feet. He kneeled down and gently lifted the woman's head. A low groan escaped her lips and her eyes fluttered open, beckoning his help. He retrieved his engraved silver flask from his pocket and offered her a drink of water. She took several sips, and then her eyes closed once more.

Nathaniel gently laid her back down on the wooden boards, unsure of what else to do, and looked up at the churlish sea captain looming over them.

"I will take her off your hands, for a price." Nathaniel could hardly believe the words that spilt from his mouth.

"A price, aye?" The man chortled. "Ye think I don't have my wits about me? I'm the one who's selling her contract."

Nathaniel's mouth went dry. He thought to reach for his flask again, but it was nearly empty now. At last he mustered up a response. "She is worth nothing to you like this. I will take her as she is."

"She still cost me her passage. I'll get recouped for that at least. She's a comely lass, at least she was when she commenced the voyage. If'n she recovers she'll be worth a good deal," the trader said.

"She will be worth nothing dead. Let me get her some help."

"Nathaniel." The ever-deepening voice of his adolescent brother, a younger, leaner version of himself, yet already as tall, caught his attention. The lad's eyes held a look of confusion.

"Alden, there you are. I need your assistance."

Alden stared at the unconscious woman. "I see that. Who is she?"

Nathaniel's glare demanded an answer from the captain.

"Her name is Constance. Starling, I believe. But it's my name you ought to be concerned about." The haughty man stood straighter and clamped his ring-laden fingers around his lapels. "Magnus Smout at your disposal, owner and captain of the good ship *Fortuna*. I'm the one you're going to compensate."

Alden looked more confused than ever.

"Never mind him," Nathaniel said as he tugged off his cravat. "Give this a soak so we can cool her face. And fetch some fresh water if you can." He handed Alden his flask and the lad fled.

Nathaniel smoothed his hair back and tugged on his queue as he tried to think of what he could do next. He had little coin on him, perhaps a few shillings, having spent what he had on supplies. He certainly wasn't equipped with the funds a ship's captain selling a contract of indenture would accept.

Perusing the merchant ship, Nathaniel noticed the figurehead of a seahorse attached to the bowsprit. It was quite damaged, one of its legs broken and the other altogether missing.

"This is your vessel?" Nathaniel asked.

The man issued a proud nod. "That she is."

"And a fine-looking vessel at that. But I see your figurehead has met with some misfortune. 'Tis a shame. She won't get far without her legs." Nathaniel cocked his head and grinned.

Captain Smout grumbled. "A shame is right, though she did come by her wounds honorably and survived a dandy storm."

It seemed he cared more for his figurehead than the young lady lying unconscious there on the quay.

"Then you have found good fortune, Captain Smout, befitting your ship's name. I happen to be a journeyman figurehead carver. I apprenticed under Phineas Cushing, one of the best master carvers in the commonwealth."

"Indeed?" Captain Smout rubbed his beard.

"Indeed." Nathaniel lifted his chin. "I will barter the woman's contract for a full repair. I'll even give your figurehead a fresh coat of paint."

"Where is your shop located?"

"About ten miles downriver. Glassenbury." Nathaniel dared hope. The man was taking his bait.

"How are you traveling?" the captain asked.

"Another brother delivered us by means of his own brig on his way up river this morning. I mean to hire a conveyance for our return trip."

"It might take you half the day to get back. Why bother when I can deliver you in an hour's time—for a price."

The thought of boarding a ship with this unsavory curmudgeon incensed Nathaniel, and he despised the thought of putting Miss Starling back on that vessel. But Nathaniel had little choice—he must get the girl some help. Soon. He might find a doctor here in Hartford, but that he could not afford. 'Twas the best solution. Another hour and they would be home.

He exhaled. "Agreed. But you have to go down to Glassenbury for the repair. What is it to you to have us aboard?"

"It is worth your silver flask, I say."

Nathaniel gritted his teeth. "I cannot do that. It was my father's."

The captain extended his arm toward the sickly woman and frowned. "What's worth more to you? A sentimental token, or this young woman's life?"

Could this man not have one iota of decency?

A short time later all the legalities had been resolved and all were aboard the *Fortuna*.

Contemplating his decision, Nathaniel leaned against a keg of rum, one of many that Smout's men had loaded into the hold below. What should have been an uneventful trip to Hartford for supplies had turned into a situation that could change the course of his life. He glanced at Miss Starling, who, after briefly wakening was now sleeping again. A thick braid of light brown hair draped over her shoulder. Unkempt tendrils clung to her dampened alabaster face. He studied her delicate cheekbones, an elegantly shaped nose, and the graceful curve of her neck. How could someone so lovely be subjected to such a fate?

His thoughts turned to his younger brother, uncertain of the kind of example he was setting for him today but grateful for his unquestioning assistance.

"You did well, Alden. You will make a good apprentice someday—you've a cooperative disposition. I am sure Uncle Phin would be glad to take you on when you complete your studies. But perhaps I shall take you on as my own apprentice," he teased. "I know, your heart is set on Yale. Dr. Hale seems to think you have the aptitude and disposition to make a good physician someday." As the eldest brother of four, Nathaniel had always been most concerned for Alden, who had had the least time with their late father. Nathaniel hoped his remarks would please his youngest sibling.

Alden looked over at Miss Starling and turned back to him. "You did the right thing, Nathaniel."

"You think so? I hope Uncle Phin will understand."

Alden shrugged his shoulders. "You had no choice. He'll come 'round. What will become of her though?"

"Let us hope Mother can restore her to health. She is good with herbs. Then mayhap Miss Starling can be of help to her." All else remained a mystery.

Once aground at the shipyard, Nathaniel set to the task of getting his new charge to safety. "I will take her directly to the inn. You unload the supplies and bring them to the carving loft. At least I have a few days to prepare my explanation before Uncle returns."

Nathaniel lifted Constance in his arms. Barely awake, her limp form rested against his chest. He could feel the warmth of her feverish body through his garments. The sound of shallow breathing alarmed him all the more. She was getting worse. "Stay with us, miss. You will be in good hands soon."

Miss Starling's head drooped and her arm fell lifelessly, dangling at her side. Nathaniel's breath caught in his throat. "No, Lord."

Alden's eyes widened and locked with Nathaniel's. "Is she. . . ?"

Nathaniel gazed down at the unknown woman cradled in his arms and observed the rise and fall of her chest. "No. . .not yet."

Alden stood tall, his countenance resolute. "I'll go for Dr. Hale. He will know what to do."

Nathaniel only hoped there was yet time enough. "Make haste, Alden. Make haste!"

# Chapter 2

*Glassenbury, Connecticut, Connecticut River Valley*
*July 1753*

Her fever has broken." Constance made out the muffled sound of a man's voice and tried to pull herself out of her daze.

"There now. You're awake." The warm smile of a woman, about the age her own mother would have been, greeted Constance as she attempted to focus.

An authoritative-looking man wearing a gray wig and spectacles stood beside her bed, offering his own greeting. "Welcome to Glassenbury, Miss Starling."

"Where?" she rasped.

"You are at my home, the Red Griffin Inn, at Glassenbury in the Commonwealth of Connecticut. . .in America," the woman said.

Connecticut. America. It began to come back to her. They had docked at Hartford. Captain Smout. Captain Smout. . .

Her eyes darted around the unfamiliar room. There was no sight of him. Could she be safe at last? But who were these new caretakers?

The woman wore a ruffled cap, with dark hair and wisps of gray peeking out from it. "I am Mistress Ingersoll, and this is Dr. Hale," she offered.

The man took Constance's wrist, felt for her pulse, and counted in silence. "Still weak but improving." He laid her hand back down on the covers and eyed her with concern. "Mrs. Ingersoll has been keeping vigil for some four days now. If not for her constant care and her prayers. . .well, let us just say you are in good hands, young lady."

Constance rubbed the soreness on her arm and noticed some circular-shaped bruises. She looked up in confusion at the doctor and then met Mrs. Ingersoll's kind but tired eyes, a familiar-looking blue-gray.

"Dr. Hale is much to be thanked. That is from the cupping."

"To restore the humors, dear," Dr. Hale said. "The marks will fade in time."

"I'll put another plaster on her arm, if you wish, Doctor," said Mrs. Ingersoll.

The man nodded.

"Take a sip, dear. 'Tis meadowsweet tea," said Mrs. Ingersoll. "I shall have our maid, Lucy, bring you a caudle from the hearth. What you mostly need now is nourishment."

Constance took a sip and moistened her lips. "How did I get here?" she managed.

"That would be my son Nathaniel's doing. If he had not the good sense to get you away from that lowly captain of the *Fortuna*, who knows into whose hands you might have fallen. You owe my son a debt of gratitude, but that should be settled as you serve out your contract."

"Contract?"

"Of your indenture. He is your master now."

Though tears threatened, Constance protested. "I've only one Master, and that is my Lord and Savior."

A deep voice came from the doorway of the bedchamber. "I'm afraid He is not the only one, Miss Starling." A stalwart young man entered the room, a parchment document in hand.

"Constance, this is my son. Nathaniel Ingersoll."

᭜᭜

Nathaniel stood in the doorway, shifting from one buckled shoe to the other. He should have waited. The poor girl was still recovering. "Good day, miss. . .uh, I do beg your pardon, I will come back later." He retreated into the hallway.

"Stay," she croaked, albeit with an authoritative air.

He turned back and looked into the room, Dr. Hale peering up at him over his spectacles. "You heard the young lady. She requests your company."

Nathaniel arched a brow. *Requests or requires?*

"I will see to that broth now, if you would be so kind as to remain here until I return, Dr. Hale," Mrs. Ingersoll said.

"Certainly." Dr. Hale pulled a timepiece from his pocket. "Then I must examine her and be on my way."

Nathaniel assessed the peaked young woman propped up in the large bed in one of the unoccupied guest rooms. Her hair was now tucked beneath a cap, revealing the pleasant shape of her face. Her full lips formed a pout. Her large brown glistening eyes met his, beckoning for answers. He swallowed hard and shifted his attention to the doctor. "How is Miss Starling, Doctor?"

"I am pleased to find Miss Starling faring well, though she must not overexert. If you are asking to find if she is fit for work. . ."

"I am asking out of concern, as her mast—as the one responsible for her. I do, however, wish to discuss the matter of this agreement." He rustled the paper in his hand. "I believe she deserves to know, if she is up for it."

Constance dried her eyes and took in a deep breath, triggering a raspy cough. "Has it not occurred to you gentlemen that you may speak to me directly?" She sat more erect and pulled the bedcover up under her chin.

"In fact, Mr. Ingersoll, I would like to thank you for seeing to my rescue from the clutches of Captain Smout. But I fear he was successful in his goal of selling my indenture. . .unrightfully so. I was taken against my will and demand to be released."

Nathaniel felt as though an anchor dropped into his gut. What trouble had he wrought upon his family?

᭜᭜

Constance realized she was in no condition to be making such requests, but she must get these people to understand her plight.

Mr. Ingersoll shook his head. He looked up, dragging his hand over his hair as he spoke. "I assure you, miss. You are no prisoner here."

The intense expression that crossed his chiseled face and his sincere declaration almost convinced her of its truth. Perhaps he was, indeed, unaware that she had been spirited away from England and was not a redemptioner.

"Heavens, no," Mrs. Ingersoll said cheerfully as she reentered the room carrying some linen. "She is our guest. At least until we sort it all out." A maid followed her, carrying a tray of steaming broth. The young woman set it down with a reassuring smile and then took her leave.

Constance's captor—or rescuer—folded his arms across his broad chest. Cocking his head to one side, he addressed his mother. "You heard?"

Mrs. Ingersoll stepped toward Constance and took her hand. "That she has been brought to this country and indentured against her wishes and is now in our custody?" His mother's compassionate look fell upon Constance. "Have you any way that we can verify this, dear?"

"You have my word," Constance said.

The sound of a chair scraping against the floor announced Dr. Hale as he stood. "If you will excuse me, folks, it appears that you have much to discuss. I will be back in a few days' time. Please send for me if need be." Mr. Ingersoll shook the young doctor's hand and thanked him before he departed, receiving a warning in turn. "Be mindful that she is still recuperating."

Mrs. Ingersoll brought the bowl of aromatic broth toward the bed, but Constance held up her hand, halting the attempt when a wave of nausea overcame her. She squeezed her hand into a fist, willing the nausea to pass. With eyes closed, she took a deep breath and the queasiness abated.

The kind woman set the bowl back on the side table. "We will talk later."

"No. Please. It mustn't wait." She looked up at Mr. Ingersoll with pleading eyes.

His mouth drew into a grim line, but he gave her an affirming nod. "Tell us what happened."

✺

Nathaniel could hardly believe this fate that had fallen on Constance. . .Miss Starling, and himself. He listened intently to her account of the dreadful afternoon. She disclosed that she had been walking with a friend in the vicinity of a London port to deliver a gift of charity. When the sky gave evidence of an approaching storm, she and her companion had briefly separated to finish their errands in haste. Apparently then, Captain Smout's men accosted her and dragged her back to his ship to sell her indenture in America with the intent of earning a tidy sum for her passage. He forced her to sign the contract with a threat of starvation. She resisted for days, but at last relented for fear of her demise.

Now she lay fast asleep, with the promise that she would be cared for and given the opportunity to earn the funds for her passage back to England. No one should have to suffer such an ordeal, especially one so lovely. Nathaniel would honor this promise, even if it cost him everything he had. And most likely it would.

✺

"Lord we beseech Thee on behalf of this, Your child, to heal and restore her body, soul, and spirit."

Constance bolted up, heart pounding. She clutched her chemise close to her chest when she realized that a man in a dark suit hovered over her bed. His eyes flashed open, as did Mrs. Ingersoll's, Lucy's, and Nathaniel's.

15

"Am I dying?"

"Oh dear! I hope not." Mrs. Ingersoll placed her hand over her mouth to hide her apparent amusement. "We are praying to the contrary. Sorry to have alarmed you. This is Reverend Ashbel Woodridge, our minister."

"A pleasure to meet you, sir. Thank you for coming." Constance was moved by their thoughtfulness, yet she contended with her own thoughts. How could she ever repay them for their kindnesses? More so, how would she ever earn her freedom?

# Chapter 3

After several days of convalescing, Constance sat at a small writing desk in the corner of the bedchamber, having penned two missives. She set the quill pen back in the ceramic inkpot, folded the paper, and applied the sealing wax. She hoped the letters would find their way back to England to inform her friend and her future employer of her whereabouts and seek their advice. If they could not help. . .well, she could not afford to think such thoughts.

She wandered to the glazed window and peered out toward the road. What lay in each direction? She had no concept of her location and was feeling restless after so many days lying abed. She surveyed the bedchamber once again, though every aspect of it was a permanent fixture in her mind's eye. The green-painted wainscoting with the hue of buttercups above. A wing chair upholstered in a paisley fabric. And the large full tester bed, covered with an emerald green brocade fabric, evidence of this family's bygone wealth. Her strength was returning, and she must find a way to be useful and help repay them for their good graces and hospitality. They had even brought the minister here to pray for her, and that meant a great deal to her. Although if the Lord were truly watching over her, how could she be in this quandary at all?

A knock at the chamber door announced Lucy, who entered carrying a gown. *Her gown.* Lucy laid the garment on the bed along with hose and garters and a petticoat Constance had not seen before. "The mistress had me launder and repair your gown, miss, and now that you are feeling better and have bathed, she sent some extra things for you as well," Lucy said.

Constance sorted through the items, including a dimity apron and short gown—suitable for housework. Was Mrs. Ingersoll expecting her to do chores at the inn to pay for her expenses? She had hoped that the mistress of the inn would not have to ask, as she had already decided to offer her services. Yet a contract still remained between her and Nathaniel. Would he require her services elsewhere? She picked up the clean gown and pressed it against her body.

"It is a lovely gown, Miss Constance," said Lucy as she tidied up the room.

"Thank you, though this is one of my plainest." Constance grew silent, recalling how the men accosted her and tore her gown and grabbed her by the ribbons of her hat, almost choking her. The basket of food had spilled over the cobbled streets. "I was wearing it that day. . .it has a matching hat, a lace cap. . .they are gone now." As was her freedom.

"Now that you are faring well, we will move you to another chamber in the back of the house, in the garret over the kitchen lean-to. Mistress informs me that we are expecting extra guests and are in need of this room."

"Do you mean this is a guest chamber, not a family bedroom?" Constance asked.

"Indeed. You have been treated as a royal guest, for I sleep in the chamber off the kitchen, and they treat me as part of the family, they do. I've been with the Ingersolls for nigh onto eight years now, since I was a girl of twelve."

"Where does the family sleep?"

"The sons have rooms on the third floor, but Mrs. Ingersoll retains her room here on this second level."

"Three floors? What type of dwelling is this?"

Lucy laughed. "I forgot, you have not yet been about, inside or outdoors. 'Tis a fine home, some call it a mansion. Captain Ingersoll was a wealthy merchant who traded along the Connecticut River Valley."

"Was?"

"Ah yes. The good man departed this world several years ago, and that is when it became the Red Griffin Inn. As the eldest, Nathaniel is the rightful owner. He inherited the house and property two years ago when he came of age at one and twenty, though he continues to let his mother operate the inn for her livelihood. He is a fine man, that Nathaniel." Lucy removed the vase of fading flowers that Nathaniel had picked from the garden. It occurred to Constance that she had not seen him for several days.

"And the others?" Constance asked.

They are mostly men now, except for Alden, who is yet sixteen. He and Nathaniel have rooms under the gambrel roof."

"Jonathan is twenty and one, a merchant trader like his father. He is away a good deal, and when he is home he sleeps upstairs as well. But Micajah who's nineteen—Micah as they call him—is apprenticed to the baker and lives there."

"Will you help me dress, Lucy?"

Lucy's cheerful laugh filled the air. "That is what you are used to, methinks. I can tell you are a fine lady. I've never been a lady's maid before, though I have assisted Mrs. Ingersoll and some of the dame guests when asked."

"Thank you, Lucy. I only hope to be as gracious as you have been to me."

☙

In the keeping room, Nathaniel rested his elbows on the long oak table and stared at the contract of indentured servitude. Perhaps there was a clause he had missed that could sever the binding legal document.

"Let me take a look at that." Uncle Phineas took the paper from Nathaniel's grasp and sat down at the head of the table in the high-backed armchair. He took out a handkerchief and cleaned the lenses of his wire-rimmed spectacles before setting them on his bulbous nose. He mumbled aloud as he read through the bond. Nathaniel pushed back from the table, his chair scraping across the wide, planked floor. He stretched out his legs and stared at the flecks of sawdust on his shoes while his uncle perused the document. Dare he look up and partake of his Uncle's wrath? It would come either way.

"Whatever were you thinking?" His uncle looked up over his glasses, enunciating each word with impending judgment.

Nathaniel sat up straight. "I was attempting to save a young woman's life, sir."

Uncle Phineas frowned. "You did not count the cost of your decision."

"She did not cost much. I did not need to pay the captain more than. . ."

Uncle Phin interrupted. "Did you spend the money I sent with you for supplies?"

In truth, he had considered it, but instead. . . "I used my own coin and bartered the rest."

His uncle pulled a silver flask from his waistcoat and planted it on the table.

"My flask!" Nathaniel reached for it, but Uncle Phin clutched it underneath his arthritic but brawny fingers.

"Not now."

"How did you. . . ?"

"I stopped at Mosely's Tavern when I came in from my trip and encountered an ornery sea captain raising it up in the air as he was bidding his farewell. I immediately recognized it and followed him out. I had to make a good bargain to retrieve it. I'll explain the terms later."

Nathaniel's shoulders slumped as he heaved a deep sigh.

"You may have it again, but you will have to earn it back. In the same way you need to earn back my trust."

Nathaniel tossed his palms upward.

"I don't think you realize the burden you have put on this family. You've imposed a cost on your mother, on me, and on yourself. One that you cannot afford." Uncle Phin gripped the edges of the table and leaned in, rising slightly from his chair. "Have you even considered the payment to the doctor, her medication, the expense to this household to provide for the waif's needs—her clothing, food. . . ?"

Nathaniel's ire rose, but he restrained his tone as he spoke. "She can work for that."

"Now that she lives. For what? Your mother already has hired help. You cannot be giving things away if you want to be successful in your craft, in business. Your time. Your labor. Your possessions. . ." Uncle Phin slid the flask back into his coat pocket. "Everything has a price."

Nathaniel had heard the speech before. But this was a unique instance, and he had needed to make a fast judgment. Did he really err? "Is not this woman's life worth anything? I was compelled to do what was right. As my father taught me. As you have taught me."

Uncle Phineas huffed. "Right?" The frustrated man found his handkerchief again and wiped the perspiration from his brow.

Nathaniel waited for him to speak as the clock on the mantel ticked. And tocked.

"You will have to do the extra work on your own time."

"That is what I intended, Uncle."

"Your time and talent are valuable. You need to learn that lesson."

A lesson he had been learning for many years under his uncle's tutelage—and scrutiny—learning the art and magic of ship carving. What would his future hold now?

"How much did you say she cost?" Uncle Phineas grumbled.

Nathaniel exhaled. "Apparently, too much."

# Chapter 4

Constance peered into the large, pleasant room with half-paneled walls. Rain tap-tapped against the paned window glass. The chill of the dismal day was offset by a low fire crackling in the massive hearth.

Still, her heart froze at the hurtful words that fell upon her ears as she approached the room. It was not that she expected Mr. Ingersoll to value her, but since her parents' deaths during her childhood, she had often felt like a burden. After Uncle Chauncey's death, she had to depend on the kindness of her friend's family, and now this.

"Dear, do come in and sit." Mrs. Ingersoll entered the room behind Constance. Obviously she had not heard the men arguing.

Mr. Ingersoll looked up from the dining table at the end of the room where he sat in conversation with an older, stout-looking man. The older man's mouth drew into a tight line and he shook his head. Nathan immediately stood.

"Is this how you treat a servant?" Phineas muttered, but loud enough for all ears to hear.

"This is my brother, Phineas Cushing. Phineas, please stand and greet our guest, Miss Constance Starling," Mrs. Ingersoll said.

"Guest, you say?" Mr. Cushing made an elaborate bow.

Constance glanced at Mrs. Ingersoll, who glared a look of warning at the pompous man. "Here, dear, sit by the fire. You mustn't catch a chill—you are still recovering, after all. I beg your pardon at my brother's unseemly attitude. He has recently returned from a long trip and is quite exhausted."

"Thank you, Mistress Ingersoll," Constance said quietly as she sat on the settee.

"Phineas, we are still trying to establish the role of this young lady. As for now, we treat her as a guest, and I will expect nothing less from even you," his sister chided. "There is no need to be such a crosspatch."

"By all means. Do forgive me, miss. From England, are you?"

"Aye sir. 'Tis a pleasure to meet you." Constance lowered her gaze and clasped her hands resting in her lap.

"She has gone through a terrible ordeal and is just now gaining her strength." Constance looked up and met Mrs. Ingersoll's kind smile. "I am so glad you decided to join us downstairs this evening."

Mr. Ingersoll spoke. "Uncle Phin, Miss Starling claims that she was taken against her will and put on that scoundrel's ship. He obtained her indenture against her will. She was from a respected family in England and was spirited away from all she knew and loved."

The man's wiry eyebrows rose, nearly touching the edge of his wig. "How can we know this is true? Even so, you paid for her indenture. By law she cannot be released from the contract until the terms are met and her freedom taxes have been paid. What of your future? And what kind of example is this to your brothers—especially Alden, who looks up to you so much? Before you take matters into your own hands, you should consult the rest of the family when your actions affect us all."

As if on cue, Alden entered the room. "You should have seen her, Uncle Phineas—she was almost dead. We saved her life." His face colored. "We, and the good Lord, with the skill of Dr. Hale of course."

"Alden, decorum." The tall young man whipped his head around at his mother's sharp retort. Mouth agape, he laid eyes on Constance. "Oh Miss Starling. You are looking well." Alden stepped toward his uncle.

"Pardon my interruption, please, but Uncle Phineas..."

"Alden dear, we are in the midst of a discussion," Mrs. Ingersoll said tersely.

Mr. Cushing regarded his sister. "Let the boy speak, Dorothy. Alden, what say you about this affair?"

"Thank you, sir. Isn't it our duty to show Christian charity in a time of need?"

"This charity is an expense to the family that it can hardly afford, especially with your desire to attend Yale College. It is one thing to give when there is a surplus but quite another when there is not." Mr. Cushing then muttered loud enough for all to hear, "Why you cannot learn a trade like your brothers..."

"Please, Phineas, let us stay on course. You know Alden is going to study medical arts. We have already settled that matter," Mrs. Ingersoll said.

"I—I will work to repay you and will not leave here in your debt," Constance asserted through the oncoming tears she attempted to resist but to no avail.

Palm pressed to her face, Mrs. Ingersoll shook her head. "No wonder you have never married, Phineas. Please be more sensitive." She reached into her pocket and found a small embroidered handkerchief and handed it to Constance.

Constance wiped at her tears and sniffled. How had this trial come upon her? Only a few months ago she had been looking forward to finally moving on in her life after dealing with the aftermath of her uncle's death. The debt he left from his business failings had left her almost penniless, and she at last had accepted her lot. All was not lost. She had arranged employment as a lady's companion, and she could retain some modicum of respect in society. Yet now...

Mr. Ingersoll stood. "Enough of this. My judgment may have been poor in your eyes, Uncle Phin, and perhaps I was wrong to presume to rely on the good graces of this family. I promise to make restitution to all of you and further, to aid this unfortunate lady as far as it depends on me."

"Miss Starling." Mr. Ingersoll held out his hand and helped Constance from her seat. Unlike the gentlemen of England, his hand was rough and calloused. Yet the warmth that exuded from his firm grasp proffered her the feeling of protectiveness and assurance—and something more? *Foolish thoughts.* She must keep her sensibilities intact. Mayhap her illness had addled her brain.

"Where are you going?" Mr. Cushing demanded.

"We have some things to discuss, in private."

"You can continue to say whatever is needed right here in this room."

21

"Nay, Uncle Phineas. This inquisition is over."

"I will speak to you about this later," the curmudgeon replied.

"Mother, have we anyone occupying the guest parlor?"

"Not at present, dear," she said.

Mr. Ingersoll gestured toward the door. "Miss Starling, please come with me."

Constance stood and gave a departing glance to her judge and jury. Although she had held her chin high during the encounter, when she met Mrs. Ingersoll's compassionate nod, she promptly lowered her head to hide the moisture forming again in her eyes.

"Across the way, please," Nathaniel said.

❦

As Constance crossed the front hall, she took a few deep breaths to regain her composure. Upon entering the parlor she faced a beautiful cabinet-top scrutoire and sighed. The writing desk was similar to the one her uncle had owned before it was sold off, along with the rest of his belongings. A hasty inventory revealed grander furnishings than those in the family hall. An ornate half tester bed, folded up on its hinges, stood against the far wall. Covered with lavish curtains and coverings of stunning crewelwork, apparently this bedstead on display was used for their most honored guests. Wallpaper, depicting a pastoral scene, covered the wall above the painted wainscoting, and the hearth wall was fully paneled. An oil painting of an impressive looking man in his middle years, resembling Nathaniel, hung above the fireplace.

"My father."

Constance startled when Nathaniel spoke.

"He would have dealt with this situation reasonably, as I hope to. Come and sit, and we will attempt to achieve that goal."

❦

Nathaniel led Miss Starling to a small carpet-covered table. "I apologize for my uncle's demeanor. He is not usually so abrasive, though he is always very attentive to my mother's interests."

"And yours?"

"Yes, and mine. I am not sure if you know, but I apprenticed under him for years and am now a journeyman at his ship-carving loft. This did not please my father, who desired for me to follow in his footsteps. Yet, as I said, he was reasonable and eventually relented when Jonathan expressed a desire to follow his direction as a ship merchant on the Connecticut River.

"Miss Starling, I know little about you, only that you seem sincere." Nathaniel tried not to be distracted by the way her eyes glistened from the light of the fire as the evening drew nigh. "I wish to help, but I need to know how."

Miss Starling retrieved two letters from her pocket and set them down. "I would like to send these in the post, if I may. They are to my acquaintances in England, requesting their assistance."

"I'll see to it." He drew the letters toward his side of the table. "The post rider should be through again soon. Still, it will take three months before you receive a reply. In the meanwhile, we must come to terms with this arrangement."

"There is nothing to arrange, Mr. Ingersoll. I will work for my keep. I have little experience, though I shall do my part."

"You are not accustomed to much work then?"

"Our servants took care of my late uncle's estate. Though I am adept at needlework."

"You will work for my mother. Perhaps you can help her with the mending and such." Though Nathaniel wondered what the *such* might be.

"Certainly, Mr. Ingersoll."

"There are more than enough men with the surname of Ingersoll in this house. You may call me Nathaniel. You should be addressed by your Christian name, as is fitting for a household servant. I would not wish to offend Lucy. She is dear to our family, and mother would box my ears if I upset her." Nathaniel grinned.

Constance gave a little laugh, and one of her delicate eyebrows rose.

"How else do you think she keeps four sons and an ornery brother in line? She puts up with precious little nonsense."

"I've seen." Constance smiled. "And what about the servants?"

"The ducking stool." Nathaniel issued a wry grin. He stared across the table at the comely woman before him, admiring the transformation at her expression of mirth.

The tall clock in the front entry chimed. This would be a long three months.

☙

Constance slid her hand over the Red Griffin Inn's roadside sign featuring a large hand-carved griffin. "This is a lovely sign. Surely it must draw attention to the inn." She looked at the stately crimson-colored clapboard house with rows of windows and impressive central stack chimney. "Though I imagine such a fine house draws enough attention on its own. Are all the homes in this area as grand?"

"Not all, though many are, especially here along the main street, Country Road." Lucy pointed north, to her right. "Colonel Thomas Welles has built a fine home up past the church for his son John and his soon-to-be daughter-in-law, Jerusha Edwards. She is the niece of Judge Pitkin of the Supreme Court in Hartford, you know. The Welleses own one of the shipyards down at Log Landing, before you get to the ferry and the tobacco fields. That is where Mr. Cushing's carving loft is."

Constance nodded, her gaze lingering down the road. "That is where Nathaniel works?"

Lucy turned left, shielding the sun from her eyes. "Yes, about a mile or so from here on the river."

Constance adjusted her borrowed straw hat. "It's close then."

"Yes. Country Road meets High Street up ahead. At the bottom of the hill we turn left onto Tryon Street, which leads right to Pease Lane. It's a pleasant walk down to the river. They specialize in figureheads, though they also do other ship carving. Sometimes other projects such as architectural features and business signs." Lucy turned and pointed above the double front doors. "Mr. Cushing created that broken-scroll pediment over the door."

"That is very nice." *Even if he is not.* Constance chastised herself for the errant thought.

Lucy placed her hand on the edge of the sign. "And this is Nathaniel's work. He made it for his mother a few years ago. The red griffin is from the Ingersoll family crest."

Constance tilted her chin. "He is very talented."

"Mmm. Yes he is. Handsome, as well." Lucy's coy smile caused Constance to wonder what the young woman was implying.

Constance looked toward the rear of the property. "I think it would be nice to plant some flowers around the sign post. Might it be possible to transplant some from the garden out back?"

"Why don't we go take a look? I am sure the mistress will not mind. In fact, she will probably be quite pleased with the idea."

The two walked around the back of the property, and Constance marveled at both the fenced-in kitchen garden and the flower garden beyond.

"You may bring some in for the dinner table, if you wish," Lucy said.

Constance gathered a bouquet of the summer blooms and lifted them to her nose, taking in the fragrant scent.

Mrs. Ingersoll strolled toward them from the kitchen door. "Ladies, I do not mind your being friendly, though our patrons may not be if we are not ready for the midday meal. If you continue to eat the bread of idleness, our guests will have no bread to eat."

"We will be in by the by, mistress, after we collect some herbs for the stew." As the proprietress went back inside, the pair went into the herb garden and cut sprigs of parsley, thyme, and rosemary. Lucy looked up from her task and said to Constance in a low voice, "We shall ask Mrs. Ingersoll about the flowers for the sign later this afternoon. . .when chores are done."

As Constance stepped into the kitchen, the smells of spices and smoke greeted her. From the ceiling beams hung dried herbs, salted meats, fowl, and cookware. A myriad of hooks, pots, and utensils filled the wall-sized hearth, where Mrs. Ingersoll leaned over tending the fire, humming a tune. *A hymn*, Constance thought. The woman looked up and smiled. "Those are lovely blooms. You will find a vase in the buttery along with the knives."

"Knives?"

"Yes, I thought you might begin by helping Lucy prepare the duck. Make sure you remove all the feathers."

❧

Constance stared at the headless duck sitting on the worktable in front of the hearth. She had never touched such a thing in her entire life. In England, all their meat and fowl had come from the butcher and was prepared by their cook. With knife in hand she proceeded to cut off a few of the tail feathers. There, not as difficult as she thought.

Mrs. Ingersoll passed by the kitchen door, peeking in. "Constance dear, you must *pluck* the feathers out, not cut them off the bird. Lucy will be back in a moment as soon as she is done assisting me upstairs. Please try to have it done by the time she returns. Then she will show you how to carve it up."

Constance felt as though the heat from the fireplace set her cheeks aflame. She kept her eyes lowered, fixated on the mallard. "Yes, mistress."

But how exactly one plucked feathers from an unfortunate creature such as this she could only guess. With nimble fingers she tugged on one, but it did not release. Placing her other hand atop the bird, she tried again, exerting a little more force.

"Oh dear. I saw mistress in the hall and she said I had better see how you are coming along." Lucy felt the duck between her hands and chuckled. "That bird will sooner come to life and fly away than you will have success that way. Why, you've not even dipped it yet to loosen its quills."

Lucy grabbed the bird and dipped it into a pot of boiling water hanging from a hinged rod inside the hearth. She retrieved it with iron tongs and placed it back on top of the table. A few moments later, Lucy demonstrated her pulling technique. "You shall find it much easier this way. Go ahead then." Under Lucy's scrutinizing eye, Constance gave it a try and removed feather after feather with relative ease. "There, now. You finish that and I shall return shortly."

"Thank you, Lucy. 'Tis new to me, these tasks."

Lucy shrugged and retreated from the kitchen, mumbling to herself.

At last the task was done and Constance tidied up the area to prepare for the next step. The poor bird lay naked on a platter. She took the bowl of colorful feathers of varying sizes and dumped them onto one of the small fires in the hearth. She took a poker from a hook and attempted to hasten their consumption. The smoldering feathers released a malodorous stench and smoke began to fill the space.

Mrs. Ingersoll and Lucy came rushing into the kitchen, faces filled with alarm. "That smell! Constance, what have you done?" Lucy inquired, fanning the smell away from her nose.

Their bewildered gazes instantly turned toward the smoky hearth. "What have you put in the fire?" Mrs. Ingersoll flapped her apron. "Open the windows, before the whole inn takes on that horrible smell." Constance scurried toward the two small windows and lifted the glazed panes. She then unlatched the door and a black-and-white cat skittered past her.

"It's the feathers, mistress." Lucy said, as she covered the blaze with ashes. It only made the smoke worse. Mistress Ingersoll coughed as she neared the hearth and aided Lucy in shoveling the disastrous lump of feathers into a metal bucket. Lucy retreated out the door toward the wood line to dispose of it. If only Constance's blunder could be so easily removed.

"The quills! We never dispose of those. They are used for Alden's schooling." Constance had never heard Mrs. Ingersoll raise her voice, but now the mistress of the Red Griffin Inn simply stared at her in anger...disappointment...sorrow. Tears sprung to Constance's eyes. Mrs. Ingersoll took a step toward her, and Constance tried to utter an apology, but her words were frozen upon her lips.

Mrs. Ingersoll wiped her hands on her apron and reached for Constance's hands. As she took them in her own, Constance noticed the contrast of the older woman's work-worn hands with her own, smooth and pale. "My hands were once fair as yours. Before my husband died, I had servants enough to run my home...when it was not necessary to keep it as a place of lodging." Mrs. Ingersoll's countenance softened as Constance's eyes met hers apologetically. "You needn't apologize for your inexperience, dear. But we must rectify the situation, as there is much work to be done in a busy inn such as this without having to take extra time to repair errors."

Constance wondered what other tasks she might muddle up, but at least she now knew how to pluck the feathers off a duck.

❧

"When are you coming home? She is trying mother's patience."

Nathaniel set his chisel down and looked up from the carving.

Micajah shoved a pasty into Nathaniel's hand. "You have been gone for days. Be glad I brought you some food from the bakery. Have you even been eating?"

"Enough." Truth be told, he fell asleep on the cot in the back room of the loft each night too tired to eat, especially since Uncle Phineas bargained with Captain Smout to do extra carving on his ship. He could not make sense of his uncle's actions these days. Yet, who was he to complain? His own behavior had him befuddled. Constance was ever present in his thoughts. He was drawn to her and could not explain the feelings that pervaded his mind. But now with the increased responsibility of an indenture contract with taxes to pay to set her free, he must focus all the more on his work. This, far easier while not in her presence. "Mmm. This is pretty good. But I suppose anything would taste good about now," he garbled, as he munched on the sweet meat-filled roll.

Micah tossed a rag at Nathaniel.

"So how is it going at the bakery?" Nathaniel asked his brother.

"I'm not here to talk about that. Mother is worried about you. And Constance is trying Mother's patience. Lucy has to teach her everything, and mother is concerned that Lucy may leave us."

"Lucy will never leave us," Nathaniel said.

"Well, when Constance set duck feathers on fire the other day it put Lucy in a "'fowl'" mood." Micah cracked a grin.

Nathaniel almost choked on his pasty. "Really? I did not realize. . . ."

A laugh escaped Micah's lips, and then he sobered. "It is not only that. Mother is also worried about Uncle Phin. His arthritis is getting worse. She has a great deal on her mind."

"Aye, I've been concerned for Uncle. He never complains to me about it, but I have noticed my workload increasing on items that require more intricate carving. He is not as adept as he once was, and I know it bothers him." Nathaniel poured some cider from a jug and took a sip. "As for Mother, I never meant to burden her so. I hoped Constance might be useful, not a source of contention."

"The Red Griffin has not been the same since she arrived, Nathaniel."

*Neither have I.*

# Chapter 5

Constance marched toward the shipyard recounting her mishaps. Burnt molasses. Scorched puddings. Broken pottery. Singed bed sheets. Angry guests. She could not even coddle eggs. When she timed them with the recitation of the Lord's Prayer, as Lucy had instructed her, she lost track of her thoughts and ruined them. Her prayer had turned real as she petitioned the Lord regarding her situation—praying for her own daily bread, to forgive those who trespassed against her, to be delivered from evil. Was her situation truly the Lord's will for her life?

Mayhap Nathaniel could offer some advice. The basket of food that Mrs. Ingersoll had given her to deliver to her son presented the perfect opportunity.

Constance arrived at Log Landing, the place where logs were floated downriver and collected for lumber to be used in building ships. The area provided an ample view of the Connecticut River. In the distance, she could see the shipyard's several buildings and the wooden skeleton of an enormous vessel. But in this quieter section, the building for Cushing's Ship Carving was not difficult to find. A bust of a figurehead was mounted to a shingled structure. She went inside and found that the lower level was a nautical instrument and clockmaker's shop. Behind the counter, a man stood with his back turned, and she noticed a girl sweeping the floor. "I am looking for the ship carver's shop." The girl smiled and pointed to a stairway.

Constance entered a loft at the top of the stairs. Immediately the smell of freshly cut wood assailed her, and she was surprised that she found it rather pleasant. Her eyes scanned the rustic-looking room, which she guessed spanned almost the entire second level of the building. Curls of wood shavings and sawdust littered the floor, some swept into piles. Ample light filtered in through several windows, illuminating a multitude of dust motes in the air. Carved displays hung on the walls as well as all manner of tools. Upon several worktables rested more tools with a variety of half-carved pieces, projects in the making. Bins of lumber and a large block of wood awaited the workers' skillful touch. A large wooden eagle was propped in the corner, and she marveled at its beauty. Was it the craftsmanship of Nathaniel or his uncle?

Constance set the food basket down on a dusty workbench. She picked up a rag and began to wipe the surface. She set the rag down, afraid she would disturb something or cause some kind of damage as she seemed to have a propensity for doing. Tears stung her eyes at the thought, and she buried her face in her hands.

A strong grip latched onto her shoulder and she jumped. When she turned she found Mr. Cushing standing there.

"I did not mean to startle you, miss. You are a timid thing."

The untrusting glare she returned to him would hopefully tell him that she was not, but instead tears streamed down her cheeks. She had never been one to cry so much, yet of late the tears seemed to frequently lie in wait.

He offered her his handkerchief. "There now, it is not all that bad, is it?"

She blotted her moist face, noting his attire was much different from the first day they met. His work clothes consisted of a blue-and-white patterned shirt, a worn waistcoat, and light-colored trousers. Gone was the wig, replaced by a Monmouth cap, and his weathered face was dotted with white stubble. "Would you really like to know, sir?"

"Yes, dear, I would. I would also like to offer an apology for being so harsh with you. It was uncalled for. My sister informs me that you are trying very hard to please her and do what you can to meet your goal of returning to England."

Constance sniffed. "She told you that?"

"Why, yes. And I have something to tell you as well. I have been investigating the matter of this Captain Smout and his transgression against you. The authorities have told me that if you can provide evidence of who you are and that your intent was not to come to the colonies as a redemptioner, that the indenture might be nullified. Further, it may be possible to bring charges against him and seek restitution."

"You have done this for me?" Constance beamed. "Mr. Cushing, how can I thank you?"

His gray eyes twinkled. "You can begin by sharing with me the contents of this food basket. Is it something you made?"

"Be grateful it is not. Lucy has prepared some pies and other foodstuffs for you and your nephew. I have no doubt that they are quite tasty, yet had I cooked them, that may have been another matter. I do not seem to be equipped with that particular gift."

Mr. Cushing picked up a small block of wood from the workbench. "We all have our talents, Miss Starling. And like this piece of wood, the carving process will reveal the design for which it was intended. I suspect you, too, will soon discover what you are fashioned for and how to best be of service."

"I suspect that you discovered this piece of wisdom through your own experience."

"Indeed I have, though I doubt it will take as long for you as it did for me before the design of your life takes shape." He winked. "By the way, if you are looking for my nephew, I believe you might find him hanging about somewhere by the river."

❧

Constance shielded her eyes beneath her straw bonnet as she tipped her head up toward the prow of the *Fortuna*. The ship was secured to the wharf alongside the river, and Nathaniel dangled from some sort of scaffolding off the bowsprit.

"Ah, good day, Miss Starling. Constance," Nathaniel called out to her.

"Good day, Nathaniel," she called back.

He put his paintbrush inside a pail that hung from a rope beside him. "How do you fare this pleasant day?"

"I am greatly improved, I am pleased to say," she said.

"Indeed?"

Constance smiled brightly. "Aye."

"I am happy to hear it." Nathaniel nodded with a smile of his own.

"Are you certain that you are safe up there?" Constance asked.

"I have done it a great many times and assure you the chains hold well." He glanced down to gather up his supplies. Was he coming down to see her?

Constance focused on the *Fortuna*'s mythological horse figurehead that Nathaniel had repaired and had been painting. "You have fixed her up quite well, restored her legs, and now she can gallop across the ocean."

"It would not be so easy for you." The unmistakable sound of Captain Smout's gruff voice hissing in her ear announced his unwanted presence.

Constance spun around. "Captain Smout."

He dipped his hat. "Miss Starling. 'Tis a pleasure to see you looking so well."

"Leave her be, Smout," Nathaniel yelled down.

The incorrigible sea captain released a haughty laugh. "I dare say you are in a bit of a precarious position to defend this lady's honor, Mr. Ingersoll."

"Be careful, Captain, or I will paint your figurehead black!"

"Ha! We can't be having that, or my crew would have my neck. Bad luck that is." Smout turned to Constance. "Just as you have been to me," he sneered.

He toyed with the ribbons of her hat. "Should have waited. You'd fetch me a greater fee now that you have some life in ye."

"I am warning you, Smout." Nathaniel cranked the scaffolding in haste and a rope came loose. The plank he sat upon tipped and he fell into the river with a splash.

"Nathaniel!"

Constance looked back at Captain Smout. "Help him!" The man was laughing so hard he began coughing. He obviously had no intention of coming to Nathaniel's aid.

Constance lifted her skirts and ran down the dock. She looked at the dark water but saw nothing.

✥

Nathaniel gasped for breath as he surfaced in the frigid river. He pushed his wet hair from his face and wiped his eyes. Constance stood on the edge of the dock, her hands pressed against her cheeks, framing her pursed lips. He swam the few feet to the dock and climbed up the side. She grabbed his arm to help him ascend to the platform.

He took in a deep breath, shook his head, and discovered his hair tie missing. His wet locks hung to his shoulders. "Thank you. It looks like this time you rescued me."

Her eyebrows rose. "Rescued? I fear it was my fault."

"Not at all. I shouldn't have been so careless." He looked around. "I'm glad to see Captain Smout has left."

Constance sighed. "As am I. Are you all right?"

He cocked his head. "A little embarrassed is all." He shook off a chill.

Constance looked down at her hand and saw her palm smeared with red. She gasped and stared at his arm. "You are bleeding!"

Nathaniel glanced down at his sleeve. He looked up at her concerned face, that beautiful face, and grinned. "Paint."

"Oh." Her face relaxed into a serene smile and she laughed softly.

Nathaniel's gaze passed over her. Even in what he recognized as one of Lucy's faded old aprons and borrowed gown, Constance was a vision to behold. Something about this woman exuded an inner beauty he was not sure she herself was aware of.

He glanced away, breaking the spell, and spotted a small bucket of water sitting by a post. He carried it back to her. "Hold out your hand."

Nathaniel trickled water over her upturned hand and rubbed her paint-stained palm with his thumb. He noticed the pale satin skin on the inside of her wrist and longed to touch that, too. His heart beat hard inside his chest. He thought he heard the soft sound of her breath catching. His eyes met her dark orbs and a little grunt escaped from his throat. His fingers trailed lightly down her fingers and back again, and he rubbed her palm again with his thumb. "That is better."

She looked down at her clean palm and pulled it back, holding it to her stomach with her other hand.

A breath swooshed through Nathaniel's clenched teeth. "I suppose I should get out of these wet slops. I am glad that I have another set of clothes up in the loft."

Constance's eyes wandered over him, and then she averted her gaze. Just as quickly she glanced up again, meeting his view. "I best be going."

"Constance. You never said what brought you here today."

"Why, you, of course." she said coyly. "You shall find a food basket in the loft, if there is any left. Your uncle found it first."

Nathaniel laughed as Constance turned away and headed back to the inn. His fall into the river must have addled his senses. He feared this Constance Starling was going to be his undoing.

# Chapter 6

Nathaniel quietly entered the kitchen through the buttery door. He sneaked up behind his mother and planted a kiss on her cheek.

"You thought I did not hear you come in, did you?" She planted her fists on her generous hips and laughed. "It is high time you showed that handsome face of yours. I have been concerned about you. You are working too hard."

"I am doing what I must." Nathaniel sat down at the work-worn kitchen table. "Thank you for sending the food. Where is Constance, by the way?"

"Lucy took her to a public vendue to obtain some much needed clothing."

"Oh?"

"The Hodges' daughter-in-law passed away, and their son is selling her belongings to help pay for the medical and funeral expenses and care of the new baby."

"'Tis a shame," Nathaniel said. "How is Lemuel caring for the child?"

"His mother is helping, and they have hired a wet nurse. He has moved back into his parents' home for the time being and has decided to let his house until he finds a new wife."

"A new wife?" Nathaniel wondered at the possibilities of him finding one here in Glassenbury.

"It would be best for him and the child," Mother said.

"Still, it is kind of his mother to help for now."

His mother puttered around the kitchen as she spoke with him. "I'm sure it is a happy burden."

"Mothers are a gift from God," Nathaniel said.

His mother walked over to Nathaniel and wrapped her arm around his shoulder and planted a kiss on his cheek. "As are their children. Even the grown ones." She chuckled.

"How will Constance pay for her new frocks?" Nathaniel asked.

"I sent her with a silver candlestick. Lemuel can redeem it at the silversmith's."

Nathaniel's voice rose. "That is too much."

"I felt led to contribute that to the Hodges to help in this time of need. The vendue was a good excuse, otherwise he might decline the gift."

"Mother, I am astounded by your generous spirit. Leave it to you to find a way to help the Hodges and Constance at the same time. And you have already done so much."

"The gift is not from me. 'Tis from the good Lord. All we have comes from Him."

The room grew quiet, and a gentle breeze drifted through the window. Nathaniel smiled at his mother. "You seem content today. I had been concerned that you were feeling upset."

"Is that what Micajah told you? He mentioned he had stopped by to see you."

Nathaniel yawned. "He said there was some difficulty."

"Yes, I suppose that is true. This has been a time of adjustment for us all." Mother grew thoughtful. "Yet the other day I was sitting in the parlor looking up at your father's picture. The Lord encouraged me with the remembrance of the time before your father and I were married. Jonathan Edwards came to Glassenbury, and we heard him preach. He said something that has stayed with me ever since, though of late I had seemed to have forgotten. He said, 'I assert that nothing ever comes to pass without a cause.' There is a purpose in all of this, and I thank the Lord for allowing our family to be a part of His plans."

Nathaniel nodded and considered his mother's words.

"Though she is not accustomed to much work and has little knowledge of household chores, Constance is really quite amiable and eager to help," Mother said.

"Is she learning?" Nathaniel asked.

"Yes, and it will prepare her to be a housewife someday." A slight grin spread across his mother's face.

"If you are thinking. . . That is not feasible. . . Not. . ." He bit into a molasses cookie and nearly cracked a tooth. "Ow!"

"Oh dear. Where did you find that? I thought that batch was given to the pig."

"I hope you soaked them first." Nathaniel grinned. "Did Micah make these? I heard he was going to supply the inn with the baked goods from now on."

"Yes, he is, and that will be a great help to us." Mother frowned. "I'm afraid that Constance baked that cookie."

"So, she is that bad, eh?" Nathaniel grimaced. "I think she added too much ginger."

"It is not as bad as all that," Mother said. "I am assessing her skills and trying to build her confidence by allowing her to utilize them."

"What can she do?"

"She is good at serving, though I think she is more accustomed to being served. Yet, she is very attentive to our guests' needs. And she enjoys gardening and putting fresh flowers in the guest rooms."

Nathaniel recalled the flowers that he had picked for her when she was ill. He hoped they brought her joy, especially now that he knew she was so fond of flowers.

"She also planted flowers around the sign out front. Did you notice when you arrived?" His mother planted her hands on her hips. "Nathaniel?"

"Um, yes, Mother?"

"The flowers around your sign. Did you see them? They complement it very nicely."

"I shall take a look."

His mother placed a plate of pumpkin bread and a cup of milk on the table for him. Then she walked over to the settle by the hearth and picked up a small stack of linen towels. "And Constance is especially adept at needlework." She pointed to the corner of the cloth.

Amusement filled Nathaniel's face. "A red griffin. She did this?"

"Yes. She suggested it herself. I have asked her if she might also label the bed linens the same for the laundress."

Alden tromped into the kitchen and grabbed a piece of pumpkin bread. "Hello, Nathaniel." He turned to their mother. "Has Constance returned yet? She promised to help me with my Latin lessons."

Nathaniel looked at his mother and the two began to laugh.

"Will wonders never cease!" Mother crossed her arms.

"What is so humorous?" Alden asked.

Nathaniel could not help but see that Miss Constance Starling had found a special place in his family's hearts. And If he were not careful, his heart would be lost to her as well.

*

Constance and Lucy walked down the tree-laden street on their way home from the vendue.

"It was kind of Mr. Hodge to offer to deliver the garments to the inn when he goes on his errand this afternoon," Constance said.

"You acquired a whole wardrobe. Petticoats, short gowns, long gowns, stays, stomachers, kerchiefs, shoes, even some gewgaws. The departed Mrs. Hodge had fine taste, and she was a very kind Christian lady."

"I am glad you found a few nice things as well." Constance adjusted her new cotton mitts. She admired the embroidery on the fingerless gloves. "Yes, all of the articles are very comely. Though, I must confess, I am not accustomed to wearing secondhand clothing. It is not that I am not grateful, as I am. . . . I am sorry." Constance buried her face in her hand and shook her head.

Lucy stayed her hand on Constance's arm. "There is no need to apologize. I understand what you are saying."

"Mrs. Ingersoll has been very kind to me, and I do appreciate everything she has done."

"I know you do, and she knows as well. She will be pleased to see that you have sufficient things to wear now. You even have a new gown for church." Lucy chattered on. "That Lemuel doted on his wife, but now he has so many expenses and has no reason to keep her wardrobe. There are no female family members nearby that would benefit from them. I imagine he could have kept them for a new wife, or mayhap he already has found one."

"Lucy Goslee, what are you implying?"

"Did you not notice his awareness of you?" Lucy teased.

"I only observed a man who looked disturbed to see his deceased wife's garments being auctioned off," Constance said.

"He could not keep his eyes off you, Constance. Mayhap he was contemplating a courtship."

Constance tilted her head toward Lucy. "I do believe you are either jealous or simply daft. But what of I do not know. I am in no position to consider marriage nor instant motherhood. I know nothing about babies or children."

"'Tis what mothers and mothers-in-law are for," Lucy said.

"The terms of my indenture do not permit me to marry," said Constance.

"Unless, of course, you were to exchange your bond for the bonds of matrimony." Lucy giggled.

Constance let out an exasperated breath and swatted her hand in the air. "Lucy! What in heaven are you implying?"

"You cannot tell me you have not noticed how handsome the Ingersoll men are. Fine men at that, Connie."

"I have not been called that since my childhood."

"Do you mind if I call you that then?"

"It would be nice for a friend to call me Connie. That is what my papa called me."

"Were you very young when your parents died? My parents are both gone, too. That is why Mrs. Ingersoll treats me as her own daughter."

"My mother died when I was very small, and my father died when I was ten. That is when I went to live with my uncle and my aunt. Uncle Chauncey treated me very well, but when Aunt Silvia passed away, he was never the same. He became somewhat reckless in his business ventures and was taken advantage of by his partners."

Lucy shook her head. "Oh Connie."

"When my uncle died earlier this year, his estate was absolved to pay his debts. My sole means of support expired, and I went to live with friends. I am—was—to be retained as a lady's companion for a Lady Bennington in Devon." Constance sighed and gathered her shawl around her shoulders. "I prayed most earnestly that God would provide for me. I never expected to find myself in this circumstance. On another continent. Subject to a master."

"A kindly master," Lucy said softly. "If you do not mind me saying, I detect some bitterness. Do you not appreciate what the good Lord has wrought?"

Bewildered, Constance stopped on the side of the road and faced Lucy. "What He has wrought? This? Here? Against my will?"

"But what of thy will? Can ye not see the handiwork of God? In all things He works together for the good of those who love Him. Connie, doest thou love Him?"

# Chapter 7

On Sunday, Lucy helped Constance dress then styled her hair with a crimping pin. This was to be her first time in church wearing the new garments she had received from the Hodges. If only she did not have to face Mr. Hodge wearing one of his dead wife's gowns!

During the service her mind wandered back to Lucy's question. *"Doest thou love Him?"*

In England, Constance dutifully attended worship services and said her prayers. In fact, she thought, her prayers had been more frequent from the time of Uncle Chauncey's death to this very day than they had probably been over her entire lifetime before. Yet, the idea of loving God seemed too personal, intimate. How did one love God?

She expected it was through works of service, and she thought of the years she had helped the needy by conducting obligatory charity work. But when she went to live with her friends after her uncle's estate was sold off, she found special joy in the acts of charity that she participated in with them. Their attitude showed their love of God. Constance tried to emulate the same, and her reward? She was kidnapped and forced into servitude. Did she love a God that allowed that to happen? Did He love her?

Uncle Phineas coughed loudly, bringing her attention back to the service in time to hear Reverend Woodridge offer the benediction. "Now, may God who 'is able to make all grace abound toward you; that ye, always having all sufficiency in all things, may abound to every good work.'"

She pressed her hand to her chest as realization dawned. His grace. Even in the midst of her dreadful ordeal, God loved her, supplying her every need including settling her with a loving family.

Mayhap she could try again by acknowledging this grace and trusting that God would continue to provide for her and enable *her* to abound in every good work, just as Reverend Woodridge said. This would be her love offering to God.

⁂

The congregation stood and made their way out of their enclosed pews. As Constance exited her row, a familiar face greeted her.

"Miss Starling, I believe." Lemuel Hodge took her hand and offered a slight bow. His mother stood nearby, holding the baby and smiling.

"Mr. Hodge. A pleasure to see you again."

He cleared his throat. "You look very becoming today, Miss Starling."

Constance smiled and glanced down. "Thank you, Mr. Hodge. It is kind of you to say so."

Lucy approached Mrs. Hodge and began doting on the infant. But Mr. Hodge seemed to barely notice Lucy's presence and attention to his baby. 'Twas a shame, Constance thought. Though plain, Lucy had a radiant smile and her demeanor was so sweet and kind. She certainly had extended extraordinary grace and patience toward her. Lucy was loyal and hardworking and, by the looks of it, adored babies.

"Was that one of my wife's gowns?" Mr. Hodge asked, drawing Constance's thoughts away from Lucy.

Constance did not expect this awkward inquiry and tried to keep her discomfiture from showing. "It is, sir."

"I am glad to see it of use." He stared at the gown, overly long, and blinked at the sound of his mother's voice.

"Excuse us, dear," Mrs. Hodge said to her son. The elderly woman handed the babe to Lucy and took Constance aside. "Dear, please don't be uncomfortable to be seen wearing these clothes. We are happy to see them be of use. My daughter-in-law's appearance contrasted very much to yours, so be not concerned. Many of the garments we gave you she had never worn. That *robe à l'Anglaise* is very attractive on you."

Constance looked over and saw Nathaniel heading toward them, looking so dashing in his blue coat, buff breeches, brocade waistcoat, and crisp, white stock around his neck. His fine silk stockings showed off his shapely calves. Suddenly she felt warm all over and fluttered her fan.

"Thank you, Mrs. Hodge. You are kind to put me at ease, but if you will please excuse me. . ."

She made her way past the congregants to the side door of the church. She exited and scurried around the back, where she leaned up against the white clapboards. A torrent of tears threatened to release, but she refused to succumb to them. Her feelings for Nathaniel were growing, and now Mr. Hodge was taking an interest in her, when Lucy would be a perfect companion for him and his child. Nothing seemed to be working out for her, despite the words of Reverend Woodridge. God's words. Oh, that she could trust them. She took several deep breaths to regain her composure and rejoin the others at the front of the church. She started walking around the building, but as she was about to turn the corner, she heard voices.

"Hodge, I see you have taken an interest in Miss Starling. Perhaps you are unaware that she is newly indentured to me."

"This I know," Mr. Hodge said.

"Then you also know that she is bound to me for the entirety of her contract, which does not permit her to have alternative loyalties. I hope you understand. If you have a mind to seek permission to court her, it will not be allowed," Nathaniel said.

"Perhaps you should let her speak for herself," said Mr. Hodge.

"As I have said, what my servant wants is inconsequential."

Constance could not believe her ears. Was Nathaniel really that callous? If he was, had she misinterpreted his subtle nuances? Or was he merely putting up a front for Mr. Hodge? She inched closer, staying close to the wall of the church, and could now see the pair standing near a tree.

Mr. Hodge chuckled. "Now, Nathaniel. I do not believe for one moment that you have become such a tyrant. I have never seen you so vexed, man. What is this about?"

Nathaniel let out a swoosh of air. "I am merely being protective of Miss Starling. It is my right. My duty."

"It is also your right to seek her for your own wife. That is what you want, is it not?" Mr. Hodge grinned. "While you contemplate that, let me assure you that I have already taken an interest in your mother's hired girl, Miss Goslee. She has taken to my young one so naturally, and I know her to be a virtuous and kind young woman."

Nathaniel patted him on the shoulder. "Pardon my foolishness, Lemuel. It pleases me to know you have your sights fixed on Lucy. She has been with our family for many years. A girl with such remarkable qualities is rare, and I have never seen a more cheerful and capable one. At least that is how I think of her, but I suppose she has come of age. I wish you both much happiness." Nathaniel extended his hand.

Mr. Hodge nodded with a large smile and shook Nathaniel's hand. He looked over Nathaniel's shoulder, catching Constance looking at them. She froze.

"Thank you. As for the apology, if she has heard all that we said. . ." Mr. Hodge pointed his chin in Constance's direction, "I think you ought to send it that way."

Nathaniel turned and his countenance fell. "Constance. I. . ."

She could not bear it. She clutched her silk skirts and fled.

🙢

Nathaniel heard a sharp cry come from around the corner of the church. *Constance!*

He ran and found her fallen in a heap. He stooped down by her side. "Constance, are you hurt?"

She hugged her knees, her pretty stocking-clad ankles peeking out below her petticoats. He averted his gaze and noted her fabric-covered hat with her pretty brown curls spiraling down onto her shoulder. The hat remained tilted down, concealing her face entirely. Tiny whimpers were muffled beneath it.

He tipped her hat upward and lifted her chin with his fingertip. When her eyes met his, the hurt he saw there almost did him in. "Constance. . .I am so sorry."

Her lashes collected her tears and her lower lip trembled, yet she said nothing. He tried to steady his heart. If they were not at the church, he might very well take her in his arms and confess how precious, indeed, she had become to him.

"Can you stand?"

She nodded.

He rose and took her hands, gently pulling her to her feet. She stood upright, somewhat disheveled, her gown having collected an array of tiny sticks and leaves. He reached out to wipe a smudge of dirt from her jaw.

She slapped his face with her kid glove, sending his cocked hat to the ground.

Nathaniel rubbed the sting from his cheek. "I suppose I deserved that."

But before she could reply, a voice bellowed. "What is going on here?"

"You may ask him." Constance marched past Reverend Woodridge, leaving Nathaniel to fend for himself.

Nathaniel explained the misunderstanding, painfully recounting the conversation that he had had with Lemuel. It had been embarrassing enough when Constance had heard, but he was mortified to have to confess all to the minister. He knew Reverend Woodridge would expect full disclosure of the incident, especially after he saw a disheveled Constance slap Nathaniel, tears streaming down her face. Strangely, Nathaniel felt somewhat relieved to have unburdened his frustrations. But nothing subdued the regret he felt over hurting Constance's feelings.

When the family walked home from church together, Nathaniel trailed behind them in his misery.

Alden trotted back to join Nathaniel. "Brother, what keeps you? You are walking like an old dame. Come up and join me and Constance. She could use the company. It seems nothing I can say will cheer her."

"Alden, I fear if you cannot cheer her, no one can." *Least of all me.*

# Chapter 8

The last light of dusk came through the small window of Constance's bedchamber as she lit the candle on the table by her bed. The narrow chamber with a slanted roof was plain but adequate and brightened by a pretty bedcovering that Mrs. Ingersoll had given her.

Constance sat on the edge of her bed and reached for *The Art of Cookery, made plain and easy: which far exceeds anything yet published* that Mrs. Ingersoll requested that she peruse. She opened the small book, determined to become more adept in the kitchen.

*To the Reader. I believe I have attempted a branch of Cookery, which nobody has yet thought worth their while to write upon: but as I have both seen, and found, by experience, that the generality of servants are greatly wanting in that point, therefore I have taken upon me to instruct them in the best manner I am capable; and, I dare say, that every servant who can but read will be capable of making a tolerable good cook, and those who have the least notion of Cookery cannot miss of being very good ones.*

But as the scent of the bayberry candle filled the room, Constance's thoughts drifted back to the events of the morning, and she let out a heavy sigh. She had suppressed her feelings most of the day, enough to make it through the afternoon's activities. Mrs. Ingersoll was in the habit of asking Lucy and Constance to join them for the family dinners on Sundays—so long as there were no guests at the inn that needed attention. Why did today of all days have to be one such day?

She wasn't sure if it was Reverend Woodridge's presence as he visited with the Ingersolls this afternoon, or simply the recollection of his poignant benediction, but Constance tried to take his words to heart to help her endure the day.

Yet, she knew she had failed miserably when put to the test in the incident with Nathaniel that occurred after the morning service. She was not sure what sin she had committed when she slapped him across the face, if any at all, though she did regret it.

After dinner he returned to the loft, with a gentle reminder from his mother not to work on the Lord's Day, but Constance knew he was also painfully enduring the day for his mother's sake. Once Nathaniel left, Reverend Woodridge invited Constance to sit with him on a bench in the garden to discuss what had happened during her encounter with Nathaniel.

Constance related the conversation she overheard Nathaniel and Mr. Hodge having and how hurt she had felt upon hearing Nathaniel speak of her desires as "inconsequential." To him, she was nothing more than a lowly servant. When Mr. Hodge had asserted that Nathaniel might wish to pursue her for himself, Nathaniel disregarded the comment entirely. The duel changed course, and the men proceeded to praise Lucy for her many virtues, which all the more illuminated the fact that Constance was lacking.

How different things were here in the American British colonies than in England, where gentlemen fought for her attentions. But when she all but confessed that she was falling in love with Nathaniel, somehow she sensed the kind reverend already knew.

Constance wondered how Nathaniel's conversation had gone with Reverend Woodridge this morning. The wise and compassionate man must be the keeper of many secrets. And she still had one of her own.

🍂

The following morning, outdoors behind the carving shop, Nathaniel prepared the trunk of a tree that exceeded his nearly six feet, for the carving of a new figurehead. He scraped off a length of bark and stood. He braced his hands on his lower back to stretch and felt the perspiration through his loose-fitting shirt. He took a drink of cider and anticipated the forthcoming meeting that he and Uncle Phin would have with an important customer to discuss further details of the project. Nathaniel was relieved to at last be done with the work on the *Fortuna* and to return to his regular duties. But he was especially glad to be rid of Captain Smout. As much as he had complained about the man, Nathaniel could no longer imagine what it would be like if Constance Starling had never come to Glassenbury, even at the price of his and his family's convenience. *Lord, please help me to trust You for my decisions, right or wrong. And I pray that You will help Constance to trust You also. I am sorry for hurting her when You have entrusted her to my care.*

He stepped back to assess the huge piece of oak and wiped his brow. The prospect of commencing a new piece usually excited him, but Nathaniel's sense of ambition had waned. If only he had some inspiration. As he stared at the ground, he caught a flicker of something out of the corner of his eye. His gaze traveled the ground until it met a pair of ladies' shoes. Then his gaze continued to slowly ascend over a familiar skirt and apron, at last landing on the beautiful face of Miss Constance Starling.

Nathaniel tightened his lips and lifted his brow. Her lips parted as if to speak, but then she closed them again. She offered a shy smile.

"Constance."

"Mr. Ingersoll."

Their salutations tumbled over one another.

"Mr. Ingersoll?" Nathaniel cocked his head. "We are back to that, are we?"

"Yes, I mean, no. . . Nathaniel, please. I have come to apologize."

"My dear Constance, I am the one who owes you the apology. I never meant for you to hear that conversation."

"Your true opinion of me was revealed, and I shall have to accept it."

"Not in its entirety." Nathaniel took a step closer.

Constance's head turned at some commotion by the river. Nathaniel turned to look and saw his brother's ship, with the figurehead of a bright red griffin, moored by the shore. "Jonathan! Come, let us go greet my brother."

Constance followed closely on his heels as they made their way toward the docks.

"Nathaniel!" Jonathan shouted.

The brothers embraced. "You were gone much longer this time. I hope your trip was a success." Nathaniel looked out toward the ship.

"Indeed, it was. I brought some cloth for Mother and some more spices. My crew is seeing to them now." Jonathan regarded Constance with curiosity. "And who have we here?"

Nathaniel glanced at Constance and back again at his brother. "Forgive me. Miss Constance Starling, this is my brother, Captain Jonathan Ingersoll."

Constance held out her hand. "A pleasure to meet you, sir."

"Indeed, the pleasure is mine." Jonathan turned his head and winked at Nathaniel.

Nathaniel's chest tightened. "Jonathan, Constance is a new servant at the inn."

Jonathan appeared confused. "Has Lucy left us?"

"No, nothing like that. It is a long story, one which I shall tell you about later if you will come back with me and help me hoist up a new tree trunk for carving." Nathaniel draped his arm over his brother's shoulder. "Let us go surprise Mother. She will be glad you are home in time for the fall muster on Saturday. She would not want you to get fined."

"Has she forgotten that I promised to take us all up the river to Hartford for the occasion?" Jonathan asked.

Nathaniel shrugged. "Mayhap. Well, let us go assure her that you are present."

Jonathan offered Constance his arm.

"Thank you, Captain Ingersoll," Constance said with a smile.

"You may call me Jonathan," he said with a roguish grin. And now Nathaniel was not sure if he was glad his brother had returned or not.

"The family calls me Constance."

"I do hope you will be joining us on Muster Day, Constance."

"Of course she is. I will not allow her to miss it."

Constance craned her neck toward Nathaniel and shot him an angry glance. Mayhap he should take some lessons in charm from his brother.

❧

As they sailed up the Connecticut River toward Hartford, Constance marveled at the first signs of autumn, already displaying an array of color on the tree-lined shore. The reflection of God's glorious handiwork in the glistening water caused her to hope that her life would reflect God's love to those around her.

Nathaniel walked up and stood beside her.

"'Tis beautiful," she said.

"Beautiful, indeed." But Nathaniel was not looking up the long winding river. His eyes were fixed on her.

Constance sighed, and tried not to blush. "This journey is much more pleasant than my first."

Nathaniel leaned against the rail. "Forget about Smout. He is long gone by now."

"A fine morn," said Jonathan as he sidled up to them. He made an impressive-looking ship's captain. Nathaniel's younger brother matched him in height and build, though his hair was not as dark and his eyes were a hazel brown.

Jonathan looked out into the deep blue river. "The Nayaugs called the Connecticut

River *Wahquinnacut*, meaning 'bear-of-a-long-river' or 'great river.'"

Constance turned to him. "Nayaugs?"

"Indians."

"Oh." She nibbled the corner of her lower lip. She had heard about the Indians in America and wondered if they were still a threat to the colonists.

Micajah joined them. "Do not fear, Miss Starling. We have a ship full of militiamen at your service."

"I am glad to hear it, Micah." The three brothers made a dashing trio. And she found that she much preferred the attentions of this troop of men to the stuffy aristocrats in London's ballrooms.

She looked around at the crowded deck, of men dressed in makeshift uniforms and ladies in fancy dress and children playing together. Mrs. Ingersoll and Lucy were chattering away on the opposite side of the ship. "Where is Alden?" she asked.

"I believe he's bending Dr. Hale's ear," Nathaniel said.

"He will make a fine doctor someday."

"With thanks to you for helping him master his Latin," Nathaniel said.

Constance pointed up the river. "Look, more ships!"

"Yes, all of Hartford County is convening for today's Fall Muster," Jonathan told her. "Our regiment alone includes Glassenbury, Westhersfield, Middletown, and Kensington Parish. We normally muster on the village green, except when the entire regiment is gathered. Traveling the river is the most expeditious way to get there."

Before long they had arrived in Hartford. Nathaniel took Constance by the hand and helped her down from the ship onto the quay. She looked around and sighed. Nathaniel gave her an acknowledging glance and squeezed her hand ever so gently before releasing it to join his regiment.

The morning passed quickly as the women visited with one another while preparing the noon meal. Girls played with their hoops and dolls, while boys of all ages held stick muskets and practiced formations of their own.

The sound of fife and drum announced the parade. The Sixth Regiment Connecticut Militia marched by, garbed in a variety of colors, many in their hunting garments. Muskets hung from their shoulders, along with their haversacks and powder horns. Despite the motley uniforms, they presented an impressive assembly.

The Ingersoll men marched in unison with their company, led by Colonel Thomas Welles, a Glassenbury shipbuilder.

Mrs. Ingersoll pressed her hand to her chest. "This is Alden's first year and possibly Phineas's last. It pleases me to see all the men I love assembled here and looking so valiant."

"Hmmm." Constance nodded absently, but she had eyes for only one soldier.

After a forenoon of drill and maneuvers, Nathaniel joined his brothers and uncle for a picnic with the family. They ate ham, poultry, squashes, beans, fruits, breads, puddings, and pies. New cider was served to all, as Mother would abide no rum.

The Hodges joined them under the shade of a large elm tree. Lucy sat jostling the baby in her lap, Lemuel beside her, being particularly attentive to both.

Mother looked at each of her sons and smiled. "You boys made a fine display on this important day. I am proud of all of you." Her eyes grew misty. "What is more, your father would have been proud to see his four sons ready to serve their country. We have much to be thankful for; we are living in times of peace. Yet it is good to know that we have such able bodies at the ready to protect us—my courageous young men." She smiled toward Mr. Hodge and Lemuel. "And that goes for the Hodge men, too. . .including that precious baby boy who will join these ranks someday."

As laughter filled the air, several colorful leaves floated onto the blanket, adding to the spirit of merriment. The spicy, sweet scents of cinnamon, nutmeg, cloves, and molasses tickled Nathaniel's senses as he lifted a piece of cake. "Thankful we are, as well, Mother. You outdid yourself with the muster gingerbread this year." He took a bite and licked his fingers.

His mother smiled and issued Constance a knowing grin. "You may send your compliment to Miss Starling."

Constance arched an eyebrow and smiled. A slow blush appeared on her face. "May I serve you another piece?"

"Please!" Nathaniel would eat gingerbread all day if it would make her happy.

After the meal the crowd gathered for artillery demonstrations, fistfights, footraces, marksmanship, and other competitions. Food booths and tents were set up, vending peanuts, cakes, and rum.

As the day wore on, Nathaniel hoped he would have a chance to talk to Constance about a matter of importance, though she seemed to have disappeared. She was probably chaperoning Lucy and Lemuel, as he noted the elder Hodges minding the sleeping baby.

Nathaniel wandered the green, and Jonathan caught up beside him. As they walked along they talked, joked, and discussed the recent news from Jonathan's copy of the *Connecticut Gazette*.

Jonathan held up the paper. "Listen to this headline, Nathaniel—'Ship's Carver Enamored of Indentured Servant.'"

Nathaniel grabbed the paper from his brother's clutches and whacked him on the shoulder. Jonathan took off running and Nathaniel pursued, playing a game of cat and mouse. The two finally stopped, huffing and puffing. Jonathan's laughter roared. Nathaniel leaned over, hands on his knees, trying to catch his breath.

Jonathan stood and patted Nathaniel on the back. "Truly, Nate, I have seen the way the two of you look at one another. What is holding you back?"

Nathaniel grunted and pulled on his queue. "It is complicated—too much so, although I may have a plan."

A flash of Constance's cheery yellow gown caught Nathaniel's attention. "I refuse to be a pawn in your game, Nathaniel Ingersoll. I am not one of your little toy soldiers." Constance marched off.

Bewildered, Nathaniel looked at Jonathan. "How does this happen? She always catches me unawares, and at the most inconvenient times."

Nathaniel went after her. She had found refuge back under the elm tree, rejoining the family. It was obvious that she refused to budge.

His mother looked up at him. "She is obviously upset, Nathaniel. Whatever you have to say may be stated in our presence."

"Very well, then." Nathaniel exhaled. "Constance, I only wish to release you from your indenture. I have an alternative arrangement that I would like to propose."

All gazes shot to Nathaniel faster than a lead musket ball and then ricocheted over to Constance. Then she whizzed off the blanket like a cannon on fire—straight into Jonathan's arms.

# Chapter 9

L et her go!" Nathaniel demanded.

Constance spun away from Jonathan, embarrassed that she had run to Nathaniel's brother for safe harbor.

"Nathaniel, calm down," Jonathan ordered, releasing Constance and stepping toward him.

Nathaniel pulled back his arm and plunged his fist into Jonathan's jaw. The men fell to the ground and rolled about furiously.

Constance cried out. "Nathaniel! Stop! Jonathan, no!"

Micajah and Lemuel appeared, seizing the brothers and pulling them to their feet.

Colonel Welles approached the scene. "I trust this diversion is all in good sport, men?"

"Yes sir," they said in unison.

"Very well, then. I would hate to have to put you in the stocks." The colonel turned to Constance. "What say you, Miss Starling?"

Constance glowered at Nathaniel for a moment. "Mayhap this one."

Colonel Welles arched his heavy eyebrow.

"'Tis tempting," Constance said. "But you may leave him to me."

The colonel issued a warning scowl and then dismissed himself from the incident.

"Let us leave Constance to her peace, Nathaniel. Jonathan," Micajah said.

"No. I mean, I should like to speak to Nathaniel now," Constance said.

"You are certain?" Jonathan asked.

"Yes. Thank you for your aid, gentlemen."

The troop marched away.

Nathaniel wiped the dirt and blood from his split lip with the back of his hand. Letting out a deep breath, he hung his head, his hair hanging loose. Then he glanced up with stormy eyes, waiting for her to speak.

Constance sighed. She took a few steps toward the nearby stone wall to hide her pending tears.

Nathaniel walked up behind her. "Constance, please," he said—his voice raspy yet seemingly sincere.

Constance turned and crossed her arms over her embroidered stomacher. "I will not abide an obligatory marriage. I refuse to take further charity—the union we already have is taxing enough. Besides, I am already betrothed."

Nathaniel worked his jaw. "To Jonathan?"

"Of course not!" *What was he thinking?*

"To whom then?" Nathaniel stood straighter. "I have not given my consent."

"If you must know, I have a previous arrangement to wed a Mr. Polsted in England. I am unavailable to be otherwise attached, and thus your consent is not required."

Despite her protest, Constance's heart plummeted. She refused to cry. She had already spent too many precious tears since coming to Connecticut.

Nathaniel's countenance stiffened. "Constance, please. I had only hoped that you would remain and work for wages."

Had she misunderstood? Her resolve threatened to crumble, but she stood fast. "I assume that is an expense you can hardly afford, since you are trying to build your future. I have already inconvenienced you enough, Mr. Ingersoll."

Nathaniel removed his cocked hat and held it contritely in front of him. "Please listen. Lucy and Lemuel are to be married. She will be leaving her position at the inn, and Mother would like to hire you in her stead."

"She need not hire me—I am already her servant."

"If you accept this, it will relieve me of the expense, and it should be a great relief for you as well."

"What of the freedom taxes you must pay?" Constance asked.

"I will manage in due time," he said.

Constance tucked some errant strands of hair under her cap and straightened her hat. "I will continue to work to repay the expense I have already caused your mother, and you."

Nathaniel shook his head. "You confound me, Constance."

"It is simple, really. Did you not know? Your Uncle Phineas has offered to hire me on my day off to do some chores and grind some pigments for the paint at the carving shop. I refuse to be an expense to your mother, even if that means continuing to be a burden to you."

❧

A new week had begun. Nathaniel stumbled out of the back room into the loft, tucking his shirt into his breeches.

"Good gracious, you look like a shipwreck," Uncle Phin growled.

Nathaniel grunted.

"Your mother sent you some leavings of ham and biscuits from this morning's breakfast. There is hot coffee on the woodstove." Uncle often started the stove to take off the morning chill, even in the summer, despite how warm the loft became by the heat of the afternoon.

"Thank you." Nathaniel took his apron from a hook on the wall and wrapped it around his waist then poured a mug of coffee. Uncle Phineas seemed to eye his every move.

"When are you going to start sleeping at home in the comfort of your own bed? You would be better rested and ready for work in the morn." Uncle Phineas gathered up some tools and placed them by the grindstone. "That being said, I should like to have a word with you."

Nathaniel turned to grab a trencher of food and muttered under his breath. Uncle Phin may have been up since before dawn this Monday morn, but Nathaniel's day had just begun. He glanced at the small clock on a shelf. Half past seven—no wonder Uncle was champing at the bit.

A gouge clattered to the floor at Uncle Phin's feet, and he stopped peddling the small machine. "This grindstone is losing its power," he grumbled. But Nathaniel knew that Uncle Phineas had difficulty with the repetitive motion required to keep the grindstone turning. He had also noticed, for some time, that his uncle had been having increased difficulty holding the small-handled instruments with his arthritic hands.

Nathaniel picked up the tool and set it back on the workbench. "I will sharpen those later. I would like you to review the plans for the new figurehead with me, if you have a mind to." Hopefully that would distract Uncle Phin and help him to feel useful at another task.

"Indeed. Show me your diagram," the master carver said.

Nathaniel spread out the sheet of foolscap. His illustration depicted an image of a woman in a flowing gown, poised confidently under a bowsprit. "I plan to do scrollwork on the trail boards as her base, extending the design upwards toward the lower portion of the drapery of the gown. I have already calculated the angles."

Uncle Phineas rubbed his chin. "I inspected the form you have begun to shape. That is a fine section of timber you chose—methinks you will do fine with the one piece and not have to add to it. Let us hope he has not changed his mind and decided on a lion or a dragon." Uncle Phin flattened his lips.

Nathaniel slowly shook his head. "Oh no. The contract stated a woman, and a woman he shall get."

"If you are going to inherit this business someday, you shall have to learn to please your customers."

"That I shall. Yet I will be clear on the elements of my work beforehand, as you are. In return for a man's cooperation and funding, I will grant him a satisfactory and expedient product."

Uncle Phineas laughed and patted him on the shoulder. "That is what I wanted to hear."

Nathaniel squinted. "Did I hear you correctly concerning your plans for this business?"

"Indeed, you did." Uncle Phin looked Nathaniel square in the eye. "I cannot do this type of work forever. You have worked diligently with me over the past nine years, first as an apprentice and now as a journeyman. I would be pleased to pass this shop on to you, in due time. There is only one thing lacking."

Nathaniel listened intently, his heart filling with excitement. How long he had waited for this moment. Hoped. Prayed. Worked.

"You are ready to create your masterpiece, as I did, so that you can be recognized as a master ship's carver."

"Uncle Phin. I do not know what to say."

"Say you will."

"I will!" Nathaniel beamed with exuberance.

Uncle Phineas tapped his nubby finger on the diagram. "This will be your master-piece, nephew."

Nathaniel smiled and shook his uncle's hand. "I will do my best to please you."

"That, you already do, Nathaniel," Uncle Phineas said. "You made a fine show with the regiment at the muster."

"What of my poor behavior? I fear I failed you all, once more."

" 'Twas your own pride that altered the latter part of the day."

Nathaniel rubbed his aching shoulder and wondered if his brother had been injured, though Jonathan had said nothing on Sunday. In fact, they spoke little to one another yesterday, and he was thankful that Mother had been distracted enough by her guests not to notice. Though, mayhap she did.

Nathaniel looked out the window toward the river. "I should go apologize to Jonathan."

"You will have to wait on that. He set sail on the *Rivier Handelaar* at dawn." Then a twinkle appeared in Uncle Phineas's gray eyes. "I remember what it was like to be young and in love."

Nathaniel grinned. "Uncle Phin, you never mentioned that before."

"It is a thing of the past. I lost my chance at love because of my own pride. Beware of that. 'Tis the only reason that I mention it."

Nathaniel looked down at his scuffed leather shoes and kicked some wood shavings on the floor.

"No need to be so downcast. You might still have time to redeem yourself with Miss Starling."

Uncle Phin headed for the stairs. Then he turned back. "Clean yourself up. Captain Cyprian Andruss is coming by to discuss the figurehead he commissioned. I shall be here with him this afternoon."

᳐

Nathaniel looked up from his carving to see Uncle Phineas, accompanied by the ostentatious captain attired in a maroon suit trimmed in ruffles and lace. The captain removed his fancy three-cornered hat and perched it under his arm.

"Good day, sirs." Nathaniel brushed off his apron and walked over to greet them.

"Captain Cyprian Andruss, as you recall. My nephew, journeyman carver Nathaniel Ingersoll. He will carve the figurehead and nameboard for your new barque. We have a fine piece of oak selected for you."

"Capital! I have seen some of your handiwork, young man, and admire your talent." The stout gentleman eyed Uncle Phineas. "Cushing, you will be overseeing the project, I presume."

"I oversee all work at my shop, but I have every confidence that Nathaniel's work will exceed your expectations."

Captain Andruss surveyed Nathaniel stem to stern. "Very well, then. Now, what have ye in mind?"

Nathaniel brought out his sketches and showed the wealthy merchant the preliminary drawings, which were received with all manner of "mmms" and "ahhhs."

Then Captain Andruss wandered toward a window, looked out on the water, and mused aloud. "I see it now. . .a beautiful maiden facing the sea, embracing all obstacles, surviving all storms, calming the seas—"

The captain turned as Constance appeared at the top of the stairs. She stepped into a stream of light from one of the windows, which encompassed her in a heavenly glow.

"It is she!" Captain Andruss approached Constance. He walked around her, inspecting her, as if she were the finished product itself. "Have you ever seen such beauty?"

"Certainly not, sir. She cannot. I am sure we can find another model." Nathaniel had not expected that his pledge regarding how to deal with customers would be so soon put to the test, though he feared that this supercilious gentleman was accustomed to getting his own way.

"Surely this young lady is of unmatched beauty. Do you not agree?"

Nathaniel cast Constance a furtive glance. "Yes. . ."

"Then it is settled. The figurehead will be carved in her image."

❧

Constance's confused gaze darted from Nathaniel to Mr. Cushing and back again to the captain. She could not escape the feeling of another impending abduction. "I beg your pardon, sir, I should like to be consulted in this matter."

"Forgive my exuberance, young lady. Captain Cyprian Andruss, at your service." The man took her hand in his and kissed it almost humbly. "I only mean to borrow your likeness, miss. 'Tis too sweet not to share with the world. And what is your name, dear?"

"Constance. Constance Starling."

The captain threw his hands into the air and offered a broad smile. "What providence! My ship is named the *Constant*."

"It is?" Mr. Cushing asked. "I thought your new vessel was yet to be named."

"It is named now!" Captain Andruss turned to Nathaniel. "I hope you will carve the sign and gild the letters, as is fitting. Now, let us settle this issue at once." He clasped his hands behind his back and widened his stance, ready to issue his orders.

The captain continued with the ruminations that Constance had overheard when she had ascended into the loft. "Her hair is blowing in the wind, her eyes looking toward the future, with flowing hair and fair bosom."

*Not that!* Constance had seen figureheads before with women partially clad above the waist. If he was implying—she drew her arms over her chest, pressing her palm against the muslin modesty piece tucked into her bodice. Her eyes darted toward Nathaniel, and he seemed to sense her discomfiture as she nibbled her lower lip.

Nathaniel planted his hands on his hips. "Captain, if I may be so bold. Miss Starling is a lady."

Captain Andruss's face turned crimson. "Oh, I did not mean. . ." He let out a nervous chuckle. "Miss Starling, I simply would like the honor of having Mr. Ingersoll carve your beautiful face and form into the figurehead for my new ship. When I set ashore in England, one and all will be in awe of the angelic sentry at my helm." He addressed Nathaniel and Mr. Cushing, to gain their support. "It could be good business, gentlemen."

Mr. Cushing looked at Constance. "It is up to you, my dear."

Constance contemplated the captain's words. "England?"

"Why yes, miss. I will return there before I embark on my voyage to the West Indies."

Constance tilted her chin. "Then I would like you to consider my plight, and mayhap we can come to some terms."

"You have my attention," Captain Andruss said.

"A short time ago I was taken from my home in England aboard the *Fortuna* and forced into indentured servitude here in America. I have been under the protection of Mr. Ingersoll and serving his family. Yet, he has recently offered to release me from my contract." She glanced toward Nathaniel for affirmation that his offer held true, but he remained silent, his gaze intent. "Moreover, I have no means to obtain a passage back to England. Although Mr. Cushing has been kind enough to offer me additional employment—and thus my visit here today—I am certain that a ship's passage is well beyond my means in the foreseeable future. If Mr. Ingersoll will still consent to release me"—her eyes flitted toward Nathaniel—"I would like to barter with you, Captain Andruss. You may use my image for your figurehead if you will pay my freedom taxes and provide me with a safe and comfortable passage to England."

"Then it is agreed. Mr. Ingersoll will release you from your indenture and I will pay all necessary fees. It will further be my pleasure to provide your passage back to England."

Constance smiled and sighed great relief. "Thank you, Captain Andruss." Her eyes moistened. She was going back to her former existence—and away from Nathaniel.

# Chapter 10

Constance regarded the massive piece of timber which hung at an angle from a large beam with the aid of a heavy chain and pulley. Roughly hewn, she could neither imagine it as a tree nor as a ship's ornament, much less one that would look like her.

She had come early so that she could tend to some chores, but Mr. Cushing told her that was no longer necessary. He had hired a boy since she now had another occupation as the model for the figurehead. He had forgotten that she would be coming, however, and had made an appointment with another customer.

"I will be back momentarily." The old ship carver grabbed his coat and hurried off.

As Nathaniel approached, Constance felt a fluttering sensation in her chest. How could someone in a faded linsey-woolsey waistcoat look so handsome? His light blue eyes contrasted with his dark brown hair, and she had to resist the urge to remove the small wood shaving that was stuck there.

"Since you have come, why not stay and we can get started?" he asked.

Constance glanced down at her unkempt short gown and worn petticoat. "I am not properly attired."

Nathaniel grinned. "It matters not. At this stage I only need to do some preliminary sketches and make some markings."

Constance assessed the wood. "It is very large."

"Yes, she is over six feet tall, though some are even larger, depending on the size of the ship. That is why it is important to draft the correct proportions." His eyes crinkled. "You will stay?"

"Yes, I shall."

Nathaniel stacked several crates in a steplike fashion. "Would you please climb up here? I would like to have you pose in the proper position."

Nathaniel offered her his hand, assisting her as she climbed upon the platform he had assembled. His strong, warm grip sent a startling sensation up her arm. "Please stand on this crate and take a right step up onto the next crate. Do you have your balance?"

"Yes."

He continued to hold her hand and with careful steps moved around and faced her. "Now your other hand, please. I am going to step backward and pull you toward me at the proper angle. Is that all right?"

Her eyes widened. "Will I fall?"

Nathaniel chuckled. "Not at all, and if you should, I will catch you."

"Are you sure?" Constance asked.

"Do you not trust me?"

51

"Yes, Nathaniel Ingersoll, I trust you with my life."

"That is good to know." Nathaniel grinned. "Ready?"

Constance nodded. Nathaniel gently drew her arms back, causing her to lean slightly forward.

"Now, you may drop your hands to your sides."

Nathaniel stepped back to assess the results. He stepped closer again, and as if it were a tool, he held his outstretched finger at the base of her neck and gently guided it to an upward tilt. And he did not even ask—nor did she mind.

He walked away and sat down on a stool and began to sketch, glancing up at her intermittently. A few times he got up and went to the timber and made some markings, returning again to complete his sketches. Constance admired the passion he seemed to have for his craft.

Nathaniel returned to her platform. "You may relax now. I hope that was not too uncomfortable." He took her by the hand once more. "Here. Let me help you down."

Constance stepped down from the upper crate to the main platform and turned, finding herself face-to-face with Nathaniel. His gaze would not let her go.

"Constance," he whispered. He took a slow, deep breath and swallowed.

Her breaths were shallow and mingled with his as he leaned toward her. He traced her neck and the curve of her jaw with his featherlight touch. His eyes never left hers. . .until he backed away. "Forgive me, I believe you are already spoken for."

*Several awkward weeks passed by, and Constance rarely caught sight of Nathaniel. He worked the span of daylight, and if he did come home to eat or sleep, somehow he managed to avoid her, save briefly passing and seldom uttering a word. Constance worried that he was working too hard and prayed for him to remain well and able. Would the carving be done soon?*

When might she find the opportunity to tell him that she really was not betrothed? She had refused to marry William Polsted, her uncle's insidious business partner, despite the cad's threats and insistence that they had a binding agreement. If not for Nathaniel's strange behavior on Muster Day, she might never have even mentioned it, yet it was the only weapon within her reach. *Father in heaven, I beseech Thee, please grant us all the freedom only You can provide and help us to follow Your will. Amen.*

One afternoon, after delivering a basket of food, Lucy returned from the carving shop with a message from Nathaniel. He requested that Constance come to the loft so she could pose for the carving. Might this be an opportunity to set things right? "Will there be a chaperone, Lucy?"

"You are needing a chaperone now, aye?" Lucy giggled. "Be not concerned. Methinks Mr. Cushing's new boy is there."

When Constance arrived, a boy passed her on the stairs and announced that he was on his way to chop some wood. What could she do? Nathaniel was expecting her.

As she stepped into the loft, she beheld the figurehead and went near. The sculpture had an elaborate scrollwork base and precise detail to every flowing curve and niche. The beauty of the figure that emerged from the bulk of ordinary wood nearly made her cry.

Nathaniel stood at a workbench honing a curved gouge. As he looked down at the tool, the sound of Constance's sighs rose above the sound of the friction. He angled his head and peered at the demure Miss Starling as she inspected the hanging figurehead.

Constance's eyes met his, and if he was not mistaken, she blinked back tears. But why? He was trying to give her the respect she deserved and would not let his feelings for her complicate her life further.

"What is your impression?" he asked.

"It is difficult to compliment something that is in the likeness of one's self."

"Then compliment the craftsman," Nathaniel said with a wink.

Her pretty brown eyes glistened. "It is wonderful."

Nathaniel dipped his chin and eyed her earnestly. "Truly?"

Constance looked back at the sculpture and then again toward him. She placed her index finger on her chin. "One thing seems to be lacking."

Nathaniel chuckled. "You mean the face?"

"Yes." She patted her cheeks and smiled. "It seems that if I have one, this effigy must as well."

"The very reason I asked you here today." He set his honing strap down and stepped toward her, tool in hand. "Now that I have carved the drapery of the gown, I need to study your hands, your face, and hair."

He carefully removed her cap and arranged her hair over her shoulders, the silky locks slipping through his fingers. She smelled of autumn flowers and spices.

And just as the shape of a beautiful lady emerged as he released the figurehead's shape from its prison, he hoped with all that was within him that he could find a way to draw from Constance the love he knew she had inside for him.

"Are you to sketch me again?" she asked softly.

"Yea, though first there is something between us that must be reconciled. You need to know that the burden I carry concerning you weighs upon me greatly. . . ."

"This you have said."

"But there is more."

Constance and Nathaniel turned to the sound of someone running up the steps. Alden burst into the loft trying to catch his breath. "Uncle Phineas sent me for you. There is a visitor at the inn, and he says it is of utmost importance." His eyes widened. "It is the magistrate. He says it concerns Constance and Captain Smout."

The trio hurried out and boarded the wagon that Alden had driven to Log Landing and traveled in haste to the Red Griffin.

Mrs. Ingersoll greeted them with a knowing smile and ushered them into the parlor. The white-wigged magistrate sat at the table with Mr. Cushing, who promptly stood and made introductions. "The Honorable Judge Wiggins, Miss Starling. And my nephew, Nathaniel Ingersoll."

Constance greeted the magistrate with a curtsy, mortified to have left her cap at the loft. "Do sit. We have good tidings," the magistrate said.

The impressive gentleman continued. "I have consulted with Judge Pitkin of the

Supreme Court at Hartford regarding the matter concerning your indenture. . .your abduction, rather."

Constance's heart leaped at the acknowledgment of the terrible injustice that had befallen her. Yet now she could hardly believe her good fortune—God's providence. Her eyes roamed about the room, meeting many heartfelt expressions. Nathaniel nodded and offered a taut smile.

"Captain Magnus Smout of the *Fortuna* has been jailed for kidnapping and awaits sentencing," Mr. Cushing interjected.

"You see, when Mr. Cushing requested an investigation of your situation, we learned that several others had also petitioned the courts with a similar complaint," Judge Wiggins continued. "Captain Smout had also sold the indenture of other passengers against their wills at locations along the Connecticut coast and up the Connecticut River."

"I know there were other passengers aboard the ship, but I was kept in a secluded cabin. I never knew what became of them." Constance winced with concern. "Will they be freed as well?"

The judge clasped his hands on the table. "Yes, they shall. But there is something else."

Mrs. Ingersoll reached for Constance's hand, trembling in her lap. "What is it, sir?" Constance inquired.

"Captain Smout confessed that an unsavory gentleman named William Polsted was his accomplice, the mastermind behind your abduction. He claimed that Polsted sent you away when you refused to marry him, with the intent of appropriating Chauncey Starling's unresolved assets. Apparently your uncle's estate is of greater worth than you may have been led to believe. Word has already been sent to London for Polsted's arrest and imprisonment at Newgate."

Mrs. Ingersoll squeezed Constance's hand. "Praise be the Lord."

Constance sighed. "Indeed." It was all so much to take in. But at last she was free.
*Free.*

The figurehead for the *Constant* was nearing completion. Once it was painted and mounted on the ship, she would sail for England. Tears flooded Constance's eyes. She could hardly bear the thought of leaving those she had grown to love and serve with joy, yet she knew she had to reclaim her life. And by virtue of Nathaniel's lack of encouragement in the matter, she knew that, sadly, it did not include him.

❧

Nathaniel anxiously watched Uncle Phineas inspect the finished figurehead mounted proudly under the bowsprit of the *Constant* and awaited his verdict.

Uncle Phineas grabbed Nathaniel by the shoulders and gave him a broad smile. "You have done a remarkable job, Nathaniel. 'Tis a masterpiece indeed!"

Nathaniel returned the manly embrace, latching on to his uncle's forearms. His heart soared. "Thank you, Uncle Phineas. I learned from the best."

"You make a fine master ship's carver."

Nathaniel exhaled and donned a great smile.

"I would like to congratulate you by offering you to partner with me in my business." Uncle Phin turned and pointed.

Nathaniel's mouth dropped open. Nailed across the carving shop was a new sign—CUSHING & INGERSOLL SHIP CARVING. "I am deeply honored, Uncle Phin."

The men shook hands, and then Uncle stuffed his hand into his coat pocket. "And I have a little something else for you." He winked.

Nathaniel accepted the silver flask that had belonged to his father and swallowed hard. "Thank you, sir."

"I trust you will take good care of that now, nephew." Uncle Phineas slapped him on the back. "Come along, your mother has a fine dinner cooking in the hearth."

As the pair walked out of the shipyard, Nathaniel looked back at the figurehead—a vision of loveliness, so like Constance. Though no longer betrothed, she would soon be gone. But her image would be forever ingrained in his mind and on his heart. If only she had room in her heart for him. He glanced at Uncle Phineas, limping along beside him, and wondered what his uncle's life would have been like had he given love a chance. Was it already too late for Nathaniel?

🐝

Wrapped in her cloak, Constance stood on the quayside on the chilly October morn, as mist rose from the river. Soon she would board the *Constant*—reminding her that God was her only constant in this world—but once she embarked Captain Andruss's ship, her life would change forever. England was an ocean away and so, too, her dreams would be.

She had said good-bye to Lucy last night and rejoiced with her that her wedding banns had been read. Lucy would soon be married, with a family of her own. Yet, parting from the Ingersolls was so hard that Constance could hardly bring herself to say farewell, except by means of a letter.

Constance faced the three-masted barque, admiring the intricate workmanship mounted on the prow. The brightly painted figurehead, fashioned in her likeness, was an image of a brave and free woman—just as she had become. A thought dawned—that not only was she free to leave Glassenbury, but she also was free to remain. And why not? Mayhap the Lord had brought her here to stay. Why she had not considered this until now she knew not, though the very realization of what the Lord had wrought in her life by allowing her to come here inspired new hope in her heart. Might that she would, she could freely offer her love to Nathaniel, if only he would accept it.

Autumn leaves rustled on the wharf, and the sound of rapid footsteps drew near.

"Constance! You are still here."

'Twas the sound of Nathaniel's voice. He attempted to catch his breath; his hair hung loose; and stubble darkened his jaw. "What think thee of the figurehead?"

"It is sublime," she said, her smile demure. "Magnificent, in fact."

"Thank you, good lady."

"How did you complete it? You never called me back to finish your drawings."

"Constance, my dear, I believe I have every lovely detail about you etched upon my heart."

"'Tis kind of you to say."

"'Tis my masterpiece—you were my inspiration. What shall I do if you go?"

"You said I am a burden."

"You are God's masterpiece and no burden to me. All that I carry is the love I have for you, waxing brighter even now, deep within my heart." Nathaniel moved closer. "I am confident that God had a special plan in bringing us together. Miss Constance Starling, I ask you not to leave but to stay and become my beloved wife."

Tears of joy streamed down Constance's face. "Oh, Nathaniel. I love you and could never leave you."

As the sun began to rise, light filtered through the trees, casting its glow upon the river. Nathaniel took Constance's hands, drawing her into an embrace. Woodsmoke lingered on his garments, and she could feel the warmth of his body. He kissed her neck and buried his head in her unplaited locks, whispering, "I have always loved you, Constance. And I always shall. Come home with me, and together we will carve a future."

# MUSTER DAY GINGERBREAD

The following recipe is taken from *The Art of Cookery made plain and easy* by a Lady, 1747 (Hannah Glasse was discovered to be the authoress in the 19th century).

*To make Ginger-Bread.* Take three quarts of fine flour, two ounces of beaten ginger, a quarter of an ounce of nutmeg, cloves, and mace beat fine, but most of the last; mix all together, three quarters of a pound of fine sugar, two pounds of treacle, set it over the fire, but do not let it boil; three quarters of a pound of butter melted in the treacle, and some candied lemon and orange peel cut fine; mix all these together well. An hour will bake it in a quick oven.

## MUSTER GINGERBREAD
(A modern version for you to try.)

⅓ cup shortening
½ cup brown sugar
½ cup molasses
1 egg
2 cups flour
1 teaspoon baking soda
¾ teaspoon ground ginger
¾ teaspoon ground cinnamon
¼ teaspoon ground cloves
¼ teaspoon salt
½ cup water, boiling

Cream shortening and sugar until very light. Add molasses and egg, beating well. In a separate bowl, stir together flour, soda, spices, and salt. Add to creamed mixture alternately with boiling water, beating after each addition. Bake in a greased 8 x 4 x 2-inch loaf pan at 350° for about 50 minutes. Cool a few minutes before removing from the pan, and wrap. This cake mellows and tastes best the next day.

Author's note: The treacle mentioned in the first receipt, as recipes were then called, is molasses. Muster Day gingerbread, sometimes called Training Day gingerbread or simply muster gingerbread, was usually prepared as a loaf cake. I discovered a variation of this recipe that was rolled out and baked as a cookie.

Muster gingerbread was traditionally washed down with rum after militia training, though I recommend a nice glass of apple cider or fresh milk.

New Englander **Carla Olson Gade** writes from her home amidst the rustic landscapes of Maine. With eight books in print she enjoys bringing her tales to life with historically authentic settings and characters. An avid reader, amateur genealogist, photographer, and house plan hobbyist, Carla's great love (next to her family) is historical research. Though you might find her tromping around an abandoned homestead, an old fort, or interviewing a docent at an historical museum, it's easier to connect with her online at carlaolsongade.com.

# TRADING HEARTS

by Amber Stockton

# Dedication

To my husband, for willingly assuming the *Mr. Mom* role so I can meet my deadlines. To my readers, for your support which enables me to continue doing what I love.

# Chapter 1

*Connecticut River Valley*
*October 1754*

I believe this is the last of what you requested, Mr. Yancey."

Jonathan Ingersoll set the final crate in the back of the shopkeeper's cart, nodding to two of his crew to return to the ship. He thanked the good Lord for this substantial order to go with the other orders he'd filled today. It would tide him over during the coming winter months when the frozen river made his normal trade route impassable. Trade hadn't come easy lately. He turned to face Yancey only to see the man had moved to the side of the cart.

"Hmm," the shopkeeper replied, sounding distracted.

"Is there something amiss, sir?" Jonathan knew the order was accurate. He'd double-checked and verified it himself. But the man's wrinkled brow and pursed lips made him second guess his careful calculations.

"No, no," the man finally said. "Everything is in order." He held up a pouch cinched closed with a cord and dropped it into Jonathan's hand, the coins inside clinking against each other. "You are a good man and an honest trader, like your father before you." Covering Jonathan's hand—coin pouch and all—with his own, Yancey gave a nod. "I am certain you still feel the loss of such an honorable man. But it is a pleasure to continue doing business with your family."

"The pleasure is mine as well, Mr. Yancey." Jonathan withdrew his hand and turned toward the wharf. His father had taught him everything he knew. How could he not honor him by continuing in his trade? No time for melancholy thoughts though. He had a schedule to keep, and the tide waited for no one. "I shall return after the spring thaw," he said.

"Headed back up to Glassenbury?"

Jonathan looked over his shoulder. "Yes, I am."

"Keep a watchful eye on the water levels up that way," the shopkeeper said. "The shoreline, as well, where the river narrows." He grabbed hold of the horse's reins and turned the cart toward town. "We have had some unseasonably heavy rains of late, and there have been reports of swollen riverbanks."

"It will remain uppermost in my mind," Jonathan replied, tucking the coin pouch into the leather satchel at his hip. "I shall instruct my first mate and crew likewise. You have my gratitude."

Without any further word, he and the shopkeeper parted ways. Jonathan made haste down the path to the river's edge, where some of his crew waited. As the seaman rowed the launch toward the ship, the *Rivier Handelaar*, Jonathan stared at his awe-inspiring vessel. His crew was among the best to be found. They worked in rhythm as well as the ebb and flow of the daily tides. And his ship stood like a beacon in port, beckoning to all who gazed upon it. From the red griffin figurehead at the stem that Uncle Phineas had carved, all the way to the stern, every mast, sail, deck, and hatch gleamed to perfection. It told all who beheld the Dutch *fluyt*, this belonged to a successful merchant tradesman. That man was once his father. Now it was Jonathan, and he intended to do everything within his power to continue the notable legacy.

After accepting the hand of his boatswain as he crested the rail, Jonathan made his way to the upper deck.

"What is our next destination, Captain?" his second mate asked, ready to give the orders to again set sail.

Yancey's words rang foremost in Jonathan's mind as he looked upriver. Once again, the steady droplets of rain fell. The gray clouds and precipitation had been a constant companion for several weeks. For a brief moment, Jonathan considered making port right there in Saybrook. But he might as well push as far north as possible.

"Let us press on toward Selden." Jonathan pointed to the mark on the map his second mate held splayed out in front of him. "We have several deliveries there," he said, tapping the dot, "and lightening our load will undoubtedly be a benefit to us as we enter into the swollen waters farther north."

Shouts rang out, commands floated on the air, and all crew on deck scrambled to heed the orders. Every man knew his duty and did it without complaint. In fact, they seemed to thrill to the task. Yet another reason to thank the Almighty Lord for the favor granted to him and his ship. The sails caught the damp, chilly breeze, and the ship made its first jerk as it headed for the mouth of the Great River.

Two hours later, with their most recent round of deliveries made and customers satisfied, the ship continued on its way toward Glassenbury. Each mile brought Jonathan closer to home. He could almost smell the fresh bread his brother Micah baked, and the aroma of his mother's onion pie tantalized his taste buds even without the actual presence of the fare. No matter how long he was away from the Red Griffin Inn, or how often he had to travel his trade route, the welcoming warmth of home called to him and made each journey that much more satisfying. Only two more stops this day before he could genuinely give the orders to make way toward their home port.

"Captain," his second mate called. "You might want to come have a look at this."

Jonathan made haste to the bow, his trained eyes taking in the scene before them. Yancey had made no mistake in his warning to take heed of rising waters. They were less than a thousand yards from the next village, and what he saw ahead signaled significant danger. He knew the shoreline of the Great River in this segment like he knew his own ship, and it was much wider than normal. To the left and right, where familiar trees usually stood sentinel over the banks, the murky water now encased their trunks, hiding the tall grasses from view.

Howling wind whistled through the branches and across the deck. Darkness descended on them in an instant, and the ship was tossed against the choppy water. His crew scrambled on deck, holding tight to the rigging and adjusting the sails in an attempt to maintain control. A jolt nearly threw Jonathan off balance.

Oh no! They had scraped the shallow river bottom. He mentally judged the distance to the shore. They were too close. Another jolt and another scrape. He had to do something fast, or they *would* run ashore. There was no way they could fight the current and remain in the center of the river.

"Chambers!" he hollered above the ominous winds.

The first mate rushed to Jonathan's side, slipping on the soaked deck and righting himself. "Yes, Captain?"

"We need to make port now. The winds are too strong, and the tide is hurling the ship to and fro. We cannot risk pressing through this." Jonathan looked off to the right, where the flickering lanterns in front of what appeared to be a quaint inn fairly beckoned to him. "There," he said, pointing toward the faint outline of the building. "We will anchor the ship and take refuge at that inn."

"Right away, Captain." Chambers saluted and barked out the orders to the crew.

Twenty minutes later, soaked to the skin and fighting against the blustering winds to maintain his footing, Jonathan and a third of his twenty-seven crew members approached the front of the inn. It might not be the Red Griffin—his home—but with its whitewashed front and painted black shutters, at least it appeared clean. He shivered. At this point, anything offering a blazing fire would be a welcome sight.

Lifting the brass knocker, Jonathan gave the door three swift raps. A moment later it opened, and a petite yet sturdy maiden greeted them with a warm smile that traveled from her delicately bow-shaped lips to her shining gray eyes. With her ruffled cap slightly askew and several tendrils of wheat-colored hair escaping the confines of her single braid, she looked a great deal younger than what he presumed her age to be. The aromas of beef, baked ham, and what smelled like onion pie assailed his nostrils. His stomach rumbled in response, earning a charming giggle from the maiden before him.

Sweeping off his hat and tucking it beneath his arm, Jonathan bowed. "Good evening, miss. My name is Captain Jonathan Ingersoll, and I command the *Rivier Handelaar*. The flooded river has forced us to lay anchor about two hundred yards south, and this dismal rain has us all soaked through. My crew and I would be in your debt for a hot meal, if you have it to spare."

The young girl curtsied and swung the door open wider, gesturing with her arm in a sweeping motion toward the main room of the inn. "Do come in, Captain Ingersoll. My name is Clara Marie Preston. My father is the proprietor. Welcome to the Higganum River Inn."

Jonathan stepped aside and allowed the first wave of his crew to precede him. He glanced over their heads into the main room. They weren't the only ones to whom this inn had beckoned in this dreary weather. His men would have to eat in shifts and most would likely have to sleep in the hammocks below deck.

"I invite you to choose your tables from those available," Miss Preston said once they were all inside, "and I will notify my father of your arrival."

Jonathan touched the cuff of the maiden's sleeve, and she paused midturn.

"Did you need something more, Captain?"

"Is that perhaps onion pie that I smell?"

"Yes." Miss Preston smiled. "I baked it myself this afternoon."

As the maiden walked away, a grin came to Jonathan's face. Based upon how the skirts of the simple dress fell around Miss Preston's feminine curves, he'd been fairly close to the mark in his conjecture on her having attained at least ten and seven years. And she could bake the very pie he considered to be his mother's best dish. This meal just might be the next best thing to eating at the Red Griffin.

Taking a seat at the nearest table, he allowed his gaze to roam the room. So much of the decor reminded him of the Red Griffin. Well-scrubbed floors were dotted with bright rugs. The furnishings showed obvious signs of wear, but they appeared to be of good quality and well cared for. Flickering flames from the chandeliers hung from the beams above cast an ethereal glow about the room. The teasing aroma of that baking ham hung in the air. A scent like that would entice every weary traveler within ten miles to seek lodging at this establishment. If they had to be forced ashore earlier than planned, at least the resulting destination was one possessing a great deal of appeal. . .in more ways than one.

🐝

Clara peered out from behind the swinging door leading from the hallway to the main room, her eyes scanning the occupied tables. When her gaze landed on the handsome captain, her breath caught in her throat. He certainly cut a dashing figure, from the polished black boots and fawn-colored breeches that hugged his long, muscular legs, to the broad shoulders encased in a fitted, navy overcoat, every button fastened and gleaming. That brought her to his face, where the rain-glistened brown hair was tied back in a queue, and high cheekbones gave way to warm, hazel eyes that had caught her attention the moment she opened the door. Well, that, and the rather loud rumble emanating from the captain as soon as he smelled the food cooking.

He sat at a table at the far edge of the room, leaning back in his chair with a nonchalant air, taking in the room with measured observations. Clara self-consciously smoothed her hands down the front of her apron and reached up to check her wayward tendrils. A whoosh of air escaped her lips as she felt the loose strands of hair around her ears and cheeks. She must appear a sight, for certain. Tucking as much as she could back into her braid, she then inhaled and slowly released her breath.

"Clara." Her mother's voice sounded from behind, making Clara straighten. "Have you discovered the number of gentlemen accompanying the captain for the evening meal, and what meat they would prefer?"

"No, Mama," she called over her shoulder. "I am on my way right now."

"Very good, my dear. Our guests need our attention. We do not have time to dawdle. Please also determine how many will be requiring a bed for the night. I am certain we cannot provide rooms for them all, but we shall do our best."

With another deep breath, Clara pushed through the swinging door and headed straight for the captain. As her eyes met his, a congenial smile formed on his lips. Had she imagined it, or did he immediately look her way the moment she stepped into the room? The way he watched her as she approached certainly made that reality a possibility. He seemed very aware of her every move, and Clara couldn't decide if that excited or unnerved her.

When she stood just a few feet from his table, Captain Ingersoll greeted her with a nod. "Miss Preston."

Clara bobbed a quick curtsy. "Captain Ingersoll." She folded her hands in her apron and shifted from one foot to the other. "Mama has asked that I inquire after the meal choices of your crew and how many might require a bed for the night."

The captain leaned back in his chair and smoothed his thumb and ring finger down the sides of his mouth. "Ah yes. I suppose it would be helpful if we told you what we would like to eat, for I am certain you cannot divine our thoughts."

The mirth in his eyes and the teasing slant of his lips drew out an answering grin from Clara. My, but he was charming. And if she didn't miss her mark, he knew it as well. Quite a dangerous combination but appealing nonetheless.

"Well, do allow me to set your mind at ease. My men will take a healthy serving of whatever you have readily available or in abundance. And only six or seven of them will be sleeping here tonight. The rest of us will bunk down on board the ship."

The rest of *us*? Clara's shoulders fell. Did that mean he wouldn't be staying at their inn? She had hoped to see him for longer than the evening meal. It didn't appear as if that would happen though.

"After all, I cannot leave my goods and merchandise unattended, especially in this weather. Who knows what unsavory sorts are lurking about the river, waiting for the opportune moment to strike."

Merchandise? Goods? "Oh! Are you a merchant trader?" she asked.

"As a matter of fact, I am. Just like my father before me."

Her brother, Samuel, was a trader, too. Before his accident, anyway. But he was in town tonight. And considering his attitude of late, perhaps that was a good thing. Then again, maybe it would benefit him to talk with Captain Ingersoll. Perhaps the captain could help.

"Clara!"

Clara turned to see her mother standing in the doorway, an expectant look in her eyes and a stern expression on her lips. Oh! She'd done it again. She must see to the matter at hand. They had a room filled with waiting guests.

"Coming, Mama!" she called in return, pivoting on her heel.

"Miss Preston?" the captain beckoned softly. She again looked in his direction. "Do forgive me for keeping you from your duties. Please," he said, gesturing vaguely toward the expanse of the room, "see to your other guests. I am certain to be here for quite a spell and intend to make good use of your inviting fire."

She nodded, unable to voice a reply. That last statement filled her with such delight. And she was impressed by the captain's need to apologize, even though he had done nothing wrong. She could easily while away the hours enjoying his company. Oh how she prayed the evening would last far longer than usual.

# Chapter 2

Just as Clara had prayed, the hours seemed to lengthen. Although she tried to resist it, her eyes continued to seek out Captain Ingersoll throughout the evening meal. And almost every time, she caught him watching her as well. The wind continued to howl outside, and the rain pelted the windows, presenting a cold and dismal landscape just beyond the sturdy walls of the inn. But inside, the fire blazed, and despite the weather, the resonant chatter from the guests lent a cheerful air. And the warmth creeping up Clara's cheeks was from more than the heat in the fireplace.

Not long after they finished eating, the guests retired to one of the other public rooms for continued diversion. Clara and her younger sister, along with two servant girls, kept them supplied with cups of steaming tea, hot cocoa, or water, as well as a selection of delectable pumpkin bars, applejacks, and orange-spiced scones. She made certain to be the one serving the room the captain had chosen.

Clara now stood at the preparation table, staring at the wall in front of her. If someone had told her that morning how her day would play out, she never would have believed them. The good Lord and good fortune certainly smiled down upon her with the rise of the river and from the moment Captain Ingersoll knocked on their door.

"Clara." Her mother's voice interrupted her musings. "Are you going to stand and stare at that wall for the rest of the night, or will I benefit from your assistance in preparing additional sweets for our guests in the other rooms?"

Clara straightened and blinked several times. Adelaide Preston was nothing if not hardworking and generous. She expected her children to be the same. Clara had to bring her mind back to the present. There was work to be done, and she needed to be aware enough to complete it. The precious time she wanted would only slip away from her with her daydreaming.

"I'm here, Mama. Tell me what you need me to do."

Mama passed a large, wooden bowl down the kitchen table to her. "Separate the flour into equal portions for the mixing bowls. When you are finished with that, you can move on to the sugar." She turned to give directions to the other servant girls in the kitchen.

"Mama, can I help, too?"

Clara's ten-year-old sister, Molly, missed the step down into the kitchen from the hallway and stumbled into the room. Nine-year-old Garrick was right on her heels and braced himself on the doorpost to keep from knocking her down. At one time or another, every Preston child had worked at the inn. But now Clara's oldest brother and older sister were married, living in the village proper. And Samuel had returned to the inn just a few short months ago.

"Garrick, you can go find your papa and help him with whatever he is doing. You are more than ready to start taking on more responsibility."

"What can I do, Mama?" Molly clasped her hands in front of her and looked up at Mama with an angelic expression. Clara's heart warmed at the sight.

"You, my little angel," Mama said as she tapped Molly's pert nose, "can help me cut pieces of cheesecloth for these canisters."

Mama often said children were a sign of the good Lord's favor and blessing. And she at one point had a houseful. Clara hoped she'd be equally blessed when the time came for her to have a family. As she sifted through the flour and portioned out equal amounts for each bowl, her mind once again drifted to the captain.

How was it that she had never before encountered him or made his acquaintance? Their inn sat in a very noticeable location, and it had always been a popular resting spot for many a weary traveler. As a merchant trader, Captain Ingersoll no doubt traveled the waterways from the mouth of the Great River at Saybrook up north to where the waters became impassable by the larger ships. From the way he carried himself, he was not new to the trade. So why then had he only just tonight appeared at their door? Perhaps if she found a way to listen to more of the conversation in the room where he sat, she could learn the answer to her question.

The moment the next batch of scones was ready, Clara snatched the tray and rushed from the kitchen. After taking a moment to compose herself before bursting into the parlor, she stepped through the doorway with calm assurance, doing everything she could to make certain her racing heart could not be detected. As soon as she approached, Captain Ingersoll looked up and smiled. She smiled in return. He lifted the empty tray from the table in front of him and took the full one from her, placing the empty one in her hands.

Charm, confidence, grace, and a servant's heart. The captain was amassing an appealing list of qualities. His easygoing manner and awareness of others reminded her so much of Samuel—before—and that made him seem all the more familiar to her. Stepping to the side table, Clara retrieved the water pitcher and filled the empty cups, moving to pour tea and cocoa next. A low tone caught her ear as she approached the settee.

"Have you heard the news of General Washington?" one of the inn's guests asked of the captain.

Captain Ingersoll held up his hand and inspected his fingernails. "Do you mean in regard to the two battles against the French at Fort Dusquesne and Fort Necessity?"

The man nodded. "Yes. Are you aware of what is to happen next?"

The captain crooked one corner of his mouth. "From what I have learned, the Duke of Newcastle has been in negotiations in the months since those two battles took place. I am not certain what has taken him so long, but I hear tell he has finally decided to send an army expedition not long after the new year."

"And Major General Edward Braddock has been chosen to lead the expedition."

"Major Braddock?" The captain leaned forward, resting his forearms on his knees. "Wasn't he just granted the colonelcy of the 14th Regiment of Foot last year?"

"One and the same," the other man replied. "It seems he has served Britain well, and as a major general, was the obvious choice. I cannot help but wonder what King

Louis XV is going to do should he learn of Britain's plans."

The captain's face grew grim. "Let us pray he does not discover those plans, or any attempt on Britain's part to thwart the French will be destroyed. And it could drastically affect my trade success along the river, should the French shipping industry be attacked."

Their conversation volleyed back and forth for several more minutes, but Clara's primary interest in the news of the battles was how the situation might affect them there in the river valley where they lived.

"So tell me, Captain," the man she had identified as Mr. Coulon said, "how is it you have never made port near this little village prior to this evening?"

Clara stopped in her tracks. This was exactly what she wanted to know. Now she could hear the answer to her unspoken question.

Captain Ingersoll leaned back against the settee and folded his arms across his chest. "In all honesty, I cannot say for certain one way or the other. In fact, when my first mate alerted me to the peril of the risen waters through this area, it was the first time I had actually taken notice of the existing village flanking the river."

"But from what I have gathered in what you have shared this evening," Mr. Coulon pressed, "you have been traveling this section of river for several years, even before you assumed control of your father's ship. Were you not aware of this village even then?"

Clara had asked herself the same thing not long after learning Captain Ingersoll was a merchant trader. Ships could only venture so far along the river, and they all frequented the ports in Saybrook on their way out to the ocean and other ports along the shore. So, why not Higganum or Haddum?

The captain shrugged. "Unfortunately, beyond the fact that I had no cause to make port in this area, as none of my current customers reside here, there is no other answer to your inquiry. And I do not believe my father had cause to trade here either, or I am certain I would have remembered stopping along the route." He uncrossed his arms and rested his hands on his legs. "If I had to make a conjecture, I would say the residents of this village and the residents nestled in this little nook have been trading with other merchants or getting their supplies from a trader along the post roads. There are far too many towns along my route for me to possibly service them all. But I am available to all who make a request of me."

So, that was it. And the explanation made perfect sense. The captain was right. He could never fulfill the needs of everyone along the trade path of the Great River. But perhaps now that he had stopped here and made some acquaintances, he would see fit to return and offer his services. Clara would have to speak to Mama and Papa at the earliest opportunity to discover who provided them with their supplies.

"Now, if you will excuse me, Mr. Coulon"—the captain's voice broke into Clara's thoughts—"I believe I am going to partake of the heat from the fireplace in the great room. The stove here is sufficient, but there is nothing quite like the heat from a fire to warm you through. And despite the length of time my crew and I have spent inside, there remain areas of my clothing that are not yet fully dry." He stood. "The fire is sure to remedy that."

The captain was about to head in Clara's direction! That meant he would pass directly in front of her if she did not move from where she stood.

Coulon waved his hand in the air as a dismissal. "Of course, of course. Thank you for your engaging conversation, Captain. I do hope to see you again sometime."

"And I you, Mr. Coulon, if for no other reason than to discuss the ramifications of Britain's military actions in the Ohio Valley and France's response. I have a feeling this is only the beginning."

A moment later, Captain Ingersoll closed the distance from the settee to the doorway in four long strides. Clara could do nothing but watch him as he approached, unable to avert her gaze or find anything else to occupy her attention. The captain commanded attention no matter where he stood, and his effect on her was doubly compelling.

He paused as he stood in front of her and smiled down, the flecks of green in his hazel eyes shimmering with mirth. Had he somehow discovered her attraction to him? Or was the delight she saw borne of genuine kindness and respect for the service she provided? Based upon how he had treated every person who had served him this evening, Clara assumed the latter.

"Miss Preston, might I presume upon you to bring me a fresh slice of that bread you served with the meal earlier this evening? And some butter as well, if you have it at the ready?" He placed his hand just below his ribs. "I must confess, that was the best bread I've tasted since I last enjoyed a loaf baked by my own brother, Micah."

Clara beamed. Little did he know she was the one who had baked that particular loaf. "Thank you, Captain. I shall be certain to notify the one who baked it and share your appreciation." She preceded the captain through the doorway and turned in the direction of the kitchen. "Please, do make yourself comfortable by the fire. I shall have a warm slice with butter brought out to you there."

The captain raised his hand and bowed. "You have my undying gratitude, Miss Preston."

❧

Jonathan watched Miss Preston disappear into the darkened hallway alongside the public sitting rooms. She had been quite attentive tonight. As she saw to each table and each guest, her winsome smile and pleasant attitude only added to her quality service. He enjoyed the liberty of observing her from a distance most of the evening. And the other guests seemed rather taken with her as well. Not that it surprised him. Her beauty flowed naturally from within and bubbled out as it brought joy to others.

He turned and continued on his way toward the stone hearth on the opposite side of the great room. He passed in front of the broad staircase leading to the rooms on the upper floors and walked by the desk where he had earlier signed the register. A shelf behind the desk caught his attention. How had he missed that before? Even the light from the candles in the chandelier made the items adorning the shelf stand out.

He took a few steps closer and peered at each glass figurine in turn. Whoever collected these had an affinity both for fine craftsmanship and the wild animals of the great outdoors. In fact, he had only seen such delicate work performed in one town along the ocean coastline. He had two similar figurines on board his ship at that moment. One was intended for his mother, but the other he had purchased on a whim with no specific recipient in mind at the time. Now he knew why. And he had to retrieve it.

Once he had the glass animal in hand, he made certain the ship was secure and returned to the inn. He would be back on the ship all too soon, but only after he enjoyed what he could of the warm fire before spending the night in the cold and lonely captain's quarters.

As soon as he reentered the inn, he glanced toward the hearth and saw a piece of bread with a dollop of butter beside it on the plate. Miss Preston had done as she'd promised. He only regretted not being there when she delivered it. . .if she had been the one to do so. Of course, judging from the way she appeared wherever he chose to sit, he had no doubt it *had* been Miss Preston who provided him with the additional bounty.

But he had a greater purpose to attend to. After casting a careful look about the room to make certain no one would see his actions, Jonathan stepped behind the desk and stood in front of the shelf. He carefully withdrew the swan figurine from the pouch at his hip and placed it on the shelf in an empty spot near the end. Taking two paces backward, he admired how well the swan blended with the other figurines nestled there. The lack of dust on the collection showed its owner took great care to keep them polished. Yes, this figurine had found a new home.

Nearly half an hour later, Miss Preston returned to collect his empty plate and refill his cup one more time.

"Thank you. The bread was just as delicious as the first taste I had, and the hot tea has sufficiently thawed me to the core."

"The pleasure has been mine, Captain Ingersoll."

Miss Preston bobbed another curtsy and graced him with a genuine smile as well. A smile that had a greater effect on him than all the tea he'd drunk that evening. She left him then, walking toward the parlor. Jonathan returned his attention to the dancing flames in the fireplace, stretching his hands toward the warmth.

"Oh!"

The sudden gasp made him twist around to the source of the sound. As he and Miss Preston had been the only two in the main room, it took but a second to identify the reason. There she stood, holding the figurine he'd placed on the shelf only moments before.

"How beautiful," she exclaimed, running her finger along the delicate curves of the swan's neck and back. "It is simply exquisite."

Jonathan watched her marvel at the newest addition to her collection. He'd had an inkling she would be the owner, and now that he knew for certain, he found an even greater pleasure in knowing what he'd done. Should he admit to being the party responsible? Why not? What did he have to lose? He stood.

"I thought the same thing when I first saw it in the shop window in New Bedford, Massachusetts."

Miss Preston spun to face him, her hand going to her chest. "Captain Ingersoll? This was yours? You're giving this to me?"

Even from this distance, Jonathan could see the sheen of unshed tears glistening in her eyes. It was all he could do not to go to her, but propriety kept his feet firmly planted on the wooden floorboards.

"Thank you," she said and sniffed. "Thank you very much."

Jonathan dipped his head then raised it and met her gaze from across the room. "Miss Preston, this time, the pleasure is all mine."

He didn't know what else to say, but it was obvious no further words were needed. Miss Preston replaced the swan in its new spot and backed away toward the parlor, bumping into the wall on her way. Other young maidens would have rushed from the room after such a blunder, but not her. Instead, she shrugged, a most beguiling and sweet smile gracing her lips, as she once again left the room.

The blustery wind howled just beyond the windows, and Jonathan shivered involuntarily at the thought of venturing outside once more to spend the night on his ship. The rain had ceased hours before, yet the cold remained. But just thinking of Miss Preston and her charm warded off the chill. The memory of the way she cherished his gift would stay with him for a long time to come.

# Chapter 3

Clara pressed the brief missive to her chest and closed her eyes. Although saddened when she ventured downstairs this morning to find the captain and his crew already gone, pleasure immediately replaced the sadness when she discovered he had left this note. She had read it so many times, a tiny hole had formed in the crease. Unable to resist, she unfolded the piece of paper and read the note again.

*Dear Miss Preston,*

*I am sorry I will not be here when you awaken, but we rose early and discovered the waters had receded sufficient enough for us to be on our way. As we suffered a delay yesterday, we felt it imperative that we make haste in continuing on our journey. But rest assured, that delay was made quite enjoyable by your presence and your family's service, and I cannot imagine any other delay I might wish to repeat than one which would bring us back to your inn.*

*Although the coming winter months will soon make passage along the river impossible, I will continue my trade via wagon cart and do my best to return by whatever means necessary before the spring thaw. In the meantime, I trust the newest addition to your figurine collection will take my place until I can return.*

*Yours sincerely,*
*Captain Jonathan Ingersoll*

The captain had left a brief note for Mama and Papa, too, but it lacked the personal touch he'd included in his note to her. It was equally as cordial, and the sentiment echoed what he had written for her alone. Nevertheless, she enjoyed reading between the lines and interpreting a deeper meaning, even if he hadn't intended one. Most would call her foolish. She didn't care. Captain Ingersoll's note was hers to keep and hers to interpret as she wished.

"I do believe, Mr. Preston, our daughter has become smitten by a certain dashing captain who joined us last eve."

"Yes, Mrs. Preston. I would have to concur with your assessment." Her father paused. "I do wonder, though, how she will serve our guests if her eyes are constantly watching the front door for this gentleman's return."

"Perhaps," her mother continued, "we should relegate her to the kitchen in order to remove the temptation."

Clara glanced up into the amused faces of her parents. "Mama, Papa. You do not need to speak of me as if I were not present in the room." Nor did they need to restrict her duties in any way. "And I assure you, I am perfectly capable of seeing to our guests without distraction. You have no need to be concerned."

Mama reached out and placed her hand over Clara's. "Oh, we were not concerned, my dear. At least not more for the guests than we are for you." She patted Clara's hand. "However, this is the first time your father and I can recall you being so enamored." Mama smiled. "We always knew this day would come, but we cannot help but wonder. Why this man?"

Papa snapped his fingers. "It is the uniform, is it not? Even I must admit, a man in uniform commands attention."

Clara shook her head. Oh how she loved her parents dearly, especially their penchant for the occasional lighthearted banter. "Captain Ingersoll is not the first seafaring guest we have had at our inn over the years. Nor is he the first in uniform. And I am certain he will not be the last."

Mama nodded. "This is true. But why this captain?"

In her mind's eye, Clara brought back the captain's image. Every detail, right down to the tiny scar on the lower left side of his angled jaw. Even now, the depth of his hazel eyes and his self-confident grin drew her like a mouse to molasses. And she would willingly endure the sticky situation for another opportunity to speak with him. All of a sudden, the captivating eyes blurred, only to be replaced by the expectant expressions on her parents' faces. Now, what was it Mama had asked?

"I am not certain I can answer that question, Mama." Clara leaned her forearms on the registration counter in front of her and shrugged. "What I do know is the captain possesses a quiet strength and inner peace that fascinates me. In the brief moments I had to observe or speak with him, he demonstrated kindness, genuine concern for others, and an awareness of everything and everyone around him." She straightened and turned to retrieve the glass swan he'd given her last night then faced her parents once again, cradling the figurine in her palm. "He had a way of making me feel special, of looking for that one thing that would say he noticed me, and doing it without hesitation."

Papa pressed his lips together. "Now, those are good reasons to be enamored of someone. They are admirable qualities to possess. No doubt about it." He propped an elbow on the counter. "Of course, his family's reputation and the stellar integrity his father possessed do not hurt his prospects either."

Family reputation? Clara set the swan on the counter in front of her. "Are you saying you know Captain Ingersoll, Papa? That you have met his father?"

Mama cleared her throat. "*Knew* the elder Captain Ingersoll, Clara dear. He passed away several years ago."

Captain Ingersoll's father was dead? And he had been a trader, too? That meant the captain had followed in his father's footsteps and probably even taken over his ship. Oh, how difficult that must be—to live every day on a ship serving as a reminder that his father was no longer with him. Clara's heart went out to the captain.

"And now," Mama continued, "I do believe this is my cue to take my leave and return to the kitchen. The midday meal is not long off, and there are several items on the menu which need my attention." She reached out and gave Papa's arm a loving squeeze, sliding her hand down and touching her fingertips to his. "You two have a nice little chat."

Papa watched Mama walk across the room and disappear behind the swinging door to the central hallway. Even after all the years they'd been married, the love he felt for Mama shone in his eyes. Mama's, too. Neither one of them made any attempt to hide it. Clara prayed daily she would find someone to look upon her with the same level of affection.

"Yes, I did make the acquaintance of the elder Captain Ingersoll on more than one occasion." Papa turned to face her, leaning again on his elbow. "We did not engage in any business transactions, as I had already arranged for the delivery of our goods from another trader. However, there were a handful of times when he would take a meal with us, or I would encounter him in the village as he made deliveries."

"So, there was a time when the Ingersoll ship did trade with the people here in Higganum?" From what Clara had learned last night, the captain had never stopped here. But now she was learning his father had. Perhaps he'd done so when the captain had been too young to accompany his father.

"Oh yes. In fact, about fifteen years ago, he was responsible for the majority of trade conducted via the Great River's waterways."

"What happened?"

Papa looked up and narrowed his eyes. "I am not 100 percent certain, but I believe another trader arrived and was determined to overtake the business Captain Ingersoll had established with the villagers here."

"But how could he do that? Wouldn't the captain have agreements with those villagers? And wouldn't it be rather difficult to steal a customer?" Clara didn't even know who this other trader was, but from Papa's tone of voice as he talked about him, the trader couldn't be half the man the captain's father was.

"As I said, I did not know the elder Captain Ingersoll well. However, from what I can recall, this other trader began to falsify the captain's reputation and sabotage his trade agreements through attacks on the captain's character. I do not know how the trader accomplished it, but he must have had other men working for him. And it was a devious yet carefully orchestrated plan. Before long, many of the residents in the villages began to believe the lies and shifted their loyalties to the new trader."

"But that was not fair to the captain. He had done nothing wrong." The incident might have happened a little after when Clara learned to walk, but it still incited a great deal of anger inside of her. She clenched her fists and gritted her teeth, regardless of how unladylike she might appear.

Papa chuckled at her reaction and covered her fist with his hand. "You are correct. The captain *was* completely innocent of all charges against him. But that didn't change the minds of the villagers. This other trader had so effectively besmirched the captain's good name, continued trade with Ingersoll was out of the question."

"Oh, that was truly awful." Clara frowned, trying to imagine what it would be like to have someone lie about her in such a manner. And for what purpose? The guaranteed trade of a few tiny villages? It hardly seemed worth all that trouble.

"Yes," Papa agreed, squeezing her hand as she relaxed her fist. "But, from the reports of the dispute, no matter what that other trader said or did, Captain Ingersoll remained calm. Rather than verbally rebutting the falsehoods, he continued to do trade and conduct business as he had always done. And he never once raised a hand to the other trader or called the man out for his actions." A pleasant expression crossed Papa's face, as if the incident he recalled brought back fond memories. "When the time came to cease his dealings with the villagers here and remove this port from his route, the captain did so without a word. Any other man might have engaged in a round of fisticuffs or possibly even returned devious intent with an equally devious action. Instead, the captain walked away, his integrity still intact."

"That must have been extremely difficult for him." Clara could only imagine what she would do if that had happened to her. "But thank you, Papa, for telling me. I can see where this captain," she said, touching the glass swan, "gets his noble character. He comes by it honestly."

Papa nodded. "Yes. He does. And now you see why I said earlier that the character traits you mentioned were good reasons to become enamored of someone." He smiled. "If this Captain Jonathan Ingersoll is anything like his father, he is welcome at our inn anytime."

Clara smiled, feeling the effects all the way to her eyes.

"Now, that is enough stories for today. As your mother often says, this inn will not run itself." He grinned and reached out to trace a finger down Clara's cheek. "Besides, I have a feeling we will be seeing this captain again very soon."

As Papa headed outside, Clara paused and stared at the swan again. She carefully replaced it on the shelf and ran her finger across the arched back. Oh that her father's words would come true.

# Chapter 4

Jonathan's crew strained against the frigid waters of the river. They had resorted to making use of the sweeps in order to navigate in the still winds. And the oars were even used on occasion. In the shallower areas, ice had already begun to form. It wouldn't be long now before the entire river was too frozen for ship travel. But he said he would do his best, no matter what it took. And he intended to do just that.

Three hours after leaving Glassenbury that morning, the town of Haddam came into view. Higganum was a little farther down. As his crew maneuvered the ship toward a place where they could make port, Jonathan's spirits lightened at the thought of seeing Miss Preston again. It had only been three weeks, but right now that felt like an eternity. He was over the rail and descending the ladder to the launch before his crew had even dropped anchor. Let them tease him. Jonathan didn't care. After all, he paid their wages. They would do well to remember that when the urge to mock him came upon them.

He rushed from the shore the moment his boots touched land, his long strides eating up the distance. Only a few more steps and he'd be knocking on the front door. But just as he set foot on the bricked stoop, the painted door swung open wide and there stood the young lady whose image had been uppermost in his mind since the day he left.

"Captain Ingersoll," she greeted with bright eyes and a smile. "How delighted I am to see you again."

Jonathan regarded Miss Preston for a moment before he spoke. Something about the fair maiden captivated him. Perhaps it was her guileless nature or her winsome smile. Maybe even that glimpse of her engaging personality he'd caught on his first visit. Whatever it was, he was glad he had come. If only he could prolong his stay. But the river wouldn't wait. He had to get the *Handelaar* to the South Cove at Saybrook and docked for the winter.

He swept off his hat with a flourish and bowed. "Miss Preston, as promised, I have returned." He glanced up at the gray clouds, threatening snow. "And once again, I am accompanied by less than desirable weather," he said with a grin.

She giggled. "It is not within your power to control the weather, Captain Ingersoll, but one does have to wonder about the good Lord's affinity for bringing you here under such dreary conditions."

"It is only to better accentuate my bright presence."

This time, she laughed. "When juxtaposed against the backdrop of bleak and gray, how could it be anything but?"

Jonathan pressed his hat to his chest and feigned offense. "You wound me, fair maiden. What must I do to return to your good graces?"

Miss Preston lowered her lashes and tucked her chin against her chest. "I dare not say, for it would be presumptuous of me to do so."

Ah, a sense of humor *and* modesty. Two quite admirable traits. Jonathan extended his hand. "Then, would you do me the honor of accompanying me outside for a spell? Do be certain to wear your wrap. It is rather chilly out here."

She glanced over her shoulder where her mother stood watching their exchange. A silent nod from the matriarch communicated her approval. Miss Preston reached for her wrap, but when face-to-face with him again, she hesitated. He turned and offered his elbow to her. She eagerly accepted.

With her hand tucked securely in the crook of his arm, Jonathan led her down the brick path toward a stone bench beneath a towering sugar maple.

"Shall we?" He extended a hand toward the bench. She sat and tucked her skirts beneath her, folding her hands in her lap.

The faintest of breezes stirred a few wisps of hair against her cheek. Jonathan started to reach out to tuck them behind her ear, but he closed his fist instead. That would be far too forward. A moment later, she took care of it for him, tugging at a lock of hair as it rested across her shoulder.

Jonathan had the feeling it was up to him to start the conversation, but what should he say? Yes, he was the one who had invited her to join him, but beyond that, he hadn't thought of much else. Talk of traveling his trade route or sailing his ship to Saybrook would likely not be of much interest to her. Perhaps he should talk about the inn. With the Red Griffin Inn run by his mother, that was a topic he knew well.

"So, tell me more—"

"What is it like, living—"

They both laughed as their words tumbled over each other's.

Jonathan gestured for her to continue. "Please."

Clara dipped her head then returned her gaze to his. "Your life on board a ship for most of the year affords you a certain advantage. I have overheard bits of conversation between Papa and several guests, along with my brother Samuel, that have piqued my interest, but they tell me their affairs are not for a young lady's ears." A beguiling pout drew Jonathan's eyes to her lips. "I do not wish to pry, but I am fascinated by what little I do hear and long to know more. And you spoke with one of our guests at your last visit about a Major Braddock, so you must be aware of what is happening."

He had best tread carefully, both in his errant thoughts and on this subject. As her brother and father said, much of the life of a seaman as well as military talk was not meant for maidens to hear. And he did not wish to anger either of those men in her life. But if he said too little, he would risk disappointing this very attractive young lady. Neither outcome held much appeal.

Jonathan shifted his attention back to her eyes and away from the more engaging area of her lips. "Tell me first how much you already know about the life I lead and the developments to the west."

Clara chewed on her bottom lip and gazed over his shoulder. He took advantage of that moment to observe her. Waves of wheat-colored hair were gathered with combs and fastened under a lappet cap. Eyes the deep gray of the wet sand along the cape near Saybrook hinted at wisdom beyond her years; yet, at the same time, her manner bespoke a youthful innocence that increasingly intrigued him. He presumed her to have nearly attained her eighteenth year but not quite. If more, then the men of this town should be brought to question for not seeing the beauty before them.

The object of his scrutiny shifted her focus and caught him staring. A becoming blush stained her cheeks, and she averted her gaze. Innocent indeed. A characteristic he found both refreshing and appealing. Unable to resist, Jonathan gave a light touch to her cheek. The warmth in her eyes chased away the embarrassment, but the doe-like innocence remained.

"Do forgive me. I must apologize for causing you discomfort. Please share with me what you know, and I will endeavor to supply the necessary facts to satisfy your curiosity."

His young companion brightened, and her enthusiasm once again took hold. "Over the years, Papa and Samuel have often spoken of the many ships that lay anchor in the harbors at the mouth of the Great River. I have only had the good fortune to see them once, many years ago. From the way they speak, the community there is fairly teeming with the latest information, commerce, and industrial developments. It all sounds so exciting. But here"—she made a general sweep of the property where the inn sat—"I am like a bird in a cage, seeing the world, yet unable to be free enough to explore it. What little I do know, I gather from the conversations of the guests at our inn."

Jonathan nodded. "I can see how your life might seem constrictive, but consider the diversity in the guests you meet every day. I would hazard a guess that you know more than the average villager."

"Perhaps. I do know there has been talk of the developments in the Ohio Valley and as far north as the St. Lawrence Valley. I understand the dispute over who owns the land beyond the mountains has led to the animosity with the French, but I am unclear about how all of these recent events interconnect."

A sweet face paired with an intelligent mind. That was a combination Jonathan didn't often encounter in the women he knew.

He took a deep breath and exhaled. "Basically, both the French and the English claim all the lands from the Alleghenies west to the Mississippi River. While the area along the St. Lawrence River has also been under dispute, the Ohio Valley has recently become the main focus of this conflict."

"Papa says the Ohio Territory is beautiful. From his description, I can almost see it—majestic rolling hills and valleys with glimmering crystal streams, how the rising and setting sun casts color and shadow across the landscape, and all of it stretching as far as the eye can see."

Not only intelligent but a poet as well. He must learn more about this charming lady.

"Such a vivid imagination you possess," he said with a smile. "The problem is the French claim they discovered this land, while we English claim it is ours by charter and by our alliance with the Iroquois."

Clara pursed her lips. "If this land is as valuable as it is beautiful, any man would be foolish not to want it for his own." She tracked the progress of a lone brown leaf as it fell to the ground. "This land here, west of the Great River and east of the Hudson, has a beauty all its own. I would gladly fight for it if someone challenged me to its ownership."

Jonathan straightened, astonished to have found such a kindred spirit. She had no idea how much he longed to find someone in whom he could confide; someone who didn't have an obvious vested interest in the militant developments. Because he often associated with fellow seaman, trade customers, and the occasional riffraff he encountered in various taverns, Jonathan hadn't met many beyond his own brothers who could hold a passable conversation with him. Never in his wildest imagination would he have expected to find such compatibility with a young lady here in Higganum.

Clara's attention remained with the single, dead leaf, and she didn't seem to take note of his pause. "That is the exact source of the dispute," he murmured. "If the French have their way, we English will be confined to this narrow space between the Atlantic and the crest of the Alleghenies. On the other hand, if we have ours, the French will be hemmed within a small portion north of the St. Lawrence."

The sudden flight of two late-migrating swallows overhead caught their attention. When the birds flew into a nearby pin oak, a squirrel chattered in protest. The birds only flapped their wings, chirped a few times, and remained where they landed. Accepting defeat, the squirrel scampered down the trunk. Bounding over to another oak, he raced up it to resume his previous activities. Clara shared a smile with Jonathan at the little animal's antics before bringing their conversation back to the matter at hand.

"Why cannot England and France simply come to an accord on this issue?"

Jonathan sighed and shook his head. "In my opinion, greed is the force that blinds them to any compromise."

Impulsively, Jonathan covered Clara's hand with his then quickly withdrew it, conscious of propriety. She didn't seem to notice, or at least showed no signs that she did. No need to cause her undue distress by making advances that would be seen by a guest at the inn or either one of her parents. Better yet, they should move from this somewhat secluded spot.

"Will you walk with me?" He rose and extended his elbow.

She stood and again placed her hand in the crook of his arm. The pressure of her touch sent his mind wandering in another direction, but he quickly reined in his thoughts. It was enough to handle, simply escorting such a lovely young lady around the property.

Once they reached the path leading to the back of the inn, he continued. "Our current situation is tenuous at best," he said. "Hostilities have risen to an alarming level. England continues to launch attacks against the French, but we are suffering more loss than gain."

Clara turned her attention to him and furrowed her brow, as if attempting to piece together everything she knew and had learned. "We have been aware of the disputes, but we have had no awareness here of how critical the situation has become." She pointed past him, where the sails from his ship could be seen through the barren trees. "Not even our trade or the cost of goods has been affected as of yet. Colonel Washington's journal published in the *Maryland Gazette*, where he shared the details of his July encounter with the French near the Great Meadows, was our first indication."

Jonathan nodded. "The French commander and nine of his men were killed, which led to the colonies rallying in fear of the French threat. And as you overheard from my last visit, we should be receiving support soon from England. None of the bloodshed has trickled this far east, and for that, many of us are extremely grateful. But if this conflict continues to escalate, as I fear it will, it will not be long before we are unwillingly drawn into the midst of it all." He pressed his lips together then relaxed them. "If I had to hazard a guess, I would say this coming year will be critical in the decisions that are made regarding the potential for war."

Jonathan returned his attention to Miss Preston's face. Lines furrowed across her brow, and her mouth was pressed in a thin line, upsetting her delicate features. She seemed so vulnerable at the moment. How could he tell her he had to leave? That his ship and his crew awaited his return? But he had no choice.

He pulled his arm away and reached inside his coat for a note he'd penned, but in his haste he pulled out other papers with it. The pages fluttered to the ground at their feet. "Miss Preston, I must go."

"Go? But must it be so quickly?"

Biting her lip, she bent to stop the scattered papers from blowing across the grass in the breeze. He hastily dropped to one knee to help. As they reached at the same time, they bumped heads.

Brilliant. He was as couth as a drunken sailor. Hoping a smile would soften the abruptness of his announcement, he got to his feet, rubbing his head ruefully. He bent to take her hand, and she straightened to stand before him, regarding him gravely.

"Forgive me, Miss Preston. But, as you can see from the condition of the river, the ice is already forming." He quickly took back the other papers and left her with the note. "If I do not make haste toward Saybrook, there will be irreparable damage done to my ship."

She clutched the note to her bosom. "And that would cause undue hardship on your trade business as well."

Jonathan nodded. "Yes. So you see why I cannot tarry." She started to respond, but he stayed her words with his hand. "I have enjoyed every moment of our conversation, and I do not wish for things to end here. But I cannot guarantee my availability during the coming months." He took a breath and prayed for courage, nodding toward the lone page she held. "I have written my request in that note to your father, but now I am asking you as well. Might I have permission to call on you after the spring thaw?"

"Yes of course," she answered without hesitation.

"And would it be presumptuous of me to ask that you write?"

Her lashes swept downward, and a light pink colored her cheeks. She raised her gaze once more to meet his. "It would please me to have your permission."

In spite of knowing that spring was nearly five months away, a thrill lifted his spirits. He reached into his coat for a pencil, but before he could find it, she thrust one into his hands. He raised one eyebrow in question.

She colored prettily. "I keep a pencil with me at all times."

Jonathan knew the significance of what he was about to do, but he could no more resist than he could deny himself food and water. Already he felt the absence of her company at the thought of the long, solitary journey back to Glassenbury after he secured his ship. He quickly scrawled his address onto one of the papers, tore it free from the full page, and placed it with the note he'd penned, praying she'd write.

Clara held tight to the two pages from him, their hands barely brushing. She glanced down at the address he'd given her. "I shall write at the earliest opportunity."

Jonathan lifted her hand to his lips and brushed a kiss across her knuckles. "And I shall eagerly await the receipt of your letter."

He forced himself to turn and stride in the direction of his ship. Unable to avoid a final look, he glanced back over his shoulder to find Clara watching him.

She held the papers to her chest, and sadness softened her features. He gave a cheerful wave and tore his gaze from her as his measured steps put more distance between them.

Although hesitant to admit it, he left a part of his heart behind.

# Chapter 5

C lara raised the tambour on her escritoire and reached for the quill lying next to the paper. She dipped it in the inkwell and started to write.

*Dear Captain Ingersoll,*

*This will likely be the final missive you shall receive from me, as the spring thaw is nearly upon us. I have greatly enjoyed the written exchange we have shared these past few months, but it pales in comparison to knowing you will soon be here again. I am pleased to learn of your many successful ventures during the winter with your cart and horse, although I am certain it lacks the thrill of sailing aboard the* Handelaar *and navigating the waters of the Great River. Perhaps upon your return, I might experience firsthand standing on board your main deck and receive a tour of your ship.*

*Business has slowed, as expected, here at the inn, but we have not been for want of a consistent flow of guests. As I shared earlier, many of them have been integral in keeping me informed of the happenings beyond this river valley. I appreciate you sharing what you have learned as well, despite the grim nature of the news. It concerns me to hear of more soldiers crossing the land here in New England on their way to the Ohio Valley, but from what you wrote, the increased activity and need for supplies has been good for your business. So how can I not at least be happy for you?*

*I anticipate the coming spring, knowing the thawing of the river will not only breathe new life into the bleak landscape and bring forth the colorful blooms, but it will also allow you to travel the waterways once again. You are no doubt anticipating that moment with greater expectancy than I. But until that day comes, I shall continue to watch and wait for your return.*

*Fondly your servant,*
*Clara*

After reading it over once more, Clara folded the note and sealed it with melted wax then pressed a stamp with her initial into it. The courier from the village would arrive tomorrow, and her letter would be on its way. She prayed the captain would receive it before he departed for Saybrook to retrieve his ship.

"I cannot fathom why you would continue to correspond with this Captain Ingersoll." Samuel's voice held the predictable blend of disdain and bitterness as it always did when he spoke of what once was his life. "Knowing what you do about the merchant trade business."

Clara pivoted on her stool to face her brother, who stood in the doorway. He took several labored steps into her room, leaning heavily on the cane that had been his constant companion for almost a year, and stopped right in front of her.

"Father told me about your affection for this captain." His eyes narrowed and his eyebrows dipped into an angry point. "How could you possibly allow yourself to develop feelings for this man when he could very well be one of the traders responsible for the attack on my ship?"

Clara wanted to jump to the captain's defense, but that would only anger Samuel further. And she had no intention of succumbing to his cynical bait. Despite Captain Ingersoll's many merits, Samuel responded with retorts of how no trader could possibly be that virtuous.

"Samuel, you do not even know if Captain Ingersoll and his ship were anywhere in the vicinity when you were attacked." At least she hoped he hadn't been involved. Everything she knew about him gave rise to his innocence, but what if she was wrong? No. She couldn't be. "As I recall, you were the one to say his normal route and location at the time failed to line up."

"That does not mean he is innocent of being involved in some way. I was well on my way toward establishing a rather successful venture in this region before those men attacked me. It stands to reason that he might be in league with those who wanted to see me stopped." He shifted his weight to his good leg and gestured at the sealed note. "Tell me, what do you really know of this man beyond what he has told you himself?"

"I know what Papa has said about his father and the integrity he no doubt passed on to his son. And I know from the brief time I spent with him that he could not possibly be connected to any of the men you seek."

"Well, I am not so certain," he growled.

"Please, Samuel." Clara reached out and touched his injured arm. "I promise you that this captain is innocent. If you would take a moment to step outside of your anger at your circumstances, you would see that."

He yanked his arm away from her and glared, animosity and disapproval fairly shouting from his expression. "What I see is that you have completely disregarded what has happened to me and allowed your emotions to muddle your sensibilities. You care more about this. . .this nobody trader," he said with disdain in his voice, "than you do your own flesh and blood."

Now he was being simply absurd as well as ill-mannered. "His name is Captain Jonathan Ingersoll, and as he has done nothing to you. He deserves your respect."

"I do not care about his formal name or about your defense of him. You say he has done nothing wrong. I say that has not yet been proven." Samuel pinned her with his intent gaze. "And until this matter is fully resolved, you would do well to avoid men like him. Do you not realize the potential danger in which you have placed yourself?"

"But Samuel, that is what I am trying to tell you. There is no danger." Why was he being so bullheaded and narrow-minded about this? Even Papa had given his consent to the forthcoming courtship. Surely that should make a difference in her brother's mind. "Captain Ingersoll is a man you can trust. I promise you. And if you would take a moment to absorb everything I have told you, you will no doubt find that I am correct in what I say."

"There is nothing you can say that will change my mind." Samuel threw back his shoulders and thrust his chin into the air. "Perhaps I should have a talk with Father about all of this. See if he feels the same about your relationship with this man once he hears my side of the story once more."

Furious at her how her older brother attempted to exert authority over her, Clara jumped to her feet and stood toe-to-toe with him.

"Captain Ingersoll has always been the perfect gentleman in my presence, and he has never demonstrated anything other than respect for everyone around him. In fact, he even asked after you in one of the letters he penned to me this winter."

Samuel broke their visual standoff and stared out the diamond-paned window. "And you no doubt supplied him with all the details of my sad and lonely state."

"As a matter of fact, no, I didn't," she countered. "Instead, I wrote to him about how much you used to love the sea and sailing and that maybe one day you will return to it, once you are able to truly put the past behind you." If only her brother could move beyond this hatred. It was eating him alive and poisoning everything he did or said.

"The only way I am going to put this behind me is if I track down and discover who did this to me," he said, gesturing to his leg and arm. "When that day comes, and I can mete out equivalent justice, *then* you can talk to me about sailing once more."

"Well, do not interfere with our relationship unless you have solid evidence to prove that Captain Ingersoll was involved. I do not want your venomous distrust of all seamen destroying what could become a permanent arrangement."

If Samuel had been younger, he might have cowered beneath her anger, but at almost twenty-two, he had no reason to fear her. And by the look in his eyes, he was not about to allow his sister to speak to him that way. . .no matter the circumstances.

He jammed his index finger into his chest and stared at her. "*My* distrust? I am brutally attacked, my ship is burned, my potential future is completely destroyed, and *you* are angry at *me* for what I *might* do should I be present the next time this captain appears?" He huffed. "I am only looking out for your best interests and do not wish you to get hurt. You?" Samuel jerked his thumb toward the folded note. "You are only concerned with what you see and your own feelings. You do not even want to acknowledge the possibility that your captain might be less than what you perceive."

"That is not true!"

Samuel brought his face within inches of hers. "I dare you to prove it."

Clara knew she would never succeed with her brother if they remained angry at each other and allowed their emotions to get the better of them. She took several deep breaths and tempered her ire then pressed forward.

"I actually will not have to prove anything. And I know the captain is exactly how I perceive him. You will be able to see it for yourself the moment you meet him. The type of men who attacked you do not conduct themselves with the integrity the captain possesses. And when you realize this, you will also see that his intentions toward me are completely honorable. Even Papa has approved."

Her brother remained silent for several moments, his mouth rigid and forming a tight line as his eyes narrowed. Clara shifted from one foot to the other. Maybe she was actually getting through to him. But then he stiffened and tightened his grip on his cane.

"We shall see who will arise the victor," he threatened, limping from the room faster than Clara thought possible.

It was like the story Papa had told her about Jonathan's father all over again. Only this time, the trader attempting to sabotage Captain Ingersoll was her own brother. And his reason wasn't to steal away customers. No. It was to thwart the captain's chances of success so his eligibility to court her would be diminished. Clara had to do something. But what?

☙

Jonathan turned at the long shadow appearing in the doorway of the stables, and there stood his older brother. Jonathan nodded to the groomsman who readied his horse. Thank the good Lord he didn't have to tend to the animal himself. He much preferred the ropes of the rigging to the leather of the reins, but he rode when necessary.

"Ah, the day has finally arrived," Nathaniel announced. "The dismal winter is behind us, and you can again set sail for the high seas."

"I am not certain the high seas are what I would term the location of my sailing." Jonathan chuckled. "But I cannot deny the thrill in my blood knowing in just a few hours, I will see my ship again."

Nathaniel grinned. "Are you certain that excitement is not due to the young maiden awaiting you in Higganum?"

How could he deny it? Nathaniel, more than their younger two brothers, understood the pull of a lady's affection. His wife, Constance, even now worked with their mother overseeing the inn.

"Yes, you know me all too well, brother." He gave Nathaniel a sheepish grin. "I confess, the prospect of seeing Miss Preston again holds an equal measure of draw as returning to my trade route." Grabbing hold of the reins, Jonathan led his horse toward Nathaniel. "And how fares your bride these days?"

"Her time is nearly upon us." Nathaniel sighed and ran a hand over his chin, then from his chin to his hair, leaving several dark brown strands standing on end. "I am not certain who is more worried about the coming little one." Jonathan walked with him out into the bright morning. "And it is a good thing Mother is experienced in these matters, because it seems everything I do or say is the wrong thing."

"Have patience." Jonathan dropped a hand on Nathaniel's shoulder. "It will not be long now, and then you shall have the squalling bundle stealing your sleep at nights."

"When you state it in that manner. . ." His brother grimaced. "It does not hold as much appeal as Constance has intimated."

"Do not take my word on it." Jonathan laughed. "Remember, I have no more experience than you in these matters."

"No, but it might not be long before you do."

And with that, the sweet face of Miss Preston came to Jonathan's mind. He wanted to ride right now to Higganum to see her. His work had kept him far too busy for social calling the past few months, leaving his desire to see her that much stronger. But he must see to the *Handelaar* first.

"And if your face is any indication, that young lady will be unable to resist."

Jonathan grinned and dropped the reins to take his brother's hand between both of his. "From your mouth to the good Lord's ears. May it be so."

⁂

"I have kept each and every letter you wrote in a bundle tied with twine in my writing desk." Clara pressed her hand in the crook of Captain Ingersoll's elbow as they walked the brick path in front of the inn. The first glimpses of color were just starting to peek up from the ground, and tiny green buds were right on the edge of bursting open. "Going back to read them helped the long, cold days of winter pass more quickly." She'd never been happier to see spring arrive.

"Yes." The captain chuckled. "The words in those letters did have a way of keeping me warm." He smiled down at her. "Although I must say, gazing upon your face again far exceeds the warmth gained from your words."

Clara felt heat from her neck to her cheeks. She glanced away from him. It felt good knowing his affection had developed at the same rate as hers during their separation. But where did that leave them now? He had yet to declare a formal suit, although he had hinted at it when last they spoke and more than once in his letters. Would he follow through with that today?

He grazed her fingers with his free hand. "You mentioned a little bit ago that you had something you wished to share with me." His soft voice compelled her to again look at him. "It sounded important. Is now a good time to discuss it?"

Perhaps, although Clara would much rather pursue the topic of courtship than discuss her brother and his nefarious plans.

"Yes." She sighed. "Better now, before something happens."

The captain halted, and the instant tug made her stop as well. "Is everything all right?" he asked. "You are not in any kind of trouble are you, Miss Preston?"

Clara looked up into his soft eyes, mostly brown this evening, and a part of her heart melted. "No, no. I am not in any trouble." She sighed again and closed her eyes. *Dear Lord, please give me strength.* "But you might be."

The light touch of his finger on her chin caused Clara to open her eyes, and she allowed him to raise her face toward his. "Miss Preston, please tell me what is amiss." He lowered his arm but placed his hands at her elbows, the warmth of his touch bolstering her enough to continue.

"You recall from my letters how I mentioned my brother and the brutal attack he suffered last year?"

"Yes." The captain nodded. "And as a result, he has been unable to sail since, blaming those men for all he lost."

"His bitterness has gotten worse, I am afraid to say." Clara's throat tightened and moisture formed at the corners of her eyes. No. She couldn't cry. Not now. She must get this out. Taking a deep breath, she continued. "Samuel came to me two weeks ago, ranting about you being involved and how I was not thinking clearly about my relationship with you."

He glanced to the left and right then gently turned her to walk with him toward a bench. "Please. Let us sit."

Clara obeyed and angled her body toward his as soon as he sat down.

"Let me see if I understand correctly." His brow furrowed. "Your brother believes me responsible in some way for his attack? How can that be? I knew nothing about it until you told me."

"That is what I attempted to explain to him, but he refused to listen. Instead, we exchanged a few heated words, and he ended the argument with a remark about seeing who would emerge the victor." Even now, Clara couldn't quite make sense of what her brother had said. She only knew it didn't bode well for the captain. "One thing you should know about my brother—he can latch onto something like a dog to a bone sometimes. And he will not let go until he believes the matter is settled."

The captain tapped his forefinger to his lips and lapsed into silence for several moments.

Clara wrung her hands in her apron, chewing on her bottom lip as she waited. She only needed a word from him, a single sentence that absolved him of any possible connection. Finally he spoke.

"You say he was attacked in June of last year?"

Clara nodded.

"My ship was north of Glassenbury at that time. Yet, he believes I am somehow involved?"

Praise be to the good Lord. The captain hadn't been nearby after all! But that didn't clear his name yet. "Yes, and Samuel is determined to prove it." The moisture in her eyes pooled, and a lone tear slipped down her cheek. She didn't want to see the captain hurt by her brother's blindness to the truth.

Captain Ingersoll reached out and captured the tear with his thumb then smoothed her cheek, pushing a few tendrils of hair behind her ear. The tenderness nearly caused more tears to fall, but she held them in check.

"If your brother is seeking revenge on his attackers, he is likely to lash out at anyone in the shipping industry, but especially other merchant traders, if he believes the attack was of a premeditated nature to destroy his business."

"So, what is there to do?" How she wished she could steer her brother away from the captain, redirect his ire at someone or something else. But that didn't seem possible.

The captain placed his hands over hers, where they rested in her lap, and leaned toward her, maintaining a respectful distance. Everything in his expression spoke of confidence. She had done the right thing, confiding in him, even at the risk of alienating her irrational brother.

"Allow me to make a few inquiries along my route, and we shall see what I can discover." He squeezed her hands. "Oftentimes a level head can discover the truth more easily than one who goes forth in rage."

"Thank you, Captain." Clara mustered up as much of a grin as possible and sniffed. "Telling you this has not been easy for me."

He smiled, a soft light entering his eyes and making the green flecks more prominent. "I realize that, but I am glad you have trusted me enough to share it." He again touched her cheek, and she leaned against the pressure. "I promise, together we shall find the truth."

The truth. Would her brother accept it if it were found?

# Chapter 6

Ah, Captain Ingersoll." Samuel approached from around the side of the inn. Clara and the captain jumped to their feet.

"We meet again."

The tone of her brother's voice might come across as cordial, but Clara knew better. The captain took an almost imperceptible step closer to her and placed his hand at the small of her back. His touch soothed her.

She closed her eyes, praying her brother would conduct himself in a respectful manner. He had made it clear the other day, though, that he intended to ferret out the truth regarding the captain's potential involvement in the attack last year. And Samuel's dogged determination usually got him into more trouble than not. If he went too far, she might adapt that same resolve where the captain was concerned.

"Good evening, Mr. Preston," the captain greeted, his own cordiality sounding forced. "Are you out for a stroll as well?"

Samuel groaned. "Do not attempt to hide behind false pleasantries, sir. I know you have spent sufficient time in my sister's company this evening, and she has undoubtedly warned you about me." He raised his cane and aimed it in the captain's direction. "So let us dispense with the formalities, shall we?"

Captain Ingersoll nodded.

"Our father has already spoken of your intentions toward my sister, but I wonder if you have told her the truth about the work you do."

"Samuel—"

"No." Her brother shifted his eyes to look at her. "Clara, you deserve to know. And if this man possesses half the integrity you claim he has," he said, glaring at the captain, "he should have no trouble answering."

The captain pressed the lapel of his buttoned coat against his collarbone before meeting Samuel's gaze. "I will be more than happy to oblige, although I believe your sister is quite intelligent and aware of what I do. What exactly do you feel she should know that she might not?"

"To start, have you informed her of just how many days and nights you spend traveling the river at one time? Or that you might be gone for many days should you need to venture out into the bay and journey to some of the larger ports around New England to acquire supplies?"

"Mr. Preston," Captain Ingersoll said, speaking in measured tones, "given the time lapse between the visits your sister and I have been able to enjoy, I am certain the length of my absences is obvious. She is well aware of what she will be facing."

"And that does not bother me in the least, Samuel," Clara spoke up. "I am certain there will be more than enough work to be done to keep me occupied while

Captain Ingersoll is away."

They were speaking in such future terms, as if it were a foregone conclusion that their relationship was going to take on a more permanent nature. He still had yet to officially declare his suit. Was the captain aware of how their words sounded, or was he only seeking to satisfy Samuel's interrogation?

"What about your activities when you lay anchor for the night? When you seek repast at a local tavern or seek to quench your thirst?"

Samuel was baiting the captain. Clara could see it. Why was he so bound and determined to find something that might paint the man in an unfavorable light? Had the attack so turned him against the merchant trade business, he wanted to make certain no one he cared for got involved in it?

"Mr. Preston, I will not lie to you." The captain glanced down at Clara. "Or to you, Miss Preston." He looked back at Samuel. "There are several members of my crew who make it a habit to visit every tavern that exists in the ports where the *Handelaar* stops. And I have, on occasion, needed to escort them back to the ship personally, sometimes carrying them when they have imbibed beyond their limitations." He flattened his palm against his chest. "But I myself have never once been too deep in my cups that I was unaware of my surroundings or required assistance to walk."

Samuel snapped his fingers. "So, you *admit* to drinking on occasion."

"I do not know of a single man who does not." Captain Ingersoll shrugged.

He had a point. Even Papa kept a small supply of sherry and brandy available for guests when they requested it.

"And which taverns exactly, have you frequented?" Samuel pressed.

"Mr. Preston. . ." The captain sighed. "If you are attempting to manipulate the facts to appease your desire to somehow connect me to the scene of your attack, you will not be successful."

"So, you refuse to name the taverns then. That must mean you are withholding something for fear of being discovered."

"Or it could mean I will not engage in theatrics with you when you are so bent on sullying my character."

"There would not be any way to sully it if you were truly innocent." Samuel raised his cane again and nearly jabbed it at the captain. "You have all but admitted repeated visits to taverns, yet you refuse to name the ones where you have spent some of your nights."

Clara wanted to speak up on the captain's behalf, but it was not her place. Not yet, anyway. Captain Ingersoll was handling himself rather well, all things considered. She was quite impressed. But just how long would her brother continue with this ridiculous tirade?

"Believe what you will, Mr. Preston," Captain Ingersoll replied. "I stand by my word."

"I intend to make certain our father knows the truth." Samuel pressed his lips into a thin line and inhaled rather loudly through his nose. "Perhaps then he will rethink his compliance with your intended suit of my sister."

Clara gasped. No! Surely her brother wouldn't go that far. The captain's hand at her back formed a fist. She opened her mouth to protest but stopped and looked up at him.

"Mr. Preston, you should be aware that I will not stand idly by while you bear false witness against me. For every lie you tell, I shall be right there proclaiming the truth."

Samuel narrowed his eyes. "So you intend to challenge me, then? You, Captain, are not worthy of my sister's affections."

Captain Ingersoll stiffened, his eyes darkening and his jaw tightening. "And you, sir, are a cad!"

Samuel took a step back at the captain's harsh words. Clara also stared. She could hardly believe Captain Ingersoll had gotten so upset. When her brother hurled his worst accusations at him and attacked his integrity, he remained placid. But threatening to cause division between him and Clara had obviously been the tipping point.

"Now do you see what I mean?" Samuel jerked a thumb toward the captain and glared at Clara. "He not only undoubtedly knows several of the other merchant traders whose ships were near mine the night of the attack, he also admits to sharing company with drunken seamen and has gone so far as to insult me in your presence."

Clara shrugged. "And how is that any different than what you have been doing to him these past few minutes? You have been attacking his very character and paying no heed to me."

"So you are going to take his side over your own brother's?" Samuel's fist curled around the top knob of his cane. "And I thought you had more sense than that. Clearly, I was mistaken."

"The only sense I have right now is to realize you are merely speaking out of your anger and making empty threats."

"A lot of good my threats will do. I have already—"

Jonathan cleared his throat. Clara and Samuel turned their attention to him.

"I believe it is best if I take my leave now and return to my ship. It is clear my presence is a source of hostility, and I do not wish for family members to engage in an argument because of me." He reached for Clara's hand and raised it to his lips, pressing a soft kiss on her knuckles. "Miss Preston, I do apologize for any problem I have caused you this eve. Please forgive me and remember what I said." He spoke softly, his eyes communicating what his mouth could not, at least not in front of her brother.

Clara wanted to stop him, but she knew it would only cause further trouble. "I will," was all she said as she watched him walk off into the darkening dusk. This evening had certainly not gone the way she had imagined it would. Once she could no longer see the captain, she turned on her brother.

"How could you do that?"

Samuel feigned innocence. "I have not the faintest idea what you mean."

"Do not play those games, Samuel." Clara clenched her fists. "You know exactly what I mean." She waved her hand toward where the captain had disappeared. "How could you treat the captain in such a disrespectful manner? He has done nothing to you other than be employed in the business of merchant trading. And despite your personal vendetta, that is no reason to transfer all of your hatred onto an innocent man."

Her brother pressed his cane against the ground and moved it in a circular motion. "You saw it and heard it yourself, Clara. Captain Ingersoll refused to be honest."

"No, he refused to be baited. And I admire him for that. Any other man might have engaged you in a round of fisticuffs for your tainted accusations." Clara wanted to continue her lecture, but it would not reach a conclusion anytime soon. She sighed and shook her head. He might be acting unreasonable, but Samuel was still her brother. And she did not wish to say something she might regret or risk causing irreparable harm to their relationship.

"And just who would you like to see be the victor in such a duel?"

"Samuel," Clara groaned. "I do not even know who you are anymore. You have become so controlled by your vengeance, I can no longer see the real man underneath." She turned and glanced back over her shoulder. As much as it pained her, she had to say this. "Until you can make peace with all of this, I do not wish to speak with you again." And with that, she walked away.

"Mark my words, Clara," her brother called to her back. "I intend to impede your captain's trade business in every way possible until he either proves his innocence or confesses to being involved. The truth is going to be revealed, one way or another. You will see."

Yes, the truth would be revealed. And when it was, Samuel would be the one who would be forced to apologize. At least she prayed that to be so.

❧

Jonathan spoke to other merchants, ship captains, and seamen as he traveled his route. For the most part, what he learned didn't help him piece together the mystery of Samuel's attackers any more than the details with which Clara had provided him. The passage of time since the incident didn't help matters either. If only he had met Clara last summer, he might have been able to help more.

It had been weeks. Every time he found someone with information, he would ask one question too many, and the party would all but clam up. He knew most of those who avoided him were being intentionally evasive or silent. And that usually meant fear of someone else. To complicate matters further, with every delivery he made or every conversation he had, Jonathan found himself defending his integrity and countering a passel of lies that had been spreading throughout the river region. He knew exactly who was to blame, but that issue would be resolved when he found the answers to his questions.

And perhaps those answers would come tonight.

Jonathan pushed open the heavy door of the dark tavern and cringed at the loud creak it made as it swung in on its hinges. He ducked and winced then peered into the dimly lit interior. No one even looked up at his entrance. He stepped farther into the room and scanned the tables. A tip from the barkeep at the tavern across the river had led him here. All he had to do was find the informant. The barkeep said he'd described Jonathan to the man, but how good was his description? Jonathan moved to the side and out of the way, praying this man would come find *him*.

"Pardon me." A gravelly voice spoke not two minutes after Jonathan found an inconspicuous place to stand and watch the room.

Jonathan turned toward the sound. A rather burly man stepped out from the shadows near the wall and gestured at the small, square table nearest them. He looked

91

like any other seaman, from the unkempt beard and bandanna tied around his head to the motley mismatch of apparel ending in a pair of buckled boots. Only his doublet decorated with braids indicated he might have attained a position of rank. Jonathan took a seat across from the man.

"Did I hear you might be looking for some information?" he said, barely speaking above the din of other voices.

"As a matter of fact, I am." Jonathan wanted to lean forward to hear the man better but hesitated. Best to be cautious until he could gauge if this man could be trusted. He touched the scar on his left jaw. An overzealous mistake had given him that scar. He didn't intend to repeat the incident. "What have you heard?"

"I remember this man, this Samuel Preston you have been asking after." The seaman scratched his beard. "This would be what? Around mid-June last year?"

"Yes. That is exactly when the incident in question occurred."

The seaman looked to the left and right then leaned in close. "You did not hear this from me, but there is a small band of river pirates who sail on the ship *Dominion*. They run their operation under the guise of merchant tradesmen, when they are really on the lookout for any loot they can steal, pillage, or plunder. And it does not matter to them how they come upon this merchandise. If someone gets in their way, they dispose of them." The man again cast a look around him. "If what I hear about this Preston fellow is right, he got in their way."

At last! He finally had a lead, something with which he could approach the river authorities in Essex. Jonathan extended his hand, but the man didn't move.

"I hear you are supposed to have some payment for me?"

What else should he have expected? It wasn't as if the man would readily give away his identity or make any effort to be cordial. The other pirates would string him up for something like this.

Jonathan reached into his satchel and pulled out a small purse of coins. He dropped it into the seaman's beefy hand.

"Now, you never saw me, and you never spoke to me."

"This conversation never occurred." Jonathan nodded. "You have my word."

# Chapter 7

Clara straightened and pressed two fists into the small of her back as she arched and tilted her head to gaze up at the cloudless sky. She had already scrubbed seventeen bed sheets and three times as many towels. On the personal clothing items of their guests, she had lost count. Hunching over the washtub once more, she plunged the last of the shirts into the murky but soapy water then slapped it against the washboard.

"Clara!"

Mama's voice called from the kitchen, and Clara looked up to see her mother peer around the doorjamb a moment later.

"Would you come into the parlor as soon as you can make yourself presentable?"

Presentable? Why would she need to take additional pains with her appearance? Unless. . .

"Of course, Mama. I will be in directly."

She twisted and worked out the kinks in her spine. At last, a reprieve. And if Mama made a specific request for her to appear respectable, that could only mean they had a noteworthy guest waiting inside. She always made certain to be clean and satisfactory, but this time was different. Could Captain Ingersoll have returned? Would this be the moment when he made his courtship official? Only one way to find out.

Twenty minutes later, Clara approached the parlor, only to find the doors had been pulled almost closed. Mama stood just inside and peeked through the opening just in time. She pushed the door open far enough for Clara to enter then pulled them completely closed.

"Ah, Clara. How good of you to join us," Papa announced. "Please, come take a seat."

Clara's heart jumped when she locked gazes with Captain Ingersoll. He smiled, looking resplendent in his navy velveteen doublet with gleaming buttons, silk braids, and satin trim on the cuffs. His tricornered hat rested on his lap on tan breeches that disappeared into nearly knee-high polished boots. His hair had been combed and fastened with black cord at the nape of his neck. The captain had certainly taken great pains with *his* appearance. And now, Clara felt rather dowdy in his presence.

That was when she noticed that an equally well-dressed gentleman sat across from the captain in a chair next to Papa. Her brother Samuel stood near the stove, his arm propped on the mantel above it.

"Clara?" Papa spoke again. "If you please?"

The only available seat within respectable distance of those gathered was next to Captain Ingersoll. She quickly took her place, careful not to sit too close. What was all of this about?

Papa looked to Mama, who nodded and took a seat near the door. They obviously did not wish anyone to disturb them.

"Very well." Papa cleared his throat. "Now that we are all present, let us not forestall the matter at hand any longer."

This sounded far more ominous than what Clara hoped to be the topic of conversation. As the unknown gentleman's dress resembled the captain's in many ways, and as Samuel had been invited as well, the matter Papa referenced must be connected to Samuel's attack.

"Judge," Papa encouraged. "You have the floor."

Clara looked at Captain Ingersoll, but his mouth remained closed.

"Thank you, Mr. Preston," the other gentleman said. "For those present to whom I have not been introduced, my name is Captain James Wells. I serve under Colonel John Austin and reside in the town of Essex as a councilman and judge for the Connecticut Assembly." He extended an open palm toward the captain. "Captain Ingersoll is responsible for my being here today, and the reason involves Mr. Samuel Preston."

At the mention of his name, her brother straightened, his injured arm falling from the mantel to his side.

"Father?" Samuel's brows dipped toward the center. "You were aware of this?"

"Mr. Preston," Judge Wells said, directing his address to Samuel, "no one but Captain Ingersoll is aware of what I am about to say."

Clara glanced sideways at the captain. To most, he might appear completely relaxed, but she noted the subtle differences. The way he tapped his boot on the rug. The way his fingers drummed on the edge of his hat. Even his shoulders stood more erect than usual. And then his neck. His Adam's apple bobbed several times, and his tongue darted out to wet his lips more than once. Whatever this judge had to say, if he did not hurry, Captain Ingersoll might say it first.

"Are you going to appease our curiosity, sir," Samuel asked, "or shall we all remain in suspense?"

Clara wanted to know the same thing, only she dared not voice it.

"Perhaps the first bit would be better if it came from Captain Ingersoll," Wells replied.

"I came to know Judge Wells," the captain said as he stood, "as a result of the inquiries I made regarding the attack summer last on Mr. Samuel Preston."

Samuel groaned low in his throat, but a glare from Papa kept him silent.

"It was not easy," Captain Ingersoll continued, looking at Samuel, "but I eventually managed to find the answers I sought, and that led me to the men who attacked you." The captain swayed forward. "From that point, it did not take long to assemble my men and infiltrate the crew of the *Dominion* while they celebrated rather boisterously in one of the local taverns in Essex. Their inebriated state made confining them quite easy."

"And that is where I became involved," Judge Wells added. "The captain managed to locate me and provide me with the details of his inarguably daring act, but I did not believe it until I stood on the deck of the *Handelaar* and witnessed the scene myself." He grinned across the room at the captain. "Every crew member of that river pirate band sat on board deck, their ankles and wrists bound, and gags in their mouths." He laughed. "I am still puzzled about how you managed such a feat, Captain, but the end result made my job far easier than it could have been."

"So I was attacked by a band of river pirates?" Samuel stepped away from the stove, using his cane as support. "Not merchant tradesmen?"

"That is correct." The judge nodded.

"And their ship, the *Dominion*. It is nothing but a ruse?"

"Again, you are correct." Judge Wells stood and approached Samuel. "I am aware of the many months you have spent seeking out these men who committed such heinous acts against you." He placed a hand on Samuel's shoulder. "But you were looking for the wrong men. At least in the wrong line of work," he added. "And you have Captain Ingersoll to thank for discovering the truth."

Samuel looked between the judge and the captain. His shoulders drooped, and his eyes lost all the fire that had been a constant companion to his pinched face these many months. Next, his gaze went to Papa, who nodded. Clara knew what had to happen next, but would her brother follow through with it? She prayed he would.

"Captain," her brother began with a sigh. "It appears an apology is in order, and it must come from me. I also owe you a great deal of thanks."

"I appreciate it, Mr. Preston." Captain Ingersoll dropped his hat to the settee. He extended a hand, which Samuel took, shifting his weight to his good leg. "And I accept your apology. I know how difficult this is, so I will not cause you to suffer any further." He raised one eyebrow and angled his head toward Samuel, a slight grin forming on his lips. "I will, however, ask that you set to right the rumors you have you been spreading regarding my business practices and ethical behavior." He gave Samuel's hand a single shake. "Otherwise, I might be forced to command my crew to mete out the same punishment they delivered to those pirates who attacked you."

Clara bit her lip to keep from laughing at the thought of her brother trussed up, bound, and gagged. It might do him good to sit that way for a spell, but it wasn't likely to happen. Mama, Papa, and the judge weren't as successful at containing their mirth. And although she couldn't see the captain's face from this angle, her brother must have read something in the captain's expression that told him the captain *would* follow through.

"I believe time spent at the pillory or a few dips on the ducking stool would also suffice," the captain added with a smile.

"You have my word," Samuel rushed to reply.

"Very good." Captain Ingersoll withdrew his hand and clapped Samuel on the back. "Now, there remains one more person to whom you owe an apology." He stepped back and both gazes landed on her.

Clara inhaled quickly. An apology? To her? But she hadn't been wronged. Not directly, anyway. A spark flashed in her brother's eyes but dimmed when he reached for his cane and took several steps toward her. She stood.

"Clara," he began. "I know my behavior of late has been reprehensible. And I said a number of things in anger that I now regret." He dipped his head. "I confess my wrongdoing, especially where the captain is concerned. It was not fair to you, placing you in the middle." He raised his eyes and looked at her, penitence reflecting in the eyes that matched hers. "Will you forgive me?"

Although a nagging part of her screamed to deny him his request, a still, small voice told her she should. He was her brother, after all, and despite his actions, he remained a good man. She had no doubt his guilt would be punishment enough. It was not up to her to levy judgment on him. The good Lord could handle that far better than she.

With gladness in her heart, she met his gaze. "I do forgive you, Samuel, and I pray the next time you are tempted to act in haste, you will learn from your mistakes, not repeat them."

He nodded but didn't reply. On impulse Clara embraced him and kissed his cheek.

"It takes a great man to admit his mistakes." She placed a palm against his chest. "I am happy to have my brother back."

Papa stepped forward then, his hands in front of him, pressed together at their fingertips. "I believe we have settled what we all gathered here to accomplish." He turned to Captain Wells. "Judge, I appreciate you making the journey to be here today. If you will find a seat in the main room, our staff will see you receive a hearty meal before you must return home."

The judge patted his stomach. "Now, that offer I will not refuse," he said with a grin, nodding at Mama, who pushed open the doors and allowed him to pass.

"Samuel. Adelaide, my dear," Papa continued, moving to stand next to Mama. "Captain Ingersoll and Clara have a few things to discuss. Let us adjourn and grant them some privacy."

Her brother turned to face the captain. "You do right by her."

The captain nodded. "I will make it my priority."

And with that, her brother and parents took their leave. Clara turned her head from the doorway to where Captain Ingersoll still stood and sat again on the settee. A moment later, he regained his seat, tossing his hat on a low table. With a twinkle in his eye and a crooked grin, he reached for her hands.

"Before I say what is uppermost in my mind, might I have your permission to address you by your given name?"

"Of course." It seemed like such a natural request. Clara was surprised he hadn't made it sooner.

"Very well. Clara," he said and paused, as if testing the sound of her name on his lips. "And I would like it very much if you called me Jonathan."

She could only nod, the tightness in her throat making it impossible to speak.

"I made you a promise when last we spoke. . .and I have now kept it," the captain said. "I know it might take some time before your brother fully trusts me, but at least he can lay his anger to rest and return to a life of normalcy." He brushed his thumbs across her knuckles, and she had to quell the shiver that threatened to travel up her back. "Now, that leaves the matter of us and a certain courtship I promised."

Again, Clara could not force any sound past the lump in her throat. She licked her lips and swallowed several times.

"I see I already have rendered you speechless." Jonathan grinned. "That makes what I am about to say much easier." He raised her hands to his lips and placed a lingering kiss on the back of each. "Clara, would you accept my suit and travel back with me to Glassenbury to meet my family? I have taken the liberty of asking one of your servant girls to accompany you as your maid. At last I heard, my older brother and his wife were about to have a baby. I would like for you to meet that newest addition."

Clara bit her lip then took in a few labored breaths. He had finally said it. Had finally done it. She was certain he had already approached Papa. Otherwise Papa would never have left them alone. Nor would he have been certain the captain had something to discuss with her. Now all that remained was her answer.

"Yes, Jonathan. Without a doubt, yes." She squeezed his fingers. "I would be honored to accept your suit."

"Splendid." Jonathan again kissed her hands, only this time they were quick pecks. "Now, after we tell your family you have agreed, I do believe we have a tour of a certain ship to take, and then we shall be on our way. Your mother has already begun to pack your trunk."

He had thought of everything. She could hardly wait to get started.

# Chapter 8

Pain-filled screams reached Clara's ears the minute she placed her hand on the front door latch of the inn.

The baby!

She burst through the front door of the Red Griffin Inn without even waiting for Jonathan to accompany her. After scanning what she could see of the main floor, her eyes immediately landed on the staircase leading to the second level. But the screams came from a room to her right. So the baby had not yet arrived. With only a second's hesitation, Clara raced toward the sound.

As soon as she entered the room, the familiar scene met her eyes. A woman Clara could only assume was Jonathan's mother kneeled beside a woman who had to be Constance, a wet cloth pressed to her forehead. The matriarch wore a ruffled cap over dark hair streaked with silver. But the penetrating power of the blue-gray eyes she turned on Clara was mesmerizing.

"You are Miss Preston, I presume?" It was more a statement than a question, but Clara nodded.

"How can I be of service?"

"The pains came on rather sudden and they have lasted for a bit more than an hour now," the mother said. "I have already sent for the midwife."

Constance had a death grip on the sides of the bed frame where she lay. From the look and sound of things, the woman might not last until the midwife arrived. Clara felt compelled to do something. She'd seen many babies born at the inn. She'd even assisted in the birth of her younger brother. Of course, that was nearly ten years ago. Nevertheless, some things a person never forgets.

"Have you ever been present for a birth?"

"Yes, I have." Clara boldly took a step closer. "Several, in fact."

"As have I." Mrs. Ingersoll nodded. "And with that said, I am certain you realize the midwife might not arrive in time."

"What can I do to help?"

"I have already set water to boil and instructed one of my servant girls to bring a basin of cold water as well." Mrs. Ingersoll removed the cloth from Constance's forehead, dipped it in the cool water, wrung it out, and replaced it. "If you would not mind fetching the boiling water and bringing some fresh towels as well, I will begin preparations."

"Very well," Clara replied, turning to go in search of the kitchen.

"Take the second hallway on your left, just before the stairs," Mrs. Ingersoll called.

While she found a basin for the water, Clara also had two servant girls prepare some nourishment for Constance. As soon as the baby arrived, the woman would need something to help her regain her strength. Clara located the extra cloths and tucked them into the waist of her apron; then she grabbed hold of the basin and made her way back to the room, careful to avoid sloshing the scalding water.

Mrs. Ingersoll had rolled up her sleeves and surrounded Constance with an abundance of towels.

"Miss Preston, we must work in great cooperation with each other. Are you certain you are ready?"

"Yes, Mrs. Ingersoll. I shall do whatever you need."

"Everything is proceeding just fine, Constance." Mrs. Ingersoll placed a hand on her daughter-in-law's forehead and smiled. Constance returned a weak smile, her eyes half-closed and perspiration dotting her upper lip.

Clara closed her eyes. *Lord, we could use Your divine assistance this day.* And that was the last thought she remembered.

In no time at all, the squalling baby entered the world, and as far as Clara could tell, without complications. She raised her eyes to the ceiling and smiled.

"Heavenly Father, thank You."

"Amen to that!" came Mrs. Ingersoll's reply. She held the baby over a makeshift table by the wall, using the hot water to wash the newborn. A minute later, she swaddled the child and made her way back to Constance. "We never would have accomplished this without His help," she said, kneeling on the floor beside the makeshift cot which held the new mother.

Clara peered over the woman's shoulder. The infant squirmed and fidgeted within its confines. Only whimpers escaped the tiny lips as Mrs. Ingersoll settled the baby into Constance's waiting arms with a smile.

"Constance, you have yourself a healthy baby boy."

The wonder and the joy of life. A miracle. Constance was so peaceful, and the little boy knew his mother held him. What had begun as so much pain ended in wonder and delight. The circle was complete.

"If you do not mind, Miss Preston, I do believe an anxious father is waiting outside." Mrs. Ingersoll chuckled. "You might wish to let him know he is welcome to come in and meet his son."

Soon the entire family crowded into the little room. Clara had no trouble identifying Jonathan's three brothers. They all shared the same blue-gray eyes of their mother, and two of them also shared the dark hair. Jonathan and the one Clara assumed to be the youngest son had lighter brown, and only Jonathan had hazel eyes. He must have gotten them from his father.

"Although Miss Preston and I have already gotten to know each other"—Mrs. Ingersoll spoke up, causing the quiet conversations to cease—"perhaps now is a good time to exchange introductions?" She gave Jonathan a pointed glance, and he immediately responded.

"Ah yes." He moved to stand behind Clara and placed his hands on her shoulders. "Mother, I would like to introduce you to Miss Clara Marie Preston." Jonathan shifted to catch Clara's eye. "Clara, my mother, Mrs. Ingersoll."

He then went on to introduce each brother in turn. From the eldest, Nathaniel, to the third in line, Micah, and down to the youngest, Alden, each one of Mrs. Ingersoll's sons stood tall and strong. Clara could easily see the family resemblance, in more ways than one.

"Nathaniel," Jonathan explained, "works as a master carver at Cushing & Ingersoll Ship Carving down by the river." He pointed at the third brother. "Micah is an apprentice for the town baker, but he never lets us forget the dislike he has for the man. So, he spends as much time here as possible, providing our guests—and us—with delicious baked goods. And that leaves Alden. He will be entering Yale College in the fall, studying to become a doctor of medicine."

Clara looked at each brother in turn and then at Mrs. Ingersoll, whose eyes shone as she beheld her sons. Each one had established a reputable trade or pursued it at present. Any mother would be proud of that.

Replacing his hands on her shoulders, Jonathan then addressed his family. "Clara works at her father's inn in Higganum." He gave her shoulders a squeeze. "She does not know this yet, but I hope to bring her here to work with you, Mother, running the inn."

Here? At the Red Griffin? Running it? That would be a dream come true. She had always thought she would take over for Mama, but this prospect held far more appeal. Clara twisted her neck and gazed up at Jonathan from the corner of her eye, smiling. He winked down at her.

"There is just one problem." He looked again at his older brother. "You have owned the inn since you achieved your twenty-first year. And now, with your family, I could not possibly ask you to give up that right."

"I believe I can answer that," Nathaniel spoke up from the edge of the bed where he sat cradling his wife and newborn son. He reached behind his lapel and withdrew an envelope, extending it toward Jonathan. "You are aware Uncle Phineas passed on about a month ago."

"Yes." Jonathan withdrew two pieces of paper from the envelope and held them in front of Clara for both of them to read. She did not follow a lot of what was written, but from what she could decipher, his uncle had solved the dilemma already.

"As you will see from that signed document, Uncle Phineas left the house and shop to me, with the provision that you have ownership of the inn if you live here with your future wife and allow Mother to live here still. Alden, too, as long as necessary." Nathaniel nestled his chin against his wife's hair. "Constance and I will be moving into Uncle Phineas's house at the earliest convenience."

"So, it appears to be all arranged." Jonathan stepped from behind Clara. "Except for one thing."

The knowing grins on the faces of Jonathan's brothers and mother alerted her to what Jonathan was about to do. Still, she thrilled at the prospect and allowed him time to kneel in front of her.

"I suppose the answer is quite obvious, but for the sake of propriety, I must ask." Jonathan flicked his gaze up to meet hers and took her hands in his. "I realize I have only recently asked your permission to court you, but Miss Clara Marie Preston, will you do me the honor of becoming my wife?"

"Yes! Yes! A thousand times, yes!" As soon as he stood, she jumped into his arms.

She could hardly believe it. Just this morning she'd conducted life as usual. Now, she would soon become Jonathan's wife and manager of a beautiful inn. The good Lord truly looked down upon them with favor.

"I have prayed for years," Mrs. Ingersoll said from the other side of the bed, "that each of my sons would grow to find and marry women of good character and possessing a strong faith." Tears glistened in her eyes as she looked first at Constance and then at Clara. "Two have done so. There remains but two more."

"And that may be a little while longer yet, Mother." Laughter rumbled in Jonathan's chest as he hugged Clara to him. He pulled back just enough for her to see the sparkle in his eyes. "At least I have performed my duty." His expression softened as he studied her lips. Clara smiled, inviting his touch. Locking her arms more tightly around his neck, she sealed their vow with the unconditional acceptance of their two lives soon to be joined as one.

"Very good," Mrs. Ingersoll spoke up once her son had stepped back. "Who would like a piece of my onion pie?"

Clara smiled at Jonathan, remembering when he asked about that the day he arrived at her inn.

"I would," they both said in unison.

# ONION PYE

From *The Art of Cookery Made Plain and Easy*
by Hannah Glasse, 1747.

1 pound of potatoes
1 pound of onions
1 pound of apples
2 pie crusts
½ pound butter
1 ounce of mace
1 nutmeg, grated
1 teaspoon pepper
3 teaspoons salt
12 eggs
6 spoonfuls of water

Wash and pare some potatoes and cut them in slices. Peel some onions, cut them in slices. Pare some apples and slice them. Make a good crust and cover your dish. Lay a quarter of a pound of butter all over. Take a quarter of an ounce of mace, beat fine, a nutmeg grated, a teaspoonful of beaten pepper, three teaspoonfuls of salt, mix all together. Strew some over the butter, lay a layer of potatoes, a layer of onion, a layer of apple, and a layer of eggs, and so on, till you have filled your pye, strewing a little of the seasoning between each layer, and a quarter of a pound of butter in bits, and six spoonfuls of water. Close your pye and bake it an hour and a half.

**Tiffany Amber Stockton** has been crafting and embellishing stories since childhood. Today she is an award-winning author, speaker, and a freelance website designer who lives with her husband and fellow author, Stuart Vaughn Stockton, in Colorado. They have a daughter and a son and a vivacious Australian Shepard named Roxie. Her writing career began as a columnist for her high school and college newspapers. She is a member of American Christian Fiction Writers and Historical Romance Writers. Three of her novels have won annual readers' choice awards, and in 2009, she was voted #1 favorite new author for the Heartsong Presents book club.

# OVER A BARREL

by Laurie Alice Eakes

# Dedication

To my sister for letting me use her dining room table.

*Trust ye in the LORD for ever:*
*for in the LORD JEHOVAH is everlasting strength.*
ISAIAH 26:4

# Chapter 1

*Glassenbury, Connecticut Colony*
*October 1758*

The barrel was too light. Under no circumstances could the keg that Micajah Ingersoll had dragged from its corner of his storage room contain a hundred and ninety-six pounds of flour. Less than half of that at an immediate guess.

Bending his six-foot frame, since stooping had become impossible thanks to a French musket ball wound in his right leg, Micah examined the lid of the barrel. No seal. The wax poured around the edges had been neatly cut.

"Who would sneak in here and take flour?" He spoke to a room empty of everything save the ingredients for breads and the occasional pie—flour and sugar, the sourness of the yeast starter and sweetness of apples, the tartness of dried fruits and the exotic perfume of spices in their locked chest.

The spice chest was the only lock in the bakehouse Micah used. He kept the shop open so townspeople could use the ovens, in the event he was occupied elsewhere and they needed to bake. Glassenbury residents had always proven to be an honest lot, leaving money on the counter for the consumption of firewood or any other supplies they used, with the exception of the spices too expensive and too difficult to obtain to share as he did a pound or so of flour. He had been known to share as much as five pounds in an emergency. Micah had his small inheritance from his Uncle Phineas. He didn't care about giving away a few shillings' worth of flour.

"But half a barrel and more's worth?"

With a sigh at the idea that he might have to start locking up the bakehouse while he slept the few hours of the night his leg and the Glassenbury baking needs allowed him, he tipped the barrel onto its side and started to roll it into the more brightly lit bakehouse to better examine the pilfered barrel.

A squeak emanated from inside the wooden staves.

Micah froze. Surely he was mistaken. Mice could be enterprising when they wanted food. Because of the quantity of flour and grains he kept on hand, he fed a veritable army of cats just enough to keep them near his business, but not enough they wouldn't hunt the local rodent population away from his supplies. In the past six months, he hadn't seen so much as one mouse dropping in the storage room or bakehouse, and in his entire life he had yet to meet the mouse who could apply a knife to a wax seal. Chew through it, most certainly. Slit it with the neatness of a tailor cutting out a shirt pattern, never.

There it was again, a squeak; a rustle now, too.

And a whimper?

"Egad." Micah dropped onto the lid of another barrel and plowed his fingers through his cocoa brown hair. It tumbled loose from the black grosgrain ribbon holding it away from his face, and he lowered his hands to his leg, rubbing the right calf so obviously smaller than the left. Too obviously smaller than the left below his knee breeches. Despite the leg's shrunken muscles, the pain was absent most of the time now. Surely he had enjoyed enough sleep to not be losing his reason as happened to some other soldiers wounded in the war on the frontier.

No, more likely one of his brothers was playing some sort of trick on him, exchanging a barrel full of flour for a barrel full of rodents. A few dozen mice squeaking at once might come through the wooden sides like a whimper in the stillness of the predawn hours.

Not wanting to release the vermin inside the bakehouse, Micah struggled to his feet and gave the keg a push toward the outside door. He would roll the thing right down to the Connecticut River and then pretend to his brothers that he had experienced nothing odd during that night's baking.

A thump and a cry rose from within the barrel.

A bang of his heart sinking into his guts, and a groan of dismay rose from within Micah. No mice squirmed and scrabbled inside that barrel. It was something much larger—larger than a mouse anyway. Larger than a mouse and much smaller than his tall, broad form.

Feeling more lightheaded than even the surgeon's laudanum had made him, Micah tipped the barrel onto its end again. Another thump and cry slammed against his ears.

"Lord, please do not let me find what I think I am about to find." He shot up a prayer, perhaps the first one in months, and slid the blade of his ever-present knife between the edge of the barrel and the lid. The latter popped up on one side. Micah grasped it and tossed it aside. It clattered onto the floorboards with a resounding roll. His heart felt as though it clattered to somewhere near his boot soles as he saw exactly what he had prayed not to see.

Two large dark eyes gazed up at him. A wide pink mouth spread even wider and let out a shriek loud and piercing enough to frighten a bobcat.

Micah flinched. "How did you get in there?"

He gripped the edge of the barrel to stop himself from covering his ears before the cries deafened him. Better not to concern himself with the hows right now and stop the yowling before it deafened the entire town.

"I am not going to hurt you." He doubted the creature heard him over her own keening. He couldn't hear himself. "Will you let me pick you up?"

No response but more howls, perhaps even louder.

Hard-working Glassenburians were not going to appreciate this kind of a ruckus in the middle of the night. If these cries grew any louder, the British navy would be sailing up the river thinking the French and their Indian allies had managed to invade this far east.

No help for it. If he had any hope of quieting things, he must act.

He reached inside the barrel, fully expecting to be bitten, and lifted the little girl into his arms.

Yes, certainly a girl, complete with flowing dark hair, somewhat the worse for wear with its matting of flour, and ruffled petticoats and gown. Little was not such an accurate description. She was small enough to fit into the nearly two feet across and higher barrel, but she was sturdily round and beyond the toddling-about stage.

But not beyond the sobbing-in-gasping-bursts-too-staccato-to-be-comprehensible-words stage. Five or six years, surely.

He tried to comfort her against his shoulder. "Where did you come from, little one?"

Hiccup. Hiccup. Hiccup.

He patted her back. "Where is your mother?"

Not that a woman who would abandon her child in a barrel deserved to be any child's mother.

The girl pushed against him, showing him a red and tear-streaked face. "I—" Hiccup. "Want—" Hiccup. Hiccup. Gasp.

He needed his brothers Nathaniel and Jonathan or their wives. They had children. They would know what to do. But walking through the streets of Glassenbury with a sobbing child in the middle of the night would do nothing good for his reputation. Likewise, neither would taking her to his mother at the Red Griffin Inn.

He could not, however, let her continue to cry like this. Surely it wasn't good for her. He knew little of children. A bachelor, he had only a passing acquaintance with children save for his nieces and nephews and the one or two who came into the bakeshop to buy the family bread.

And then he had encountered a few on the frontier while fighting for the English army. The less he thought about them the better. They had never sobbed like this. They were quiet in their fear and grief. Far too quiet for children.

Nothing about this young miss was quiet. If anything, her howls grew louder with each passing moment that Micah dithered about what to do with her. If the ruckus continued, he wouldn't have to think what to do with her—the entire town's worth of ladies would descend on him to discover what he was doing.

Or perhaps they would simply think his collection of cats had decided to yowl at the new moon.

He would rather have an encounter with ten cats than continue to hold on to this child. She pounded on his chest with tiny and ineffectual fists and continued her incomprehensible tirade. "I want" were the only words that emerged comprehensibly.

"Yes, well, I want a few things, too," Micah muttered. "Like to know how you got into my barrel and where the flour went. Like what to do with you."

Above all, he would like to know how to stop her crying.

He began to walk. He recalled Constance walking one of her babies when it wept inconsolably. From storeroom to bakehouse, he limped around and around, from door, to ovens set into the hearth, and back to the door. Still she sobbed. Still she struggled against his hold. Still her wants proved unintelligible. He could guess—she wanted her mother. So did he, or whoever was supposed to be in charge of her—the irresponsible, unfeeling, unnatural creature that she must be.

Beyond the window of the shop, the night remained black enough for the grayish glass to reflect his progress, his unbalanced gait, the protesting child, the light from the lamps flickering with the breeze of his passing, or perhaps the exhalation from the child's wails.

He paused at the window, allowing his body to block the light inside so he could peer out. Surely something along the street would give him insight as to where to take the child.

The only hope for him was to take the girl to Mother. She would know what to do. As an innkeeper since their father's death, Mother knew how to manage people of all ages. One small girl would be no trouble for her.

He turned from the window—and caught a flash of movement from the corner of his eye. He swung back, nearly overbalancing. Nothing moved in the darkness now. Down the street, a lantern in front of the inn glowed, welcoming the weary anytime of day or night. Outside his bakehouse, the street lay silent and still. Yet he had seen something, a flash of white like a face on the other side of the glass.

He headed for the door, an idea, a hope, warming inside him. Not until he rested his hand on the latch did he realize that the child had stopped wailing.

"Did you see it, too?" he asked her. "Is it your—"

No, he dare not ask her again about her mother. He didn't dare risk setting her off again. Besides, she hadn't been facing the window. She wasn't facing the window now. She stared at something behind him.

He turned and noted a tray of sweet biscuits resting on the counter. How foolish of him not to think of a sweet to quiet the girl.

"Do you want one?" he asked.

She nodded "Please."

One perfectly clear word from her. Clear and perfectly polite.

He closed the distance to the tray and handed a cinnamon-dusted biscuit to her. She crammed as much of it as possible into her mouth, chewed, swallowed, took another enormous bite.

The poor thing was starving.

A flood of tenderness washed over him as it did each time he found a starving or wounded creature. Abandoned, hungry, no doubt frightened to death of him, a person more than five times her size, and all he had thought of was his annoyance over the noise she was making.

"Let me take you someplace with food," he suggested.

Mother would have ham, bacon, eggs, and bread left over from the previous day. There would be nothing fresh today if he didn't get rid of the child and get to work.

The first biscuit had vanished. He gave her another one and headed for the door. If he could keep her quiet for the hundred-yard walk to the inn, all would be fine.

She began to sob the instant he opened the door to a rush of crisp, autumn air. "No. No. No."

Micah groaned. "Hush."

The girl cried louder as he turned from the bakehouse. The biscuits seemed to have given her renewed strength. Her wails sounded louder. Already a light bloomed in the ironmonger's shop across the way.

"Want. My. Momma." This time her words rang out as clear as bells warning of disaster. "Momma. Momma. Momma."

For a flash, Micah considered returning her to the barrel while he fetched his own mother. Then he simply felt like yowling for her to come to him, too.

Someone *was* coming to him. Footfalls clattered on the stone walkway. The light, quick footfalls of a female. One of the townswomen wondering what wild animal he had rescued this time, ready to lecture him on the dangers—

A hand grabbed his arm—hard. "Where are you taking my daughter?" asked a voice like a honey-coated razor.

# Chapter 2

**M**y child." Sarah Chapman grasped the big man's arm with both hands. "Where are you taking my child?"

"Momma." Eliza ceased wailing and lunged toward Sarah.

She caught her child, staggered under her weight.

"Not so quickly, madam." The man stepped back, pulling Eliza out of Sarah's hold.

"But she is my daughter." Sarah tried to wrap her arms around Eliza again. The act brought her into an uncomfortable proximity with the man, and she stepped back, trying to pull Eliza with her. Eliza began to wail again.

"You can see she is my daughter," Sarah cried above her baby's sobs. "Please." Her throat closed. Tears sprang into her eyes, and she blinked hard to hold them back. "Please let me have my little girl."

"You were not so concerned when you abandoned her in my storeroom." The man took another step back, forcing Sarah to follow or let go of Eliza. "And I do not see in the least how she is your child."

"She called me momma." Sarah lost her battle with tears. They poured down her cheeks, likely streaking the dirt and flour smudged over her face.

Raven-haired, brown-eyed Eliza favored her deceased father in looks, if not in temperament, a complete contrast to blond-haired, green-eyed Sarah. Sarah had more than once been mistaken for the girl's nursemaid rather than mother.

"You left her in my storeroom." The man enunciated each word as though Sarah were a mooncalf and couldn't understand him otherwise. "No mother would do such a thing."

Sarah dashed the corner of her shawl across her eyes. "She would if she were afraid of having her harmed."

"Indeed." A world of doubt and disdain rang from that single word, quiet yet audible past Eliza's sobs.

Words of explanation, of defense of her actions crowded into Sarah's mouth. Her lips refused to cooperate. They parted but nothing emerged. She could scarcely breathe, let alone talk. Her limbs shook, and her head felt stuffed with uncarded wool. Worse, they were no longer alone in the formerly quiet street. The flicker of torches grew brighter, drawing nearer.

"What is amiss here, Micah?" someone cried out.

Eliza began to weep again, not deafening wails this time, but deep, racking sobs. Sarah's arms ached to be holding her baby. She reached up to take Eliza away from the big man holding her, but he took another step back, let out a grunt as though of pain or surprise, and reeled back against the door of the bakehouse.

It didn't hold. His shoulder struck the wooden panel, sending it flying back against the wall, and he followed. With Eliza gripped in his arms, he couldn't catch himself.

Sarah lunged after him to grab her baby. She ended up with her arms around both Eliza and the man. At least as far around them both as she could reach. He was broad and not an ounce of it excess flesh. He couldn't be the baker. Bakers were fat, were they not? He felt like all muscle and—

She jerked away, her face heating despite the chill of the autumn night. "I—I am so sorry. I thought. . . I intended to. . . Please just give me my daughter, and I'll be on my way."

"Doesn't look like her daughter." The torchbearer stood behind Sarah, the light flickering over Eliza's pale and tear-stained face, and the man's chiseled features twisted as though in pain, his cool, blue-gray eyes belying any hint of weakness of body. "Stolen, do you think?"

"I do not know what to think." Micah fixed those autumnal-chill eyes on Sarah. His features smoothed out. "I think I should fetch the sheriff."

"No, please." Even as the words left her lips, Sarah knew they were a mistake, but she couldn't hold back the protest, which surely gave away her fear of being discovered.

Micah's eyes narrowed. "I think I should indeed."

"I will fetch him for you," the torchbearer offered. "He will be as angry as a hornet, being waked up in the middle of the night, but if she's stolen this child or something, she should be—"

"I did not steal her." Sarah was gasping with the notion of being separated from Eliza. "She calls me momma. You heard her." She fixed a pleading gaze upon the bakehouse man.

His expression didn't change. "Children are gullible. They can be convinced to call a body anything."

A wave of murmurs rose behind Sarah.

"I could just fetch your mother," someone from the onlookers suggested.

Laughter ran through the small crowd.

A shiver ran through Sarah. This man must have a formidable mother if someone suggested her rather than the sheriff. And yet another woman might see the mother and daughter bond between Sarah and Eliza, be convinced she told the truth.

"Do not disturb the sheriff," Micah said. "I will get an explanation from this lady before we decide whether or not to notify the sheriff of her presence." His face softened. "No sense in separating them if she is telling the truth."

"I am. Eliza, tell the man who I am."

Eliza took a long, shuddering breath and buried her face against the man's shoulder.

Sarah's own next breaths entered her lungs in constricted bursts. Her head spun. She grasped the doorframe and blinked against encroaching blackness.

"She's going to faint," someone called.

"No." Sarah steeled herself against the desire to collapse. Eliza needed her strong despite the fact she had not eaten for a day and a half. "I am not a weak female who faints."

"She looks half-starved." This was a softer, gentler voice, a woman's voice.

Sarah blinked and looked around. An attractive woman of late middle years approached the bakehouse doorway.

"I am Mrs. Drake, the ironmonger's wife." The woman smiled at Sarah. "Please come into our shop and let me get something warm into you."

Sarah wanted to hug the woman and cry, "Yes, yes, yes." But the man called Micah still held her baby. She sent him a pleading glance and hated every second of the eye contact.

"Of course I will bring her," he said. "You scarcely look strong enough to carry her ten inches, let alone ten yards."

"I have carried her all the way from—" Sarah snapped her teeth shut. She was too fatigued and hungry to be able to speak without giving information away. She bowed her head. "Thank you."

"Come along, child." Mrs. Drake slipped her arm around Sarah's waist and guided her forward. "The rest of you go back to your beds."

"But your man is away, and we don't know if she is a thief or not," someone shouted.

"She's got flour all over her," another man said. "Like as not she's been stealing from the baker."

"I didn't steal—" Sarah sighed. "Not much anyway."

"What did you do with nearly two hundred pounds of flour then?" Micah asked in a tone too calm and quiet to be trusted as genuinely unconcerned about his stores.

Sarah brushed at the telltale white powder on her nearly threadbare skirt. "I got most of it into a sack."

"Huh." He drew his rather nicely arched brows together over a high-bridged nose. "And how did you manage that without making a mess?"

"I cleaned up. I wanted no trace..."

"For the thief catchers?" Micah asked.

"Hush all these questions, Micajah Ingersoll," Mrs. Drake admonished. "Your mother would be ashamed of you for being so inhospitable."

"Mighty strange to me, madam, that she would take out all that flour to hide her daughter in one of my barrels. She could easily have just put the child in the sack instead."

Too obvious a hiding place. Sarah wouldn't say that if she could avoid it. The clandestine implications of the situation would confirm his worst suspicions. Eliza had been directed to remain quieter than a mouse. But no five-year-old child could remain perfectly still, and movement was less noticeable in a barrel. Besides, the barrel was more solid, safer.

Eliza was quiet now. Too quiet, clinging to the man like he was a lifeline in the middle of a stormy sea.

"And why weren't you closer at hand, unless you intended to abandon her?" Mr. Ingersoll pressed.

Sarah flinched. Eliza burrowed more closely to him, probably convincing him that Sarah had meant her baby harm.

"I never intended to abandon her. Eliza, what did momma tell you?"

"Momma?" An edge formed in the softness of Mr. Ingersoll's voice. "You are from south of here, are you not?"

Sarah bit her tongue. More speech would only convince him he was right.

"Micah," Mrs. Drake scolded, "no more. Can you not see she is unwell?"

"She would be more unwell in the jail." Despite his remark, Mr. Ingersoll stepped into the street, pulling the bakehouse door behind him, and started toward the building across the way. He limped badly, poor man. No wonder he was so ill-tempered. He must be in pain from that leg and carrying Eliza, small as she was. He couldn't possibly lift those heavy barrels of flour. Though perhaps he could with those shoulders and arms, muscles bulging against his—

Sarah pulled up her thoughts. She shouldn't notice such things about a man, not with her husband barely a year in his grave. She fixed her gaze on the ironmonger's shop door and light beyond that promised warmth and perhaps shelter, if shelter were something God would grant her at last. He hadn't provided much thus far, sending her north in the autumn, colder and colder nights, barely warm days.

She shivered.

Mrs. Drake tightened her hold on Sarah. "You'll come straight through to the kitchen. A shop full of nails and hammers is no place to rest."

It smelled of iron, rust, and turpentine. Despite the glow of the lantern in the window, the tools and paints seemed to radiate chill.

Not as much as the blue-gray of Micah Ingersoll's eyes.

If those eyes ever warmed, if his fine mouth ever smiled, he would be heart-stoppingly handsome.

Fortunately for Sarah's conscience, he did neither as he carried Eliza into the kitchen behind the shop and placed her on the settle with the tenderness of a mother laying her own child in its cradle. "Sleep there, little one," he said in a voice so tender Sarah's eyes burned. He then removed his coat and laid it over her daughter and turned to poke the smoldering fire into a blaze.

"You sit down, Miss—Missus—" Mrs. Drake frowned. "What is your name, my dear?"

"Sarah Ch—" She bit her lip. She should have a pretend name ready, but she had changed it in every town through which they passed between Virginia and Connecticut. She didn't think she should use any of them again, and her mind rang hollow from a lack of new ideas.

Which, naturally, made the suspicious Micajah Ingersoll even more mistrustful of her.

"Do, please, seat yourself, Mrs. Sarah." He gave her a mockingly deep bow.

Sarah wished she possessed the strength to stand, snatch up her daughter, and run to another hiding place. Her legs, however, wobbled, and she dropped onto the settle beside Eliza. "Are you all right, precious one?"

"I tried to be quiet, Momma. But that barrel rolled and rolled, and I thought I might be sick." Tears pooled in Eliza's dark eyes, and she popped her thumb into her mouth.

"That's all right." Sarah tugged the thumb free. "I didn't know the man would come to his shop so early."

"When do you think I bake bread? Sunrise?" Mr. Ingersoll slammed the poker into its stand and reached for a bucket of water standing beside the hearth. "Do you wish to heat this, Mrs. Drake?"

"Yes, but I'll lift it." Mrs. Drake bustled forward and snatched the bucket from Mr. Ingersoll. "I am still strong enough to lift water. You needn't hurt yourself lifting anything that heavy."

Despite his injured leg, Micajah Ingersoll was strong enough to move those barrels of flour. Mrs. Drake's remark must have wounded the man's pride.

A muscle jumped at the corner of his jaw, and he turned away, not saying a word. He didn't even look at Sarah, but crossed the kitchen to lean against the worktable, arms crossed over his chest. "While Mrs. Drake does her Christian duty and serves you tea, you can tell us why you placed your child in a barrel that had recently held flour and then left her behind."

Sarah needed the tea first. Her throat felt as dry as that barrel of flour. She swallowed and tried to speak. Nothing emerged. The kitchen fell silent save for the crackle of the fire and the splash of water gurgling into the iron kettle suspended from a hook to swing over the flames.

"I'm waiting." Mr. Ingersoll speared her with his gaze.

Sarah crossed her arms over her chest in imitation of his posture and tilted up her chin so she could meet and hold his gaze while she spoke the absolute truth. He would accept none of her truths cloaked in subterfuge. "I am a widow, a very wealthy widow, with a very bad man insisting he will have me to wife so he can get his hands on my plantation. He nearly caught us a few days ago, so I headed inland to get away. I hid Eliza in the barrel while I looked for a place to hide for the daytime. I—I did not know that you would come to work so early, or I would have gone elsewhere."

"Indeed." No expression changed the strong lines of Mr. Ingersoll's face. "Is that all?"

"Yes." Flour was too damp to describe the texture of her lips, her tongue, her throat. More like chalk not quite ground into powder. "That's all."

"A pity." Mr. Ingersoll uncrossed his arms and straightened. "Because I do not believe a word you said."

# Chapter 3

Micah had read of more believable dramas enacted on the London stage than the tale this flour-daubed woman had just told him. Runaway widowed heiress indeed. With Mrs. Drake there frowning at him, he managed not to snort with derision, and he believed Sarah Ch-something as far as he could throw her, which, alas, was not as far as he could throw before he ran off to fight for the English army. Not that he was still as weak as he had been when he returned home. He was still not able to cut logs for fires, as could other men, as he didn't have the balance, but he was not weak in body or mind. And his mind told him that this woman before him, pretty despite her disheveled state, could not be telling the truth.

Yet the fear twisting her delicate features tangled a knot inside Micah. Fear of him sending her to the town jail as a thief, or fear of someone chasing her.

Ah, yes, the chasing part.

"I should amend my last remark," he conceded. "I do believe you are being chased. But by whom is the question. Perhaps you stole that child, or perhaps—"

"I never." Sarah surged to her feet. All color drained from her face and she swayed, flailed one hand toward the back of the settle.

Micah caught her hand and pressed it to the solidity of the wood. Despite its generally grimy appearance and flour caked beneath her nails, Sarah's hand felt soft beneath his. Soft and warm from the fire.

He snatched his fingers away. "Sit down before you fall down." His tone was harsh, in response to the tightness building inside him. "Mrs. Drake, I dislike imposing upon you, but if you have some bread for this. . .female, I will bring you a fresh loaf whenever I manage to get to my baking."

"Of course I have bread, and no need to replace it unless I come over to buy." Mrs. Drake fixed him with a sharp gaze. "It is nothing less than my Christian duty to feed the hungry."

Micah flinched at the barb.

"I do not wish to be any trouble." Sarah sank onto the settle again and covered the little girl's hand with hers.

The child's mother or not, she did hold affection for the girl. Only someone who acted on the stage could pretend that kind of spontaneous tenderness. Of course, she might have been playing some role for so long she had learned to act the part. The little girl looked nothing like her and, despite calling Sarah "momma," had not seemed particularly eager to go into the woman's arms. Still, if she was the girl's mother, he had no right to separate them. . . .

And the longer he dithered there in Mrs. Drake's kitchen, the later the bakeshop would open, the less money he would make, and the more annoyed with the female he would grow. He needed to find somewhere to put her. The jail made sense, and he would not have hesitated a moment if it were not for the child. A prison was no place for a little girl. Separating her from the only person she knew in town, mother or not, was also wrong.

He glanced toward the window cut into the wall across from him. Light bloomed in the eastern sky, far too late for him to not be at his baking. But not too late for Mother to be awake and bustling about the inn, preparing breakfast for the guests and supervising the maids to clean rooms or the myriad other tasks involved in running the family business.

"If you will ensure this female remains here," Micah said abruptly, "I will fetch my mother and see if she can take her in at the inn. There is that room Constance used a few years ago."

He referred to his now sister-in-law, who had been near death when his eldest brother, Nathaniel, bought her indenture papers and carried her to Mother for care.

Huddled before the fire beside the sleeping child, her hands wrapped around a mug of tea, Sarah Whoever needed care, too.

"I'd take her in," Mrs. Drake said, "but I have no space once my husband and sons return from bringing the supplies up from New York City."

"No one needs to take me in." Sarah's voice sounded weak with fatigue or perhaps defeat. "I can survive on my own a bit longer."

"I think not." Micajah limped to the door.

Mrs. Drake bustled forward and laid her hand on the latch, preventing him from leaving. "You are not going to get the sheriff instead, are you?"

"No, I am getting my mother as I said." Micah glanced toward the window. "I do not want to let her leave, but neither do I want a female and child in the jail."

"Please." Sarah struggled to her feet. "Just let me leave. I am sorry for the trouble last night. I—I am certain that...man is gone now, and I can be on my way."

Micah did not respond. He had announced his intentions, he would not change his mind or go back on what he said. Mrs. Drake knew him well enough to understand that and stepped aside at last, with a nod and a tight smile.

"Of course you will go to your mother," she said. "I never should have questioned it."

"And I will bring by bread later."

"Too much later," he muttered as the ironmonger's door closed behind him.

He strode through the morning, noting frost lying over the plants and the vapor of his breath clouding the air before him. Winter approached with a rapidity that never failed to remind him of that horrible winter with the army in the western hills, never warm, never dry, never enjoying a full belly. The bakeshop from which he had been a runaway apprentice sounded like heaven on earth then. At that moment, five years later, it still looked like heaven, with light glowing dimly in the brightening dawn and the promise of warm ovens and warmer fires.

First things first.

He traversed the block of buildings to the inn with its weathered clapboard and shining windows, smoke from the two chimneys puffing vapor against the rising sun, and aromas of frying bacon drifting through the doorway. He rounded to the rear, to the kitchen, and pushed open the door.

Mother; his sister-in-law, Clara, wife to his second-eldest brother, Jonathan; and two maidservants swarmed around the large kitchen with platters and jugs nearly flying from hands to tables and back to other hands that carried them through the doorway into the dining room. Micah stood in the doorway for a few moments, not wanting to interrupt the rhythm of the morning routine, waiting for someone to notice him.

Mother did first. She paused on her way across the chamber bearing an enormous ham. "Micajah, what are you doing here, and with empty hands? We need at least three dozen bread rolls."

"Your guests will have to do without until dinnertime." He glanced at the other females, now all paused to watch and listen to him. "I. . .have a bit of a dilemma here." He flashed a glance at the door to the outside, hoping she would understand he wanted to speak to her alone.

Being his mother, who had singlehandedly raised him and his three brothers for a quarter of his life, she understood at once and thrust the ham into Clara's hands. "Carve this up thin. I'll be back in a trice—perhaps." She followed Micah into the innyard to where sunlight had reached a patch of the kitchen garden. She paused with her hands on her hips and her face tight. "You are not telling me you are quitting the bakehouse, are you? You are not nearly well enough recovered from your wound to—"

"I am not running off again, Mother." He interrupted with a gentle smile. "But someone has run off, and I do not quite trust her story."

Mother's blue-gray eyes sparkled. "Another one?"

"You mean like Constance? No. This one is not a potential bride for me or Alden."

"You cannot know that if you just met her."

"Mother, please." Micah suppressed his sigh of exasperation with his mother's constant desire to see her four sons wed and settled. "This woman, I assure you, is a bane, unlike Constance or Clara."

Mother's face softened. "Yes, they have been a blessing. But what of this female, and how did you find her?"

"She found me. Well—" Micah hesitated, organizing his thoughts. "I found her daughter, or the child she says is her daughter, but they don't look a thing alike. The child is dark and the mother fair."

"Golden hair?" Mother cocked her head. "And blue eyes of course?"

"No, her eyes are green. A pale, bright green like spring gr—" Micah's cheeks grew warm in the chilly morning air.

Mother started to laugh. "Pretty, is she?"

"Perhaps she is, under all the dirt and flour." Annoyance left his voice harsh, his tone hard.

"Ah, so you are not attracted to her." Mother sighed. "I will keep praying."

"Do, please, Mother, be satisfied with having two of us married off already." He tried to smile to soften his words.

She did not smile back. "You, of all my sons, need a wife most. You concern me greatly since you came home."

"With all due respect, ma'am, I am naught for you to be concerned about."

119

Her gaze flicked to his leg.

He clenched his jaw then forced it to relax so he could speak. "You know no woman here wants a lame man for a husband; thus, I am looking for no woman to take to wife."

"The right—" Mother stopped and sighed.

They had endured this discussion since he returned home from Albany in the New York colony, feverish, close to having his leg amputated. All Mother seemed to think about was getting her four sons married to good, Christian women. Micah had seen the pity in the females around Glassenbury. He wanted none of that.

"This does not in any way meet your specifications," Micah said. "She has told me a tale like some drama out of London and acted badly at that. Indeed, she is the last sort of female I would take to wife, if I were in the market for one. Now then, to practical matters. . ."

# Chapter 4

M y mother will give you a place to sleep." Micajah Ingersoll stalked into the Drakes' kitchen and began to talk to Sarah without greeting.

Half asleep before Mrs. Drake's warm fire, her stomach full for the first time in a month, Sarah jerked upright at the sound of the baker's voice—a melodious timbre that should belong to a preacher—and banged her elbow on the arm of the settle. Her breath hissed through her teeth. "I was asleep." Sarah rubbed her eyes for emphasis. "What do you want me to do with your mother?"

"It is what my mother will do with you." His gaze skimmed over her. "Clean clothes and water perhaps will do as an introduction."

"Micajah." Mrs. Drake bustled in from the ironmonger's shop. "You know better than to talk to a lady that way."

"I'm sorry." He didn't sound as though he were. "I am in a bit of a rush. The baking is already hours behind."

"I will make up for it." Sarah stared at her filthy hands, the fingernails black with dirt and whitish gray with flour. "I can bake."

"Never heard of an heiress who could." Despite the words, a hint of interest sparked in his blue-gray eyes. "And if you speak truth, we may be able to work on an agreement. What can you bake?"

Sarah dropped her gaze to her filthy fingernails again. "Cakes. Fine sugar cakes."

"I would be welcome of that for a special reason," Mrs. Drake said.

"Perhaps you would be interested, but I can't see too many others in Glassenbury thinking the cost would be worth the effort." Despite his words, Mr. Ingersoll's eyes still held a gleam of interest. "Of course, if they are. . ." He trailed off and bent to pick up the still-sleeping Eliza from the settle. "We must be on our way. I am losing money by the minute."

So money drove this man. He was angry with her because she was taking away from his baking time.

"I told you to let me go," she murmured. "You could have been about your baking without troubling yourself with me."

"And leave you to steal from my neighbors? I think not."

"I have not stolen—" Sarah sighed.

No doubt the bit of flour she had wasted convinced him she was a thief.

"Where does your mother live?"

"At the inn." Mr. Ingersoll headed for the door.

"She is a fine lady," Mrs. Drake said. "She will be kind to you."

"Not possibly as kind as you have been, ma'am." Sarah dropped the older woman a curtsy.

Mrs. Drake laughed. "I have never been curtsied to before. We do not hold much with that sort of thing up here."

No, of course they wouldn't. Sarah's cheeks grew hot, and she scurried after Mr. Ingersoll, her head down.

Sunlight tinged the horizon, burning through morning mist. Sarah shivered in her now threadbare shawl and the gown that should be held out with several petticoats but now hung limp and a little too long over just one, as she had sold the others to buy what little food she could purchase with the pittance the once-expensive garments had gained her.

If Mr. Ingersoll could see the lace she had traded for bread, he would believe her an heiress. Or perhaps not. He might think she wore her mistress's cast-off clothing, as Sarah had once so blithely passed a mended gown or petticoat to her serving women. Serving women who likely now thought her tucked away in a home in town, while they took orders from Benjamin Woods's appointed overseer, and Woods himself chased after her.

Even the thought of the man's name, the image of his handsome but dissipated face in her mind, sent a shiver up her spine that owed nothing to the morning chill away from the warm fire. Striving to keep up with Mr. Ingersoll, she glanced around, certain she would see her husband's factor skulking in a doorway, an alleyway, ready to pounce. She knew she had seen him the previous day, coming after her himself, not trusting to an agent, so he could force her to be his wife without delay. Surely she hadn't been imagining things. That face, those black eyes, looked like no one else she had ever encountered.

She saw no lurking shadows of a man spying on her movements. He might not have followed her inland, up the river, to this town. He might have thought she would push north to Boston and her late husband's grandmother in the hope the woman would take her in for the sake of Eliza.

They reached a large clapboard house with the sign of the Red Griffin swinging above the door without encountering anyone. Woodsmoke and the aromas of frying bacon drifting through the street announced that the townspeople were awake and readying themselves for the day. In the distance a bucket clanged, and a horse whinnied close at hand.

"We will go around to the back," Mr. Ingersoll announced. "I will not parade you before any guests who might be at their breakfast. This inn holds a fine reputation."

And she looked disreputable. Sarah understood that implication.

"Momma?" Eliza lifted her head from Mr. Ingersoll's shoulder.

"I am here, child." Sarah reached up to stroke her daughter's soft tangled curls. Her knuckles rasped against Mr. Ingersoll's jawline, a line of whiskers he had missed beneath his chin. An odd thrill ran through her at the familiarity, and she jerked her hand away, pulling Eliza's hair in the process.

The child cried out.

"I–I'm sorry." Sarah glanced around, feeling as though she needed a bolt-hole, a place to run and hide. Nowhere presented itself to her. Two horses being hitched to a wagon by a groom stood between her and the stable. Other buildings rose around the inn on three sides. Most important, Mr. Ingersoll still held Eliza.

He shot her an impatient glance. "Are you coming?"

"Yes." Sarah hastened to keep up with him.

They rounded the end of the building and a tall, well-favored woman of middle years emerged from a kitchen doorway on a wave of apple and cinnamon scent. "Is this they?" she asked Mr. Ingersoll.

"It is. More trouble for you, ma'am." He set Eliza on the ground. "Can you walk from here, little miss?" Again his tone held that tenderness that brought a lump to Sarah's throat.

Eliza giggled. "Of course I can walk, sir. I am not a baby."

"No, I expect you are quite old enough." He spoke to Eliza but shot Sarah a glance of returning frost.

Old enough for what? Sarah would not ask him. She didn't have the time to ask him. His mother glided forward, graceful in her black bombazine gown and snowy apron. "You know they're no trouble, Micajah. For shame you even saying so."

"We do not know that yet, ma'am." He straightened, his features pinching for a moment as though the action brought him pain. "I will be off to the bakery. No one will have any bread this morning." He strode away, fast, yet limping badly.

His mother gazed after him, her brows furrowed. "He works too hard for a man who hasn't yet recovered."

"I never asked for him to carry my daughter." Sarah stooped to gather Eliza close to her.

But Eliza had caught sight of a black-and-white cat striding from the stable and ran forward with a joyful, "Magpie!"

"No, Eliza, that's not—" Sarah started after her child but hesitated. Too many people rushing at a strange animal might make it flee, in which case Eliza would give chase. Or it might attack. Either way, Eliza would make a fuss and draw more attention to Sarah than she had already garnered in the past few hours.

"It will be all right." Mrs. Ingersoll laid a gentle hand on Sarah's arm. "She is a friendly cat."

"She looks like one Eliza played with in the garden at home."

"And where is that home, my dear?" Mrs. Ingersoll asked.

Sarah hesitated then decided she should be perfectly honest with this lady. If she could convince her, though her son had been dubious about the veracity of her words, Mrs. Ingersoll might be more willing to help Sarah get to Boston. Once there, surely she could pay her back.

"I came up here from Virginia, ma'am." Sarah wrapped her shawl more tightly around her shoulders and kept her gaze on Eliza now kneeling to pet the cat.

It rubbed its head against the child's hand as though enjoying itself.

"It is not a pretty tale," Sarah admitted.

"I expect not, but you are a very pretty young woman." Mrs. Ingersoll smiled. "Despite the grime. Would you like a wash for you and the child?"

"The child," Sarah said with cool dignity, "is my daughter. She has five years, and I have three and twenty."

"Ah, you wed when you were. . . ?"

"Sixteen, ma'am. My father died and Mr.—Mr.—" She sighed and bit her lip, reluctant to give her full name, but knowing she must to earn this woman's trust. "Mr. Chapman was my friend from childhood and had just come into his inheritance. He needed a wife. I needed a guardian, so we wed."

"And he has gone to be with the Lord?"

"Last September. He caught a chill."

"Which you are about to." Mrs. Ingersoll opened the kitchen door. "Do come in. I already have water heating. Your child's name is Eliza?"

"Yes." Sarah reached out her hands. "Leave the cat and come here, sweeting. We are going to have a wash."

"And an apple?" Eliza remained on her knees beside the cat, which had toppled to its side and rolled onto its back, all four paws waving in the air, claws sheathed.

"I want an apple," Eliza announced.

"Eliza, no, you mustn't. You must wait until someone offers you something."

"But I am hungry." The hint of a whine crept into Eliza's voice. "I want—"

"Eliza, enough." Sarah wanted to crawl into the hayloft with mortification. She offered Mrs. Ingersoll a tight smile. "I apologize for her poor manners. Before—before last month, I am afraid we all spoiled her. I thought. . . We thought. . .she would have a different sort of life." Sarah marched to her daughter and bent to pick her up. "You must listen to me, Eliza. I told you that."

Eliza's lower lip puffed out.

"Do not cry. Remember what I said when we ran away from the bad man?"

Eliza's lip quivered, but she scrambled to her feet and took Sarah's hand without a word. When Sarah rose and turned to Mrs. Ingersoll again, the woman's eyes had narrowed in speculation much like her son's, without the coldness.

Sarah wished she could stick out her lower lip and pout and weep like a child. Perhaps stamp her foot, too. Nonsense. She knew God was punishing her for living a life of leisure, doing as she pleased and showing little heed for how the nursemaid and other servants spoiled the beloved daughter of the house. They liked Sarah well enough. She was kind to them and didn't ask too much; however, Eliza was everyone's pride and joy. Only a son of the family would have brought more joy to the plantation. Sarah was paying for it now, with Eliza and she being too poorly acquainted as mother and daughter for anyone here to believe her claim of maternity. And thus they didn't believe anything else she said either.

"I was spoiled, too," Sarah admitted.

"Let us make you more comfortable," Mrs. Ingersoll responded. "Then you may tell me your whole story, and I will make my own decision about whether or not I believe you tell the truth."

"Because your son does not?" Sarah did not move toward the door in the older woman's wake.

Eliza tugged on her hand. "Please, Momma? I smell apples."

"Hush, baby." Sarah did not go toward the house. "Is he going to have me put into the jail?"

"Not yet." Mrs. Ingersoll opened the door to the inn, and a wave of fragrant warmth spread into the yard. "He's acquiring the *London Connecticut Gazette* first to see if you fit the description of any runaway servants."

"I am not and never have been a servant," Sarah insisted.

"Even if this is true and, judging by your hands, I suspect you are telling the truth, he has suggested that we keep the child close here at the inn while you help in the bakery."

"What?" Sarah could scarcely breathe. "But she is my daughter."

"Aye, so she is." Mrs. Ingersoll nodded, the ribbons adorning her cap fluttering in the morning breeze. "So you will not be running away without her. If you do, then we shall know that all you've said is an untruth."

# Chapter 5

Micah's mother brought Mrs. Chapman to the bakehouse three days later. Micah had seen her every evening when he took his meal with Mother and often Jonathan and Clara, too. She conducted herself in a quiet and composed manner and avoided Micah's eyes, though if someone spoke to her first, she responded to them, and even greeted the inn maids by name. To Micah, she said not a word, as he pretended she wasn't there—a rude action, he knew and his mother and brother pointed out—but he couldn't help himself. Mother must not gain ideas of matchmaking with this female about whom they knew nothing. Simply because the previous week's *Gazette* said nothing about a runaway servant or wife did not mean the notices simply had not arrived in Connecticut yet.

And she was just too fine to look at for his comfort. Dressed in a clean black gown and apron, her face and hands scrubbed clean, Sarah Chapman was a much different looking lady than the vagabond who had rushed up to him in the street in the wee hours of the morning. Beneath a bleached cap, her hair shone as gold as an English guinea, and her complexion glowed as pale and smooth as a pearl. In truth, she was more than simply a pretty girl. She was beautiful, and his heart skipped a beat or two before he got it under control and focused on his brother.

After the second day of Mrs. Chapman's presence, Jonathan and Nathaniel took Micah for a walk along the river. They ignored the protests of their womenfolk. Neither of Micah's elder brothers believed him incapable of a walk, though he sometimes gritted his teeth against the pain caused by having to keep up with them.

"Why don't you trust her?" Jonathan asked. "Clara says she's quiet and gentle—"

"And scarcely pays attention to her child," Nathaniel broke in.

"Which is why I don't trust her to be telling us anything other than a faradiddle," Micah said, gazing at the undoubtedly icy water of the river and thinking how its chill would soothe his aching leg. "Constance and Clara are always talking to or at least looking after the little ones. Mrs. Chapman scarcely seems to know her child."

"They do things differently in the southern colonies." Nathaniel looked thoughtful. "It would seem like proof that she is an heiress if servants did all the work."

"Not a wife for you then." Jonathan clapped Micah on the back.

He snorted. "Tell that to Mother."

The brothers laughed.

Still, Micah began to observe Mrs. Chapman more closely, especially when little Eliza joined the family in the big inn kitchen. When they prayed, Mrs. Chapman took the little girl's hand. Often, she stroked the child's forever-tangled curls, and sometimes she gazed upon Eliza with a tender glance that put odd notions into Micah's head, such as how much he would like a wife who gazed upon their children as though they were a wonder.

In that first week of being near Mrs. Sarah Chapman, Micah began to believe that she was the girl's mother after all, and had not stolen her from her rightful home and merely convinced Eliza to call her Momma. He also found Mrs. Chapman to be soft-spoken and polite, yet too reluctant to answer direct questions such as those Mother posed to her about her home, its location, her late husband.

Chapman, apparently, was a common name in the Virginia colony. It might not even be this woman's name. She might have taken it from her master, were she a runaway servant, or from a name she knew would not be easy to trace to its original family without going to the colony itself.

The one thing Micah believed about Sarah Chapman without a hint of a doubt was that she was running and hiding. She refused to go into the inn itself and rarely emerged into the yard unless needing to chase after Eliza, who in turn chased after one of the stable cats each time an opportunity presented itself. She worked in the kitchen without having to be asked, washing dishes, scrubbing pots, rolling out crust for a meat or onion pie. But when Mother asked her to carry a platter of chicken into a group of guests, Mrs. Chapman refused.

"I will turn the ham on the spit." And she turned her back on Mother and began to do just that.

"I am sorry I brought her to you if she is always this defiant," Micah said. "Perhaps she should earn her keep in the bakehouse instead."

Mother hefted the platter of roasted fowl. "And hide in your storeroom?"

"If she likes."

The stiffening of Mrs. Chapman's shoulders told Micah she heard every word they said.

"Bring her tomorrow," he said.

"I would rather stay here," Mrs. Chapman responded.

"But Mrs. Drake has been asking about those cakes you said you can make," Micah reminded her.

Mrs. Chapman gave the spit another turn. "I can bake them from here."

"I don't have a good oven as Micajah has," Mother pointed out then vanished into the inn.

"Tomorrow," Micah repeated.

He and the widow stood alone in the kitchen, the first time they had been alone since they met. Though ten feet separated them, he experienced a discomfort that few females gave him. Likely from the fact she never looked directly into his eyes. Until that moment, when she turned her head and held his gaze for no more than a breath, a heartbeat, both of which seemed to snag in his throat.

"I have to look after Eliza."

"And how long have you been doing that?" he asked.

"Not as long as a mother should." She gave him a view of her slim, straight back. "I was too occupied with frivolities. That's why I can bake fine cakes and nothing else."

"We shall see." He attempted to maintain his chilly demeanor toward her, but something in her honesty about herself softened his heart just a bit.

So much, though, that he procured a copy of the *London Connecticut Gazette* the next morning to have a second look at the notices of runaways—servants, slaves, and even wives. Nothing appeared that matched Mrs. Chapman's description, which proved nothing one way or the other. News traveled slowly from the southern colonies to the northern ones then up the Connecticut River to Glassenbury. Yet she said she had been on her way north for five weeks.

On her way north to what? He really needed to ask her. When she came to the bakehouse. If she came to the bakehouse.

Which she did not do anytime that day. His leg aching from an onset of cold, wet weather, he didn't take dinner at the inn, but ate leftover bread and cheese in his quarters above the bakehouse. Later in the evening, he presented himself at the kitchen door in time to find Mrs. Chapman scrubbing a stain from the pine kitchen table.

"I will pay you a fair wage to work in the bakehouse if you can indeed produce cakes," he said without greeting.

She didn't pause in her work. "I will not leave my daughter without someone to care for her."

"My mother or Clara will look after Eliza," Micah said. "I cannot have you slipping out the storeroom door with her when I am otherwise occupied."

Her scrubbing grew powerful enough to reduce the surface of the work space to splinters in a few more minutes. "And of course you have no reason to take my word that I will not."

"Will you give it if I say I will?"

"I need the money," she admitted, still without looking at him. "I will be there."

Accompanied by his mother, she arrived early the next morning before many folk in the town had awakened. Cap frills fluttering, she marched up to the serving counter, bringing the clean, sweet fragrance of lavender and rosewater with her, mingling with the aroma of baking bread. "I have arrived, and if anything happens to my daughter because I am here, it will be on your head."

"You promised to bake cakes for me to earn your way." He spoke more harshly than he intended, but something seemed to be wrong with his breathing. "Can you keep that much of your word?"

"The Lord will provide for you for doing your Christian duty in helping her," Mother said.

"That remains to be seen." Micah glanced at the *Gazette*. "There's still nothing in the newspaper, but I would rather have you close at hand, whether you are telling the truth or not. If you are, you are safer here than at the inn."

The instant he said the words, he realized they were foolish. He could never defend her if a villainous man were indeed chasing her. No doubt Micajah Ingersoll would get in the way of her renewed flight rather than fend off an assault.

Another reason why no female in town wanted him—defending their honor or possessions with a loaf of bread sounded like something from a pantomime or farce.

"I will agree to stay as long as my daughter and I are safe." Mrs. Chapman gave him a steady gaze. "Where do you want me to start?"

He smiled at her. "Where you started here before—in the storage room. Find the ingredients you need for your cakes."

"Do you have any spices? Nutmeg or cinnamon or ginger?"

"I do. I keep them locked away. Tell me when you need them."

"Eggs?"

"In the storeroom."

"All right." She rounded the counter and headed back to the storage room. Though he rarely needed them, he had purchased a basket of eggs just that morning, counting on her appearance.

"I'm willing to give her a chance," he said to his mother.

"Good. I believe her."

"How can you? We do not even know her true name."

"I do." Mother rested her hands, fine hands with long fingers, but a little red and rough from work, unlike Sarah's hands, smooth and white now that they were clean. "Her name is Sarah Chapman."

"Or so she says."

"Aye, and I believe her. She, as you know, was widowed last September. A month ago, her husband's factor abducted her and her daughter, trying to force a marriage."

"I have never heard of anything like that, not even up in the New York wilderness."

"It happens in the southern colonies where they do not have many preachers. People do not. . .er. . .get married with the blessing of the Lord or the Crown outside the cities unless they have a great deal of money."

"And she said she is an heiress."

"She is, but this Woods is not a rich man. He only wants to be."

"As I said," Micah scoffed, "a drama right off the London stage. London back in England, that is. Sounds preposterous to me."

"It does." Mother nodded. "But so preposterous, I believe it is true."

"But I will keep looking for runaway servants in the paper. This one is a week old." Micah folded the sheets of print and set them on a shelf below the serving counter. They worked well for wrapping up loaves of bread.

And he had loaves of bread ready to come from the oven. Though he had acquired a clock with the bakehouse, he had gotten so he could know if the bread was ready by the way it smelled.

These loaves he pulled from the oven built into the side of the hearth were a perfect golden brown. He used a long, wide blade to lift them onto a wooden rack so they could cool. While he worked, Mother waited quietly on the other side of the counter. From the storeroom, Sarah's voice rose and fell in quiet recitation, as though she repeated a recipe again and again. Then her footfalls sounded on the wooden floorboards and she came into the shop.

He glanced down at her shoes for the first time. Foolish of him. Shoes told stories of a man's—or woman's—life.

Though the leather of Mrs. Chapman's shoes was scuffed and scratched, it had once been fine, expensive material, though her shoes were nothing anyone should walk in for long. They appeared more like the hour glass-shaped heels ladies wore when dressed in their finest. The buckles were real silver, as any lesser metal would have tarnished. She could have sold the buckles for passage or food, but she might not know she could fasten shoes with twine. Or maybe she wasn't willing to sink that low.

A servant given her mistress's cast-off shoes would use string or perhaps ribbon to fasten them.

Gripping the doorframe, Mrs. Chapman raised one foot with the sole toward him so he could see the trodden-down edge of the heel and the thinness of the leather bottom. "The heels are worn down, too. Ridiculous shoes to run away in. I told your mother I was a pampered wife. I had nothing more sensible."

Another note in her favor.

Micah couldn't help himself. He laughed. The short guffaw sounded rusty to his own ears, and he couldn't recall the last time he had so much as snorted in mirth. He didn't trust this female to be telling him the truth, and yet her indomitable spirit, her courage, even if she were a runaway servant, impressed and, yes, amused him.

And amused his mother. She grinned broadly and turned toward the door. "I will leave the two of you to bake without my supervision. I need to oversee the inn. We have several guests heading into the mountains for the autumn hunting at present."

"You work too hard, Mother." Micah tried to hurry forward to open the door for her. He led with his right leg, a lifetime of habit, and his knee buckled. His right hand shot out to catch a solid surface for balance.

His fingers closed on a feminine arm instead, small-boned, yet smooth. No sleeve covered the delicate forearm. She had tucked up the sleeve ruffles to protect them. Only a light dusting of flour graced her fine skin.

"Will you forever be covered in flour?" He intended to sound exasperated but sounded amused instead. He barely suppressed a groan. Mother probably thought this banter was a sign he had decided Mrs. Sarah Chapman might be exactly what she said and, more, that he had decided to get to know her better.

He wished his mother weren't right.

# Chapter 6

As Mrs. Ingersoll closed the door behind her, a peal of laughter drifted back into the shop.

Sarah snatched her arm away from the warmth of Micah's strong fingers curved around it. "I—I am sorry. The bread. You were about to grab the bread."

"Considering how many customers I owe loaves, that would have been a disaster." He stared at the crusty bread rather than her. Beneath his shining dark hair, his ears burned red.

"How did it happen?" Sarah asked.

Mr. Ingersoll stared at her. "I beg your pardon?"

"How did you injure your leg?"

A bold question for her to pose to him, yet the limb obviously gave him trouble, so she may as well also have that honesty between them.

Still not looking at her, he gave an offhand shrug. "I ran off and joined the Sixth Connecticut Militia and fought in this nonsensical war with the French. A French musket ball found me."

"I am so sorry. Is that why you became a baker? I mean—" Her cheeks heated as though she were too near the fire. "I mean, I thought bakers were old and fat, not young and hand—" She started to clap a flour-dusted hand over her mouth.

He caught her wrist before her fingers touched her face. "You cannot continue to waste my flour on your face. Your skin is pale enough."

He reached out his other hand toward her cheek, as though about to smooth a fingertip over her skin. "How a runaway could keep her skin so fine, I cannot imagine."

Fingers tingling where he gripped them, Sarah stared at the scuffed toes of her once-expensive shoes, imported from Italy. "I had a hat until the day before I arrived here. I traded it for a penny loaf."

"Is that all?" Mr. Ingersoll's gaze flew to her hair, where one of his mother's frilly caps perched. "It must have been in poor condition."

"It was not, but I was hungry and Eliza was crying from the pain in her stomach." Speech delivered, she spun on her heel with a flurry of cap ruffles and wide skirt and hastened back to the storeroom. She tried to lose herself in blending eggs and butter, flour and sugar, while her ears pricked to the sound of Micajah Ingersoll moving about the bakery—the slight drag of his right leg over the boards, the *slap, slap, slap* of those broad hands with their long, strong fingers working the dough. Her mind's eye saw him reaching toward her face, a strange light in his eyes, a glow that made her feel too warm, made her want him to caress her cheek.

"Don't like him," she warned herself. "At any moment, you will have to run again."

She wished she didn't have to. The days at the inn had been a welcome respite of warmth and good food, clean clothes, and Eliza crying less than she had since that dark night when Sarah snatched the child from her bed and fled from the plantation before Benjamin Woods could carry out his plan to force her into a marriage without the sanction of the church or Crown.

The family was kind. Even Micah had softened toward her. If her cakes turned out well and sold, he might soften more, might help her get to safety in Boston.

She needed the precious spices to make the batter complete but waited until a band of customers left the shop. Just because the entire town knew her name didn't mean they had to know where to find her. In the warmth of the storage room, surrounded by barrels of flour and loaves of sugar, tins of salt and bowls of yeast, and, most of all, with Micajah Ingersoll between her and the only unlocked door, she felt safer than she had since her husband's death. If only Eliza were there, close at her side, ready to flee if necessary.

A man with a bad leg couldn't chase them—another reason to feel safe in Mr. Ingersoll's company. Only Woods, not tall but strong and whole in all his limbs, could catch up with them. If only he had gone to Boston, followed the false trail she had tried to lay.

The shop door closed behind the last customer, and Sarah rushed from her thoughts of Woods's handsome but florid face to request the key to the spice chest.

"I won't waste any, I promise." She didn't look at him. She couldn't. She had been unable to do so often, for every time their gazes met, a jolt like the sensation of an imminent lightning strike raced through her. "I only need a pinch of cinnamon and nutmeg. And—and tomorrow I'll make macaroons—if you have any almonds, of course."

"I do not, but my mother may. We shall see how the cakes sell first." Mr. Ingersoll gave her the key to the spice chest. He, too, only looked at her from the corner of his eye.

Because he felt the same jolt?

Hoping the cakes would not sell and she could return to the inn kitchen, warm and friendly and close to Eliza—even if it were not as safe as the bakehouse and its sad proprietor—Sarah slipped into the bakeshop with a bowl filled with fragrant batter and a request to use the ovens. "And a pan to bake these upon."

"There are irons aplenty beside the hearth." Mr. Ingersoll stood at a table kneading more bread, his hands never ceasing their rolling, pushing, lifting motion, the fingers flexible, the wrists beneath the folded-back cuffs of his shirt, supple.

Who cared if a man had one bad leg when he possessed hands and arms like that? Hands strong enough to turn a mound of dough to the texture of satin, gentle enough to sooth a fractious child.

Sarah's insides felt as soft as the butter she smeared onto the iron sheet before she scooped the thick cake mixture into mounds upon the pan and carried it to the oven.

"I became a baker," Micah said abruptly, "because I loved cakes and thought I could have them all the time if I baked."

"But you don't make anything other than some sweet biscuits." Sarah concentrated on not tilting the sheet of cakes. "What do you call those cinnamon sweets?"

"Snickerdoodles. They are Dutch. I learned how to make them when I was in Albany on the way to the fighting. They are a stiff dough that stays put."

"Ah, I understand." Sympathy tightened her chest.

He did not make cakes because his gait was too uneven and he might tilt the pan, causing the batter to run all over the sheet.

"You could make wafers," she suggested. "The iron keeps the batter inside."

"The occasional sweet biscuit is all anyone wants," he snapped out. "I expect you will use my ingredients for naught."

"Perhaps, and I told you that cakes and macaroons are all I know how to bake."

"Of course, you are an heiress." He didn't keep the hint of sarcasm from his tone.

"I was not always. I should have learned more practical baking." She closed the oven door with a gentle clang of metal against metal but did not turn to face him. "But my father wouldn't allow it. He had plans for me to marry Ralph Chapman nearly since I was born."

"I expect you were not opposed to the notion of becoming wife to a rich plantation owner."

She shrugged. "I was not opposed to marrying Ralph. He was gentle and kind, and we had been friends all my life, it seemed. My father was his tutor, you see. We grew up together on the plantation, like you must have with girls here in—" Sarah stopped and darted into the storeroom as though she had forgotten something vital, which, of course, she had—the way the females in Glassenbury treated Micajah Ingersoll now that he had come home a wounded militiaman.

"I despair of him ever finding a wife," his mother had bemoaned. "The older females are married and the younger ones think a man with a lame leg cannot be a good provider."

Silly females. Money did not make a happy marriage. Sarah had not been unhappy, and she and Ralph remained friends, but she never felt the tingling warmth, the melting joy her friends described or she read about in the poets' works.

Inside the bakeshop, Mr. Ingersoll kneaded the bread again, though the force of the pounding of the dough sounded more like he tried to tan a hide than blend the ingredients to the perfect texture for bread. It was an angry sound, or the sound of a man in pain trying to focus that anguish on something else.

Sarah cringed in the storeroom, waiting for the baking time for the cakes to pass. She cleared away her mess from mixing the batter. She inspected Mr. Ingersoll's stores to see what else she might bake. She tried not to hear him beating the bread dough beyond submission.

She succeeded at the first three tasks. She failed at the last one. Her ears strained toward the sound of his uneven footfalls, the way he swept the floor with smooth, even strokes, the rumble of his deep voice when he spoke to customers.

That voice made her feel as though he sang ballads to her. If any female were wise enough to listen to him talk, she wouldn't care for a moment that he might not be able to hunt or carry anything abnormally heavy or dance at a festival. Yet the females who came into the bakery treated him with a cool politeness that suggested he was nothing more than a mere acquaintance.

She began to tidy up the shelves of the storeroom, rearranging jars and small casks, dusting the shelves. On one shelf a pile of old newspapers lay. Micah used them for wrapping up bread and rolls and those cinnamon sweet biscuits he made sometimes. She began to straighten the stack so every corner was even.

They were at least a week old and some appeared a bit too handled around the edges. She removed those sheets from the stack. She could make fire spills out of those and keep the clean ones for wrapping.

She saw the notice in the third paper down. No wonder Mr. Ingersoll hadn't seen a notice of her being a runaway in any recent paper. It was in an older paper, an advertisement requesting the return of a runaway wife and child, "For she may not be in her right mind."

The description fit Sarah perfectly.

How Benjamin Woods had gotten the information into a Connecticut newspaper so quickly took Sarah a few minutes to work out. Of course he had come north ahead of her, had likely ridden, so he moved faster than she with a child who hadn't obeyed well until recently. He had expected Sarah to go north to Ralph's grandmother. He had simply lain in wait and no doubt peppered the papers with notices to have her returned to him.

"But you're not my husband, whatever you claim," she growled to herself. "We never shared so much as a house, however much you lie."

Yet who would believe her?

Quickly she began to tear the newspaper into curled twists of paper for starting fires. But this belonged to Micajah Ingersoll. She couldn't destroy it. Newspapers were expensive, were they not? Paper certainly was, and this appeared to be several sheets' worth. She could simply hide it, tuck it at the bottom of the stack. By the time he got that low, she would be long gone with Eliza or have convinced him she was telling the truth.

She must start out by proving she told the truth about being able to bake delicacies. Sarah wanted to avoid any of the customers seeing her now she knew a notice had been posted, but she needed to remove the cakes from the oven. Head down, Sarah scurried out to the hearth and wrapped a linen cloth around her hand so she didn't burn herself opening the oven door. The instant the iron grate separated from the box, the aroma of spices swept into the bakehouse.

"What is that?" Mrs. Drake cried. "Not apple pie. I don't smell apples."

"Currant cakes," Mr. Ingersoll said. "My new assistant is trying to prove her worth."

"I want one immediately," Mrs. Drake insisted.

"I need to test them first." His footfalls approached Sarah. "Must ensure they are fit for consumption."

Despite the potential unkindness of the words, his tone suggested a hint of teasing instead, as though he believed her cakes would be fine.

They looked good, a perfect honey gold bursting with the dark, dried berries. Still, Sarah bit her lip, and her hands shook a little as she set the pan on the table. If they weren't delicious, she would have no way to earn her keep. His mother didn't need Sarah's services at the inn. She would have to take Eliza away, head north without any money, before the winter snows arrived. "Well?" Mr. Ingersoll prompted.

"We are all eager to have cakes we can buy," Mrs. Drake said. "I know we can all make them ourselves, but it is so much better to buy them from someone who has mastered the art."

"They should be cool enough," Sarah murmured. She lifted one from the pan, thanking the Lord that it didn't stick.

Mr. Ingersoll took it from her hand. For a moment their fingers entwined. Sarah fought the impulse to hold on, beg him to give her another chance if this one failed. "I—I have not baked since my husband died," she whispered.

"They smell very good," Mrs. Drake said. "Micajah, do hurry and give us your opinion."

Mr. Ingersoll lifted the cake to his lips, leaving Sarah's entire body cold despite the heat inside the bakehouse. He took a small bite with strong, white teeth, and chewed slowly. His expression remained bland.

"Well, how are they?" Mrs. Drake demanded.

"Passable." Mr. Ingersoll's blue-gray eyes twinkled at Sarah and he laughed. "Better than passable. You have a light hand, Mrs. Chapman."

"Then I will take half a dozen," Mrs. Drake said.

In minutes, she departed with several cakes wrapped in paper and her coin shining on the counter.

"I do believe," Mr. Ingersoll said in his melodious voice from close behind Sarah, "your cakes are a success and you will be worth keeping on at least as long as the ladies of Glassenbury think them worth the cost."

Or he found the paper she should have destroyed rather than hidden.

# Chapter 7

"You have changed your mind about her, have you not?" Mother waylaid Micah the instant he entered the kitchen door of the inn.

Quickly he glanced around in search of Sarah Chapman, assuring himself she couldn't hear his mother's declaration nor his response. "I have changed my mind about her not telling the truth about being able to bake and no lady in Glassenbury willing to pay for the sweets."

Indeed, in the week since Mrs. Chapman had begun to bake her currant cakes, Shrewsbury biscuits, and almond macaroons, every female in Glassenbury had slipped through his door, even several who baked their own bread. Despite the cost of the sugar and other expensive ingredients, he had made more money in the past six days of work than he had made in the previous six weeks.

"I will pay her a fair wage for her time," he said, "and expect she will run away from us."

"But not for any ill reasons." Mother drew Micah into the yard despite the cold, late October day. "I do not believe for a minute that she is a runaway servant or wife and think you do not either."

Micah shrugged.

"Stop making that rude gesture in front of me, young man." She tapped his arm and gave him an exaggerated frown. "You are one of my sons, which means you are not weak-minded. You know what you think."

"I do, and I continue to read the *Gazette* for notices."

"Stop it. She is a lovely young woman, and Eliza is a sweet child."

"She is naughty."

"She is spoiled. Servants were given care of her and never made her do anything she did not want to."

"Which does not speak highly of Mrs. Chapman—if she is Mrs. Chapman."

Mother sighed. "Micajah Ingersoll, will you give no one an opportunity to make mistakes and learn? You know God gives us a second chance in life after we have been sinners and come to Him."

"And does that mean we do not pay for those mistakes?" He cast his gaze down at his right leg.

"Sometimes we do," Mother admitted, her face softening. "I believe Sarah is paying for her mistakes with Eliza in that you and others do not believe she is her daughter."

"I beg your pardon?" Micah gave Mother his full attention. "What are you saying?"

"You may ask her. Indeed, I think you should take her for a walk this evening. The moon is full."

Micah glanced into the sky, clear and bright with stars. In the east, a moon hung as heavy as a filled grain sack, nearly as yellow as the sun. "A good reason not to take her for a walk. But I will go on one myself if you will excuse me." He turned on his heel and strode away with as much speed and dignity as he could muster.

If he didn't leave, he knew what the next words from his mother would be: "She is perfect for you."

She wasn't. Just because she had increased his profits and had proven a tremendous help, not to mention good companionship in the bakehouse, didn't mean she was someone he would want to marry. He couldn't, by law, marry a servant who had run away and certainly couldn't even consider a courtship with a woman who might still be married. Or married again. How Mother could think he should, baffled him, or proved how desperate she was to see him wed. Just because the ladies of Glassenbury pitied him rather than fawned on him as they had before he went off to war didn't mean he needed to grab the first female who came along and take her to wife.

He should have reminded Mother how she always told them that God would provide a wife when the time came. Odd she would forget her own words of wisdom and try to foist Mrs. Sarah Chapman onto him. Perhaps she, like God, had given up on him, on trusting that God would oversee his future.

He would oversee his future, however lonely that might be, in his rooms above the bakeshop, suppers with his mother and married brother, visits from his nieces and nephews as they grew older.

Walking past the businesses and homes of the town, seeing families enjoying the company of one another, Micah's future felt as bleak as a January night—cold and dark. He should go home and sleep, but the idea of his empty rooms, cold from the fire being out all day, prompted him to take advantage of the clear night and bright moon for a walk. Walking strengthened his leg and felt good after mostly standing all day.

He turned toward the river, and footfalls clattered behind him. He paused, glanced back. Pale gold hair shining nearly as bright as her white cap in the moonlight, Sarah Chapman dashed toward him.

"Mrs. Ingersoll sent me." She caught up to him, panting. "Mrs. Jonathan Ingersoll, that is. I was to be sure to tell you your mother did not send me."

"And why did Clara?" Reflexively, he offered her his arm.

She took it and laughed. "The same reason, I expect."

"I am sorry. So you know they want to matchmake?"

"I know. It it foolishness of course."

His perverse heart clenched inside his chest at her words. Even a desperate female didn't want him.

"You do not believe my story," she continued, "and no one can have even a friendship based on distrust like that."

"I am not sure what I believe anymore."

Not when he liked the feel of her hand on his arm, the whisper of her skirt swinging against his leg as they walked, the light, slow speech of her voice.

"Then I would like to be on my way to Boston as soon as I have earned enough money." Her fingers clenched on his arm for a moment. "That is, if you will let me go."

"You are not a prisoner. I cannot stop you."

"But you should if I am a runaway."

"For your own safety."

She said nothing until they reached the river. A few boats bobbed at anchor in the water, but no lights bloomed on their decks. The only brightness shone from the moon reflected in the rippling dark surface. It was the sort of autumn night about which poets wrote, the sort that made a man think about a female at his side throughout the coming frosts and then snows of winter and beyond. The sort of thoughts he would not allow himself to have. He should pull away now before he decided he trusted her.

"Why did you run away and join the militia?" she asked abruptly.

He started, glanced down at her upturned face. "I was bored. That's the best explanation. Perhaps I was rebellious. I didn't like the baker all that much. He would not let me do more than sweep up and stoke the fires, when I wanted my hands in the dough or wanted to create recipes." He let out a harsh bark of mirth. "I like to cook. My brothers used to tease me about it, and yet I find something satisfying about creating food that fills a man's—or woman's—belly with satisfaction."

"So you just left the baker without assistance?" she asked.

Micah hesitated, remembering that last night, that last straw. "I did, but it was not mere selfishness."

"No?" she prompted.

He started to shrug, remembered Mother telling him that was rude, and turned his face away upriver to where he thought he'd find freedom and adventure. "I never told anyone. It would have made my brothers angry and my mother—well, she likely would have ruined the man from ever working in the colonies, and I couldn't let that happen. So I just left, encountered a friend who was joining up, and went with him."

Again she gave him that gentle pressure on his arm. "What did the baker do?"

Micah hesitated a moment then decided anyone knowing, now that the man was in his grave, wouldn't matter. "The baker had spilled oil on the floor and expected me to clean it up, but I did not know about it. When I carried in a load of wood, I slipped and dropped it. Some shavings got into a batch of dough and ruined it."

"I expect he was furious."

"Quite." Micah shifted his shoulders in memory of the rage, the result. "He grabbed the nearest object to hand and started striking me with it."

"Which was?"

"A poker."

"Mic—Mr. Ingersoll, that is terrible! He could have killed you."

"I am not sure he did not want to. I lit out and did not come home until last year, when I was nearly dead from my wound."

"And he was gone."

"He had been for years. Had an apoplexy not long after I left, so the bakehouse stood empty. People used the ovens for baking their bread, as most people do not have their own, or not big enough for more than a meat pie. I started helping with the baking, as I could not do much else, and eventually took over the entire shop again."

"For which the women of Glassenbury have been most grateful, I am certain."

"Yes, I believe they are."

"I always appreciated having a servant to bake and one to cook and one to do everything else for me, I thought. But now..." She paused and ground a scuffed toe into the soft earth near the river. "I believe I like having a reason to get up in the morning. The way these hardworking women look so happy when they bite into one of my macaroons or York cakes or puddings... It's more satisfying than reading poetry and writing letters when there was little about which to write that wasn't gossip. Though I do miss visiting the poor." She gazed down at her ruined shoes and laughed. "I guess I am the poor now."

"What happened to your inheritance?"

Surely what she answered would reveal some of the truth of her past.

"It is still there along the James River. Prospering, no doubt. Mr. Woods will be seeing to that, as he wants it, but I cannot go back." Her fingers dug into his and she added, "I cannot risk being at his mercy again. Please."

She was shaking hard enough for him to feel it, and he covered her fingers with his free hand. "Unless you are a runaway, I do not have to send you back. If you are, Mrs. Sarah Chapman, I do not have any choice."

"I am not a runaway." Despite her declaration, she bit her lip and looked away.

Shame? An admission of guilt? Definitely an evasion.

Heart heavy, Micah turned toward the road home. "I need to be getting to my rest. Tomorrow is a workday."

Despite the silent and tense ending to what had begun as a pleasant stroll, Micah wanted to repeat it as long as the weather remained cold but mostly dry. Walking with the calm and understanding presence of Mrs. Sarah Chapman at his side felt far more pleasant and natural than walking alone.

Too pleasant and natural. So much so, he avoided any more than necessary contact with her for several days. Yet for every minute of every day, he felt her presence, smelled her lavender and rosewater fragrance from Mother's handmade soap, heard the rustle of her petticoats, caught a flash of gold hair beneath the white cap. She remained out of sight from customers most of the time, preferring to keep herself occupied in the storeroom, cleaning or mixing or reading through the newspapers he kept in there for wrapping bread if the customer didn't bring his or her own sack. She read every paper he purchased, and he purchased the few that came up the river, enjoying the news from the other colonies and his own, curious, in spite of his experience, in the progress of the war with the French and their Indian allies.

The latter didn't seem to be progressing at all. The other news remained much the same. Life in America meant hard work and was generally a pleasant way to live. Some fretted at England's control and lack of understanding that life in the colonies was different than life in England.

He also looked at the notices. Still nothing appeared. And with each listing of runaway servants, children, and spouses he encountered, a nugget of hope began to expand, rise like yeast.

But she spoke of nothing but going to Boston and the home of her late husband's grandmother. "I would like to get there before you all get the snows for the winter," she said at the family supper that evening. "When will I have earned enough money?"

"I expect within a week or so," Micah admitted.

The reluctance with which he spoke came through, and Mother and Clara glanced at him with wide smiles.

He shook his head. "Now, ladies, with all due respect—" he rose abruptly—"I do not think I banked the fire properly; we were so late closing up the bakeshop this evening."

With this half-truth drifting behind him, he strode from the room and into the drizzle of the night.

"Meow," one of the stable cats greeted him.

He bent and stroked the damp fur. "You should go inside. The weather outside is no place for a cat to be, and you will not find any mice." He continued across the yard, leaving the yowling cat behind him.

The bakeshop would be warm, dry, empty. It was always empty these days, no longer the haven of solitude he had needed after military life. Just solitary. Seeing Jonathan and Nathaniel so happy emphasized his loneliness. Alden didn't mind his bachelorhood. He was still young and knew what he wanted to do—become a physician first and then find a bride.

"All right, Mother," he said to the solid walls of the bakehouse, "I admit it. I want a wife and family now."

Mother had always told them to pray for mates. Micah had as a young man. No more. He had gone to war against everyone's advice, broken his promise to the baker, and now God showed him with every disinterested female that he had sacrificed his future as a husband and father. Still he prayed but didn't trust God to listen to him now.

Weary of the silence, he set out a stack of clean papers and bread starter for the next day, noting the former was growing low, then banked the fire properly and headed for the steps leading to his rooms above the shop.

A knock sounded on the door then it opened. "Mr. Ingersoll?" Mrs. Chapman's voice rang to him soft and clear. "Mr. Ingersoll, are you here?"

"Yes." He pivoted on his left leg, grabbed the handrail, and made his slow progress down the steps. "What are you doing here so late?"

"I am sorry." She wrung her hands at her waist. "We—we cannot find Eliza." She started to cry. "I am such a terrible mother. I never should have left her."

"Where did you leave her?" Stumbling a little over the bottom step, Micah rushed to her side and rested a hand on her shoulder.

As fragile as a bird's wing, it shook with her silent sobs. "In—in her bed. She was asleep in our room off the kitchen. I thought she was safe."

Though he had considered her to be a terrible mother when she abandoned her child in the barrel, regardless of her reasoning, he now found soothing, reassuring words spilling from his lips. "You are not a terrible mother. You thought she was sleeping."

"But I was not near. I was not watching over her. Oh Mr. Ingersoll." She clutched his arm and gazed up at him with wide, bright eyes. "What if he—if Benjamin Woods took her?"

Either her fear was real or she was indeed an actress of the finest order. For whatever reason this Benjamin Woods was chasing her, the man did exist, Micah believed wholly now.

He covered her hand with his, finding it ice cold. "Let us go back to the inn and begin the search."

"Everyone is out looking for her now. I cannot believe she would go far. She never does. She plays in the innyard with the cats or sometimes with other children, but she has never gone away." She snatched her hands free and covered her face. "I should never have left her alone. God is punishing me for being such a terrible mother all her life. I left her to servants because I was so selfish."

"I do not think God punishes us for sins we have repented of." Micah found himself using his mother's words. "That was what Jesus' death on the cross was for."

"I know, but I've only thought of myself." She turned toward the door. "Perhaps she would have been better off if I had stayed on the plantation with all the servants who love her and care for her."

Though she began to walk swiftly, Micah caught up with her and pulled open the door then clasped her hand and headed back toward the inn with her. "Why were you so against marrying this man?"

*Or being married to him?*

He shoved the thought aside. "Was he cruel to you?"

"Not physically. But he said things that frightened me. He's a fine factor. At least, the plantation prospered under him. But even if I didn't so dislike him, I don't. . .love him."

"And you want to love your husband?"

"Yes, foolish female that I am." She wiped her eyes on the edge of her shawl. "If I did not think I should be able to marry a man I love, rather than another *mariage de convenable*, now that Ralph left me the plantation entire, Eliza would be safe."

"We do not know that she is not." Micah squeezed her fingers and released her hand as they entered the innyard.

Two cats began to wind themselves around his ankles, nearly tripping him. He stopped to gently shoo them out of the way and let out a sigh. "Looks like we will be getting more kittens soon. Now tell me where everyone has begun to look?"

"All the different streets and down—down to the river. There could have been a boat. Ooo." She pressed her hands to her middle.

"Where is Mother?"

"In the kitchen."

"Good. Go join her. I—oh, that silly cat." It planted itself in front of him, meowing. "Go into the barn where it is dry."

The cat didn't move.

"I want to look, not stay here."

"But if it is this man who has taken her, he could grab you, too."

And Micah didn't want that to happen. He didn't want her to be a runaway servant, property of another man at least for the length of an indenture.

"You may stay with me," he decided.

"Thank you." She clung to his arm. "But where to start?"

"Micah, you cannot be out in the wet," Mother called from the kitchen doorway.

"You are barely well again, and if you slip. . ."

Micah cringed with embarrassment.

"I am with him, ma'am," Mrs. Chapman said. "We'll be near at hand in the event the others find. . .something." She wiped a mixture of tears and drizzle off her face. "If only we knew where to start instead of everyone scattering about."

"Ye–es." Micah stared down at the obviously expectant cat. The second one had disappeared, presumably into the stable. But the soon-to-be mother cat prowled around the door, no doubt begging for scraps of food.

"Eliza likes the cats, does she not?" he asked.

"She adores them, and they are so gentle with her. But they never go far—oh." Her eyes widened. "Could we be that silly?" Hope brightened her face in the dim glow of a lantern over the kitchen door.

"Perhaps."

As one, they headed for the stable.

"She has always liked animals." Mrs. Chapman spoke more quickly than her usual drawl. "She had several cats and made pets out of my husband's hunting hounds on the plantation."

The stable was dry, warm, and fragrant of horses and hay. A single lantern hung above the outside door, casting a dim, shadowy light inside. The horses of guests munched or shifted in their sleep with a rustle of straw. One roan fellow poked his head over the door of his box and poked Mrs. Chapman's shoulder as they passed.

She reached up and patted his nose with an affection that said she liked animals as her daughter did. "Have you seen a little girl, you beauty?" she asked the horse.

He blew through his nose.

"Eliza?" Micah called.

Hay rustled and a cat meowed from a nearby empty stall.

"Eliza," Mrs. Chapman called, "are you with the kittens?"

They peeked into the stall. Two cats lay in a bed of clean straw, but no little girl joined them there or anywhere else.

"Eliza?" Mrs. Chapman called again, an edge to her voice now. "Are you here?"

Another rustle brought wisps of hay drifting from above.

Micah glanced up, caught a pale blur and a whimper.

"Are you up there?" he asked calmly.

"Ye–es." Now he heard the sniffles.

"Eliza." Mrs. Chapman headed for the ladder to the hayloft. "Eliza, how did you get up there?"

The ladder was steep and narrow, and the rungs surely too far apart for a small child to climb. Yet she must have.

"I heard babies up here," Eliza called down. "But now I'm scared."

"You should have thought of that when you went up." Mrs. Chapman stared at the ladder.

He could guess what she was thinking—climbing it in a gown and petticoats would be difficult at best. Climbing it with his lame leg might be more difficult, coming down with the child worse. Yet he had to do it. He had to do something for her after how he had doubted her.

He took a step toward the ladder. "Mr. Ingersoll?" Eliza's face peered over the edge for a moment then shrank back. "Momma, come get me."

"Do not watch," Mrs. Chapman said. "I will have to tuck up my skirt."

"No, I will retrieve her." Micah grasped one side of the ladder then waited, expecting her to say he couldn't do it.

She gave him a brilliant and grateful smile. "Thank you."

"Please," Eliza whimpered.

"I will be there in a trice." Or two

Micah began to climb. One rung then two. His left foot up then his right. Left, right. Weight on the left, not the right. If he remembered that going down...

He reached the top and held his arms out to the child. She ran to him and clung. "You saved me again. I couldn't climb down."

"You should not have gone up at all," Mrs. Chapman said from the stable floor.

"But I had to see the kittens. Babies." Eliza clung to his neck.

She was a sturdy thing, hard enough to carry on a flat street, harder down a ladder. If he dropped her, she would surely break something. If he fell, he could injure his leg again. Sarah Chapman would look at him with disgust or pity, certainly not admiration.

He wanted her admiration. He fully admitted it. But his breathing grew rough, his heart rate faster.

"Hang on tightly," he murmured.

Left foot first. Leave his weight on the left. The right wouldn't fully bear his weight, let alone his and the child's. But Mrs. Chapman never doubted for a moment that he could do this.

Slowly, one step at a time, concentrating, he descended the ladder. He didn't realize he held his breath until both feet stood on the solid floor and Eliza wriggled for him to let her down.

"Kittens, Momma." She ran to her mother. "Babies with closed eyes."

"You should never have gone up there." Mrs. Chapman's tone was gentle but firm.

"But you should see them."

"The only thing I want to see is you in your bed where you're supposed to be."

"Why? I didn't hurt myself." The lower lip protruded.

Her mother pursed her own mouth, and Micah realized how full and pink her lips were. Soft looking, too, giving him notions.

He turned his face away. "Do you wish me to carry her?"

"No, she can walk." Sarah took Eliza's hand. "If you will excuse us, I need to talk to my daughter about her disobedience."

Eliza began to cry.

Mrs. Chapman's lips quivered, too, but her footsteps were firm as she stalked from the stable towing the dragging child.

Micah followed and waited in the kitchen while Sarah entered the bedchamber off the kitchen usually reserved for a maid who lived in. Though faint behind the thick door, voices rose and fell, one pleading, the other lecturing. The child cried. The mother waited until silence fell. The others returned, and Micah told them where Eliza had been.

"You climbed up?" Nathaniel looked surprised.

Mother just smiled. Micah guessed what she was thinking—"I told you so." Nonetheless, he waited for Mrs. Chapman to emerge into the passageway outside the kitchen.

"I told her to never leave the inn without someone with her. Perhaps she will listen to me now." She held out her hands to him. "Thank you for fetching her down."

He took her hands in his. "I was happy I could do so."

"Why could you not? Oh." She flicked a glance to his leg. "It did not stop you from going up."

"And you are learning how to be a good mother, judging from the scolding you gave her."

"I love her. I have always wanted nothing but to keep her safe."

And he loved Eliza's mother, Mrs. Chapman. Sarah. He wanted to keep her safe. He knew in that moment, holding her hands, the aromas of baked meats and lavender drifting around them, her hair a shining cloud about her cheeks, her face turned up to his with her pretty lips parted.

He bent his head and kissed her. She drew in her breath, and for a heartbeat he feared she would pull away, but then she relaxed against him, into the arms he circled around her. She slid her fingers into his hair, pulling it from its queue to make a curtain about their faces.

The click of footfalls on the kitchen floor sent them staggering apart, but if his expression was anything like Sarah's—dazed and dreamy—whoever exited the kitchen would know in an instant what he'd done. What they'd done.

"Do I apologize?" he asked.

Sarah shook her head.

"Good, because I'm not going to."

Mother walked out of the kitchen, glanced from one to the other, and laughed. "Very good. Tomorrow after the shop closes, we'll discuss my son giving you a proper proposal."

"Oh no, he needn't. I shouldn't have." Hands to her crimson cheeks, Sarah fled back to the room she shared with Eliza.

"Of course I will." Heart singing, Micah strode to the door without a bit of hesitation in his walk. "And you can say I told you so all my life, Mother."

He barely felt the rain pouring down outside, the cold wind off the river, the pavement beneath his feet. Of course Mother was right. He had been attracted to Sarah from the beginning—to her audacity, her courage, her gentleness. He would indeed propose to her the next day, and in the morning not the afternoon.

But in the morning, while he wrapped the first loaves of bread in paper, he found an old newspaper with a notice about a runaway wife. It fit Sarah's and Eliza's descriptions to perfection.

# Chapter 8

The instant she arrived at the bakehouse, Sarah knew something was wrong. Micah didn't greet her when she walked through the door shortly after sunrise. He simply pointed to a chair then returned to his kneading. She opened her mouth to ask what was wrong then saw the paper lying on the counter and closed her lips, folded her hands on her apron, prayed.

God had brought her this far, had given her shelter through the Ingersolls, had given her a man she wanted to love within days of meeting him. He would not let her down now unless she was wrong and she was not to remain with Micah.

But Micah had kissed her. He had held her and kissed her.

Her heart pounded so hard her stomach hurt. And still Micah didn't speak until he divided the dough into loaves and washed his hands free of flour. Then he faced her, his arms over his chest. "You lied to me. I have fallen in love with—I have kissed another man's wife. You knew it and you kissed me back."

"Will you believe me if I tell you the notice is a lie?" Sarah ventured in a small voice.

"Then why did you hide the paper?"

"I could not destroy it. Paper is expensive. I thought you would not notice."

"But you hid it. Oh Sarah, Missus—whatever your name is. . ." He swallowed. He speared his fingers through his hair, pulling it loose from his queue as she had the night before. He turned his back on her. "Come along."

Sarah didn't move. "Whe–where are you taking me?"

"Where I should have taken you the first night—to the sheriff."

"And you cannot believe me?" She sprang from her chair and rushed across the room to face him, blocking his path to the door. "You say you love me, and yet you do not trust me to be telling the truth? And here I trusted you to fetch my child from that ladder when I know no one else believes you can do as much as any man. I believed you loved me when you kissed me. I believed you were a fair man worth loving."

"No woman believes I am worth loving." He started to step around her.

Sarah grabbed his arm. "No, Micajah Ingersoll, it is you who thinks you are not, who believes you are being punished because you ran away. And now you think everyone who runs away from a terrible situation should be punished. But you are wrong."

"You are the one who is wrong. I only think you should be returned. If I had been younger, if someone had returned me—" He stopped, gazed past her shoulder. "You need to face your life, Sarah, not run from it."

"Then don't run away from me." She stepped close to him. "From us."

"We cannot be, you and me. You belong to another man."

"You only believe that to justify going in the opposite direction from loving me. But you have to trust I am telling the truth and trust that God knows you are sorry about the past and forgives you." She touched his cheek, his skin smooth from the morning's shave. "But you are right. I must return to the plantation and risk encountering Benjamin Woods so I can prove to you I am telling the truth." Running, she left the bakehouse and headed for the inn.

Where she found an uproar because Eliza had vanished again.

Micah trotted after Sarah as fast as he could. Not until that moment, when he couldn't run after her, did his leg injury bother him so much. Not the pity from females who had once cast eyes at him, not the way others tried to do things for him he knew he could do for himself, not since he returned to Glassenbury humiliated did he care so much that he was lame. By the time he reached the inn, neither Eliza nor Sarah could be found.

"The child was in the yard with the cats," Mother said, "and then she wasn't. Then Sarah came running in here like a mad hound was after her, and the minute she heard Eliza was gone, she vanished out the door."

"We have to find her." Micah gave no explanation for his actions, simply climbed the steps to his mother's private quarters, took his father's old pistols from the high cabinet in which she kept them, ensured they were primed and loaded, and returned downstairs. "She's in danger," he said as he exited the inn.

"Wait." Mother rushed after him, cap flying from her head. "Micajah, you cannot go after her. Let me fetch your brothers."

"She is my lady. I will find her."

If he hadn't been too much of a fool for her to still love once he did. If he didn't stumble at a crucial moment. If—

"If You want us to have a future together, Lord, You will guide my steps." For the first time in the year since he'd been wounded, Micah placed his complete trust in the Lord.

Then he began to ask everyone he passed if they had seen Eliza or Sarah.

"Saw a big man carrying a little girl 'bout an hour ago," a river trader said. "Noticed 'cause she was screaming."

And so it went. Some had seen the child, some Sarah. They had gone toward the river. The river meant a boat and—where? Down toward the sea or north toward the hills?

Downriver. Benjamin Wood would take Sarah and Eliza back to that southern colony that paid little heed to the recent English marriage laws requiring licenses and preachers giving the blessing over the union. He needed a boat. He could row perhaps faster than someone could sail. Nathaniel would have one.

He didn't ask for his brother's permission. He simply took the boat from its mooring.

"Micah, wait." Nathaniel sprinted from his workshop. "You cannot go rowing."

"I can." Micah bent his back to the oars. It was strong. His arms were strong. His need to catch up with Sarah stronger.

The current helped, carrying him downstream. It would help Woods, too. He didn't know what the man looked like. He should have asked Sarah. He should have asked her a great deal.

Upriver, Nathaniel gestured and talked, haggling with some men for the use of their boat. Behind him, smoke from cooking fires spiraled into the sky, reminding Micah he'd left the bakehouse fire blazing on the hearth. He prayed for no fire to damage the town. If the bakehouse burned, he wouldn't care. He and Sarah could rebuild together if she would have him.

He rowed harder, faster. He scanned every craft he drew near, every one that passed whether propelled by sail, oar, or paddle. Nothing. No one. No golden-haired lady or raven-haired child. Many strangers. He called to several, asking if they had seen the woman and child. None had.

Micah's arms began to ache, his back throb. The pistols lay heavy against his thighs, close at hand, ready for him to use. He could shoot. He would shoot straight.

"Micah." Nathaniel's voice rang across the sunlit water. "Farm."

Nathaniel, in a boat with a friend of his, gestured toward shore.

Micah glanced around. A farm sprawled down to the water's edge with its own landing. Two boats bobbed there. One lay empty. The other lay too low in the water to not hold a passenger, but Micah could see no one above the gunwale.

A man stood on the narrow jetty, short, broad, muscular. A well-enough looking fellow, save for a thin tightness to his mouth that suggested cruelty. "Keep moving," he barked. "My property here."

"No, it's not." Micah drew alongside and threw the painter over a mooring post.

The man reached to toss it back.

Micah cocked one of the pistols. "Do not touch it, fellow."

"I don't want you here." Despite the defiant words, the man froze.

Micah smiled. "I will move along as soon as you give me the lady and child."

"I don't know what you're talking about." But the man glanced toward the boat.

Micah could still not see inside. No help for it, he had to step out of the boat. Too easily, this man could shove him off-balance and into the river. If Micah had to fire the gun, the recoil might throw him off-balance and into the river. Between the cold and the current, he was unlikely to survive.

For Sarah's sake, he must take the risk.

He led with his left leg, one hand on the mooring post, the other gripping the pistol. "Do not try to push me off, or I will fire."

"She is my wife," the man insisted.

"She says she is not."

"She is mad. She stole our child and—" The man lunged toward Micah.

With one leg on the jetty and his weak leg still on the thwart of the boat, Micah fired. The man reeled back, clutching his arm. Micah teetered then flung himself forward and hauled himself onto the jetty. He landed with one knee in the middle of the man's belly.

"Are you Woods?" he demanded.

"I need an apothecary." The man's arm bled freely.

"You may have one. What is your name?"

"All right. I am Woods and she is my—*ooph*."

Micah's knee drove the air from the man's lungs.

Now he saw into the other boat. Sarah and Eliza lay there tied together and gagged. Eliza wept, but Sarah's eyes were wide and as clear a green as new spring grass.

Leaving Woods for Nathaniel to take in hand, Micah knelt and leaned forward to cut their bindings. "And while I am on my knees," he said with a smile and duck of his head while he worked, "may I beg your forgiveness and ask you to be my wife?"

Free from her gag and bindings, Sarah laughed and hugged a sobbing Eliza then rose on her knees and grasped Micah's hands. "You came even when you were not certain I was telling the truth."

"You were telling the truth. I was just a fool who thought I am of no use as a husband, so let myself believe lies."

"But you trust me now." It was a statement, not a question.

He leaned forward and kissed her then gathered Eliza into his arms to lift her from the boat.

"I want a snicker biscuit," she said.

"I do not have any," Micah said.

"But we can bake some," Sarah added.

Micah stared at her for a moment, suddenly ill. "Since you were telling the truth about everything, I just realized that you are an heiress. You will not want to work in a bakeshop when you have servants to do that for you."

"Money and servants kept me from my child. I will not let them keep me from you, and if that means baking cakes the rest of our lives, I will bake cakes the rest of our lives."

"You are certain? I could go to the plantation, but I know nothing about farming. And my family is here."

"I am certain."

"But it is hard work."

"Micajah Ingersoll," Sarah scolded, "are you trying to run away from me?"

"No, I will run to wherever you are."

"And that means back to Glassenbury and family and work baking cakes." She perched on one of the thwarts so she could kiss him. "I can think of nothing sweeter."

# Macaroons

The following recipe is taken from *A New and Easy Method of Cookery* by Elizabeth Cleland, 1755.

*To make Macaroons.* Blanch and beat a Pound of Almonds very fine, keeping them wetting with Orange-flower Water: Take an equal Quantity of fine Sugar, pounded and sifted, then beat up the Whites of eight Eggs, and mix them all together; place them handsomely on Wafers, then on Tin Plates or Papers. Bake them In a slow Oven.

Author's Note: After some digging into eighteenth-century dictionaries and cookery books, I deduced that a "wafer" was a special iron implement designed to produce thin, flat biscuits or, what we now know as cookies. Think the crispy part of an Oreo.

If you wish to try this recipe, you can use an ungreased cookie sheet in a low oven, probably around 300 degrees, though I have seen modern macaroon recipes calling for an oven as low as 250 degrees.

You can substitute vanilla extract for the orange-flower water, or, if you like, use a few drops of orange extract.

By the way, the word *cookie* comes from a Dutch word meaning "little cake."

Award-winning author **Laurie Alice Eakes** has always loved books. When she ran out of available stories to entertain and encourage her, she began creating her own tales of love and adventure. In 2006 she celebrated the publication of her first hardcover novel. Much to her astonishment and delight, it won the National Readers Choice Award. Besides writing, she teaches classes to other writers, mainly on research, something she enjoys nearly as much as creating characters and their exploits. A graduate of Asbury College and Seton Hill University, she lives in Texas with her husband and sundry animals.

# IMPRESSED BY LOVE

by Lisa Karon Richardson

# Dedication

To Joel, Ethan, and Olivia, you make me want to be a better me.

# Chapter 1

Phoebe flinched as another round of cannon fire slammed into *Aries*'s hull. The crew answered the blow valiantly, their great guns spewing round shot and fire. A muted cheer went up from one of the gun crews. Their ball must have found its mark. But it wouldn't be enough to save them. The French ship of the line had twice as many cannon.

Lips moving in silent prayer, Phoebe paced the confines of the gun room to which she had been relegated. There must be some way she could help without getting in anyone's way. She was an Englishwoman after all. Should she stand by and raise not a finger to defend the ship?

She heaved open the door and stepped into the companionway just as another barrage from the French punched holes in the ship's stout timbers. Her foot caught and she tumbled forward, striking the bulkhead as a cloud of splinters filled the air. She flung up an arm to cover her face. For a long moment she crouched on the deck, making herself as small as possible. Blood pounded so loudly in her ears she could hear nothing else.

It took her awhile to realize that the men were cheering. Had they beaten the French back? Phoebe dared to peek, then straightened to her feet. Beneath her the frigate seemed to dig into the water like a thoroughbred gaining purchase for a final sprint.

Thinking to return to the gun room, Phoebe turned, but a gaping hole marked the place where the door had been. A jagged crevice in the deck opened to the bread room below. Her mouth went so dry she couldn't swallow. The choice had been made for her. She couldn't go back, so she would go forward.

She made her way up and out into the waist of the ship. Something warm dripped onto her arm, and she raised her hand to her forehead. Blood. She must have been scratched by a shard of flying wood. She reached into her sleeve for her handkerchief, but it wasn't there. Instead she dabbed at the cut with the back of her hand. How was she going to be any good to anyone if she didn't even have sense enough to carry a handkerchief?

She stayed where she was, out of the way of the toiling gun crews, until at last she caught sight of Uncle John on the quarterdeck. He stood tall and proud, the gold lace on his captain's uniform gleaming in the afternoon sun, his sword slung at his side. Deep in discussion with his first lieutenant, Mr. Loring, Uncle John motioned toward the shoreline looming closer and closer.

For an instant, Phoebe thought he meant to run the frigate aground in order to keep her out of French hands, but then she realized they were aimed toward the mouth of a river. Wily Uncle John. He must hope to escape by navigating waters too shallow for the larger vessel. She grimaced. God grant that the waters weren't also too shallow for *Aries*.

Behind them, the French ship's chasers barked and spat. The cannon fire tore through the rigging, showering the quarterdeck with tackle and wicked splinters. Phoebe plastered herself even closer to the bulkhead.

When she looked again, Uncle John had collapsed to the deck. Heedless of the danger, she raced forward and hurled herself up the ladder.

Uncle John was conscious and trying to regain his feet.

His lieutenant held him down. "You musn't, sir. I've sent Midshipman Hollis for the surgeon."

Phoebe sank to her knees next to her uncle. Her gaze shied away from the stain spreading across his coat. "I am here, Uncle. We will take care of you."

He didn't seem to hear her. He grasped Mr. Loring's arm. "Take us. . .Glassenbury. They've—" His words broke off in a grimace. His breathing grew reedy as he struggled to master the pain. "Shipyards."

Gasping and pale, the midshipman appeared. "The surgeon is dead, sir."

Phoebe's gaze locked with the lieutenant's. Tight as her throat was, she managed to squeeze out a plea. "We have to get him to a physician."

Mr. Loring nodded. He stood and gave orders to the helmsman.

One thought pulsed through her. *Please, God, do not take someone else I love.*

❧

He musn't forget the laudanum. Alden turned on his heel and paced back the way he'd come. He unlocked the medicine cabinet and selected a dark bottle. Carefully he stowed the tincture in his bag.

The front door burst open, but he didn't glance up. "I am coming, Connor. Your father will be fine."

"Are you the doctor?"

Alden snapped his head up at the unfamiliar voice. "Who are you?"

A tall bruiser in white duck breeches and a blue jacket stepped inside. "We need the physician." Behind him three other fellows crowded into the doorway, each as seedy looking as the first.

"I am afraid I am on my way to another call." Alden hefted his bag. "If the matter is urgent, you had best call upon the surgeon. If it can wait, I will attend you once I have treated my neighbor." He moved to usher them out, but not a one budged.

The tall fellow yanked off his hat. "Listen, mate, our captain's hurt bad."

Alden removed his spectacles and put them in a breast pocket. "Your captain?" He rubbed the bridge of his nose.

"Had a nasty scrape with a French ship of the line, we did. Had to come up the Connecticut to get away from them frogs."

A fellow wearing a disreputable straw hat stuck his head around his taller companion. "Our surgeon was kilt."

The men were obviously deeply concerned for their captain. Alden modified his tone. "My neighbor has fallen from his roof. When I have tended him, I will come straightaway."

The tall fellow looked at his mates, unspoken communication crackling between them like heat lightning. "That's not good enough, sir."

"It will have to do, lads."

"No sir." The big fellow took a step forward. "You're coming with us."

Alden planted his feet, refusing to back up. "I think you better go now."

The other intruders stepped forward as well, making a wall.

"No sir, I hate to have to do this, sir. It'd be a lot easier if you'd just come with us nice and easy like."

Surely they weren't so deluded as to think he'd allow anyone to dictate which patients he'd see. "I think not."

The fellow sighed. "Then I got no choice. See, we're Royal Navy."

Alden tasted something bitter at the back of his throat. "I have asked you politely. Now get out of here before I raise a hue and cry."

The fellow said sadly, "Afraid I can't do that. You're being pressed, boy'o."

*Impossible.* For a moment, Alden's mind went blank as a fresh-washed slate.

He shook his head. But the men closed in on either side, despite his attempt to deny reality. His fingers clenched around his bag, ready to thump someone.

The shortest of the lot, a stout fellow with impressive side-whiskers and a red neckerchief, moved in to grab Alden's arm. Alden swung the bag and caught the lout under the chin, snapping his head back. Alden spun and jabbed his elbow into the biggest bruiser's solar plexus.

But there were too many of them. He was overwhelmed in a matter of minutes. One of the brutes pulled his arms behind him and clamped manacles around his wrists.

The bewhiskered fellow picked up Alden's medical bag then led the way out of the office. Alden considered his options, but with two men on either side, there was little chance of escape.

Connor Martin moved to intercept them. "Dr. Ingersoll, Papa needs you!"

"Run for the surgeon. I will come when I can."

Tears shone in the child's eyes. "But he's hurt real bad. He could die."

*That tears it.* Alden grunted and yanked the chains free of his captor's grasp. He darted past the boy. "Run, lad!"

He made it less than a hundred feet before a blow caught him above the ear and the world became a wash of swirling color and pattern. He pitched forward into the mud of the street.

The sun flickered like a candle in a draft and winked out.

☙❧

"You shouldn't have hit him so hard. Now what good is he?" The voice was feminine— lilting but with an edge of tension.

The sound of a man's response was engulfed in throbbing pain that radiated from the side of Alden's skull. He swallowed against nausea and squeezed his eyes shut. A groan escaped his lips and at the sound the woman spoke again.

"Oh! I think he must be rousing." The voice came closer. "Dr. Ingersoll?"

As appealing as the voice was, Alden wished it would go away.

"Dr. Ingersoll? Are you feeling better?" The whisper brushed his cheek.

It startled him and his eyes popped open. He immediately regretted the rashness of that act and closed them again but not before his brain had been imprinted with an image of the loveliest creature he'd ever seen.

Mahogany curls, pert nose, and coffee-dark eyes looking at him expectantly.

He wasn't in the street anymore. Where was he? And who was this woman?

An altogether rougher voice shattered the quiet. "I wouldn't have hit him at all if he'd come quiet like. He'll come 'round any minute and won't be worse for wear."

Recollection snapped his eyes open again. The view was far less enchanting this time. The big Royal Navy fellow loomed above him.

It wasn't just an effect of the blow to his aching head; he really was swaying. He was on board a ship.

"I protest." It didn't come out as strongly as he wanted. More a kitten's mew than the lion's roar he intended. He tried again. "I protest!"

❧

Phoebe looked pointedly at the bosun who suddenly seemed to find the stitching on his hat fascinating. She turned to the physician. "Dr. Ingersoll, I must apologize for the manner in which you have been handled. Mr. Harcourt here did as he thought best. I hope you will forgive him."

The doctor made to rise, and instinctively she moved to assist him. The feel of warm muscle bunching beneath the linen of his shirt brought with it the burning revelation that she'd never touched a man in such an intimate fashion.

Humiliation stung her cheeks, and she knew she was turning as crimson as a marine's uniform. As soon as he was upright, she pulled her hand free and clasped it tightly in her other hand to make certain she didn't make some other impulsive and inappropriate move.

"I don't think you understand, Miss—"

"Carlisle," she supplied.

"Miss Carlisle. I was on my way to tend a patient."

"I am afraid that is not possible. My uncle has been gravely injured in a battle with the French. He needs your help."

"There is a prior claim on my attention."

Harcourt cleared his throat. "Badgering the lady won't help you a jot. Not now. You've been pressed nice and legal."

The doctor stared at Harcourt as if he were speaking a foreign tongue.

"I am afraid it is true, Dr. Ingersoll," Phoebe said. Her heart hammered in her throat and she wiped damp palms against her skirt. There was no way to soften the blow. "You serve at the pleasure of His Majesty's Navy."

An angry wash of red swept up past his loosened cravat and bled across his cheekbones. "And if I refuse to treat your captain?"

The bosun grabbed for the doctor. "Then I'll keelhaul you myself, and that's after I take the lash—"

156

Phoebe forestalled Harcourt's threats with an upraised hand. "Please, Dr. Ingersoll, as a physician, you must be a man of compassion. My uncle is dying." The tears she'd tried to keep at bay overran her defenses. Blinking rapidly to keep from humiliating herself, she covered his hand with hers where it rested on his chest. "Surely even righteous anger is worth little in comparison to a man's life."

He glared at her for an interminable moment. Just when she thought he would demand to be keelhauled instead, he sighed. "Take me to him."

Sweet relief rushed through her along with the realization that she was holding his hand. She pulled away. "Thank you."

His stern expression melted a bit. "There may be little I can do for him."

Phoebe had to look away from the grave truth mirrored in his eyes. "I understand." But she didn't want to understand. No, she had to believe that God had provided the physician they needed for a reason.

# Chapter 2

The world spun around Alden as he tried to stand. He clutched at the side of the berth to keep from falling. After that clout on the head, he had more business being a patient than treating one. Still, the sooner he took care of the captain the sooner he could leave. Surely they wouldn't keep a man of standing in the local community. They just meant to force his cooperation. He put his feet experimentally to the deck.

He swallowed hard as the ship rolled beneath him. Prickles of sweat beaded his forehead. He would not be ill in front of these people. Especially not Miss Carlisle. Lips clamped tight, he took a step forward and reached for the door.

"Would you care for tea?" Miss Carlisle stood at his side, brow furrowed as if she'd bought a faulty clockworks doll and was trying to think how to return it to the shop.

"No." It came out harsher than he'd intended, and Harcourt stiffened. Alden fumbled for his glasses. Let the brute try something. One-on-one, Alden could give as good as he got. He hadn't grown up with three older brothers without learning a trick or two.

"Then my uncle is in the orlop deck with the other wounded men." She swept around him into the companionway, leaving him to stumble along in her wake.

The deeper into the bowels of the ship they went, the fouler the air grew, until it seemed a physical presence as real and wicked as a pair of hands wrapped around his throat. Just when it seemed he could bear it no more, they descended into the orlop deck and the stench doubled. No, trebled.

He covered his mouth with his hand. He might as well have tried to turn back fog with a lady's fan. There was no masking the reek. Alden staggered and grabbed for the bulkhead. Miss Carlisle plucked a handkerchief from her sleeve and shrouded her nose and mouth.

*This is where they keep their injured and ill?* It was a wonder any of them survived. "Where is he?" He managed to grate out the question.

Miss Carlisle pointed at a table against the far wall.

At least they didn't have the fellow in one of the hammocks strung throughout the low-ceilinged compartment. Alden set his jaw and picked his way through the crowded aisle to the captain's side.

The man's complexion held the gray pallor of dirty linen. A befouled bandage encircled his head. Alden put his ear to the captain's chest. His breathing was shallow and erratic. In the light of the swaying lamps, Alden could tell little of the wounds. But if the state of the bandages was an indication, they were grave.

"He must be moved out of this squalor."

Miss Carlisle motioned for Harcourt. "Could you see that he is moved back to his cabin immediately?"

"Where will you sleep, miss?"

"Perhaps the carpenter could replace the bulkheads and partition the cabin so I may stay near him."

"Righto." Harcourt motioned for a young man wearing what looked like a butcher's apron to help him. Together they shifted the captain. The man moaned and a grimace twisted his features.

Alden glanced back at the wounded men still lying in the foul recesses of the ship. Who would see to the poor wretches?

Miss Carlisle soon outstripped her uncle's bearers, darting up the ladder and out into the light and air. Alden followed more slowly. The others weren't his responsibility. If he tried to treat them all, he'd never get off this ship. He'd take a look at the captain, prescribe a treatment, and then they'd surely let him leave. He'd pray for these fellows. And if the ship was still in port after he'd seen his patients, perhaps he'd come back.

He hurried up the hatchway after his newest patient. The poor fellow looked as if the coffin fitter ought to be called.

How would this crew take it if their captain didn't recover? The near silence of the ship took on a sinister air. Officers and sailors alike followed his progress with their eyes. Alden glanced up into the rigging. Even the men in the tops had their attention focused on him rather than their duty.

Right. Well, he'd just have to do everything in his power to see that their captain recovered. He adjusted his spectacles and stepped into the captain's cabin.

Phoebe opened the door and held it wide as Harcourt and the loblolly boy carried in Uncle John. She took in the cabin with a more critical eye than she had employed in months. The guns had been cleared away, but the carpenter's crew had not yet replaced the bulkheads, and the compartment was one long chamber. Still, windows banked the far wall, letting in light and air. The decking had been swabbed clean, and the sea cot rehung. Surely this would satisfy even the fastidious Dr. Ingersoll?

That gentleman bent slightly to clear the doorframe. He surveyed the chamber. "I suppose it will do."

Feeling like a hostess whose offerings have been snubbed, Phoebe let the door bang shut with the motion of the ship. The doctor moved out of the way just in time. The look he cast her showed he had no idea why she might be piqued.

Was he really the best physician in the town? This fellow was handsome, but that was no indication of professional skill. And he seemed closer to her own age than a learned physician ought.

Dr. Ingersoll leaned over Uncle John and gently began to unwind the bandage wrapped haphazardly around his wound. A grunt revealed his dissatisfaction with what he found.

Imperiously he held out a hand. "Where are my instruments?"

"Your. . .instruments?" Phoebe looked around, at a loss for why he might think she had his instruments.

Harcourt tromped toward the door. "I'll get 'em."

Dr. Ingersoll turned his attention back to Uncle John. Phoebe stifled a gasp as he removed a dressing and revealed a half dozen angry red wounds.

"Your presence is not required, Miss Carlisle. If you are uncomfortable around the injured, do not distress yourself by staying." The doctor did not look up as he spoke. "I do not need another patient to tend."

Phoebe blushed. "I am not some ninny likely to faint away at the sight of a little blood."

"As you wish." The doctor continued his inspection.

Phoebe planted a fist on her hip. A bad habit. She jerked it away. "Can I be of assistance?"

At last the infuriating man deigned to look at her. "I believe the bosun went for my bag."

"I am capable of more than fetching and carrying."

He sighed. "The loblolly boy is here to assist me. And in truth, I do not know what I am going to do yet."

"What?" Phoebe couldn't keep the sharpness from her tone.

Dr. Ingersoll straightened with wintery hauteur. "Your uncle is suffering from several different injuries. To begin, he has a broken clavicle. Not an uncommon injury but painful to the patient. There are half a dozen serious cuts and gashes that will require stitching, the worst of which is a laceration to the brachial artery in his left arm. The tourniquet was properly applied, which may have saved his life, but he will certainly lose the arm. And then there is this head wound. I do not know that he will ever wake up. He has undergone a terrible shock. I cannot promise he will recover."

Phoebe could feel the blood drain from her face. Her eyes grew hot and prickly. She squeezed them shut. When she was sure she would not cry, she opened them again. "Just tell me what to do."

His expression softened. "This is no job for a lady."

"The loblolly boy has his hands full with the other injured. Would you rather leave them unattended?"

"Surely there is someone else on this blighted ship who can assist me."

"They all have tasks, and as you can see, I am idle. He is my uncle. I want to help him."

"Say a prayer for him."

"I will, but I would like to do something practical as well."

"I cannot imagine what would be more practical than prayer." He held up a hand. "I will need a man of some strength to help keep him still. Besides which, I doubt your uncle would appreciate you being exposed to such sights."

The comment cut off her protests. He was right. Uncle John wouldn't want her to see him in the agony that was to come. He deserved to retain his dignity.

Lips pressed hard together, Phoebe left the captain's quarters as Harcourt returned. She paced the deck outside the door, her hands kneading one another, her lips moving in silent prayer. Surely God would heed her. He must.

Jimmy, the loblolly boy, came and went a half-dozen times.

The sun set with its usual burst of brilliance.

Lieutenant Loring joined her. "The captain has a remarkable constitution. He'll be shipshape in a fortnight."

Phoebe couldn't quite force her lips into the expected smile. "The physician said he would need to remove Uncle John's arm."

"We're lucky he did not balk at performing a surgeon's task. Don't worry, miss. Many a naval man has done without an arm. It will not signify to the admiralty."

"What am I to do if he dies, Mr. Loring?" The question spilled out.

"Don't fret." He patted her arm awkwardly. "I shall take you to your family in Halifax as your uncle intended. They will welcome you with open arms."

Phoebe brushed away hair the wind had blown into her eyes. At least there were still people around to map out her future. She would never be expected to make a truly important decision. Though she'd sought the reassurance, it irritated her. "I wanted to stay and assist, but Dr. Ingersoll would not allow it."

"I'm sure he was wise. Let the physician go about his business without interference."

The cabin door opened and Phoebe swung toward it, her pulse hammering in her throat like a maddened woodpecker.

Dr. Ingersoll stepped out. His apron was covered with blood, but he must have rinsed his hands. He removed his spectacles and rubbed the bridge of his nose.

❧

Alden already regretted his harshness toward Miss Carlisle. He could not prolong that look of wide-eyed terror, though he feared it might soon return and would not be so easily banished. "You may go in now, Miss Carlisle. I have dosed him with laudanum, so do not try to rouse him."

She snatched up her skirts and darted past him.

The officer who'd been standing with her put his hands behind his back. "Good work, Doctor. I trust everything possible has been done."

"Everything my skill can devise."

The man nodded and made to move away. Alden reached out to detain him. The lieutenant glanced at the hand on his arm and then back up at Alden with a look of reproof so strong Alden immediately let his hand drop to his side. It couldn't stop him from speaking, however. "I've treated your captain, and I will agree to come and check on his progress. May I go now?"

The lieutenant stiffened. "I'm afraid that's not possible."

Alden replaced his spectacles. "I have patients on shore who require my care."

"Dr. Ingersoll, you have been impressed into the British navy. You have no patients outside the confines of this vessel. You have no home outside this vessel. You serve at His Majesty's pleasure."

"You are not going to let me off this tub?"

The man scowled at the denigration of his ship. "While the captain yet lives, it is not a decision I can make. But we are in desperate need of a good medico, and you were highly recommended."

"You cannot do this. My whole life is in Glassenbury. Everything I have worked for, everything I care about."

The officer met his gaze, though the line of his jaw relaxed a fraction. He softened his voice. "It's already done, I'm afraid. I cannot release you without being party to desertion." He clasped Alden's shoulder. "It isn't such a terrible life." He raised his voice again. "Mr. Harcourt."

The odious bosun emerged from the captain's cabin. "Sir?"

"Keep an eye on the good doctor here."

"Yes sir."

With nowhere else to go, Alden all but dove back into the captain's cabin. How was he going to fix this?

# Chapter 3

Alden did not immediately see Miss Carlisle. When his eyes adjusted to the relative gloom, he realized she was kneeling next to her uncle's berth. He plopped wearily onto a stool and let his head fall into his hands.

How was he going to get out of this mess? Did his family yet realize what had happened? He had promised to dine with Mother at the inn this very evening, but if he didn't arrive she would assume he had been called away to tend an emergency.

Perhaps she could rally the mayor to demand his release. There must be something that could be done. These people couldn't simply spirit away whomever they liked on a whim.

But of course they could.

The war still limped along, and as long as it did, these sailors could enslave any man they pleased.

"God, I'm going to need Your help."

The words were a bare murmur, but Miss Carlisle turned toward him.

"I'm sorry?"

He raised a hand. "I was just. . .joining you in prayer."

"Thank you. I fear he needs it."

Alden rose and joined her side. He had done an elegant job, if he did say so himself. The head wound had been neatly stitched and bandaged. As had the arm stump. He had even managed to realign the clavicle with the help of a bolster under the captain's back and a push on his shoulders.

Still, Captain Carlisle looked even paler than he had before. Alden checked his pulse again. The captain was cold to the touch, despite the warmth of the day, and his pulse sped like a fury.

"Is there anything else you can do?" The girl's question was tentative, as if she didn't really wish to know.

"I. . ." Alden ran a hand through his hair. "He has lost a great deal of blood."

"But is that not a good thing? You will not have to bleed him."

"In this case, I fear it has gone too far. The humors are unbalanced, to the opposite extreme."

"Is there any sort of treatment?"

He continued to stare at his patient's pale visage. "I have been reading of some experimental treatments developed in London and Paris nearly a century ago. They involve transfusing blood from animals into the injured."

"That can be done?"

"It was not always successful, which is why the treatment fell by the wayside. I have theorized that it would be more effective to transfuse blood from a family member

163

rather than an animal. They do say that 'blood will tell.'"

"I am a family member. Could you do it for Uncle John?"

Alden wheeled to look at her. "You must be joking!"

"If he needs blood he can have mine." She spread her hands. "I am sure I am due for a blood letting after all the excitement aboard ship. Why ought it go to the leeches if there is the slightest chance it might help him?"

"I have never attempted such a thing."

"How does it work?"

"A small incision is made in the veins of both patients and a tube is connected. I do not recall all the details. I never expected to actually employ the technique. I will not do it."

"Please, Dr. Ingersoll. I beg you to reconsider. There can be no real danger. Do not let him die for lack of something I could freely give."

Alden scrubbed his face with his hands. Could this day get any worse? What had he been thinking to mention transfusion at all? He'd wanted to sound erudite and well-studied in front of a beautiful young woman. He was daft. That was all there was to it. But he'd never have expected her to jump at the notion so eagerly.

Although. . .she had a point.

The captain's need was grave.

With a sinking sensation, he knew he was about to give in. He gave a final gasp of protest. "I would need several medical texts from my office, and the first lieutenant has made it abundantly clear that I cannot leave the ship."

"I will gladly fetch anything you require."

He smiled. "I thought you disliked fetching things."

In spite of herself, Phoebe smiled back. "I merely said I am capable of more."

❧

Phoebe clutched the list of books in her hand as if it were a ten-pound note. The pair of ten-year-old midshipmen who had been sent along as escorts were having trouble keeping up with the pace she set, but she didn't care if she left them behind entirely. Time was of the essence.

The town had appeared charming from the ship, but now with night firmly in control of the horizon, she could see nothing beyond her thin circle of lamplight. Appreciation of Glassenbury's attractions would have to wait. She had a task to fulfill.

The door to Dr. Ingersoll's office hung slightly ajar. He had indeed been taken in haste.

Despite the open door, the interior of the office was tidy as a monastery. Inhaling the pungent scent of herbs and books, she walked through the front room to an examining room where she found the glass-fronted bookcases Dr. Ingersoll had described. He had a surprisingly large library for a colonial physician—at least a hundred volumes. She perused the spines. And not all medical texts either. Dr. Ingersoll had a wide range of interests. She handed the requested volumes to Midshipman Hollis.

Her gaze lingered on the remaining books. What sort of man owned these disparate works? She found everything from a slim volume of Gray's poetry to the works of the famous historian, Herodotus, to a *Robinson Crusoe* that her fingers itched to open and delve into. She spun on her heel and marched toward the door. It wasn't any of her business what kind of reading material the good doctor enjoyed.

She stopped short, making the midshipman do an awkward hop to the side so as not to collide with her. The stairs to the private quarters were right in front of her, and Dr. Ingersoll had been snatched from his home without any sort of notice.

She made a decision. "Hollis, take those books back to the ship. I will follow along shortly." It would be kind to bring Dr. Ingersoll some clothes and personal effects. He wouldn't be ready to do the transfusion until he'd gone over his references anyway.

Taking up her skirts, she mounted the stairs. She pushed away all doubts of the propriety of her actions. Surely the law of kindness was more important, and it wasn't as if she were visiting a man's chambers when he was in residence.

The rooms were well proportioned and comfortably furnished. A broad mantel crowned a brick fireplace. It held several small, carved images. She approached and found the artistry impressive. A handful of human faces looked as if they might speak at any moment. But there were others as well: a miniature dolphin and an eagle, wings spread as if he were diving after his prey.

Perhaps the doctor passed long winter nights by whittling. Her fingers brushed the glossy wood. These were finished though. The work of a craftsman. Even if it was not his own work, he obviously appreciated beauty. The doctor certainly was turning into something of an enigma.

She was dallying. Reluctantly she turned from the intriguing bits of statuary.

In the bedchamber she found a wide bed, its hangings pulled back to reveal a plump pillow and skillfully embroidered counterpane. A table beside the bed held yet more books and what must be a spare set of spectacles.

Phoebe took up the spectacles and the first volume of *Tristram Shandy*. The doctor's clothes hung from a neat row of pegs along the far wall. Folding the garments tidily on the bed, she focused on the task at hand rather than considering the advisability of her actions. Though her cheeks burned, her hands were steady as she added clean linens and stockings to the pile. Now, what to carry it all in?

In the kitchen she found a marketing basket. She sighed. It was no sea chest, but it would have to do. She carried it back up to the bedchamber and placed the garments inside before adding the book and glasses. Hands on her hips, she made a final survey of the room. There must be something personal he would want to remind him of home.

Then she spotted it. No carvings adorned the mantel here. Just a single miniature. Phoebe took up the painting and held it to the light. Small enough to fit in her hand, it nevertheless captured an inordinate amount of detail. It depicted a young lady with eyes the color of the Atlantic after a storm, lustrous skin, and dark, luxurious hair. She held a posy of violets and appeared delighted with the world.

Dr. Ingersoll must have a sweetheart. Or a wife.

For some reason the thought had never occurred to her. But of course, such a man must be attached. Phoebe sighed and sat on the edge of the bed. The girl was lovely. Phoebe hesitated. Perhaps it would cause more pain to be reminded of this girl when he could not be with her? Phoebe would never be able to compete with such a prize.

Catching the drift of her own thoughts, she sprang to her feet. She tucked the miniature into the basket and snatched up the burden. She was being ridiculous. She had no intention of competing with the young lady in the picture.

❧

Alden closed the last treatise and rubbed his eyes. Why had he allowed himself to be persuaded into this scheme? The procedure seemed fairly straightforward, but what if he managed to botch things and killed both the captain and Miss Carlisle? Harcourt would devise something far worse than keelhauling.

Bowing his head, Alden said a prayer for wisdom. While he was at it, he mentioned the captain and his niece, too. His further plea that God would help him figure a way out of the British navy was interrupted by Miss Carlisle's return.

She hauled a basket with her that looked—familiar. She thrust her burden at him. "Here. I thought a few things from home might make the situation easier."

"You went through my things?" He spoke slowly, trying to decide whether to be angry at the intrusion or grateful that he once more owned something other than the clothes he stood in.

Her cheeks blossomed pink. "I did not mean to pry. Only to make you more comfortable in your new circumstances."

Alden accepted the basket and peeked inside. Mother's miniature lay on top and he pulled it out. Had she yet heard what had happened? Would she be able to rein in his brothers when they heard?

He said another quick prayer that they didn't attempt anything foolhardy.

"I thought you might wish to have that with you. She is very lovely."

He nodded. "Always was the belle of the ball."

"I am sorry you will not be able to see her for a while."

"I do not know what she will do when she hears what has happened."

"But surely she loves you?"

Again he nodded, his eyes fixed to the tiny portrait. "Of course."

"Then I am sure she will wait for you."

He glanced up. "Wait for me to do what?"

The becoming pink in Miss Carlisle's cheeks spread. "Come back and marry her."

He laughed and turned the portrait so she could see it as well. "This is my mother."

"Your mother?" She clapped a hand to her mouth. "I am so sorry. I convinced myself I was not prying, and look at what I have done."

Alden suddenly made up his mind not to be offended. "I am pleased you brought the portrait. It will remind me of home."

"Are you ready to try the transfusion?"

The question jolted Alden, returning him with a profound thump to the deck. "Are you certain you want to go through with this?"

She looked at her uncle. "If I do not, he will die."

"Not necessarily." Alden grabbed for the text he'd been reading. "We could try it with a lamb."

"Doctor."

He stopped flipping pages, compelled by her quiet steadiness to meet her eye.

She continued, "Please let me do this. I am not frightened, and I must do something to help him."

He sighed. "All right. We will do the procedure here rather than transfer him back to the orlop deck. The jostling would not be good for his wounds."

Miss Carlisle nodded.

Alden licked his lips. "He still might die, you know."

"At least I will know we tried everything."

# Chapter 4

While Dr. Ingersoll made arrangements, Phoebe changed into her nightdress and wrapped herself in her dressing gown. With quick, neat movements honed by years of practice, she took down her hair and plaited it. At last, prepared and with nothing else to do to stave off unease, she knelt by Uncle John's sea cot. Her prayer was simple but heartfelt.

A knock at the cabin door proved prelude to Dr. Ingersoll's return. The loblolly boy held the other end of a high, narrow table, and they maneuvered it through the door awkwardly.

They placed the table next to Uncle John and Phoebe stared at it.

"I need you to lie on top."

"I. . .see."

She rested a hand on the table considering how she was meant to get up there.

"Let me help you." He encircled her waist with one arm and scooped her up with his other hand behind her knees.

Phoebe stiffened and threw her arms around his neck. Then she laughed. "You took me by surprise."

Dr. Ingersoll's cheeks reddened but he laughed with her. "Apologies. I should have warned you." He settled her atop the table and withdrew.

"No apology is necessary." Trying not to feel like a suckling pig, Phoebe lay with her hands clasped across her abdomen. He spread a coverlet over her and placed a small bolster under her head, his touch gentle but with the swift assurance of a practiced physician.

He pushed his spectacles up on his nose. "I would dose you with laudanum to deaden the sensation, but it would slow your pulse."

Phoebe licked her lips. "I understand."

The door smacked open. Lieutenant Loring stalked in. "What is this I hear? You're performing experiments on the captain and Miss Carlisle now? I'll not hear of it."

Phoebe pulled the coverlet higher about her neck. "Mr. Loring, I have reque—"

The lieutenant bowled through her words as if they were skittles. "Don't think that you could ever get away with harming an officer of this vessel because you dislike having been pressed. I'll have you brought up on charges—"

"Mr. Loring!" Phoebe sat up.

He paused and glanced at her. His cheeks turned scarlet at her dishabille.

Phoebe snatched for the blanket and moderated her tone. "I appreciate your concern, Lieutenant. However, I have *asked* Dr. Ingersoll to proceed with this treatment. It is none of your affair."

"Miss Carlisle, during your uncle's incapacity, I feel as if I must act as your guardian."

Phoebe lifted her chin a notch. "You overstep, Lieutenant. I owe you no obedience other than that of a passenger on your vessel. I owe my uncle a great deal more."

Loring looked to Dr. Ingersoll as if he might now expect aid from that quarter. "You must know this is a ridiculous risk."

The doctor straightened to his full height, a good four inches taller than the lieutenant. "The captain is failing. You can see for yourself."

For a moment the lieutenant's eyes shifted to take in Uncle John, who lay still as death and twice as pale.

Dr. Ingersoll continued, "The transfusion may indeed be the best option to help him."

The lieutenant threw up his hands. "Don't say I didn't warn you." He turned on his heel, but his sword caught between the table legs and he had to do an awkward sidestep to pull free.

Phoebe met the doctor's gaze as the door banged shut. She smiled, and an instant later they were laughing together. "Forgive me. I must not make you mock a superior officer."

"I have yet to find my sea legs in that regard. I—I still cannot imagine that I will not be going home when your uncle's treatment is concluded."

The raw disbelief Phoebe heard in his voice grated across her conscience. Her amusement faded and she lay down again.

Doctor Ingersoll turned his gaze to the instruments the loblolly boy had laid out. "It will not take long, Miss Carlisle."

Phoebe trained her gaze on the planks directly above her. She didn't want to see what was happening.

☙

Alden took up a lancet. He'd placed Miss Carlisle on the table so she would be slightly higher than her uncle, and gravity would help rather than hinder them. She flinched as he made the incision but made no sound. It took only a moment, and then he placed the stripped quill that would act as funnel and bound it in place.

Now for the captain. Another incision and he inserted the other end of the quill.

In essence it was a simple procedure. There wasn't much more to do but sit back and wait. Alden looked from one patient to the other. If it worked, perhaps he could use the circumstance to his advantage and persuade the captain to release him.

His gaze settled on the view through the windows. The green of the woods beyond the town offered a refuge. If he could escape the ship he could take to the woods. There were families outside town who would take him in until the British were gone and it was safe to return to his life.

Loring had made it more difficult by ordering Harcourt to watch him. Alden wasn't the only impressed man on board, and the lieutenant had suspended shore leave due to the risk of runaways. No one would be willing to turn a blind eye, since he'd resent someone else gaining their freedom.

Maybe he ought to wait until dark. He could simply jump over the side and swim like mad for shore. But guards were posted at night. At the splash the sailors would be on his trail in a trice. There'd be no chance to find a safe haven. Alden sighed.

"Is everything all right?"

Miss Carlisle's soft inquiry startled him from his reverie. He jumped and jostled the quill. She winced.

"I am sorry, Miss Carlisle. I was woolgathering. Does it hurt much?"

"No more than a normal bleeding."

Alden nodded, then cast about for something more to say. "What brought you aboard a Royal Navy vessel?"

She closed her eyes. "My grandmother died. I lived with her in Kent since my parents and younger brother died from the smallpox in 1750. Because I have no closer relations, I am on my way to live with Uncle John's family in Halifax."

"A long trip."

"Excessively." She closed her eyes, opened them again, and a sad smile twisted her lips.

"I have never been more than a hundred miles from home," he said.

"Did you grow up in Glassenbury?"

"Yes. My mother operates the Red Griffin Inn."

"Do you have any brothers or sisters?" she asked in a dreamy voice. "I always wanted a sister."

"Three older brothers. I am the youngest of the family, and they teased me incessantly." She smiled again, so he continued. He'd long ago learned how to chatter so as to take patients' minds off their discomfort.

Her eyes drifted shut again. "Doctor." She interrupted the flow of his words. Her own words were slurred. "I feel a bit. . ."

When she didn't continue he checked her eyes. They'd rolled back. She'd fainted. He all but ripped out the quill and had her arm bandaged well before he thought to breathe again. He waved the smelling salts under her nose. She didn't so much as twitch.

❧

Phoebe blinked. The world spun like the time that dreadful neighbor boy had twisted her swing until she'd gotten sick. As sick as she was about to be. She rolled to her side. A bucket appeared in front of her, and she emptied the contents of her stomach.

Someone rescued her braid from danger of being fouled. The same hand rubbed her back in gentle encouragement. With a groan she at last lay back. Her eyes met Dr. Ingersoll's, and she realized that it had been him ministering to her at such a moment.

She squeezed her eyes shut. If she tried hard enough perhaps she could disappear. Why, oh why, did it have to be him?

He was a doctor; he'd probably seen worse things.

But not from her.

She groaned.

"Are you feeling better, Miss Carlisle?"

"Hm? After that you may as well call me Phoebe. My physician back home always did. I tend to get ill after being bled. I ought to have told you."

"The reaction is not uncommon. I was ready." He nudged the bucket with his foot.

"You are very kind, Dr. Ingersoll."

"Just Alden will be fine. If I am to use your given name, you ought to have the liberty of mine."

"My previous physicians would disagree."

He bent a little closer. "Your previous physicians are not here."

"You are right. They would never have let me proceed with the transfusion."

"Then they might have lost your uncle."

"Is he well?"

"Not well, but I believe he may mend. The rhythm of his heart has slowed, and his color is a touch improved. We will see how he fares when he wakes from the laudanum."

Warmth spread through Phoebe. Perhaps, at long last, she had done something really worthwhile. "Is there anything more I can do to help?"

"You have helped enough. For the rest of the night you are a patient."

That wasn't so terrible. Movement still made her head spin. "May I stay near Uncle John?"

"For the time being. If I need to operate again, I'll have to have you moved."

"Thank you." The knife of guilt flayed her conscience. He had been so kind to her, and not at all condescending as most physicians. He had even acted as a surgeon to save Uncle John's life. How would he feel if he knew it was her fault he was here?

# Chapter 5

Alden awoke in the tiny surgeon's berth with a crick in his neck from the hammock and no notion of the time. How did men survive years of this life? At least he wasn't bedding down with the sailors. Those poor wretches were packed in like stacked firewood.

A knock sounded at his door and one of the midshipmen, he couldn't tell them apart, poked his head through the door. "Lieutenant Loring's compliments, sir. And he would like to see you."

"I am coming." Alden groaned and hoisted himself out of the hammock. He dressed. God bless Miss Carlisle for fetching clean garments. Scraping a hand through his hair, he decided his appearance would have to do then presented himself to the quarterdeck, where the lieutenant was holding court.

"Ah, Doctor. How fares the captain?"

"Better, I believe. He regained consciousness in the wee hours and we spoke briefly. He was lucid, with no lingering hallucinations from the medication. Barring infection or fever, he will mend well enough."

"That is good news. And Miss Carlisle is well after her ordeal?"

"I believe she suffered no lasting ill effects."

"I'm glad to hear it. And what of your other patients?"

"My other patients?"

"The sailors injured in the fighting."

"I have not seen any other patients."

Lieutenant Loring clucked his tongue. "Doctor, I know you weren't pleased to be brought on board, but I hadn't expected you to be remiss in your duty."

Alden stiffened, his jaw settling into a hard line. "I was kidnapped from my home to tend your captain. I have done that."

"No sir. You were impressed into the Royal Navy to replace our surgeon. I suggest you get about the task."

Alden whirled and stomped away without another word. He didn't trust himself to speak. If he once let loose with what he thought of that officious. . .smug. . .son of a sea hag, he'd be hauled up and flogged. He ground his teeth at the unfairness.

He slammed into the captain's quarters to check on his patient.

Miss Carlisle—Phoebe—was sitting next to her uncle's cot with a book open in her lap. The sun gilded her form until she seemed to glow like a Renaissance madonna. She was easily the most beautiful thing he'd ever seen, and his breath hitched in his throat.

The sight of her cooled his fury slightly. Her smile as she looked up heated his blood in a different way. The lieutenant didn't matter a whit. Just a few days more tending the captain for Phoebe's sake, and if need be the crew, and then he'd escape into the woods.

She motioned to a bowl on the table beside the captain's sea cot. "I fed him some broth, but he fell back asleep after a few minutes."

"The body requires a great deal of rest while it heals." Alden checked the bandage. Noted with pleasure the sight of laudable pus and wrapped a fresh cloth around the wound. Many physicians didn't bother changing the bandages, but it seemed to help the smell.

"I would like to help tend him today, if I may."

"That may be a good idea. I have been informed by Lieutenant Loring that I have neglected my duties." Alden nearly spat the words, his temper rising. "As if he has a right to assign me any task. I am a free man. A landowner. He has no right."

Phoebe paled, and he wanted to kick himself. Of course, Loring had the right by virtue of his position. By virtue of laws written a world away and the sovereignty of a king Alden had never seen. His outburst put Phoebe in an awkward position. Her loyalty must lie with the navy, of which her uncle was a part.

He ran a hand through his hair. "I am sorry, Miss—Phoebe. I should not have spoken to you thus."

"Oh Doc—Alden." Tears shimmered on the edges of her lashes. "Please, I should be the one to apologize. I—I did not realize at the time. It was all happening so fast. And I was so worried. But it is all my fault."

⁂

Phoebe could hardly breathe with the weight of guilt pressing against her heart. The doctor's handsome brow furrowed. He'd likely never smile at her again. Those eyes of his would never light up with wit and friendship, at least not for her. But she couldn't go back now. He deserved to know the truth. If he kept blaming Harcourt or Lieutenant Loring, it would only lead to trouble.

"When our ship put in, I made inquiries for the best doctor in town."

He drew back.

Phoebe sucked in a breath. "I learned your name and where your office was located. But then I feared that you might not come with me. So I asked the lieutenant to send a few men." She swallowed. "I even suggested that if you were not amenable, they could press you, though such a thing is not usual with surgeons."

He looked at her as if she'd struck him. "*You* did this to me?"

Mouth as dry as ship's biscuit, she nodded. "I never considered. I never thought of the consequences to you. I was just so worried—"

"You will excuse me, Miss Carlisle. I have patients to tend."

She might have been Medusa, the way his face had frozen in hard planes. Back rigid, he turned and stalked away. She wished he had slammed the door behind him. It would hurt less if she could be angry rather than ashamed. Once again she searched in vain for a handkerchief. She'd have to do without. Just as she'd have to do without the doctor's approbation.

Her tears spilled over, and she covered her face with her hands. Why hadn't she just asked him to come herself? He surely would have obliged. Then he wouldn't be trapped here. But instead she'd wanted her own way above everything. She certainly hadn't prayed and gotten God's approval on her machinations. Father had always told her that just because she could get her way didn't mean she should. This was what he must have meant.

"What can have my girl so upset?"

Phoebe jerked upright at the sound of her uncle's voice. Thin and scratchy as the day's growth of stubble on his chin, it nevertheless sounded marvelous.

"Oh Uncle John. You are going to be all right, are you not?" It came out as more of a question than the affirmation she intended.

He groaned. "I do not think you will be rid of me quite yet."

Phoebe grasped his remaining hand and brought it to her lips. "I am so glad. So glad."

Her tears rained on him and he sputtered. "It would be a pity to drown now after escaping the French."

Phoebe instantly pulled back and smiled. "I am sorry."

"What has you weeping?"

"Everything. The doctor, and my own wretched hubris, and you, and grandmother."

"What has the local doctor to do with your troubles?"

"That's just it. He is not just the local doctor. He has been pressed into the navy, and it is all my fault."

Uncle John's eyes drifted closed. "You rousted him with a billy club no doubt."

"Go ahead and laugh, but it is the truth. Please, can you discharge him? Once you are better of course."

He reached to squeeze her hand. "I told you when you came on board not to question the running of the ship."

"This is different." Phoebe poured out the tale. Uncle John would have words of wisdom to share. He could set things right. If she could just find the right words, she might even win back the doctor's regard by securing his release.

She glanced over to Uncle John. His eyes were closed, his breathing deep. He'd fallen back asleep.

Phoebe closed her own eyes. There'd be no help from that quarter.

❧

Alden took refuge in his cabin. He paced the confines for a good five minutes. How dare she meddle? Did she think she was some sort of deity that could toy with people's lives? He'd thought her possessed of Christian feeling, but that couldn't be. Not with that level of disregard for her fellow man. She had been the one bright spot in this whole farrago. The sense of betrayal stung nearly as much as the offense.

He slammed his fist into the wall of his cabin. A howl of pain and rage escaped him. It had been stupid. He stared at knuckles split open from the force of the blow. "Physician, heal thyself," he muttered.

He retrieved a roll of bandages from his case and awkwardly bound the wound.

The change of watch sounded. Alden rubbed his forehead. It was time to see about his other patients, before Loring took it in his head to inspect the sick bay. With the orlop deck stench fresh in his memory, he tied his handkerchief around his mouth and nose. He breathed in deep and said a prayer. God was going to have to figure out this mess.

With the gunports open to catch the breeze, the air in the sick bay wasn't as fetid as the orlop deck. He lowered the handkerchief and made the rounds with Jimmy, the loblolly boy, at his side. His patients were a miserable lot, with a range of illnesses and injuries that would make a heartier constitution than his quiver. It seemed the treatment had mainly consisted of grog and gruel, with the lad making a special effort to remove the worst of the splinters if they were easily reached.

It was going to be a long day. Alden put on one of the surgeon's leather aprons.

When the worst of the injuries had been handled, his mind began to wander. Surely it couldn't be so very difficult to get off the ship without anyone noticing. The eyes of the lookouts couldn't be everywhere at once.

After he ministered to these poor men he could escape this ghastly tub with a clear conscience. He'd forget about Phoebe Carlisle as soon as he was free. His cheeks heated with a renewed sense of betrayal every time he thought of her. The sooner he could get away, the better.

The bit of him that always subverted his best attempts at self-pity spoke up. He muzzled it. But whenever he turned his attention elsewhere, the little voice piped up again. *She was trying to save her uncle's life. She didn't know what she was doing to you. She's naive. What would you do if Mother needed help? Would you be any less ruthless?*

The voice kept at him, an incessant pricking. He might just go mad before he had a chance to escape.

She didn't deserve forgiveness, he assured himself. And he'd find a way off this ship. An idea occurred to him. His eyebrows rose, lips pursed. It just might work. He could use Miss Carlisle's regret to his advantage. She would help him escape without ever knowing she had.

# Chapter 6

Phoebe looked up from her prayer at the sound of the door opening. She hoped it would be Dr. Ingersoll, but it was her uncle's steward with another bowl of broth. The fellow placed the tray reverently on the table by the head of his cot, and when Phoebe insisted she would feed the patient, he nodded gravely and departed with the assurance that he would bring her meal directly.

Phoebe touched her uncle's shoulder. "Uncle John, you need to take some nourishment."

He groaned in response and made to turn away from her. But the movement seemed to cause him pain. His face contorted in a grimace of agony.

"Uncle John!"

His eyes popped open, the whites showing his alarm. "Phoebe?"

"Uncle John, are you all right?"

"No, I am not all right. An arm I no longer have itches, and the stump feels none too pleasant. My head aches as if Cerberus is gnawing on it, and this infernal collarbone hurts like blue blazes."

Perversely, Phoebe smiled. Uncle John had ever been known as the worst possible patient. He was generally so robust that any infirmity put him in a foul mood. He wanted nothing of drams and doses. He wanted to get back to commanding his ship. Enforced idleness wore on him like no amount of work could.

In other words, he was becoming his old self. "Pipe down, Captain Carlisle. You will be able to hound your crew only when you are better. So you might as well take some broth and stop your grumbling."

She stood and piled bolsters behind him to prop him up. He harrumphed and would likely have crossed his arms if one had not been missing. But he opened his mouth and allowed her to spoon in some soup.

"You are too slow." He took the bowl from her and slurped the contents without resorting to niceties such as a spoon. "There," he said, handing it back. "That's efficient."

Phoebe leaned forward and kissed his cheek. "I am so glad you are on the mend. You had me worried."

He patted her shoulder. "Truth be told, my girl, I was a mite concerned myself."

The door opened again and Phoebe turned, anticipating her lunch. Instead Dr. Ingersoll stooped to enter. He said not a word to her but examined his patient with every appearance of concern and skill.

Phoebe sat by silently, listening as he instructed Uncle John on the importance of his diet, bed rest, and fresh air. It was a good thing she was here, or Uncle John would promptly disregard everything the doctor said.

"You are making good progress, Captain, but you will be weak for several days, possibly weeks. The headache should gradually wane as the swelling within your skull reduces, and the stitching without heals. The transfusion was a remarkable success. I—"

Uncle John's eyes, which had been drooping, popped open. "What?"

"I employed a treatment known as transfusion. In fact, your niece helped."

"What has Phoebe to do with any of this, other than playing nursemaid?"

Dr. Ingersoll colored as if he knew the answer would not be well received. "It is a process by which blood is funneled from a healthy person into an injured person. I assure you there is precedent for the treatment."

"You asked my niece to do what?" Uncle John struggled to sit up.

Phoebe intervened, placing a mostly gentle hand on his chest and helping him to lie back. "I insisted, Uncle John. It was no different than being bled for some ailment."

"But you were not sick. You might have thrown your humors out of balance and made yourself ill."

"Nonsense. Every doctor I ever met seems to think we are all in need of a good bleeding. Now, if you do not get better, we may have to do it again."

"Not under any circumstances." He shook a finger at the doctor. "I do not know what kind of quack you are, but do not let her do it again, or I will send her to the masthead and you to the brig."

Phoebe planted herself between them. "You would do better to thank us both kindly for saving your life."

Uncle John snorted and glowered, but within a few moments had fallen asleep again.

The doctor turned to leave.

Oh no. He wasn't going to get away that easily. Phoebe reached out and touched his arm. "Dr. Ingersoll, please. You have every right to be angry with me, and I do not intend to try to talk you out of it, but please, is there any way I can make amends?"

❦

Alden hesitated. That had been too simple. He had been braced to manipulate her into making such an offer. But it appeared God was smoothing his way. It had to be a sign that this trial was nearly over. He'd be free and home in a day or so. He could be patient for that long. But he was getting ahead of himself. "Do you think you might see your way to performing a small service?"

"Anything."

"I wrote a letter to my mother explaining where I am." He drew it from his waistcoat pocket. "And bidding her farewell." *And instructing her whom to contact about finding me a hiding place once I gain shore.*

"I would be delighted to deliver your letter. If Jimmy can sit with Uncle John, I will go now."

"I will sit with him." Alden gave her directions on how to find the Red Griffin and handed over the letter, ignoring the pinch of conscience. He wouldn't have been forced to such an action if she hadn't had him practically kidnapped. At least he could be sincere in his gratitude for her cooperation. "Thank you."

Miss Carlisle ran her fingers over the makeshift seal he'd managed to produce from candle wax and his thumbprint. When she looked up, there was no mistaking the reproach in her eyes at his lack of trust. "Is there any other message or token you would like me to take to her?"

Alden bit off an apology. "No, but if you could wait for a reply?"

"Certainly." She stood and moved around him with a circumspect swish of skirts, as if afraid of brushing too closely.

The captain stirred and she looked back anxiously.

"We will take excellent care of him while you are gone."

She nodded. "I will just fetch my cloak. Is there anything further I can bring you from your home?"

The thought enabled him to harden his heart. He shouldn't need to pack up the detritus of his life. He should have the freedom to return to his things and his life. And if he didn't go soft in the head and blurt out his plan, he would be going home. The pause was stretching too long. He forced a grim smile. "You have already brought me everything I require."

She nodded and departed so quickly it was obvious she was glad to escape his presence.

Alden sighed and dropped into the chair she'd vacated. As much as he hated to admit it, even to himself, he wanted her to smile at him again. But there was little chance of that now. Especially after she found out he had duped her.

🕸

Phoebe took only a moment to tie on her cloak before requesting the use of the jolly boat for the afternoon. Lieutenant Loring was exceptionally accommodating, and she had to decline his escort rather more forcefully than she might have wished. She had an idea there might be naval prohibitions against an impressed man communicating with his family while in his home harbor. Well, if there were, she preferred to remain in ignorance.

She kept the letter tucked safely out of sight and carried with her a large, empty basket that implied her desire to visit the shops. Feeling like a traitorous spy, she sat staring at her clasped hands as the oarsmen pulled steadily toward the dock. When at last she was handed ashore, she turned her gaze to the town.

It was a handsome, prosperous-looking place. Its tall clapboard buildings looked as if they were pleased with themselves but not smug, merely content. Late flowers still bloomed here and there despite the nip in the wind.

Unlike in London, numerous trees lined the walkways. A few of these grand old dames were already changing their fashions for the reds, oranges, and golds of autumn. With Dr. Ingersoll's precise directions, it didn't take long for her to find the inn his mother owned.

It was perhaps the most charming establishment she'd ever seen. Vibrant orange chrysanthemums, russet helenium, and snowy-white asters filled window planters and mounded along the walk. The building itself was painted a cheery red, brighter than brick, but in no way showy. Spotless windows were flung open to welcome the sun's rays. All in all, an air of cheerful bustle promised excellent housekeeping and a staff that knew what they were about.

Phoebe hesitated on the stoop. Alden had asked her to wait for a reply. What if they expected her to make conversation? There would be no way to avoid the questions that would come her way.

The decision was made for her when a neatly starched young maid flung open the front door. The girl yelped and hopped back. "Oh glory, miss. You gave me a fright."

Phoebe apologized and asked for the mistress of the establishment.

"I'm afraid I can tell you we're full up this evening."

"I am not in need of lodging. It is a personal matter."

"Oh, well we've got all the staff—"

"And I am not in search of employment. I have brought her a message."

Curiosity blazed in the girl's eyes. "I'll fetch her down."

"Thank you." Phoebe stepped into the front hall. Her fingers kneaded the wicker handle of her basket.

The Red Griffin was as pleasant as she had expected. Well-scrubbed floors were dotted with bright rugs. The furnishings weren't new but appeared to be good quality and well cared for. The aroma of roasting chicken and something else delectable hung in the air. The scent alone would entice every weary traveler in the district to lodge at this establishment.

The maid returned and opened the door to a small sitting room. "Mistress invites you to have a seat in here. She'll be down directly."

Phoebe went through and perched on the edge of a settee. This chamber didn't look like a public room. A secretary desk bursting with papers occupied one wall. Sketches and paintings hung in joyous abandon, some straight, others less so. The mantel held carvings similar to the ones she'd found in Dr. Ingersoll's home.

In spite of herself, Phoebe crossed the room to examine them. She was almost certain these came from the same talented hand, perhaps a member of the doctor's family. Above the fireplace a series of four charcoal sketches caught her eye. The artist had limned the faces of four young men. A younger version of Alden was captured in the drawing on the right. The others must be the brothers he mentioned. Phoebe stared at the sketch of Alden until it seemed it might speak. He looked more at ease than she had ever seen him. His smile warm and open, not tinged with bitterness as it was aboard ship. Had circumstances changed his smile before he came to the ship? Was this the way he looked at home? Or was the loss of that ebullient grin her fault?

A sound behind her made her spin.

The lady who had materialized in the doorway wasn't so different from her miniature. Plumper, perhaps, and wearing a mobcap over dark hair that was now streaked with silver. But the penetrating power and good humor of those blue-gray eyes were as self-evident in person as they were in the painting.

"I always did like those drawings of my boys. The artist did an excellent job of capturing their personalities."

Phoebe murmured agreement.

"Now, what might I do for you, young lady? Marianne said you have a message for me?" Mrs. Ingersoll's glance swept Phoebe's person, obviously taking in the quality of her garments and marking her down as a most unlikely messenger.

"Yes ma'am." Unsure whether or not she should explain herself, Phoebe pulled Alden's letter from its hiding place and handed it over.

Lips pursed, his mother slipped open the seal, removed the letter, and began to read. The color drained from her face. "Alden!"

Blindly she groped for a seat. Phoebe stepped forward, but the woman collapsed onto the settee before Phoebe could offer assistance.

Mrs. Ingersoll couldn't seem to tear her eyes from the letter. She held it in trembling hands. Eyes wide with more emotions than Phoebe could name or even guess at turned suddenly toward her.

"What do you know about my son?"

# Chapter 7

Phoebe cast about for words, an explanation, anything to turn those baleful eyes away. Though in truth, she deserved the reproach radiating from the woman. "I. . .I believe he explained in the letter." What had he written?

Mrs. Ingersoll turned her attention back to the letter. Her eyes seemed to devour the lines of neat script, darting across the page and back again.

Phoebe willed her feet to remain planted. They wanted so badly to flee the cozy inn that they ached. She hadn't considered how difficult this interview would be. Just another headlong tumble into trouble. Why couldn't she ever look before she leaped?

She had to stick it out. She'd promised Alden she would wait for a reply.

A bit of color seeped back into Mrs. Ingersoll's cheeks, though they were nowhere near the comfortable rosy shade she'd exhibited when she entered the room. Abruptly she stood and pointed a finger at Phoebe. "Wait here." Then she turned on her heel and marched from the room.

Phoebe heard a tiny crack as the handle of her basket gave way beneath the pressure of her fingers. She loosened her grip instantly. Her cheeks burned. Her throat was tight enough that she might never swallow again, and her vision seemed to shudder. She couldn't focus. Every bit of her wanted out of this room and safely back on *Aries*.

Safely? Why had she thought that? Did she really think Mrs. Ingersoll meant her harm? What if the woman decided to hold her as a hostage in exchange for the doctor? It would be illegal of course, but that would be little consideration to a mother in danger of losing a beloved son. England was at war, after all. Phoebe hadn't just signed the doctor up for a pleasant cruise down the river. *Aries*'s battered condition was proof enough of that.

No. She was being ridiculous. No one meant to kidnap her.

In the hall she could hear the scurry of rushing feet. Lowered voices murmured just below what she might have overheard. Somewhere a door slammed.

After an eternity that the mantel clock insisted on calling a mere quarter of an hour, the door opened again. Phoebe swallowed convulsively, though it did no good. Her mouth and throat were parched. Mrs. Ingersoll entered first, followed by two men, their faces flushed, their postures intimating tightly leashed anger. Both of them wore aprons over working clothes. But whereas one was dusted with flour, the other was flecked by sawdust. The befloured man walked with a limp and had maple-colored hair. The other looked more like Mrs. Ingersoll, with darker hair and sea-washed eyes. Phoebe glanced at the drawings to confirm her guess. Yes. These were two of Alden's elder brothers.

Mrs. Ingersoll spoke first. "I haven't questioned her yet. I wanted you boys with me." The sawdusted one eyed Phoebe like she was a louse, though his remarks were addressed to his mother. "How long do you think it will take for Jonathan to get here?"

"I do not know. I sent Marianne to fetch him, but it will depend on whether he is out on the river or not."

"Perhaps we ought to start without him. I am sure that Miss. . ." The other brother looked at Phoebe.

"Carlisle," she said.

"Miss Carlisle must be wishing to return to her uncle."

Phoebe nodded eagerly. "I should very much like to get back to the ship."

Mrs. Ingersoll was less conciliatory. "I have a few questions first. Tell me exactly what has happened to my son."

Whalebone from her stays prodded Phoebe in the ribs. Or was it guilt? She ought to tell the full truth and simply accept the consequences. She had wronged these people nearly as much as she had the good doctor.

She licked her lips, trying to find a way to make them understand that she had been frantic. She couldn't say that she hadn't meant to do what she'd done. She'd planned it out. But she was sorry. She had failed to take into account the physician whose life would be upended.

"I ought—"

The door to the sitting room flew open and another young man marched in. Three handsome young women entered hard on his heels. Mrs. Ingersoll was engulfed in hugs. Noise and movement and energy filled the room. Everyone was talking at once, either demanding to know what had happened or busy trying to explain. Several small children joined the chaos, and with them an energetic little puppy.

Phoebe tightened her grip on the arms of her chair and stayed very still as the storm raged. Was this how normal families acted? She could hardly recall. Her own upbringing had been one of straight spines, stiff upper lips, and cold dinners alone with a nurse in the nursery. Grandmother had not believed in noise.

For all the clamor, there was a good-naturedness about the madness. They obviously cared for one another.

One of the younger tykes began to cry when she heard that Uncle Alden had been taken from them. Tears came to Phoebe's eyes as well. God forgive her for what she'd done. Was her uncle more important than this child's? Why hadn't she thought things through?

At length, Mrs. Ingersoll raised her hand, and the room quieted by degrees. The children were sent outside and the adults took seats, ranging around the sitting room in a comfortable sprawl of familiarity.

"Now," said Mrs. Ingersoll, "we were just about to listen to what Miss Carlisle can tell us of Alden."

Phoebe's hands were becoming sore with the constant kneading. "Dr. Ingersoll was impressed aboard *Aries*. I"—her voice quavered—"I'm afraid it was my idea. My uncle is the captain and he was terribly injured. Dr. Ingersoll saved his life. But I am so sorry that I never considered what impressment would mean to him or to his family. I want to make amends."

The family members looked one to another. Phoebe tried to decipher their emotions. Doubt, suspicion, worry, fear, anger, a host of others, but none pleasant.

Where was the relief that confession was meant to bring? No one would look at her. It was almost worse than when they'd all been looking at her. Phoebe jumped to her feet. "Perhaps you would like to discuss matters? I will wait outside for your answer."

"I think that would be best, my dear," Mrs. Ingersoll said, her voice quiet.

Phoebe hastened outside. She could not stop trembling. On the stoop she realized she'd forgotten her basket, but it would have taken an army to make her go back for it.

Staring at the flagstones that Alden must have traversed a thousand, nay, a hundred thousand times, she made a decision. It might mean betraying her uncle and *Aries*, even the laws of England, but she was going to help Alden escape. She had to make matters right.

❧

Alden rubbed his temples. Would the carpenter and his crew never finish with their infernal hammering? His head now pounded as much as they did.

He'd made his rounds after lunch, checking on each of the sailors and allowing three to return to their duties. Then he returned to the captain's cabin and dismissed Jimmy.

A hand to his patient's wrist established that he had a steady pulse. A touch rapid. But not nearly the frenzied race it had been on the night before. His color was better, too. Still wan but without the waxy quality of a man begging entry at heaven's gates.

Gently he unwound the bandage around the captain's arm. When the wound had been exposed, he examined it. Pleased with the look of it, he took a breath and opened a jar of ointment he had made. Compounded of wool wax and comfrey, it had a unique stench that made his eyes water and his nose hair sizzle. He ought to have opened the windows before he started this.

His patient groaned.

Alden hesitated.

"What is that?"

Alden held up the jar so the captain could see it. "An ointment. I know it reeks, but I assure you, I have used it before with great success."

The captain grimaced in a way that Alden thought might have been meant as a smile. "Lad, a sailor thinks the more unpleasant a medical treatment, the more effective. Smear away."

Alden did so, eager to be able to close the jar. "I think your arm will do. You show no signs of infection."

The captain grunted.

As soon as he closed the jar, Alden applied a fresh bandage. If nothing else it would muffle the stench of the ointment. "You will still be weak for at least a fortnight. It would be best if you remained abed for at least that long."

"I have a ship to command."

Alden squinted at his patient then realized why the man was so fuzzy and put his spectacles back on. British captains were supposed to be nearly godlike in their powers over the lives of their men, but Alden was well used to recalcitrant patients. "Lieutenant Loring is doing a fine job of seeing to the repairs, and you are at safe harbor. Your vessel will not fall apart if you take time to recover your health."

The man snorted. "Discipline might."

"What good would it do your crew for you to kill yourself by early exertion? The choice is yours of course. You need only listen to me insofar as you wish to get better and stay better. Although I will say that I hate to have my good work ruined by ungrateful patients."

"Me, ungrateful? You allow my niece to participate in quack medical experiments, and I am considered ungrateful?"

Despite his own misgivings on that score, Alden sensed that if he gave so much as a particle of ground, the captain would insist on his own way. "She saved your life with her gift. Yes, I would say your attitude is ungrateful."

Clearly, Captain Carlisle was unused to disagreement. He harrumphed and shifted in his berth. "I am grateful to Phoebe of course. You are the one that ought to have put a stop to that ridiculous procedure."

"If I had, your niece and crew would be attending your funeral today. Now, take this." Alden handed him a dose of laudanum.

The captain accepted the cup but did not raise it to his lips. "Where is my Phoebe?"

"She has been here almost constantly." Alden was not about to admit to the favor he had asked of her.

Captain Carlisle nodded. "She needs to rest."

"And so do you. Drink the medicine."

The captain grimaced but obeyed. "You are an impertinent young man."

"I have not yet become accustomed to naval life."

"Well, in spite of everything, I appreciate that you came aboard to treat me."

"I was press-ganged, sir. I had little choice." Alden regretted the words immediately.

The captain's eyes widened. "My men impressed you?"

*At your niece's bidding.* Alden restrained himself and said neutrally, "They were greatly concerned for you."

Subdued, the captain lay back and swallowed his dose of medicine. "I believe I recall Phoebe mentioning it. But then this must mean our surgeon has passed? I had hoped she merely insisted on a physician."

Alden nodded.

"And the men? God forgive me, I have been remiss in considering any pain but my own." Captain Carlisle rubbed his head. "Was the butcher's bill very high?"

By the time Alden finished giving his report of the wounded, the captain's head was nodding. His eyelids closed once more, and before long a gentle snoring filled the cabin.

Alden sighed and crossed to open the windows. Then he took the seat Phoebe had vacated. He'd taken no pleasure in giving the captain bad news. It was apparent the man cared for his crew as much as they cared for him.

They had all been right that their captain would die without assistance, and when he had refused to come with them, they must have felt their options limited indeed. Some of the resentment smoldering in his gut fizzled.

"Lord, help me to know what to do. I do not know why You brought me here, and I want to go home. But please, help me not to overlook Your guidance due to my anger." He lifted his face to enjoy the breeze off the water. His eyes drooped closed. His head bobbed and he shook it, trying to clear it of cobwebs. He was just so tired. He'd had at most two hours of sleep in the past thirty-six hours. His eyes were so heavy. If he rested them for a moment, he could go back to figuring out what God wanted with him. His eyes shut.

"Doctor?" A sweet voice plucked at him. A small hand squeezed his shoulder. "Are you well? Should I call the boy?"

Alden fought to free himself from the tentacles of sleep. With an effort he managed to pry his eyelids apart. "No. I am all right. A little sleepy."

"You ought to be." Phoebe settled beside him. "You have been run off your feet since coming aboard."

Alden shrugged. "Were you able to see my mother?"

"I was. You have a lovely family."

"You met them all?"

She nodded. "Most of them, I think. How many are there?"

He snorted. "At times it seems like too many."

A dreamy look crossed her face. "I think I would enjoy having a large, close-knit family. It was just Grandmother and I for so long that the silence became oppressive."

He met her gaze and felt the heat of shame burn his cheeks. He was trying to get back to them all. How could he pretend they were anything but a blessing in his life? "Did they give you a reply?"

She pulled a letter from her basket, along with a paper-wrapped parcel. "You mother sent this along as well. She said likely you were not eating right and wanted you to have something from home."

Alden accepted the package and opened it to find an apple, a slice of ham, an entire loaf of bread, and three crullers. He shook his head and sighed. Mothers. At least she hadn't sent along clean drawers.

Cheeks warm, he glanced up to find Phoebe smiling at him. He shrugged. "She worries."

"Of course she worries. You are her son."

"I am also a grown man."

"I am not sure that matters."

His raised his eyes from the package and was surprised anew at how beautiful she was. The urge to stroke that petal-soft cheek overwhelmed him.

"Dr. Ingersoll, I . . ." She moistened her lips with the tip of a pink tongue. "I have to apologize. I am so, so sorry, for what I have done to you. I—no excuse is good enough. But I will try to make it up to you." Tears glittered in her eyes.

Unthinking, Alden stepped closer. He reached forward and cupped her cheek in his hand. She leaned into his palm.

"It is all right, Phoebe. Of course you wanted to save your uncle. It is all right. I forgive you." His fingers moved to stroke her hair. He might be starting to see why God brought him here.

She lifted her face and met his gaze. And the urge was too much. Still gently cradling her head, Alden lowered his lips toward hers.

❧

The breath caught in Phoebe's throat. Her lips tingled in anticipation. And then his lips were on hers. Somehow both firm and soft at the same time. He moaned a little in the back of his throat and pulled her closer. Willingly she yielded and wrapped her arms around his neck.

She'd never been so swamped by sensation. Eyes closed, she raised herself on tiptoe to better welcome his mouth on hers. Nothing existed outside the contact of her body with his.

Uncle John snorted and mumbled something, and almost at the same time the cabin door opened to reveal the chaplain. Phoebe sprang away from Alden.

Breathing hard, she brushed her lips with the back of her hand.

Eyebrows raised, Reverend Malcolm nodded a polite greeting. "Good day, Miss Carlisle. I hoped to be able to offer some small service to the Captain, if only to sit with him. I do hope he is feeling better."

Lips still feeling the force of Alden's kiss, Phoebe nodded. "I am certain he will appreciate the company. He was just stirring."

Alden had turned to inspect the instruments and bottles that had accumulated on the table. She wished she could see his face. What was he thinking?

Did he regret kissing her?

She didn't regret it, except. . .it was going to be even harder to help him escape when she really wanted to keep him near always.

Looking at the rigid line of his back, she knew she had to try at least. He deserved to be happy. And she was the one who had to make certain he could go home where he belonged. Hand pressed to her chest as if to calm her racing heart, Phoebe hurried into her cabin and shut the door.

It was time to begin planning.

Really, it oughtn't to be so hard. They were, after all, within hailing distance of the shore. If she could just get him to town, he would be able to find shelter among his friends and family. He was well loved.

Phoebe nearly smacked her head on a beam. The new cabin that the carpenter's mates had knocked together for her was a good deal smaller than her former lodgings. She turned on her heel and resumed pacing.

Could Alden swim? She sighed. There were so many unanswered questions. Well, she wasn't going to let that stop her. She retrieved a book of foolscap and began to write out her ideas. There had to be a way.

186

# Chapter 8

Over the next week and a half, Alden found himself falling into step with the routine of the ship. The life wasn't so unpleasant. If he had been starting out, he might almost have enjoyed the demands of shipboard life. There was something to be said for routine and discipline. But every time he went on deck or glanced out the gun hatch toward Glassenbury, longing for his home and his family seared him.

On the other hand, every time he caught a glimpse of Miss Carlisle, he ached to hold her again. To have her near. To touch her hair and hear her say his name.

One thing was clear. He couldn't have them both. If he was going to escape, he didn't have long to figure out why God had put him aboard *Aries*. The repairs were almost complete, and the frost was coming thicker and thicker every night. Captain Carlisle and Lieutenant Loring were worried about the early ice on the Connecticut River. They could not afford to wait too long and end up trapped. Alden could sympathize.

Not only that, but it seemed the townsfolk had heard of his impressment and most had refused to do business with *Aries*'s crew. The officers had a hard time refitting and replenishing their stores. And the men had been discouraged from going ashore by the hostile reception they received.

His attention was caught by the scrape and bump of a boat coming alongside. The bumboats had largely disappeared from *Aries*'s vicinity. The occupants were either angry about the press or fearful of being pressed themselves. He craned his neck to see what was going on through the gun hatch.

Phoebe sat in the bosun's chair. He'd never seen a back so stiff, and she clutched the ropes with fingers that looked to be made of white marble. Without stopping to put on his greatcoat, he bounded out of his cabin and up on to the deck. She freed herself from the apparatus and stood with a manner so regal that he could only imagine some insult to her dignity. Her eyes were suspiciously bright and her color high. Had she acquired a fever? Pain pierced him at the thought of her falling ill.

But no, the midshipmen swarming aboard via the nets looked like they had been in some sort of tussle. Clothes disarranged and torn, they looked like they'd wallowed in a pigsty.

As he drew closer he realized that her cloak had been decorated with splotches of some sort of noxious substances. There was no fever. This was in a way worse, because it was personal. Someone had targeted her. The fearful pang of worry that had squeezed his heart twisted into searing heat. He'd never so desperately wanted to be ashore.

Dear God, if he could just get his hands on the ruffians who had done this he would teach them a lesson, and he wouldn't even care if it took splitting his knuckles open again. He tried to catch Phoebe's eye, but she hurried down to her cabin immediately.

Alden turned to where the captain had been taking the sun on the quarterdeck. The man struggled to his feet and might have fallen if his lieutenant hadn't been there to catch him. Knowing that his place was with his patient, Alden allowed only his gaze to follow Phoebe's retreating form.

The captain refused Alden's steadying arm at first but relented enough to allow himself to be assisted down the ladder.

"Shall I see you to your cabin, sir?" Alden asked.

"No. I want to speak to Phoebe."

"I am sure she would be happy to wait on you."

Captain Carlisle snorted. "Then you do not know Phoebe as well as you think you do. She does not want to wait on anyone at the moment."

Alden tilted his head and looked sidewise at the man. "Then perhaps she ought to be allowed a bit of privacy."

The captain stopped short. Glared at Alden. Sighed. "Oh all right. Take me to my room and then send in my steward."

Alden nodded understanding. "Shall I tell him you want tea?"

"No, but you can tell him to have cook make some of those sweetmeats Phoebe likes."

"Yes sir."

Alden opened the door and helped him negotiate the stoop. The captain shook off his hand then and moved to take his favorite seat. Alden turned to go.

"You know what happened to her is your fault, don't you?"

The caustic tone halted Alden in his tracks. He turned. "I feared so."

"Your presence has complicated what should have been an easy stay in a pleasant port."

"My mother would tell you that I have the tendency to complicate a good many simple things. It is one of my greatest flaws."

"You are impertinent, too."

"Another of my flaws. I beg you to excuse me."

The captain grunted and waved Alden to a seat. "The worst of it is that my Phoebe is taking the brunt of this. She has taken it into her head that she is responsible for seeing you pressed. I tried to tell her that my men do not take orders from female passengers. In the absence of orders from a superior officer they rely on their own judgment and experience, but she will not hear a word of it."

Alden was all too aware of Phoebe's determination to retain her guilt, but he didn't know what to say.

Captain Carlisle continued, "She blames herself for everything from the ill feeling in the town toward our crew, to depriving you of the home and practice you have built. She would blame herself for the French attack if she could figure out just what she did to put them on our track."

Alden looked up from studying the worn leather of his shoes. "Sir, I did try to convince her that I do not hold her accountable. That I have forgiven her. I think the Lord may have put me here to some purpose, I just do not know what it is." *Or how long I'll have to stay.*

The captain regarded him for a long, appraising moment.

"If there is anything further I can do or say to try to convince Miss Carlisle that I bear no grudge, please—"

The captain moved his stump in a gesture of dismissal. "I believe you. You have given every indication of. . .kind feeling toward her." Something unsaid in the captain's demeanor made Alden blush. "Guilt is a vicious master, however. Even though she understands your protestations with her head, she has not forgiven herself enough to let them into her heart."

"What would you have me do?"

It was the captain's turn to sigh. "I wish I knew, lad. I wish I knew." He sounded more fatigued than he had in days, and Alden rose to check his pulse. The captain flapped at him. "I am all right. Just go fetch my steward. And do not stir the pot. For Phoebe's sake."

Alden nodded and all but ran from the room. His errand took only a moment, as he met the steward in the companionway and passed on the message. Then he sought out Reverend Malcolm. He found the clergyman in the gun room and begged an audience. The good reverend immediately set aside the volume he had been perusing. "Certainly, Dr. Ingersoll. I am in need of a distraction. It is a pity to find the folk of the town so poorly disposed to us."

"Yes, well. That is a bit of what I wanted to talk about, I suppose."

The reverend patted his arm. "I am afraid the gun room is not conducive to private conversation. Follow me." He led the way out and up onto the main deck and then began to climb the rigging as if he were one of the hands.

Alden raised an eyebrow, but he knew his way around a ship and grasped hold of the ropes. The farther he climbed from the ship, the freer he felt. Perched on the platform, he gazed down on both the ship and the town.

Reverend Malcolm smiled. "Now, what is it you wanted to talk about?"

With a few hitches and starts, Alden poured out the conflict tearing at him. "I would feel better about it if I knew what God wanted me to do here. As it is, I cannot seem to find any peace."

The reverend nodded sagely. "It sounds like the problem may be that you are looking in the wrong place."

"In what way?"

"Simply put, any peace you have based on circumstances will be fleeting. True peace arises not from the pleasantness of our situation but from our relationship with the Creator."

"But I do believe in Him. I try to follow His guidance."

"Ah, but you tell me that you cannot tell what He wants from you."

Alden shook his head. "I know what I want. I don't know what He wants."

"But you believe He placed you here."

"He must have. I'm here."

"Then why are you so anxious to leave the place He's brought you to?"

Alden swallowed. "I. . .if I don't get off this boat before they sail on the tide, the chance of escape almost disappears. I'll be stuck for years, and who's to say I won't get turned loose just to be taken to serve another captain?"

"You know, when we sign up to follow the Lord, we give up many of the rights we hold so dearly. All of them, in fact. Except the right to follow the Lord and do His will. You have the right to be angry for the way in which you were brought aboard this ship, but you can choose to set that aside and consider why God has allowed it. You never know what might happen if you abandon your rights and your will. He has a way of working things around that never ceases to amaze me."

"But what if He does not?"

"Then you will still have been obedient."

"But what if He wants me to take a stand—to escape?"

The reverend pantomimed looking around. "Obedience is the key, no matter the call."

Alden sighed. "I thought for a bit that I might know why He brought me here. But the more I think on it, the more ridiculous it seems. I do not stand a chance, and even if I did, it would mean leaving everything I have ever known."

Reverend Malcolm winked and stretched. "Nothing is impossible with God." He lowered himself through the lubber's hole, leaving Alden to ponder.

Alden stared at the scarred platform, scored by the blades of innumerable bored midshipmen. If God had brought him here, did he have any right to demand to leave before God opened the door? The more he thought on it, the more he realized his turmoil came not in the decision to leave the ship, but in leaving Phoebe.

He had to admit it to himself. Somehow in the few days he'd known her, he'd fallen in love. She was everything he could desire in a wife, and much more.

Alden swung himself out to the ropes and climbed down. He headed to the orlop deck, where he took out his frustration on dried herbs, grinding them to powder in the mortar. It didn't work. He slid to the floor, letting his head fall back against the bulkhead. He covered his eyes with his hands. He would stay. He would wait on the Lord, and he would enjoy what time he could with Phoebe. She would leave the ship in Halifax, and he'd likely never see her again. But either way, he'd trust the Lord to direct his steps.

"God, I hope You can work through all this. I just don't see any hope for us to be together."

⁂

Phoebe paced her cabin. Her hands had stopped shaking an hour ago, but she couldn't seem to sit still. She had never been treated so dreadfully in her life. And though a part of her felt she deserved to be reviled, most of her ached to slap those schoolboys. They didn't know anything about her.

And besides, she was working to make things right.

She kneaded her hands as she considered her plan once again. It ought to work. Her only difficulty might lie in distracting the midshipman on watch. With good weather and a friendly harbor, there wouldn't be many men on duty. It should all be a easy as flicking open a fan.

How she would miss him. It seemed impossible that he should occupy so much of her thoughts and heart when they hardly knew one another, but he did. His departure would leave a hole in her life. But considering only her own desires was what had brought her here. For once it was time to consider someone before herself. If she loved him as she suspected, then she should seek his happiness. She would have to trust God to fill the gap in her heart that Alden would leave behind.

Phoebe sucked in a breath of fresh air through the gun hatch and stared out at handsome little Glassenbury.

Evening seemed to take an inordinately long time to arrive. When she finally did, it was as a fashionable lady, late to the ball but trailing a gorgeous gown of stars. Her escort, the moon, was only a sliver, high above and far away.

Good. Phoebe didn't want too much light. They would need every advantage they could possibly gain. Though it hadn't been officially announced, everyone knew this would likely be *Aries*'s last night in Glassenbury.

The watch would be on their guard for an escape attempt. But they wouldn't suspect her. She prepared for supper with exquisite care. She wanted to look her most fetching. Ostensibly to appeal to any guards she met, but also, truth be told, because she wanted Alden to remember her looking her best.

At her suggestion, he was to dine with them. She'd also invited the chaplain and Lieutenant Loring, to mask her intent.

The dining table had been spread with Uncle's second best. But it gleamed and glowed enough to assure the guests of their welcome. The men stood at her arrival, and Phoebe self-consciously took the seat Lieutenant Loring pulled out for her.

She glanced over at Uncle John and he winked. He was looking almost his old self. If nothing else good came from all this, at least God had used Alden to save her uncle's life. She really couldn't ask for more.

Covertly she looked to where Alden sat, wearing his best coat, with his dark hair pulled back in a queue. His spectacles perched on his nose, and his linen glowed snowy white in the candlelight.

He looked like. . .he looked like a thoughtful Adonis. That was it.

But when he met her gaze, he affected her more like Zeus slinging a lightning bolt that stole her breath and pinned her to her chair. His smile, at once tender and determined, also held something more ineffable.

"Is something wrong, Miss Carlisle?" Lieutenant Loring's voice brought Phoebe back from the ether in which she had been floating.

"No, of course not." She realized her hand had been poised over her fork for several long seconds without picking it up. Snatching up the utensil, she launched into trivial conversation. The first course was presented and consumed without any blunders. Then came the next course and finally the pudding. Phoebe's heart beat faster as the time for action drew closer. But her bright smile never slipped.

At last it was time to drink the loyal toast. The men stood and raised their glasses.

Phoebe did likewise. Then with a little moan she sat heavily back in her chair.

191

The men clustered around her. She raised a hand and spoke faintly. "Dr. Ingersoll, suddenly I do not feel well. Would you see me to my cabin and perhaps prepare a draught for me?"

"Certainly, Miss Carlisle. Do you feel well enough to stand?"

"I. . .I think so." She fluttered her eyelashes and sagged against him.

He put a hand under her elbow.

The look of concern in Uncle John's eyes made her cringe, but she couldn't turn back now.

Alden nodded to the officers. "Please excuse me, gentlemen."

In the companionway, Phoebe straightened. "Come with me. I have a plan to get you out of here," she whispered.

"What?"

"Do not worry. It will work." She grasped his hand, tugging him forward. They couldn't afford to dally.

The cold on deck slapped her cheeks and seared her lungs.

"Miss Carlisle—"

Phoebe shushed Alden. "We do not have time for you to argue."

"Now stand over here." She pushed him into a shadowy corner and moved to intercept the bosun. "Mr. Harcourt, I believe the captain wishes to speak with you."

The bosun's eyebrows rose a bit in surprise that a ship's boy hadn't been sent with the message, but he nodded and headed toward the hatch. Good. That just left the midshipman. Phoebe whirled to fetch Alden, but he was already at her back.

"You were supposed to stay hidden," she hissed.

"Miss Carlisle. I have decided—"

A light from below allowed an eerie glow to edge along the deck. They were wasting time. She grabbed his hand and tugged him toward the waist of the ship.

Up near the bow, a chorus of a drunken song erupted. Feet thundered on the deck toward the disturbance. Alden straightened, his head cocked toward the tumult. Phoebe made sure the midshipman had abandoned the quarterdeck and dragged Alden up the ladder.

A hiss sounded from the dark and she peered over the rail to find Jonathan Ingersoll in a small skiff. Beside her, Alden peered down into the darkness, too, and his jaw dropped. "Did my brothers put you up to this?"

Phoebe began uncoiling a rope over the side of the ship. She forced a tremulous smile. "I put them up to it. Now all you have to do is climb down."

Alden took her hand. "I do not want to go. Not if it means leaving you." He drew her closer.

Below, Jonathan hissed again and motioned for him to hurry.

Alden ignored him. "I believe God brought us together for a reason. I love my family, but I cannot leave you."

All the feeling in her hands seemed to have drained away. The rope fell from her fingers. The deck felt suddenly unsteady. "You would stay for my sake?"

He nodded.

"You do not resent me?" Her eyes prickled with the heat of imminent tears.

"How could I? You only acted to save your uncle."

"But what of your practice?"

"People get ill everywhere. When I am discharged from the navy, we can settle wherever you like."

She shook her head. "I cannot let you do this."

"I am afraid you have no choice. Unless you intend to reject my suit."

She stared at him, almost wishing she could find the strength to deny him, for his own good. And then she threw her arms around him. "I want to, but I cannot."

Their lips met in a sweet, soaring kiss.

Alden's lips moved along the line of her cheekbone until they nuzzled her ear. "I love you, Phoebe. I will go anywhere for you."

A light flared over his shoulder, blinding her. She jerked away from him and her foot tangled in the coil of rope. Before she could so much as gasp, she hurtled overboard. Arms flailing, she hit the water on her back. It forced the air from her lungs. Almost as quickly, the frigid water snatched at her skirts and dragged her down.

# Chapter 9

For an instant, Alden's heart seemed to stop. Behind him came the sound of shouts and curses. He kicked off his shoes and vaulted over the side of the ship. Fingers plucked at him. Caught his shirt, tried to hold him back. But he was free. His body knifed through the air after Phoebe.

The water closed over his head in a rush of cold that sent a jolting shudder through him. He kicked, driving himself deeper into the river. Trying to find Phoebe by touch alone. *God, grant me light! Help me find her.*

A warm glow of lantern light filtered to him from above. Below him and to his right, Alden caught a glimpse of something pale. It was Phoebe. Hands clawing at the water, she was yet dragged toward the bottom. Air bubbles streamed from her mouth. Her eyes were open, silently begging for help.

His lungs burned, threatening to burst, but he pushed forward until he could catch the cloth of her skirts in his grip. With every bit of energy he could muster, he hauled her up toward the light.

His head broke the water, and he sucked in a lungful of air. Men's voices battered him, but he couldn't heed the angry tumult. He found Phoebe's face in the mass of fabric from her dress and held it above the water. All the while prayer pulsed through his veins. *Don't take her, God. Please let her be all right.*

Rough hands snatched at him and pulled him from the water by his collar. Other hands pried Phoebe from his grasp. The wind made him realize how cold he was, and his body convulsed in shivers. Somehow he landed in a pile on the deck. He scrambled to his feet looking around wildly for Phoebe.

She lay huddled on the deck, looking tiny and fragile. He lunged forward, but arms prevented him from moving. He scrabbled at them, trying to free himself. Men clustered around Phoebe until he couldn't see her anymore. Everyone seemed to be shouting.

A bellow cut through the chaos. "What is the meaning of this?"

Harcourt shoved Alden forward. "He tried to take a runner, sir. And knocked Miss Carlisle in when she got in his way."

Still shuddering and gasping for air, Alden could only say, "No!"

The blood leeched from the captain's face until he looked as ill as he had when Alden first saw him. His eyes burned like live coals when he stared at Alden. "Throw him in the brig," he roared.

"No. That's not what happened."

Hands clamped on Alden's arms and he was dragged away.

Reverend Malcolm joined the captain. "Sir, you might want to have the doctor tend her before you lock him up."

"Turn her on her stomach. Loosen her stays," Alden shouted over his shoulder. "Get her warm." A fist struck the side of his head and set his ears ringing.

Still he struggled.

Lieutenant Loring appeared at his side. "We've got your brothers, Ingersoll. Looks like we'll have three more fine new hands."

Alden shook his head. It couldn't be happening. *God, where are You?*

There was a gasping, choking noise and someone retched. It was the sweetest sound Alden had ever heard. The men cheered.

"Phoebe, are you all right?" Desperately he yanked free of his captors. He didn't make it far.

A whispery imitation of her voice scratched at the air. "Alden? Alden!"

The men holding him slowed, looking at one another questioningly. Alden stilled as well. "I am here, Phoebe."

The men parted and he saw her. She still lay on the ground, but swathed in blankets, her uncle kneeling by her side. She turned her head to Alden.

He ached to run to her. Instead, he met the captain's gaze. "Sir, I did not knock her into the sea, and I was not trying to escape."

"What? No!" said Phoebe. Her voice still achingly weak. A grimace twisted her features as she tried to sit up.

Uncle John pressed her back down. "Calm yourself, my girl."

"It is my fault," she rasped. "I fell." Her hand fluttered out from under the blankets and extended toward Alden.

He took a step toward her, and this time no one restrained him. He kept moving until he, too, knelt by her side. He looked up at the captain, who appeared confused. "We need to get her out of this wind and into dry clothes."

"In my cabin." The captain stood with difficulty.

Alden gathered Phoebe into his arms and followed.

⁂

Phoebe leaned her head against the hollow of Alden's shoulder. So this was what it felt like to be cherished.

If only she could enjoy it.

But someone was attacking her head with an ice pick, and her throat and chest ached. In the great cabin he lowered her into a seat. Uncle John's steward appeared at her arm with a clean, dry dress. The gentlemen departed so she could change.

The warm cloth stilled the worst of her shivers, but she retained one of the blankets. When she opened the door she found Alden also wearing dry clothing.

"Phoebe." Uncle John's voice sounded as it had when she was eight and he had caught her in some infraction. "I think it is time for you to explain."

He settled behind his desk and gestured for her and Alden to sit. The pent-up story tumbled out in a swirling eddy of words.

Uncle John's face remained stony until she came to the part where she fell over the side. "That would seem to clear up the matter of Mr. Harcourt's allegations. Doctor, please accept my apologies for the accusation."

Alden bent his head in grave acknowledgment.

At some point during the interview, she had reached for Alden's hand. They now sat linked together as they awaited the captain's judgment.

Uncle John sat back in his seat and rubbed his face. "My darling, do you love him?"

Feeling as if she were tumbling through space again, Phoebe turned to meet Alden's gaze. "I do."

"And you love my niece?"

"With all my heart." Alden squeezed her hand.

"You would be willing to stay as our surgeon?"

"I will do anything to stay near her."

The captain nodded. "That is what I wanted to know." He pushed away from his desk and stood. He stuck his head out the door and ordered the steward to fetch Reverend Malcolm and Lieutenant Loring.

The lieutenant arrived first.

"Mr. Loring, please prepare the ship for sail. We will go with the tide on the morrow."

The lieutenant's curiosity radiated from him like a skunk's stench, but he saluted and left to attend his duty.

The reverend arrived. "You asked for me, Captain?"

"Yes, Reverend. I have need of your services. Do you have your prayer book?"

Reverend Malcolm patted his pocket. "Always."

"In that case, we are in need of a marriage ceremony."

Phoebe jumped to her feet. "Uncle John, do you mean it?"

He raised an eyebrow.

She looked to Alden. "Is this what you want?"

"More than anything."

She flung her arms around his neck. "As do I. But not like this. Reverend, you may put your prayer book away just for a bit."

Alden cocked his head at her, eyebrow raised.

"You must have your family here."

In short order, Alden's brothers were procured from the brig. They filed in, each holding his hat before him like a penitent schoolboy. Uncle John announced that he wasn't going to hold them, and some of the tension eased from their shoulders. Then Alden announced his impending marriage, putting his arm around Phoebe's waist and pulling her to his side.

Silence as the brothers gaped, and then there were cries of congratulations and a round of backslapping. Phoebe's hand was shaken, and she sensed each one covertly inspecting her.

As dawn lit the sky, Alden's mother and sisters-in-law and what seemed at least a dozen nieces and nephews were helped aboard.

Mrs. Ingersoll embraced her son fiercely, driving the air from his lungs in a whoosh. Phoebe clapped a hand over her mouth to stifle a laugh at her suitor and then decided that, upon occasion, impulsiveness might not be so terrible. And she allowed her joy to well up into a full-fledged laugh.

Mrs. Ingersoll stretched a hand toward Phoebe. "I knew in my bones I would be seeing more of you when I first spied you in my sitting room."

"Then the thought of this wedding is not too distasteful to you, Mrs. Ingersoll?"

"Bless you, child, I raised my boys to listen to the Lord's voice. I am just glad Alden finally found someone. He is the pickiest one of the bunch."

The comment sparked laughter from the surrounding family.

From the basket hanging over her arm, Mrs. Ingersoll produced a bunch of helenium and asters from the Red Griffin garden. "These are for you. Every bride ought to have flowers."

Phoebe accepted them, tears brimming in her eyes.

"And call me 'mother,' if it suits you, dear."

"Oh, thank you." Phoebe embraced the older woman.

Chattering and laughing, her new sisters took her hands. "You must get ready!"

They accompanied Phoebe into her makeshift cabin and helped her dress her hair. Then she donned her best gown.

When at last she was deemed properly enchanting, she was led on deck. Alden's smile when he met her eyes was even broader and more engaging than in his mother's sketch.

It wasn't the wedding Phoebe had ever imagined, but it was perfect.

A wedding breakfast was prepared, and Phoebe reveled in her new family's noisy, joyous festivities, so different from her grandmother's mausoleum of an existence.

When at last the breakfast drew to a close, Alden gave his mother a hug. "I will be back to visit when I can."

Uncle John approached and put a hand on Phoebe's shoulder and one on Alden's. "I have not given you your wedding gift yet. You are hereby discharged from His Majesty's service."

Alden looked to Phoebe, his eyes shining. "What do you want to do?"

Phoebe's heart was so full it felt as if it might burst. "We have to stay here. Your life is here, and my life is with you."

She flung her arms around Uncle John. "I will miss you."

His one-armed hug was still tight enough to catch her breath. "I will miss you, too. But I thought you might say that." He gestured over the side at his cutter, which had been lowered into the water. It already contained her trunks.

Tears misted her eyes. "I love you, Uncle John. Thank you."

He nodded and turned to hide his reddened eyes. "Now I am about to miss my tide. Be off with you."

Within minutes the entire Ingersoll tribe stood on shore. Phoebe waved and waved as *Aries* grew smaller and finally disappeared.

At last she turned to find her husband gazing at her with a complicated mixture of pride and worry and love. He kissed her temple. "Are you ready to go home?"

She smiled. "I cannot wait."

## Apple Fritters à la Bavarre

*The following recipe is taken from A Complete System of Cookery in Which is set forth a Variety of genuine Receipts collected from several Years' Experience under the celebrated Mr. de St. Clouet, sometime since cook to his Grace Duke of Newcastle.* by William Verral, Master of the White-Hart Inn in Lewes. Suffex, 1759.

Pare and quarter some large pippins, lay them to soak in orange juice, fine sugar, cinnamon and lemon-peel, and toss them often. Your dinner being almost ready, dry them in a cloth, tumble about well in fine flour, and fry them all very tender in hogs lard; dish them up, and sift plenty of fine sugar over them, color nicely with a salamander, and send them up.

Author's Note: Nowadays a salamander is a super broiler mostly used in restaurants, but traditionally it was a long utensil with a flat metal head, which was heated very hot. Sort of like a branding iron used to caramelize sugar.

Influenced by books like *The Secret Garden* and *The Little Princess*, **Lisa Karon Richardson**'s earliest writing attempts were heavy on boarding schools and creepy houses. Now that she's (mostly) all grown-up she still loves a healthy dash of adventure and excitement in any story she creates, even her real-life story. She's been a missionary to the Seychelles and Gabon and now that she and her husband are back in America, they are tackling new adventures—starting a daughter work church and raising two precocious kids.

# WHEN THE SHADOW FALLS

by DiAnn Mills

*For I the L*ORD *thy God will hold thy right hand, saying unto thee,*
*Fear not; I will help thee.*

ISAIAH 41:13 KJV

# Chapter 1

Ninette Curvier peered up at the gray skies and realized Papa would be angry. She had allowed the day to slip by without checking the beaver traps, and now a storm raged in the distance. She didn't know which fury she'd rather face.

Grabbing a heavy hunting knife, she raced out into the afternoon toward the water's edge. Heavy air nearly stole her breath away, and perspiration rolled down her forehead and stung her eyes. Early June, and such a sultry day. A wisp of wind swept up leaves and debris and tossed them into the air as though an invisible child frolicked about. A faint coolness embraced her face and offered a moment of reprieve.

Signs of a vibrant summer from budding spruce, maple, and oak trees to white trillium, bright pink lady slippers, and blue forget-me-nots usually lifted her spirits, but not today. She lifted her face to the ever-graying sky while a robin's song serenaded the quiet island. Its sweet warble would soon fade with the fast-approaching storm.

She slowed to step over fallen trees and avoid the rough terrain on the small hills leading to the traplines. Several feet away, beyond white and red pines, were the beaver dams. Papa's steel traps lay in and around these areas, all secure with a chain in the deep water. This first one sat at the base of a slide where the beavers swam under to pass through. Some of the traps were partially submerged to catch the animals that crossed over from one dam to another, and a few other traps were anchored at den entrances.

She moved closer to where Papa had jabbed a branch dipped in beaver scent at the side of a trap. The trap was gone, and her gaze swept to the deep water. A beaver must have decided to explore the scent and stuck its paw into the jaws of the trap. As it attempted to swim for safety, the weight of the chain pulled the animal down and drowned it.

How many times had she checked the traps, and still she loathed the task? All of them needed to be checked. And if they held beavers, she had to spring the trap and carry the animal home. As much as Papa's livelihood depended upon the fur pelts of the fox, beaver, muskrat, and otter, she wished he had chosen fishing or another way to live off the wooded island.

Ninette cringed at both the idea of the dead animal and hauling it up from the water's depth. She stepped out onto a log over the water and tugged on the heavy chain. The muscles in her upper arms burned. Oh, how she detested the times Papa left Michilimackinac Island to venture the five miles across to the mainland. On rare occasions, she accompanied him, but as usual, he'd requested she stay and watch the traps. He planned to sell their animal pelts to a merchant who'd be leaving the fort soon.

During his absence, without anyone to talk to, she quickly became disenchanted with the isolation of their island home. At times, friendly Indians wandered onto the island. Ninette spoke enough of their language to converse a little. However, Indian women did not travel with the men, and so once again, she yearned for the companionship of other women. Better still, she wished Papa would move them to the mainland where people were plentiful. Her infrequent trips to the fort offered brief encounters with the women there, and she relished every one. But Papa didn't want her near the English soldiers.

Slowly she brought up the chain. From the weight, the beaver must weigh seventy pounds. A brisk wind blew around her shirt, which cooled her slightly. She balanced her footing on the log in hopes she wouldn't fall in. The first sign of the beaver was its scaly, wide, paddle-shaped tail and then its webbed hind feet. She refused to look at its face, although Papa said she should be used to dead animals by now. Once she successfully dragged the animal to the shore, she loosed the jaws of the trap. This part offered fewer pleasantries than pulling up the chain.

Lightning flashed, and a rumbling of thunder followed. In the heavy humidity, her dress clung to her body. Suddenly the heavens appeared to burst with a downpour of rain that felt refreshing, until the needlelike drops pierced her body. But before she could seek shelter, the trap needed to be reset and the rest pulled up for inspection.

With the branch coated in beaver scent intact, Ninette moved out onto the log to drop the chain. Thunder reverberated in the distance, and it sounded like musket fire. She watched her step to make sure she didn't slip. Once she'd traversed across to the proper point, she released the chain. With a sigh of satisfaction and relief, she turned her body just as the chain caught her right ankle and plunged her into the water. Frantic thoughts raced with the possibility of a trap beneath the chain trapping her foot. She'd be mangled like the lifeless beaver. Coughing and sputtering, Ninette struggled to the water's surface with the weight of her waterlogged dress and burdensome shoes. Her heart pounded hard against her chest, reminding her of the plight of the beaver.

Frustrated and shaking with fright, Ninette pulled herself back onto the log and across to the bank. Snatching up the dead animal, she struggled across the rain-soaked path to the cabin. With the animal deposited inside the doorway of the shed, she changed into clothes more befitting a man and smoothed out her dress to dry. The other traps had to be checked, no matter what the weather.

*Papa, where are you? It's been three days.*

Only the forces of the storm replied. Papa hated dealing with the English, even more so since they'd seized control of the formerly French-occupied land. Usually he traded the pelts for supplies and hurried back. She prayed nothing had happened to him. Knowing Papa's temper with the detestable English, he might have had too much to drink, and. . .well, she didn't want to think about it.

☜☞

*Mainland: Fort Michilimackinac*

Neal gazed out over the crowd of soldiers and Indians. A gray sky, combined with hot temperatures, had not dampened their jovial mood of celebrating the king of

England's birthday. However, Neal's despairing mood continued. He adjusted his hat and smoothed the jacket of his red uniform in hopes no one noticed his dismal temperament and accused him of not being loyal to the king. The garrison had long since needed a little merriment. At least Neal did.

He heard laughter, and a man began to play his fiddle. The spirits flowed freely, and with the strong drink came loud voices and the frequent foolhardiness of those who partook of it. Neal had never acquired a taste for strong drink. His dear mother had expressed her views of its evils ever since he could remember, and he rather enjoyed the jingle of coins in his pocket rather than spending it on whiskey. Besides, the liquid burned all the way down, and the behavior of men never improved with its usage. Honoring his mother's wishes was the one thing he could do for her.

But he refused to acknowledge her French heritage.

A curse. Neal glanced on both sides of him and wondered if one of the soldiers recognized him as half French, half English. Yes, he'd been cursed since the day he was born.

"Neal, are you going to watch the Chippewa and the Sauk play a game of *bag'gat'iway*? They invited us. I'd like to wager against the Sauk."

Neal swung his head to the familiar face of William Rogers, a private like himself. From the looks of his friend's reddened face, the excitement of the celebration had seized him. "I've considered it." He nodded at the sky. "Do you think it'll rain?"

"I think not, but even so, it would feel quite good."

"A game of bag'gat'iway, you say? I've only seen the game one other time. And then the Chippewa appeared to be the better players." Neal laughed. "I like to make sure I'm shouting for the winning side, so I'll join you at the match after I check on the canoe that plans to depart tomorrow for Detroit."

"You and your diligence to work. Do you ever take a rest?" William shook his head. "Perhaps I should tie you up and make you accompany me."

Neal grinned and noted the Indians inside the fort appeared to be enjoying the festivities. The sight of them made him incredibly nervous, and rumor had it that nearly four hundred more roamed outside the fort.

Two Chippewa walked past them. Neal smelled the outdoors on their bodies and the scent of animal. Those characteristics did not bother him, but the stench of whiskey that trailed after them made him wonder about the wisdom of supplying the Indians with drink. Four hundred Indians against ninety soldiers and three officers did not sound encouraging. Of course, the English merchants and French families housed within the fort weren't included in that number, but how much did they know about real combat with Indians anyway? A moment later, Neal conceded that his misgivings had produced the same sensation as a knife in his stomach.

"Why are you frowning?" William asked. "This is a day to celebrate. The Indians are friendly, and we've shown the French our mighty force. Tomorrow we can go back to being soldiers."

"Of course." Neal caught sight of three Indians who examined a merchant's tools. "I've noticed the Indians have been purchasing axes. What do you think of that?"

William lifted his red hat and combed his fingers through dark brown hair. "Just as many are looking at other provisions and supplies. Hey ole chap, the Indians don't carry weapons. They're harmless."

Neal tightened a grip on his musket. Uneasiness swirled about him. He'd experienced the same anxiousness when he spied on the French for the English. He shrugged. He needed to relax. "I'll join you soon. I think you may need me to win your wager."

This time, William laughed. "I'm going after a little ale, and I'll wait for you at the gate. I hear it'll be open for us to watch." He slapped Neal on the back. "We'll have a jolly time of it at the match." He strode away with a lift in his walk.

Neal sighed. Were his fears simply ghosts sent to plague him and weaken his mind? Idle time always did that to him—stamped a heavy measure of guilt and fear about his past. The Indians were indeed friendly and appeared eager to learn English ways—a peculiar twist of events since they'd fought alongside the French during the recent war.

He wove his way through the crowd and out the fort's gate to where the Chippewa and Sauk had gathered to play their game. Already it progressed with much vigor. The game was played with a ball and a four-foot-long limb. The piece of wood curved in such a way that it closely resembled a beaver's tail. Neal stood near a post that belonged to the Chippewa; another post in the distance belonged to the Sauk. From what he could make of the game, each side desired to get the ball to the adversary's post.

Neal watched a few minutes more and noted that the Indians moved closer to the fort as their game continued. Of course, several soldiers watched from the open gate and welcomed a closer view. He turned to hurry along to the water's edge.

Dense woods lay beyond the Indians' game. He walked along the edge en route to the river. A shiver raced up his spine with the thought of four hundred Indians lurking in the shelter of the trees. He whirled around to peer into the dark fortress. *Nonsense. Rumors. Just rumors.* This was a fine day to spend with William and forget about his troubled world. He set his sights on the river to make sure the merchant loading at the river's edge received a letter destined for his father in England.

Several yards away, birch canoes rested along the Straits of Mackinac loaded down with animal pelts, trinkets for the Indians, supplies, and provisions. Neal waited patiently while a French trapper bartered with the English merchant. The Frenchman's voice rose, and in apparent frustration, he replaced English with French. Neal swallowed a laugh. The trapper had no idea the English soldier beside him spoke fluent French.

"You'd steal from your mother's grave," the trapper said.

"Speak English," the merchant said. "I can't understand your gibberish."

"I said my furs are worth more than what you're offering to pay," the trapper said in English.

"No, I've given you a high price. Have you lost your senses? Must have been the time spent in the stockade for insulting an officer."

The trapper blew an exasperated sigh. "You're robbing me like the English stole our land," he said in French.

"I don't understand you," the merchant said. "Take my price or go elsewhere."

The trapper clenched his fist. "I said you're robbing me like the English stole our land. I must have more money. These furs are the finest quality."

"No better than others. I refuse to alter my price."

"Your king is a knave." The trapper punctuated each English word.

The merchant dropped the pelts and raised his fists. "This is the king's birthday, not a day to insult His Majesty."

"Gentlemen, fighting will not solve your problems," Neal said.

"And you call yourself a soldier?" The merchant asked. "A real soldier understands the honor of a good fight and the king's honor."

Fury settled in Neal's bones. The crack of musket fire ripped through the air. Then another. Shouts from the fort seized his attention.

"What is going on there?" The French trapper whipped his attention toward the fort. "Fighting? Is it the Indians?"

The foreboding sensation that had been with Neal all day came to realization. He squeezed his musket. "You two men need to follow me."

The merchant shook his head. "I'm leaving. This is not my war."

Neal wanted to ask him about his words of courage spoken only moments before, but he dared not waste his time if the Indians had turned hostile.

"I have a daughter to look after," the trapper said.

"Cowards," Neal said. "I'd shoot you myself, but you're not worth England's consideration." He raced toward the fort, leaving the men behind him.

Once Neal caught sight of English soldiers being cut down by the Indians, he raised his musket. Friendly Indians did this? The game had been a guise to lure his countrymen from their duties. Anger tore through his frenzied thoughts. He should have been here to defend the fort. He heard a scream and saw a man being scalped alive. *William!* Neal raced toward the Indian and aimed his musket.

Before he could fire, white-hot pain pierced the back of his head and sent him sprawling onto the ground beside two slain soldiers. He struggled to take a breath. An instant later, blackness enveloped him.

# Chapter 2

Neal woke with an agonizing throb in his head. He wanted to open his eyes but feared Indians observed him. Better they think him dead than to subject him to torture. He listened, but only the sounds of nature's tiny creatures buzzed around his ears. His head cleared somewhat. He heard birds and recognized the savagery of vultures picking at the soldiers' bodies. The men needed proper burials and prayers for their families. His stomach lurched, not a normal reaction for Neal, and he fought hard to not move. The memory of the massacre played vividly before him. He saw the painted faces of the Indians who had masked their hatred for the soldiers until the time came to strike. They'd hid in the woods. How clever of the Chippewa and Sauk to use the king's birthday celebration and a game to massacre the soldiers.

The longer Neal lay with his eyes closed, the angrier he became. Rain splattered around him, and he envisioned water mixing with the blood and slowly washing away the lives of those he respected. But the memory of what had happened here would never erase from his mind. How unfair this world. He'd dedicated his life to England. He'd committed treason against his mother's people because of his love and devotion to her. Now...

He slowly opened his eyes. Not an Indian was in sight. Slowly he lifted his head, but the pain brought tears to his eyes. The rain increased. A moan escaped his lips. On both sides of him trickled blood. His blood. A tomahawk must have pierced his head. Why had his life been spared? Why hadn't he been scalped like so many others around him? He brushed against one of the soldiers lying beside him. Open eyes stared back at him.

*William. I've got to find William.* He'd seen his friend's attacker just before being struck down. Neal tried to ignore the incessant hammering in his head, although the roar reminded him of a waterfall. Then again, rushing water from a mountainside was beautiful. Breathtaking. Not painful. He must be dying to have such peculiar illusions.

But before he succumbed to death and the judgment of God, he had to find William and see if his friend had survived. Gritting his teeth, Neal crawled on his belly to where he believed William lay. Twice Neal thought he'd fall under the waves of blackness, but each time he mustered the strength to move forward. What greeted him proved worse than death in and of itself. William had died a cruel death, one Neal could never forget or forgive. *Oh God, why?* He wanted to shout at God, scream at the unfairness of it all, but instead, he swallowed his emotions. He'd been spared, but for what purpose? Revenge cloaked what was left of his mortal body.

He touched the back of his head and gingerly brushed his fingers along a huge gash. Blood matted in his hair. Somehow he needed to make it to the water's edge. Maybe the merchant or the trapper still lingered there. Surely they would help him. Neal turned his body around and crawled back toward the water. He refused to let the Indians return and find him alive or allow vultures to pick over him. A tree branch lay to the right of his path. If he could stand, perhaps he could lean on the branch and walk. Moments later, he wrapped his fingers around the wood and gripped it. Perspiration dripped down his face as he forced it into the ground for support. Exhaustion took its toll. He began again, determined not to let the Indians have one more body to claim.

With sweat dripping from his face, he managed to pull himself up to his knees. His stomach lurched, and he forced the bile back down to his stomach. *I am a soldier for the king's army. I will live to fight another day.* He began the slow process of standing. His head... *Merciful God, help me.* Dizziness swirled about him as though he were caught in a whirlpool, and the urge to scream swept over him repeatedly. Each time the thrust of pain threatened to overtake him, he denied his body's cry for help and continued on through blurred vision. At last, he caught sight of the water's edge. The men were gone. Where there had been three canoes, two remained.

A blessing. Life had become a gift, and birch-covered canoes were a sure sign that he would not die. Neal would find help, and he'd return to bury the bodies and avenge the dead. Finally his fingers touched one of the canoes, and he pushed it into the water. His worst fear came that it would sail without him. Reaching for the side, Neal tumbled in and yielded to the blackness that beckoned his body and soul.

Ninette woke with a start. She'd slept later than she intended, and so much work needed to be done today. Throwing off the thin coverlet, she hurried to dress. The thought of tasting warm fresh milk moved her faster, and in a few moments, she had the cow tied to a post with a bucket beneath.

With each *ping* of milk that hit the bucket, she contemplated what to do after breakfast. Weeds had sprouted up in the garden and threatened to choke fledgling corn, green bean, and tomato plants. With the rain and sunshine, juicy berries were ripe for picking in the woods. And then she must deal with the rising number of animal skins that piled up inside the shed. The dead animals would soon have a horrible odor, especially as the sun heated the day.

*Papa, where are you?* Her anger from the previous day had dissipated to a gnawing fear. He'd been disgruntled with life ever since the English took over the lands around them from the French. Ninette used to be able to make him laugh. Now she counted each smile as a blessing. Oh, that her father was safe and had not done something foolish.

She would make him a lovely berry pie. She would catch fresh fish this afternoon, too. Glancing up at the sun, she prayed for enough hours to get everything done—and for the Lord to bring Papa home safely. Once the cow was fed, along with the pig and chickens, Ninette stored the milk in the cool ground along with fresh eggs. She sliced into a loaf of bread, baked the day before, and then poured a mug of milk. She shouldn't fret so about Papa. He always spoke of how he detested leaving her alone. Something had detained him at Fort Michilimackinac, and he would explain later. God knew Papa's whereabouts; she simply needed to have faith.

Sensing comfort from those thoughts, Ninette stepped boldly into the day's work; however, she could not stop the glances toward the woods where Papa would likely appear. When she moved to higher ground or near the water, she continually studied the mainland in the distance.

With her mind set that Papa *would* be home before dusk, she weeded the garden in no time, cleaned up the cabin, and even considered skinning a few of the animals.

Once late afternoon arrived, she set a pail of wild berries inside the cabin. She could almost taste the sweet pie. Everything had been accomplished, except for the fishing. He loved trout, but a bass would be a welcome meal, too. Though her back ached and an hour's respite from the heat of day tempted her, she instead snatched up the wooden pole and set her sights on a feast for Papa.

The path to the fishing hole held wildflowers off to the left. On the way back, she would pick her favorite forget-me-nots for the table. Lifting her head to the treetops, she smiled at the sun filtering through the utmost limbs in sparkling fingers of light. She loved the island, but she'd love it more if someone shared it with her during those lonely times when Papa was gone.

Ninette's mind sped off in another direction. Romantic notions filled her head, but none of the nearby Frenchmen interested her, and Papa would shoot an English soldier if he even so much as looked her way. She sighed. God needed to bring her someone before she grew too old. She glanced down at her dirty clothes, and her nose detected she needed a bath. Before the evening meal, she'd bathe and wash her hair.

The path wound through the trees and out onto a narrow beach. Seagulls glided overhead and called out to each other. Her gaze trailed to the beach. Startled, she covered her mouth. A lifeless man lay beside a canoe.

"Papa!" Ninette raced toward him. She stopped within several feet of the body. The red uniform signified an English soldier—and he looked more dead than alive.

She stood paralyzed, not knowing what to do. Papa's words rang through her mind. *"Every Englishman should be shot. I should have fought with the French. Maybe I could have done something to prevent the surrender."*

Had Papa done this? Dread settled on her like a fever. Surely not. Papa wouldn't have hurt this man and left him to die…unless Papa fought for his life. She remembered the thunder yesterday that sounded like musket fire. She may have been too overcome with her own problems to distinguish the sounds clearly.

"Papa, are you here?" Only silence met her, and despite the heat, she shivered.

Ninette inched closer. The soldier lay facedown, and he had been hit in the head with what looked like an ax. Or a tomahawk. Her gaze flew toward the mainland.

The Chippewa and the Sauk were friends. Surely they wouldn't have done this. She swallowed hard at the realization. The French and Indians had fought alongside each other to rid the English from their soil, but they'd failed. Had they tried again? What if they arrived at the island and found her with an English soldier?

Ninette focused her attention on the man. If he was still alive and she tried to help him, Papa's fury would ring beyond Fort Michilimackinac. But if she didn't try to tend to him, he'd surely die, and Ninette could not knowingly let any man die.

*Dear God in heaven, what shall I do?*

With caution ruling her every step, she bent at the soldier's side to examine his head wound. Dried blood mixed with light brown hair hid the extent of the gash, and she moved a strand of hair back to see the slice taken in his head. It must be cleaned and sewn together, or he would die. She stared up into the sky and asked for strength and guidance. No doubt the man had found the stamina to climb into the canoe. Perhaps he'd find the same will to live awhile longer.

"Sir," she said softly. "Sir, can you speak? Have you seen a French trapper?" She searched her mind for a few English words, but none came to mind that lent themselves to asking poignant questions.

With trembling hands, she grasped beneath his shoulders and turned him over to face her. His pallor frightened her. She brushed back her hair and laid her ear on his chest. A faint heartbeat filled her with hope.

"Sir, you are alive. Praise God."

If only a muscle twitched. He did indeed look dead. She quickly examined the rest of him for injuries, but he appeared fine except for his head. She must get him back to the cabin. But how? Finding no way to lift him, Ninette grabbed beneath his arms and began to drag him toward the path leading home. Many times she fell with the burden of his weight. All the while, she prayed for the soldier to live and for Papa to come home. Never mind that an English soldier shared their cabin. She'd gladly face Papa's wrath than worry another minute about losing her precious father.

# Chapter 3

Neal woke to incessant pain filling his head and numbing his senses. He tried to concentrate on what had happened to him for some clarity of thought, but sheer torture denied it. He blinked, for darkness shrouded his vision. As his thoughts slowly cleared, he realized he no longer lay in the canoe, but in a cabin. For a moment, he feared the Indians had found him and waited until he awakened to torture him. Neither a knife nor fire could be any worse than the blow inflicted to his head. Somehow he must find a way to escape. He willed his eyes to open.

Then he saw her. A young woman with chestnut-colored hair and luminous dark eyes peered down at him. A splatter of freckles dotted her nose and cheeks. Surely she must be an angel sent from God to nurse him.

"*Monsieur, comment vous vous sentez? —*Sir, how are you feeling?"

His former thoughts betrayed him. He was under the care of a French woman? He fought to keep his eyes open. Aye, the French. Heathens, all of them. They most likely had assisted the Indians in the hideous massacre. He tried to move.

"*Monsieur, vous êtes la blessure. Vous devez vous reposer. —*Sir, you are hurt. You must rest." Her tiny hands pushed on his shoulders.

If not for the pain, he could have easily overcome her. Dare he reveal his knowledge of her language?

"*J'ai traité votre blessure. —*I have treated your wound."

She must not be among the enemy. Why else would she nurse him? He must find out if they were alone, but he had no strength to make the inquiry or twist his head to look about. A cherub smile greeted him. He nearly gasped at her beauty, and the freshness she invoked caused him to cast aside the pain for one second more. Oh, why must the enemy be so lovely? Perhaps Lucifer had disguised himself as a woman to drive him mad. Indeed, it could easily happen. The truth, like a battle cry, sounded out his despicable life. He deserved whatever the future held—but not without a fight.

A list of the many guises he'd used to deceive the French marched across his mind. To the French, he was a traitor; to the English, a hero. And his dear, sweet mother had gone to her grave knowing her son betrayed his kinsmen. Neal deserved to die for his mounting sins against God. Confusion over his life, his family, his injury, and the angel nursing him continued to plague him until he drifted into sweet oblivion.

☙

Ninette fretted with her patient. She'd applied an Indian potion to his wound, one she'd learned from the Chippewa. It was made from the trunk of a young white pine boiled, then mashed. Some Indians claimed it could be made into a type of hot tea, and she would administer it to the soldier if necessary. Papa said he'd seen the potion remove gangrene from an Indian's leg, and that was proof enough of its powers.

She tilted her head to watch him sleep. He should be lying on his stomach so as not to disturb the wound she'd tended, but she feared he couldn't breathe with his face down. She'd cleansed the area and stitched his head with thread from her sewing basket, then carefully turned him onto his back. For pain, she'd prepared a hot brew from Indian herbs, the origin of which she knew not, but Papa said the concoction eased the worst of anguish. By leaning the soldier's head back, she managed to dribble a few spoonfuls down his throat. If he became feverish, she would prepare a cup of catnip tea. In the meantime, she waited and prayed.

The soldier couldn't understand her, but Papa had forbidden her to learn English. No matter that Papa himself spoke the English language. Sometimes Papa's ways confused her. Perhaps when she grew older, she would find more wisdom about such worrisome topics.

Thinking of Papa brought a fresh onslaught of tears. With the language barrier between her and the soldier, she had no way of finding out about Papa or learning what had happened to the man lying desperately close to death. She shuddered at the thought of Papa's demise. She didn't want to think of living another day without his love and protection.

She took a deep breath. The cabin smelled of berry pie, and Ninette so wanted Papa there to enjoy it. Fish had been substituted for smoked pork, another one of his favorites. Now as evening fast approached, she fretted more about where he might be—and if he were alive.

Seeing that the soldier had drifted off to sleep, where pain no longer snapped at his body like a wild animal in torment, she stood and stretched. She must keep awake in case her patient needed attention. . .or Papa returned. Her gaze focused on the soldier's face, a matter she hadn't been able to help but notice before. Wide-set eyes, high cheekbones, and thick hair the color of honey were quite fetching. Not a scar touched his face—and such broad shoulders. If not for his dreaded uniform, she could have looked upon him with more than casual interest.

Ninette discarded her girlish thoughts and rushed outside to complete her chores. She longed to hear Papa come whistling up the path calling out to her. He'd have a trinket for her in his pocket or a piece of ribbon for her hair.

"What do you have cooked for me?" he would ask. "I haven't had a fit meal since I left for the mainland."

She'd throw her arms around his neck and scold him for giving her such a scare. *Oui*, such was the homecoming she wanted for Papa. No talk of fighting or people killed, just Papa home safe and unharmed, and maybe happy again, as before the French and English War. Joy is what she wished for him, more than anything on earth.

Long after the sun eased down into the west, Ninette waited by candlelight—for Papa, and for the soldier to awaken. She dozed in a chair facing him. The day had been long, and her body cried out for rest. . . .

The door creaked open and startled her.

"Ninette?" Papa called.

She rushed to the door and wrapped her arms around his neck. The smell of him, a mixture of outdoors and animals, reinforced her joy. She laughed and cried while the

213

words refused to come. His stocky frame, so strong, comforted her. Finally it occurred to her that he might be hurt. "Papa, are you all right?"

"Oui, daughter. A terrible thing happened at the fort, and I could not get back to you. And you are fine?"

"Of course. I feared as much for you. I thought I heard musket fire, and when you didn't return, I knew something detained you."

"I'm so very sorry. I worried for you, but I had to believe our God in heaven would keep you safe."

"Thank you, Papa, and He has. Please, sit. Are you hungry? I have food for you."

"Bless you. My stomach has cried out all day, but I dared not eat until I knew my *petite fille* had not been harmed."

She stepped back from the doorway. His endearing name of "little daughter" always touched her heart.

Papa startled and walked to her straw mattress. "Who is this?" He picked up the candle with its flickering light. "An English soldier? Why is he here?" He bent over the man. "Is he dead?"

"I think he's still alive." She took a deep breath. "I found him at the water's edge this afternoon. I dragged him here and treated his head. Looked like a tomahawk."

"He can't stay here." Papa's voice shook the cabin. He whirled around and grabbed her shoulders. "He's an English soldier."

Ninette trembled. "He's an injured man who needs help."

"Having him here may cost our lives. We can't risk the danger."

"Would not our Lord tend to him?"

Papa released her and swung his attention back to the soldier. "He may die anyway and solve the problem."

"Papa, how can you say such things?"

He slowly turned back to face her. He clenched his fists in the shadows between them. "Let me tell you what kept me away from you. The Chippewa and the Sauk planned a clever attack on the soldiers. While the soldiers celebrated their king's birthday with festive events and strong drink, the Indians played a game outside the fort. The Indians moved closer and closer while the soldiers watched through an open gate. When the time was right, they pulled out tomahawks and knives. Even the women had axes and tomahawks hidden in their garments." Papa shook his head. "Praise our heavenly Father that I did not have you with me. I thank Him for sparing your young eyes from seeing such a hideous sight. The Indians offered no mercy to the English soldiers." He pointed to the wounded man. "Save this one." He hesitated. "I was with an English merchant at the time—at his canoe—when we heard the fighting begin. The merchant jumped into his canoe and got away. I hid in the brush, but one of the Indians found me. They did not harm me, or any of the other French that I know of, but they made me go with them far inland to their camp. I was forced to stay there overnight. When they finally let me go, I checked on the situation at the fort and learned the French had buried the English."

"Oh Papa, how terrible."

He pulled her to him. "Don't you see? If the Indians make their way to the island

and find this soldier, we'll be killed."

Ninette heard Papa's words, understood what he meant, yet she could not bring herself to abandon the man lying on the brink of death. "Were the Hurons among them?"

Papa shook his head. "They remain true friends to the English and French."

"Wouldn't they help us, hide this man if need be?"

She heard Papa's heart beat strong against his chest. "Daughter, you know how I despise the English. Already, prices for pelts have dropped. Our livelihood is at stake, as well as our very lives."

"I know, Papa, but this is a man who will die without care. Is this not like the Good Samaritan? Would not our Lord want us to put our prejudices aside?"

For several long moments, he said nothing. She knew he pondered her words. Ninette broke free from his embrace. "There is no need to answer me yet. Let me get you something to eat." She smiled. "I have a berry pie, baked this evening."

He brushed his hand over her hair. "I would do anything for you," he said. "But putting aside my hatred for the English and placing your life in danger is more than I can give."

She pressed her fingers to his lips and felt his prickly whiskers. "Pray for wisdom, Papa. Do not burden yourself with any of this tonight. The Indians would not come until daylight, and they've not been here yet."

# Chapter 4

Neal woke to the tantalizing aroma of smoked pork, eggs, and fresh bread. Heaven could not smell much better to a hungry man. But as soon as he began to relish the thought of food, the pain in his head hit him full force. He'd survived the night. But why, when those he respected had been killed?

He remembered the day before. . .the king's birthday celebration. . .painted faces of the Chippewa Indians. . .the savage attack on the fort. . .the hideous war cries. . .the slaughtered. . .the canoe. . .and the curious young French woman. His eyes opened easier than before. A dreadful taste enveloped his mouth. Perhaps he'd been poisoned.

"The soldier is awake," a man said in French.

"Papa, don't be angry at me because of this. I did what I thought was best."

"Another reason why I should have been here. I'd have rolled him into the water and let the lake claim him."

Neal closed his eyes. So he'd come between a man and his daughter. Not exactly a good position for two men who despised each other.

"Papa, please, let me tend to him until he's stronger. I've been praying for the Hurons to visit us. They'd take the soldier and keep him until he's well."

"Must you vex me so?" The man's voice sounded familiar, yet Neal couldn't place him.

"Papa, eat your breakfast, and then we can talk more."

"Ninette, our problems will not vanish when I have a full stomach." *Ninette.* The name haunted him. What was God doing?

"But you'll have a better temperament," she said.

"For one who never saw her mother, you have many of her ways." The man grumbled as though angry with her.

"Then you'll allow me to nurse him?"

"I haven't made a decision yet."

Neal heard what he thought was a quick kiss. No doubt, Ninette believed she'd won the dispute. He heard light footsteps and knew she stood over him. He couldn't help but stare up into her face, if for nothing more than to once again feast on her beauty.

"Good, you are awake," she said. "I know you don't understand me, but I need for you to drink more of this tea. So far, I've managed to get a little down you, but more will help ease the pain."

He opened his mouth.

She eyed him curiously but said nothing. She stirred the contents of a mug and offered him several spoonfuls. Ah, the origin of the bitter taste in his mouth.

"I think I'll have him try a little broth," she said. "His body needs nourishment."

"To make our lives miserable?" the man asked. His metal plate rattled on the table. "The food was good, and I appreciate your work; but I think it was all done to appease me."

Ninette smiled into Neal's face. Today her hair had been pulled back into a long braid down the middle of her back, although a few curls surrounded her face. "Papa, would I try to change your mind about something by appealing to your hunger?"

"Why not, my petite fille? Your mother used it quite often, and successfully, too." She continued to smile.

"I'm going to skin the animals." He tramped across the dirt floor and on outside. *This man is the trapper who refused to help the soldiers.*

"I'll be out once I finish inside," she said. "Thank you, Papa." She turned her attention to Neal. "Now, for your broth, but I do believe you understand me."

He kept his gaze focused on her face.

"Remember? When I said I needed to give you tea, you opened your mouth."

Neal rethought Ninette's words. In his pain-filled stupor, he'd revealed himself. It must have been her name that caused him to cast away caution.

"An English soldier who understands French is indeed peculiar. I wonder how Papa feels about such a thing." She shrugged. "He might like you more."

She whirled around, and he caught sight of her slender figure...narrow waist...petite. He should feel ashamed for noticing such things. A moment later, she stood over him with another mug.

"The pain is lessening, correct?" She smiled and a spark of mischief met his gaze.

He couldn't stop the return of her smile.

"Odd, about the Indian ways," she said. "Those people can do terrible things—like at the fort—then they have wonderful medicines. Of course the so-called civilized English and French kill each other, too. Most people will kill to preserve their homes and families." She shrugged daintily. "The treatment for your head and the pain medicine is Chippewa."

She'd used heathen potions on him. He'd rather die...no matter that the pain had subsided a bit.

"Stop frowning and open your mouth. I know what you're thinking, but the Indian medicine saved your life. I made this broth, so you shan't be poisoned."

*Does she read my mind also?* He opened his mouth.

She laughed and fed him a few spoonfuls of chicken broth. His stomach rumbled and gave away his hunger. She laughed again. The sound had such a sweet ring to it.

"Let's begin with your name. Don't be too stubborn about it."

"Neal Wellington," he managed.

"Very English. My name is Ninette Curvier, and Papa's name is Chapin."

"We're on the island?"

"Yes sir. But you are not safe here."

"I heard, but I haven't a solution."

"Neither do I, but I'm praying for God to show us a way."

How odd to hear a French woman make such a statement. He'd assumed they were all heathens, but then he'd not taken the time to befriend any of these people at the fort.

"How did you come to know the French tongue?"

"I learned it from a dear woman." She needn't know the whole truth.

Her face softened, and her dark eyes filled with compassion. "I am sorry about your friends at the fort."

"*Merci.* —Thank you."

"Papa said the French gave them a proper burial."

"They were spared?" He couldn't disguise the sharpness.

"I would think you'd be glad innocent men, women, and children escaped death and injury. The shedding of blood makes no sense to me. If only we could all live together as our Lord desires."

A rarity that he'd seen only in his mother. His mother had not shared in the same theology as his Christian father, but his mother loved the Lord. For a moment, Neal wondered if he'd passed into a strange world where souls lived in another body. *Preposterous. Absurd. Blasphemy.* His mind must be toying with his logic. Such things did not exist. He'd merely found a coincidence of culture and name. Nothing more. He closed his eyes and drifted toward sleep. His wound needed to heal so he could escape the clutches of this obscure woman and her father.

☙

Ninette finished washing the plates from breakfast, scrubbed the cooking utensils, and tidied up a bit before joining Papa. Her mind spun with the unexpected news about the soldier. She wanted to believe Papa might have a hint more sympathy for him since he spoke French. However, as difficult as her father could be, it might make the situation worse.

While Neal slept, she made her way to the back of the shed where Papa worked.

"I saw some good pelts there," she said. "The beavers were fat."

"With the price I received for the last ones, these have to be excellent."

His grumpy mood had continued, and she ignored it. "I could scrape the skins for you." One of her worst chores, but she'd do it to soothe him.

He eyed her and pointed to the ones he'd finished. She picked up a sharp-edged rock and a pelt, then moved into the sunshine where she could stake the pelt to the ground with the flesh side up. Beginning from the inside of the skin, she scraped toward the outside. Once it dried and stretched in the sun, she'd scrape again.

All the while, her mind spun as she tried to figure out Papa's thoughts. Needling him about the soldier would make him angry for sure, but she itched to have the matter settled. After all, the Chippewa could choose to pay them a call. With blood on their hands and the possibility of whiskey in their stomachs, they could be a fierce lot.

"Have you considered the Hurons?" She continued to work at the pelt.

"I will not leave you. Not ever again. I lost your mother, and I will not lose you." He sucked in a breath.

Never had she observed such emotion in him. "Papa, it is not my intent to cause you such distress. I love you too much to upset you, yet surely the journey would not be long."

"No."

The finality of his tone should have dissuaded her, but she'd never been known to give up easily. "If you'd tend to him, I'd go."

"Ninette!" His voice roared.

She shivered. "What must I do? I am torn between my love for you and what our Lord requires of us."

Papa raised his knife from the beaver and sank the blade into the ground. "Put the scoundrel into the canoe he arrived in and send him on his way."

"I will not live with his death against my soul. There has to be another way."

Several long moments passed. He sat back on his haunches. "We could move him to the cave. I don't believe he'd be discovered there."

"Good. I can nurse him without fear of the Indians."

"You will not stay there with him alone. His strength will return fast enough."

"Oh Papa, I can take care of myself."

"Such naivety, daughter. Men can be evil."

She raised a brow. "I understand. Then you'll join us in the cave?"

He scowled. "Tell me one good thing about the English soldier."

*Dare I tell him?* "He speaks French."

He stiffened. "For what purpose?"

"You could ask him." *Surely his knowledge is for good.*

"For ill gain, I'm sure. When did you learn this?"

"While giving him medicine this morning. His name is Neal Wellington."

"I don't care about his name. He's one of them." With those words hurled like a spear, he rose from the ground and stomped toward the cabin. "Better a man dead than to come between a father and his daughter."

Ninette gasped at his words. She well recognized Papa's intense love for her—and his hatred for the English. She dropped the rock and scurried after him. He swung around to face her.

"This is between the soldier and me. I deny you little, and I expect you to obey me."

Her eyes widened, and she nodded. *Dear Jesus, in my zeal, have I goaded Papa to sin?*

❧

Neal woke to the sound of Curvier bellowing his name.

"Wellington, I want a word with you."

He blinked. The roar of the trapper's tone secured his attention.

"And since you speak French, then so shall I."

A myriad of thoughts flashed through Neal's mind as to Curvier's topic. None of which sounded like something Neal could handle now. "Have the Chippewa arrived?"

"I'd be happy if they had, for then I would turn you over to them."

"Finding me in your cabin might cost your life and your daughter's." Neal realized the gamble he was taking, yet he did not want to sound foolish in light of his physical condition.

"Ah, we are balanced, I see. What stops me from ridding our island of you?"

"Ninette."

Curvier's face reddened. "Have you already sought to trap her affections and use them against me? The Indians should have skinned you alive."

"No sir. I am an English gentleman."

"No Englishman is a gentleman!" Curvier leaned toward Neal. "But mark my word—if I learn of any talk or actions that prove you otherwise, I will pierce your heart with a dull knife and twist it."

"Should I attempt such inappropriateness, I would deserve it." Talking tore at Neal's strength.

Curvier peered at him. "Now that we are in agreement, let's talk of what to do with you."

Neal waited. He'd long decided to fight death until his last breath. "It's not good that I remain in this cabin where your daughter's life is at risk."

"True, and I have an idea."

Neal searched his face. "Do you plan to take me back to the fort?"

"I can't take the chance of a Chippewa realizing you've been here and finding your wounds were tended. There's a cave on the island, one that's hidden. The Chippewa know of it, but unless you were spotted in the canoe, they have no need to search for you."

"I understand, and I appreciate your hiding me."

"Humph. Don't thank me. I'm merely honoring my daughter's wishes."

Perhaps Ninette was an angel. He must thank her properly.

Curvier glanced about. "Can you walk?"

"Yes." Neal doubted if he could move his legs from the bed.

"It's about two miles from here."

"I'm ready." Neal believed the trek would kill him. The pounding in his head had returned as fierce as yesterday, but he would try.

Curvier flung open the cabin door. "Ninette, we are taking the soldier to the cave."

*Thank You, Lord, for this blessing. With Your help, I'll live to tell of Your greatness.*

Curvier lifted him from the bed with no mercy. Ninette bit into her lip, but she said nothing.

"Clean up everything of his, and I want you to cover our tracks as we walk," Curvier said.

"Yes, Papa. What about food and supplies?"

"I'll return for those things later. Right now, we need to hide this man."

Neal attempted to walk with Curvier aiding him, but he made such poor time that the trapper grumbled and dragged him along through the woods and over thick underbrush. Ninette and Curvier did not talk, and Neal used all of his strength to keep from passing out.

At first, Neal kept track of the landmarks in case he needed to escape, but with the pain whirling in his head, he gave up. After what seemed to be hours, Curvier stopped in front of a heavy growth of trees and laid Neal atop a blanket of green ferns. The man disappeared between the trees. Neal thought he needed privacy.

"We're here," Ninette said. "Be thankful, very thankful, that you did not end up back in the canoe."

"I am." Neal did not elaborate on the grievous state of his body. A soldier must endure all manners of discomfort, and he was a soldier.

Curvier returned and partly carried Neal through the trees. "Make sure our path is not marked," he said.

As Neal's eyes adjusted to the shadows of the cool cave, he took in the human bones and skull in a corner. Whatever had happened to the poor chap would not happen to him. "Merci," he said, once Curvier laid him onto the damp ground. "I am deeply grateful for your risking your life."

"As I said before, this is for my daughter, not you." The trapper turned to Ninette. "Stay here. I'm going back to the cabin for food, supplies, and medicine. We'll all stay here for a few nights."

"Yes, Papa. What if the Chippewa arrive while you're there?"

"They have no quarrel with me."

"But won't they question my whereabouts?"

"I'll tell them I've sent you away."

She nodded. "Be careful, Papa. I'll be praying all the while you're gone."

A smile rose to the whiskered man's lips. He stroked her cheek. "So much like your mama. Stay inside until I return. I won't be long." He pulled a knife from his sheath. "If the soldier gives you any trouble, use this on him."

"Of course, Papa."

*How comforting.* Neal could not condemn Curvier. He loved his daughter. A man would have to be blind not to see that. The Frenchman drew Ninette into an embrace, and Neal's heart ached to know such love, especially with a rare flower like this young woman.

# Chapter 5

Ninette stared out into the light that splayed through the trees and brush. Again, as in days past, she longed to see Papa. An unsettled feeling lay heavy on her heart and kept her leaning against the cave's wall, watching for him to push his way through the trees and brush.

"He'll return soon," Neal said.

She turned in his direction and gave him a faint smile. "He's been gone too long."

"Did he have work to do at the cabin?"

She shrugged. "Skinning the animals and scraping the pelts, and there are always other chores."

"Your livelihood is important to him."

*"Stay inside until I return. I won't be long."* Papa's words were like the sun rising in the east. "This is not like him." She made her way to Neal's side. In her self-absorption, she was neglecting his care. "How is your head feeling?"

"Like the tomahawk is still there."

In the shadows, she saw perspiration drip down his face. She felt his forehead.

"Fever?" he asked.

She smiled. "No, but you need something for the pain. Papa will have all those things." She gently moved his head to view each side. "You're not bleeding, but you will have a nasty scar."

"My hair and hat will cover it. I'm glad to be alive."

"Are you a Christian?" she asked.

"Yes. The Church of England."

Ninette wanted to laugh at his seriousness. "Our Lord will not ask us on Judgment Day to what church we belong." His scowl did not deter her. "He will ask if we know His Son."

"When have you read the Bible?"

"Papa has one. From it, he taught me how to read. Did you think because we're trappers that we don't know how to read or write?" His silent admission angered her. She stepped back. "Have you read the scriptures?"

"Yes, indeed."

"How commendable. So where does it say the Church of England is the only church Christ loves?"

He said nothing and turned his head.

"So a French woman has challenged you about your faith?" She took a deep breath to keep from saying regrettable things. Jesus treated everyone with respect and love. Did He understand how difficult she found the task to follow His example and do likewise? An image of those who were clearly sinful flashed before her eyes. The world was such a confusing place.

🙰

Neal had angered Ninette. He shouldn't care, but he did. A part of him admitted she was right about England's church, but theology had been engrained in him by his grandfather, a minister of the king's church. No one ever questioned Grandfather Wellington, even when he disowned Neal's father for marrying a French woman. Needless to say, Grandfather had not met Ninette Curvier.

"I'd not thought about religious matters in those terms," he said.

"Papa says it is good for us to think on things of God."

*Must she always look so fetching?* "I think your treatment of me is like the Good Samaritan." There, he'd said it.

"Merci. I hope you can one day help someone in need. Then again, as a soldier, I'm sure you help many." She wrapped her arms across her chest and stared out beyond the cave's entrance.

A moment ago, he despised Ninette's questions, and now he wanted to hear everything in her pretty little head. He imagined her in a fine gown instead of the patched dress that hugged at her curves. A slip of a thought grabbed hold of his mind and traversed to his heart. Was this how his father had felt when he first glimpsed his mother? For certain, Neal had no desire to be captured by love from any woman, least of all a French one.

She touched a finger below her eye. The mere idea of Ninette in tears troubled him. Oh, his mind perplexed him with this woman. He'd rather sleep and forget about her, but his head pained him far too much.

"Do you like living on the island?" he asked.

She turned and pressed a finger to her chin, the one that had just wiped away a tear. "Most of the time. It's beautiful with its hills and greenery. Then the cold in winter and the heat in summer can both be severe."

He smiled. "What about this place does not please you?"

"Ah, when Papa is gone, I find it quite lonely. I'd like to live among more people, but our island suits him fine."

"I've never seen you at the fort." And he was sure he would have remembered.

She stood and paced the cave to his side. "Neal, you know how Papa feels about the English. He much prefers for me to stay here and look after the traps. After the trouble from the Chippewa, he'll never let me go there again."

He'd feel the same way if such a treasure belonged to him. "I've heard talk of building a fort here," Neal said.

"Papa would not be happy with that news. Please don't tell him."

He chuckled. "You have my word. Do you know what *Michilimackinac* means? Seems strange that is the name of the fort and the island."

"It means 'big turtle.' The Chippewa named it. If you look at the island from a distance, it resembles one. The Indians say the turtle emerged from the water with the earth on its back. It gave a place for all living creatures to live."

"What other things do you know about the Indians?"

"Which tribes?"

"All of them."

"Why?"

He shrugged. "It's important to learn all one can about the enemy."

"Is that the reason why you talk to me?"

He swallowed hard. Her question had hit his mind and his heart. If he said yes, he'd lose her friendship. If he said no, he'd lie. What was the truth? He knew not, and it tormented his mind. Once he healed, he'd fight for England and resume his role in His Majesty's army. "I'm not sure." His words were honest. "I'm obliged to you for saving my life; however, the mystery is why."

She smiled and appeared to ponder his words. "Who you are and what you've done in your life matters naught to me. I saw a child of God who needed help. If you'd been one of those Indians, I'd still have nursed you."

"I think you have foolish ideals."

"Do I, Mr. Wellington? Or do I simply spend my hours viewing life as our Lord and Savior desires of us?"

"What if one of those Indians had hurt or killed your father? How would you feel about nursing one of them?" Her insistence on what the Lord required of man had gotten the best of him. Naivety could get a person killed.

She held her breath and whirled her attention back to the cave's front. "The English and the French fought a bloody war."

"But that's over. I'm talking about now."

She stiffened. "I am merely stating what our Lord requires of us."

Long moments followed.

"You see, Miss Curvier, one must practice what one professes. To love as Christ is honorable, but He calls for our obedience, too. You must do both, and by your own silence, you admit it is a difficult task. You can't pick and choose which laws to follow." When she failed to respond, Neal sensed no satisfaction in having the final word. In fact, not one drop of holiness or honorability raced through his blood in pointing out Ninette's misgivings.

❧

Ninette watched the light from the cave's entrance fade into shadows and blackness, and still Papa had not returned. She feared the most horrible of all nightmares had befallen him. Why else had he stayed away?

Neal slept fitfully. His head must have him in agony, but she had no medicine—or food and water either. She'd prayed a hundred times this day for Papa to be safe, and she must trust he would return. Papa said to stay in the cave, and she would oblige him until morning. And she hoped Papa brought a shovel so she could dig a grave for those horrifying bones in the corner. The idea of hers and Neal's joining them needled her mind.

Neal's rebuke bothered her. Papa had said more than once that, until she lived in the ugliness of the world, she should not judge others. Now, after pondering how she truly felt about anyone who killed good people, she had not been able to draw a conclusion. The Lord commanded her to love, and He demonstrated love in His dealings with all kinds of people. The answers refused to come. She had tended to Neal, but what if he had tried to hurt Papa? What if she were in a situation where she had to hurt someone or be hurt? How very hard to consider the right thing to do. Ninette leaned back against the wall of the cave and closed her eyes.

A hand touched her shoulder. "Ninette." Papa's whisper woke her from a light sleep.

"Papa."

"Hush. The Chippewa are on the island. I must leave these supplies and get back to the cabin."

"Why? You're safe here."

"They've seen me, and we've talked. If I disappear and my canoe is still here, then they will search the island."

"Are they hostile?"

"It's not worth the chance. Many of them have been drinking."

Her heart pounded until it hurt. He needn't say more. She well knew what whiskey did to the Indians—to any man. Papa unloaded food, medicine, and water. What could she say to make him change his mind?

"Could you hide our canoe and Neal's, too?"

"Ah, my sweet daughter. They're camped not far from mine."

Ninette held her breath to keep from shedding tears. "I'm afraid for you."

Papa pulled her to him. "The Lord has always taken good care of us, and He will continue. Remember when you were a little girl and you were frightened of the wild animals roaming the island? I told you God had you in the palm of His hand. Nothing's changed."

She nodded and laid her head against his chest. "I'm finding life can be frightening."

"Yes, it is. And this is something I never wanted for you." He held her from him and lifted her chin with his finger. "I must talk to Wellington and hurry on." Papa stepped across the cave.

"I heard you come in," Neal said.

"I need to have your word on a matter," Papa said.

"Tell me more."

"If I don't return, I must have your word that you will look after my daughter."

Ninette gasped at Papa's request. Surely the danger with the Chippewa was graver than he indicated.

"I will, sir," Neal said without hesitation. "She kept me alive, and you did not refuse her."

"I want her with people—people who'll love her. She's lonely here."

"Yes sir."

Ninette covered her mouth. *Papa, don't talk so. You'll be fine.*

"There's a knife and a musket." Papa pointed by the cave entrance. "One more thing. I have friends among the French. If they learn you've abused my Ninette, they'll kill you."

"I give you my word," Neal said. "She'll be well taken care of."

❧

Neal lay back down in the inky blackness and deliberated if he'd truly gone mad.

*Promised to look after Ninette? A French woman?* Curvier had been gone for over an hour, and still Neal pondered the words between them.

"I'm sorry Papa burdened you with my care," Ninette said.

"It's not a burden, and I'm sure your father will be fine." What would he do in the event of Curvier's demise? He was a soldier not a guardian.

"If something does happen to Papa, I can take care of myself. I would not want to interfere with your duties in the English army." Her voice quivered, and Neal was glad for the darkness between them.

"It's the least I can do."

"But it's not a task befitting a man bound to the army. I can manage by myself," she said. "I am nearly seventeen years old."

He thought her much younger. "I gave my word." He heard her soft weeping. "Don't cry. I'm sure your father will be fine."

She sniffed. "Of course. I'm being silly here."

"Try to rest. Daybreak will come soon enough."

In the short time of their acquaintance, Ninette had come to mean very much to Neal. As he continued to deliberate the young woman's plight, he recognized a part of his heart had been given away. He no longer saw her as one of the French or one of the heathens or as a woman who shared the same characteristics as his mother, but rather as a compassionate young woman who had nursed him to health. God help him, but in a matter of hours, he'd grown to love her. He glanced about the black cave, trying to make some sense of what was going on around him.

*When the shadows fall is when a man finds his faith and courage.*

"Ninette."

"Yes."

"I want to tell you something. . . . My mother was French, and her name was Ninette."

# Chapter 6

Glimmers of light trickled into the cave as the sun slid up from the horizon into an orange-and-pink sky. Ninette had tried to rest despite the burden in her heart and the hard dirt floor of the cave. She'd prayed and cried throughout the hours until finally drifting off to sleep. Now, with morning ushering in a new day, her body ached from the damp cave. Or maybe she ached because of her fear of losing Papa. The last few days had plagued her with worries, of which she could do nothing about.

Papa had forced Neal to take on an unwanted responsibility. In the event that something happened to Papa, she could care for herself. Although she secretly admitted the curious thoughts that rose in her mind about Neal looking after her, the idea of an English soldier looking after a French woman would arouse gossip. How dreadful.

She rose to her feet and stepped out of the cave for a few moments of privacy. The dew-kissed wildflowers and beads of water on leaves were a reminder of how nature seemed unaffected by the turmoil of man. She hadn't considered these things before. Life had taken a twist toward a darkness not present in her life before.

*I must think of more pleasant things. Worry is a sin, and I do trust God's provision.*

Sin. How she hated it, and yet it continued to happen all around her. Up until a few days ago, she wanted to believe the best of everyone. The French and English War had not reached their island, and Papa didn't speak of what men did when they warred against each other. Now she had experienced the fear and horror of men inclined to kill each other. It shook the foundation of her faith.

Back inside the cave, Ninette made her way to Neal's side. His confession during the night had left her scrambling for words. His parentage must have been difficult for him. Obviously he'd chosen to live as his father did. But what about his mother? Did he have contact with. . .Ninette Wellington?

He opened his eyes and smiled up at her through the shadows. "Good morning," he said. "Did you sleep well?"

"A little."

"I understand. Because of you and your father, I'm feeling much better this morning." He searched her face. "I prayed for your father's safety."

"Merci." She smiled. "I'm sure he'll be back tonight. He and the Chippewa are friends."

He propped himself up on his elbows. "I want to start moving about. If trouble comes, your father will need help."

*How strange two enemies must stand together.* "In the past, the Indians have not stayed here more than a few days at a time."

"Ninette." His words caressed her like a soft breeze. "I am a soldier, and I'm trained to fight if necessary. I saw what the Indians did on the mainland; so did your father. If they have been drinking or have decided that all white men are enemies, the situation

227

here could be dangerous."

"Why are you telling me this?"

"I want you to be prepared and cautious for any problems. Stay inside the cave. Your father and I will protect you the best way we can."

Rather than argue, she nodded.

Slowly Neal managed to stand. When she attempted to help, he declined. "You have taken care of me for the past few days. Now it's my turn to return the favor and resume my role as a soldier."

He shuffled across the cave's floor to the opening. "I will return in a little while. I'm leaving the musket for you, and I'll take the knife." He leaned against the rock wall and removed his red jacket. His shoulders rose and fell.

"I can tell your head pains you," she said. "I can mix a little of the tea in tepid water."

"When I come back, I'll take some. I can't allow anything to dull my senses. Right now, I want to scout the area to see if I can detect the Indians' whereabouts. Do you know how to fire the musket?"

"Yes, Papa showed me."

"Don't be afraid to use it."

The thought of Neal venturing very far from the cave frightened her. And the question rose in her mind as to whether she feared for him or for herself. "Be careful."

His gaze lingered on her face. "Indeed, I will."

Ninette's cheeks burned, and she stepped back so he would not see. Neal had a peculiar effect on her. Even the sound of his voice raised a chill on her arms and a quickening in her heart. *Don't give away your heart to an Englishman. Even one whose mother is French and shared the same name.*

"You'll be all right while I'm gone?" he asked.

"Oh yes. I'll prepare us something to eat, without a fire. And Papa brought his Bible for me to read."

Neal disappeared through the underbrush. His venture out might be premature. He could lose his balance and topple out of sight or hurt himself again. Neal and Papa, her mind tossed with worries about them both. Would life ever become peaceful again?

Once she'd tidied up their meager surroundings and read from Psalms, Ninette sat with her knees drawn up to her chest and stared out into the filtered sunlight—always looking for Papa or Neal. The morning proved long. The thought of checking on traps had more appeal than the not knowing what lay beyond the cave's edge. Her gaze swept back to the bones in a dark corner. She shivered and reached for Neal's musket. At last, she dozed with her head on her knees, dreaming of fishing for Papa's dinner and a garden full of ripening vegetables.

❧

Neal bent behind a thicket of trees and watched the Chippewa scout around a far hill. They were either hunting or looking for someone, hopefully not Curvier, Ninette, or him. Knowing their unique ability to track down anything crawling, he did not want to expose himself. He no longer had just himself to consider but Ninette and her father also.

Her image rose in his mind, and he did not push it away. With his word to her father, she'd taken on new meaning in his life, and he welcomed it. Yes, welcomed the responsibility if need be—not that he took any pleasure in Curvier meeting death but of taking care of his daughter.

For a moment, he feared losing his senses. He'd grown too quickly attached to the young French woman. How would they ever fare? His parents had found no real home to call their own: Neither the English nor the French had accepted them. Then his mother died during the French and English War, and Neal's father returned to his family's fold. Father had the opportunity to remarry but said he could not replace Neal's mother.

Frustrated with his thoughts lingering on Ninette, he studied the Indians. None of them had a fresh scalp tied to their waist. He breathed a sigh of relief. Chapin Curvier had not fallen. He waited a few moments longer and crept back toward the cave. His stomach rumbled, and his eyes longed to catch sight of Ninette. Snatching up a handful of ripened berries, he made his way back into the cave.

"What a feast you have here," Neal said. He kept his voice low in anticipation of the Chippewa.

"Smoked fish and stale bread is not exactly a feast," Ninette said. "Survival best describes this."

*I think it is the sharing of your presence that pleases me the most.* "The bite of berry pie is most tasty."

She laughed. "I think you are a starved man, or your wound has caused you to take leave of your senses."

"Do you know what it is that a soldier calls a meal?"

"No, but I think you are about to tell me."

"Hard bread, tasteless meat, and the promise of a few scant vegetables or fruit."

She wrinkled her nose. "I think the English army needs a cook."

"We have one." He bent closer to her. "I think the man was brought from an English prison."

Her horrified look amused him. "Aren't you concerned he might poison you?"

*The poor chap is probably dead, but I shan't be gloomy.* "It would be hard to tell from the taste of his cooking."

She took a deep breath, and her look of mirth became one of seriousness. "I think you miss the army, even if misfortune has fallen upon your friends."

"Yes, I do miss the regimented way of life. I believe in England and fighting for my country. It suits me well." But he knew already that he would miss the fair Ninette when he returned.

"Have you ever considered any other way of life?"

"My father wanted me to be a bookkeeper."

"I can't picture you laboring over ledgers and numbers."

He chuckled. "Neither could I. Father was displeased at my choice, and Grandfather even more displeased."

"Why is that?"

"Grandfather is a minister, and he had his heart and mind set on me following in his footsteps."

She tilted her face. "Serving the Lord is an honorable profession, but so is defending your country."

"Even if I'm English?" He tested her. He recognized it, and yet he couldn't stop himself. Where were Ninette's loyalties?

"You are a child of God. He doesn't look at the color of your uniform or where you were born." She sighed and placed her hands in her lap. "I despise what the English have done to our French friends and the war, but I never knew an English soldier as a person. It makes deciding loyalties very difficult, especially with Papa's sentiments. . .and you."

The softness of her voice blended with the bird's singing outside the cave. He searched her face, but she'd glanced down as though staring at her hands. "What of me?" he asked.

"I mean you were an enemy, but now you are a friend."

"What a compliment you've paid me, Ninette. I shall treasure it always." His words must have coaxed a smile from her, for her lips turned up slightly.

Once they finished eating, the sun disappeared and thunder roared outside the cave.

"I usually enjoy a summer storm," she said. "But today the thunder reminds me of what could be going on with Papa."

"Then concentrate on why you like a storm."

"It's the reminder of how God is in control of all the earth. I see a flash of lightning or hear the thunder, and I'm helpless to all that power. The rain is like a blessing." She shrugged. "I'm talking on like a silly girl. I simply enjoy a good summer storm and the rain that follows."

"No need to explain," he said. "I enjoy listening to your perspective on things. My mother and father used to debate books and principles from the Bible. I enjoyed hearing what each one had to say. Even when she lay dying, the two spent hours conversing."

"I'm sorry about your mother," she said.

He thought about his mother often. Her parting words clung to his conscience. "She was a beautiful woman. And yours?"

"I don't remember her. She died when I was a baby."

"You have a true loss. At least I have fond memories."

"Papa has told me many things about her. He even tells me I look and act like her." She laughed lightly. "He misses her terribly. I can see it in his eyes at times when he looks at me."

Neal no longer knew what to say for fear the fondness growing in his heart for Ninette would surface. He must talk himself out of this idiocy. To contemplate a future with Ninette was absurd. A soldier had no time for family, and he would surely face the opposition of his father's family. Yet Father had fallen in love with a beautiful French woman, and he would not criticize.

Ninette had nursed him back from near death, and he was grateful. But the gratefulness now ventured into forbidden territory. She liked him, he could tell. Yet, if she knew what he'd done to the French during wartime, she would despise him. After all, he loathed himself for the terrible wrong.

*My son, how can you betray your own people? Is winning a war more important than the blood that flows through your veins?"*

# Chapter 7

The long day with no sign of Curvier had left Neal restless. Every time a bird sang outside the cave, his thoughts tossed between a reminder of a promise made to Curvier and the possibility of the Indians calling to each other. He glanced at Ninette.

"You're frowning," he said.

"How can you tell in the shadows?"

The sound of her voice soothed him. "By studying your pretty face."

She startled. "I don't know what to say."

"Ah, I was bold, and I apologize. But it is the truth." He hesitated. "I wish there were a way I could make things good and right in your world."

"Only God in His wisdom can help all of us."

"If He'd only tell me what to do," Neal said. "A man can yearn for such glory, for to be used by God is to fulfill his life's purpose." How rare of him to state noble themes when his life had been hard-pressed for honor.

"You are a fine man, Neal Wellington."

"In words maybe, but on too many occasions, selfishness has dominated my actions."

"We're all self-centered." Ninette's gaze cast toward the ever-increasing darkness. "I believe that is the worst trait of all people. Look at the despair selfishness has caused over the past few days."

"True. Are you always contemplating the hearts and minds of men?"

"Are you teasing me?" The sadness so evident in her voice made him want to strive for a spark of goodness deep inside himself.

"Not at all. I admire your desire to see the finer attributes of life."

"I think mine is all naivety," she said. "My ideals have been shattered with the realization of the evil around us."

"Doesn't the Bible tell us good triumphs over evil?" If only he believed this, then perhaps the nightmares plaguing him would vanish.

"Indeed, it does. My faith needs to be stronger amid this turmoil. God understands our plight, and He has a perfect solution for us."

"Such a wise young woman," Neal said.

Ninette shook her head as though disbelief reigned in her thoughts. Yet she said nothing and continued to stare out in the fast-approaching night. To read her thoughts meant so much to him, and he longed to reach out and pull her close. Surely she must be ready to weep for the misfortune around them. As much as disgust ruled Neal's opinion about the French, he did want Chapin to return safely.

Such a peculiar change of heart for an English soldier.

He made his way back to the other side of the cave for fear he'd do what his mind warned. Plans needed to be made. He had responsibilities as a soldier, and that meant getting back to the fort to see if any other soldiers had escaped. Other English forts must be warned about the hostile Indians and measures taken to protect the people and the holdings of the king. Neal understood his duties. Soon he must leave this glimpse of heaven with Ninette and return to his old life. The comprehension filled him with dread.

How ironic to see an image of paradise with the daughter of an enemy in a cave where the bones of a dead man rested in the corner and bloodthirsty Indians roamed outside.

*Oh merciful God. I need Your wisdom in this plight—not for me, for I've filled my life with sin—but for this young woman whose innocence fills my life with peace.*

🍂

Once again, Ninette watched the morning sun peek through the horizon with streaks of color. Never were two sunrises the same, for she memorized them. She'd been in this same spot yesterday morning, and the gloom of spending another day worrying about Papa was more than she could bear.

Neal had wakened before dawn. They'd spoken briefly, but neither seemed to be in the mood to dwell on Papa's whereabouts.

"As soon as the sun is up, I'm looking for your father."

"Do you think that's safe?" she asked. *I can't bear to lose both of you.*

"I have to. Staying here when I could help him is cowardly. We need fresh water and food." His voice, spoken barely above a whisper, soothed her, even if his words frightened her.

"Will you promise me you'll be wary of danger and return to rest when your head pains you?"

"I'm a soldier. I'm trained to forget about my own needs when others are in peril." He touched her face, and her heart beat furiously. "I have not forgotten my promise to your father, and I'll be careful."

"That's all I can ask."

Ninette swallowed her tears and fought the tightness in her throat. She must be brave.

🍂

Neal crept through the thick woods. He tried to watch where his boots touched the fern and undergrowth, but the Chippewa could follow him regardless of how he tried to hide his tracks. So far, he'd seen nothing, and he'd walked a good two miles from the cave, following the woods. The cabin would be an obvious place for him to go, and if the Indians were in the area, they'd most surely have it watched.

He wondered about Curvier. Not a sign of him either. What would Neal do if he were Ninette's father? Leading the Indians away from the cave would be a priority. But how? Befriending them? Praise them for the surprise attack on the fort? Feed them? Giving them whiskey didn't make sense; they could turn on him.

Then Neal realized the best deterrent was to fool the Indians, especially if he knew they trailed his every move. Fighting the pain in his head, he blinked back the dizziness and then embarked upon a trek to the water's edge near the cabin. Up and down the banks, he looked for canoes. Granted, the island had plenty of areas for him to search, but it made sense that the Indians would land near the cabin. Curvier had said their canoes were near his.

He rested for a moment. His body cried out for water and something to take away the hammering in his skull. Licking his dry lips, Neal willed the agony tearing at his body to flee. No matter how many times he tried to convince himself that he endured the torment to his body because of his soldier responsibilities, he knew Ninette was the real reason. Soon all of the turmoil here needed to end, so he could slip back into his old ways.

Not a pleasant thought for a man who hated his past and wanted the present to be his future.

The sun beat down hot on his back, and sweat soaked his face, neck, and shirt. His red coat lay in the cave, and he wished his red trousers were there, too. At times, the bright color exposed him for several yards. But the island appeared deserted. With an air of caution, he proceeded around most of the perimeter of the island, staying close to the water's edge where canoes might be hidden.

By midafternoon, Neal discarded the thought of finding the Indians' canoes. But, he did find the canoe that had brought him from the mainland. He moved closer to the cabin and knelt down in the brush. For the next hour, he watched for movement. By the second hour, he crept to the shed. Flies buzzed around it, and the stench filled his nostrils. Neal feared the worst. The animals and chickens roamed about, as though nothing had changed in their surroundings.

With only his knife in his boot and a thick limb in his hand, he made his way to the door and opened it. Dead beavers lay everywhere—not Chapin Curvier's body. *Thank You, Lord.*

A curious thought swept over him. Why hadn't the Indians taken the animals or the animal pelts? And where was Curvier? His gaze swept to the path leading to the cabin. No moccasin or boot prints embedded in the ground. Neal stole around to the cabin entrance. He neither heard nor saw anyone. His mind toyed with the strong possibility of a trap on the other side of the door. He lifted the latch and flung it back. Nothing. No one.

Once convinced that Curvier had not been back to the cabin, Neal continued to look for canoes. As the day lengthened, he became more convinced the Indians and Curvier were missing from the island. Where had they gone? Had they left together?

When hunger clawed at his stomach, he retraced his steps to the cabin and gathered up a few potatoes, dried pork, and one nearly ripe tomato from Ninette's garden. If he'd evaluated the situation correctly, they could return to the cabin tomorrow. It made no sense to him that the Indians had not taken the Curviers' food and belongings.

After drinking fully from the well, he drew water into an animal skin to take back to the cave. Weariness tore at his body. He'd taxed himself today, but at least he had information to give Ninette, even if he didn't have all the answers. Sunset had fallen by the time he reached her. The moment he approached the cave, she rushed from its secluded depths.

"Neal, I worried so for you."

The mere sight of her eased his discomfort. "I've been scouting the island." He held up the bag of food. "And I've been to the cabin—twice."

Her eyes widened. "Did you find Papa?" She peered behind him.

"No sign of him anywhere. And unless you know where he hides his canoe, I couldn't find it either."

She turned her head as though pondering his words. Worried lines creased her forehead. "You mean he's gone?"

"I think so. The Indians are not here either."

She shook her head. "Let's get you inside before I have to carry you. Then we can talk about this."

He inwardly chuckled at the way she sounded like one of his commanding officers. Except Ninette was far easier on the eyes and her voice much sweeter.

Neal slumped to the cave floor, exhausted and in pain. Yet, he was strangely at peace, satisfied that his endeavors today did not focus on his military career, his obligation to England, or how his superior officers might view him. Instead, he sought to relieve the burden placed on one young woman and determine the whereabouts of her father.

"Do you know where your father might be?" he asked.

"If not for the problems on the mainland, I'd assume he'd go there."

Neal shook his head. "Fort Michilimackinac may not be safe." It made sense Curvier would deliberately lead the Indians away from the island. "But, according to your father, the Indians did not harm the French."

"Then perhaps he may have gone there." She paused. "He did this to protect me. I'm sure of it. Not very long ago, one of the Chippewa wanted to purchase me for his wife. Papa told him no. Said I was spoken for, which I'm not. The man was not pleased and offered more in trade. He could have tried again."

Anger swelled in Neal. He clenched his fists. "You may be right. Your father could have led them to believe you'd married and left the island. Then again, the Indians may have forced him to join their band. The whole situation is confusing, because nothing at the cabin has been taken."

"Not the pelts, the animals, or my garden?"

"I checked for anything missing. The cabin looks the same as when we left it."

"I want to go to the mainland. I have to make sure Papa is safe."

Neal nodded without hesitation. "I'll take you."

"And what if the Indians are there?"

"I'll borrow your father's clothes. After all, I speak French, remember?" He smiled in hopes of easing her fears. A man did strange things when love ruled his actions.

"Shall we return to the cabin?" she asked.

"Oh Ninette, I know this cave is damp and uncomfortable, but I think we should stay one more night. In the morning, I'll make sure we're the only ones on the island before we return to the cabin." He groaned and glanced toward the corner of the cave. "I meant to bury that poor fellow's bones before I left today. I can take care of it tonight, if you like."

"Tomorrow's fine." She glanced at the skeleton. "We had a bit of a conversation today, although he never had much to say."

Neal started to laugh. The image of his Ninette, in all of her beauty and innocence, speaking to a pile of bones struck him as incredibly funny. He laughed until his side ached, and when he peered into her face, he saw she'd covered her mouth to control her own laughter. He reached for Ninette and drew her into his arms. The moment her small body touched his, all mirth ceased. Neal realized he'd never be the same again. He'd fallen in love.

She lifted her face to his, as though sensing his emotions and questioning what it all meant. He wanted his lips upon hers, He wanted to hold her tighter. He wanted to tell her of the love growing in his heart.

But he'd promised Chapin Curvier he'd take care of his daughter, and Neal could not give in to a single kiss unless he could promise her a lifetime of more.

# Chapter 8

Ninette bent to put a small bouquet of forget-me-nots on the freshly dug grave and made the sign of the cross. Early this morning, before the sun appeared on the horizon, Neal left for the cabin and returned with a shovel to bury the bones. Now they had a final resting place; however, she'd never forget how frightening they looked when Neal left the cave and she spent hours alone. At the time, she believed death mocked her, and the same threat weighed upon her still.

*Papa, are you alive? Will I ever see you again?* "Should we pray over this man?" she asked.

Neal moistened his lips and wiped the sweat from his brow. "I can." He knelt beside her and took her hand. His touch emitted strength. "Lord, we know nothing about this fellow, but Thou doest. We pray he did not suffer when he died and his family and friends were comforted in his absence. And, Lord, we ask Thee to protect Chapin and grant us wisdom as to what we should do. It is in the name of our Savior Jesus Christ we pray. Amen."

"Merci," she said and spread the flowers over the mound of dirt. Her gaze met Neal's, and he helped her to her feet.

Since the preceding night, when she felt certain he wanted to kiss her, Ninette realized their relationship had changed. And now, she considered her every word to him. Her face warmed. She rubbed her palms together.

"We can go back to the cabin," he said.

"Good." She took a deep breath to still her trembling heart.

"I apologize."

She stared toward the path home and blinked back a tear. "There's no need."

"Yes, I must. I've ruined our friendship."

She swung back to him. "Not at all. I'm simply not sure how to act...or what to say."

"Are you repulsed?"

She gasped. "Never. You are the finest man I've ever met."

"I'm not much good, Ninette. I've committed many acts for which I bear shame."

She placed a hand on his shoulder. "As a soldier, you are obliged to obey your commanding officers."

"I'm not referring to those kinds of offenses."

Had he partaken of loose drink and committed adultery, as she'd heard women speak of at the fort? Some of the women reported unspeakable acts among the soldiers. "I'm not prepared to hear...your confession."

His face softened. "I understand. My intentions with you are honorable. Please believe me."

"I do." Her heart quickened. Love blossomed, and it seemed so precious and beautiful. Dare she reveal her own heart or wait to see what the future held?

He grasped his musket and swung a bag over his shoulder while she carried the shovel. They headed toward the cabin when a rustling several feet away from them caught her attention. A beaver raced through the woods with a brown bear after it. The beaver's helpless groan was a familiar sound.

Neal grabbed Ninette and shoved her behind a tree. "We don't want that bear to decide he'd have a better feast with us." He clasped her hand firmly into his. "Hurry, before it picks up our scent." She left the shovel behind as they raced through the woods. He tugged on her hand and glanced backward. "It's after us. Run, Ninette. I'll take care of the bear."

"I can't leave you."

"Go, now!"

The force of his words propelled her to run faster than she could ever remember running before. She pushed aside the brush and limbs in her path, scratching her face in a mad flight to safety. What about Neal? He had the musket, but was it ready to fire? Too frightened to form the right words to pray, she cried out with a solitary plea for help.

A briar caught her dress and ripped the skirt. Still she ran, waiting. . .begging God for the crack of musket fire.

Then it came, and the sound exploded through the air. Ninette caught sight of the cabin. She thought her lungs would burst from her chest. If only Papa waited there. He'd help Neal. Her trembling hands touched the door latch, and she swung it open wide. For the first time, she turned and searched the path for signs of Neal.

*Oh please, God, help him.*

Long moments passed. Her breathing slowed, but she continued to pray. She blinked, then stepped from the cabin door.

"Neal?" Ninette snatched up the hoe leaning against the side of the cabin. "Neal, are you all right?" The silence frightened her. "Neal, if you're alive and not answering me, I'll shoot you myself and leave you for that bear."

Laughter rang around her. "I'm answering, Miss Ninette. Please don't feed me to the bear."

Ninette saw the familiar figure moving slowly toward her. She lifted her skirts and hurried toward him. He caught her waist, and they nearly fell, laughing as though the bear chasing them meant nothing.

"You killed it?" she asked.

"Yes, got it right in the neck. It's waiting back there for you to skin."

"How dare you say such a thing? I was worried sick, and now you want me to skin a bear?"

"Hmm, and cook it up, too. Haven't had bear in a long time."

"Do you want me to tan the hide while it's cooking?"

"I wouldn't want you to work too hard."

He pulled her close, and she relished the closeness of him. "It would bring a fine price." His words grew softer. He moistened his lips and released her waist. "This is getting harder, Ninette. I want to hold you and kiss you." He glanced around them. "I'd like nothing more than to stay right here on this island with you forever."

She touched his face, so unlike nursing him when she checked him for a fever.

"Would staying here be wrong?"

"Didn't you say you wanted to live on the mainland with other people?"

"I did." *But I'd be happy here with you forever.*

"And your papa. We must find him."

Reality washed over her. "How selfish of me when I have no idea where he is—or if he's unharmed."

"I'll not rest until I have the truth," he said. "And then, maybe then, we can talk about you and me."

Ninette lifted her gaze to meet his. Her pulse quickened. "I'll wait for both of you."

Neal's face softened. "I love you."

🐾

Once Neal skinned the bear, he cut off a generous slab of meat, and Ninette added it with herbs to a simmering pot. More than once, he found himself thinking about living on the island with her. He'd marry her today, if she'd have him. They'd raise a fine family according to the Bible. The thought filled him with more happiness than he'd ever experienced.

*Foolishness. She doesn't know what you've done. Ninette may look at you with adoring eyes now but not after she's learned the truth.*

She walked toward him with a flask of water. Her smile. Her sway. The innocence of a woman-child. He envied her pureness. If only he could change his past.

"You must be somewhere other than on the island." She bent down beside him.

"I am, and then I'm not."

She turned her face, the quizzical image of a little girl through a splattering of freckles. "Can you tell me?"

His shoulders lifted and fell as he scraped the flesh away from the bear skin. "I'm working as diligently as though I lived here instead of you—as though we weren't leaving here tomorrow."

"So you have regrets in leaving?"

"I have regrets in leaving what I've found here. For the first time in my life, I'm thinking of someone other than myself."

She paled, then moistened her lips. "One of the women at the fort said love brings out what God intended for all of us to have."

"A wise woman. Did she say how to work out the problems of two people who love each other, but who are from different cultures? Or where these two people could live where prejudice would not cause them to lose sight of their bond?"

She shook her head. "I have been asking God for the answers to those questions."

"I pray He answers soon. The anguish is worse than when the Indian sank a tomahawk into my head."

🐾

Neal reached for Ninette's hand and helped her into the canoe. She'd chosen to take only a few things, much less than he expected for a woman. Perhaps it was her optimism in finding her father that held her back. In any event, they'd spoken few words this morning. The uncertain future clung in the air as thick as the fog lifting from the water.

Things needed to be said, and he must find the courage. At this moment, he believed her knowing his past far outweighed the consequences of his actions.

"I have to tell you the truth about me." Neal lifted the paddle and dipped it into the water. "I love you, Ninette, and you say you love me—but the past haunts me."

"Nothing will change how I feel," she said.

*My sweet, this is so ugly.* "Save your words until I've finished, for your opinion of me will change. I'm not sure where to begin, but I've told you about my French mother." When she nodded, he continued. "Living in England with my parents, those around me criticized my father for his French wife. I grew angry at their disrespect, but something else happened within me. I began to see my father as a weakling because he didn't fight those who viewed my mother as an outcast. I sided with them and became ashamed of her." He paused in an effort to recall why he'd ever viewed his dear mother as anything but good and kind. "As soon as I was old enough, I enlisted in the king's army." He sighed.

"*Angry* best described me—and also *coward*. I didn't have the courage to stand up for my mother, and so I turned against her. I took my knowledge of the French and my ability to speak their language and spied on them. In essence, I turned on my own people." He shook his head, no longer able to look at her. "Many fine men died because of my espionage."

She gasped and turned her attention toward the water. The canoe bounced over the waves, rising and falling. "You betrayed your own people."

"Yes. At the time, I justified my actions because I was a soldier. I even thought God wanted me to use my French background to aid the English, when in truth I did it all out of hatred for myself."

"I don't quite understand."

He'd never spoken aloud of this, and the verbal telling of it brought back the sting of truth. "I placed my value according to English standards instead of God's."

"And now?"

"I've confessed my sins repeatedly and know my sins are forgiven. . .but forgiving myself is another matter."

Long moments passed between them.

"Did your mother learn of this?" she asked.

"Yes, and she died before I made my peace with God or her."

Ninette stiffened.

"I understand you need time to ponder over what I've said." He waited for what seemed like an eternity.

"This. . .this is a hard thing for me."

"I love you, Ninette. I want you to be with me for as long as God allows. I want to find a way for us to be happy, but I will abide by your wishes."

"I love you, too, but I need a little time."

He drew in a heavy breath. "I understand." He listened to the oar dipping rhythmically in and out of the water. "I made two promises that I intend to keep. One was to your father to look after you, and the other is to find him for you."

Ninette's wide brown eyes held such sadness. He'd put the melancholy there, just as he'd done to his mother. But with God's help, the outcome would be different. He'd fulfill both promises with no thought of selfish gain.

# Chapter 9

The canoe rested against the sandy soil of the water's edge. Ninette's mind raced with thoughts of Papa, Neal, the people at the fort. . .and the Indians.

"I'd like for you to wait here while I investigate the fort," Neal said.

She glanced at him in Papa's trousers. He did look more French than English. "I'm going with you. I refuse to stay behind."

"Ninette, please. We don't know what is ahead."

She shook her head. "I'm going with you. If people need help, I want to be there. And if Papa is here among the French, I want to be the first to see him."

"All right, but at the first sign of trouble, you must return to the canoe." His gaze rested upon her, and she could almost read his thoughts, sad ones for what he'd revealed.

They followed the path toward the fort. It looked deserted. She blinked. Splotches of blood pooled the ground. She thought the rain would have washed it away. In the next instance, a man called out in French. She strained her ears to listen.

"Are you alone?" the man called.

"Oui," Neal said. "Is it safe?"

The man walked toward them. She'd seen him before but did not know his name. "Yes. The Chippewa have been gone for three days now."

"And the English soldiers?" Neal asked.

"Four are still alive. We are caring for them."

Ninette breathed a sigh. *Praise God for sparing them.*

"I have Chapin Curvier's daughter. Have you seen him?"

"No. I assumed he was on the island."

She swallowed a sob. "Do you know where he might be?"

The man, a tall fellow with strands of gray in his hair, shook his head. "No, miss. He helped us bury soldiers, then left. I assumed he went home. I don't know if this will help you or not, but we did find an empty canoe yesterday. A fellow said it looked like Chapin's."

"We're trying to find him," Neal said.

The man held out his hand, and Neal shook it. "The name is Jacque Dupire. Come with me. My wife and I will get you something to eat. We can talk about where Chapin could have gone."

Neal glanced at Ninette, then at Dupire. "I must continue searching, but I'd be grateful if you'd look after his daughter until one of us returns." He took a breath. "If I don't make it back, will you see to it that she is cared for?"

She started to protest, but the stern look on Neal's face stopped her.

"I'd be glad to," Dupire said.

Neal lifted Ninette's bag from the canoe and handed it to her. "I intend to keep my promises."

She wanted to say something, but the words died in her throat. She loved this man, but his ways. . .his past confused her. She took the bag and joined Dupire.

🙠

A lump rested in Neal's throat. Telling Ninette about himself had been a mistake, but he would never have been able to live with himself if he'd kept the truth from her. He'd find Curvier, and he'd make sure she was taken care of. For once he had chosen the honorable road.

He ventured farther down the coastline. His eyes fixed for signs of Indians or Curvier. How far would a man go to protect his daughter? His life?

With each beat of his heart, the hammering in Neal's head attacked him. Much like the old memories. His thoughts turned to Ninette. She was so trusting of God's Word, and even when he'd pointed out her contradictions, her faith didn't waver.

Questions repeated in his mind. *How far would a man go to protect his daughter? His life?* The ponderings brought forth how far God went to protect His children. He'd given His Son's life so all who called on His name could be forgiven.

Lack of forgiveness had torn through him for too long. God had forgiven him, but he couldn't forgive himself. Neal startled. Was he denying God's gift of life by refusing to forgive himself? Did this mean Christ had died for nothing? Remorse wound its way through Neal's mind. He was guilty of both pride and selfishness. How long had he wallowed in self-pity and remorse instead of drinking in the fullness of life? He thought back on all the times he'd been moody, ill-tempered. *God, forgive me. You gave me a way out of my sins, and I refused it.*

With the admission of his wretched actions came a new sensation—one of hope. He no longer had to live in desperation but in freedom. And what joy filled his soul despite his mission to find Curvier or the knowledge that Ninette might never be his. For the first time in his life, Neal experienced real peace.

🙠

Ninette helped Mrs. Dupire bathe her two young children and dress them in clean clothes. She adored little ones and outwardly displayed her enthusiasm, but inside she ached for her hard heart.

She hadn't even told Neal good-bye. All of her talk about living as God directed meant nothing when she couldn't soothe a man's tormented mind. He might be killed in his search for Papa, and he'd never know how much she truly loved him. The poor man could not forgive himself, when in truth, if she'd voiced her compassion, his burden might be lighter. How foolish and naive for a woman who expressed her love of God. She had so much of life to learn.

*I'd go after Neal if I knew where he'd gone. God, forgive my foolish ways.*

The following day, Ninette's misery for the two men in her life seemed to increase with each passing moment. She wanted to leave and search for them, but which way did she venture? Late morning, she walked to the fort's gate. Everywhere there were reminders of the soldiers. She shivered. Just like Papa and Neal. . .reminders had taken root in her heart. As she had waited at the cave's opening on the island, so she took vigilance at the gate. Hours passed. She swiped at her tears. Papa would want her to continue on with life. She turned to walk back to the Dupires' cabin. One more time, she stared out over the surrounding land. In the distance, a lone figure moved her way.

Ninette held her breath. A beaver's cap bobbed on the man's head. Papa! It was Papa! She rushed through the gate and raced toward him.

"My petite fille," he said. "You know I always come back to you."

"But must you break my heart while I wait?" She clung to his neck and sobbed—for him, for her, and for Neal. "Where did you go?"

As Ninette had suspected, the Chippewa man had wanted to purchase her.

"I told him you were married. I knew if I stayed away from the cave long enough, Wellington would come looking for me, so I left." He glanced about. "Where is he now?"

"Searching for you. He promised me he'd find you."

Papa lifted her chin and gazed into her eyes. "Do I see something else in your eyes?"

Ninette held her breath. "Oui, Papa, you do."

His shoulders slumped. "What am I to do? I've never wanted this for you. My wish has been to see you happy among the French. Yet, my highest goal is to see you happy."

"I'm happy with Neal."

"I see the same sparkle in your eyes that your mother used to give me."

"Then you do understand, Papa?"

"Oui, I'll find him."

"And I'll go with you."

He pulled her into his arms. "Is he on foot?" When she nodded, he held her close. "We'll track him down."

❧

Neal ventured deeper into the mainland. He'd slept well the night before, better than he could remember. Odd, when his world was crumbling around him, he'd found peace. He hoped to find a settlement soon or come upon the Huron Indians. They might know where Chapin had gone. For certain, he refused to give up. The thought of facing Ninette without her father was inconceivable.

The weather warmed. Without his soldier's uniform, he realized the French would be more sympathetic in helping him. For once, he looked forward to seeing his mother's people—his people.

Neal walked for miles with no signs of anyone. Food rations ran low, so he fished on the shore. He relished the beauty of the lake and the untouched land around him. No wonder Chapin preferred the solitude of the island. Here, settlers would come and inhabit the area, but the island offered respite.

By late afternoon, the pain in his head had increased, and he stopped to rest. He realized he'd pushed himself in his search, and now he must pay the price. He stole back into the trees and leaned back against an oak. In a few moments, his body relaxed.

Something poked at his shoulder. Neal startled and opened his eyes. Three Indian braves stood over him. He couldn't tell what tribe, but fear raced through him. His musket lay to the side of him, and he'd slid his knife into his boot.

One of the Indians pointed at him and said something to the other—so stoically that he couldn't tell what they discussed or what they intended to do with him. Their faces were not painted, and no scalps hung from their waists. Would he live to see another day?

One of the Indians pulled Neal to his feet and motioned for him to follow. Another Indian grasped his musket; Neal had no choice but to accompany them. They walked deeper into the woods. His thoughts turned to Ninette. He might never see her again, and she'd never learn of his repentance. On he walked with the Indians until he wished they'd end his life rather than continue. They reached a clearing.

He blinked. Chapin stood there with Ninette. She whirled around. A smile spread across her face.

"Neal! The Hurons have found you!"

She hurried toward him and stopped short a few feet in front of him. "I'm sorry. Will you forgive me?"

The sight of her was like a soothing balm. The mere sound of her voice rallied his strength. "There is nothing to forgive."

"Ah yes, my pride. You left, and I couldn't say I love you."

Neal's gaze swept to Chapin who had walked behind his daughter. He raised a brow. "Your intentions with my daughter?"

"To love her all the days of my life, sir. If you will grant her hand and she is willing."

"I believe she is willing." Chapin sighed. "This will be a difficult journey for you two. I am concerned about both the French and the English making your life hard."

"With God on our side, we can combine the best of both worlds."

Neal glanced down at Ninette. He brushed a single tear from her cheek. "Will you have me, Ninette?"

"Oui, today, tomorrow, and always."

**DiAnn Mills** is a bestselling author who believes her readers should expect an adventure. She combines unforgettable characters with unpredictable plots to create action-packed, suspense-filled novels.

Her titles have appeared on the CBA and ECPA bestseller lists; won two Christy Awards; and been finalists for the RITA, Daphne Du Maurier, Inspirational Readers' Choice, and Carol award contests. Library Journal presented her with a Best Books 2014: Genre Fiction award in the Christian Fiction category for Firewall.

DiAnn is a founding board member of the American Christian Fiction Writers; the 2015 president of the Romance Writers of America's Faith, Hope & Love chapter; and a member of Advanced Writers and Speakers Association and International Thriller Writers. She speaks to various groups and teaches writing workshops around the country. She and her husband live in sunny Houston, Texas.

DiAnn is very active online and would love to connect with readers on any of the social media platforms listed at www.diannmills.com.

# NEW GARDEN'S HOPE

by Jennifer Hudson Taylor

# Dedication

To my husband and daughter, thank you for your loving support. To my Quaker ancestors who began at New Garden Meeting in Greensboro, North Carolina, thank you for inspiring this story. And finally, to my Lord, thank You for making all things possible.

# Chapter 1

Josiah Wall looked as if he were about to propose, but he'd just done the opposite and postponed their wedding—again. Ruth Payne cringed as the empty void inside deepened.

He bent on one knee in front of her. She sat on a wooden swing, hanging from a large oak tree. Beneath the shade of a black wide-brimmed hat, his hazel eyes searched her face. She wondered if he could see the ache in her expression. Even though she'd known him all her life, right now he seemed like a distant stranger.

"Ruth, say something. . .please."

Josiah covered her hand where she gripped the rope, but his touch seared her, almost as much as his words. She jerked away and stood, slipping from his grasp. The swing swayed between them as his sensitive eyes blinked in surprise. Her gaze drifted to his brown locks around his ears and to his sideburns.

Her heart stammered through denial, anger, and then pure gut-wrenching pain. She wouldn't plead and cry like last time. She turned, clenching her teeth, and stared at her parents' white two-story house. Brown leaves tumbled in the breeze across the yard. The midmorning sun shimmered through shifting tree limbs in the crisp fall breeze.

"What is there to say?" Ruth asked, still avoiding his gaze. "The first time thee said it was because we needed our own home. Now that the new house is built, thee claims it must be after the presidential election. The only thing I can say is that I don't understand."

Ruth closed her eyes to shut out the threatening tears. She wouldn't humiliate herself again. Pride may be a sin, but she needed to preserve some of her self-respect, didn't she?

Josiah stood to his full height, at least a half-foot taller than she. He slipped his thumbs under his black suspenders. A robin swooped from the tree, flapping its wings. Josiah ducked and righted his hat.

"I was afraid thee wouldn't understand," he said. "But Ruth, I'm working with the Federalist movement, and it's imperative I give my full attention—at least through the 1808 election. I can't allow myself to be distracted by wedding plans."

Anger burst inside her. Ruth opened her eyes and whirled to face him. "We're not like the rest of the world. Quakers have simple lives. We have plain weddings and homes. Thee is making this much more complicated than it should be."

Ruth linked her trembling hands in front of her charcoal-colored dress. It contained pleats at the waist and long sleeves with white trimming. The drawstrings of her bonnet suddenly felt tight under her chin. She cleared her throat and leaned her palm against the bark of the tree trunk.

"It's only for a few months," Josiah said. "By then most of the house could be furnished. Right now it's too bare." He stepped around the swing and leaned close.

Ruth stepped back.

His eyes widened as he lifted a dark eyebrow. "Don't be angry," he said. "To prove my commitment, let's reschedule the date for the second month on the twelfth."

Ruth laughed. "Dates mean naught to thee. When that time comes, thee will only change it." His wounded expression pierced her, but she wouldn't take back the words. As far as she knew, they were true. "In fact I'm not even sure thee really loves me—if thee ever did."

"Of course I do!" Josiah stepped toward her but halted when she stiffened and leaned sideways. He gulped, his eyes pleading. "Be patient with me a little longer. I love thee, Ruth—even when we were children. I knew thee was meant for me that day in the school yard when I forgot my lunch and thee gave me an apple." He offered a handsome grin, but she managed to resist him by averting her gaze.

"Are none of these Federalists in thy group married?" Ruth laid a hand on her quivering stomach.

"Of course, but that's different. They're already settled. When thee becomes my bride, I intend to give thee all my attention. I want things to be perfect."

"Josiah," Ruth sighed. "I fear thee has some misguided notion about marriage. Either thee cannot love me or thee is afraid to make a commitment. Seek God and allow Him to show thee what to do. Right now I'll not agree to another date."

His mouth dropped open in disbelief. He touched the top of his hat, paced a few feet, and then came back. "What is thee saying? Is thee breaking our engagement? Ruth, don't do this. Please, I beg thee." Josiah's breath released in rapid gasps. His brows wrinkled and he rubbed his eyes as if they burned.

Ruth wanted to console him but feared she'd lose the tiny thread of self-control she still possessed. How many times could she allow him to do this? If he wasn't sure about his love for her, how could she be so selfish as to trap him into a lifetime of marriage? No. She couldn't do it. In spite of the pain it would cause, she'd sacrifice her own happiness to give him his.

"Josiah Wall, I release thee from our engagement."

෨෨

The bell on the front door of the Wall Brothers Seed and Feed store rang, alerting Josiah to an arriving customer. He stopped stacking the new feed sacks he'd gotten in that morning and left the storeroom.

Matthew Payne, Ruth's father, strolled up to the counter. He had a healthy physique for a man of his age, with broad shoulders and a slightly bulging belly. Beneath his broad-brimmed hat, his gray hair was brushed to the side of his forehead.

"What can I do for thee?" Josiah tensed as he set his palms on the counter and forced a smile. Would Matthew Payne be angry he'd hurt Ruth by postponing the wedding again? Guilt sliced through his chest, causing him to take a deep breath. He hadn't meant to hurt her. He'd give anything to see her happy. That's why he worked so hard to make their future better.

"I was wondering if my cattle feed had come in yet?" His gray mustache moved with his lips as he spoke.

"It came in just this morning. If I remember correctly, ten feed sacks, right?" Josiah raised an eyebrow and rubbed his chin.

"That's right." Matthew Payne nodded and scratched his side-whiskers. He glanced at the parallel rows of goods on the wooden shelves. "I can't remember a day this store wasn't organized and immaculate. Thee and thy brothers have carried on and accomplished no small feat in thy father's shoes."

At the mention of his father, Josiah stiffened, his gut twisting like an angry tornado. Three years ago his father had turned fifty and couldn't stop talking of all the things he'd never gotten to do. As a lad he'd always wanted to be a seaman. Josiah used to enjoy the stories his father read to him about seafaring adventures. All those years sharing his father's love for ships and the sea, Josiah never imagined his father would one day disappear and choose such an adventurous life over his own family.

Josiah forced the unpleasant thoughts to the back of his mind, reminding himself that Matthew only meant it as a compliment. "I'm sure my brothers would agree in our thanks. I've always respected thy opinion—even more than my father's."

"I was looking forward to having thee as my son-in-law, Josiah, but Ruth returned from a long walk yesterday, weeping and saying the engagement is off."

She'd been crying? Hope lifted Josiah's heart. When she refused to set a new date, she'd appeared so calm that it frightened him. If she was upset, perhaps she wasn't serious about breaking their engagement. *Lord, please let that be the case.*

"I don't want to break the engagement. I asked to postpone it. I'd hoped for more time to make additional furnishings for the house and be able to give Ruth my all after the election."

Matthew nodded as he slipped his thumbs under his suspenders. "Son, thy reasons are sound and logical—for a man. Now a woman, she's going to think down a much different path. That's the main thing I've learned during all my years of marriage."

"I love Ruth, and I still want to spend the rest of my life with her. She says I don't love her, but that isn't true."

"Thee need not convince me, but her." Matthew's gray eyes pierced Josiah.

"I intend to try," Josiah said. "I was hoping Ruth might be in better humor today."

The elder man shook his head. "I can vouch thee might wait a few days for her good humor to return."

"I see." Josiah slouched against the counter, disappointed but thankful for the warning. "Thanks for letting me know." It would be disastrous to visit today and make things worse. He'd give Ruth time for her anger to subside, and then he'd try to reason with her again.

"Well I'd better get back to the farm to care for my cattle and livestock," Matthew said. "Now that Caleb is twelve, I plan to supervise the lad in fence mending this afternoon."

"Give my regards to everyone." Josiah pointed to the front of the store. "Did thee park the wagon out front or on the side?"

"In front. Shall I pull it around?"

"No." Josiah shook his head. "I'll bring the feed sacks out in a wheelbarrow." He stepped into the storeroom.

The bell rang. Josiah assumed it was Matthew leaving the store. Taking a deep breath, he closed his eyes, seeking a moment of peace. *Lord, I know that everything happens for a reason. It must have been Thy will for Matthew Payne to come in this morning and warn me about Ruth. Even though I long to try to mend things, I'll trust in Thy judgment. Give me strength to obey Thee.*

Josiah stacked the feed sacks in the wheelbarrow and rolled them from the storage room.

"Just the man I'm looking for," said a high-pitched female voice. Josiah looked up to see Sarah Goodson saunter toward him. Her blond curls framed her face beneath her white bonnet, her blue eyes sparkling in spite of her gray dress. Sarah's animated personality always outshone her plain appearance.

Dread pooled in Josiah's stomach. He'd better let her know he was with a customer, or he'd never break free to finish with Matthew.

"Good morning, Sarah Goodson. I need to load these feed sacks on Matthew Payne's wagon, and then I'll be right with thee."

"Oh! He passed me on the way out. I'm in no hurry. I only came to pick up some feed for the chickens."

Josiah moved on, but before he reached the door, footsteps rushed up behind him and a hand grabbed his arm. "Josiah Wall, I wanted to tell thee how sorry I am about thy breakup with Ruth."

"How does thee know?" Josiah's blood ran cold as he gulped in surprise.

News had always traveled around the community of New Garden at a fast pace, but this was unbelievable. Josiah gripped the handlebars so tight that his knuckles whitened on the wheelbarrow.

"She was in a very sour mood at the quilt meeting this morning, and when I asked her what was wrong, she told us—all of us."

Alarm spread through Josiah as a wave of fear prickled the skin along his arms. His anger faded to a dull ache that engulfed the back of his head, seizing his thoughts. Ruth was a private woman. If she'd shared the news with others in such a manner, this wasn't a small argument she needed to overcome, as he'd hoped. Ruth was serious. Their engagement was over.

Josiah's heart plummeted.

# Chapter 2

Ruth slid the drapes aside and glanced at the sun-drenched landscape of faded grass the color of hay. The row of poplar trees along the narrow dirt road displayed an array of orange and golden leaves. It was a beautiful day for a long walk, but she couldn't bring herself to leave the house.

What if Josiah came by? Granted, she wouldn't agree to see him, but she couldn't help wondering what he was doing and thinking. Was he hurting as much as she? Or had he moved on with his life?

She sighed, leaning her forehead against the glass. It had been two whole days since she'd seen him. With her heart shattered, there were moments when her chest felt so heavy she could hardly breathe.

"Ruth, that's the third time thee has looked out the window in the past hour," her mother said. "If thee has changed thy mind, why not send Caleb to Josiah Wall with a letter?"

"I don't wanna get in the middle of their lover's quarrel." Caleb wrinkled his nose and eyebrows, his blue eyes glaring at her. "Besides I promised Father I'd finish mending the fence we started the other day."

"I haven't changed my mind," Ruth said, dropping the drapes. "I need another project to keep me occupied."

"Well don't include me in any more of thy projects," Naomi said. "My arms are sore from scrubbing the floors yesterday." Her sister crossed her arms and rubbed them, her brown eyes surveying Ruth. "I've told thee before Josiah Wall loves thee. How can thee doubt him after all these years?" Her blond curls bounced as she shook her head in disbelief. "I don't understand."

"Well at fifteen I don't expect thee to understand. I love Josiah Wall, but he doesn't love me like a wife. He's in denial. I'd be selfish if I allowed him to wed me under such a falsehood, especially now that I've come to realize it." Her voice choked as tears pooled in her eyes. Ruth turned away, hating how her heart squeezed at the mention of him.

"I'm only three years younger than thee," Naomi said. "Old enough to judge Josiah's character. I don't understand why thee insists on torturing thyself this way."

"Girls are so strange," Caleb said, walking across the hardwood floor. "I'd rather be outside working."

"The attic hasn't been cleaned out in a while." Her mother's gentle voice echoed across the living room.

Wiping a few stray tears, Ruth nodded. "A good idea. I'll see to it."

Ruth climbed the stairs and walked down the long hallway to the half-size door at the end. She turned the brass knob. It creaked, and the bolt slid from its hold, allowing her to swing the door open. She peered into the dark hole, lifting the lantern to reveal a steep incline of narrow steps.

Gathering her skirts, Ruth ducked then plowed up the stairs. She came to a small room lit by only one rectangular window. It had been ages since she was here. She hoped no rats, bats, or spiders showed themselves. A rare shiver passed through her spine.

She shoved a hand on her hip and strode to the center of the attic, and then ducking her head, turned full circle. Dust littered all the boxes, discarded toys, and old furniture. Her gaze landed on two cedar chests by the window.

She bent to her knees in front of the large one and lifted the lid. The hinges groaned as they locked in place. A brown leather Bible lay on top of several quilts. The volume was so large and heavy she had to use both hands to lift it. She remembered seeing it years ago; her mother had since relied on a more recent Bible that was smaller and easier to carry.

Ruth hauled the book onto her lap and flipped open the cover to the inside. Various messages had been written in slanted cursive, along with a list of names in the Payne family, and dates extending back to the late 1600s to Sussex, England.

She sat on the floor so long reading her family history that her tailbone began to ache. She shifted to the side to ease her discomfort and caused the Bible to slide off her lap and thump to the floor. The edge of a piece of paper slipped out from the middle.

Ruth dug her fingers into the spot and shoved the stack of pages to the other side. She unfolded the thick brown paper, a handwritten recipe for gingerbread that required a measure of molasses, sour milk, vegetable oil, wheat flour, a dash of salt, and a tablespoon of ginger.

How long had this recipe been in her family? Ruth scraped her teeth over her bottom lip as she pondered what to do with it. The original was too important to remove from the family Bible. She would copy it, and if she had time, try it out this evening.

"Josiah!" Caleb called from below the attic window. "Wanna go fishing?"

Ruth paused, realizing Josiah must be walking toward the house. She leaned over the chest and scrambled to her knees to look outside. The lid slammed on her fingers where she gripped it for support. She yelped and bounced back. Her head slammed against a low beam. Pain sliced across her left temple as her legs crumbled beneath her. The voices below faded with her sight.

☙

Josiah glanced up at the sound of a woman's scream. "Who was that?" He looked to Caleb for an answer.

"With two sisters in the house, there's no telling. One of them may have found a spider." Caleb shrugged, his mouth twisting in a grin as he followed Josiah's gaze.

"Caleb!" His mother hurried out of the house, clutching a cream-colored shawl. She breathed heavily, trying to catch her breath. "Go fetch the doctor. Ruth has taken a terrible fall and is unconscious."

The lad's blue eyes widened as he gulped.

"Go! Hurry!" Elizabeth Payne waved him away, her brows wrinkled in worry.

"Is there something I can do?" Josiah asked. He wanted to go see Ruth for himself, but he managed to keep his feet planted out of respect for her mother.

"I thank thee, Josiah Wall. Please, go find her father and her brother Elijah. I believe they are out in the pumpkin patch, loading a wagon for market."

She disappeared back into the house, where he assumed Naomi attended Ruth. Josiah ran past the swing on the oak tree to where orange pumpkins grew in long rows. The Payne's wooden wagon was half full from the harvest of four rows.

Over an hour later, Josiah paced the living room floor, his boots clicking a steady rhythm. He hoped they didn't kick him out, but he couldn't be still. His gut twisted in agonizing knots as he waited for news—any news. Voices echoed from upstairs, but he couldn't hear what they said. He rubbed his hand through his hair. His hat was somewhere around here. He was always losing the thing.

Footsteps sounded on the front porch. He rushed to open the door. Dr. Edwards, carrying a black bag, removed his hat. His plump form almost hid Caleb.

"Where are they?" Dr. Edwards asked, his brown eyes searching Josiah's.

"Upstairs." Josiah nodded toward the steps in the foyer, and the doctor rushed past him.

"Is she awake, yet?" Caleb asked.

"I haven't heard her voice." Josiah shook his head. "This is pure torture." He bit the knuckles of his fist as he paced the floor again. A discarded sewing basket lay on the couch with a threaded needle stuck in a shirt. He wondered if the work belonged to Ruth.

More footsteps sounded on the stairs. Josiah whirled and hurried to the foyer. Naomi followed her elder brother, Elijah. Grim expressions marred their faces.

"Mother asked me to offer thee some tea or coffee," Naomi said, looking up at Josiah. "I'm about to make a cup of coffee for Dr. Edwards."

"Has she awakened?" Josiah asked.

Naomi nodded, her eyes focused on the floor as she gripped her hands in front of her. Why wasn't she more happy? Why did she look so uncomfortable?

Behind him, Caleb breathed a sigh of relief.

"Did she say anything?" Josiah asked, stepping closer.

Naomi met his hesitant gaze then looked away. Confused, Josiah glanced at Elijah for an explanation. Two years Ruth's senior, he and Elijah had become close friends while growing up. But over the last year, Josiah had focused more of his attention on Ruth. At times Elijah seemed annoyed by it, but not today.

"She asked if thee was here." Elijah's blue eyes peered into his, an older version of Caleb's. "And she doesn't want to see thee." Elijah shook his head. His hair was a shade darker than Caleb's. "I'm sorry, my friend."

"May I at least stay until we hear a verdict from the doctor?"

"Of course." Naomi glanced up. "Mother said to make sure thee is comfortable. I think we could all use some coffee." She strode to the kitchen.

"Indeed." Josiah sighed, reeling from Ruth's rejection at such a time as this. When would she forgive him and get over his delaying their wedding? Would she have asked if he was here if she didn't care? Hope surged in his battered chest.

He joined the others in the kitchen. They all sat around the table while Naomi made a pot of coffee. The brewing pot smelled delicious. As he finished drinking his coffee, he heard Dr. Edward's voice in the foyer. He stood and followed the sound of the voices to the bottom of the stairs.

"It's a minor concussion, but she should be all right by this time tomorrow. Make sure she gets plenty of rest." Dr. Edwards turned from Matthew Payne, grabbed his hat, and headed for the front door.

"Thank thee," Ruth's father said, still standing on the bottom step. He rubbed his chin thoughtfully as Josiah approached with Ruth's siblings. He looked older, the wrinkles around his eyes more prominent. He met each gaze with lengthy silence.

"Here is thy coffee." Naomi handed a steaming cup on a small saucer to the doctor.

"That smells delicious." He nodded, gave her a grateful smile, and set his black bag on a table. He sipped the black brew as steam swirled around his bald head.

"Please have a seat and join us a bit longer." Matthew Payne gestured to the couch.

Dr. Edwards shook his head and sipped more coffee. He swallowed. "I appreciate the offer, but I have more stops I need to make."

"On that note, I'll be taking my leave as well," Josiah said. "Please tell Ruth that I was here, and I hope she recovers quickly."

"We will." Matthew slapped him on the shoulder. "Never fear. Ruth will come around eventually."

Josiah's heart thumped with optimism.

# Chapter 3

The next morning Ruth woke with a searing headache. She touched the side of her temple and winced at the tender bruise. Thoughts of Josiah assailed her, and she groaned in embarrassment. If she hadn't been acting like a foolish schoolgirl upon his arrival, she wouldn't have lost her balance and hit her head like a simpleton. How could she face him in such humiliation? In her weakened state, she would have succumbed to his consolation and wept upon his shoulder like a lovesick fool.

Ruth washed from her basin and dressed. She pulled her hair up in a braided bun and opened the curtains in her room. Having a corner chamber afforded her two windows, one by her bed and the other in front of her writing desk. A fireplace with a simple mantel graced the opposite wall. The bottom half of her walls were taupe, while the upper half were adorned with pictures of various flowers she and Naomi had painted last summer.

Downstairs, the smell of biscuits, frying bacon, and fresh coffee made her mouth water. As she passed through the living room, her parents' low voices carried from the kitchen. A slight chill made her shiver, and she rubbed her arms. She noticed Caleb's shirt where she'd carelessly left it on a chair. Thoughts of Josiah had distracted her when she'd mended the unfinished seam.

Ruth lifted the shirt to move it to a table so no one would sit upon the needle that poked out of it. Josiah's black hat lay discarded beneath. A sentimental wave of affection overflowed her heart and brought tears to her eyes. The back of her throat ached. Her fingers curled around the brim, and she hugged it against her chest. The familiar scent of his musk and soap drifted to her nose. She closed her eyes and basked in it, trying to ignore the nagging thought of never again hugging the real man as she now hugged his hat.

"Ruth, is that you?" her mother called from the kitchen.

Jerking to attention, Ruth tossed Josiah's hat on the chair. She took a deep breath, lifted her chin, and straightened her shoulders before entering the kitchen.

"Yes, Mother, it's me." She attempted a smile, but the muscles in her jaw and the throbbing at her temples intervened.

Her mother rose and came to her, a concerned expression wrinkling her dark brows. Gentle hands cupped Ruth's chin as her mother's brown eyes surveyed hers. "How is thee feeling this morning? Did thee sleep well?"

"Yes, and I had no dreams to interfere with my rest."

"What about the bump on thy head? Let me have a look."

Ruth tilted her head for her mother. When her fingers stroked the sore spot, Ruth winced.

"I'm sorry. It's still swollen." Elizabeth Payne bit her bottom lip.

Realizing her mother considered calling upon the doctor again, Ruth laid her hands on her shoulders. "I'm fine. Dr. Edwards said there would be swelling for a few days. Right now I'd like some breakfast. I'm starving."

"I think a hearty appetite is a good sign." Her father's soothing and encouraging voice carried across the table, his own plate was half full. "Elizabeth, fix her a plate. Naomi, pour her a cup of coffee."

"I can do it," Ruth said, but her mother motioned to her usual chair.

"Ruth, what does thee have planned for the day?" her father asked.

"I found a gingerbread recipe in the old family Bible and thought I'd try it."

"Is that what thee was doing in the attic yesterday?" Her father sipped his coffee, staring at her over the cup's rim.

"I was supposed to be cleaning, but the trunk caught my attention. Mother, does thee know who the recipe came from?"

"Indeed." She nodded. Her brown, silver-streaked hair swayed as she laid down a steaming plate of bacon, eggs, and biscuits in front of Ruth. "It came from my great-great-grandmother and traveled all the way across the sea from England."

"How interesting!" Naomi set a warm cup of coffee next to Ruth's plate. "Did thee find anything else?"

"There's so much history written in the pages of that Bible, generations of our family, with names and dates. It's a treasure." Ruth picked up her coffee and sipped the strong brew. The liquid flowed down her throat and settled in her stomach, startling her awake.

"I want to help thee make the gingerbread," Naomi said.

"That's a good idea. I don't think Ruth should be up and about, doing too much today. Dr. Edwards said she should rest." Their mother glanced from Naomi to Ruth.

The side door opened, and Elijah and Caleb walked in, their shirtsleeves rolled up to their elbows. Elijah carried a pail of milk in each hand, and Caleb, a basket of brown eggs.

"The animals have been fed, and we already washed up outside," Elijah said. He glanced over at Ruth. "I saw Josiah walking up the driveway."

Ruth choked on a mouthful of eggs. Her mother rushed over and slapped her back. A tingle raced up her spine as she imagined seeing him in a few moments. She couldn't. She wasn't ready.

"Is thee all right, child?" Mother bent over her, but Ruth kept her gaze on her plate and shook her head as she covered her mouth.

"No, my head hurts. I believe I'll go lie down." Ruth rushed from the kitchen as a sturdy knock sounded on the front door. She paused on the stairs where Josiah couldn't see her and leaned against the wall, her hand on her trembling stomach. How was it possible that he could do this to her without even seeing him?

Ruth rested her head back and tried to ignore the pain lashing from her temple across her forehead. *Lord, please help me be strong so I can do what is best for Josiah.*

❧

Unable to leave, Josiah accepted breakfast and offered to assist the Payne men with their day's work. They said Ruth had gone to her chamber with a headache. He hated to think of her in pain, and he wanted to be as close to her as possible. His brother had offered to take care of the store, and so he was free. As he and Elijah each swung an ax outside Ruth's window, he couldn't help glancing up, hoping for a glimpse of her. A couple of times he thought he saw someone move the curtain aside but then wondered if he'd imagined it.

"It's exciting to know we'll soon be incorporated as a real town," Elijah said as he tossed two pieces of split wood on the pile. "I think it fitting to name the town after General Nathanael Greene. If it wasn't for him and the Patriots fighting for our freedom years ago, we'd still be under the British Crown. And us Quakers would have forfeited our lives in refusing to bow to a king's unfair demands."

"True." Josiah raised the ax over his shoulder and swung it in an arc, his breath gushing at the effort. A hearty satisfaction raced through his gut as the blade sliced through the oak with a jolting thud. One piece of wood tilted, and the other toppled over the stump, where his ax now lay buried.

"I like the name Greensborough," Elijah said. "It has an official ring to it." He paused, staring off into the distance.

"Have they sold all the lots around the courthouse?" Josiah asked, wiping his brow on his arm, his sleeve rolled up at the elbow.

"Yes, that's why I know it won't be long now before we're an official town." Elijah grinned and set another chunk of wood on the tree stump. "Our little New Garden community will benefit from the new people a town would draw. Folks are calling it New Garden's Hope. Has thee thought about relocating the store within the town limits?" Elijah raised a dark eyebrow.

"We'll stay right where we are—and we won't be building a separate residence in town. I won't allow all these changes to cloud my judgment on foolhardy decisions. The house I've built for thy sister is solid and not too far away when she has need to visit."

Elijah's grin faltered, and his eyes flickered before he looked away, rubbing the back of his head.

Josiah paused, recognizing his friend's hesitation to voice what was on his mind. "What? Thee might as well say it. Does thee think me naive to harbor hope that Ruth will change her mind?"

"I'm no fool, Josiah Wall. I know thee hasn't been out here helping me finish loading the pumpkin wagon and chopping firewood for fun. Thee hopes to see my sister and speak to her."

"I won't deny it. I've been worried about her injury, and while I take thy family's word for her condition, I'd feel better if I could see her." Josiah shoved his hands on his hips, paced a few feet away, and came back. "I need to talk to her. Help me. Please?" He rubbed his face. "Tell me, is she avoiding me?"

"I don't know for certain, but perhaps." Elijah averted his gaze. "I'm sorry, my friend."

A cool breeze lifted around them. Leaves fell from the trees and blew across the yard. Josiah lifted his face to the welcoming caress, realizing it felt similar to the hot summer day when Ruth had waved a fan in front of him.

The sound of Elijah splitting more wood jarred him to the present. "I figured she might be. If I could get her to talk to me, I'm sure I could convince her to change her mind. We belong together. Everyone knows it. I can't understand why she'd think differently just because I postponed the wedding."

"Does thee really think thee can change her mind?" Elijah picked up the wood he'd sliced and tossed it on the growing pile.

"I do." Josiah nodded. "She only needs to know how much I love her. It's all a misunderstanding."

Elijah nodded as he tilted the ax on the stump then leaned on the handle. "Why not stay for supper? I know my sister, and she doesn't like hiding out in confined spaces. After being in her chamber all day, I daresay she'll want to emerge for supper tonight."

"Is thee sure? It could be uncomfortable to the family to have me stay for supper, especially after breakfast. I don't want to overstay my welcome." Josiah flashed a grin at his friend.

"Thee is my friend as well as Ruth's. I may invite whomever I please to supper. My parents feel the same way, I assure thee." Elijah stepped back and lifted his ax. "Now let's finish splitting this wood before we lose more time. I'm working up a mighty big appetite."

"Agreed." Josiah felt the skin on his neck prickle. He had the sensation they were being watched. He glanced up to see a slender hand holding aside the lace curtains. The nerves in his stomach danced in glee. He recognized Ruth's blue gown but couldn't see her face. Feeling bold, he lifted a hand and offered a reconciling smile.

The curtain jerked closed, and the figure disappeared, leaving a black hole in the thin space in the middle, much like his aching heart as more pain burrowed deeper and deeper.

# Chapter 4

Ruth's stomach grumbled as she finally left the sanctuary of her chamber. The smell of burning wood drifted to her senses from the living room, where her mother read a letter by the fire. The orange flames crackled in a gentle motion as a wave of heat warmed the atmosphere.

At the sound of Ruth's footsteps, Elizabeth Payne looked up and smiled. "How does thee feel? Get enough rest?"

"Yes." Ruth sat in a chair across from her mother and inhaled the scent of roast beef drifting from the kitchen. "Supper smells good."

"Naomi is finishing up the cooking so I can read the letter thy father brought home."

"Is it good news?" Ruth folded her hands in her lap, starved for conversation and company after lingering alone in her chamber all day with a headache.

"I think so." Her mother stacked the loose sheets of paper and folded them along the crease. "Cousin Dolley is coming for a visit."

Ruth leaned forward, excitement lifting her spirits. Even though Dolley was her father's age and his first cousin, she always told the best stories. She traveled all over the country and lived in Washington DC, where so much happened. It had been years since she'd last seen Dolley at Grandma's house in Virginia. Ruth wondered how much she'd changed.

"It appears that her husband, James, is stopping at the new town of Greensborough on his campaign trail." Mother shifted in her chair and, with a brilliant smile, reached out her hand. Ruth accepted her warm hand as her mother's eyes sparkled in the firelight. "Even though Cousin Dolley has chosen to leave the plain ways, we must welcome her with loving arms."

"I feel for her. She's endured so much ridicule for marrying outside the Quaker faith, but she's followed her heart. And her place is now by her husband's side," Ruth said, gazing into the fire as images of Josiah came to mind, the only man she could ever think of as her own husband.

"And just think how much influence she might have if James Madison is elected president. He'll make decisions regarding the laws that govern this great land. I can't help but think of our Dolley Madison as a modern-day Esther."

"Exactly! Why didn't I think of that?" Ruth squeezed her mother's hand. "Will they stay here?"

"Yes. Would thee mind sharing Naomi's chamber while they're here? I must make the same request of Elijah to share Caleb's room. Thy father and I will give James and Dolley the master chamber on the first floor. We must make room for their servants and traveling companions."

"Mother, I'm afraid we don't have enough space. They'll feel horribly cramped."

"My dear, we don't have any choice. There isn't an inn around here for miles. Tomorrow I'll write Dolley and ask her for the number of servants and guests who will be traveling with them."

"Since we never got around to trying out the gingerbread recipe, Naomi and I could make it for them." Ruth clasped her hands in front of her waist. "After all, they're part of the family, too. Dolley may want a copy for herself."

"I think that's a splendid idea." Mother folded the letter and tucked it in her pocket.

Footsteps sounded at the front door. Mother glanced at the foyer then back at Ruth. "Please, don't say anything about this to Josiah Wall," she whispered. "As a Federalist, his views differ from James Madison's, and I don't want any political arguments at the supper table."

"He's still here?" Ruth took a deep breath with her increasing pulse and tried to ignore the distress it caused her.

Her mother nodded as the door opened and men's voices carried on the cool air that instantly filled the room. Ruth shivered, but it had naught to do with the sudden draft and everything to do with the dark brown gaze that searched the room, landing on her like an owl that didn't miss a detail. Ruth broke from his luring gaze and pulled her shawl tight around her.

He started toward Ruth, but Mother's voice interrupted his charge. "Josiah Wall, I'm glad thee has decided to stay for supper."

"I thank thee for having me." He halted, awarding her mother with a handsome grin that began to thaw Ruth's insides. "I regret I must leave early. I've a meeting in town at eight o'clock."

Ruth's head swung up before she could check her behavior. At the motion he turned and caught her gaze. Warmth flickered in his eyes as his lips curled in a grin that threatened to fray her nerves. "I hope thee is feeling much better. I've been praying for thy recovery and looking forward to seeing thee."

"But thee is leaving early for a meeting?" she asked, wondering where he could be going.

"I've a meeting with the Federalists. We won't be holding so many meetings after the presidential election."

The temporary warmth inside her evaporated with her waning hopes. If it wasn't for this Federalist group that occupied Josiah's mind day and night, they might be married by now. A sharp pain sliced through her and dulled to a deep ache. He'd unknowingly given her confirmation in making her decision to break their engagement.

"Please excuse me." She stood. "I need to help Naomi in the kitchen." She stepped around him, but he grabbed her arm.

"Ruth, we need to talk. Please—"

She shrugged her arm away and met his gaze. "We've naught to say. Enjoy thy meeting. It's the path thee has chosen. I hope it gives thee all the love and support thee traded me for."

An eerie silence pierced the room, but Ruth didn't care. She needed to get away.

Her heart pounded in her chest, but her lungs wouldn't open and give her air. She strode from the room, leaving him to stare after her.

"Josiah, I'm sorry." Her mother's voice echoed over the threshold.

Elijah spoke, but Ruth couldn't make out his words as she hurried down the hall. Footsteps stormed after her.

"Ruth, wait! What does thee mean?" Josiah asked.

A hand landed on her shoulder and whirled her around. She would have collapsed if he hadn't held both her arms steady. She gasped and finally caught her breath. Her head began to throb where her injury was still sore, and she lifted her hand to the area.

Josiah followed her action and touched the spot on her head. "It's still swollen. Thee should be in bed. Let me help thee. . .please." His voice gentled as his eyes searched her face.

"I'm fine. I missed lunch is all. I'm hungry."

"Then the last thing thee should be doing is helping thy sister in the kitchen. Sit down and rest." He touched his hand to her back as if he intended to lead her back to the living room.

"Don't touch me!" Ruth shoved him away and took a ragged breath. It was his fault she had this aching concussion. If he hadn't been outside the window, she wouldn't have lost her concentration or her balance. The man had a way of making her lose all reason and purpose. Feeling weak, she stepped back and leaned against the wall.

"Leave me be. Thee has made thy decision, and now thee must live with it."

He lifted her chin and looked into her eyes. "I don't know what decision thee believes I've made, but allow me to say this. I love thee, Ruth Payne. I asked to postpone our wedding, not break our engagement. This separation. . .this misunderstanding is killing me. I want things to go back to the way they were."

"That's the problem, Josiah Wall. I don't want things to be the way they were."

☙❧

Still reeling from Ruth's cold rebuff, Josiah approached his friend's house and kicked a small stone with the toe of his boot. How could Ruth say that she didn't want things to be the way they were? Their relationship had been so perfect—practical—affectionate. The only thing that could have made it better would be marriage, to make it a permanent situation.

The cold air nipped his ears and face as he secured his horse to a tree. He rubbed his hands and blew on them. His heart throbbed in denial as he pondered Ruth's uncharacteristic behavior. Right now the last place he wanted to be was this Federalist meeting. He couldn't muster his usual enthusiasm for the cause, and the election was around the corner, in only a fortnight. Yet he'd promised, so he would put in an appearance and slip out as soon as possible. He was hardly in a position to advise others if his own life continued to crumble around him.

"Josiah, how did the day go at the Payne farm?" Andrew called from the front porch, where a lit lantern hung above his head. Their younger brother, Samuel, stood on a lower step beside him.

"Confusing," Josiah answered with a sigh. "I don't know what has gotten into Ruth lately. I was sure I could convince her to change her mind if I had a chance to talk to her." He paused, looking up at them. "Thanks for working in the store."

"It was my turn. Samuel came in and helped this afternoon." He grabbed their younger brother on the shoulder. "We had a steady flow, so the day's profits were good."

Josiah nodded. He hadn't even thought about the store profits. Consumed with Ruth, he hadn't been able to concentrate on anything else. Only the grace of God had reminded him about tonight's meeting. Even though supper had been awkward after his heated exchange with Ruth and the tension between them at dinner, Josiah hadn't wanted to leave with things unresolved.

On three occasions he'd felt his cheeks warming when he tried to engage her in conversation, as if Ruth's blazing looks seared his skin. He touched a cold palm to his jaw. He'd taken fist shots that hadn't pained him as much.

"Sarah Goodson stopped by the store to see thee. I think she was quite disappointed thee wasn't there," Samuel said. "If things don't work out with Ruth, I'm sure Sarah would be happy to take her place."

"No one could take Ruth's place—ever." If the hard edge in his tone didn't give them a hint to drop the subject, his lack of presence would. Josiah climbed the steps and pushed past his brothers. He wasn't ready to admit defeat, regardless of what his brothers thought.

Inside, dense lanterns lit the parlor of George Osbourne's home. As the Federalist leader of their local group, George was deeply committed to their cause, and no doubt disappointed in Josiah's lack of participation of late. George had a way of making a fellow feel guilty for not doing his share. Josiah agreed to attend tonight only as a favor to his best friend. It wasn't that he didn't support the Federalist movement, but right now he had more pressing matters draining him.

For the next hour, he would try to concentrate on political issues. As he approached, George looked up from his conversation with Nathan Hyatt. They stood in front of the roaring flames in the fireplace, their elbows on the mantel's edge.

"Look who finally decided to show up." George uncrossed his booted feet and stepped toward Josiah with a pleased grin. They shook hands. Josiah greeted Nathan with another handshake.

The moderately sized room contained about fifteen men, and a few more stood in the foyer, talking under the brass chandelier. Additional light shone from two candelabras. The dark paneled walls increased the need for light.

"Looks like there's a good turnout," Josiah said.

"Yep." George nodded, a dark lock of hair falling over his forehead. "The numbers keep growing the closer we get to election, even among the Quakers. Did thee hear the latest news?" He raised a dark brow.

"No, I spent all day at the Payne farm."

"Rumor has it James Madison is coming through here on his campaign trail back to DC and plans to make a visit to the new town of Greensborough," George said in a low voice.

"We aren't incorporated as a town yet," Nathan said.

"But we will be," George said. "It's only a matter of time now. Mr. Mendenhall already drew up the streets on a map, and the new lots have been sold. Construction on the courthouse will soon begin."

"They're even building a new jail—with a whipping post." Nathan shook his head as if he didn't believe it. "Can we Quakers prevent the whipping post?"

"There isn't much we can do about it. Sounds like the others are doing what they please. They view discipline differently than we do," Josiah said.

"And slavery, don't forget about that," Nathan said.

"Gentleman, back to the topic at hand," George interrupted. "The point I intend to make tonight is that we be ready to welcome James Madison when he arrives—the Federalist way."

# Chapter 5

Ruth wrapped her gray cloak around her as she sat between her mother and Naomi on the church bench. Men were lighting the fireplaces around the large sanctuary, eager to warm the chilly air. On the drive to New Garden Friends Meeting, white dew had layered the grass and bare tree branches lining the dirt road.

She loved attending New Garden every Sunday morning. It gave her a chance to see old school friends and distant family, and to worship in fellowship in the loving grace of God. This morning was the first time she'd ever felt apprehensive at the idea of attending meeting. Josiah would be here with his mother and brothers. Ruth thought highly of Pearl Wall and had looked forward to being her daughter-in-law. She prayed things wouldn't be awkward between them.

"Thee has hardly spoken all morning. Is thee all right?" Her mother whispered in her ear, her warm breath carrying in the frigid air like white smoke.

Ruth nodded, rubbing her gloved hands together to heat her fingers. She longed to go over and stand by the fire. But she remained on the hard bench, seated with the women, divided by a partition from the men, who sat on the other side of the room.

Families continued to arrive in a steady flow, filling up the benches and greeting each other with nods and smiles. Most of the women were garbed in plain dresses of black, gray, brown, or dark blue. Their bonnets covered their heads and shielded their expressions in shadow. The men wore brown or black pants, white shirts, black jackets, and the familiar round-brimmed hats.

Someone touched Ruth's shoulder. She turned. Pearl Wall smiled, her green eyes shining with warmth as she perched on the seat behind Ruth and swept a strand of silver hair beneath her white bonnet. No animosity or haughty judgment lingered in her demeanor.

"Good morning, Friend Ruth Payne. How has thee been lately? Josiah told me of the fall thee took. I worried about thee, but I knew thee would be in good hands with Dr. Edwards."

"I'm much better. I had a slight concussion, but the swelling is gone. And thee?" Ruth forced her gaze to meet Pearl's eyes, so she wouldn't be tempted to look around the sanctuary for Josiah.

"Same as usual. Although I'm looking forward to purchasing a few of thy father's pumpkins to bake some pies. It's Josiah and Samuel's favorite."

"What's my favorite?" Samuel paused in the aisle, his mischievous brown eyes full of youth and wit.

"Pumpkin pie," Ruth answered, grateful he wasn't Josiah.

"Not me, mine is cherry," Andrew said, walking up behind Samuel.

Ruth stiffened. Where was Josiah? He couldn't be far behind them. She allowed her gaze to drift to Andrew's tall frame.

"Good morning, Ruth Payne." Josiah walked up and stood beside Andrew. While they were of equal height, Josiah was thinner and his shoulders not quite as broad, since he spent more time in the store and Andrew worked hard at farming out in the fields. Had Josiah lost a bit of weight in the last few days? His eyes were bloodshot, and faint circles framed his dark brown eyes. She wished they were outside where the light was more telling.

"Good morning, Josiah." She clenched her teeth to keep from blurting out questions of concern. Their gazes crossed. His eyes were searching and penetrating, aching and soaking up every minute detail about him.

"The pastor is going up front. We'd better get seated," Andrew said, nodding toward the men's side. He and Samuel walked away, while Josiah lingered and stepped closer.

"Thee looks beautiful, Ruth." Josiah lowered his voice. Sadness lingered in his tone, piercing her heart like a double-edged sword. Doubt cast a spell in her mind, weaving a web of confusion as he strode away.

Pastor Gray stood and, with his hands folded, waited until all conversation faded. "Let's bow our heads to pray and let the Lord lead us."

Throughout their fellowship meeting, Ruth struggled to concentrate on her relationship with God. Raw pain sank her spirit deeper into despair. The last thing she'd wanted to do was hurt Josiah. If he truly loved her, why did he have such a hard time marrying her? Josiah was a decisive man who never acted on impulse. He planned every action. He would have given careful consideration to his decision to postpone their wedding a second time. Knowing this made his paltry excuses harder to bear.

Soon the meeting ended, and all the Friends filed out of church. Ruth kept her head down, avoiding eye contact. She didn't feel like engaging in pleasantries.

"Ruth Payne!" A man called her name, but she didn't recognize his voice. She took a deep breath, forced a smile, and spun around. Surprise lifted her mood as she watched Solomon Mendenhall take long strides toward her. He'd been away at the University of Chapel Hill for two years.

"I thank thee for giving me a moment," he said. He glanced at the members of her family who'd paused with her and nodded to each one in greeting. "A pleasure to see thee again, Matthew Payne, Elizabeth Payne, and Friends Naomi, Caleb, and Elijah."

"Welcome home." Ruth's father extended his hand with a wide smile, and Solomon shook it. "Is thee home for good, or is this only a short visit?"

"I'm home for good this time. I plan to set up an attorney's office in the new town of Greensborough." His bright blue eyes drifted to Ruth. "In fact, I wanted to ask if I may stop by for a visit sometime."

If Solomon had been looking at her mother and father when he asked the question, perhaps it wouldn't have felt so personal. But since he continued to stare at her as if he wanted her permission, Ruth's neck grew warm, and she felt her face flush.

"Thee is always welcome at the Payne home," Mother's voice said behind Ruth, rescuing her, and her mother laid gentle hands on her shoulders.

"We're going home to a big Sunday meal. Why don't thee invite thy family over?

We'd enjoy thy company," Father said.

"My parents and sister have already accepted an invitation to my uncle's house. I would be the only one free to accept thy offer."

"Then come on over. I'd like to hear the news from Chapel Hill. Elijah is intent on taking over the farm, but Caleb has a great interest in learning. I'd like to hear thy thoughts on the university there," Father said.

"I'd be delighted to help in any way I can," Solomon said. "I'll walk with thee to the buggy then grab my horse. I rode to meeting on horseback this morn."

"Thee brought thy stallion?" Ruth asked.

"Indeed. I thought he could use the exercise." He walked beside Ruth as they followed her parents. "Would thee like to see him?"

"Perhaps when we return home."

A motion caught her attention. She glanced to the right. Josiah paused before climbing aboard the buggy with his mother and brothers. He stared, his rigid back went slack, and he turned, but not before she witnessed the raw hurt in his dark brown eyes.

Guilt ripped through her. She knew he'd misinterpreted her walk with Solomon. She had no interest in anyone else, but would it do any good to try to convince him of it, now that their engagement was no more? Maybe it was better this way. She looked down at the grass and blinked back scorching tears.

☙

Josiah's gut clenched as Ruth walked by with Solomon Mendenhall, their arms a mere inch apart. When her gaze paused in Josiah's direction, her lips fell into a frown, and a tiny dimple formed on her chin. She crossed her arms over her middle and rubbed them—a sign of discomfort.

His head swam in a jealous rage as anger ripped through his battling chest. Torn by the desire to march over and interrupt them and the fear of upsetting Ruth, Josiah held back. If he caused a scene, winning her forgiveness might take even longer.

He stepped forward but pivoted on his foot, turning around in a circle. What should he do? He couldn't just stand by and watch Solomon take his place—especially now, when Ruth felt unloved.

At thirteen Solomon had started hanging around Ruth, teasing her, and walking her home from school. It was the first alarm Josiah had ever felt at the prospect of losing her to someone else. He'd always assumed they'd grow up and marry, until Solomon came along and shook up his confidence—then and now.

How could he have gotten so comfortable and sure of himself that he'd taken their relationship for granted? Wasn't Solomon supposed to be at that fancy law school in Chapel Hill? Perhaps Josiah could wait it out until the fellow returned to school and was no longer a threat. He didn't need a smooth-talking lady's man flattering Ruth.

"Does thee plan to stand there and gawk after Ruth Payne long after she's gone?" Samuel asked.

"I wonder when Solomon Mendenhall came back and how long he'll be here." Josiah rubbed his chin and shifted his weight from one foot to the other.

"Sarah Goodson was looking for thee after the meeting, but thee had already left the sanctuary." Samuel winked, a teasing expression on his face as he raised an eyebrow.

Josiah sighed in frustration and turned to walk away. He didn't need his brother's taunts right now.

"I thought thee might like to know—" Samuel's words chased him. "I heard Sarah telling Mother that Solomon is home for good. He graduated and plans to set up a law office in the new town of Greensborough."

"Is thee sure?" Josiah paused in midstride and closed his eyes.

"Yes." Samuel cleared his throat. "What will thee do?"

"I'm not sure." Josiah shook his head, glad his hat sheltered his eyes. He blinked several times, willing the sting away as he turned to face his brother. "Right now I'm going for a walk. Tell Mother I'll be home later."

Josiah didn't wait for a response. He set out with the cool breeze and kicked at the brown leaves tumbling onto his path. With no destination in mind, he let his feet carry him to the house he'd built for their marriage. He stood outside and surveyed the white two-story structure, a dream he'd envisioned for almost a year.

While everything on the outside looked finished, Josiah knew the rooms on the inside were bare and in need of furniture. He'd wanted everything to be perfect when he carried Ruth over the threshold. She'd worked so hard all her life. This was one gift he wanted to give her—without her having to work for it.

He slipped his hands inside his pockets and climbed the three steps to the wraparound front porch. He pulled out a key, inserted it into the lock, and turned the knob. The bolt slid and clicked into place.

The door opened on the newly oiled hinges without a sound. He stepped inside and sniffed the fresh scent of pinewood flooring. The empty foyer with the white-painted walls greeted him like a barren castle. His satisfaction of accomplishment vanished in the realization that it meant nothing without Ruth.

If she didn't come back to her senses and renew their engagement, he couldn't live here. The dream would be incomplete—a reflection of his failure—a constant reminder.

His booted heels clicking against the floor was the only sound as he strolled into the living room then the dining room. Perhaps if he filled this house with the furniture they'd talked about making, and brought her back to see their dream had become reality, she'd realize how much he loved her, and she'd understand.

Josiah shrugged out of his black jacket and laid it on a counter in the kitchen. He'd start on the dining room furniture today. If he worked out back in the shade, no one would see him laboring on the Sabbath.

Hadn't the Lord used the analogy of going after a lost animal even on the Sabbath if it strayed? How could he do any less? His love had strayed under some misguided perception. All he needed to do was prove he still loved her and lure her back. What better way to do that than show an act of faith—provide a finished home, fully furnished, and ready for a new family—theirs?

# Chapter 6

The sound of an entourage of carriages and the clip-clopping of horses traveled up the drive. A flutter of excitement spiraled through Ruth as she placed the last gingerbread cookie on a plate piled high for their guests.

"They're here!" Caleb called from the living room.

"I hardly can recall what Cousin Dolley even looks like," Naomi said as she bobbed up on her tiptoes and leaned out the kitchen window in anticipation.

"I daresay," Mother said, straightening her cap and adjusting her collar, "she won't recognize any of my children. Everyone is so grown up." She gestured to Ruth and Naomi. "Come, let's meet our cousins."

Ruth untied her apron, hung it on a peg, and followed them outside, where they joined her father and brothers. A black coach hitched to six proud horses, along with a brown buggy, rolled to a stop. Several horsemen surrounded the carriages like guardsmen.

"Whoa!" The coach driver pulled the reins and set the brake. The door opened and out stepped James Madison, Dolley's husband. His hair, which hung straight down his neck, was whiter than Ruth remembered. Although she knew him to be considerably older than Dolley, she hadn't expected him to have aged so much. Even from a distance of ten feet, James wore wrinkles around his eyes and mouth when he smiled. He turned to assist his wife.

A gloved hand slipped into his, and Dolley stepped out wearing a bright smile, a silver turban headpiece, and a royal blue cloak. She rushed to Ruth's father, gripped his hands, and kissed his cheek.

"Dear cousin, it's so wonderful to see you again, and in such good health, I see," Dolley said. Ruth smiled as her father's face and neck darkened to match his nose, reddened by the biting cold.

"And thee, Dolley Madison." Father nodded, and his eyes lifted to her husband, who stood tall behind her. Dolley moved on to Mother while the two men greeted each other with a handshake.

She threw her arms around Mother, tears warming her dark eyes. Though Dolley and Father were first cousins by blood, it was Mother she wrote and confided to in her monthly letters.

"Elizabeth Payne, it has been too long." She squeezed Mother's hands and sighed. "Oh, we've much catching up to do."

"Indeed." Mother's white cap bobbed with her nod. "But first let's get thee into the house where it's warm. I know thee must be tired from traveling. Elijah and Caleb will see to the servants and thy luggage."

"But first let me greet them." Dolley clapped her hands once as she made her way down the line greeting Elijah, Caleb, Naomi, and then Ruth. She grabbed Ruth's hands in hers. "My, how you've grown. You were just a little girl the last time I saw you." She stepped back and looked Ruth up and down. "Now you're a young woman about to be married."

Ruth looked down at her feet, unable to hide the despondency that filled her. They hadn't had time to write Dolley with the news of her broken engagement. Now she wished they had.

"Ruth, what is it?" A very perceptive Dolley lifted her chin.

Ruth met Dolley's deep brown eyes, knowing she'd find wisdom and compassion, but now wasn't the time to unload her burdens. "We'll talk more once thee is settled in," she said.

"She's not marrying Josiah anymore," Caleb said. "But Solomon Mendenhall came to call the other day."

"Caleb, hush!" Ruth glared at her brother. "Dolley, I made some gingerbread cookies from an old family recipe I found in the attic. I'm sure they'll taste great with a warm cup of coffee."

James stepped beside Dolley and bowed to Ruth. "Good to see you again, young lady." He winked at Dolley. "You've grown into a stunning beauty."

Ruth's cheeks grew warm in spite of the freezing weather. A beauty she was not, nor did Quakers bow and curtsy to others, so she wasn't sure how to respond. She didn't want to offend him, so she glanced at Dolley for help.

Dolley grinned and looped her arm through her husband's. "I do believe some warm coffee and fresh gingerbread cookies would suffice."

The boys helped the servants unload the luggage while the rest of them strolled into the house. Dolley unbuttoned her cloak and slid it off, revealing a long-sleeved and high-waisted, silver muslin gown with royal blue floral prints. Next she pulled off her turban cap. Her brown hair was crowned in a bun, loose curls lining her oval face. She looked quite elegant but simple, compared to some fancy women Ruth had witnessed in Greensborough.

"Matthew, I'll need to practice my speech tonight, right after dinner. I hope you don't mind," James said, settling in a chair near the hearth.

Ruth took Dolley's cloak and hat, while Mother directed her to a wingback chair by the fire, across from her husband.

"Of course not. Let us know if there's anything we can help thee with," Father said.

"You're already doing plenty. You've opened your home and offered to feed us. We couldn't ask for more," Dolley said.

"I believe I remembered to make it the way thee likes it." Mother handed Dolley a steaming cup.

"Thank you." She smiled, accepting the brew. Dolley closed her eyes, sniffed, and then sipped.

"And so tomorrow is the big celebration? New Garden will finally have its very own town—Greensborough." James rubbed his hands together over the fire. "I'm honored to be speaking to the fine, upstanding citizens here. It has been a long campaign. I never imagined I'd run for president."

"Friend James, I feel I ought to at least warn thee. Not all Greensborough citizens feel the same way as we do, regarding our political allegiance," Father said.

Realizing the discussion would now turn to boring politics, Ruth stood and offered Dolley a plate of cookies. Dolley took one, and Ruth moved to James, grateful to have something to do.

"That's to be expected, Matthew. I find pockets of resistance all over my travels around the country." James bit into his cookie.

"Yes but we've our very own Federalist movement in favor of Charles Pinckney." Matthew leaned against the mantel and crossed his booted feet. "Ruth's ex-fiancé is one of the local leaders."

Ruth's hand shook as she laid the plate on the table. She'd known Josiah was part of a political group, but he never liked to talk about it since he knew how she hated politics. Now she wished she'd paid closer attention. The reminder that Josiah's loyalties went against her own family brought a fresh sting of betrayal to her scarred heart.

"Oh Ruth, I hope that isn't why you broke your engagement." Dolley lowered her coffee and sought Ruth's gaze. All eyes turned toward her, some questioning, others in sympathy.

What could she say? That she hadn't believed Josiah's political aspirations were that important? That she'd been a fool? That she was still a fool?

She opened her mouth to respond, but words of denial clogged her throat. Crossing her arms and rubbing them, Ruth felt her knees weaken. What had Josiah been planning all those times he'd left early to attend a meeting? No doubt plotting a way for her cousin to lose the presidential race. Everyone in her family knew it, but they'd said naught about it—willing to accept Josiah into their humble family—regardless of where his political loyalties lay.

Her throat stung. She swallowed with difficulty. "Please—" Ruth cleared her throat in an attempt to speak above a whisper. "Excuse me." Tears blinded her as she rushed into the foyer and up the stairs. She needed privacy. She needed to disappear.

❧

Josiah stood in the crowd beside his brothers and George, listening to Isaac Mendenhall, the new mayor of Greensborough. He hovered in his black overcoat, adjusting his top hat. If only it covered his exposed ears, perhaps his head wouldn't feel so numb.

White ribbon stretched between two trees where the new courthouse would be erected. The speakers stood on a wooden platform built for the occasion. George nudged Josiah's arm and tilted his head toward the front.

Mayor Mendenhall waved to a white-headed man, motioning him forward. He introduced him as James Madison, the 1808 presidential candidate, in their midst.

George moved with smooth caution, careful to blend in with the crowd. Josiah followed.

James Madison rose from his chair and shook Isaac's hand. He turned to address the crowd. George and Josiah slipped into the front row.

"Repeal the Embargo Act!" George called.

"The Embargo Act hurts American businesses and will cause unwanted war with Britain!" Josiah yelled above the startled and grumbling voices around them.

"No embargo!" Federalist men chanted, strategically scattered throughout the crowd, so they couldn't be assembled easily and silenced. The chants grew louder and more succinct.

James Madison smiled and raised his hands, motioning people to calm. When they didn't cease, a gun exploded. A man climbed the wooden steps to the platform with a smoking pistol in his hand. He gazed at the crowd.

The chants faded as people murmured and whispered among themselves. Silently the man stepped aside, allowing Mayor Mendenhall to face the crowd.

"I'm ashamed of you all," the mayor said. "Regardless of our political differences, we've always been a community that welcomed our visitors. This isn't a political rally. We're here to celebrate the incorporation of our new town as Greensborough. James and Dolley Madison are here visiting family. They agreed to speak today to share in this momentous occasion with us. Some of you may not know this, but Dolley was born here. Is this how you will treat her?"

Heads bowed, and smiles faded into frowns. Conversation buzzed again as people looked at each other, and several glared at George and Josiah.

Feeling properly reprimanded, Josiah cleared his throat. "We meant no disrespect, only to exercise our rights as a democracy. How else will James Madison know our concerns if he wins? We may never get another chance to meet him again."

The mayor opened his mouth to respond but paused when James Madison lifted his hand. "I would answer, please." He met Josiah's gaze. "You're right. We're blessed to operate under a democracy, and I'll do my best to honor the integrity of it. I'll always listen to the people, but we must recognize we'll have a difference of opinions, and the majority will rule."

Several people clapped. A baby began crying from the back. Josiah could feel his toes going numb from the cold in spite of his black boots.

"Therefore if the majority elects me, I've a responsibility to them in carrying out the promises I pledged during my campaign—to support the Embargo Act that President Thomas Jefferson put into action a year ago, so we can ensure peace."

"It's causing conflict with Britain, not peace!" George blurted out. A series of conversations erupted all at once. In the midst of the chaos, a shiver passed through Josiah that had naught to do with the biting temperature. With a feeling of foreboding, he glanced around, tuning out the rising voices. A pair of solid-brown eyes glared at Josiah beneath a crisp, white bonnet.

*Ruth.*

His heart skidded to a halt, momentarily stealing his breath. Politics forgotten, Josiah slipped around George, determined to close the distance between himself and Ruth.

Her lips thinned in obvious anger. How long would she stay angry with him? He'd never known Ruth to be a grudge holder. This wasn't like her. The image of Solomon Mendenhall escorting her from church on Sunday came to mind. Could Solomon be the reason Ruth continued to find fault with him?

Josiah braced himself to confront her. He needed to know the truth behind her behavior these last few weeks. Until he understood what motivated her, he had no idea how to defend himself and convince her to think differently.

Ruth clutched her cloak at the neck and whirled in an attempt to disappear in the crowd. He edged closer, maneuvering between people, careful to keep Ruth within sight. He wasn't about to let her go so easily—at least not without speaking to her.

She slipped by a burly man and a woman carrying a child. Another man stepped in Josiah's way, paying him no heed. Josiah pressed on around him, determined to keep Ruth in sight. Where was she going? Surely she wouldn't leave her family here and try to walk home by herself. The distance was several miles.

Josiah increased his pace. He would run if he had to and not care who witnessed his pathetic plight. Reconciling with Ruth was all that mattered.

She broke free of the crowd, lifted the hem of her dress, and ran toward a black carriage waiting by a weeping willow tree. Josiah pursued her, pumping his arms and legs.

"Ruth!" Josiah grabbed her elbow in an effort to slow her. "Please—I only want to talk."

"How could thee do it?" She turned to face him, her high-pitched voice and gasping breath surprising him. "How?" she demanded.

"How could I do what?" Josiah blinked, no longer cold. His blood flowed through him like hot lightning. "Thee will not even speak to me, so how in the world could I have done something new to upset thee?"

"Thee humiliated our family in front of everyone. Dolley and James Madison are our cousins. They're staying with us, and we're glad to have them." She looked back at the crowd. "Although now I'm not so sure they're glad to be here."

Remorse shot through Josiah as his skin crawled with prickles. Nausea swirled in the top of his stomach. "I'm sorry, Ruth. I didn't know."

"Josiah, I've never been more disappointed in thee than I am right now." She turned and left him standing in the cold wind, haunted by her words, and wrestling with self-loathing.

# Chapter 7

Ruth hurried to the carriage, her heart pumping. She glanced back to see if Josiah followed. He stood where she'd left him, scratching his forehead.

If she waited in the carriage, he could still find her, but she didn't want to talk. Right now she was too angry and worried she would say something she'd later regret.

Her gaze landed on a weeping willow behind the carriage. She slipped under its limbs, which hung like swaying vines, wrapping her in its cocoon. Ruth settled herself on the opposite side of the tree trunk, out of sight. She crossed her arms, sliding her hands under them to warm them against her body.

"Ruth?" Josiah opened the carriage door then closed it. "Where is thee?"

She closed her eyes and leaned against the hard bark. At least her bonnet provided some protection and warmth.

"Ruth, please don't do this. I didn't mean to embarrass thee. Please—forgive me for everything."

She clenched her teeth. She could feel the confused tension mounting inside him. He sighed in a deep breath.

"I know thee is listening, so this may be the only chance I get to say this." Josiah's voice filled the air, each word gnawing at the defenses of her heart. "If I'd known how thee would react the second time I postponed our marriage, I promise thee, I'd have never done it." His voice cracked. He cleared this throat. "It wasn't worth this. Naught is worth losing thee." The timbre of his tone lowered.

Warm tears stung her eyes and slipped beneath her lids. She dared not sniffle aloud as her throat constricted. Should she believe him? Again?

*Oh God, please help me. I don't know what to do.*

"Even if thee never accepts me as thy husband, I pray thee will forgive me," Josiah continued. "And know that no matter what thee decides, I'll always love thee, Ruth Payne."

Footsteps faded. Ruth took a deep breath, now free to weep. How could Josiah love her if he was afraid to wed her? Afraid to commit his entire life to her? The man was a walking contradiction. He'd always been so sure of himself and his goals. How could she be the only thing in his life where he wavered? It didn't make sense.

"Lord, please show me what to do. I forgive him, but I don't know if I can trust him again," she whispered.

Ruth prayed until her heavy eyes closed, and she drifted to sleep. A while later someone called her name.

"Ruth?" It was Elijah's voice. "Mother and Father are worried."

"No one has seen her." Caleb ran up, breathing hard.

"I'm here." She swallowed, trying to rouse herself. "I fell asleep."

Elijah and Caleb stumbled through the weeping willow branches, their eyes wide with surprise and concern.

"Why is thee here?" Caleb raised a brown eyebrow and twisted his lips.

"Hiding," Ruth said, scrambling to her knees.

Elijah strode over and helped her up. "From Josiah, no doubt." He shook his head as they ducked to leave the cover of the tree. "He apologized to the whole family, including Dolley and James. I believe he even mentioned that thee was angry at him."

"Embarrassed and angry. Lately I don't understand him, Elijah."

"Yes thee does. He believes with all his heart that the Embargo Act will cause another senseless war. If that happens, lives will be lost over a simple disagreement. At least his heart's in the right place." Elijah looked down at her as they walked toward the two waiting carriages. "Whatever thee must think of him now, Josiah is still a man of his convictions, and I believe he still loves thee."

"Would thee keep postponing marriage to a woman thee loves, or would thee be inclined to hasten it?" Ruth's glance willed him to help her understand the mind of a man.

"I don't know." He shrugged. "I do know that I'd want to be in a position to properly take care of her and a family."

"Josiah has a whole house with plenty of rooms for our children. That's more than many other couples have starting out," she said as they walked.

"True, but every room in that house is empty. He wanted to give thee a furnished house. I can understand that, so does Mother and Father."

"Did it ever occur to anyone that I'd have enjoyed helping him furnish the house? He doesn't have to make every single piece as a wedding gift. I feel like I'm being left out of everything. Dolley ordered all the furniture in her house."

"Indeed I did." Dolley leaned out the carriage window with a bright smile and twinkling brown eyes. "But neither of my husbands had the desire to determine the furnishings of our home. Your young man sounds like a very special gentleman. Come, Ruth." She slid over and patted the seat. "Join me on the ride home. I've been married twice now. Perhaps I can give you some insight."

Elijah opened the door and helped her inside.

"I'm so glad they found thee. I was beginning to get a little worried. It isn't like thee to go wondering off," Naomi said, sitting across from them.

Dolley slipped an arm around Ruth's shoulders like a mother, comforting her. "I imagine you had a lot to think and pray about."

"Does thee still pray, Dolley?" Naomi asked with wide, innocent eyes.

"Naomi!" Ruth admonished her sister with a stern look.

"It's all right." Dolley gave Ruth's shoulder one more squeeze and released her. "Yes, prayer will always be important in my life. I prayed a lot about my decision to marry a man outside the Quaker faith, and I believe this is how God wants to use me. Just because I've been dismissed by the Quaker church and I no longer keep the plain ways, doesn't mean I don't believe."

Elijah returned. "Now that Caleb is settled in the other carriage, there isn't enough room for me. May I ride with thee, ladies?"

"Of course," Naomi patted the seat beside her. "We've plenty of room."

Ruth tucked Dolley's words away in her heart and pondered them on the way home. Could it be that, like Dolley's faith, Josiah still loved her even though he'd acted differently than she expected?

❧

Josiah sat by the living room fire, contemplating his choices. After his encounter with Ruth, he'd gone to the house, worked on more furniture, and prayed. Usually prayer made him feel better, but tonight restlessness still stirred in his heart.

His mother glanced at him as she took up her sewing and settled in her favorite rocking chair across from him. "Thee has that same brooding look thy father had before he left."

Josiah closed his eyes and rubbed his face, dreading the promises she would now expect from him. Their father's sudden departure brought many burdens and a deep void, but the one thing they could never escape was her fear that one of them would disappear one day as he had. She needed constant reassurance.

"Mother, Josiah has Ruth on his mind and naught else." Andrew stirred the fire and added another log. The new bark crackled in the heat. He sat on the couch beside Josiah. "I spoke to Mayor Mendenhall today. He said they might have a place for me on the new town council, but I'd have to limit my involvement in the Federalist Party, so I don't give the perception of bias."

"Of course they're going to say that." Josiah sat back and gave his elder brother a level stare. "It's their way of controlling thee. While thee can still vote the way thee wants, their goal is to prevent thee from persuading other men to the Federalist side."

"And that would have some credit with me, if the campaigns were not over and the votes cast. In a few months, we'll know the results, and we'll have to make peace with whatever is done." Andrew shook his head as if he felt sorrowful. "Thee must learn to let things go, Josiah. What is done is done."

"Thee knows thy brother, Andrew." Mother pulled her needle through the fabric she held and tugged until satisfied it was secure. "He has a tenacious will of iron."

"And it's the very thing I'm worried might destroy him." Andrew crossed his booted ankle over his knee. "Josiah has succeeded so much that he doesn't understand failure. There comes a time when a man must give up and move on."

An image of Ruth as she ran to escape him came to mind. A gaping hole ached within him. He rubbed his chin. "Thee is no longer talking about politics, but Ruth Payne."

"Thee has taken to obsessing over her, Josiah. I'm worried. Thee isn't thyself lately."

"If this is about the store, I'm sorry I haven't been there much. I'll do better. I promise."

"No." Andrew leaned forward with his elbows on his knees, linking his fingers in the middle. "This isn't about the store. It's about the weight thee has lost. The circles under thy eyes. The other things thee has given up. Brother, thee may be present with us in body, but thy mind and spirit are far from us."

"I'm not giving up on Ruth." Josiah stood and paced around the room. "This is all a misunderstanding. I know her. She still loves me. I could tell by the way she looked at me today."

"She ran from thee!" Andrew's voice exploded. "Has thee gone daft?"

"Thee doesn't understand. Thee has never been in love like this before. Without Ruth, I'm naught. . ." Josiah couldn't go on. Frustration raced through him until his nerves itched to pound something. Instead, he forced his legs to move across the carpet, his boots clicking against the wood floor at the edge of the room.

"No, but I've been in love," Mother said, her voice calm. She lowered her sewing and stared up at him with a concerned expression. "And I've lost the one I dearly loved. It makes one feel like dying inside. The pain is so raw and fierce that I can hardly find the words to describe it. But son, I know what thee is feeling, and I want to remind thee that we are naught without God. Ruth is not thy God. Don't allow thy love for her to place her where she doesn't belong."

His heart constricted with conviction as a pain shot through him. She was right. That's why he hadn't felt the peace he'd sought after prayer earlier today.

*God, please forgive me.*

"When thee feels ready, go to Ruth and find some way to show her what *she* means to thee. Separate her from thy goals. Right now I suspect she feels like naught more than another goal that thee has set."

"Mother, thee is encouraging him to keep chasing after Ruth?" Andrew leaned toward her. "He must accept her decision and move on."

"He needs to know that he's tried everything before he gives up. He'll never be content if he doesn't." She turned to Josiah. "A woman senses another woman in love, and I've seen the way she looks at thee. Don't give up, son. Now is not the time. Make peace with God, and the rest of thy life will fall in place."

With hope rekindled in his heart, Josiah kissed her cheek, warmed by the heat of the fire. The room glowed in a way it hadn't before. "Thank thee. I'll repent and pray on my way to Ruth's house."

# Chapter 8

Josiah needed time to think and pray as he walked to Ruth's house. When he reached the long drive leading up to the Payne house, he felt more peaceful than he had in a long time.

The late afternoon sun slanted in the sky, casting an orange halo over the land. He kept his hands buried in the pockets of his long overcoat. His warm breath blew smoke in the air each time he breathed.

The aroma of meat roasting and of gingerbread lifted the air. He ignored his rumbling stomach and watering mouth. No doubt they were preparing a nice dinner with their guests.

Guilt ripped through him at the reminder of what he'd done that morning. While the Payne family had accepted his apology, they hadn't invited him to the house as usual. Matthew Payne had turned from him as if dismissing him from their conversation.

Josiah wanted to knock on the front door as he'd done countless times before, but he wasn't sure he'd be welcome. Instead he walked around the corner and leaned against the side of the house. He wondered if anyone had seen his approach through the front window. The barn and stables were on the other side of the house. Here he had a perfect view of the well, where most of the women would go. It would be his best chance of catching Ruth. He'd wait here until nightfall if necessary.

After a while his legs grew weary. Josiah crouched into a sitting position and bent his knees. Soon the smell of pumpkin pie teased his nose. How many desserts would they make? At some point they would need water. He folded his arms around his knees and rested his chin on them.

He closed his eyes and listened to the birds chirping. The leaves rustled in the slight breeze, and his hands began to freeze. He rubbed warmth back into his fingers. The back door squeaked open and Josiah paused.

Someone stepped out onto the wooden steps. A woman laughed as a door closed on female voices. Josiah rose to his feet, careful not to give away his presence. A woman wearing a brown cloak and white bonnet descended the steps, carrying an empty bucket. Since he couldn't see her face, he could only assume it was Ruth or Naomi. He studied her walk and the way she carried herself. She walked with Ruth's confidence. Waiting until she was a good distance from the house and couldn't easily run back inside to escape him, Josiah followed.

He took a deep breath. "Ruth?"

She gasped, clutched her hand over her chest, and whirled. "Josiah, thee frightened me!"

"I'm sorry. I didn't mean to." He slipped his hands in his coat pockets, watching her pale face turn a rosy glow.

"What is thee doing out here?" Her tone changed to slight irritation as her dark eyes surveyed him.

"I wanted to talk to thee."

"Why not come into the house like normal folk, rather than hovering out here in the cold?"

"I considered it, but would thee have spoken to me?" He raised an eyebrow, daring her to deny it.

Her gaze dropped from his, and she turned toward the well. "I won't lie. Probably not."

He kept pace beside her and tried not to let her answer bother him. While it wasn't a surprise, the confirmation of what he already knew made the sting dig deeper.

She set the bucket on the stone well and cranked the handle, lowering the roped bucket, avoiding his gaze. "Now that I'm here, what does thee want?"

Josiah longed to reach out and pull her to him or tilt her face so he could see her better, but he dared not. Although he'd known Ruth all his life, this was a side of her he'd never seen. Where was the Ruth he'd come to love so much? The woman he'd always been able to persuade and tease back into his arms? A dull ache seized him, and he clenched his coat pockets to keep his hands to himself.

"I want thy forgiveness. . .please." The words nearly choked him, but he managed to say them anyway.

"I forgive thee." She raised the filled bucket to the surface without looking at him.

"Ruth, if thee truly forgives me then at least give me the courtesy of looking at me."

For a moment she said naught, only poured the water into the bucket she'd brought with her. Setting it aside, Ruth turned. Strands of sandy-brown hair fell across her forehead. He didn't expect her eyes to be so red and swollen. Dark circles matched her brown irises. His gut twisted.

"Josiah Wall, I forgive thee for everything. I forgive thee for postponing our wedding and for embarrassing my family at the town's celebration today." She sighed but held his gaze as moisture gathered in her eyes. "I could never stay mad at thee for long. At least that's one thing that hasn't changed."

Relief washed through him, and the burden upon his shoulders lifted with his next breath. "Thank thee. Does this mean we can resume our engagement?"

She shook her head, biting her lower lip. "I've given thee my forgiveness. That doesn't mean I'm willing to give thee my heart again."

Pain sliced through his chest as he stared at her. He gulped, clinging to the one positive thought enticing him to hope. She'd forgiven him. Wasn't that a good sign? A new beginning?

"Ruth, be honest with me. Is it Solomon Mendenhall? I saw him escort thee from church the other day."

She blinked in obvious surprise. "No, he only walked me to the carriage and came home to eat lunch with us at Father's invitation. He hasn't been back."

Josiah believed her. At least he didn't have to battle competition on top of everything else. There was only one thing that could be holding her back—she no longer trusted him. How could he win her trust back if she refused to let him? If only he hadn't been so dimwitted in trying to make their marriage perfect before there was ever a marriage, he wouldn't have hurt her so deeply, and their relationship wouldn't be at risk right now.

"Please give me one more chance."

"I've forgiven thee, Josiah. That's all I'm prepared to do at the moment. Now please excuse me before the others come find me. We're having a late Thanksgiving meal with Dolley and James Madison, before they leave in a few days."

"May I call on thee when they leave?"

"No." She shook her head. "I don't think that would be a good idea." Ruth shoved past him, spilling water on his arm in her haste.

❧

Josiah reached up to stock the top store shelf with more chicken feed. The door bell rang, announcing the arrival of another customer.

"Good morning!" He called over his shoulder.

"Josiah, it's me." Andrew strode toward him. "I heard some news, and I'm not sure how thee will take it."

At his brother's serious tone, Josiah paused and turned toward him, balancing himself on the ladder. As far as he was concerned, Ruth had forgiven him and the day looked bright. He was one step closer to being enveloped in her good graces again. Naught else Andrew could say would change that.

"If thee plans to tell me that George and the rest of the Federals are upset that I apologized to the Paynes, as well as to Dolley and James Madison, I'm quite aware of it. And I don't care."

"If only that were the case," Andrew said, shaking his head. "This concerns Ruth."

Josiah's chest tightened instantly. He climbed down the ladder. With his feet planted on the floor, he folded his arms and met his brother's gaze. "What about Ruth? Is she hurt?"

"No, nothing like that." He gripped the ladder. "Ruth's leaving. She's decided to go back to Virginia with the Madisons."

Cold fear clenched Josiah's gut, making his stomach coil and bile rise in the back of his throat. He swallowed and shrugged, trying not to let himself grow alarmed. "I'm sure it's just a temporary visit. Naught wrong with that, since they're family." He scratched his temple. "Perhaps she's going to spend Christmas with them."

"That's what I thought at first, but then I heard that it's an indefinite trip. She and Dolley came into town this morning and Ruth's being fitted for three new gowns. At least that's what Sarah Goodson told me."

Sarah? Josiah suspected Sarah had always harbored a secret jealousy of Ruth. She pretended to be friends with Ruth by attending their quilting parties and inviting her to dinner, but she never failed to flirt with Josiah when she came to the store or when she saw him in New Garden without Ruth.

"So Sarah's the one who told thee this?" He released a relieved breath. "I think I'll wait to hear it confirmed from a more worthy source."

"I just wanted thee to be aware of what's being said in case there's any truth to it. I'd rather thee hear it from family than someone else." Andrew removed his hat and coat.

They worked for another half hour before the bell jingled and two women entered the store. Josiah glanced up from his ledgers on the counter, and his breath caught as

279

Ruth walked over. He nodded to her and to Dolley Madison, who stood behind her in a bright red cloak and a colorful turban hat.

Even in plain gray, Ruth stood out like a canvas painting. Her sandy-brown hair curled around an oval face, ripe with cold. She must have gotten some rest last night; the dark circles under her eyes had faded, and the redness was gone. Her pink lips were prominent. Josiah swallowed, a deep ache of longing reminding him that he no longer had the right to kiss Ruth or pull her against him in a tight embrace.

"Josiah, I wanted to come by and let thee know that I will be traveling back to Virginia with Dolley and James. For the first time in years, I'll see my grandmother for Christmas."

Her soft brown eyes sparkled with excitement even as his own gut twisted and kicked in rebellion. Had he lost her for good?

"Will thee be coming back after the New Year?" He held his breath. She dropped her gaze, and his heart thumped harder.

"Actually that's why I came by to speak to thee in person." She crossed her arms and glanced back up at him. "I need time to think and consider my future—to be alone. Every corner of New Garden reminds me of thee, and it distracts me from seeking God. I'm sorry, but I didn't make this decision until late last night."

Wasn't it only yesterday he'd come to a similar conclusion? He'd been more than distracted by placing Ruth as a higher priority in his life than God. His involvement with the Federalist movement had fallen somewhere in the middle.

He searched Ruth's dark eyes. She blinked back tears. What she'd come to tell him hadn't been easy for her. No matter what, she would do what she believed God wanted her to do. It was one of the reasons he loved her so much.

If she'd come here with any other excuse, he would have protested, but not this. He wouldn't be the right man for her if he stood between Ruth and her relationship with God.

*Not my will, Lord, but Thine.*

"I'd never knowingly distract thee from God. Ruth Payne, I want thee to know I'll always love thee as a man loves a wife. If God doesn't lead thee back to me, I know in time that He'll heal me, and it wasn't meant to be."

Her chin trembled, but she held it in place and continued to meet his gaze. Ruth's eyes narrowed as they filled with tears. How could she not believe that he loved her after all this time? There was naught else he could do to prove it. The rest was now in God's hands.

"May I have a good-bye hug?" he asked, aching to hold her in his arms one last time.

Ruth shook her head in denial. She turned and strode to the door with Dolley Madison taking her arm to comfort her like a mother. Josiah's world crumbled when she walked through the door.

# Chapter 9

Once Ruth made it back to the carriage, she burst into tears. Dolley laid a gentle hand on her back and opened the door. Ruth wiped her cheeks as she climbed inside, eager to escape the view of passersby.

"I daresay you'll feel better soon enough," Dolley said.

"All I can say is I'm glad that's over."

How long would this gaping hole in her heart take to heal? She'd done the right thing, hadn't she?

Josiah would soon realize he didn't love her enough to commit himself to her, and he'd be grateful. Staying in New Garden held too many painful memories. It made sense to go to Virginia with Dolley. She needed a fresh new start on life with no reminders.

When they arrived home, Ruth excused herself to her chamber. She had no desire to talk to anyone. Over the next few days, she kept her mind occupied with work from the moment she rose until she rested her head on her feather pillow. When others brought up Josiah as a topic of conversation, Ruth told them she didn't want to talk about him.

She knew her behavior not only puzzled her family but also concerned them. She didn't know how else to handle the situation. Even harder to bear was that Josiah had stopped offering his help around the Payne farm, eagerly attempting to win her affections back. Ruth didn't know whether to be relieved in finally accomplishing her goal or disappointed that Josiah hadn't fought harder to save their relationship.

A week later she and Naomi returned to Greensborough to pick up Ruth's new dresses. Dolley stayed home to spend time with their mother.

As they walked by the barbershop toward the waiting carriage, George Osbourne stepped out with a new haircut and fresh shave. He stroked his jaw and nodded, his gaze glancing at Naomi and settling on Ruth. His eyes hardened as he straightened his shoulders and back.

"Well, well, if it isn't Ruth Payne and her little sister." He stepped in front of them, blocking their path. In the past Ruth never had any reason to fear George since he was Josiah's best friend, but now she sensed more hostility steaming from him than ever before. He blamed her for the few times Josiah had cancelled their plans or refused to join them on one of their Federalist adventures.

Why would he have any reason to resent her, now that Josiah was free to pursue all his political interests? It didn't make sense. She gave him a polite nod.

"Good day to thee, George Osbourne."

"Is it a good day? I suppose it is when thee is planning a splendid one-way trip to Virginia with one of the most famous couples in America, while Josiah Wall nurses a broken heart in Indiana—hundreds of miles away." He shrugged. "Although I'm not surprised his brother Samuel is going with him. The boy is young and eager to discover the world. Has a little bit of his father's wanderlust about 'im." His accusing eyes met Ruth's. "But Josiah? He's never had a desire to go anywhere—until now."

Ruth's heart thumped so hard she felt breathless. Josiah in Indiana? She'd never heard him mention it. Several Quakers had moved out that way to plant new roots and escape slavery, but since when did Josiah have a desire to go there? He'd spent the last three years consoling his mother, determined to never leave her behind as his father had done.

"What of his mother? Will she be going with them?" Ruth held her breath. If Josiah was truly going away without her, something was terribly wrong.

"I heard she has a sister living there, so I understand that she's going with them." George shook his dark head. "Josiah sold his portion of the store to Andrew. He's the only one in the family who's staying. Josiah also resigned from the Federalist Party, and now he's putting the house up for sale."

"Our house?" It was as if the blood drained from Ruth's head, numbing her down to the shoulders. An eerie sensation slithered through her spine, making her shiver.

"It isn't exactly thy house now that thee has abandoned it." George's tone sharpened. "What was Josiah to do with it?"

"I don't know, but he poured himself into that place trying to make it perfect. All his hard work and sweat can't be for naught." Tears stung her eyes, and Naomi laid a comforting hand on her arm.

"Thee still doesn't get it, does thee?" George shook his head in disbelief. His dark eyes pierced her with no understanding or compassion. "He wasn't making it perfect just to be making it perfect, Ruth Payne. He only did it for thee." He turned and strode away.

Ruth clutched her stomach and bent over. Tears blinded her. What had she done? Had she expected to run off to Virginia in a prideful rage, while Josiah waited here with open arms? Yes. She'd hoped that time would help him determine if he truly loved her and could commit to her for a lifetime. But this news changed everything.

What did it mean if he was willing to give up everything he'd ever held so dear? She never imagined he would go back on a promise he'd made to his mother. Surely Josiah wouldn't leave.

"Ruth, is thee all right?" Naomi asked, wrapping one arm around her shoulders while carrying a package in the other.

"I need to go to the store. See if this is true or all a lie." Ruth wiped at the hot tears spilling over her lids. "What if I was so hurt by Josiah postponing our wedding that I was blind to his love and everything else around me?" She looked up at her sister. "What if I've lost him because of my behavior and not because he didn't love me as I thought?" She groaned. "How could I allow that much pride to control me?"

"Come on, Ruth." Naomi guided her across the street to the carriage. "There's only one way to find out. I'll take thee to the store. Thee must find him and discover the truth for thyself."

"Yes, let's make haste. I must see Josiah Wall within the hour before he does anything else he'll regret."

❧

Josiah nailed the FOR SALE sign onto the oak tree in the front yard of the home he'd built for Ruth and their future family. His heavy chest felt like a loaded burden. He'd finally realized he couldn't force Ruth to change her mind and trust him again. In time he'd learn to live with his regrets, but until then he prayed God would make things more bearable for him.

He gripped the hammer in his hand and turned to go inside. A carriage rolled up the lane. Josiah paused. Who would be visiting him here? Everyone in New Garden knew the house was still empty, and by the end of the week, the newspaper ad would be out. Soon they would all know it was for sale.

As the carriage drew near, Josiah tensed. It looked like the Payne family. Matthew and his sons would have come by horseback or wagon. The only exception was on Sundays when they traveled to meeting. Today was Wednesday.

Hope filled his chest. Could it be Ruth? As soon as the thought crossed his mind, he squashed it. No sense in getting himself too excited. She might be coming by to congratulate him for moving on and starting over.

He walked forward as the horses slowed and the wheels crunched over graveled dirt to a complete stop. Naomi held the reins and set the break as Ruth scooted to the edge and prepared to exit. Her white bonnet concealed her gaze from him. With his heart nearly in his throat, Josiah offered his elbow to assist her.

To his surprise Ruth didn't hesitate laying a gloved hand on his arm. She gripped him tighter than he anticipated, almost as if she feared something. Ruth held her skirt with her other hand as she stepped down.

"I'll wait right here," Naomi said.

Ruth nodded and turned to glance up at Josiah. Worry filled her dark eyes as she continued to hold onto him even though she no longer needed his assistance. "I would like to talk to thee. . .alone."

Her hand trembled on his arm when he didn't answer right away. It wasn't that he wouldn't speak to her alone, but he needed a moment to calm his racing heart so he could trust his voice. A lump kept trying to form in his throat. Josiah swallowed it back several times before nodding. "Of course."

She led him toward the tree with the FOR SALE sign and pointed to it. "So it's true? Thee plans to sell this house?" She gestured to the white two-story structure behind them, very similar to the Payne house.

He nodded but didn't offer her an explanation.

"And the store? Is it true that thee sold it to Andrew? Will thee move to Indiana?" Her hand on his arm tightened.

"Yes, it's all true."

"But why?" She tilted her head to the side and blinked up at him in obvious distress. "Thee has put so much work into everything. I heard thee also quit the Federalist group. The house, the store, the politics." She swallowed and shook her head. "I thought they meant so much to thee. I thought they were thy life. I don't understand. Josiah Wall, I

283

don't want thee to make a mistake thee will regret."

"None of those things mean that much to me. They're not my life. God is, and next to Him, thee is." Sorrow filled Josiah's chest, and he wished he'd seen things from this perspective sooner. He covered her hand with his. "Ruth Payne, I'm so sorry." His voice cracked, but he cleared his throat and continued. "I should have shown thee how much more important thee is than all those other things. I only pursued them with such vigor to make thee happy, but I was wrong."

"And I was wrong. I see that now." Ruth stepped closer and lifted her hand to cup his cheek. "I was so blinded by hurt that thee would postpone our wedding, not once, but twice. I couldn't see beyond the pain to the truth. It took thee to give everything else up for me to realize it. Will thee please forgive me?" Tears filled her eyes, and her nose turned pink.

A huge burden lifted from Josiah's heavy chest, but he was afraid to let his guard down. "There's naught to forgive." He held himself still even though he wanted to wrap her in his arms. "Does this mean thee will still marry me?"

"Yes." She nodded as tears slipped down her cheeks. "If thee will still have me."

"Oh, make no doubt about that—ever." Josiah pulled her into his embrace and squeezed her against him. Relief gushed through him like a rushing wind, sweeping away all his concerns. Her warm body felt soft and perfect against him. He closed his eyes, savoring the moment.

All too soon she pulled back. "Would thee like to set a date?"

"No." He shook his head.

She frowned, biting her bottom lip.

"I'd like to find a preacher and marry this day. Does thee think Naomi will be a witness?"

"Indeed." She threw her arms around his neck and leaned up on her tiptoes.

Josiah could no longer resist, now that her mouth was so close. He dropped his head, allowing his lips to meld with hers. She smelled of gingerbread and felt as warm and inviting. Yes, today he would make her his. He couldn't afford to wait any longer.

When their lips parted, he leaned his forehead against hers. "What about thy trip with Dolley to Virginia?"

"Forget Virginia. I'm going with thee to Indiana or wherever thee goes."

"Let's build a fresh new start together in Indiana. We can create our own New Garden there." Josiah kissed her again. She smiled up at him, her eyes lighting with new hope.

**Jennifer Hudson Taylor** is an award-winning author of historical Christian fiction and a speaker on topics of faith, writing, and publishing. Jennifer graduated from Elon University with a B.A. in journalism. When she isn't writing, Jennifer enjoys spending time with her family, traveling, genealogy, and reading.

# NEW GARDEN'S CROSSROADS

by Ann E. Schrock

# Dedication

In loving memory of my grandmother, Mary Elizabeth Davies Phelps (1901–1980), an enthusiastic volunteer at the Levi Coffin House historic site.

# Chapter 1

Slave hunters on horseback milled around the Coffin family's rambling brick house, forming moving shadows in the gloom of a stormy winter evening.

Deborah Wall shivered as she stood next to her older cousin Katy Coffin and peered through one of the parlor windows. Katy's husband, Levi, kept some of the soul drivers talking at the front door.

Deborah's pa had left with the runaways only moments ago.

Deborah strode through the candlelit dining room and looked out the window. A narrow break in the storm clouds gave just enough light in the sunset to show that members of the posse watched every door. Her heart thudded, and her mouth went dry. She forgot all about being cold and wet from the ride from home to Newport.

One of them, a tall and lean man, his shoulders broadened by a caped riding coat, turned his horse and studied the side door.

The horse, with its solid build and stylish head and neck, caught Deborah's eye. A Morgan, a mighty fine animal for someone like that.

What if that wicked man noticed Pa's wagon tracks? Her father had figured the trees along the creek bank would hide them. They'd rushed into the night for fear the rising creek would wash out the bridge and get too deep to cross.

As if from some invisible cue, the Morgan sidestepped closer to the door. Its rider folded his arms across the saddlebow and leaned down to study the tracks.

Did he see? Did he guess who left the trail?

She heard Levi at the front door, telling the other slave hunters why—under every point of Indiana legal codes and English common law—they couldn't come in and search his house.

Cousin Katy's three daughters clustered around their mother and Deborah.

"How long does thee think they will stand and listen to Friend Coffin's message?" Deborah asked.

"I hope long enough that thy father can take those fellows clean away," Cousin Katy said. She took a deep breath and closed her eyes. Her normally cheerful face tightened with worry.

Outside, the man on the Morgan put his hand to his mouth and shouted, "Over here!"

Deborah felt blood drain from her face, leaving her dizzy. He must have seen Pa's wagon.

Time. They needed more time to get away.

The horse pivoted and took a few strides, following the wagon tracks down to the creek.

Deborah prayed for boldness then grabbed her black cloak and bonnet. "I'll try to delay them." Her mouth felt dry as sawdust and her voice cracked.

"How?" Cousin Katy gasped.

Deborah glanced over her shoulder and grinned, which lightened her fear. "As I feel led." She took a breath to steady her nerves.

Cousin Katy stepped toward her. "Truly?"

Deborah paused, her hand on the latch. What if she was wrong? No time to waste. She opened the door.

The cold wind took her breath away and sleet stung her cheeks.

The Morgan tossed its head as its rider turned toward the house and gazed up at Deborah standing in the doorway. Light from the house spilled over him. He'd be a handsome man but for his harsh countenance.

"I caution thee," Deborah said, "to beware of the water."

He stared at her. A Southern drawl slowed his voice. "Now, why would a pretty little Quaker gal be talkin' to someone like me?"

Her heart and mind raced. Were her actions so unusual that she made him suspicious? But if she kept him talking, Pa would have that much more time to get the runaways home to the farm, safely under Ma's wing.

A tart answer came to mind, and she gave him a crooked smile. "I'd given little thought to thee, neighbor. But I would hate to see any harm come to such a likely looking horse."

His quick grin showed a mouthful of white teeth, like a wolf's. "Why thank you, miss." He dropped one hand to the horse's neck and straightened its windswept mane. Then he looked into Deborah's eyes. "I know a fine filly when I see one."

Deborah ignored that. Would she be able to keep him talking about the horse? "It's a mare, then?"

"Yes, miss. In foal to—well you wouldn't—"

The storm's wind cut through her cloak, making her shiver. What else could she say? "I might, if it's from around here."

"No, miss, to a racehorse from down by Richmond."

She thought of the most notable one. "Messenger?"

"That's the one. She sure is." He studied Deborah for a long moment.

Deborah stared in awe at the mare. What a valuable foal that would be. "When does thee expect her to foal?"

"Later this spring."

Deborah edged a little farther out the door, onto the top step. She prayed for the right words. "For that reason, neighbor, thee must be careful with her. I wouldn't go any farther that direction. We just came that way, and the creek is rising fast."

"Whose tracks are these, then?"

She must keep him talking. She'd never spoken as much to a strange man, especially one of the world. "Ours. My father brought me here for another week of work. He wanted to hurry home before the creek got too high."

The stranger leaned forward and studied the mud and snow again. He raised his head and gazed into her eyes. "Lot of footprints there for just you and your dad."

Deborah inhaled sharply. "We made several trips in and out with firewood. This house uses a prodigious amount."

He glanced down at the tracks then back into her eyes. "With respect, miss, that's not what those tracks look like to me. All shapes and sizes of prints."

The front door slammed, and the mare flung up her head. The other horses and riders sloshed through the mud, joining him. The sharp smell of horse sweat made Deborah's nose wrinkle. The animals shivered and snorted.

Deborah took a shaky breath. She felt like she was on display.

The man with the Morgan smiled and took off his hat. The wind tangled his long wavy hair. "You must excuse me, miss. Business."

Before he could say more, another man, lean and predatory like a weasel, urged his horse forward. Octavian Wagner, the notorious slave hunter. He looked down at the hoofprints, tracks, and wagon ruts then turned to the group. "Well, looky here. All kinds of sign."

Deborah clutched the doorframe, reminding herself to breathe. What had she done? What would they do to Pa and the runaways? Why had she said anything?

The man on the Morgan nodded at Deborah. "Little Quaker gal there made a point of sayin' not to go that way."

Another man edged his horse forward. "Wonder if we hurried, if we'd catch 'em."

Wagner grinned. "I got a better idea. What's your name, sweetheart?"

Deborah fumbled with the door latch behind her. It swung open, and warm air from the house breezed out. Cousin Katy put her hand on Deborah's shoulder. "Come inside, dear heart."

Wagner leered at Deborah. "I know you now. You're that Wall gal. Dad's the furniture maker."

"Josiah Wall," another man said.

Fear crackled through Deborah. These men recognized her? And knew of her family?

The man on the Morgan swung the horse between her and the others, almost protectively. "Go inside, miss."

Wagner got an evil grin on his face. "I believe I can make them come right to us. Thank you so much for your help, darlin'."

Such arrogance. Deborah clenched her fists.

The posse rode down the street. A few hundred feet from the house, behind the Coffins' barn, the horses splashed into the rising creek. "Josiah Wall!" Wagner called. "Friend Wall! I have a message for thee from thy daughter!"

# Chapter 2

The slam of a door scared Nathaniel Fox's horse, and she leaped sideways. His body swung with the horse's motion as he tightened the reins and patted her neck to calm her. He shivered, waiting for the Quaker girl's father to answer. The wind might have carried his voice to the runaways or carried it away. While the others bet on what they'd find ahead of them, he looked back. The Quaker women and some children milled about inside the big red brick house, and candlelight glowed warmly in the many windows.

The sound of their plain speech made his heart ache with grief and loneliness. All he'd lost—home and family among the Friends—might as well be a thousand miles away even though it was right before his eyes. One choice had led to another, and now, here he stood, in outer darkness.

"Well? Seen anything, Fox?" Wagner asked, gruff as ever. "They ain't at the house."

"Tracks are headin' out of town."

"Good enough."

The horses' hooves punched through thinly iced mud puddles, crunching and cracking. Some of the men swore as cold muddy water spurted up.

The rushing wind overhead rattled the limbs of cottonwoods and sycamores along the creek banks, and snow and sleet pelted down. Nathaniel's feet had gone numb.

They rode farther, toward the creek itself. The sound of roaring wind and water gave Nathaniel chills. The surrounding houses and barns were dark, though a few dogs barked and hens cackled. The group halted their horses. The storm and darkness upset the animals, which tried to turn back from the flood. The sudden thaw over the past couple of days, plus several inches of rain, had melted most of the snow.

Wagner leaned back in his saddle and sighed. He pointed to the dark water foaming through willow thickets. "If they drove into that, prob'ly all drowned by now."

The men murmured in agreement. Wagner motioned for them to turn around.

Nathaniel faced the water. That girl's father was out there, in danger. Nathaniel's world had ended when his pa was killed. He hated to imagine another family suffering like that. "We don't know that. We ought to try and find them."

"Bah! If slaves get clear up here to Newport, they up and disappear." Wagner sounded cross. "No sense goin' any farther. Old Man Wall took his chance."

The group turned to go, starting a long, miserable two-hour ride down to Richmond, the county seat.

Nathaniel made the restless mare stand. How could they turn their backs on someone in danger? That must be the way of the world, as he, and the Prodigal Son in the scriptures, had discovered through sad experience. "I don't know about you all, but I want to know what happened to them."

Wagner shook his head. He was just another dark blob in the whiteness of the falling snow. "Ain't ridin' into that mess in the dark," he said, nodding toward the water.

"Listen, boys, I've a mind to go and see where those tracks lead," Nathaniel said. "You all going with me?"

The others shook their heads.

"You'll learn better, once you been at this trade as long as I have," Wagner said. "No night for man nor beast. You won't find nothin' tonight. Catch up with us when you can. We're headin' down the Richmond Pike."

Deborah wiped up the snow she'd tracked in, wondering if that liar had tricked Pa into turning back.

When he came into the dining room, Friend Coffin folded his arms and gave her a stern look. The tall thin man in a gray suit reminded her of a great blue heron, especially when he trained his keen eyes on someone. "Thee should have left me to speak, Deborah Wall. This misadventure frightened poor Katy."

Cousin Katy put her hand over her heart and added, "That man could have grabbed thee and taken off with thee."

They were right. Deborah looked down at the floor. Mama's cousin might be upset enough to send her back home. With younger children still at home, Friend Levi's elderly mother, and so many fugitives in and out, Cousin Katy had welcomed Deborah's help. A young able-bodied woman was such a blessing, she'd often told Deborah, who began working for them after one of the Coffin girls died of a fever.

Friend Coffin sighed. "Thee has heard the saying that 'zeal without wisdom is folly.'"

Deborah nodded and glanced quickly at him.

His gray eyes twinkled. "I grant thee does have zeal. Why did thee feel led to speak out like that?"

"I thought to delay them, although I haven't had near as much practice as thee and Cousin Katy at confounding the slave hunters." She paused thoughtfully and then added, "I might have relied too much on my own understanding."

Cousin Katy breathed deeply. "Let us pray for thy father and those with him."

Deborah leaned against the fireplace mantel, closed her eyes, and prayed silently for safety for Pa and the runaways.

Sleet rattled against the windowpanes. Where were they? Crossing the flooded creek could have been a trial. Surely the bridge withstood it, but the rising water on either side might have gotten even wilder.

Did she hear voices from outside? Was that possible over the stormy winds?

# Chapter 3

Nathaniel fought with the mare as she snorted and backed away from the churning water. The falling snow lightened the darkness enough to see the flooded creek rushing over its banks, already rising to the mare's knees. The bridge ahead looked to be solid, had they reached it. Sleet and snow stung his face. The wind roared through the sycamores, and water thundered at the bridge.

Mr. Wall and the wagon must be just ahead of him. If they'd wrecked, perhaps he could help them out and soothe his own soul, troubled as it was over this brutal trade. Wagner had made it sound like easy money, and Nathaniel had wanted to save for a farm of his own, make a fresh start in Indiana, somewhere other than the Friends' settlement. His relatives who'd moved up here would no doubt disown him, once they realized all the bad things he'd done since losing Pa and Ma.

He tightened his legs around the horse, urged her toward the bridge. She took a few reluctant steps. The icy water had risen to her belly and soaked through Nathaniel's boots. She reached the end of the bridge, stopped again, pawed at the swirling water. The current shoved her sideways; she lurched and stumbled to regain her footing. She put her head down for a moment then flung it up.

Nathaniel took a deep breath. "Come on, Brandy!"

A voice swirled on the wind, shouting, "Bridge out!"

Nathaniel looked over his shoulder but saw no one. "Mr. Wall?"

No answer. Must have been the wind in the trees or his imagination.

The mare tried to turn back, but Nathaniel made her face the bridge. He wouldn't rest until he knew what had happened to the other travelers. He hated to resort to spurs but touched her with them.

Brandy flung up her head, almost rearing, and then leaped forward into the surging water. She landed with a huge splash but lost her footing. Nathaniel gave her her head and knotted his hands in her mane as she struggled to stay on her feet. The horse fell. The icy water took his breath away. They slammed into the railing of the bridge. The mare crushed Nathaniel's knee into the side. With a crack, the post, rails, and floor gave way.

Nathaniel and his mare fell over the side into the flood.

Brandy would break his back or both legs, pin him under the water—not even a chance to pray. The horse's body slammed him deeper into the rushing water, which filled his nose and mouth, tore at his clothes. Trapped. The struggling horse's weight crushed him. Debris battered him. He had to breathe, had to get clear of the horse, anything to get his head above water and get some air. The flooded steam carried him away into darkness.

🐝

Pounding at the door surprised Deborah. She set down her candle and turned around.

Friend Coffin strode to the door. "Yes? Who's there?"

"A Friend. . .with friends."

At the password, Friend Coffin flung open the door. "Come in, neighbors. Come to the fire."

Pa lurched in, carrying a soaked and unconscious young man in his arms.

Deborah stared at them. "Pa, what happened?"

"I had doubts about the bridge and pulled off. This man rode right past us and tried to cross, but didn't make it." The runaways behind him slammed the door, latched it, and then stood shivering.

"He might have passed away," Pa said. In a heavy voice he added, "I tried to warn him, but it was too late."

Friend Coffin picked up the slave hunter's wrist and felt it. "Still alive."

"Bring him to the fire," Cousin Katy said. "Deborah, he needs dry clothes and blankets."

Deborah hurried through the house and trotted up the curving front staircase. On the landing at the top of the stairs, she found the door that led to the attic. She opened it with a quiet click so as to not wake the girls or Grandmother Coffin. Working by feel, she located folded clothes on the attic steps. They were ice cold. Poor man. He would freeze for sure unless they let these warm up. She couldn't believe she had a shred of sympathy for that evildoer.

The commotion must have awakened the children, who rustled around in their bedroom. "Deborah? Who is here?" Little Catherine, the youngest, murmured.

"One of the slave hunters."

The girl gasped.

"He might not live the night," Deborah said. He was so alive, proud, and boastful just an hour or so ago. Where was his soul now? She shivered.

As she returned to the dining room, her father paused at the side door. "I'm going to fetch the doctor," he said.

Friend Coffin and two young black men worked over the drowned man. They'd pulled off his wet coat and waterlogged boots. Deborah handed them blankets.

One man shook his head. "I still think we should've just left him. Won't lie to you."

The other one paused for a moment. "I know, Chance, but I think the Lord would have wanted us to try."

The slave hunter coughed, making an awful noise. Was he dying, right there in front of them? What if he faced God with the blood of runaway slaves on his hands? Could the Lord save even one such as him?

She put more wood on the fire; it flared and illuminated the stranger's condition.

His paper-white face was smeared with mud, his half-opened eyes glassy, and his lips blue. He might be near her age or a few years older. Wet hair was thick and dark as an otter pelt. A full beard hid the angles of his jaw and cheekbones. Asleep or unconscious, he appeared harmless. Only the Lord knew the extent of his evil deeds.

She crossed her arms.

Cousin Katy put her hand on Deborah's shoulder. "Thee seems troubled."

She breathed deeply and let it out. "I am wondering. . . . Would the Lord redeem even someone like him?"

Cousin Katy gasped. She put her hand over her heart and stared at Deborah.

Friend Coffin glanced up from the fireside. "Tell us thy mind, Deborah."

The slave hunter's conscience must be seared as hard and black as coal. "Perhaps drowning is the Lord's judgment on him for his evil ways—and should he recover, he knows all about thy affairs."

Friend Coffin shook his head. "I'm sure the Lord would want to redeem this man, but will he accept the Lord's grace? If he lives. We should pray that the Lord's good, acceptable, and perfect will comes to pass in this young man's life." He stood and gazed into Deborah's eyes. "In all of our lives."

She looked down at the clean clothes she'd wadded into a ball. She nodded as she smoothed out the linsey-woolsey shirt and pants and hung them over the fire screen. "I'll take his wet clothes if I may."

Someone pounded at the door then opened it. "I brought the doctor," Pa said, stamping snow from his feet.

Friend Hiatt followed Pa. His brow furrowed at the sight of the injured man.

Deborah took their coats and hats then put the stranger's dripping clothes in a basket. His riding coat alone would have weighed him down. Pounds and pounds of wool soaked with water and mud made her arm ache.

The doctor got down on the floor by the victim. "Yes, yes, keep him warm." He looked up at Friend Coffin for a moment while assembling his stethoscope, a wooden trumpet-shaped instrument. "We could write an article for the medical journals about reviving patients from exposure, Friends."

"Yes indeed."

He went to work, leaning over the patient and listening. He nodded. "Wonder of wonders. Heart is still beating." He shook his head. "A great deal of fluid in the lungs." He used his thumb to gently raise one eyelid. "Ah. The pupil still contracts. Good sign. Friend Coffin, he needs a warm bed as soon as one can be prepared. Hot water bottles, too. Does anyone know if the horse trampled him? There is something amiss with his knee."

"It's anyone's guess," one of the runaways said. "Didn't see the horse after they fell."

Deborah shivered. That beautiful mare had been swept away in the flood? And the man nearly drowned. No matter who suffered that end, it would've been cold and terrifying.

Pa took her arm. "These fellows and I want to try to cross the creek again. I expect we can cross south of town. Out of our way, but we can make it over."

Cousin Katy looked troubled. "Thee's welcome to spend the night."

Deborah hoped Pa and the others would stay here. Traveling by the morning light would be so much safer. She added up how many that would be for breakfast: Levi and Cousin Katy Coffin, their three girls, Grandmother Coffin, herself, Pa, two fugitives, and the slave hunter, if he survived. Eleven for breakfast. Cornmeal mush would work out the best.

Pa shook his head. "I have too much to do at the farm. I appreciate the offer though."

Deborah put down the clothes basket and leaned against him for a moment. "Thee has had quite a trip. Take care. Give my love to Mama."

He nodded, putting one arm around her. "I know thee likes working here. Just now is the first time thee has seemed troubled."

Deborah sighed. "I've been exercised over the wisdom of helping such a one," she admitted, nodding toward the slave catcher.

Trust Pa to simplify it. "God's will is that none should perish, but repent and live."

Deborah gazed at the young bounty hunter's face. Could someone like that repent?

# Chapter 4

Warm, dry air filled Nathaniel's lungs. He was alive, still. For a long time, he didn't know any more than that.

Voices echoed then faded away. He must be in someone's house. Whose? Voices spoke of a general store, the road to Richmond, the washing for that day, mending the next, and always about the weather. Children's voices, too, came and went. From somewhere came the steamy scent of laundry. Must be daylight.

His eyelids weighed too much to open, but he could feel his heart beating, hear its slow thump in his ears. *Alive—alive—alive.* If Nathaniel had died, he would've faced God's judgment without Christ. He shivered. How would he account for himself? For all the wrong he'd done since Ma and Pa died?

But the Lord had mercy on him, and someone had rescued him. For no other reason than mercy, because Nathaniel deserved nothing from the Lord's hand.

If the Lord gave him back his life, what was Nathaniel to do? Too much to think about. His knee throbbed with every heartbeat, but the pain testified that he'd survived. He struggled to breathe. If only he could fill his lungs. His splinted leg felt heavy as a log.

Footsteps thumped on the floorboards, and someone walked over to him.

"Well, well, well. Look at that color," a man said. "Very, very encouraging."

"Indeed it is, Friend Hiatt," another man said. "Thanks be to God."

Nathaniel's eyelids felt heavy as pig iron. When he finally pried one open, he found himself on a pallet on the floor of a warm room with many windows and doors. It was a dining room, with a crane and cooking utensils in the huge brick fireplace, a table and chairs off to one side, and a braided rug on the polished floor. Not a log cabin like home, but a modern house. The blue-painted woodwork around the fireplace and chair rail looked cheerful against the white plaster walls. Nearby two middle-aged men studied him, a tall thin man with twinkling gray eyes, and a short stout man. Both wore plain clothes: white shirts, dark coats with no lapels, vests buttoned almost to the throat, and trousers of the same dark material. Nathaniel's voice sounded old, like a rusted hinge. He propped himself up on his elbows for a moment, but dizziness overtook him and he lay back down. "Why would anyone thank God for me?"

The tall man's smile showed mostly in his eyes. "For His great mercy. I am Levi Coffin, thy host, and this is Friend Hiatt, the town doctor."

Nathaniel nodded. He recognized their names. Not only had the Wagner gang spoke of them, but so had his uncle and aunt, months ago, in one of their last letters inviting Ma and him north.

The doctor asked, "What is thy name?"

He gathered his strength. "Nathaniel Fox." After taking another breath—no matter how hard he tried, he could not get enough air—he asked, "What happened to my leg, Doctor?"

Doctor Hiatt shook his head. "I believe it is not broken, but I do suspect damage to the joint."

Nathaniel's heart dropped. If he were crippled, he'd have no way to make a living. "How long will it take to heal?"

"Several weeks. Thee must give it enough time. If it heals imperfectly, thee might always have trouble with it."

Nathaniel stared in horror at his splinted leg. How could he lose weeks of work? Stranded here among the Friends meant the Wagner gang had left him behind. Some friends they were. At least his horse had some value. The mare, his pistols, and his money sewn in his coat lining—no, wait—all of those were gone, too. He sighed.

Levi Coffin watched him, tapped his forefinger over his lip. He looked off into space as though mentally going through a list of names. "Is thee related to George Fox?"

Nathaniel sighed again. His aunt and uncle now lived near Newport, but he wanted no contact with them. "Who founded the Quakers? I don't think so, Mr. Coffin."

"Who are thy people?"

"All dead, sir." He refused to use plain speech. "You wouldn't know them anyway."

Dr. Hiatt sat down by him. "May I see thy hand?"

It weighed a ton, but Nathaniel reached out to him. The doctor took his pulse then looked at Nathaniel's hand. "Thee must be a tradesman of some sort."

"Was a blacksmith for a while."

"Why did thee leave thy station to run with the Wagner gang?"

Nathaniel's eyelids felt heavier. "Money, Doctor. Each slave is worth hundreds of dollars."

The two pious old souls studied each other as though taking a moment to hide their disgust. No matter.

"The love of money is a source of great evil," Levi Coffin pointed out, as one of them was sure to do. "And so thee has pierced thyself with many sorrows."

Nathaniel shook his head. It felt as big as a pumpkin. "That's as may be. My choice."

"Let us help thee sit up to ease thy breathing," the doctor said. "He will need to put up his leg, too."

The two of them moved a couple of chairs closer to the fireplace. They each took an arm and, grunting, tried to help Nathaniel up.

Pain shot through his knee. The room tilted and whirled around him as they dropped him into the chair. The doctor propped Nathaniel's injured leg on another chair and padded it with a folded coverlet.

Light footsteps pattered, and that girl appeared in the doorway across the room. Nathaniel forgot about his knee. Even in a plain brown dress, she was the prettiest girl he'd ever seen. A white cap covered most of her shiny dark brown hair. A white cape and apron made her waist look tiny. Her eyes were dark, her face freckled from time outdoors. His heart started to race, but that made his ribs hurt.

She asked the doctor, "Does thee need anything from the kitchen, Friend Hiatt?"

She glanced at Nathaniel. Even though he tried to smile, her dark eyes narrowed slightly at the sight of him. She concentrated on the other two men. Her cheeks turned pink. A moment later her glance flickered back toward him. He tried another smile. She looked wary and turned away.

"Is thee hungry or thirsty, neighbor?" Mr. Coffin asked.

Nathaniel had to pause in admiring the dark-haired girl. "No thank you, sir. I want to know what happened to my horse though." Perhaps the runaways had stolen his coat and the horse. "Even if it's bad news, I wish I knew what became of her."

She looked over her shoulder at him before she slipped out the door.

Nathaniel tried to concentrate on Mr. Coffin and Dr. Hiatt, but he struggled to keep his eyes open.

Mr. Coffin shook his head. "As yet, there's no sign of the animal. I wish I had better tidings for thee."

"We should let thee rest now," the doctor said.

Nathaniel could hear them talking as they went into another room. He closed his eyes and sighed. He wasn't welcome here because of his wicked ways. He stared into the fire. Aside from his health and his money, the mare was the most valuable thing he owned. No one knew if his knee would heal. His whole future—gone. What would he do now?

If his father were alive, what would he say? Nathaniel let himself remember until sorrow overcame him. There was only one book in their log cabin, Mother's cherished copy of the Bible. Pa might have repeated a Bible verse. . . *"Let not your heart be troubled, neither let it be afraid."* From somewhere the remainder of the verse welled up. *"Peace I leave with you, my peace I give unto you: not as the world giveth, give I unto you."*

Nathaniel had tried to find peace in the world, but his wild ride ended here. He bowed his head and prayed silently. *Oh Lord, everything I have touched has turned to dust.*

Everything that Ma and Pa believed about God came back to mind. God never changes. He would be Nathaniel's unchanging Father—one who never grows old or weary, never leaves him desolate, always guides him, always with him, always knows the right way to go. Jesus came into the world to seek and save the lost, even a wretched sinner like Nathaniel, or that thief on the cross beside Jesus. He remembered a verse his mother liked—*"Come unto me, all ye that labour and are heavy laden, and I will give you rest. Take my yoke upon you, and learn of me; for I am meek and lowly in heart."*

Everything he'd depended on had been swept away—health, strength, money, and his horse. Only the Lord is forever.

Nathaniel finally knew peace, and it felt like that first breath of air after almost drowning. *Oh Father, heavenly Father, take me back. . . . But what do I do now? Will anyone ever believe I am Thine?*

❦

Downstairs, Deborah checked on the laundry.

The slave hunter's buckskin breeches were probably ruined, shrunken from getting soaked and dried. Colors from his bright-colored vest had run all over his white shirt. His wool riding coat might come out better than his other clothes. As it dried it appeared a streaky dark blue. Dye had splotched the brick floor as water dripped from his coat. It might dry better closer to the fire. She grabbed it, but it was so heavy she dropped it. The coat clinked as it hit the floor. When she picked it up, things spilled out.

What on earth? Gold coins glittered on the floor.

She hung the coat closer to the fire, put the money in her apron pockets, and trudged back up the stairs.

The slave hunter dozed in a chair with his splinted leg propped up. Deborah paused and studied him. The old clothes he wore were too short for his arms and legs, but the homespun fabric made him look more like an ordinary farmer with wide shoulders, muscular arms, and big hands. His shoulder-length wavy hair had dried to a chestnut brown. A thick brown beard and mustache framed his mouth. Frown lines still showed between his brows. Before his dissolution he might have been handsome, but his countenance was hardened, as though hunting humans like animals troubled him not. How would they see "that of God" even in one like him?

She cleared her throat and kept a wary distance. "Good morning, neighbor."

His eyes flashed open. They were a clear blue-gray. A brief smile brightened his pale, gaunt face. "Yes, miss—"

She held out the gold coins. "These fell out of thy coat."

He grabbed them and stared at them. "All there. Good."

Deborah clenched her fists and held her breath to calm herself. "Does thee think I would take anything of thine? Of that blood money?"

He closed his eyes for a moment. "I beg your pardon. I meant no offense. I feared some of it must have been lost when I fell in the creek."

Of course. Deborah felt petty and mean. If the Lord meant to redeem this man, perhaps she needed to show more of the fruits of the spirit, including patience. "Forgive me."

He smiled quickly. "Think nothing of it."

Deborah stole a glance at him from the corner of her eye and watched him run the coins through his hands. Why did he do that?

Cousin Katy and Grandmother Coffin joined them in the dining room. "Deborah, perhaps our guest would like some tea," Cousin Katy said. She focused on the stranger. "Good morning, neighbor. I am Catherine Coffin. This is my mother-in-law, Prudence Coffin, and my cousin, Deborah Wall. Can thee tell us thy name?"

Deborah poked up the fire, lay on more wood, refilled the kettle, and swung it back into the fireplace. She watched the stranger from the corner of her eye.

He braced his arms against the chair seat and levered himself to an upright posture but winced as he disturbed his knee. "Nathaniel Fox. Thank you for taking care of me."

Deborah gave him a curious glance as she took the teapot and cups to the table. "'An Israelite indeed, in whom there is no guile.'"

He gazed at her for a heartbeat or two, his blue eyes narrowed with a guarded expression. "Yes, at one time." He paused. "But then—" He shook his head and said no more.

Deborah pressed her lips together and tilted her head. At least he was familiar with the Bible verse. "Cousin Katy, thee must forgive me for taking so much time with the washing."

"Thee had some extra work, with the rain and all." Cousin Katy was so long-suffering, so kind with everyone.

"Mrs. Coffin," Nathaniel Fox said, the coins clinking in his hand.

"Yes, dear?"

He sighed and held out the money. "You need this. You had the doctor out on my account, and I'm another mouth to feed. . .and it bothers me how I came about it."

Cousin Katy took it and stared at the money in her hand. "If that is how thee feels led. . ."

He nodded. "I do."

Deborah stole a glance his way as she helped Cousin Katy with the tea. She hadn't expected him to give up all his money. Grandmother Coffin, tiny and drab as a sparrow in her gray dress, watched him with her bright eyes but said nothing.

Cousin Katy urged Nathaniel to have plenty of tea to help fend off illness. The mantel clock chimed nine as Deborah helped with the cups and saucers. The pink china cup looked as fragile as an eggshell in his big hand. "I thought to make potato soup for dinner."

Cousin Katy smiled and nodded. "Very good. Will thee have some soup later, Nathaniel? Our Deborah is a gifted cook."

"I'm sure she is, Mrs. Coffin." He watched Deborah. "Quaker ladies are so domestic."

Deborah wondered if he was trying to tease her. "Thee may call us Friends. Quaker is a term of mockery."

He nodded, and for some reason he chuckled. "I have heard that."

"Then why—" Perhaps he fully intended to give offense. A wise man overlooked such things. She set her jaw. "Does thee want any soup or not? I need to plan."

He shook his head. "No thank you."

Cousin Katy followed her to the basement stairs and took her arm. "I would like thee to cook it up here, my dear. The kitchen is clear full of laundry. Make some extra. I hope the scent will bring his appetite back."

"But I will have to step around him."

Cousin Katy carried the tea tray and followed Deborah down the stairs to the kitchen. As she washed the tea things, she said, "The sooner he is well, the sooner he can leave."

That did make sense. Deborah weaved in and out of the dripping laundry, gathering what she needed into a big basket. With all the rain, they had no choice about where to hang the clothes, some in the kitchen and some on the side porch. As she climbed up, to manage the sharp turn in the stairs, she put the basket on the floor above her for a moment. The angle was most unhandy for someone as tall as her. One would think the stairs could be made differently in a new house—but that might have added to the cost.

At the top of the stairs, she picked up her basket and straightened, only to find Nathaniel Fox watching her.

"I can help you peel potatoes, Miss Wall." After such a long string of words, he had to catch his breath.

"Well—all right." She sat at the dining room table, trimming eyespots from a potato and handing it to him. She glanced at him after trimming the next potato. He was almost done with the first. A thin, brown ribbon of peel spiraled away. Deborah's work looked clumsy and wasteful by comparison. "Thee must have had a great deal of practice at that."

He smiled, his face brightening, "I have."

They peeled and cut potatoes for several minutes, dropping chunks into a bowl of cold water. Every time she glanced up, she found him studying her. Even John Moore, the weaver, never more than stole a glance, never stared at her in such a forward manner. Heat rose to her face. But of course, she'd been up and down the stairs many times and had sat near the fire.

Cousin Katy came in. She must have noticed Deborah's tense posture. "My husband told me thee was a blacksmith, Nathaniel."

Deborah looked up at Cousin Katy. "If I were a man, I believe I would shoe horses."

Cousin Katy chuckled. "Thee and thy horses."

"I did enjoy it." Nathaniel smiled, his countenance softening, perhaps with happy memories.

"If thee had work that suited thee. . ." She shook her head, what a puzzle he was.

His expression hardened, his eyes narrowed, and his lips tightened. "Why did I ride with slave hunters?"

Deborah looked into his eyes and nodded.

He concentrated on a potato, elbows on the table. "Money, my dear. I was told I could get rich quick." One corner of his mouth quirked up. "No one told me what the trade was really like."

"Does thee regret it?"

"Maybe." He dropped more potato chunks in the bowl then raised his head and gazed into her eyes. She couldn't look away. "I should have counted the cost. Never reckoned on losing my horse or going lame myself."

Another coughing spell seized him; he looked miserable. She'd never seen such a worldly person, yet Christ died even for one such as him.

As Cousin Katy left them, she said over her shoulder, "Neighbor Fox, thee must rest."

He took a shaky breath. "Yes ma'am."

Deborah slipped potato chunks into the kettle of steaming water and swung it back over the fire. She stole a glance at Nathaniel. Had she ever met someone so contradictory?

# Chapter 5

Dinner with the Coffin family and Deborah was torture for Nathaniel.
Beautiful Deborah Wall helped her gray-haired cousin Katy set the table, while Mr. Coffin came into the dining room from his office in the front of the house. He helped Little Catherine wash up at the stand by the door. Grandmother Coffin came in from the parlor, where she'd been knitting. She and Mr. Coffin talked and laughed about something to do with samples for his paint business.

The Lord hadn't spared a miracle for the Coffin girl or one for Pa in his accident or Ma in her last illness. The Lord had no good reason to let good people suffer and die. The Lord also had no reason at all to save Nathaniel, just out of His great mercy. But Ma and Pa were in heaven now. Perhaps part of believing was trusting the Lord to make all those losses worthwhile somehow.

The littlest girl didn't seem to mind her condition. She stared at Nathaniel as Deborah ladled potato soup out of a large tureen. Deborah, with her long slender arms, could reach across the table and serve everyone within moments—almost as quick as a gambler stacking a deck of cards. He should tell her that sometime—when he felt well enough to enjoy seeing her dark eyes sparkle and cheeks turn pink.

Mr. and Mrs. Coffin and Grandmother Coffin talked about how soon the neighbors could rebuild the bridge. Little Catherine bumped her water cup with her shaky hands, and Nathaniel grabbed it before it spilled. The two of them smiled at each other.

"Are you home from school today?" he asked.

Little Catherine looked sad. "Maybe someday I will be strong enough to go with Sarah and Elizabeth. I pray so."

He nodded, unsure what to say next.

A moment later the little girl brightened. "In the summer Jesse and Henry might come home."

Nathaniel tried to place them.

"My older brothers," Little Catherine added.

Deborah Wall glanced at them out of the corner of her eye. When she'd served them all, they bowed their heads for a silent prayer.

How long had it been since he was in such a home? At table with a family for a meal, not having something charred over a campfire or served half raw at some tavern. So much like home in North Carolina, when Ma and Pa were still alive. Nathaniel's eyes burned, and his throat seized up. Tears? In front of these strangers? God help him. He kept his head down.

He looked up to find Mr. Coffin studying him. "I hope thy business with the Lord is profitable, Nathaniel Fox."

They all looked at him.

Should he tell them of the change in his life? Not just yet. He might give way to tears. He shook his head. "You're right. I do have business with the Lord but am not sure of His terms. I'm at a crossroads."

Mr. Coffin set his spoon down. "The Lord has said if thee loves Him, He will send the Comforter to be with thee and guide thee."

Nathaniel looked down to hide his expression. For some reason that brought him close to tears again. He nodded and cleared his throat. "I hope to be well enough to travel soon."

Mr. Coffin nodded. "Has thee anywhere to go?"

Nathaniel hesitated. How would following Christ change his plans to move on? "No sir. Well—I don't know."

Mr. Coffin paused before speaking. "Tell us thy mind, Nathaniel." He added a pinch of salt to his soup.

He watched them eat. The soup looked and smelled better all the time. "Maybe I will have some of that soup, Miss Wall."

She nodded and smiled briefly, mostly with her dark eyes, still looking bemused by him.

The hot soup eased the congestion in his chest, and its buttery scent reminded him he hadn't eaten for almost a whole day. He'd been raised with better manners but scooped it up like a hog eating corn. He let their conversation go on without him until he'd emptied his bowl.

He gathered his nerve and glanced around at them. "About someplace to stay. . . I do have family around New Garden. Somewhere. My uncle is George Fox."

Little Catherine raised her head. "Oh. Who founded the Society of Friends? I did not guess thee was that old, neighbor."

Nathaniel had to laugh. "No dear, they have the same name. My uncle is about Friend Coffin's age."

The older man smiled slightly. "As the storekeeper of course, I know most everyone, and everyone else knows even more people. I took the liberty of inquiring of Friend Fox and his wife. They said they are missing a nephew who is a blacksmith."

Nathaniel looked up from his soup again. Telling the truth made him feel free. "That would be me."

Little Catherine had more questions. "Neighbor Fox, didn't thee say thy mare was in foal to Messenger?"

Deborah had passed bread to Nathaniel, who was mopping up the last of his soup. He paused. "You overheard?"

Little Catherine looked down, her face turning pink. "Yes I did."

He chuckled. "You must be able to hear as well as an owl. Yes, she was in foal to him. But—I have little if any hope of seeing her again."

"If the Lord wants thee to have her. . ."

"I hope so."

Mr. Coffin spread apple butter on a piece of bread. "How did thee come to own her?"

For a long moment, Nathaniel stared into his soup bowl. "I bought her after a claim race. She didn't look like anything, and no one else wanted her. Despite her bloodlines."

"At a horse race." Mr. Coffin blinked.

Nathaniel took a deep breath. Other than drinking establishments, there were probably no places more worldly. "That's not how I was raised. My parents were Friends. I fear they wouldn't be proud of me at all now."

Little Catherine and Mrs. Coffin gasped and stared at him. Deborah Wall stopped, the ladle in midair, and stared at him, too. Now that they knew some of his past, they would give up any notions that he could be civilized.

Nathaniel felt worn out and ill. "Excuse me."

Katy Coffin nodded.

He got up and hopped over to his chair by the fire. The chair creaked and cracked under his weight. He couldn't sit still as his shivering grew more pronounced.

Deborah Wall left the dining room. Her brown dress swirled around her. Watching her gliding walk was almost worth getting sick again. He would love to see her expression if he compared her to a dancer.

She fetched some quilts. He managed to catch her eye and smiled at her. Even though his teeth were chattering, he had to tease her. "I thought you might throw those coverlets at me, Miss Wall."

As he'd hoped, her cheeks colored. "The thought crossed my mind, but that is not how the Lord would want me to act."

"Of course. Do unto others."

"Not quite. Rather my kindness to thee is like heaping coals of fire on thy head."

He stared up at her. His teeth chattered. "Coals of fire sound good right now. You d–d–don't have to wait on me."

"I would do the same for anyone else." She fetched out a hot brick covered in ashes from the fire and, with a pair of tongs, carried it over to him. Muscles in her slender forearms corded from the strain. "Pick up thy feet."

She arranged it for him then stood back. "Warmer now?"

He shook his head, feeling dizzier. Shivering overtook him. The hot brick felt no better than a chunk of ice. "No, not yet." He raised his head slowly. It felt like it weighed a ton. He searched her face. What would it be like for beautiful Deborah to look kindly on him? He could start by being honest. "I don't feel well at all."

# Chapter 6

Ice crunched as Deborah stepped through puddles hidden by wet snow. In these few minutes between cleaning up after dinner and starting supper, she'd begun searching the creek banks for Nathaniel's missing horse.

Every few minutes the sun broke through the torn gray clouds, their white edges glowing like molten silver against the blue sky. Red birds flitted in and out of clumps of willows. Along the creek banks, the sycamore trees' white branches contrasted with the dark clouds. The water still sped along far beyond the banks, rushing around the trees and bubbling over smaller obstacles, such as fallen limbs or the wreckage of the bridge.

Her foot slipped and went through the ice up to her ankle, over her boot top. The sting of icy water took her breath away. She was about to fall. She held on to a tree branch until she got her balance.

Perhaps that best illustrated her spiritual life: Trying to balance on her own but needing the Lord. He was the Vine; she was one of the branches. . . . And apart from Him, she could do nothing. If the Spirit guided her words and deeds, Nathaniel could see and respond to "that of God" in her.

The Spirit might not lead her to tell Nathaniel that he was a wicked sinner. That work most likely belonged to someone else. Strife and accusations were the products of worldly wisdom, not of the Lord. She needed so much help. *Lord, speak to my condition.*

She might have put the good work of helping runaway slaves ahead of following the Spirit. Perhaps she'd made an idol of helping the fugitives, since it took her mind off the looming possibility of never marrying for love. Who in the Bible was distracted with much serving?

She found a better place to stand, on a fallen log sprinkled with icy, half-melted snow. No sign of any animal up or down the creek, although she saw deer tracks and the paw prints of rabbits and foxes. Being outdoors helped her find peace. "*Cumbered about much serving. . .*" Mary and Martha hosted Jesus at their home, and He told Martha that.

Perhaps butting heads with Nathaniel Fox showed her where she'd gone wrong, how she'd lost sight of her first love for the Lord.

*Out of the abundance of the heart the mouth speaks. Lord, I had no idea I cherished such iniquity. Lord, Thou knowest how I need Thee. Forgive me for my anger. Search me, O God. . . . Guide me in right paths. Even if that means trying to show kindness to that man. Thou hast commanded us to pray for our enemies. Precious heavenly Father, have mercy on that man. Heal his leg, so he can go away soon.*

She put her hand to her eyes and studied the woods and creek banks as far as she could see. No sign of the missing horse.

The creak of a door woke Nathaniel. He opened one eye as Deborah Wall came into the dining room, her cheeks rosy from the cold. "I looked for thy horse, neighbor, but found nothing."

"You went clear out to the creek? I appreciate it."

She nodded and hung up her cloak and bonnet. "Oh yes. I was glad for a chance to go outside. And I took the liberty of bringing this for thee." She held out a dripping cheesecloth bag stained from years of berry preserves. "Ice. Plenty of it, right now. If thee is going to break something, winter is a good time to do so."

He smiled. "It hurts, but I don't think it's broken." He took the bag and draped it over his swollen, throbbing knee. The splint helped to hold it in just the right place. "Thank you, Miss Wall."

"I wish only to treat thee as I would want—or how I was treated the last time I got thrown by a horse and hurt."

Nathaniel wondered if he were dreaming. She was beautiful, she liked the outdoors, and she liked horses. He had to pause and remind himself to breathe. He could foresee falling in love with Miss Wall and embarrassing himself if he wasn't careful. What had happened to the hard-drinking, gambling bounty hunter he professed to be? "You got thrown by a horse?"

She smiled ever so briefly, but a real smile it was. "Oh yes, we used to ride all the time before there were roads. When my folks came, Indians still lived around here. As long as the Friends wore their plain clothes, the Indians recognized them as peaceable people, even during the War of 1812."

"Was your family from New Garden? In North Carolina?" What if Deborah's family or the Coffins knew of his family? He could almost feel connected here.

"My family came in 1808, I think. The Coffins came later." She studied him and the ice pack. "I think thee could use a towel or two."

Someone rapped on the door that faced Mill Street. She strode across the room, her brown skirt and white apron swirling, peeked out, and then threw open the door. "Pa!"

A tall, thin, dark-haired man came in, took Deborah Wall's hands, and kissed her cheek. "Hello, dear one."

Nathaniel stared. Did he know the man?

Then he recognized the voice—one he thought he'd heard last night.

Deborah's father was purposeful. "Hello, neighbor. I'm glad to see thee looking well."

Nathaniel gripped the sides of his chair and tried to stand up, but the room slid sideways and started to go in circles. Deborah and her father lunged forward and grabbed him. They helped him back to his seat. "Not perfectly well, sir, but better than last night."

Mr. and Mrs. Coffin joined them. "Friend Wall, how good to see thee," Mrs. Coffin said.

Deborah's father smiled in return. "I brought these. We prayed thy guest would soon be well enough to use them." He held out a pair of crutches. "I trust our Deborah won't need these again for a while."

She looked down and shook her head at some memory.

"Thank you, sir." Nathaniel propped them near his chair.

Mr. Coffin cleared his throat. "The goods thee received recently, Friend Wall—"

"Oh yes. Loaned them out already." Mr. Wall smiled.

Mr. Coffin nodded as though that pleased him.

What did they mean by that?

Mr. Wall, still wearing his coat and hat, focused on Nathaniel. "I also believe I have good tidings for thee. A stray horse came to the farm—a brown mare with a star. She looks like she might be in foal. Would that be thy horse?"

Nathaniel sat up. "Must be her! How did you know?"

"I caught a glimpse of her last night."

Nathaniel put his hand over his eyes and took a deep breath. That led to a coughing spell. "Answer to prayer," he sputtered.

They all looked at him with a variety of puzzled expressions, except for Deborah Wall, who looked at him suspiciously. She must think his change of heart was an act. Maybe someday she would know that he wouldn't turn away from his heavenly Father. He'd made his decision and finally felt peace. *Thank You, Lord.*

Mr. Wall cleared his throat. "We have room in the barn and plenty of hay. I would be glad to keep her for thee until thee is more settled, neighbor."

"Thank you, sir." He smiled wryly. "I don't know how long that will take or where I'll end up."

# Chapter 7

After supper Friend Coffin and Cousin Katy got ready to go to an antislavery discussion at the meetinghouse. Deborah and the girls waved to them as the horses leaned into their collars to pull the buggy through the mud. Ordinarily they would take one horse on such a short drive, but the roads were so heavy from all the rain that they needed two.

Little Catherine linked arms with her sisters, Sarah and Elizabeth. "I wish we could have gone to hear the speaker tonight."

"I do dislike having all of us scattered like this," Grandmother Coffin said. "I wish we were all under one roof. I think keeping everyone at home is best."

Deborah wondered if the older lady was thinking of the other children. The older boys had been apprenticed out.

"I am curious though, what the visitors will say," Little Catherine said.

Deborah closed the curtains. A chilly north wind rattled the windowpanes, making the gingham curtains shiver. As she put more wood on the fire, she said, "Perhaps another time when the weather is better. Come sit with Grandmother by the fire, girls."

Little Catherine glanced over her shoulder. "Nathaniel Fox, would thee like to join us in the parlor?"

The drowsy man raised his head. "I would be pleased to. Although I'm not very good company." He levered himself out of the chair, tucked his crutches under his arms, and stepped slowly toward the parlor.

Grandmother Coffin sat on the bench, her back to the window that looked onto Winchester Road, the main road through town. One pale, wintry sunbeam streamed through the window. Grandmother held her Bible up to the light. "Oh good. All these young eyes can help me read."

Nathaniel Fox limped across the room. He paused by the fireplace and ran a fingertip around the pretty woodwork. He'd never been in such a beautiful new house. "May I join you, Mrs. Coffin?"

"Of course. Would thee like to read to us?"

He set aside the crutches and hopped over to the bench. "Where does it say, 'Let not your heart be troubled'?"

"John, chapter 14. Does thee know that verse?"

Deborah arranged the wood in the fireplace, and then she and the girls sat in other chairs. She picked up her knitting—they always needed clothing to replace the rags worn by the fugitives—and glanced at Nathaniel and Grandmother Coffin. What would he answer?

He held the Bible up to the fading light and read the passage. After a moment he said, "My mother and father quoted that to each other often."

Deborah paused in her knitting. How had he lost his family? She shouldn't care. She made herself concentrate. She could knit by feel and didn't need to light a candle. Matter of fact, it was nearly time for the girls to go to bed. Such a pleasant change from yesterday's storm and the travelers.

Grandmother Coffin nodded. "Tell us about thyself, neighbor."

Nathaniel closed the Bible and gave it back to her. "My family came from New Garden, in North Carolina. Mother and I started up here after my father died, but she died on the way."

Deborah paused when she heard that. How sorrowful.

Nathaniel went on. "After that, I did blacksmithing for a while. Was told I could make more money by capturing runaway slaves. I was very useful at working with chains and shackles and such. I always meant to write to my people up here but never did."

Perhaps his conscience bothered him and he didn't want to reveal his shameful life to his relatives.

"What will thee do now?" Grandmother Coffin asked.

Nathaniel glanced over his shoulder, out the window. The Coffins' store, other buildings, and bare trees across Winchester road blocked the sunset's glow. "I don't know."

Someone tapped on the door. Deborah put down her knitting. They'd received no word of travelers tonight.

She went out to the dining room and hesitated at the door. "Yes?"

"Aunt Deborah, it's me, Tom," called one of her nephews. "Thee should know we have company coming."

"Friends?"

"Yes. I'll run back to the meeting now."

"Thanks, Tom." She went back in and picked up her knitting, trying to think what to say. She looked into Grandmother Coffin's dark eyes. "We might have company tonight."

Little Catherine understood. "Perhaps someone is coming home with Mama and Papa."

Grandmother nodded.

Deborah put away her knitting. "I should build up the fire and put the kettle on."

"We can put ourselves to bed," Little Catherine said.

"How will you get up the stairs, Little Catherine?" Nathaniel asked.

She giggled. "All kinds of ways, neighbor."

Deborah went out to the dining room, put more wood on the fire, and slipped down the stairs to refill the water pitcher from the well. She took a coal from the fireplace with tongs and lit a candle lamp. She tied back the window curtain then set the light in the window. With a sigh she looked at the roll of blankets Nathaniel had used last night. She wanted him out of the way, but where to put him?

His crutches thumped on the wooden floor. He paused in the doorway, casting a big black shadow in the firelight. "If they're going to be in the dining room and parlor, perhaps I should go somewhere else."

"There is a daybed in Friend Coffin's office." She looked over her shoulder. "It might be too short, but at least thee will be off the floor."

He chuckled. "The floor might be more comfortable." His smile softened his features. In the candlelight he looked cheerful and good natured.

She picked up the blanket roll and handed it to him. He draped it over his shoulder and hobbled out through the parlor. One of the girls pointed him to Friend Coffin's office across the entryway from the parlor, and he shuffled in there. Furniture bumped and scraped on the wooden floor as he settled in.

Deborah sighed with relief. He was out of the way. Hopefully he would sleep through any commotion.

"I will put the girls to bed, Deborah," Grandmother Coffin said. "Good night. Thee knows it might be hours."

"I know. I will just wait up."

She gathered her knitting and sat down with it at the dining room table. Now she had too much time to think as her knitting needles clicked. The yarn and movement kept her fingers warm. Nathaniel Fox was such a puzzle. Where did he stand with the Lord? He seemed to have changed, but he also seemed so worldly with his fondness for horseracing. His recent companions were men of violence. No denying he was a handsome man, but what was he on the inside?

☙

Once again voices woke Nathaniel. He found himself in a dark room with bookcases and a big desk. The fire had gone out, and wind rattling the windows and shutters made the room more dark and cold.

Voices and footsteps echoed from the kitchen. Deborah Wall sounded upset. "Oh no—oh look at thy foot. Perhaps we need the doctor."

"Ma'am," a man's voice replied, "if we could just get the manacle off somehow." A chain clanked on the wooden floor.

Manacles and chains—must be more runaways, maybe the rest of the group the Wagner gang had pursued and lost and recaptured all the way up here from Kentucky. What would the Lord have him do? He couldn't pretend to sleep through this.

He grabbed his crutches, straightened his clothes, and limped into the dining room.

A crowd of runaways dressed in rags and covered in mud and burrs stared up at him with wild eyes. One of the men recoiled. "You!"

Nathaniel's heart dropped. "Aaron—"

Deborah Wall stared at him then at the runaway. "Thee knows him, neighbor?"

Aaron clenched his fist, took a deep breath, and then opened it. "You tell the lady what you done, soul driver. What's he doin' here?"

"He was hurt. This is the nearest house, so we brought him here." She gave Nathaniel a long look. "All God's children are welcome here."

If Aaron could've grabbed something, he would've probably hit Nathaniel over the head. Nathaniel's voice sounded unexpectedly calm. "I put that on you. I can take it off."

Aaron narrowed his eyes and stared at him. "Why would you help me now?"

"It's the right thing to do. Deborah Wall, is there a file hereabouts?"

"Out in the barn."

"Maybe we best move on. If he's here. . ." one of the others said.

Light footsteps sounded on the back stairs, and Grandmother Coffin came into the dining room. She looked fragile. "Stay and rest, neighbors. There is nothing to fear here."

Aaron pointed at Nathaniel. "Him. You know what kind of man he is?"

Grandmother Coffin nodded. "We are all the same before God. Dreadful sinners."

Aaron looked down for a moment.

"I don't know where Neighbor Fox stands with the Lord, but we must look for 'that of God' in everyone," Grandmother said. "Have no fear, friends. He will do thee no harm."

As she put on her wraps, Deborah paused in the south door and looked over her shoulder at him, as though wanting him to hear that. She slipped out across the porch and disappeared into the night.

Nathaniel grabbed his crutches. "Aaron, sit by the fire. Let me see your leg."

"Friends, come to the kitchen," Grandmother Coffin said. "There is a good fire down there. Plenty of room. Let us find something to eat." They followed her down the stairs, several staring at Nathaniel as they passed.

Aaron limped to Nathaniel's chair and winced as he sat down. He propped up one leg and sighed.

Nathaniel stared at Aaron's leg. Swelling appeared above and below a shackle tightly clamped just above the ankle. Nathaniel had put that on Aaron only a few weeks ago, when they'd captured some of the family and tried to drag them back to Kentucky. But the runaways had escaped again. Seeing some drown in the Ohio River had sickened Nathaniel. He tried not to think about it. What to do? He lit a candle, turned a chair around, and leaned over Aaron's leg.

The other man could easily kick him in the face or hit his bad leg.

Nathaniel sat up and thought out loud. "This will be painful. I wonder if we should have the doctor out. Can you feel anything of your foot?"

Aaron's face was a study. "Little bit. Likely froze, too. Why are you helpin' me now?"

Nathaniel gazed into Aaron's narrowed dark eyes. "It's the right thing to do."

"Won't bring anybody back. Bein' kind now won't make you right with God."

Nathaniel nodded. "I know that very well. Only Christ can make someone right with God the Father."

Hoofbeats thudded outside, but Nathaniel didn't hear carriage wheels or trace chains. He turned toward the window. Someone came on horseback. He limped to the window. Outside were horses and riders, men with guns. "Wagner's gang."

❧

In the barn Deborah gave each of the horses and the milk cow a handful of grain to keep them quiet while she searched for the tools. She found the file in the freight wagon toolbox, and when her fingers brushed the cold metal of a hammer and chisel, she decided to take those, too.

The neighbors' dogs started barking. Hoofbeats echoed.

She peeked out the barn door. The Wagner gang had returned.

Fear jolted through her. She almost couldn't breathe. The children, Grandmother

313

Coffin, and the runaways were all in the house with no one to protect them. Nathaniel Fox might choose that moment to betray them. Such a big group must be worth thousands of dollars. Why had they trusted him? Once he let them in, they would tear through her dear ones like a pack of wolves with a flock of sheep.

She slipped out into the shadows and froze. Her pounding heart shook her whole body. If she went along the path, she could hide in the grape arbor between the house and barn, and then slip onto the porch and through the side door to the dining room. Fright sharpened her eyes. Every detail, every frosted blade of grass, and every buckle and button on the horses and riders appeared magnified in the starlight.

She leaned on the doorframe and prayed. The path looked a mile long. Her legs shook. If the gang stayed on the street, she would be safe. If the barn door made no noise, that would help, too. She slipped through and eased the barn door shut. The few yards to the grape arbor were wide open. The horses and riders clustered at the front of the house, but a few came down Mill Street. Waiting for them to turn around took forever. She strode up the path and slipped into the grape arbor, praying the tangle of vines would hide her.

She clutched the tools to her, hands trembling. If she dropped one on the brick path, the clatter would alert the slave hunters.

Finally she reached the side porch and crossed it in a few quick, quiet strides. The side door opened. Nathaniel Fox grabbed her arm and pulled her inside.

He loomed over her, his warm hand on her arm. "I started to worry, Deborah Wall."

"I brought the tools." Her voice shook.

"In a minute." He hobbled over to the other door. With a scrape he picked up the fireplace poker. "If any of them get past me, Aaron, use this."

"Thee would use violence?" Deborah's voice sounded choked.

"To protect a houseful of women and children, I would. I only wish I hadn't lost my pistols."

"Against thy friends?" What if he meant to deceive them and betray them?

He leaned forward a fraction of an inch to look into her eyes. In the dim light, his eyes looked big and dark. "They aren't my friends, Deborah Wall. I don't want them in this house. I know what kind of men they are."

Deborah gulped. He sounded so grim. *Lord, help us.*

Someone pounded on the front door. Nathaniel took the hammer from Deborah, nodded to Aaron, and then limped to the door. "Who's there?"

"Octavian Wagner. I got writs to serve here for multiple fugitive slaves."

"No slaves here," Nathaniel called as Deborah joined him at the door.

"Don't split hairs with me, Coffin."

Nathaniel laughed. "He's not here. Don't you know me, Wagner?"

Deborah put her hand on his solid arm. "What is thee about, Nathaniel Fox?"

"Not letting them in."

"Who's there?" Wagner called.

"Nathaniel Fox."

Several men swore in amazement. "We heard you was drowned," one called out.

"Not quite."

Wagner laughed. "The fox is guarding the henhouse. Open up. You'll get a double share of the money, I promise."

Deborah shivered. Nathaniel had pounced on those gold coins earlier. She stared up at him. What would he do? Was he tempted?

"Not my house. I can't do that."

"Then we're comin' in."

Deborah held her hands over her mouth, hardly breathing.

"Don't. The Friends won't put up a fight, but I will. You know I'm a pretty good shot."

Deborah's heart pounded harder and harder. He wouldn't, would he?

"You only got a couple of pistols."

"You don't know what I found in here though. Maybe a shotgun or somethin' else very useful."

"Octavian Wagner, you and your men are disturbing the peace," a voice interrupted. "I'm ordering you to disperse."

Deborah sighed with relief. Her knees went weak for a moment.

"Who is that?" Nathaniel whispered.

"The constable."

"I got papers here—" Wagner argued.

"We'll read 'em in the morning, see if they're any good. Now go away."

Hoofbeats sloshed around outside, saddles creaked, horses snorted, and men muttered as they turned around.

Deborah took another deep breath. "Bless the constable. He needed a bank loan recently, and Friend Coffin, since he's one of the principals of the bank, helped him obtain it."

"I can't help but admire Mr. Coffin." Nathaniel chuckled.

Little Catherine called down from the girls' bedroom. "Deborah, have they gone away?"

"Yes, dear ones, everything is all right. Your mama and papa will be home soon."

They turned to go back into the parlor, but Nathaniel tripped on a rug. Deborah held his arm to steady him. "Is thee all right?"

"Yes, thank you." He organized his crutches. "I didn't mean to frighten you, Deborah, with all the talk of fighting and guns."

Deborah paused before she answered. She might have to change her mind about him. "I gather that was how thee felt led." She realized she'd left her hand on his arm and pulled away like it was red-hot iron.

"Yes it was. Now we need to tend to Aaron."

They found the black man in the dining room leaning against the window, the curtain pulled out a fraction of an inch so he could see. "They gone for sure?"

Nathaniel nodded. "They are indeed."

Aaron smiled when Nathaniel told him about the constable's bank note.

"Now let's see what can be done for you and your leg," Nathaniel said. "Deborah, what about some warm water to wash this up?"

Aaron hobbled back to his chair, dragging links of chain across the floor.

Deborah went to the fire, poured hot water from the kettle, and then added ice water from the pitcher on the washstand. She took the bowl to Nathaniel, who worked gently on the manacle.

Aaron winced, gripping the sides of the chair. She watched as Nathaniel bent over Aaron's leg. Had he changed that much? Would it last?

# Chapter 8

Deborah guided Nathaniel's mare behind Ma and Pa's buggy. They were on their way to meeting at New Garden.

Nathaniel had told Deborah the mare's previous owners called her Brandy, a name he wouldn't have chosen. He hoped to open a blacksmith shop and fix up a stable and fences for the mare, as soon as his knee healed.

A dry week meant the muddy ruts of the road were frozen solid enough to travel easily. Crumbling snowdrifts lingered on the shadowed sides of trees and fences along the way, but the pale sunlight hinted that spring was coming. The road curved away from the Winchester Richmond Pike, past the few remaining cabins of the original New Garden settlement. Most families had moved a mile or so north to Newport, once they'd discovered better water at that site.

Her brothers rode along, too. As long as the mare traveled with the herd, Deborah didn't foresee problems with her. Last week Brandy had hardly blinked when Deborah first tried Ma's old sidesaddle on her; someone might have ridden the mare aside before. An easy trip over to meeting and back would be good for the horse's health. The old saddle creaked and squeaked in rhythm to the mare's strides, but even that was enjoyable. What a merry company.

The ride buoyed her spirits, too. She'd been exercised over her attitude ever since Nathaniel Fox came to the Coffins' home. Some of her anger about the fugitives' treatment might have been righteous. But vengeance was the Lord's, not hers, and when accusations came she remembered that the Lord had forgiven her. Did she owe anything to Nathaniel since she'd wronged him?

His aunt and uncle had taken him to their home to recover, leaving Deborah to wonder what would become of him.

Her nephew Tom jogged along on his gray gelding. "She's a good mover, isn't she?"

"Yes, I like her very much."

"Too bad thee has to give her back to that Fox."

"I have been dealing with covetousness, truly." Deborah sighed. What would happen to him? She was sure she'd seen "that of God" in Nathaniel's life when he helped the runaway slave, Aaron. But had he truly changed?

Tom chuckled as they rounded the curve in the road that led to the meeting-house. Tall trees stood around the long frame building. "Someone's bringing a farm wagon."

Deborah looked down the road toward the bridge that stood among bare trees. A team and wagon jolted over the bridge on the other side of the meetinghouse. "So they are."

She and Tom followed Ma and Pa, turned toward the hitch rack, and then greeted her older brothers and sisters. Tom reached up and helped her down. When she'd tied the mare, she looked past the animal to watch the farm wagon roll in.

A couple about her parents' age sat on the bench. A third person in a dark coat sat in the back of the wagon, sun gleaming like copper in his tousled brown hair. Deborah didn't recognize them at that distance.

Pa greeted them and helped with their team, and then walked around the back while the driver helped his wife down. Now she knew them—George and Martha Fox. They waited at the back of the wagon while the passenger scooted to the end, set down a pair of crutches, and slid out the back.

He looked up and stared at the mare then at Deborah.

She gasped. Nathaniel Fox. Clean shaven and his long hair cut. His countenance had changed. Now he looked cheerful with a quick, easy smile.

They all shook hands, and then Pa held his hand out to Deborah and the mare.

Nathaniel swung over to them on his crutches.

Deborah stared up at him. He looked so much better. The frown lines between his brows and on the sides of his mouth had eased. With all his whiskers gone, his face looked handsome as well as cheerful. Out in the pale spring sunlight, his eyes looked sky blue, and the cold, fresh air colored his cheeks. His dark blue riding coat was unbuttoned. He wore his travel-worn plaid vest, white shirt, flowing black tie, dark trousers, and boots as though he hadn't given up his worldly and brave apparel.

Even so, she held out her hand. It trembled. He looked wonderful. "Neighbor Fox."

He took her hand. His hand made hers feel small, protected. "Hello, Deborah Wall. How is the mare working out for you?"

"We thought an outing would be good for her."

He nodded. "I'm sure you are right."

Deborah kept staring up at him. She should say something kind and encouraging. "Thee is joining us?"

He gazed into her eyes, ran a hand through his unruly, close-cropped hair, and then smiled. "My aunt said I must or she won't feed me. Thus I cannot neglect attending meeting." He paused for a moment, still smiling at her. "I assumed you might have a comment."

Deborah tried to think of what to say. She smiled and opened her mouth. Then closed it and thought again. "I'm sure thee doesn't want to risk missing a meal. I'm glad to see thee here. And looking well."

He looked down for a moment, and instead of boldly studying her, he stole a bashful glance. Perhaps all these changes threw him off balance. Raising his gaze he asked in a low voice, "Truly glad?"

This might be the first step toward making amends. Deborah nodded then started to smile. "My integrity will not allow me to say otherwise."

He nodded and adjusted his crutches. "I'm thankful to be here. I was glad when they said unto me, let us go up to the house of the Lord."

Deborah could only stare at him. If he'd changed that much, would he join the Society?

# Chapter 9

The air smelled like spring as Nathaniel drove his aunt and uncle to meeting at New Garden. Leafy trees arched over the road. Many of the fields had been plowed by now.

"I'm sure thee's thankful for the Sabbath, Nathaniel," Uncle George said. "Thee had a busy week."

He nodded as their pacing horse ambled along the road. "This ground is sure different from North Carolina. Plenty of rocks to break plow points and all. Reckon I won't run out of work anytime soon."

Uncle George chuckled. "How is thy knee? I wondered if thee was limping by the end of the day sometimes."

"It hurts once in a while, but I'm all right as long as I keep moving."

Aunt Martha cleared her throat. She was so soft spoken. "We are glad as always to have thee come with us to meeting, Nathaniel."

Nathaniel chuckled. "Given that I like to eat, I'm still very pleased to join you in exchange for room and board."

"But I'm sure thee heard something of value at the Methodist meeting."

The horse tried to swerve around a low spot, but Nathaniel made him drive straight ahead. "They do preach the Bible, but there's so much busyness about it that I was distracted." He said nothing about all the pretty girls in fancy dresses, none as appealing as Deborah Wall in her plain clothes and bonnet.

"I did hear that some of the Methodist women are also sewing things for the runaway slaves," Aunt Martha said. "In many ways we are in one accord."

"I heard that last bunch that came through needed almost everything," Uncle George said.

"All Aaron and his family wore were rags, and it still felt like winter. Town needs a shoemaker. Almost none of the travelers have shoes."

"I wonder where those people are," Uncle George said.

"I hate to ask too much when I see Friend Coffin at the shop. You never know who might be passing by. But I heard they stayed several weeks until the lame one could walk. Then someone took them to Cabin Creek. Don't know if they stayed in Randolph County or went on."

Aunt Martha breathed deeply and let it out. "I don't think we give thanks enough for having our homes and families."

"You are right." Nathaniel had to admire the Coffin family. Mr. Coffin tended to his business activities and involvement in New Garden meeting while hiding and caring for runaways. Mrs. Coffin showed each group the same calm hospitality she'd shown Nathaniel, and the runaways were probably more agreeable company than he'd been.

Nathaniel had opened a shop east of the main crossroad in Newport. Katy and Levi Coffin returned most of the money he'd given to her, providing he used it for the shop and tools, they'd said. He included a set of shoeing stocks for draft horses and oxen. Deborah Wall's father had hewn the beams and built the stocks for him.

He often saw Deborah from a distance but seldom had opportunity to speak to her, or words to say if their paths did cross. Of all people she remembered most clearly how he used to be. Some of the argumentative things he'd said to her made him wince with embarrassment now.

They pulled up near the frame building under the tall trees; only a few horses stood at the hitch rack. He looked for the Walls, but they hadn't arrived yet.

Aunt Martha liked to be early, which suited Nathaniel. He could find a seat in the back of the meetinghouse, put his leg up, and watch for the Wall family to come in. He liked to see Deborah, but did no more than nod and smile if she said hello. He knew her father, brothers, and nephews better through business.

Little Catherine Coffin was still his friend though. When the family came in, the little girl hobbled over to tell him what all had been going on. Now she could add, subtract, multiply, and divide fractions. One of the barn cats just had kittens, and as an afterthought, she told him about a group of Friends who came all the way from England. They'd stayed with her family and met a big group of runaways.

Someone like that, devoted to abolition and helping the slaves, might take Deborah Wall away. His chest tightened at the thought.

Little Catherine jumped up to join her mother and sisters. The seams of her gray dress showed her curved back. It might have gotten worse over time. He wished he could do something to help her.

Levi Coffin sat down by him. "Welcome, neighbor. How is business?"

Nathaniel smiled. "Busy right now, sir. Even shoeing some oxen."

"So the shoeing stocks were a good investment." He nodded. "I am pleased to hear thy good report."

"Thank you, sir."

The older man nodded. "I'm always glad to hear of thy progress. Excuse me—I need to move closer to the front to be sure I can hear."

Nathaniel nodded and stole a glance toward the doors as the women and men separated and went to their own sides. Their silence and dark, plain clothes helped him clear his mind and focus on the Lord.

The ministers and worthy Friends sat in benches on the platform at the front of the meetinghouse, facing the other members. Unlike the Methodist church, there was no cross, no pulpit, and no preacher in ceremonial robes. No music either. Now that was something he wished the Friends would reconsider.

Deborah Wall came in with her mother, older sisters, and nieces. Nathaniel's business with the Lord ended abruptly. Most of her family wore gray dresses, but Deborah preferred brown still. She was tall and willowy, almost as tall as her dad, and taller than her younger brothers. Her best dress was made of shiny material; her bonnet and cape were spotless.

Another man slipped into the pew beside him and blocked his view of Deborah.

The man took a long look at her. Nathaniel took a deep breath. He had no claim to Deborah. Someday she was sure to marry one of the Friends. Her life was so different from his. A future with her was too much to hope for, although he knew his heavenly Father knew his heart, and Deborah's.

As she and her family found their seats, she looked his way. Nathaniel froze and then reminded himself to smile. She glanced at her mother and nieces, and then back at him. Wonder of wonders, she smiled at him. Nathaniel's heart started racing.

The Friends settled down for several long, quiet moments. Deborah's father went to the facing benches and sat at a desk. He was the clerk for today's meeting. A minister on the platform made announcements, and another led out in prayer. Afterward they spoke of progress at the Friends' school that used the meetinghouse during the week.

Following a long, thoughtful pause, someone raised an objection to using the meetinghouse for antislavery meetings, but no one else felt led to speak one way or another. The topic died out, but the members were disquieted for several restless moments.

Friends who had called on members that needed help or spiritual guidance reported on the outcomes of their visits. One, John Moore, the weaver, was the angular man who had sat down by Nathaniel. How could he be a match for Deborah? What would they have in common?

*Lord, help me listen.* Several members had been appointed to attend various weddings among the young people. All the events had taken place decently and in good order.

Weddings. If he and Deborah were to marry, who would the Friends appoint—no, he couldn't think about a future with her.

Sadly some others reported that members who had broken fellowship wouldn't be reasoned with and were to be dismissed. At the mention of another girl's name, Deborah's lower lip trembled, and she blinked as though holding back tears. The girl had married someone outside the fellowship. Several people sighed and murmured among themselves at the bad news.

The members became silent for long moments after that. Through the open windows came the sound of birds, a breeze in the trees, and water rippling through the creek bed.

Someone else felt led to speak about the dangers of being unequally yoked in marriage or in business. Nathaniel mulled that over. If both were Christians, were they truly unequally yoked?

During the next long, peaceful silence, Nathaniel recalled the previous year. Perhaps only such hard times could turn his heart and mind back to the Lord.

Finally the minister sensed that the meeting was over. He stood and shook hands with the others on the platform. Everyone else stood and shook hands all around. Nathaniel waited for the others to leave so his limping pace wouldn't delay them.

A short, stocky man with a jowly face and thick white hair spoke to Deborah's father. Nathaniel overheard Mr. Wall greet the man as Friend Smith. He was the other man who wanted to call on Deborah. Nathaniel found himself walking out with Josiah Wall, Deborah's father.

"I'm glad to see thee well, neighbor," the older man said. "Thee's moving a little more slowly today."

"Lots of plow horses and oxen to shoe this week."

"Glad of that. My family and I have a concern, Nathaniel."

"About what, sir?" He held his breath. What if he'd noticed Nathaniel staring at Deborah?

"Thy mare seems to be getting closer to foaling. We wondered if thee would like to come out and take a look at her."

"I would. When would it suit you all?"

"Even today, if thee's concerned about her. Our Deborah believed thee would be interested. She and Mother planned on one more for dinner."

Nathaniel grinned. "I'll tell my uncle and aunt."

Out by the hitch rack, he found the Walls sorting out who would ride in which of two buggies. The boys had ridden their horses over to the meeting. Nathaniel found himself in the buggy with Mr. Wall. Deborah drove the other horse, a high-spirited gelding. She managed it as well as any man, better than most.

He and Josiah Wall talked about the weather and farming as the horse trotted eagerly back home. They went north on the Winchester road through Newport, past the big, white tavern favored by the Wagner gang, past the potter's shop, harness maker's, cooper's, wagon maker's, doctor's house, and the Coffins' store. They turned east at the main crossroad. A few hundred yards from the creek stood Nathaniel's blacksmith shop. Since it opened, he'd been within sight of the Coffins' house and had even seen Deborah from a distance many times, but he didn't try to push friendship on her.

The horses and buggy clip-clopped over the new bridge. Only smears of silt on the trees showed the height of the earlier flood.

The first farm next to the creek belonged to William Smith, the widower interested in Deborah. Nathaniel studied the farm as they went by. A tall, square house stood at the end of a long lane. Behind it stood a big barn and pastures enclosed with rail fences. Milk cows and oxen lay chewing their cud among tall grass. Like every other farm here, woods edged all the fields and lined the horizons, showing where the first settlers had chopped fields out of forests.

The brick house had rows of windows and massive chimneys. Making enough money to build such a place of his own would take years, and Deborah would have married someone else by then.

"Nathaniel, I have a concern," her father said.

"What is it, Mr. Wall?"

"I hear good things about thy work and thy character. Thee attends meeting consistently. I wonder if thee has considered rejoining the Friends."

Nathaniel shook his head. "I don't feel led that way, sir. I am a Christian, but I differ from the Society's teaching on several points."

Mr. Wall nodded. After a long pause he said, "We are called to be in the world but not of it. How thee works that out in thy life is between thee and the Lord."

"I appreciate your concern, Mr. Wall. It's something I've been thinking about."

"Truly?"

"Yes sir. If I did rejoin the Society, I'd want to be settled in my mind that it's for the right reasons."

Mr. Wall gave him a long look. "Thee's very thoughtful."

"I have a lot of time to think while I work." He didn't want to admit how much he thought about Deborah.

# Chapter 10

Deborah turned the reins over to one of her brothers when they reached home. She watched Pa and Nathaniel in the open buggy. What had they talked about?

All these weeks he would only smile at her, never saying anything. He either didn't like her at all or thought she didn't like him, or he was trying to avoid giving offense. Most likely he didn't like her because of how she'd treated him while he was at the Coffins'. Every time she remembered her harsh words and cruel thoughts toward him, she felt pricked in the heart and prayed about it again.

If she'd given offense, she needed to make it right, one of the most difficult things she had to do as a Christian. Perhaps asking Nathaniel's forgiveness would give her peace.

After he'd helped Pa and the boys with the horses, Nathaniel limped into the house, the last to enter, and said hello to her mother. He turned to Pa. "I didn't see the mare. Is she out on pasture?"

"Down by the creek, most likely."

Nathaniel looked over his shoulder. "Very far?"

Deborah resisted the urge to speak up and tell him where to find the mare. If they walked out there together, she might have a moment to apologize to him for her conduct earlier. "I can guess where she would be. After dinner we can look for her."

During the meal Deborah hardly tasted the corn dodgers Mama served. Nathaniel talked and laughed with her family as though he'd known them for years, but he barely talked to her. What if she was right and Nathaniel had been offended all these weeks? After the meal she hurried up into the loft of the double log cabin and changed into her old homespun dress and apron.

Nathaniel waited for her on the back porch. "I hope it's not too far."

"No, it will be a pleasant walk." She led the way to the gate. Nathaniel dropped the rails and put them back.

At the edge of the woods, redbud trees looked like pink clouds. The dogwoods' white blossoms glowed in the woods, and the dark shapes of the horses and cows were visible at the end of the green pasture.

Despite the soft blue sky and warm air, Deborah shivered, gathering her nerve before speaking. "Nathaniel Fox, I have something to say to thee."

His deep voice was soothing. "I'm glad. It's been a long time since we talked." He turned and gave her a hand as they picked a path around mud puddles. His hand was warm and his arm solid.

She took a deep breath and held it. Admitting to doing wrong wasn't easy. "About that—if I did anything to offend thee, with harsh words or how I acted toward thee when thee first came here. . ."

He stopped and studied her for a moment then smiled wryly. "Harsh? I think you were justified. Somewhat. Although there were times when you looked at me like I was pond scum."

She burst out laughing then gazed up into his eyes, sky blue in the spring sunshine. She had to be as direct as possible. What was she going to say? "But still—"

He put his finger over her lips. His sudden warm touch almost stopped her heart, but then it started to race. "You have done nothing to offend me."

"Thee has said nothing to me for weeks."

He looked down and started worrying a clump of grass with his boot toe. "I shouldn't speak to you. It would make you look bad, harm your reputation. People would talk."

"I have my integrity." She held out her hand and sighed. "Let's go look at the horses." Once she told him the worst of it, he might never forgive her. She hated to risk that. Her thoughts toward him startled her again. If he never forgave her, they'd have no future. She'd allowed herself to imagine too much, that this tall, handsome man who also liked horses and farming would grow into a solid Christian, diligent in business, sober in character—someone worth marrying once he rejoined the Society.

They walked a little farther. The long grass hid stumps and roots left from when Pa and the boys had cleared the field years ago. Deborah tripped and Nathaniel caught her. Both stumbled for their balance and held each other up.

She looked up into his ruddy face. His countenance had changed so much over the past several weeks. How could she have ever thought such cruel thoughts about him? "Nathaniel, there is more I need to confess."

He closed his eyes as though bracing for bad news. "Tell me, then."

"When Pa first brought thee to the Coffins, I—" She had to take another breath to steady her nerves. "I wondered if drowning was the Lord's judgment on thee for thy wicked ways."

He breathed deeply, let it out, and then smiled.

"Nathaniel, why is thee smiling?"

"I feared worse news."

She shook her head. "What could be any worse?"

"That you planned to marry someone else."

Deborah blinked in surprise. "Marry someone? There's no one—" She cleared her throat. Her face warmed, clear up to the roots of her hair. Where did that idea come from? "Nathaniel, I wished the worst that could befall thee."

He looked down and nodded. "I'm not surprised at all. Nor offended. Tell me you haven't worried about that all this time."

"I have."

He took her hands. "Oh Deborah Wall, the Bible says if any man is in Christ, he is a new creature. But also you need to forget what lies behind."

Her voice trembled. "I was so harsh. Almost treated thee like—like—"

He kept her hands. "Like someone of the world? For all have sinned and fall short of the glory of God. You know that, as well as I do, birthright Friend or not."

She looked down and shook her head. Her voice cracked, and she paused to get it under control. "I never thought I'd act it out like that, Nathaniel."

"I never thought I'd do half the things I ended up doing either. And I was a birthright Friend, too." He held her hands then drew her after him. "We're supposed to look ahead, aren't we? I have a lot to forget, and I suppose you have an item or two you'd like to rarely recall."

She nodded. "Thee's right. Let's find the horses."

They reached the swale where a streamlet trickled toward Willow Creek. The cows were lying down chewing their cud as Deborah and Nathaniel walked up.

Two of the horses looked up then returned to grazing. The mare was missing. Deborah took a few steps farther. "I suppose, if she's off by herself, she might be foaling now."

Nathaniel nodded. "Any ideas where she might have gone?"

"There's a little clearing back here." She led him to the edge of the woods, along a muddy trail chopped with hoofprints. She glanced over her shoulder at Nathaniel. Hard to imagine he was the same person as the grim man who'd pursued fugitives to the Coffins' home.

He looked up from untangling raspberry canes from his clothes. "I wish the mare would foal about the same time as the raspberries come on."

"She's too far along. But we might see fit to invite thee back when the berries are ripe," Deborah said. She paused to study the plants, beaded with green flower buds that would yield berries in a few weeks.

"Glad of that." He smiled.

Deborah glanced back at him and smiled.

A horse snorted and a tiny voice answered. Deborah and Nathaniel exchanged glances. She took a step forward and he joined her. They pushed aside a screen of leafy branches. In the grass of the clearing, the mare stood over a tiny long-legged foal, nuzzling and licking its fuzzy coat.

Deborah looked at Nathaniel. His eyes widened and he grinned. "I thought I'd never see this. And you're here to see it with me."

She looked at him questioningly. "I'm glad thee feels that way."

He took her hand.

Deborah breathed deeply. Her hand felt so right in his—hidden, safe, protected by his strong grip. Neither John, the weaver, nor Neighbor Smith made her feel that way, because she didn't feel any closeness to them. "Nathaniel Fox, if thee has forgiven me for my harshness toward thee earlier, then do speak to me when we see each other."

He kept her hand then took her other one. Deborah's mind raced. People at weddings faced each other and held hands just like this. But wait, neither she nor anyone in her family knew him very well. "It would be my privilege."

"I think we should see if thee has a colt or filly," she added.

# Chapter 11

As spring warmed into summer, Nathaniel made many calls to the Wall farm to see the mare and her filly. Sometimes when she wasn't working, he saw Deborah, too. Every time they talked about the mare and foal, he felt more drawn to her. If only he could follow his heart, pursue her, try to win her for his wife.

Whenever he imagined marrying her, he remembered how upset she'd been when one of her friends was dismissed for marrying out of unity. What would be best for Deborah? Her entire family and all of her friends were in the Society. Love was long-suffering and kind, according to the Bible, and did not seek its own way. How could marrying him be best for her?

The open secret of the Coffins' abolition work included a sigh of relief this time of year. Everyone knew most runaways arrived over the winter, when their pursuers were reluctant to go out in bad weather. As summer went on, the days grew longer and hotter.

On a drowsy afternoon, Deborah Wall led one of the Coffins' horses down to his shop.

"Hello, neighbor," she said.

Nathaniel looked up from sharpening some hand tools, easy work in this heat. Her coarse homespun dress, sleeves pushed up on her arms, looked cool in the heat. Freckles dotted her hands, forearms, cheeks, and nose. Nathaniel had never seen such a pretty girl.

If only she hadn't seen him like this, in work clothes and in need of a shave. "Good afternoon, Miss Wall. What can I do for you?"

She tied the old gelding to the rail in front and looked around the shop. It was mostly a roof over the forge. Barn swallows darted in and out. "He has a loose shoe."

Nathaniel lifted the horse's hoof and examined the shoe. It was missing a nail. "Do you want to reset the shoes or just replace that nail?"

"Just the nail, until he needs all of them done."

"Are you in a hurry?"

She chuckled. "No, this is cheaper." She stood by the gelding and watched Nathaniel work. "I need to tell thee some other news."

He nodded.

"Neighbor Smith, outside of town, has bought a good trotting horse. Pa made bookcases for his house earlier and saw it. If thee is wondering about getting thy mare rebred, that might be a good one."

"Have you seen the horse?"

"I have. A few nights ago, I rode over with Pa."

He took a moment to gather his thoughts as well as find just the right nail. He knew Smith, a rich widower, favored Deborah. "To visit with your father or see the horse?"

She smoothed her dark hair under her bonnet. What would it look like all undone? Couldn't think like that. Or that she and her father had gone out to the Smith place. He made himself listen as she said, "Truth be told. . .a little of both."

"What do you think of that horse, Deborah Wall?"

"He's taller and has better legs than the mare. Thy mare is lovely in every way, except she toes in slightly in front. Improve that so they don't overreach or interfere at speed, and any of their foals would be even faster."

He watched, agreeing with her thoughts. "Good reason to look him over."

She nodded. "I thought thee would like to know. Good afternoon, neighbor."

Nathaniel watched her walk away. He breathed deeply and exhaled. They liked so many of the same things. They could talk about horses all day. Could he and Deborah ever have a future together? Should he even hope for that?

❧

Deborah looked over her shoulder at Nathaniel as she walked slowly back to the big brick house. As she left the shop, someone brought in a lame horse.

He worked carefully with the horse and had a long talk with the owner. The sun gleamed copper in Nathaniel's tousled chestnut hair. His face, arms, and hands were tanned. During his talk with the owner, he picked up the horse's leg and pointed to its tendons, as though those were part of the problem. The owner looked impressed. She sighed. Was she in error to hope and pray Nathaniel would rejoin the Society? She'd gotten ahead of the Spirit's leading earlier, and only the Lord's mercy had saved Pa and the runaways from the Wagner gang. She would hate to rely on her own insight again. But it was so hard to wait on the Lord's timing.

She walked up the path through the grape arbor; the fruit's sweet scent combined with the aroma of gingerbread cooling on the dining room windowsill. She'd made the cake earlier for the sewing circle.

Inside, she helped Cousin Katy and the girls open windows on the shady side of the house. They closed other windows and curtains against the sun. The house's high ceilings, tall windows, and transoms over the doors helped capture the breeze.

She climbed the narrow, twisting stairs to the bedroom she shared with the girls. She changed into a better dress then went downstairs to help prepare for the sewing circle.

Mama and her oldest sister, Ruthanne, planned to come today. The group tried to keep ahead of clothing needed by the runaways. More women came during spring and summer when travel was easier.

She steadied Little Catherine, who'd climbed into a straight chair to get to the gingerbread. "Patience, dear, thee might fall."

The youngest Coffin girl turned her head toward Deborah, but only a little because of her curved spine. "I just wished to smell it. Perhaps someone needs to sample it?"

Deborah put her hand over her lips for a moment to hide a chuckle then looked at the mantel clock. "Not long, now, dear heart." She helped Little Catherine down.

She longed to see Mama. Sometimes the fugitives' stories made her heart ache. How blessed her family was to have each other. No one could tear them away, unlike the poor slaves.

Little Catherine looked out the window. "Deborah, here is thy mother already."

Deborah opened the door and helped Mama up the stairs.

Mama took both of her hands. "Did thee make gingerbread, dear heart? I thought I smelled it. I'm surprised the whole town isn't here."

Deborah smiled. "I hope it's like thine, Mama." She refilled the teakettle and swung it over the fire.

Cousin Katy came into the dining room and held out both hands. "I'm glad to see thee, Ruth."

"Everything worked out to come a little early, Katy," Mama said and smiled at Deborah.

Mama was so pretty, even at her age, and looked so different from Deborah. Of all her sisters, only Deborah was tall and dark like Papa.

"Come in; sit down," Cousin Katy said, and then put her hand to her forehead. "I need to ask Grandmother if she remembers what we did with those fabric samples from the store. If I can find them, we can make good use of them." She went into Friend Coffin's office.

Mama held Deborah's arm. "Come sit with me for a moment. Deborah, I felt led to come early and ask if there is anything on thy heart."

Deborah sat with Mama on the bench. The big fireplace that she'd had to fill every time she turned around last winter was empty; all the ashes swept up weeks ago. Now gingham curtains fluttered at the open windows.

Deborah nodded. The Lord knew the secrets of all hearts. And Mama wasn't far behind. She sighed. "Oh Mama, I don't know where to begin."

"I must tell thee that Friend Smith has asked Papa again if he may call on thee."

Deborah froze, and her heart dropped. She shook her head. "Mama, thee knows I don't want to marry someone so many years older than me. I do not wish to be widowed."

Mama nodded. "That does make sense." She picked up the workbasket and started sorting fabric that could be trimmed for quilt pieces. Many times, they sent things with the fugitives.

Deborah picked up her knitting basket, filled as always with walnut-dyed wool for making mittens, scarves, and socks.

Mama sorted the cloth pieces by color—gray, brown, white, black. Calico samples from the Coffins' store would make a pretty addition. "I have also noticed at meeting that Nathaniel often looks for thee."

Deborah nodded. "I look for him, too. I like him very much, but I know so little of him. Thee and Papa knew each other even as children."

"Thy situation is very different. I know this doesn't seem like much of an answer, but I'm afraid thee must be patient. See how the matter ends."

Deborah sighed. Soon she would be twenty-one. So old, so soon. She kept knitting. A step of faith would be to trust the Lord with this situation. If she had no future with Nathaniel, surely the Lord had a better plan for her life. Or perhaps she would never marry, but she believed she could trust God with this situation.

# Chapter 12

On the Sabbath, Nathaniel went to the Walls' farm after meeting. Deborah let her father and brothers do all the talking with him. They talked about a neighbor boy who'd gone to a Fourth of July celebration and militia shoot. Papa and another of the worthy Friends had been appointed to call on the boy later that week and reason with him about his misconduct.

Nathaniel brought a satchel with him and after dinner told the boys it was a halter and rope to teach the filly to lead. Deborah enjoyed hearing his deep voice and hearty laugh. The boys wanted to hurry out and work with the horses. Deborah stayed back and helped Mama with the dishes.

"Is thee going to see about the filly?" Mama asked.

Deborah watched Nathaniel, the boys, and the horses out the window. "No— I would like to go for a walk." She sighed. Longing for a talk with Nathaniel had distracted her from everything that happened in meeting. Could anything clear her mind?

She went to the loft and changed into her homespun dress and apron, and then slipped down the ladder again. Outside, the grass in the cabin's shade felt wonderfully cool to her bare feet. While the boys and Nathaniel faced the other way, she slipped past the barn and into the woods.

The paths made by the cows and horses had turned to thick, warm dust that puffed up between her toes. She followed the trail to the edge of the woods and found the last of the raspberries. Couldn't let them go to waste. She plucked a few and admired the deep purple of the juice on her hands. God made such a colorful world.

Hoofbeats thudded softly on the trail behind her. She turned around. Nathaniel. The filly dawdled after him, likely out of curiosity since he'd removed the halter; she didn't see the mare.

"I thought I saw you walk out this way, Deborah. Is something on your mind? You were so quiet at dinner."

She shook her head. "It is a matter of the heart. Painful to discuss."

He nodded. "Can I ask you a question or two?"

"Of course. We should always speak the truth."

He looked down. "One of your nephews said William Smith called on your father." He took a deep breath. "This is none of my concern."

"Speak thy mind, Nathaniel." She held out some raspberries. "Perhaps this will clear thy thinking."

He chuckled as he took them.

The filly came up to them, her nose out, and snuffled at the berries. Her fuzzy tail twitched, and she stamped a tiny hoof. Nathaniel smiled and offered a berry to the creature. She mouthed it then let the pieces drop from her mouth and turned up her nose.

Out in the pasture, the mare whinnied loudly.

The foal answered in her squeaky voice. The mare galloped past the screen of trees and brush in front of them, and then slid to a stop, neighing frantically. She ran past the end of the woods then turned and thundered down the trail.

She looked wild-eyed and blinded with fright.

Deborah stared at the animal pounding toward them. The horse would not stop for anything until she found the foal.

Nathaniel grabbed Deborah and swung her out of the way. He staggered as his knee gave out, and he lurched into a tree. Deborah caught him before he fell, wrapped her arms around his waist, and then looked past his arm to the mare and foal, whickering to each other. Deborah and Nathaniel held each other up. She imagined the mare scolding the filly for wandering off.

Nathaniel took a deep breath; she felt his ribs heave. "All's well that ends well. Are you all right?"

Her head rested against his chest; his vest felt scratchy against her cheek. "We forget how powerful they are. They seem so meek."

Nathaniel looked into her eyes. He was so warm and solid, looming over her, studying her face. Was he going to kiss her? No one ever had. It would be too much intimacy outside of marriage. Deborah barely breathed, longing for him to kiss her, but knowing it was wrong. She straightened and edged away from him.

Nathaniel let her slip from his grasp. "Like our own hearts sometimes." His face grew solemn, even sorrowful. His voice sounded choked. "Deborah, are you going to marry Friend Smith?"

Deborah shook her head. She turned and watched the mare and foal. "No, Nathaniel. He is so much older than me."

"He has a lot to offer. A big farm and a beautiful home."

She shook her head. "One of my greatest fears is to be widowed. He might have many things, but he can't turn back time. I want—if I ever marry—I want to build a life together."

He nodded again. "If we are speaking the truth, then Deborah Wall. . ." He reached out and took her hand. "I have to confess, I can hardly think of anyone or anything but you. All these weeks seeing you at meeting, the times your family invited me over, how we talked about horses—wondering if we could have a future together."

Her heart leaped, and she gazed into his face. His brows were drawn. He put one hand up and rubbed his eyes. Maybe this was the answer to her prayers for leading. She held his one hand in both of hers and looked down at his big, tanned, work-worn hand. "I've wondered the same thing. But thee has said nothing of it until now."

"I'm trying to build my business and learn to be a better Christian. I felt I had no standing, no right to speak to you."

"Thee shouldn't think so little of thyself. Thee's precious in God's eyes."

Nathaniel took a deep breath. "What about in your eyes? Deborah—" He took another breath. "Deborah, I've been falling in love with you for weeks. I never thought

I'd ever feel this way for anyone, like there's a future and hope."

She touched his warm, tanned face then nodded. "I felt the same way." Was this true or a dream? The two of them together could clear new ground, build a cabin, start a farm of their own, and have a family. Tears of joy welled up in her eyes. Someday they might have a farm as beautiful as the Smith place.

He smiled, his eyes widening and his ruddy face giving his eyes a sky blue gleam. He twined his fingers through hers then raised her hand to his lips and kissed the back of it. His lips felt so warm and soft that she longed to be in his arms.

His face clouded. He looked so forlorn. "What of the Society?"

Deborah's heart raced. Surely they could work this out. "Thee only has to condemn thy misconduct."

He dropped his head. "I'm not convinced I'd be joining it for the right reasons. I question some of the Society's teachings."

She gasped. "About what?"

"Plain or lofty speech, plain dress or not, makes no difference to me." He took another deep breath. "I've been out in the world and am not convinced that a man can be completely nonviolent."

Deborah tried to understand him. "If thee trusts the Lord to keep thee—"

He nodded. "I see the logic in that. But I've seen bad things, Deborah. I wish I could trust the Lord that much."

"Perhaps such grace is given day by day, like manna in the wilderness."

"You might be right."

She took a deep breath. Her tears came from despair now. "Thee spoke the truth. I do not feel led to leave the Society."

"And I doubt my reasons for wanting to join." He rested his forehead against hers. "Oh Deborah, my hope and prayer is, someday, I'm going to marry you."

She closed her eyes, and her tears spilled over now. "But thee needs to count the cost. Both of us. I think we should speak no more of this, Nathaniel." Her breath was ragged as she shook her head. "Speak no more of this, I beg of thee."

# Chapter 13

Seeing Deborah now was bittersweet for Nathaniel. On summer days when he wasn't busy, he helped some of the neighbors with wheat harvest and putting up hay. As summer faded into fall, corn ripened and dried down. The fields faded from green to gold. Sometimes the slaves fled north at times like this, when they could easily hide in the cornfields and find cover in the woods while the trees still had leaves.

Nathaniel listened intently in meeting, and as was said in the book of Acts, like the Bereans, he searched the scriptures daily to see if these things were so.

With the Lord's help—because he'd learned to lie so fluently while in the world—he always told the truth and began rebuilding his integrity. When Uncle George remarked that Nathaniel's father would have been proud of him, his encouraging words were like a stream in the desert.

The Friends made him feel welcome, and some of the older ones even knew of his parents. But how could he be sure he was joining the Society for the right reasons, not just to win Deborah?

Deborah's life seemed to go on as before. She participated in women's meetings and kept busy helping Katy Coffin and her family. She was beautiful as ever. Her brown dresses along with her big dark eyes reminded him of a deer.

As soon as frosts came, the trees in New Garden blazed red, gold, yellow, and orange against the clear blue sky. When the tenth month arrived, the filly would be six months old. One First Day, after meeting, he conferred with Deborah's family about the horses. "I've finished the barn and fences at my uncle's, Friend Wall, so I can bring the mare home for weaning the filly."

Deborah remembered how frantic the mare had been for the filly earlier in the summer. Perhaps the process would be faster and easier if the two were separated.

Papa nodded. "Tonight might work, when we bring Deborah back to the Coffins'."

"I'll meet you at the shop."

☙

As soon as the sun went down, the air cooled rapidly. Deborah and Papa tried to soothe the mare as they led her out of the barn and hitched her to the back of the farm wagon loaded with wood.

Papa chirped to the team, and they rolled forward.

The filly whinnied for her mother. The mare dug in her heels. The wagon rattled to a stop, and the horses snorted with surprise. "Get up there," Pa called to the team.

Deborah turned on the seat and looked back. The mare's eyes were wild, and lather coated her neck and chest. Her nostrils flared as she snorted. She braced her

334

legs, and the team dragged her a few steps. "Oh Pa, I don't think this is going to work."

"Try once more," Papa said. He urged the team forward. The mare went a few steps then pulled back as hard as she could. Her halter broke, the tailgate cracked, and part of the load clattered to the ground. Just as the boys came out, she disappeared into the dark barn, whinnying for the filly.

They got down and picked up the spilled firewood. Papa sighed. "Tomorrow I'll hitch up the oxen. We can't take any more time tonight."

In town they stopped at Nathaniel's shop and told him what happened. He went around back and looked at the tailgate. "Did I mention she could be stubborn?" he said with a grin.

Deborah turned toward them, her arm over the back of the seat. He looked handsome even in his work clothes, a blue calico shirt, linsey-woolsey trousers, and tall boots. She liked his appearance better in those clothes than anything. "I have heard animals reflect their owners."

He arched his brows. "Might not be so bad." He gazed into her eyes then gave her a quick smile. "If I have my mind made up, I might be as determined as the mare."

Deborah opened her mouth but closed it again, saying nothing. He might have meant marrying her. She'd told no one, not even Mama, of his offer and her refusal. Perhaps life would be easier if he carried out his original plan and moved farther west, somewhere beyond the Friends' community. Life would be easier if she never saw him again, never saw him marry someone else.

The next day as she worked, Deborah watched for Pa, the oxcart, and the mare.

They could hear the mare before they saw her, neighing loudly for the filly every step of the way. When she tried to dig in her heels, the oxen kept going.

Deborah and Little Catherine watched from the porch.

Little Catherine studied the scene. "She has her saddle and bridle? Is Nathaniel going to ride her back to his uncle's?"

"I suppose he might." Deborah paused for a moment. What if he were hurt?

Pa and Nathaniel both took the mare's rope, fastened to her halter over her bridle. They looped it over the hitch rack and tied her. Nathaniel and Pa conferred.

The mare whinnied so loudly that she shook.

"What if they can still hear each other?" Little Catherine asked.

"Surely not."

"I believe their hearing is better than ours," Little Catherine said as the mare froze with her ears pointed to the east, toward the farm.

"Thee might be right."

Cousin Katy put her hand on Deborah's shoulder. "I know thee would like to go talk to thy papa. Why not go along now? Little Catherine can help me with a few things."

Deborah nodded. "I'll be back in a few minutes." She grabbed her wraps and darted out the door.

Both men seemed glad to see her. She held Papa's hands. "We heard thee coming."

He nodded. "She is very upset. But thee knows now, Nathaniel, she'll work out well as a broodmare for thee."

The blacksmith winced and ran his hand through his tousled hair. "If she survives weaning this one."

Pa put his arm on Deborah's shoulder. "Take care, now. I'm going to the mill to see about our corn. Soon be time to pick it. I hope all goes well for thee and the mare, Nathaniel."

He nodded. "Thank you, Friend Wall."

Deborah watched Pa as he picked up the ox goad and ordered the team to walk on. They started up the street between the edge of town and the creek, heading to the gristmill.

The mare whinnied again, and Nathaniel stood by her and tried to soothe her. He turned to Deborah.

Deborah gazed up at Nathaniel. Over the summer he'd filled out, shoulders broadened, forearms rippled with muscles. Work had marred his hands though. They were larger and more callused, but still gentle as he took one of hers. She cleared her throat. "Does thee plan to ride her back to thy uncle's house?"

The sound of galloping horses interrupted them, and a posse rounded the corner from the main road. The dogs barked, chasing after the running horses.

"Wagner," Nathaniel said. "You run along. This is no place for a lady."

A crowd of men on lathered horses slid to a stop. The leader jumped off his horse. He reminded Deborah of a snake—lean with hard, unblinking eyes. "Fox, you need to reshoe this horse quick as you can. We're in hot pursuit."

"Of what?"

"A quadroon woman worth a thousand dollars to her owner. She's a trained singer." He swung round and pointed at Deborah. "You seen anyone like that?"

Nathaniel took a half step between Deborah and Wagner.

Deborah smiled wryly at the slave hunter. "Not at my father's farm. I can't recall the last time an opera singer lodged with us."

"Never mind. Fox, put this shoe back on this horse."

"I need a dollar first."

"What? Pay you first!"

"Yep. I'm thinking of other bills left unpaid."

"All right, all right. In a hurry after all."

He nodded.

Deborah backed away. She walked up to the crossroads, thinking to go around the corner and be hidden by the buildings. There might be someone at the Coffin place who needed a hand.

Loud voices came from behind her. She looked over her shoulder.

Nathaniel set down the lame horse's foot then held up a twisted shoe. He shook his head and pointed to the horse; the horse rested the one bare foot on its toe. Even that was too much weight. It lifted its injured foot and held it in the air, trembling.

Wagner waved his hands and pointed.

Nathaniel folded his arms across his chest and shook his head.

The other men laughed and jumped back on their horses. Apparently they intended to capture the slave woman and, if they found her, cut Wagner out of the deal.

Wagner swung a punch at Nathaniel.

Deborah gasped. Would he fight back? Use violence?

He grappled with Wagner but didn't hit back. Instead he held the slave hunter at arm's length.

They thrashed through the blacksmith shop. Tools, supplies, and firewood went everywhere. Wagner flailed like a windmill but was an inch or two away from reaching Nathaniel, who kept grinning.

Men ran to the shop, including Papa, Levi Coffin, and the town constable.

Wagner grabbed a hammer off the anvil and swung it at Nathaniel's head. The blacksmith staggered and went to his knees.

Wagner untied Nathaniel's mare and jumped on her. As soon as she was free, Brandy put her head down and bolted for the farm. A cloud of dust hid them a moment later.

Deborah hitched up her skirts and raced down the hill to the blacksmith shop. She found Nathaniel sitting up, his back against one of the porch posts, his arm held over his head. With his other hand, he mashed his shirtsleeve into a cut above his eye. Despite that, blood ran down his face.

"Deborah," he said in tired voice. His eyes rolled back in his head, and he slumped over. She rushed to him. She pulled off her apron, rolled it up, and put it under his head. Perhaps he had only fainted.

He shivered. "The mare!" He tried to sit up but winced.

The constable strode after the runaway horse but turned to Levi Coffin and Deborah's father. "Men, encourage those ruffians to leave town as soon as possible. That last one though, I am taking to jail." He muttered under his breath, and his long white mustache twitched. "Can't come to my town and hit good citizens over the head and steal horses in broad daylight. That arrogant buffoon. Nathaniel Fox, are you alive or dead?"

Nathaniel groaned. "I'll be all right."

"Peace, be still," Deborah said, gripping his shoulder.

He put his bloodstained hand over hers. "I didn't hit him."

"I saw that, Nathaniel."

"Thee saw—"

"Yes. Thee did the best thee could."

"Hard not to hit him."

"I'm sure it was. Thee was sorely provoked."

"Supposed to turn the other cheek. I reckon holding him off was about the same."

The doctor arrived on his pacing horse and jumped off, quite spry for a man his age. "Well. We meet again, neighbor. May I see him, Deborah Wall?"

She moved out of the way, but Nathaniel kept her hand.

"Scalp and facial injuries do bleed considerably," the doctor announced. "Nathaniel, did thee faint for any length of time?"

"I'm not sure."

"Did thee see, Deborah Wall?"

"Yes, he did faint."

"We will treat him as though he has a concussion. Someone needs to be with him for the next several hours, so he doesn't go to sleep and fail to wake up." The doctor looked toward the road. "Now who's coming?"

"Some men went after that Wagner and Nathaniel's horse," Deborah said.

The doctor stood up, folded his arms, and watched horses and riders approach. "Well this doesn't look good."

# Chapter 14

Nathaniel's head pounded with his heartbeat, but his double vision slowly returned to normal. He sat in the parlor with Levi Coffin. A cool autumn breeze stirred the curtains at the open windows and doors.

"I haven't had a chance to converse with thee as I would've liked, neighbor," the older man said and smiled at Nathaniel.

"We've all been quite occupied."

"The Lord works all things together for good," Friend Coffin said. "Even giving me an opportunity of operating in my gift of talkativeness."

From their chairs and benches on the other side of the room, the Coffin girls giggled.

Deborah came in with tea. Over the summer, even though she surely wore a bonnet, more freckles had appeared. They only added to her appeal. Now that he'd met all of her family over the past few months, he could see she got her height and long arms from her father but had a pretty face like her mother. Friend Coffin was saying something. Nathaniel shook his head. "I'm afraid I wasn't paying attention."

The older man chuckled then grew more solemn. "How well was thee acquainted with Octavian Wagner?"

Nathaniel sighed. "Only slightly. But to think he came to such a sudden end. . ." The mare had thrown Wagner as she bolted for the farm in search of her filly. Wagner died shortly afterward.

"Perhaps he remembered something of the Gospels at the end," Little Catherine said.

Nathaniel shook his head. "If he'd ever heard them."

The little girls grew solemn. "Could anyone have never heard?"

"I fear so," Nathaniel said. "I hope I never leave something so important unsaid again." He was silent for a long, grim moment. But today's incident had cleared up something else for him. He did try to live by the Society's teaching on his own, not just when Deborah might be watching or listening. "Almost everyone in the township needs horses shod, or hinges or plow points or trammel hooks for the fireplace. In my situation I should have many opportunities to speak of our hope."

Deborah poured tea, and when she looked at him, her big eyes were solemn. But something else glimmered there. Was she proud of him?

Eventually Katy Coffin and the girls went to bed.

"Thee knows he must not sleep," Levi Coffin told Deborah. His eyes twinkled. "Perhaps thee might be troubled to talk with him until someone else can sit up with him."

She sat in the rocking bench on the other side of the parlor and picked up her knitting. "How is thee feeling, Nathaniel?"

"Tired. Head hurts. Nothing new though."

Her knitting needles clicked rapidly as mittens took shape. "I have something I need to say to thee."

Plain speech slipped out. He must be dazed still. "Please, speak thy mind. I know thee needs little encouragement."

"The Lord has made a wonderful change in thee." Her knitting needles slowed. "I have wanted to tell thee that for some time but had no opportunity."

"There's room at the other end of the bench. May I join thee?"

"Yes. Is thee using plain speech only to keep my attention?"

Nathaniel shuffled across the room. One of the Gospels talked about the Spirit giving believers the words they needed. Was this situation included? "No, Deborah Wall." The bench creaked dangerously under his weight. He put his arm over the back and turned toward her. "This is how I talk. How I was raised."

He reached over and put his hand on her hands. They felt so soft compared to his. "This is how I want to live my life."

The knitting needles stilled. Deborah took a deep breath.

Here was where he needed the Lord's help. "I wonder if thee will undertake such a journey with me, Deborah Wall?" He raised her slender hand and kissed the back of it.

"I would be pleased to do so, Nathaniel," she whispered, her voice shaky.

# Chapter 15

Deborah tried to remember the first time she'd seen Nathaniel as he took her hands in front of everyone at Ma and Pa's cabin. Today was fifth month, fourteenth day, 1841. Their wedding day.

His eyes were the same shade of blue, same brown lashes and brows, but today his wide grin and easy laugh made him seem like a different man. He was no longer angry and proud or pale and sick. Now he was healthy and strong, sober and honest. Deborah and her family were convinced that he would be a good husband.

All around were family and neighbors. Levi and Katy Coffin came as witnesses. They joined her parents, brothers and sisters and their families, the Coffin girls, Nathaniel's aunt and uncle, and many of Nathaniel's horse-shoeing customers in back. Some of the worldly ones stood respectfully in the very back but fidgeted and raised their heads to see to the ceremony. When they sensed it had started, the worldly men removed their hats; the Friends left theirs on.

The Friends looked sober in gray, brown, and black, but their eyes twinkled. Mama had made Deborah a new brown dress, white cape, apron, cap, and bonnet for this sunny spring day. The weather was clear and mild, an answer to many prayers.

Nathaniel repeated the words of the promises as she looked up at him. He never looked more handsome, wearing a wide-brimmed black hat, white shirt, and gray suit. His jacket had no lapels, and his waistcoat buttoned almost to his throat with plain dark buttons—so different from his brave, bright-colored apparel earlier.

"I, Nathaniel Fox, take thee, Deborah Wall, to be my wife. I promise with the Lord's help to be a loving and faithful husband until death should separate us."

She knew he meant every word. Deborah's hands trembled, and her voice shook as she repeated the same promises to him.

The ministers had the certificate ready for them to sign. Nathaniel's handwriting was neat and steady. She hardly could hold the pen as she signed her new name, Deborah Fox.

The Friends lined up to sign the declaration as witnesses.

Nathaniel pulled Deborah aside. "Tell me this is not a dream, Deborah Wall."

"Fox. Deborah Fox," she reminded him. She was still explaining when he gave her their first married kiss, wrapping his muscular arms around her, and pressing her to his warm, solid chest. His lips were soft against hers, and for a long moment, she felt like she was melting.

She stood on tiptoes and put her hand at the back of his neck. She rested her other hand on his cheek, smooth shaven and warm, then gave him a kiss in return.

**Ann E. Schrock** covered breaking news and features for local daily newspapers for ten years after graduating from Purdue University with a bachelor's degree in agricultural communication. She also has contributed devotionals for *Evangel*, a weekly paper published by the Free Methodist Church of North America. A native of Wayne County, Indiana, Ann and her husband are raising their three children on the family farm in northern Indiana.

# FREE INDEED

by Kristy Dykes

# Dedication

To my hero husband, Milton, who is my collaborator in the deepest sense of the word—he's believed in me, supported me, and cheered me on in my calling to inspirational writing.

# Author's Note:

In 1859, there were many black dialects in the South, including Geechee, Gullah, combinations of various kinds, even Elizabethan-sounding ones. I considered using Gullah, which is the authentic Black dialect in Charleston, South Carolina, but the dialogue would be hard to read. In an effort to maintain the flavor of the setting and time, I've sprinkled in off-grammar vernacular, the most easily-read form of dialect.

*If the Son therefore shall make you free,*
*ye shall be free indeed.*
JOHN 8:36

# Prologue

*1856, Laurel Ridge Plantation*
*The outskirts of Charleston, South Carolina*

Two important days have shaped my future, and they both had to do with freedom. I'll never forget the first day as long as I live.

That afternoon, I was helping Mrs. Williams, my master's wife, get dressed. She was to entertain her friends, and I took particular pains with her light brown hair, coiling the back into the new figure-eight style chignon, fluffing the front and sides into frothy curls. I wanted her to look her very best and had even suggested she wear her rose-colored silk, which she did. Then I refashioned her maroon velvet hat, adding ribbons and peacock feathers, something I'd seen in her ladies' magazine.

When she dismissed me, I came down the staircase of Laurel Ridge, intent on going to my quarters and checking on my little daughter, Cassie. She was asleep when I left her, and I wanted to be there when she woke up. After that, I planned to bring her to the kitchen house so I could watch her while I ironed Mrs. Williams's fine lawn underpinnings.

As I reached the last step, I lingered for a moment, thoughts of my Sweet Love Roscoe making my head swim and my heart race. My Sweet Love Roscoe lived on a neighboring plantation, and we had been allowed to jump the broom—that's slave talk for getting married—the summer of my seventeenth year, though I was still required to keep my master's surname.

Our Blooming Union, as Sweet Love Roscoe joshingly called it, had a bright spot. It had given us little Cassie. But dark clouds of despair overshadowed us when his bedeviled master issued a cruel edict after Cassie was born. He refused to let Sweet Love Roscoe see me, something that caused both of us great grief. The rare moments we spent in each other's arms were brief and on the sly.

I wept many a night over this. Other times, I got downright angry. The only things my people would ever know were ownership by other human beings and long dreary lives of servitude—if they were lucky enough not to be lashed into early graves, something that was a real possibility for my Sweet Love Roscoe.

The thought turned my stomach, as if I'd swallowed rancid meat, and I gripped the banister more tightly to steady my footing.

*Oh Roscoe,* I cried out in my heart. *Oh my Sweet Love Roscoe. . .*

I felt so woebegone, I couldn't even hang words on my thoughts. Then I shook myself. Work waited, always waited. As I proceeded across the wide hall of Laurel Ridge, I heard a door open behind me.

"Winkie?" called my master, Mr. Williams.

I turned around, my long skirts swishing in my quick movement. "Sir?"

"I've something to discuss with you. Come into my study."

"Yes sir." In moments, I was seated in front of Mr. Williams's large mahogany desk, wondering what he had to say. Though he was far different from Sweet Love Roscoe's stony-hearted master, still he was. . .my master, and inside, I chafed at this thought.

Mr. Williams sat down in his high-backed leather chair, reached into a drawer, and pulled out some papers.

Again, I wondered why he'd called me in here.

"You are a free woman," he said, eagerness in his voice, kindness in his eyes. "Here are your official papers. Winkie Williams, I'm proclaiming you free as of this moment."

I looked at him as if thunderstruck. "Free?" I finally said, trying to fathom the meaning of the word that held no meaning for the likes of me.

"I'm selling the plantation, and Mrs. Williams and I are moving back to the North. I'm freeing my slaves. You're the first one I've told because you've always been special to our family." He pushed a paper across the desk. "Here. Take it."

I reached for the document, dazed. Where would I go? What would I do? How would I support myself? And most importantly, what would this mean for my Sweet Love Roscoe and me? Living at Laurel Ridge, we enjoyed a few stolen moments here or there. When I left, I would never see him again.

Not ever.

Anger boiled in me. Of course I wanted my freedom. All of my people wanted their freedom. Now I had it in my hands. I squeezed the document, and it rustled in my grip. But freedom for me meant parting with my Sweet Love Roscoe.

A venomous chuckle roared up my throat as the irony of the whole thing struck me. Slavery had been forced on me, and now freedom was, too.

"Winkie?" Mr. Williams said, concern in his tone.

My presence of mind returned, along with my manners. "I—I don't know wh–what to say, Mr. Williams," I stammered as I stood up. "Except th–thank you, kind sir."

"Godspeed to you, Winkie."

With a nod and a smile and a confident step, I made my way across the room, but inside, I was reeling from this news. I closed the door behind me and leaned against the wall, knocking a brass sconce askew. I righted it and moved a few paces down the hall, sank into a chair, my legs too wobbly to hold me.

Tears welled in my eyes as I bunched and unbunched the fabric of my skirt, fretting over my future, a lifetime without my man. Then a thought came to me that sent thrill chills speeding down my spine.

*Strike for freedom,* I would urge Sweet Love Roscoe. *Go to Canada. We'll start a new life together, one founded in the sweet light of liberty.*

Now was our chance. We could live in Canada, where we'd been told blacksmiths easily obtained work. I knew Roscoe would do as I bid. He'd been thinking about it for months, years even.

"I'll escape to Canada on the Underground Railroad," he would say, "and you and Cassie can follow me when I get settled."

Every time he mentioned it, I would put my fingers across his lips. "No," I always said, fear gripping me with an ironclad hand. "If the slave hunters were to catch us. . ." I would shiver, and then I would say, "You know what they do if you're caught."

Now though, courage welled up in my breast, and I knew it was time for Roscoe to strike for Canada. And with my freedom granted, Cassie and I could follow him legally and unafraid. The thought comforted me like a coat in the cold.

But how would I keep body and soul together during the time Cassie and I waited on Sweet Love Roscoe to reach Canada?

My mind ran a hundred different ways. I could dress a lady. I could sew. I could take care of children. Would any of those skills help me find work once I left Laurel Ridge? I could cook. I could clean. Why, I would even scoop dung from the streets if that's what it took.

But would I be able to find work? Jobs were scarce for free people, I knew. And where would Cassie and I live? And what would she do while I worked? Who would look out for her?

The ponderations pounded in my brain until my head ached with a ferocity I had never known. If I were a lady woman, I would take to my bed with a vinegar compress on my brow. But I was not a white lady.

I was a former slave, now a free woman, alone in the world except for little Cassie, with no prospects of a job under my belt or a roof over my head. . . .

# Chapter 1

*Three years later, 1859*
*Charleston, South Carolina*

Winkie Williams stood in front of her millinery shop, sweeping vigorously. Only two hours past cockcrow, the July sun was already high in the sky, and she stopped her work and swiped at her brow with a handkerchief.

Grasping the broom handle, she stood staring at her strong brown hands, hands that had picked cotton as a child, dressed the master's wife as a girl, and were now making hats for Charleston society ladies.

She looked across the pastel-colored buildings and drew in a breath of sharp briny air drifting in from the harbor. In the distance, she could hear horns blowing, flutes trilling, drums beating, and she knew that somewhere in downtown Charleston, band members were practicing for the Independence Day parade that would soon commence.

She could picture the parade scene as if it were before her. She had watched the parade in the past, but not last year, and not today either. Today marked two years since she had gotten the awful news, and she doubted she would ever go to another Independence Day parade again. How could she celebrate when her Sweet Love Roscoe lay in a cold, dark grave?

She willed herself not to succumb to the grief that often overwhelmed her. "Think about the parade," she mumbled as a drummer banged out a fast beat.

"At the parade," she said to herself, "the streets will be lined with ladies and gents and boys and girls. Most will be dressed in red, white, and blue. Some of the ladies will be wearing hats that I made with my own hands. They're going to shake their noisemakers and toot their tin horns and sing their patriotic songs and wave their flags high in the air. They're going to shout, 'Let freedom ring.' They're going to holler, 'Liberty, sweet liberty.' They're going to say, 'God bless America.'"

She continued sweeping, intent on getting every speck of dirt off her front stoop, something she did at least twice a day. "Yes, God has blessed you, America. You are free from the bondage of your mother country. And I am free from the bondage of slavery."

She leaned down and picked dead petals off the flowers that were clumped in pots by the door. "But what good does that do?" she almost spat out. "My people will never be free men and free women, like me. They never know what it mean to have a kind master release them."

From her pocket she withdrew a cleaning rag and rubbed at a streak on the windowpane. Her musings brought to mind her dear departed mother, a slave brought over from Africa before the turn of the century, a woman whose existence had been one of unspeakable inhumanity, sorrow, and despair.

*"Burdens—that's all there be to life,"* Mama said many a time. *"We be tasked hard."*

"Mama, look—"

"Goodness, child," Winkie shrieked, dropping the rag, "I be so deep in the land of emptiness, you plumb scared the pudding out of me." She reached over and patted her six-year-old daughter where she stood in the open door, then lifted Cassie's chin and smiled down at her. "I got a surprise waiting for you, Sugarbun."

"We going to the parade?" Cassie exclaimed, her eyes lit up like the sidewalk firecrackers the white children set off every Independence Day. "Oh Mama, thank you, thank you. Just what I wanted—"

"Now what you go bringing that up for?" Winkie snapped. "I done told you my answer about the parade. It's no. *N-O*," she spelled. "Madam is expecting three more bonnets from me in the morning. I got work waiting."

She turned back to the window and rubbed the pane furiously. "Always, the work is there. There's never no letup. I be tasked hard."

Cassie grew as still as a statue, her eyes downcast, and immediately Winkie was ashamed of her outburst. She knelt down and drew Cassie to her, squeezing her in a tight embrace, head to head, heart to heart.

"Mama's sorry, Cassie, my mama-look baby. My surprise is a sweet potato pie. I made it this morning. Your favorite. Mama don't mean to be such a sore head all the livelong day. It's just that I. . .well, I got troubles pressing on my mind—"

"Winkie," a high-pitched female voice called from down the street. "I'm sorely in need of your services."

Winkie stood up, her fingers locked with Cassie's as she looked toward the lady, her girlhood friend, the master's daughter who had taught her how to read. Miss Willie was coming pell-mell down the street, her blond ringlets bouncing with every step, her bell-shaped skirts swishing and swaying with every movement.

"Why, do tell," Winkie said, when Miss Willie drew near, forcing cheerfulness into her voice. "What brings you here on Independence Day? Shouldn't you be heading to town for the festivities?"

"I'm on my way," Miss Willie huffed out. "But I had an item of utmost importance to attend to." She swooped down and tickled Cassie on the side of the neck, and Cassie giggled in delight. "Look what I've brought you, Cassie dear." From her large reticule she pulled out a charming doll dressed in an exquisite red-white-and-blue silk gown.

Cassie hugged the doll to her. "Thank you, Miss Willie. This be better than any old parade," she said softly as she turned and headed inside.

"She's a quiet child," Miss Willie said.

"Yes ma'am. Now, what can I do for you today?" Winkie looked to her left, then to her right. It wouldn't be fitten for a fine lady like Miss Willie to be seen standing in the alleyway conversing with the likes of her. "Come on in. Whatever it is you need, we be seeing to it right away."

Inside the little shop that wasn't really a shop, only a workroom with a curtained-off sleeping area, Winkie offered Miss Willie a chair, then put the broom away.

"Willie and Winkie," Miss Willie said as she settled back in the chair and smoothed her ruffle-flounced, white brocade gown. "We were a lively duo growing up, weren't we?"

"That we was."

"Had ourselves some escapades, didn't we?"

"That we did." Winkie sat down in the other chair, leaned her elbow on the table, and lightly drummed her fingers. Miss Willie's family, the Williamses, had come from the North and purchased Laurel Ridge when both girls were about thirteen.

From the moment they'd met, they'd become fast friends. Miss Willie—Wilhelmina was her given name, but everyone called her Miss Willie—had married at seventeen. That same day while the white folks' wedding festivities were going on up at the big house, Winkie and her Sweet Love Roscoe had been jumping the broom down at the quarters.

Winkie fiddled with the folds of fabric stacked neatly on the table. Growing up, she and Miss Willie had shared many commonalities. Their flair for fashion. Their interest in reading after Miss Willie taught her how. Even the similarity of their names. Willie and Winkie. Perhaps those were the things that had bonded them together so strongly.

But now one profound difference stood between them. Miss Willie had a husband and no child. Winkie had a child and no husband. She had no husband because her Sweet Love Roscoe had died fleeing the tyranny of a cruel master. Halfway to Canada, the slave hunters had captured him and dragged him back, and in the process, Sweet Love Roscoe had lost his life. And it was all because of her. She had urged him to escape.

*Oh Roscoe.* She rubbed her temple where it throbbed.

"I came by this morning to see if you'd make a few of these rosettes you made for my bonnet." Miss Willie touched the red, white, and blue fabric flowers on each side of her hat. "And sew them onto my sash." She fingered the red silk sash at her waist. "I thought a touch of red, white, and blue somewhere on my gown would look even more patriotic."

"Sure thing, Miss Willie." Winkie stood and in one quick movement gathered her sewing basket and some swatches of red, white, and blue silk fabric from a shelf overhead. Then she sat back down. "Won't take me no time."

"I knew that. Otherwise, I wouldn't have troubled you."

"No trouble at all." She could spend a lifetime helping Miss Willie, yet it would never repay her for her kindness. A few years after Miss Willie had married and moved to a plantation in Georgia, her father had decided to sell Laurel Ridge and move back to the North. It was then that Miss Willie convinced him to free his slaves.

It was then that Winkie had become a free woman.

Winkie threaded her needle, stuck it in a pincushion, cut narrow strips of red, white, and blue silk skillfully, just as her milliner patron had taught her. She would be indebted to Miss Willie for life.

It was Miss Willie who had traveled to Charleston and secured Winkie's apprenticeship with the grand milliner, Madam Henderson. It was Miss Willie who had given Winkie the guidance to set up her own shop. It was Miss Willie who was responsible for Winkie's present life—living as a free woman and productive citizen on a busy street in Charleston, even if it was a back alley.

Though the ladies of Charleston had turned up their snooty noses at her back-alley shop—causing Madam Henderson to agree to front for Winkie for a fee and no credit for her hatmaking—still, the small profits kept body and soul together for Winkie and

Cassie, and she would be eternally grateful to Miss Willie.

As long as Winkie lived, she could never do enough for the kind and gracious Miss Willie. Never. Why, there was no guile to be found in the blue-eyed, blond-haired belle, only sweetness down to the bone.

"I've come to ask a second favor of you, Winkie." Miss Willie's sparkling blue eyes were sober now.

"Anything."

"Come to the parade."

"I couldn't do that." Winkie silently reprimanded herself. Hadn't she just been thinking she'd do anything for Miss Willie? Here she was, refusing her request. But she couldn't help it.

"It's time."

"That's something I need more of," Winkie said, trying to hide the anger in her voice, thinking that she'd had far too much time to brood this morning. "I have three bonnets yet to trim."

"It's time, I repeat. I think you know what I mean."

Winkie pushed the needle into a bunching of fabric, then deftly pulled it out. In the fabric, out the fabric, in the fabric, out the fabric.

"It's been two years since. . ." Miss Willie's voice trailed off. "There's someone I'd like to introduce you to after the parade."

The first rosette completed, Winkie bit off the thread, grinding her teeth more than necessary, and rethreaded the needle. A moment ago, she'd been thinking Miss Willie had no guile in her. Now she saw a hint of pretense. *Why, Miss Willie didn't come to the shop to have rosettes made. She came to make a match—*

Winkie couldn't even finish the thought. She pushed the needle into the fabric so hard, it punctured her finger and drew blood. She hadn't done that since her apprenticeship. She wrapped her finger with a piece of cloth, stuck a thimble on it, kept sewing.

"We're going to the parade with our friends, the Fletchers," Miss Willie said. "It's their carpenter I want you to meet. Mr. Fletcher says there's no finer man of all his people. This man I'm talking about—his name is Joseph Moore—is diligent and hard working, just like you, Winkie."

Winkie didn't say a word while she completed the second rosette. She just sat there, pulling the needle in and out, biting off the thread, rethreading the needle as Miss Willie prattled on about the man she wanted her to meet, the carpenter owned by the Fletchers.

"Dolly Fletcher says the talk is," Miss Willie continued, "that Joseph hasn't found the right girl to jump the broom with. You'd be the perfect girl."

"Jump the broom?" Memories seared her mind, and she felt as though she'd been burned by an ember from the cooking fire.

"I know it's hard for you—"

"You don't know no such of a thing." For the third time this morning, Winkie felt remorseful. Silently she reprimanded herself. First, Cassie had gotten the brunt of her malcontent. Then, Miss Willie. Now, Miss Willie again. Still, she couldn't help humming loudly, "Nobody Knows the Trouble I Seen."

"Mama, look," Cassie exclaimed as she skipped from behind the curtain. "Sheena—" She held out her doll as she ran to Winkie. "Her eyes opens and closes. I never held no doll that's eyes opens and closes. Oh Mama, look."

"Come here, my mama-look baby." Winkie set aside her sewing, swooped Cassie onto her lap, and planted a kiss on each eyelid as Cassie convulsed in giggles.

All the things Winkie had thought about that morning, all the fanciful things Miss Willie was saying now—none of them mattered. Only Cassie mattered. Cassie was her reason for being. And living.

"Show Mama them eyes that opens and closes." Winkie kissed Cassie's eyelids again.

"For her," Miss Willie said, tipping her head in Cassie's direction, looking intently at Winkie. "If for no other reason, go to the parade for her. She's a child. She needs diversion every now and then. I always said Independence Day is more fun than Christmas."

Winkie fiddled with the doll's eyelids. Perhaps Miss Willie was right. Cassie rarely had the opportunity for pleasure.

"After the parade," Miss Willie said, "the Fletchers are giving a pig roast in our honor—for moving back to South Carolina." She tapped on her hat brim. "I'm so happy you'll be making all my bonnets from now on."

Winkie sat there, contemplating what Miss Willie was saying, glad Miss Willie would be living nearby. That gave her a comfort.

"That's where I wish to introduce you to Joseph Moore—at the Fletchers' pig roast. Dolly Fletcher knows of my desire, and out of courtesy to me, she's extended an invitation to you to eat with their people. There'll be children Cassie's age, and she'll enjoy their games and child play. And the food is going to be simply scrumptious. The Fletcher people have been roasting the pigs all night long. Dolly says their people make the best roast pork in all of South Carolina. She vows and declares it's the wood they cook them over. I believe she said it's—"

"Oak wood," Winkie remarked absently, straightening the doll's hair that didn't need straightening. "Oak wood bring out the flavor of pork like no other."

"And they make a special sauce—"

"Carolina gold, I'd hanker." She untied the ribbon on the doll's bonnet, then retied it, laboriously making the loops as small as possible so they'd be in correct proportion to the doll's chin. "Carolina gold be better than Carolina red by a mile."

"Won't you please come to the parade? If you won't do it for yourself, and you won't do it for Cassie, do it for me. Please? Help celebrate mine and Mr. Richard's move back to Charleston."

A half hour later, Winkie and Cassie were headed to the parade, dressed in their best gowns, matching feather-trimmed bonnets on their heads, a sweet potato pie in a basket on Winkie's arm. As they walked along, they trailed Miss Willie by a good half a block, as was proper.

"I wonder about. . .Mr. Joseph Moore, isn't that what Miss Willie called him?" Winkie said under her breath, knowing Cassie was paying her no mind.

"There won't be no mama-looks from Cassie right now," Winkie whispered. Cassie was holding Sheena—her first store-bought doll—and as the tyke walked along, she was opening and closing the open-and-close eyes. "I wonder what Mr. Joseph Moore's countenance be like," Winkie said softly.

She shifted the basket to her other arm and caught a whiff of the sweet potato pie. "Miss Willie is sweetness down to the bone. That she is." She breathed in deeply of the pleasant-smelling scent. "I'm going to the Independence Day parade and the picnic afterwards for Cassie's sake," she whispered. "And for Miss Willie's sake."

Deep down, though, she was loathe to admit that she was really going to the parade to meet Mr. Joseph Moore.

"I wonder if Mr. Joseph Moore be dark?" she mused aloud. "Or light? I wonder if he have big eyes or small? I wonder if he be tall, like me? Or short? He be smart, for sure. Double-dose smart. Miss Willie say he be so skilled at carpentering, the carpentry shop in town use his services."

Into her mind came a vision of a tall, handsome man bent over a workbench, his muscles glistening in the sunlight. Would he have understanding eyes and a compassionate soul? Perhaps this Mr. Joseph Moore would take a shine to little Cassie. That would most assuredly cause her to do a joy jig.

Then a second vision appeared, gut-wrenchingly so, of another tall, handsome man, this time bent over a blacksmith's fire, his muscles glistening in the sunlight. This man had understanding eyes and a compassionate soul, and he had loved Cassie with every sinew of his soul.

She drew in a sharp breath at the thought of Sweet Love Roscoe, her husband who'd died fleeing slavery—a word so abhorrent, she had a hard time letting it float through her mind. With brooding ponderations gnawing at her insides, she hurried on down the street.

# Chapter 2

Joseph Moore stood amidst a sea of brown faces in the proper section of downtown Charleston, his arms folded across his barrel chest, anticipating with relish the Independence Day parade that was about to commence. He hadn't planned on going with the Fletchers, but at the last minute, the master had sent word that they would need his help transporting the Fletchers' many important guests to their afternoon picnic.

"You're to oversee the carriage caravan after the parade," came the word of direction.

That set well with him. Mighty well. Who wouldn't want to look at fine bands in colorful uniforms sounding out patriotic songs as they marched in rhythmic stride? Who wouldn't want to see ships in Charleston Harbor decorated in the nation's colors? Who wouldn't want to hear cannons along the waterfront discharging, one blast for every state of the Union?

And better than all of those things, he had to admit with a wry grin, who wouldn't want a day off from their labors?

As he stood in the dense throng of people, he rubbed his jaw, which was smooth from his morning's shave. Today, the nation would commemorate the anniversary of the independence of the United States of America.

Here in Charleston, the city fathers, as well as their families, would gloriously celebrate, he knew from years past. The first part of the festivities always began with the parade, followed by cannon fire, then speeches by political figures. All afternoon, picnics would be enjoyed all over the city, from public parks to private homes, including the gala party at the Fletchers' house. The evening would be marked by fireworks lighting the skies.

With the hot sun high overhead, Joseph shielded his face with the crook of his arm, then craned his neck to see above the crowd. When would the parade reach this side of town? In the distance, he could hear the band, but just barely.

Yes, all of Charleston, it seemed, had turned out to honor the brave patriots who had given their lives for freedom.

Freedom? With a sad shake of his head, he knew that word didn't apply to him and probably never would, even though political talk had heated up recently. Despite the hot sunshine beating down on him, he shivered, thinking of the strange words that elicited anger everywhere they were discussed: antislavery newspapers, equality, abolitionists, emancipation.

Into his mind came the image of a large-bosomed black woman cradling a little boy in her arms as she taught him Bible stories and songs.

"Tell me the one about the boy with the coat of many colors, Mama," he'd said with a wide grin, knowing that the boy with the coat of many colors was his namesake.

"Someday, Joseph, I'm going to make you a coat like that," she'd said softly. Time and again she would tell him the story of Joseph-in-the-Bible and how he was sold into slavery and then unjustly imprisoned—

"But that isn't fair," the little boy would say every time at that particular place in the story.

"Life isn't fair," she would say back. "The thing that counts is always doing what's right, no matter what comes our way."

And he would beg her to finish the story because he had heard it a hundred times, and he knew something good awaited the boy Joseph.

"Joseph-in-the-Bible had the right attitude through every trial," she would say, "and in the end, God honored him. Son, hear me well. If you determine in your heart to be like that, God will honor you."

By his tenth summer, his mother had finally saved enough scraps of various-colored material and fashioned a coat of many colors. She presented it to him with great fanfare and pride.

That fall, the master sold him farther south.

He remembered the day as if it were yesterday. He would never forget his piercing cries as he was wrenched from the arms of a loving mother and thrust into the frightful unknown. Even now, he could smell her sweet scent, feel her warm breath on the top of his head.

But echoing through his mind were her words that would stay with him for as long as he lived, an admonition that had stood him well in life, an exhortation that was the reason for the sustaining peace deep in his heart: "*Son, be like Joseph-in-the-Bible. Through your trials, keep the right attitude. And God will honor you.*"

And that's how he had tried to live, even though he would always be a servant to a master. Instead of letting bitterness eat away at his soul over the inequities of life, he'd decided a long time ago to make happiness wherever he went.

And he tried to help others live that way, too. He gave them so many doses of the Holy Book, the people had taken to calling him Bible Thumper—respectfully and with admiration in their voices—a name they called ministers. Even though he couldn't read, he could quote the scriptures as good as the minister in Charleston, to his way of thinking.

He was so deep in thought, he almost jumped when he heard the loud notes of a lively patriotic song being played close by. To his left, just within his view, he saw a band marching down the street.

When only a few minutes passed, with his toe tapping to the beat of the rousing tune, the crowd closed in tighter, slaves and free people alike, all straining to get a glimpse and enjoy the frivolities of the day. He glanced around to see if he knew anyone, but the crowd kept jostling and shifting.

"Mama, Mama, I can't see," said a child to his right. "Please pick me up one more time."

"You be too heavy, Sugarbun," said a woman's voice, low and melodious. "I plumb give out from holding you."

Joseph glanced down, saw a little girl with a pleading expression on her face as she tugged on a woman's skirts. Then he looked directly at the woman, saw wide somber eyes, smooth-as-buttermilk brown skin, smart hat and gown, and he couldn't help smiling at the pleasant sight before him.

"Mind if I lend my assistance?" He tipped his head in the direction of the child. "I got mighty strong shoulders." In a playful mood, he tapped his shoulders. "I imagine they'd give a commanding view if somebody was to sit on them." He tweaked the little girl on her button nose, and she giggled, but the woman's lips were a straight line.

"Ma'am?" he asked, when the woman didn't answer. "I'd be glad to lift her up. So she can see the pretty uniforms the band be wearing."

"Mama," the little girl said. "Please?"

The woman dipped her chin demurely and lowered her gaze. "Th–thank you, sir. I–I'm sure Cassie would like that."

He tried not to stare at the woman. Was something wrong? It certainly seemed that way. She was fidgety-acting, like a filly shying at a snake in her path.

But the little girl was of another vein. Her face was one wide grin from ear to ear, and he swooped her up and settled her on his right shoulder. "Cassie—isn't that what your mama called you?—if you smiled any wider, I believe your teeth would fall right out of your mouth." He chuckled, and the woman smiled—finally.

A quarter hour passed, then another as the bands marched by, their horns blowing and their drums beating. The child was as light as a feather on his shoulder, and he knew he could stand there for hours holding her; but with a rueful sigh, he realized he had to leave and see to his duties. The Fletchers, along with the rest of the white folks, were first on the parade route, and their crowd would be dispersing momentarily. He couldn't keep the Fletchers' guests waiting. He had to hurry. If he ran the six blocks back to the wagons, he would just barely make his appointed time.

"Ma'am," he said, "much as I'd like to stay here enjoying the parade with you and your fine little daughter, I have to go." He lifted the child from his shoulders and set her on the ground, and the woman took the little girl's hand. "I have work to attend to. You know."

"Yes, I know. Work." There was a hard edge to her voice. "The likes of us," she mumbled, "is always at the beck and call of—"

"What'd you say?" He pointed toward the band and raised his voice. "The music. I couldn't hear you."

The first cannon boomed, and the crowd let out a united, "Oh." He glanced to his side, and the woman and the girl were gone. He pivoted this way and that, looked in all directions, studied every face within seeing distance. Still, there was no sign of them. The second cannon fired, then the third.

A sharp sense of disappointment—no, sadness—enveloped him, but there was nothing to do but take off on a run as the fourth cannon fired.

Duty called.

# Chapter 3

All the way to the Fletcher plantation, Winkie struggled with conflicting emotions. As she and Cassie bumped along in the seat behind Miss Willie and Mr. Richard, she gave her telltale heart a stern talking-to.

*You, who didn't care to meet this Mr. Joseph Moore, has gone into public trifling with the first man you meet. Get a grip on yourself.*

*But I can't help it,* Heart said.

*Yes, you can,* she said.

*No, I can't,* Heart said back. *He smart-looking and he handsome.*

*You been holding with the hare and now you running with the hounds. Shame, shame.*

*My, but that man be something. He have understanding eyes. And he have a compassionate soul. That be better than any kind of looksome ways, yet he have them, too—a right good plenty. Skin—rich nut brown. Teeth—so white they surely shine in the dark. Shoulders—as broad as a tree trunk. Muscles—strong enough to pick up a woman and carry her to—*

*Stop that, you hear me, Heart? Away with! Away with!*

*And the best part about him is, he take a shine to little Sugarbun.*

Tears trickled down Winkie's cheeks. *Dear heart,* she said, *we'll never see that man again. Oh, what we going to do?*

Heart didn't answer.

With a sadness that settled in her bones, Winkie whispered, "Burdens. That's all there be to life." In a quick movement, she backhanded her tears, willing herself not to let one more fall.

❦

At the Fletcher plantation, streamers dangled from tree limbs and floated in the breeze same as the gray curls of moss, and Winkie took note of the red-white-and-blue bunting that draped the porch rails.

"Mama, look," Cassie said in her customary quiet way. "It be a sight to behold."

"You got that right," Winkie whispered, drinking in the prettiness as their carriage continued up the drive that was bordered by towering oaks. The big house was whitewashed until it gleamed in the sunlight, and the windows purely sparkled. Low-growing bushes and flowers of every shade of the rainbow lined the house. A fiddle and other instruments played from somewhere not too far off, and succulent smells of roasted pork scented the air.

Her eyes continued to feast. People dressed in Sunday finery milled about, greeting each other genteel-like; and she saw little girls sitting on the velvety lawn, their pouffy skirts spread about them as they nibbled on cookies.

"Is this heaven?" Cassie asked, her eyes lit up.

Winkie sucked in a long breath of air. "It smell like heaven, that for sure." She hugged Cassie to her. "You in for a treat today, Sugarbun. You can eat till your stomach plumb hurts if that's what you want to do." She touched her midsection. Eating her fill was one of her ideas of heaven.

All afternoon, Winkie and Cassie partook of the people's festivities behind the big house. They ate to their heart's content as they listened to the lively music, and Cassie made friends with several children who were in awe of her store-bought doll.

Winkie was polite when spoken to, but she kept up her usual guard. Why be cordial with people she'd never see again?

Miss Willie had mentioned that Winkie might make some friends today. She snorted as she ate a bite of pie. There was no time for that kind of folderol. There was only time for work, pure and simple. Wasn't that all there was to a body's existence? That's all she knew, anyway.

Toward evening, she helped with the cleanup, taking her turn at the dishpan under the shade of a majestic oak tree.

"Did you get a taste of that sweet potato pie in the basket?" said the woman who was drying the pewter plates as fast as Winkie put them in her hands. "It was gobbled up first thing. I only got a sliver. For sure, for sure, it be better than Bertha's. But don't tell her I said so. She take pride in her cooking, and she would surely be offended if she heard me say that."

Winkie dropped her gaze. She wasn't used to compliments. The woman was saying she was a better cook than the cook on the Fletcher plantation.

"Why, that was your pie, wasn't it? You made it."

"Yes." For the first time, Winkie really looked at the gray-haired, dark-as-ebony woman beside her. She was kindhearted, Winkie could tell, and she reminded her of Auntie, her mother's long-lost sister. For a moment, Winkie let down her stiff reserve. "Yes, it be my pie. I glad you enjoyed it."

"It be the texture that make it so good. It light and fluffy. Kind of like a cloud." The woman good-naturedly elbowed Winkie as she laughed, her wide smile infectious, and Winkie smiled back.

"Winkie, there you are," Miss Willie said as she approached. "It's time for me to introduce you to the person I told you about."

Winkie hurriedly dried her hands on a dish rag, then rolled down her sleeves. The moment had come. She'd been dreading it and welcoming it at the same time. How could that be?

"He'll be along any moment. He's to meet us under the arbor." Miss Willie drew Winkie's hand into the crook of her elbow and proceeded toward the side lawn.

"What about Cassie?" Winkie looked at the group of children nearby.

"Let her enjoy her play."

Winkie nodded and called out a good-bye to the woman who had befriended her. Then she and Miss Willie made their way to the meeting place.

At the arbor, Winkie stood beside Miss Willie, wringing her hands. It had been so long since she'd been around a man.

*Heart, what must I do? Stand a certain way? Strike a pose? Act natural?*

Heart didn't answer.

She wrung her hands all the more as she stared toward the east, past the flower garden, into a copse of trees. What would Mr. Joseph Moore be like? Was he a swell? A coxcomb? A man about town? She hoped not. The vision appeared again of a smart, handsome man with understanding eyes and a compassionate soul.

*Heart, will he be like that?*

Still, Heart didn't answer.

"Miss Willie, I understand I'm to meet you at the arbor," said a man's voice.

The moment was here. Winkie smoothed her skirts, turned around, and got the start of her life. Standing before her was Mr. Joseph Moore. No, the man at the parade. No, the man Miss Willie wanted her to meet. She was confused. How could this be?

"Winkie, this is Joseph Moore," Miss Willie said. "Joseph, this is Winkie Williams."

With a gentle smile on his lips, Mr. Joseph Moore extended his hand.

Almost as if in a daze, Winkie extended hers.

"I've matters to attend to," Miss Willie said as she walked away from the arbor.

It was as if Winkie did not see Miss Willie. All she saw was. . .

A handsome man with understanding eyes and a compassionate soul. . .a man who held her hand in his. . .a man who had taken a shine to Sugarbun.

In response, her feet did a little dance in the dirt.

"Why, Winkie," he said, "I didn't hear the music commencing, but we can dance just the same. So, do-si-do is it, first off?"

She felt her face heat up in embarrassment. "I—I. . .n–no. . .that wasn't my intention," she stammered. "Y–you don't understand." She withdrew her hand, stood ramrod straight, trying to think what to do next, what to say.

He looked directly at her, seeming to search her eyes, but she quickly averted his gaze, glanced at her feet, ground her toe in the dirt.

Gently he lifted her chin so he could look into her eyes. "This isn't going very well, is it? Why don't we start over?" He took a step back, thrust out his hand toward her in play-acting gestures. "Winkie Williams, this is Joseph Moore. Joseph Moore, this is Winkie Williams." He bowed dramatically.

As he drew up to his full height, she saw the smiles in his eyes and felt her face heating up again. This was a man worth getting to know. This was a man who could set her feet to dancing and her face to smiling.

"There it is. A smile. I was certain it was in there somewhere." He picked a camellia off a nearby bush, placed it in her palm, and pressed her fingers around it.

Her heart pounded against her chest, and with her free hand she toyed with the button at her neckline.

*Heart, you knew, didn't you? You knew all along.*

Heart said, *Yes.*

॰॰

Under a starlit sky, Joseph drove Winkie and Cassie the two miles back to town in Mr. Fletcher's buggy. As the horse clip-clopped along, he couldn't keep his thoughts off the attractive woman at his side. She had insisted on staying to help with the cleanup, and after knowing her for only one afternoon, he found that Work was her middle name. No matter. Industriousness was a good attribute.

*"The used key is always bright,"* his mother used to say.

Winkie's busyness certainly stood him in good stead tonight, he thought with an inward chuckle. Because she'd stayed so long at the dishpan, Miss Willie and Mr. Richard had asked Joseph to deliver Winkie and Cassie back to town.

He reflected about the moment they'd met that afternoon. When Miss Willie introduced them, at first Winkie had seemed... confused? Was that the word he was looking for? Then it was like something dawned on her, and she looked straight at him. Then she did that little dance, right there in front of him, and it warmed the cockles of his heart. As she did her little two-step in the dirt, he was treading on enchanted ground.

Then she acted flustered. What was going on with her? He knew what was going on with him.

*This is a woman I want to get to know.*

A few blocks from her shop, he stopped the buggy, looped the reins, and leaned forward so he could see Cassie, who was sitting on the other side of Winkie.

"The fireworks ought to be starting soon, Cassie," he said. In the soft glow of the street lamp at the end of the block, he saw her smile in response.

Suddenly, a loud boom sounded, and Cassie jumped. Winkie let out a little shriek.

"The fireworks," he exclaimed. From their close proximity, he felt Winkie tremble, then felt fumbling and saw Winkie put her arm around Cassie protectively.

"Look, Mama," Cassie said. "That one is a wheel in a wheel."

Sitting closely beside Winkie, he was struck by how wiry she was. Why, the woman was so slight-made, he could feel her bones. Probably she ate sparingly so she could feed Cassie well.

The thought tugged at his heart.

Another set of fireworks filled the sky with bursting sprays of color, and Cassie oohed and ahed at the spectacular sight.

Joseph smiled, pleased at the little girl's obvious happiness, as he took the reins and drove on down the street.

"Thank you, Mr. Joseph Moore," Winkie said after a long span of pleasurable silence, "for giving my daughter—and me—a most enjoyable evening."

"It be refreshing for me as well." *Refreshing? No, rapturous.*

"We will never forget this night, will we, Cassie?" She patted Cassie's knee.

*I will never forget it either,* he couldn't help thinking.

"Look, Mama," Cassie said, pointing upward.

"That be the grand finale." Joseph looked skyward and saw the dazzling display. *Fireworks are not only in the sky. They're in my heart.*

# Chapter 4

Two days later, Winkie was on her way home from the fabric shop where she'd ordered some material.

"Sugarbun, don't dawdle," Winkie said. "I got work waiting. Let's take a shortcut."

Cassie didn't respond, just dutifully followed, her doll Sheena clutched in her arms, her fingers working the open-and-close eyes. Winkie took Cassie's hand and led her down an alleyway, passing rows of back doors to shops, every one of them open to let in some air on the hot July day.

The sight she beheld at one door caused her to stop dead in her tracks. In the wide opening, with the morning sun flooding in, a tall handsome man bent over a workbench, his muscles glistening in the sunlight.

The spectacle made her draw in her breath sharply.

Mr. Joseph Moore.

"Why, Winkie, Cassie," he said, looking up from the fluted piecrust table he was working on, "how good it be to see you." He jumped up, made his way to her, rubbed his palms together—sawdust flying—and stuck out his hand for a shake. Winkie shook his hand. Then he tapped the top of Cassie's head, and she smiled up at him.

"We be on our way home. I—I had to order some fabric." She clutched at her collar. *Be still, my heart,* she ordered.

"I been thinking about you." He was rolling down his sleeves, covering the glistening muscles. "And what a nice time we had the other evening."

*I been thinking about you, too.* She was thinking about him now. He stood towering over her, though she herself was tall. Even though he was wearing work clothes, he was neat, something very important to her. He was a real gentleman, she could see.

"I believe those fireworks be the best I ever saw."

She nodded. Why did the cat get her tongue every time she was around him? What was it about him that made her mute as a fish, halting of speech even?

Heart whispered the answer.

*No, Heart, it be too soon,* she whispered back.

With a sweep of his hand, he gestured toward the building behind him. "This be where I work two, three days a week. When I'm not here, I'm at Fletchers."

"Fletchers pretty good people?" she forced herself to say for lack of anything better.

He shrugged. "As good as can be, I suppose."

She studied the toes of her shoes. "We need to be going."

He tipped his head in the direction of the carpentry shop behind him. "I best be getting back to work." Then he smiled. His eyes lit up like the fireworks that filled the sky on Independence Day, Winkie noticed.

"I be seeing you," he said softly. "Soon."

The thought thrilled her as she hurried away.

The next morning, as Winkie was fixing breakfast, she heard a gentle tap at the door. She left the spoon in the jam jar and walked to the front of the shop. Who could this be at 7:00 a.m.? She hadn't even opened the door for the day in order to capture the cooling breezes.

"Must be the delivery boy bringing the fabric I ordered," she said.

She swung the door open and faced Mr. Joseph Moore. She brushed at the sides of her hair, smoothed the apron tied about her waist, and fiddled with the knot at the back. "Mr. Moore—"

"Joseph," he corrected.

She glanced back toward the curtained-off living area and a sleeping Cassie. Should she invite him in? Was he expecting that?

"I can't stay but a moment. I didn't want to disturb you this early, but I have something for you."

She saw his hands behind his back. What was he holding?

He held out a bundle. "A fresh ham."

She was taken aback. He wanted to give her something this valuable? They hardly knew each other. "I—I couldn't accept it."

"The two to three days I work in town, Mr. Fletcher lets me keep the wages. I can bear the expense."

"But—"

"I be pleasured if you'd receive it."

She bit her bottom lip. What must she do?

"Cook it for Cassie." He put the bundle in her hands. "Cassie would surely like the taste of a slice of ham, wouldn't she?"

She smiled. Then her presence of mind returned. And her manners. "I declare, Mr. Moore—"

"Joseph," he corrected.

"Joseph. You do know how to get the best of my better sense of judgment." But she was smiling. Broadly. "I tell you what. I'll accept your gift, if you'll come back and eat some of it after I get it cooked."

"I never thought of that. . . ." His voice trailed off, but his eyes were fairly dancing. "What time?" he said, eagerness lacing his voice.

"Twelve noon. I believe I can have it ready about that time."

"I see you then."

All morning long, Winkie scurried about, getting her work done, smelling the fresh ham cooking in the iron pot over a low-burning open fire on the side of the building. Not long after the ham went in, she put on a pot of turnip greens.

"Just before serving time," she said to herself as she bent over a bonnet, "I'll make a pan of cornbread."

*The way to a man's heart is through his stomach,* Heart said, giggling.

*Hush up, Heart,* Winkie said back. But she was smiling. And singing, "Birdie Went a-Courting."

Only she changed the lyrics.

"Carpenter went a-courting," rang from her lips.

🐝

On the half hour before noon, Joseph laid aside his chisel and mallet, rose from his workbench, and went to clean up. He washed in the basin, lathering the lye soap into a rich foam, then changed shirts and brushed off his trousers and shoes with a damp rag.

In no time, it seemed, he was standing in front of Winkie's open door, tapping on the doorjamb. "Hello?" he called. "Anyone home?"

Cassie bounded across the room and into his arms where he stood on the stoop. "Mr. Joseph, we got something good to eat today. Mighty good." She drew out the word mighty.

"That so?" He picked her up and swung her around, then set her down. "I come to eat with you. Your mama invited me—"

"I know. She told me. She been singing all morning."

"That so?" He folded his arms across his chest and rubbed his jaw. "Where is she, by the way?" He tried to temper the excitement he felt.

"Here I am," Winkie said, rounding the corner of the building outside, carrying a heavy pot. "I was taking the ham off the fire."

"Let me help." In three quick strides, he was at her side. He took the pot from her, being careful to keep the hot mitts wrapped around the handles. "Hmm, hmm, this do smell good."

"Taste good, too," she said, a twinkle in her eye. "I done partook." She paused and smiled at him. "But only a morsel, to see if it was any good."

"I be relieved," he joked, dramatically wiping his brow. "The hog it come off of was butchered this very morning, but you never know."

"I wouldn't want to serve spoiled meat."

He was enjoying her banter. This was a Winkie he hadn't seen before, and he liked what he was seeing.

"Come on inside." Winkie was already at the door, ahead of him. "Everything else be ready. Will you do the carving?"

"Right happy to."

Inside, his eyes adjusted from the bright sunlight to a cool dimness. He scanned the room, taking in the pleasant sight. Colorful curtains at the window. Another curtain separating the shop, probably to section off the sleeping area. A table set with stoneware plates. A single gardenia in a vase in the center. A rag rug on the floor. Folds of fabric stacked on a shelf on a far wall, millinery items beside them.

Everything was tidy, in apple pie order. And not only that, it was apparent she knew what's what. She was sharp, at home to cleverness. He resisted the urge to shake his head in awe. He was liking what he was seeing more and more.

"Set it here," she said, indicating the table.

He set the pot down, and she handed him a carving knife. After he cut up the ham until there was a heap on a large platter, she filled the drinking cups with fresh water, and the three of them took their places at the table.

"Make your manners, Cassie," she instructed. "Put your napkin in your lap." She shook the folds out of hers and did likewise.

"Would you like me to say the blessing?" he asked.

She looked surprised. After a moment, she nodded.

"Lord, we thank Thee for this, Thy bounty. Bless the one whose hands prepared it, bless her real good. Let us partake of this nourishment so we can be instruments in Thy hand. Amen."

After the bowls and platters went around the table, Winkie hurriedly cut up her food, then picked up the peacock feathers at her side. As she ate with one hand, with the other she fanned the feathers across the table, keeping the flies at bay.

"This be some big eating," Joseph said, relishing every bite. He cut another piece off the slice of ham that nearly covered his plate. "That man I bought this from, he say this hog be fed chestnuts. That—along with your fine cooking—has got to be why the eating be so good. Hmm, hmm. What kind of sauce you put on that ham when you cook it?"

"It be a secret."

"What most cooks say." He chuckled. "Hmm, hmm. This cornbread, why, it melt in your mouth. And these turnip greens, they flavored just right, and they cooked right, too. My mama used to claim that greens that wasn't cooked two hours would kill you. She used to say, 'I don't take to the scalding school of cookery.' Yes, ma'am, you have regaled me with a feast."

She smiled, apparently pleased at his compliments.

When Cassie finished eating, she jumped up and asked for the feathers. "Let me do it, Mama."

"I get the treat then." Winkie handed her the feathers and walked to a shelf along the wall, picked up a rectangular pan, and brought it back to the table. "Blackberry cobbler with heavy cream," she announced as she set it down and began ladling it into serving dishes.

"Have I died and gone to heaven? Where the hams run loose on the streets with forks and knives stuck in them dashing around crying, 'Eat me, eat me'?"

She laughed, and Cassie laughed, too. "You certainly know how to set the table in a roar."

"And you certainly know how to cook."

A look of pride filled her eyes. The twinkle he was growing familiar with was back. "Be it as good as Bertha's?" she asked.

"Better by a mile. But don't tell her or anyone at Fletchers I said so."

Winkie took the feathers, seated herself, and fanned as they ate the cobbler.

"Have you ever gone to Sabbath services at the church downtown?" he asked. "I don't believe I seen you there."

"No," she said quickly.

"That so?" He tried to read the expression in her eyes, but he couldn't make it out.

"I never have." This time her tone was soft. "My mama never took to church and such stuff. I guess that be why I never did either."

"What about Cassie? She ever been?"

Winkie shook her head.

"They sing songs and—"

"Oh Mama," Cassie said, pulling on Winkie's sleeve. "Can I go with Mr. Joseph? Where they sing songs?"

Winkie didn't say anything for a long moment, her brows drawn together as if in contemplation.

"Please?"

"We see about it, Sugarbun. We see."

Cassie jumped up, ran across the room, and within a moment or two was standing at Winkie's side, holding a frayed leather-bound volume. "Show Mr. Joseph your poetry book, Mama."

Winkie lowered her spoon, laden with blackberries, to her bowl, then took the book and ran her fingers across the cover almost reverently as Cassie skipped off to play. "It be a book of poetry. Miss Willie gave it to me when we was girls."

"Read me your favorite."

"My favorite?" Her brows drew together, another frequent mannerism, he noticed. She flipped through the book, stopped at a particular page, withdrew a paper. From the looks of the torn creases, it was apparent it had been handled many times. "This isn't in the book, and it isn't my favorite poem, but it be very important to me." In a strong voice, she read the stanzas:

THE NEGRO'S COMPLAINT
by William Cowper

*Forced from home and all its pleasures*
*Afric's coast I left forlorn,*
*To increase a stranger's treasures*
*O'er the raging billows borne.*
*Men from England bought and sold me,*
*Paid my price in paltry gold;*
*But, though slave they have enrolled me,*
*Minds are never to be sold.*

*Still in thought as free as ever,*
*What are England's rights, I ask,*
*Me from my delights to sever*
*Me to torture, me to task?*
*Fleecy locks and black complexion*
*Cannot forfeit nature's claim;*
*Skins may differ, but affection*
*Dwells in white and black the same.*

*Why did all-creating nature*
*Make the plant for which we toil?*
*Sighs must fan it, tears must water,*
*Sweat of ours must dress the soil.*
*Think, ye masters iron-hearted,*
*Lolling at your jovial boards,*
*Think how many backs have smarted*
*For the sweets your cane affords.*

*Is there, as ye sometimes tell us,*
*Is there One who reigns on high?*
*Has He bid you buy and sell us,*
*Speaking from His throne, the sky?*
*Ask Him, if your knotted scourges,*
*Matches, blood-extorting screws,*
*Are the means that duty urges*
*Agents of His will to use?*

*'Hark! He answers!'—Wild tornadoes*
*Strewing yonder sea with wrecks,*
*Wasting towns, plantations, meadows,*
*Are the voice with which He speaks.*
*He, forseeing what vexations*
*Afric's sons should undergo,*
*Fixed their tyrants' habitations*
*Where His whirlwinds answer—'No.'*

*By our blood in Afric wasted*
*Ere our necks received the chain;*
*By the miseries that we tasted,*
*Crossing in your barks the main;*
*By our sufferings, since ye brought us*
*To the man-degrading mart,*
*All sustained by patience, taught us,*
*Only by a broken heart;*

*Deem our nation brutes no longer,*
*Till some reason ye shall find*
*Worthier of regard and stronger*
*Than the color of our kind.*
*Slaves of gold, whose sordid dealings*
*Tarnish all your boasted powers,*
*Prove that you have human feelings,*
*Ere you proudly question ours!*

When Winkie finished reading, the room filled with silence.

"True," Joseph finally said of the poem. He was too overcome to say more. He lived out its words every day of his life.

A quarter hour later, with proper adieus and plenty of thanks to Winkie for the delicious meal, he made his way back to the carpentry shop.

There was a bounce in his step as he walked. He would see Winkie again next Sabbath, when he came to pick up Cassie and take her to church.

# Chapter 5

Fall was in the air, but it was springtime in Winkie's heart. The leaves were turning, changing from their glorious greens to their awesome autumn hues of orange, gold, and brown. The days were shorter and the air cooler, and Winkie put a shawl about her shoulders when she went outside. Yet down in her soul was a warmth so great it was indescribable. It abode with her day in and day out.

She had seen Joseph every Sabbath since Independence Day and a few times more when their paths crossed in town. On Sundays, Joseph picked Cassie up and took her to the downtown church.

Frequently, Winkie had a hot meal waiting when they returned, though sometimes she packed a basket dinner and they went off, the three of them together, spending the afternoon in pleasurable pursuits. Their ventures were always within walking distance. Joseph had no horse or buggy. But the afternoons were highlights in her mind.

And in her heart.

One bright, unusually warm October Sabbath, Winkie watched Joseph rig up a rope swing for Cassie, saw him push her high, heard her peals of delight. Earlier, the three of them had eaten Winkie's fried chicken and biscuits, and now Joseph was approaching her where she sat on a colorful quilt, surrounded by a copse of copper trees.

He plopped down on one end of the quilt, and for long moments, they engaged in light banter, what they did nearly every time they were together. That was Joseph's way, frolicsome-like—coquetry as some people referred to it.

Coquetry? Lightness? She certainly needed some of that in her life. She leaned on one arm. The burdens. . . They were sometimes too hard to bear. But not since Joseph. She knew that the sparking between them was on the surface, but beneath it bubbled a deep bonding.

*I'm in love.* The thought startled her but exhilarated her, too.

"How about a piece of that spice cake you brought?" He reached into the basket and withdrew a bundle in a checkered cloth. "I got a whiff earlier." He held it up to his nose. "Hmm, hmm. This do smell good."

"You like spice cake, do you?" She tried to hide the quakes in her voice. Love was on her mind.

"Grass be green?" He gestured to the expanse of lawn at his side. "Sky be blue?" He pointed upward.

She smiled at his playful antics. Joseph had never voiced his feelings about her. Just the same, she knew it was there between them, love, and she basked in this private knowing. Secretly, she'd taken to calling him her Heart Happy Joseph, not because he made happiness everywhere he went, but because he made her heart happy.

⁊ঌ

The day after Love Blossoming, Winkie had a keen desire to prepare a Christmas gift for Joseph. One of Miss Willie's friends had frequented her hat shop and placed a sizable deposit on two bonnet orders, and so she had some extra funds for Joseph's gift.

That afternoon, she made a trip to the fabric store and purchased material, two yards of blue broadcloth for a vest, three of white linen for a shirt, five of gray serge for trousers and frockcoat, a yard of elegant patterned silk for a cravat. She would make him a fine suit of clothes and present it to him on Christmas Day.

"This Christmas Day will be the best Christmas I've ever had," she told herself as she hurried home, eager to make her cuts and start the sewing.

⁊ঌ

Late at night, in the workroom off the Fletcher stables, Joseph labored by lantern glow, what he did every evening until the wee hours, what he would continue doing until Christmas. A carved blanket chest and a child's rocking chair took eons to make, yet he was determined to complete them both by Christmas.

He ran his hand over the smooth sides of the chest, making sure he had sanded them properly. "Winkie gone be plumb lit up when she see this."

Tonight he would start on the hinged top, and maybe he would get the first coat of stain on Cassie's rocking chair.

He thought of little Cassie—Starlight, he'd been calling her because her eyes were as bright as the stars in the heavens. Every Sabbath since Independence Day, he had taken her to church, and nearly every Sunday afternoon, he'd had the privilege of spending time with Winkie. On several occasions during these last few months, he'd asked her if she would go to service with him in the downtown church.

"I can't," she said each time. "I got work waiting."

The woman was a workhorse; that was for sure. But she had to be. The little monies she made went to pay rent and put food on the table, though he tried to be a help, bringing things like sweet potatoes and sacks of grits from time to time.

It was tricky, though, handling her pride. She was known to bristle, scowl even, when the subject of the lack of money surfaced, which inevitably led to the subject of their people's plight.

"The likes of us," she would say, "isn't never going to know real relief—free nor slave."

On one occasion, he confided in her about his sad past. Winkie was sympathetic, comforting even. He told her about the origin of his name and how his mama admonished him to live up to his namesake, Joseph-in-the-Bible.

Now, Joseph leaned over the long piece of cherrywood and with precision aim brought the routing plane down the side, careful to make the groove even. He thought of the poem by a writer named Cowper. She had read it to him on a few occasions, and from the first time he'd heard it, the chilling words had taken root in his brain, never to be forgotten.

No truer words had ever been penned about the despicable system of slaves and masters, to his way of thinking.

But some other words, peace-giving words, life-sustaining words now came to mind, and the poet's phrases paled in comparison.

Joseph-in-the-Bible had the right attitude through every trial, his mother had said over and over, and in the end, God honored him. "*Son, hear me well. If you determine in your heart to be like that, God will honor you.*"

He stopped routing and reached to tighten the woolen scarf about his neck. The nights were growing colder as the autumn season made its way toward winter pell-mell like a horse to a trough. Soon, Christmas would be here.

"Christmas," he said aloud. "A babe named Jesus. A woman named Mary. A man named Joseph. . .a carpenter." He brought the lantern closer. "Hmm, I never paid much attention to this Joseph. The other Joseph is the one my life be built around, the man I have always looked up to and tried to model."

He stood there marveling. "This other Joseph-in-the-Bible is a man to model, too. The angel of the Lord appeared to Joseph in two, three dreams, and every time, the Bible say he do what he bidden."

He rubbed his jaw. "What a man to look up to. This Joseph followed the leading of the Lord instead of choosing his own way. And the Lord blessed him mightily." He knew that this Joseph, of all the people in the ages before and in the ages present and in the ages to come, had been chosen to be the Messiah's earthly father.

He picked up his routing plane, and as he shaped the second edge, then the third, then the fourth, his thoughts turned to Winkie.

Winkie with her quiet manner.

Winkie with her gentle ways.

Winkie with her busy hands.

Winkie, a mother as tender as ever he saw.

Winkie, a wife as affectionate as ever he'd laid eyes on.

His wife?

He shook himself. "Be it too soon to start thinking this way?"

"It's past time," Uncle Solomon would say.

Uncle Solomon, the head groomsman at Fletcher Plantation, was well learned in the art of courtship, and many a man went to the elderly gentleman for advice on wooing a woman and winning a wife.

"It's all in how you talk to her," Uncle Solomon often said. "The rules of courtship say you got to put riddles to her. If a young miss give a man as good a answer as the question he put to her, then she be the one for him."

A warm feeling flooded Joseph's heart as he put the first coat of stain on little Starlight's chair. Was Starlight's mother the one for him? The woman to jump the broom with? Working the brush into each rung of the child-sized chair, being careful not to miss one spot of the intricate areas, he reflected on Uncle Solomon's riddles.

"Pretty miss, if there be a ravishing rose, how would you go about getting it, if you couldn't pick it, pull it, or pluck it?" the young man might ask.

"Kind sir, it would be borne on the blossoms of love," she might answer.

Every young man and woman of the peoples knew a heap of riddles. It was like a game to them, the circumlocution they went through to find out the intentions of a sparking miss or man.

371

Sometimes, if the woman couldn't answer the man's riddle, she might say, "Sir, you are a peach beyond my pear."

Then he might say, "Pretty miss, let me explain myself more thoroughly so the peach and pear can go in the cobbler together."

He chuckled out loud, musing over this ticklish business of courtship. When he proposed to Winkie, it would be in plain English. He would put the question to her in simplicity and in earnestness—this woman who had come to mean the world to him, this lady who had captured his heart. How could he live without her? He was besotted, for sure.

As if from out of nowhere, a tiny doubt crept into his mind. *She doesn't partake of your faith.*

"She will," he said in the quietness of the late hour. "As soon as she gets more customers who come to her directly, her money worries will ease up, and she'll commence going to church with me."

With force of will, he drove the doubt away, deciding in his heart the course of action he would take.

"On Christmas Day, I'm going to give her my gift. Then I'm going to declare my love. Then I'm going to ask my winsome Winkie to be my wife."

# Chapter 6

Three weeks before Christmas, Joseph sat in the balcony of the downtown church in Charleston.

"Turn to Second Corinthians," the minister intoned from his oak pulpit on the raised platform. "Our topic today is 'Be Ye Not Unequally Yoked.'"

The minister picked up his Bible. "Let us read from 2 Corinthians 6:14. Altogether now, 'Be ye not unequally yoked together with unbelievers: for what fellowship hath righteousness with unrighteousness?'"

The minister continued reading, but Joseph didn't hear another word he said. It was as if he'd been kicked in the stomach by a stallion. *Unequally yoked. Unequally yoked. Unequally yoked.* The sacred words pounded in his brain, then invaded his heart and gripped it with an iron hand.

If he and Winkie married, a wall would always be between them because of the differences in their faith. It would be like mixing grease and water, something that never worked. How could he do a thing that directly opposed the instruction of the scriptures?

*But how can I live without her?* his soul cried out. He leaned forward and grasped the pew in front of him, his spirit vexed. How could he give up the woman he loved? He had searched for the right miss for years, and when he finally found her, was he going to have to let her go?

His heart as heavy as a rock, he knew with a certainty that Christmas would not be the day of joy he had envisioned all these months. It would be a day of funereal sorrow.

Christmas would be the day he and Winkie would part company.

The elderly gentleman seated next to him twisted in the pew and let out a long sigh, and Joseph was distracted from his contemplations.

"The Bible says a man must love his wife as Christ loved the church," the minister was saying. "That is a sacrificial love, a love that makes a man think first of the woman, above himself."

*A sacrificial love?* Joseph mused. A love that made a man think first of the woman, above himself? Those were his sentiments exactly.

Precious Winkie. Winsome Winkie. He knew with a surety that she loved him. It was something tucked deeply inside him, like a secret knowledge between them. If he broke off their relationship on Christmas, the most joyful day of the year, Winkie would be doubly hurt that he'd chosen to do his ill deed on that special day.

He fiddled with his coat buttons as he formulated his plan.

*I'll wait a couple of weeks past Christmas to tell her the bad news. That be sacrificial love.*

# Chapter 7

C an you believe Christmas Day is coming to a close?" Winkie said to Joseph just as the sun went down, the two of them sitting at the table, eating another slice of sweet potato pie before he had to leave.

All afternoon they had been together, and it was a Christmas Day she'd long remember, one filled with glee and gladness. . . .

And big eating, as Joseph called it, turkey and stuffing and all the trimmings. . .

And vibrant singing, accompanied by Joseph beating on a cook pot and Cassie clanging spoons together. . .

And silly merry-making, Joseph telling riddles and stories, Cassie bursting out in fits of giggles, even Winkie laughing till her sides hurt.

Joseph. Joseph. Joseph. He was what made the day special.

As she savored the last bite of her pie, her eyes scanned the room and came to rest on the gifts. . . .

The beautiful blanket chest Joseph lovingly made with his own hands, intricate carvings adorning the cherrywood surface. The child-sized oak rocker Cassie was sitting in now, her little head slumped over in sleep from sheer exhaustion. The suit of clothes Winkie'd made Joseph, neatly folded atop the chest, waiting to be taken home with him. The red-and-white-striped bags of candy he'd brought, enough to keep Cassie in delight for weeks.

"I said, can you believe Christmas Day is coming to a close? I wish we could wrap it up like a present and open it again, don't you?" She rose from the table and picked up the pie pan, Joseph saying not a word the whole time. "Joseph?" she asked. "Did you hear me?"

He inched his plate forward. "It be a most pleasant day, Winkie."

Across the room, she stacked dishes in the tin pan on the shelf. Why was Joseph so quiet? She'd never seen him like this. He seemed to be almost. . .brooding.

What was the matter? He'd been subdued all the livelong day. True, he was cheerful when he gave her and Cassie their gifts, though he was restrained, far different from his usual frolicsome ways. And yes, he was grateful for the suit of clothes she'd made him. But he didn't jump in the air and kick his heels when he saw it, as she'd expected—a silly antic that made her laugh every time.

She pondered on this matter. What was the reason for his reserve? She touched her temple. Of course. He was going to ask her to marry him any day now, that she was sure of, and he was deciding how to go about the details. First, he needed to secure permission from Mr. Fletcher. She could picture it in her mind now, Joseph standing before Mr. Fletcher.

"Sir," Joseph would probably say, "I wish to marry."

"And who is the woman?" Mr. Fletcher would respond.

"Winkie Williams. She was here on Independence Day at the invitation of your wife and Miss Willie. She be a fine, upright woman. She be a free woman, residing in Charleston, making her living as a hatmaker. Miss Willie and Mr. Richard can vouch for her. She used to live on Laurel Ridge, where Miss Willie grew up."

"Sundays with a wife will be enough to satisfy you?"

"Have to, is all I know. You already give me a pass for that day, so the way I see it, if you be so kind as to keep that up, that be the time I spend with my new wife and child."

Now, in her mind's eye, Winkie could envision Joseph smiling at the words "wife and child." Broadly. Winkie poured water in the tin pan, lathered the rag with a bar of lye soap, and washed the dishes. She could see Mr. Fletcher sitting at his massive mahogany desk, Joseph standing before him.

"Why, that'll be fine, Joseph," Mr. Fletcher would say. "I don't see any obstacles. You can spend Saturday night through Monday morning of every week with your new family, as long as you're back at work early Monday morning. You're most deserving of happiness. If this woman will bring you happiness, if this is what you truly want, then I'll not stand in the way of it. When will this event take place?"

All the tableware washed and rinsed, Winkie picked up the first plate on the stack and dried it, then the next, her face growing warm at the thought of Joseph. What would his kisses be like? She rubbed her arms, all pimply like gooseflesh. Joseph's kisses would be dulcet yet ravishing.

Smiling shyly, she could almost hear Joseph's eager response to his master, concerning when their wedding would occur. "As soon as possible, Mr. Fletcher. Just as soon as possible."

She stared into the looking glass tacked to the wall in front of her. My, she was glad Joseph couldn't hear what she was thinking. She glanced sheepishly at him across the room. She saw his broad shoulders, his dark eyes that nearly always danced, his neat, clean clothing. She thought about his fond devotion, his gentlemanly deportment, his jolly ways.

Yes, this was a Christmas Day she would never forget, she thought as she glanced again at the tall, handsome man sitting at her table. Her Heart Happy Joseph.

Something told her a momentous occasion was soon to occur.

# Chapter 8

From the moment Joseph awoke, he knew this was the day he had to tell Winkie. Three weeks past Christmas, this Sabbath was mild, warm enough to be outside, at least long enough for him to deliver his dose of dread.

"I need to talk with you about an urgent matter," he told Winkie when he picked up Cassie for church that morning.

A couple hours later, as the three of them walked toward the outskirts of town, Winkie's basket of food on his arm, Cassie between them with hands held fast, a glorious thought hit him. If he could convince Winkie to accept the faith, then they would be compatible. Perhaps no one ever presented the Gospel to her in the right way. He would explain it in plain language. He smiled, thinking of Uncle Solomon's silly courting riddles. He wouldn't dilly-dally. He would give her a direct opportunity to accept Christ, and she would do so eagerly.

After they ate, as little Starlight swung high in the air on a rope swing, Joseph and Winkie got comfortable on her colorful quilt.

He decided to start right in. "Winkie, I have a very important question to ask you."

"I've been expecting it." Her voice was low and sweet-sounding as she leaned into him, shoulder brushing shoulder.

"Has anyone ever explained the Gospel to you?"

She looked dazed as she pulled away.

"You see, when Adam and Eve sinned, God provided a sacrifice for them. A blood sacrifice—an animal. We don't rightly know why God required a blood sacrifice for sin, but He did from the very beginning of mankind. All through the Old Covenant, man had to offer a sacrifice regularly. Then God sent Jesus, His only begotten Son, to become the last sacrifice so we would never have to offer another one again."

Impassioned by his love for the Lord, Joseph plunged on. "All we have to do is accept this sacrifice—Jesus Christ. I'm talking about a gift of salvation. All we have to do is say, 'Lord, I confess my sins and ask You to forgive me and cleanse me—'"

"Is this the urgent matter you needed to discuss?" Confusion filled her eyes as she edged to the other side of the quilt.

"Yes. You see, Christ died on the cross for us, and when we accept Him as Savior, He fills our lives with peace, and He gives direction, and He helps us, and He comforts—"

"Joseph, I don't understand. I—I thought. . ."

"I'm trying to explain."

For long minutes, they went back and forth, him almost preaching, her almost rebutting.

"I—I thought you brought me here to propose." A sob escaped her lips, but she swallowed hard, as if willing herself not to cry. "I love you with all my heart." She swallowed hard again. "You know what I've taken to calling you secretly? My Heart

Happy Joseph. You make my heart sing and my spirit soar." Tears trickled down her cheeks. "I–I'm not very good with words, I–like you are, but I can quote Burns:

*"Till a' the seas gang dry, my dear,*
*And the rocks melt wi' the sun:*
*Oh I will love thee still, my dear,*
*While the sands o' life shall run."*

Joseph's heart wrenched in his chest, and it took everything within him to bridle his trembles. In a flash, he was at her side, and he pulled her close. It was growing cooler, but it was more than that. He wanted to hold her. "I went about this all wrong."

She looked up at him, questioning, dabbing at her tears.

"I need to start from the beginning. As I was making your blanket chest, that's when I knew I loved you; that's when I decided I'd ask you to marry me on Christmas Day."

"What stopped you?" she said quietly.

"One Sunday in church, the minister preached on being unequally yoked. That means not marrying someone outside the faith."

He could feel her stiffen, but he continued on, though he felt a lump forming in his throat that made him short of breath. "I—I thought I would die, Winkie, when those words sunk into my soul. Unequally yoked. I, too, love you. . .more than life itself."

Tears formed in his eyes, but he blinked them away. "When I heard his sermon, I knew I'd have to give you up if I was to follow the ways of the scriptures."

"But that won't stand between us. The faith, you call it."

"Yes, it will." He said it emphatically, and she made no response. "I felt like I was stricken when I realized what I needed to do. I felt like I couldn't live anymore."

He continued on, telling her everything. Then he paused and held her in his arms, Starlight shrieking with joy high in the sky, the two of them not saying a word, just basking in each other's presence.

For now.

"May I ask you something else?" he said respectfully, and he could feel her nod as he held her in a loving embrace. "Won't you accept Christ as Lord and Savior and go to church with me?"

She drew a deep breath. "I've seen too much, felt too much, all of it pain, pain, pain." Her voice grew in intensity. "I hate the white man for what he did to our people."

"You love Miss Willie."

"She's different."

"The Bible says to love your enemies."

"And that's why I don't want anything to do with it," she spat out. Then the tears flowed again.

Joseph was grateful to the Lord for the calmness that overcame him. "Winkie honey," he said, taking her hand, stroking her work-worn fingers that he loved so dearly and would never touch again after today, "the Bible isn't a book of strung-together, no-account words. There be a reason for everything in it. It powerful, and it sharper than any two-edged sword, and it true, and it be food to our souls. If we partake, if we will heed its life-giving precepts, if we will sow to the things of the Lord, we will reap blessings too numerous to name."

"If that be so, then what blessings are you reaping?" She let out a snort of disgust. "What white man is doling out delights to you?"

"Oh baby." He thought his heart would break in two. Why couldn't she understand what he was trying to say, to offer her? Peace and love and joy.

"Our real struggle," he said, "isn't against a person. It be against the devil. The Holy Book say, 'For we wrestle not against flesh and blood, but against principalities, against powers, against the rulers of the darkness of this world, against spiritual wickedness in high places.' Don't you see?"

"No, I don't," she said, her jaw tensed.

With forced stamina, he resisted the urge to lean down and kiss her good-bye, knowing what he was about to say would sever all ties between them.

He cleared his throat. "You're free, but you're not free."

She pulled away from him, sitting erect, her eyes flashing fire.

"You're bound by bitterness," he said.

Her eyes narrowed to tiny slits.

"The Bible says in John 8:36, 'If the Son therefore shall make you free, ye shall be free indeed.'"

She jumped up. "Come on, Cassie." She jerked on the edge of the quilt, like she was going to start folding it with him sitting on it. "I'm ready to go. Been ready."

He rose to his feet. How would she take the last thing he had to tell her? The edict he had to deliver? The words that stuck in his throat like a bullet in a rusty gun? Finally, he said with a quiet strength, "When you let the Son make you free—not some piece of paper—you be free indeed."

"I don't ever want to lay eyes on you again, Mr. Joseph Moore, you white-lover, you."

# Chapter 9

Bundled against the winter weather, Joseph stood on the street corner, watching little Starlight walk toward Winkie's shop. Every Sabbath, he discreetly delivered her home, remembering Winkie's parting words with a sorrow unto death: *"I don't ever want to lay eyes on you again, Mr. Joseph Moore, you white-lover, you."*

He would respect her wishes. That much, he could do. Several times, he had been tempted to revive the relationship, but so far, he'd resisted.

He shivered in the cold wind, stamped his feet, blew into his clasped palms.

*Just because Winkie won't go to church doesn't mean anything,* a voice whispered in his heart. *She be a good woman, a lady who loves you. She'll make a fine wife to you and a tender mother to the children born to you.*

"She be a good woman, all right," he whispered. "She said she'd love me till the seas go dry and the rocks melt in the sun." He blinked hard as his eyes misted over, and it wasn't from the cold. He took a step toward Winkie's shop.

"No," he cried out, stopping dead in his tracks. "I can't do this." He swallowed deeply. Into his mind popped the words Joseph-in-the-Bible had said: *"How then can I do this great wickedness, and sin against God?"*

Seeing Starlight safely inside the door of the shop, Joseph walked toward home with a firm resolve. "I'm going to follow the Lord's plan from now on. I've tried mine long enough."

His own way hadn't worked. First, on the night he'd carved the top of Winkie's blanket chest, he'd made plans to propose to her despite the doubt God sent his way. *"She doesn't partake of your spiritual life,"* the voice of the Lord had warned.

Then he'd tried to force her into accepting the Gospel.

Joseph walked hurriedly down the street. A few minutes ago, he had followed the example of Joseph-in-the-Bible of the Old Covenant, and that had warded off the temptation that was dangling in front of his eyes.

"Now I'm going to follow Joseph-in-the-Bible of the New Covenant." He would do as God bid him to, just as that Joseph had. "I will bend my will to the Lord."

With a vexation of soul at losing Winkie but with a confidence that God would see him through, Joseph tramped on.

# Chapter 10

Winkie leaned over the hat in her hands, sewing with railway speed. Madam was expecting two bonnets the next day, and three of her own customers would be waiting at week's end to pick up their orders.

"Mama, look," Cassie called from where she sat on the rug, holding a book Miss Willie had given her. "See the pretty pictures?" She held it up for Winkie to see.

"Those are plumb delightful." A gentle breeze blew in the window, the curtains billowing slightly, then falling, then billowing, then falling.

"March is coming in backward," Winkie said. "It's a lamb this year. Ah, this air is plumb refreshing."

A whoosh made the curtains stand straight out, and Winkie's scraps went flying. "Well, here come the lion. Sugarbun, can you close the window a mite? We're going to blow to Kansas."

As Cassie bounded toward the window, then shut it, Winkie drew the needle in and out. *Funny. Last fall, I remember thinking, "Fall is in the air, but it's springtime in my heart." Today, spring is in the air, but it's winter down inside.*

Funny? No, it wasn't funny at all. Never had she experienced such a cold, dank feeling. *Desolate* was a more fitting word. She was pining away for Joseph. Though he was out of her sight, he would never be out of her mind. Or her heart.

Heart Happy Joseph. He was the only man who could set her feet to dancing and her face to smiling. But not anymore. These days, she rarely smiled. Counting her ills was what she did the livelong day. It all but consumed her waking moments and many of the ones she should've been sleeping.

Her mother was right. Life wasn't fair. Work was hard. There was never no letup. And her man, her Heart Happy Joseph? He had been taken away from her just like her Sweet Love Roscoe.

It was more than flesh and blood could bear, yet she couldn't cry out as she sat there sewing. She would alarm Cassie. Instead she clamped her teeth shut and kept sewing at her stitching.

"When Mr. Joseph coming to eat with us again?" Cassie asked brightly.

"Why are you always asking that?" she snapped. "I told you a hundred times. Never. N-e-v-e-r."

Cassie threw her arms around Winkie, as if she was undaunted by the outburst, as if she possessed some special something that could always bring a note of cheer to Winkie.

Winkie couldn't help smiling, and she thrust her sewing aside and gathered her baby on her lap.

"Sugarbun, Sugarbun," Winkie singsonged, "Mama's darling sweet, you thrill me dear, see here, see here—" She burst out laughing. "I can't think of anymore rhymes." For long moments, bright laughter—both Winkie's and Cassie's—filled the room.

Then Winkie sobered. "I—I don't know what I'd do. . ." She fiddled with Cassie's braids, then straightened Cassie's rumpled pinafore "If I didn't have you, Sugarbun."

Cassie kissed her once more, then jumped down and went back to her book.

Winkie bent over the bonnet. "*Out of sight, out of mind,*" her mother always said. Maybe she came to that conclusion because of the many relatives who were sold out from under her. Maybe something came over her heart, like a scab over a sore to shield it. Maybe that was her mother's protection from the wounds down inside her.

But Joseph had wounds, too. Hadn't he told her he was sold from out of his mama's loving arms? Hadn't he told her about the hardships he'd endured? But he wasn't sad, like her mother always was. On the contrary, Joseph made happiness everywhere he went.

"Be gone, dull care," she whispered. "My brain be too tired to ponder this any longer."

"What you say, Mama?"

"Nothing, child."

A tap sounded at the door.

"Help me straighten up, Cassie. Customer's come a-calling. Make haste." Winkie jumped to her feet and set the table in order while Cassie picked up her book and doll and her dried gourds with the beans in them.

Winkie brushed at the sides of her hair, then opened the door. Before her stood a fine Charleston lady. That wasn't unusual. What was unusual was the servant woman who accompanied her, tending the lady's two children in tow.

It was Auntie, a woman Winkie hadn't seen since early childhood. Dazed, yet aware of proper deportment, she greeted the fine Charleston lady, then fell onto Auntie's neck in such a tight embrace, Auntie let out a little squeal.

When Auntie explained to her missus who Winkie was, the lady graciously stood to the side, waiting for them to finish their affectionate exchanges.

As Winkie hugged Auntie's ample softness, she couldn't get enough of her. Finally, she pulled away, her eyes moist. She offered the lady a chair as she inquired about her name. Then she said, "Cassie, come, child. Show these little girls your new book while Mama waits on Mrs. Butler."

An hour later, Winkie had four new hat orders. And because of the lady's kindness, she had the pleasant prospect of a visit from Auntie.

Soon.

# Chapter 11

Weekly visits commenced with Auntie, and they were like sunshine to Winkie's soul. Sitting at the table, eating hot biscuits slathered with jam or apple slices dotted with cheese or some other such treat—Winkie quickly found out ample Auntie liked her treats—they talked about everything and about nothing.

She-she talk, Auntie called it.

Auntie was the mother Winkie needed. She petted Winkie, called her endearing names, treated her with loving regard, demonstrated tender affection toward her.

"You need a mammy," Auntie said with a gap-toothed smile on the first visit, hugging Winkie to her. "You need a mammy worse than Mrs. Butler's kids."

"I do, Auntie, I do," Winkie said back, swallowing the lump in her throat.

"I be your mammy every time I come see you. I is a good comforter."

On the second visit, after Auntie's antics died down, Winkie found out she was one of them—a church-going faith person. Same as Joseph. But Auntie didn't go on and on about it, and Winkie was grateful.

On the third visit, after Auntie's antics died down, the talk turned to the subject Winkie most liked to discuss.

The people and their plight.

Winkie pulled down her book of poems and read aloud the one on the creased paper.

After the reading of it, Auntie harrumphed loudly as she sat in the straight-backed chair. Then she pushed her half-eaten shortcake to the center of the table. "Don't you know, Winkie?"

"Know what, Auntie?" Winkie sewed away. "That your missus liked my hats and told her friends about me?"

"Don't you know, Winkie?"

"You got a riddle for me?"

"No riddle at all. It be plain as the lips on your face."

"What that?"

"There be haughty white folks and haughty dark folks. There be nice-acting white folks and nice-acting dark folks."

Now Winkie was harrumphing. Just as loudly as Auntie did.

"It don't matter what color a heart is wrapped in," Auntie declared. "They're all the same underneath."

On the fourth visit, after Auntie's antics died down, Auntie, sewing as furiously as Winkie to help her out, said, "Pride don't wear a color, Winkie. And neither does hate nor meanness nor greed. And neither does kindness nor goodness nor uprightness."

Then she said, "You keep your nose clean—even if it takes both sleeves."

"Auntie!"

Auntie's dark eyes danced, but her voice was serious-sounding. "No matter what the rest of the world do, you make sure your attitude be right. That all we be responsible for in life. If we do that, God take care of us."

On the fifth visit, after Auntie's antics died down, she said, "Winkie, the day you was borned, your mama let me name you."

"Yes, ma'am. She told me about it."

"I buried newborn twins the month before—"

"I didn't know that." Winkie set aside her sewing and touched Auntie on the forearm, trying to swallow the lump forming in her throat.

"She thought it would make me feel better if I could name you. You was the sweetest little baby, and as pretty as can be. You know what your full name is, don't you?"

"Yes, ma'am. It's Periwinkle."

"You know why I named you that?"

"Because it's your favorite flower. That's what Mama always said."

"Well, that, too. Do you know much about a periwinkle, sweet one?"

"It be purplish-blue."

"I repeat. You know why I named you that?"

"No, ma'am."

"You be finding your answer in a lexicon."

On the sixth visit, after Auntie's antics died down, she said, "You find out the meaning behind your name, sweet one?"

"It be a riddle."

Auntie's round mahogany cheeks shook back and forth, back and forth, wobbling like jelly.

Studying Auntie's nuances, Winkie ate the last bite of peach pie on her plate. That was one more thing to love about Auntie, the way she went on, exaggerated-like.

"It be plain as the ears on your head."

"No, it isn't. Miss Willie be kind enough to look up 'periwinkle' in her lexicon, but weren't nothing there about a girl's name." From her pocket Winkie withdrew a scrap of paper. "She wrote the meaning down for me, and I've read it again and again, but it be a riddle."

"Read it to me now."

Winkie looked down at the paper. "It say a periwinkle be a ground cover known for it purplish-blue flowers."

"Uh-huh." Auntie was wagging her head.

"And it say it be a trailing herb."

"Uh-huh." She wagged it again.

"And it say it be the name of a color."

Head wagging once more.

"I can't make no sense of this silliness, Auntie."

"Go on."

"That all there be."

"You sure?" Auntie's eyes were round with wonder—and with playfulness.

"All right. One more. It say a periwinkle be a shrub what be a source of medicine—"

"That it," Auntie exclaimed, throwing both hands in the air, hallelujah-style.

Winkie said nothing, just drummed her fingers on the table. When would Auntie tell her?

"What a medicine be, child?"

Winkie shrugged her shoulders.

Auntie leaned forward. "A medicine relieve pain and cures ills."

"So?"

Auntie repositioned the shawl about her shoulders, taking time to drape it in precise pleats. "The Good Book say God be the God of comfort. The reason He comfort us is so we can turn around and comfort others with the same kind we received."

Winkie folded her arms across her chest. She didn't want to hear this.

"When I named you, I looked into your big brown eyes, and I said, 'Periwinkle, one day you going to bring the healing touch of comfort to others.' Don't run from your destiny no longer, child. The Lord has decreed it. I feel it in my soul."

Winkie stood up, walked to the shelf, and busied herself by peeling a big red apple.

"The Lord be right here in this room with arms widespread, wanting to comfort you. Let Him, do let Him, sweet one. Open up the door of your heart. Just a crack. That all it take. He come in, and that peace that passes all understanding will flood your spirit and take away your pain."

Still Winkie didn't respond, just kept working on the apple until one long, unbroken peel hit the floor.

"From this day forth, I going to call you Periwinkle. You will live up to your name. Mark my words."

# Chapter 12

All morning, Winkie made ready for Auntie's visit. She straightened the shop, made a ginger cake with vanilla sauce, hurried with her sewing so she could give her full attention to Auntie when she came.

As she worked, she pondered on Auntie's last visit, three weeks ago. Why hadn't she come last week or the week before? What kept her away? Was Auntie miffed because she didn't respond to her God talk and her comfort speech?

In the afternoon, as Cassie played with her shaking gourds on the big oval rug, Winkie sat near the window to get the best light, waiting for Auntie to come, busy at her never-ending sewing. She leaned down, bit the thread above the knot, broke it off, rethreaded her needle.

As a gentle breeze blew in, she sniffed the room made sweet with ginger and savored both scents, spice and spring. She looked at the table across the room, edified by the sight. A patchwork tablecloth made from hat scraps. A cake in a serving plate. A crockery bowl filled with vanilla sauce. An earthenware pitcher holding fresh buttermilk.

When she heard a step at the stoop, she pushed her sewing into a basket and rose from her chair.

Auntie waddled across the threshold, a spray of flowers in her arms. "For you, sweet one." She thrust them at Winkie with energy. "My, something do smell good in here."

"Ginger cake." Winkie took a whiff of the colorful blossoms as she put them in a jar. "And now, flowers."

"Hmm, hmm, ginger cake. My favorite. We in for a treat this hour. I couldn't get here sooner. Mrs. Butler's had me a-hopping lately, what with all her company a-coming and a-going and all the extra childrens to tend to."

Winkie stood at the table, adding water to the daisies and delphiniums, pansies and petunias—wild jasmine perfuming the bunch, even some periwinkles mixed in. "Thank you, Auntie, for the flowers." *And thank you for not being ired at me.* She placed the jar of blossoms in the center of the table. "They'll add pleasure to our eating, for sure."

"April showers bring May flowers. Now, will you do something for me, Periwinkle?"

"You know I will."

Auntie held up a Bible. "Will you read me a few verses after we sup? Mrs. Butler gave me this a long time ago, yet I never heard it read from before."

A half hour later, though Winkie offered a myriad of excuses, she found herself reading aloud to Auntie from portions of the Book of John as Auntie called them out.

"John 14:27."

Winkie flipped through the pages and found the spot. "'Peace I leave with you, my peace I give unto you: not as the world giveth, give I unto you. Let not your heart be troubled, neither let it be afraid.'"

"Those be Jesus' words."

On and on they went, Auntie calling out selections, Winkie finding them and reading, Auntie adding a bit of instruction here and there.

"John 8:36," Auntie said.

Winkie flipped to the verse, scanned it, felt like her heart would surely stop its beating. This was the verse Joseph had quoted to her at The Parting.

"Why you quit?" Auntie said. "This be a tonic to my soul."

Winkie felt her face grow hot, remembering the sharp interchange between her and Joseph on that dreadful day. "I—I—"

"Read on. These words ease my being—" Auntie patted her round midsection. "Better than tansy mixed in honey."

Winkie swallowed hard. "Haven't we read long enough?"

"Please? Just this last verse?"

She nodded. How could she deny Auntie? Auntie was her tonic, her easement from the bitter brews of life.

"While I be thinking on it, I aim to leave the Good Book with you—"

"Oh no. That not be necessary." She didn't want to hurt Auntie's feelings, but she had no use for the Bible, felt right bristly that Auntie would do such as that.

"It don't do me no good, seeing as how I can't decipher a word. But you, you learned how. And you better give God the glory for it. He sent you a special blessing in the form of a mistress who taught you to read."

Winkie had never thought about God being the One who'd worked that out, and it set her to thinking, deeplike.

"Now, read that last verse. John 8:36."

She stared at the words on the page, feeling shaky inside. "'If the S–Son therefore sh–shall make you fr–free, ye shall be free indeed.'"

"I got a powerful potion to say to you, sweet one."

"What's that, Auntie?"

"I'm not free, but I'm free."

Winkie chewed on her bottom lip. How could this be? Not free but free—the opposite of what Joseph talked about. *"You're free, but you're not free,"* Joseph had said to her.

"I'm not free, but I'm free," Auntie repeated, leaning forward, her voice all seriousness. "Christ Jesus set me free from the chains of sin, and in their place, He give me peace, joy, and love."

Winkie looked down at her lap, her hands making hard fists, her mind studying on Auntie's words.

"Yes, I'm free indeed." Auntie smiled. Broadly. "Periwinkle, one day you going to be able to say that, too. Mark my words."

# Chapter 13

The Good Book sat on the shelf high on the wall, beside the stacks of colorful fabrics and hat trims. One day went by, then another, then another, Winkie never touching it a time.

On the fourth day, Winkie looked up at it, thinking it must have drawing powers. Seemed like every time she passed the shelf, the Good Book called out to her, making her shiver with every footfall.

That night, she couldn't sleep, and it wasn't because of Cassie's vigorous kicking. Even a pillow stuffed between them didn't bring Winkie the slumber she craved. Slowly she sat up in bed focused on the shaft of moonlight coming through the curtains, saw where the moonbeam ended.

The Good Book.

She felt herself shaking, heard her teeth chattering, touched her heart where it hammered against her chest. In a flash, she burrowed under the covers and snuggled close to Cassie. As she lay there, her heart still beating wildly, the verse she read to Auntie came floating through her mind, and she repeated what she could remember: "Something about giving us peace so that our hearts won't be troubled or afraid."

*"That be Jesus talking,"* Auntie had said.

"Jesus?" Glancing up at the Good Book bathed in the moonlight, Winkie pulled up her grit and stood. Like a miracle, her heart was strangely quieted, her soul wrapped in a cocoon of peace.

"Jesus?" she repeated. Her feet floated to the shelf, her fingers glided upward. With a flick of her wrist, she took down the Good Book, lit a candle on the table, sat on the straight-backed chair, and opened the Bible with steady hands, glad, so glad the Lord had kept her awake.

Like a starved person pouncing on a plate of victuals, she devoured the Good Book. She began with the Book of John and read every word. She flipped to the Book of Romans, doing the same.

Romans one. Romans two. Romans three. Romans four. Romans five.

"Romans 5:6," she said. "'For when we were yet without strength, in due time Christ died for the ungodly.'"

She cleared her throat. " 'For scarcely for a righteous man will one die: yet peradventure for a good man some would even dare to die.'"

She pulled the candle closer. "'But God commendeth his love toward us, in that, while we were yet sinners, Christ died for us.'"

Her heart was hammering again, only it wasn't from trepidation. It was from revelation.

"Sweet Love Roscoe," she whispered, feeling all a-twitter with new knowledge, "in a way, you died for me, a woman who loved you so. Yet it says Christ died for those who didn't even love Him. How could someone do something like that?"

The magnitude of Christ's love hit her like a shaft of sunlight, and she slipped to her knees in the dim candleglow. "Lord, can You forgive me?" she cried. "I be one of those who didn't care a thing for You, yet You died for me to take away my sins before I even asked."

She brushed away her tears. "Lord, I be sorry for being insensitive to what You did on Calvary. You provided salvation, and I accept that now. Set me free from the chains of sin, like You did for Auntie."

*"It is done,"* the Lord assured. *"I have paid the price for your liberty."*

"I'm free, Lord, truly free," she exclaimed, then lowered her voice so she wouldn't waken Cassie. "I promise to live for You the rest of my days and to proclaim Your glory to all I meet."

A peace sweeter than a honeycomb seeped over her being, from the top of her head to the tips of her toes, and she knelt there for eons, crying tears of joy, pouring forth words of love for her Savior.

Finally, Winkie quieted, basking in the Lord's presence. When she arose, her knees were stiff from kneeling on the hard wooden floor, for how long she didn't know. Then she saw the fingers of dawn peeking through the curtains.

"Ain't gonna' study war no more," she sang softly as she walked toward the bed. "Ain't gonna' study war no more, ain't gonna' study war no more-ore-ore. Ain't gonna' study war no more, ain't gonna' study war no more, ain't gonna' study war no more."

With eyes brimming with joy tears, she crawled in beside Cassie for a little shut-eye. As she settled beneath the bedclothes, into her mind came Auntie's words: *"Periwinkle, one day you going to bring the healing touch of comfort to others."*

"Lord," she whispered, wiping yet more tears away, "this be Periwinkle talking. I promise to comfort those that need comforting wherewith You have comforted me."

# Chapter 14

Y ou think I ought to go find Joseph and tell him I made it right with my Maker?" Periwinkle asked Auntie on the second visit after her Day of Liberty.

Auntie's brows drew together in contemplation. "Why not give it a few weeks, sweet one? Let the Lord work it out for you. I know He going to."

"Yes, ma'am."

"Meantime, you keep reading the Good Book and get yourself rooted and grounded in the things of the Lord."

"I am, Auntie, I am. I be eating it up."

Auntie wagged her head, saying "Um hmm" over and over. Then she paused. "The Bible say, 'They which hunger and thirst after righteousness. . .shall be filled.'" She licked her lips. "Now, have you got a dab more of them spiced apples and that clotted cream?"

*⁂*

On a bright June morning as Periwinkle took the pan of biscuits off the outdoor fire and put them on a plate, she saw her neighbor, Mercy Jones, across the alleyway.

"How goes it?" she called, friendlylike, wrapping the plate of biscuits with a checkered cloth.

"Misery, pure misery." Mercy, a freewoman and clothes washer who had previously avoided Periwinkle, walked toward her, wringing the last drops of water out of a towel. From the bunglesomeness of it, Periwinkle judged the towel held a gang of collars and wristbands that belonged to some fine gentleman.

"Misery? How so?" Periwinkle put down the plate and turned her attention to her neighbor.

"My throat be purely plugged with terror. There's talk of war and such stuff all over. Every time I make my deliveries in town, that all I hear. Yesterday, Mrs. Davis—she be one of my customers—why, she told me about a war in this country before the turn of the century, she said, where guns was shot off and innocent people was killed right and left."

Mercy let out a little sob. "I be terrible scared, just terrible. I don't want no bullet to go through my skull. I have tried turning my shoes upside down every night for weeks now, and I even made the soles face the wall. But nothing helps. The talk gets worse every day. Oh, why can't I go on to Diddy-Wah-Diddy, where we going to dance on the streets, sing and eat chitlins and possum pie all the day long?"

Mercy was beside herself, groaning and moaning, and when she dropped the towel full of laundry, Periwinkle knew how deep her despair was. Water was too hard to come by to let clean clothes fall in the dirt.

*"It's time, Periwinkle,"* the Lord seemed to whisper. *"This is your destiny."*

"Yes, Lord," she whispered back. With a gentle grip, she held Mercy's shoulders and looked into her eyes. "Mercy, the Good Book say, 'Let not your heart be troubled.' It also say, 'Thou wilt keep him in perfect peace, whose mind is stayed on thee.'"

Periwinkle hugged Mercy to her in a sisterly embrace. "Oh Mercy, Christ Jesus has set me free from the chains of sin, and in their place He give me peace, joy, and love. And He want to do the same for you, right here, right now. His peace will flood your soul like the waters that cover the sea if you trust in Him."

A quarter hour later, her biscuits cold but her steps light, Periwinkle went inside to wake Cassie.

"Yes, Lord," she said, looking heavenward, smiling and crying a joy tear at the same time, "I promise to comfort those that be in need of comforting wherewith You have comforted me."

# Chapter 15

Periwinkle stood at the window at breaking of day and smiled. "Independence Day has dawned without a hint of rain in the cloudless sky." At her light footfall across the room, Cassie bounded out of bed.

"Parade day," Cassie said, jumping up and down, nightdress jiggling. "It's finally here. It's finally here."

"Yes, it's parade day, but that parade don't start for a good three, four hours, young lady. You better get some more shut-eye, or you be too tired to enjoy it."

"I can't, Mama, I can't."

For close to an hour, as Periwinkle worked on her hats, Cassie played with her collection of gourds and then with the doll Miss Willie gave her.

At last, Cassie curled up on the rug, fast asleep. As Periwinkle pinched a piece of fabric to form a green satin leaf, she thought about the pleasant prospects of the day. First, there would be the parade. Then there would be the picnic, what she promised Cassie, on the outskirts of town. In a few minutes, she would lay down her sewing and get the chicken to frying in the vat and the sweet potatoes to baking in the hot coals. Then it would be time to wrap and pack them, and then she would get Cassie up and dressed and herself dressed, too. Then it would be time for them to head to town and commence some merrymaking.

*"I always thought Independence Day was better than Christmas,"* Miss Willie was known to say.

"Yes, me and Cassie both be looking forward to some gaiety today," Periwinkle whispered to herself.

She pulled her needle in and out of the rose-colored silk, turning the fabric just so, until a perfect rosette emerged. She remembered last Christmas and how she'd thought it was the best Christmas Day she'd ever had, except for wondering about Joseph's brooding silence. On that day, she thought Joseph was quiet because he was planning The Proposal.

A few weeks later, she'd learned the truth of the matter. He was planning The Parting.

"Oh Joseph," she said, feeling all weepy inside, "I have sorely missed you." She bit off the thread and rethreaded her needle, her hands trembling. "My Heart Happy Joseph, the man who set my feet to dancing and my face to smiling, him who made my heart sing and my spirit soar, where art thou, as the poet said?"

She glanced up. "Lord, what be Your plans for my future? Do they include my Heart Happy Joseph? Will my heart sing and my spirit soar once again? Be it possible that I might get a glimpse of him today at the Independence Day parade?"

*"I have everything under control, Periwinkle,"* the Lord seemed to whisper. *"Have faith."*

# Chapter 16

O nce again, as on the previous Independence Day, Joseph Moore stood amidst a sea of brown faces in the proper section of downtown Charleston, his arms folded across his barrel chest, anticipating with relish the parade that was about to commence.

He remembered last year's parade as if it had happened yesterday, a warm feeling flooding his heart. On last Independence Day, right here on the same corner, he'd met his winsome Winkie and her charming daughter, Starlight.

That afternoon, there had been a formal introduction at the Fletcher plantation. Their first meeting entranced him. Their second meeting thrilled him. As they shook hands under the arbor, her feet did a little dance in the dirt, and he thought his heart would burst from happiness.

He was so deep in thought, he almost jumped when he heard the loud notes of a lively patriotic song being played close by. To his left, just within his view, he saw a band marching down the street.

When only a few minutes had passed with his toe tapping to the beat of the rousing tune, the crowd closed in tighter, slaves and free people alike, all straining to get a glimpse and enjoy the frivolities of the day. He glanced around to see if he knew anyone, but the crowd kept jostling and shifting.

His mind studied on the events of the past year.

Getting to know Winkie.

Sharing meals together.

Enjoying outdoor picnics on the wayside.

Falling in love with her.

Carving her blanket chest.

Making plans for a future together.

And then. . .

The sermon. *"Unequally yoked,"* the minister had called it.

*Unequally yoked. Unequally yoked. Unequally yoked.* The first time Joseph had heard those fiercesome words as he sat in church, they had pounded in his brain, then invaded his heart and gripped it with an iron hand.

How could he live without her? his soul had cried out, his spirit vexed. How could he give up the woman he loved? He had searched for the right miss for years, and when he finally found her, he had to let her go.

Etched into his mind, never to be forgotten, were the immortal words Winkie had quoted the day of their parting:

*"Till a' the seas gang dry, my dear,*

*And the rocks melt wi' the sun:*
*Oh I will love thee still, my dear,*
*While the sands o' life shall run."*

Now, standing on the street corner listening to the patriotic tunes, his heart wrenched in his chest, and it took everything within him to bridle his trembles. How many times since their parting had he made his way to her, only to turn his steps around by sheer willpower and God's power, too? How many times had he thought of taking her into his arms and making her his wedded wife, to love and to cherish, forever and ever?

"*Trust and obey,*" the Lord seemed to say on each occasion. "*Give Me time to work.*"

"How long must I wait, Lord?" he mumbled, in anguish of soul.

"Mama, I can't see," said a child to his right. "Please pick me up one more time."

"You're too heavy, Sugarbun," said a woman's voice, low and melodious.

Instantly, he recognized the voice, and his breath caught in his throat.

"I be plumb give out from holding you."

Joseph glanced down and saw a little girl with a pleading expression on her face as she tugged on a woman's skirts. Then he looked directly at the woman, saw wide somber eyes, smooth-as-buttermilk brown skin, smart hat and gown, and he couldn't help smiling at the pleasant sight before him.

Winkie looked up into his eyes, not dipping her chin as was her custom, just staring straight at him, smiling so big, her teeth were near to falling out of her mouth.

His heart hammered in his chest as he noticed the tears in her eyes, and she drew near him and raised up on her toes, and he thought she was going to hug him, only she didn't, just leaned toward him, toward his neck, toward his ear, not touching him at all.

"My Heart Happy Joseph," she whispered so no one else could hear. "I'm free indeed."

If he hadn't been standing in a packed crowd, he would have leaped in the air and kicked his heels together. "You're free indeed, Winkie?" His heart was beating so hard, he felt dizzy for a moment. Dizzy with love.

"Liberty, sweet liberty," someone hollered out.

"Joseph, I know with a surety that Jesus paid the price for my liberty."

He understood exactly what this meant for her, as well as for them, and he reached into his pocket, withdrew his handkerchief, dabbed at her tears, holding his in check all the while. "Joy tears," he said softly as he kept dabbing, so overcome he could hardly speak.

"That be right."

"For more reasons than one?"

She nodded, smiling up at him through tear-glistened eyes.

"Oh baby." He hugged her to him amidst the jostling crowd, with Cassie sandwiched between them and embracing the both of them, expressing her joy in her own quiet way. How good Winkie felt in his arms.

"I'm sorry for the angry words I said to you—"

"Don't you worry your pretty head a minute more."

She sighed. "Wilderness wanderings come to an end. . ."

"Wedded bliss about to begin." He smiled.

She did a little two-step in his embrace, what had thrilled him when they were formally introduced, what thrilled him now.

"Kind honored miss," he said, holding her tightly, repeating one of Uncle Solomon's courting riddles, "will you condescend to encourage me to hope that I might, some glorious day in the future, walk by your side as a protector?"

"As soon as possible. Just as soon as possible."

After the parade, at the wayside picnic, she told Joseph about her new name, Periwinkle.

"That was my borned name," she said, "and that's the name I be living with from now on."

"You mean you had a name change?"

"You might say that."

"That be like Sarah in the Bible. Her name be Sarai, but when God gave the promise to her husband, Abraham, God changed her name to Sarah. It mean 'princess.'"

"That sound purely poetical. I going to read that story in Auntie's Bible when I get home."

"And when God changed her name, the Good Book say the Lord told Abraham that He would bless her and would give her a son by him." His eyebrows went up and down, his eyes danced beneath them, and his face wore a silly grin.

She laughed out loud at his antics, catching his meaning.

"Princess Periwinkle." He pecked her on the lips. "That be what I going to call you from now on."

As they made their way back to town in the late afternoon of Independence Day, Periwinkle saw a crowd gathering at a red-white-and-blue bunting-draped podium.

"Guess they going to make another speech or two," she said.

"And a few more songs, maybe?" Joseph gestured at the colorfully uniformed band behind the podium.

Through the throng they made their way, and from out of nowhere it seemed, a tall man—a plantation owner by the looks of his white linen suit and wide planter hat—bumped into Periwinkle, knocking her bonnet askew, then continued on his way as if he'd collided with nothing more than a gnat.

*I love you, white man, you,* she groused in her heart, trying to hide her grimace, *because the Bible tell me to. But I sure don't* like *you.*

"You look as if you stepped in a briar patch," Joseph said. "What you be thinking?" He stared at the man in the white linen suit walking briskly away, saw her adjusting her bonnet. "I think I know, Princess." He paused. "Baby, you got to love them."

"Oh, I will." *In the sweet bye and bye.* She squelched a chuckle.

"It be the right thing to do."

She nodded, and they continued walking, her holding his arm, Cassie at her side, thinking of Auntie's words.

*"You keep your nose clean—even if it takes both sleeves,"* Auntie had said.

*"Auntie!" Periwinkle had exclaimed.*

*Auntie's dark eyes had danced, but her voice was serious-sounding. "No matter what the rest of the world do, you make sure your attitude be right. That all we be responsible for in life. If we do that, God take care of us."*

"You be right, Auntie," Periwinkle whispered as she walked beside Joseph.

"What you say?" he asked now.

"Nothing." *Lord, I choose to obey Your Word and live by Your commandments, if You give me the strength.*

*"That pleases Me, daughter,"* the Lord said back.

"Come on, Princess. Quit dragging. We got wedding plans to make." Joseph's eyebrows went up and down, and his eyes danced beneath them, and his face wore that same silly grin.

"That so?" she said, dipping her chin.

"That so."

"Mama, look," Cassie spoke up, tugging on her mother's skirts.

"What, my mama-look baby?"

"I got something to ask you and Mr. Joseph."

Periwinkle stopped in her tracks, and Joseph did, too, and they both looked down at Cassie, waiting for her question.

"Is the peach and the pear going in the cobbler together?" Cassie was smiling so big her teeth were near to falling out of her mouth.

Joseph laughed heartily, along with Periwinkle. "They sure is," he said. "They sure is."

"Liberty, sweet liberty," someone shouted.

# Epilogue

## 1866

Yes, two days shaped my future, both of them having to do with liberty. The second one, I call my Day of Liberty. It was the day I realized I was free indeed, oh joyous thought, according to John 8:36: *"If the Son therefore shall make you free, ye shall be free indeed."*

Six years have passed since my Day of Liberty, and during those years, war came to our nation, pitting brother against brother with its terrible scourge of despair, disease, and death. Four long years of horrific tragedy passed, so tortuous I cannot put adequate words on it.

When it was going on, I often wondered if it was God's judgment against America for the sin of slavery, much as the poet Cowper suggested.

No one will ever know.

But I do know this. If I keep my nose clean, though it may take both sleeves, God'll take care of the rest.

That's come to be my philosophy in life.

And there's another thing I know, for sure. *"For I know whom I have believed, and am persuaded that he is able to keep that which I have committed unto him against that day."*

That's from 2 Timothy 1:12, another of the many verses I have committed to memory.

Joseph and I have found this verse to be true in our lives. God kept us during the war, and we came through unscathed, and Cassie, too.

And along the way, God gave us a son.

His name is Joshua. It means "salvation."

—*Princess*

**Kristy Dykes**—wife to Rev. Milton Dykes, mother to two beautiful young women, grandmother, and native Floridian—was author of hundreds of articles, a weekly cooking column, short stories, and novels. She was also a public speaker whose favorite topic was on "How to Love Your Husband." Her goal in writing was to "make them laugh, make them cry, and make them wait" (a Charles Dickens quote). She passed away from this life in 2008.

# A MOTHER'S CRY

by Jane Kirkpatrick

# Dedication

To midwives everywhere.

# Prologue

A dele Marley laid the infant on her mother's breast. The umbilical cord looked barely long enough, but something more was wrong, very wrong. Adele's mouth felt dry, and she reached with one hand still centering the child on its mother while pressing a clean cloth against the woman's birth chamber. Blood soaked the rag in seconds, staining the bedsheets, Adele's hand. Everything looked red.

"It's all right." Adele spoke to the mother, hoping as she did that she'd be forgiven for the lie. "Feel your daughter. Pretty dark hair. Fine as goose down. You've delivered a treasure to the world." The woman groaned, and Adele helped her place a weak hand on her daughter's head. "You did it."

"I did it," Serena Schultz gasped. "I did all things through. . ."

"Him who strengthens me." It was the verse Adele had given the woman for comfort all through the pregnancy. It was a prayer as well as a promise. Serena gasped in pain. In Adele's few short years as a midwife, she had never seen so much blood. "Serena? Stay with me. I'll send Arthur for the doctor. Arthur!"

The man appeared, hair up in sticks from rubbing his hands through it in worry, eyes rheumy with waiting, hoping. Adele heard Serena's breathing change. "God be with this woman, this child, this man," she prayed under her breath, so as not to alarm Serena.

"What's wrong? Serena?"

Adele touched Arthur's shoulder. "You have a healthy baby girl, Arthur. Polly, isn't that what you said you'd name a daughter?" Arthur nodded. He reached for his wife's hand. "Polly's healthy." Serena gasped, her breath shallow and short. "Go get the doctor, Arthur. I'll do what I can." She knew it was too late. Arthur hesitated.

Adele stared at the woman's face, pale as piano keys. The placenta moved from her as her breath exhaled. Adele cut the umbilical cord. Then she watched as a presence moved up through Serena's body like a breath, floating across the woman and disappearing at her eyes, passing without a sound from her body. Serena, no longer full of life and struggle, lay still, her face peaceful.

"Serena!" Arthur pushed the infant aside then, and Adele stood in time to catch the slippery babe and hold it to her breast.

"I'm so sorry, Arthur. So sorry. But you have a daughter to care for now. A beautiful child. Serena would have—"

"I did not want a child!" His eyes rained tears. "Serena—" He held his wife to him, her limp arms unable to wrap comfort around her husband or her child.

"I'll hold the baby until you're ready." Adele held back sobs.

"I have no care what you do with that child. None at all. I never want to see her again—or you. If you hadn't told Serena she wasn't too old to have a child, if you hadn't—"

"She's only thirty-two, Arthur. It was a quirk—" Adele stopped. She knew that anger was the brother of grief. Her words would only fuel the fire of loss that burned within him.

Adele swaddled the child. "I'll find a wet nurse." It was her nature to set necessary things in motion. Her own grief would have to wait. She held the baby to her and stood to heat watered milk she knew the child would need. False sustenance it was when what she truly needed was her mother's love, her father's care. Neither was to be.

🕮

*March 2, 1843. A midwife means "with woman," and tonight that was so in such a mournful way. At times I feel helpless in being "with woman" during times of uncertainty and fear. The beginning of the first stirrings of life is so wonderful, and I am "with woman" until the moment when the child cries into living, eyes staring at the candlelight, wanting to connect with someone even before they want to suck. I knew Polly, who sleeps beside me, before she was born. I was there when her mother felt the quickening. There, when she startled Serena with her kicks. She was "Paul or Polly" then; it did not matter. She was life, and I was there with her.*

*But I must not let my heart fall too deeply in love with little Polly. It is the gift of midwifery to be present at the hour of birth, to speak courage and potency to the mother, to tell her that she is capable of delivering this new life into the world. "I can do all things through Christ which strengtheneth me." That's the verse I gave Polly's mother. And she did do it, deliver this child. But midwifery is also a curse when things go wrong. Even with the child thriving, a good midwife knows never to fall too deeply in love with another's child, because that love cannot be returned in an unconditional way. Such surviving children belong always to another. No, a faithful midwife learns to love, to cry, to pray, and to say good-bye.*

# *Chapter 1*

## SOMETHING UNUSUAL THIS WAY COMES

*Western Wisconsin*
*Sixteen years later, 1859*

Adele Marley stood at the postal window, staring at the letter.
"It's from that new banker," Cora Olson, the postmistress, told her. "There."
She pointed. "The return address. Jerome Schmidt, Esquire."

"Probably a printed flyer announcing something at the bank." Adele pushed the envelope into her grip along with the German Almanac from Milwaukee and a letter from her friend in the new state of Oregon. She was careful not to disturb the thread and needles she'd purchased earlier from the other end of Cora's store.

"I haven't seen any other letters like that one," Cora said. "I'd say it was a personal message of some kind. See the handwriting? Lots of flourish. Don't you want to open it? In case you have to stop at the bank and take care of something before you head home, you know."

"I thank you for your insights." Adele looked the woman in the eye even though she wanted to stare at her broken eyetooth. Adele didn't let on that a trickle of sweat had already begun seeping beneath her corset.

"Might be a legal concern." Cora's raised voice floated as Adele reached the door. "That 'Esquire' after the name means lawyer, doesn't it?"

"You have a nice day now."

Adele hurried out to her buckboard, the boxes of supplies already loaded by Cora's husband, who lifted his hat to her. Adele nodded back, her eyes dropped in modesty beneath her bonnet. She grasped the wood smoothed by years of hands and stepped up into the seat of the wagon then lifted the reins, snapping them to let the mule know she was ready.

What would the banker want with her? The note against her farm was paid annually, with interest. She owned the land but, like most farmers, borrowed operating expenses each year, expenses paid off with the sale of her milk and butter and the occasional heifer. She had a bull that brought in breeding fees, and with selling excess wheat she grew and her midwifery, she and Polly did quite well. She'd even been able to supply a widow with five children all the milk they needed until they could afford a cow of their own. She hadn't asked for a loan extension of any kind. No, the letter couldn't be about the farm.

The new banker was a lawyer, but—*Arthur*. After all this time. Adele pulled up the reins just before crossing the bridge of the Buffalo River outside of Mondovi, the small town she and her husband had moved to in western Wisconsin five years before.

She dug in her satchel for the letter, breaking the wax seal with her gloved finger. Arthur had moved away from Milwaukee, long before Adele and John and Polly headed west. They had no idea where he'd gone. They'd left notice with a lawyer where they could be found, though Arthur had not. But this was what Adele feared, that Arthur would come looking for them or send someone else. With John gone—God rest his soul—the possibility of the loss of Polly sent a searing pain into her side. Her hands trembled as she opened the letter.

*May 2, 1859*

*Mrs. Adele Marley from Jerome Schmidt, Esquire.*
*I have a question of some urgency that I would like to discuss with you. I will arrive at your home on Tuesday, May 10, at 3:00 p.m. Tea is not expected.*
*Cordially, Jerome Schmidt, Esquire*

He was coming to her home? Tuesday—this very afternoon!

Adele stuffed the letter back in her bag and flicked the reins, her lips moving to unspoken prayers. She'd send Polly away for the afternoon. One look at the slender girl with walnut-colored hair compared to Adele's stocky frame and aging yellow strands would only remind the lawyer that Adele was not Polly's mother. Polly, such a jewel in Adele's life, full of sparkle and yes, lately, a bit of spit. Polly, reminding her of life and living and that there is a time for everything; even sadness must not last forever. Maybe being a mother didn't last forever either.

*I'm not Polly's mother. I have to remember that.*

She'd send Polly to the widow Wilson, give her eggs to take—yes, that would work. She'd deprived the girl of the trip to Mondovi for weekly supplies, telling her it was because the garden needed planting. Adele often found excuses not to let Polly be out and about. She was being protective. And there was no sense in Polly being frightened by changes blowing in the breeze. Adele would keep her composure, but she'd fight for this girl as much as she'd fought to keep Polly's mother alive all those years before. Then, forgetting her earlier promise to remember Polly's birth mother, Adele spoke out loud to the mule: "Polly belongs to me, and I'll make sure that lawyer-banker knows it."

# Chapter 2

## THE SLANTED SEAT

Jerome Schmidt preferred action. The bank ran itself, what with Miss Piggins, old as dirt, looking after reports and such. So this task came at a good time. He didn't intend to remain long in this small village, but it had given him respite. He had eyes on Oregon, but then, what adventurous man didn't? Maple leaves glistened in the light breeze, and the white bark of the birch trees gave his old blue eyes comfort. At forty-two he wasn't that old, though of late, he'd felt that way. He inhaled the scent of spring in this western Wisconsin hamlet, taking in the variety of greens popping out in the woods, lilacs primping for their May performance. He preferred this to the bustling city of Milwaukee, where a man could barely get a good night's rest with the drayage firms delivering supplies at all hours, steamships and trains blowing their whistles. Sounds of progress, yes, but constricting, too. Refuge, that's what he'd found here on the Buffalo River, and a chance to start over and keep his commitments to his family, such as it was.

He rode his big gelding into the widow's neatly tended yard, spied the stock tank at the end of the hitching rail, and dismounted, letting his horse drink as he surveyed the two-story house framed by lilac bushes. A good tight barn stood to the side with the edge of a new planting of what looked like oats in the distance. Six cows chewed their cuds lazily near the barn, surrounded by new grass. The fences could use repair. Hollyhocks would add to the bare outhouse. He tied the horse to the rail in the shade of a giant maple then approached the house. Chickens scattered. He noticed the porch post wobbled when he touched it. Yes, a little fixing might help. Before he could knock, the door opened. The woman's glare surprised him.

❧

"Mr. Schmidt, I presume?" Adele took the lead. She was glad she'd decided to do so, as his presence was imposing, with his well-trimmed beard sporting a hint of silver within the auburn and eyes as blue as her Willow plates. One eyebrow arched higher than the other, making him look. . .intimidating. He was taller than most of the farmers she knew, and he'd have to duck through the door. The seven-foot ceilings might make him feel enclosed, which was good. He had no right coming here without invitation, setting the date and time, giving her no chance to protest or even prepare. What if she'd waited until tomorrow to go to town and get the mail? He'd have shown up and she wouldn't have had time to send Polly away. It was not coincidental that Jerome Schmidt's letter offered a measure of preparation. She thanked God for that.

"I am," he said and removed his hat. He ran his hand through his maple syrup-colored hair that didn't match his beard at all.

"I only this morning received your letter. A busy woman doesn't have the luxury of picking up her mail daily."

He stepped back. "My apologies. Perhaps the letter wasn't posted when intended."

His admission surprised her, and she gentled her voice. "Yes, well, that does sometimes happen in a busy bank." She thought back to the date on the letter, a week previous. But still. Let Mr. Schmidt, Esquire, be a little uncomfortable. In fact, when they entered the parlor, Adele directed him to "the chair." It had belonged to her grandmother, who had cut the front legs down two inches so the occupant tipped slightly forward, a little off balance. Maybe Mr. Schmidt wouldn't be as likely to stay as long as he would if he could settle himself and lean back in a nice soft leather seat and take over the room let alone the conversation.

Jerome Schmidt took the seat, his knees awkward as he slanted forward. He frowned slightly but didn't complain.

"I have tea," she said. "Would you like cream? It's very fresh."

"No, nothing. I know I'm imposing."

"Nonsense," she said. "I'll have tea. You may as well, too."

"If you insist," he said. His voice was deeper than her John's had been, but not unpleasant.

At least he had manners enough to admit his imposition. She took a closer look at him as she handed him the small cup. Slender as a poplar shoot. He probably couldn't push a wagon stuck in the mud like her John could. A narrow face with a full lower lip, which she noticed he chewed, as though nervous. She decided to take the advantage.

"I know why you're here," she said. "And he can't have her. Arthur was distraught the night she was born, I know that. I've lived my entire life ruminating about what I might have done differently, and I always come up with the same answer: nothing. It was out of my hands. I did everything I could from the beginning of Serena's term until the very moment of delivery. It was tragic, mournful, awful. But I could not have prevented it. God moved in that room." She caught her breath, slowed. "He is her natural father and I waited, giving Arthur weeks, months, years, to come to his senses. I know there was grief. But now it's too late. I'll not put Polly through such a reversal that returning to a father she's never known would mean. I'll fight him in the court, I will. I'll mortgage this farm, sell my cows, whatever it takes to keep that child with me."

She'd moved closer to the man and towered over him in his slanted chair. She took a deep breath, stepped back. Color had drained from his narrow face. The arched eyebrow made him look confused.

"Am I to understand that you have the care of a child given to you at the time of her birth?"

"Arthur didn't tell you that detail?"

"My good woman, I have no idea who this Arthur is. Nor this Polly. But am I to understand this all occurred as a result of your handling the infant's delivery?"

"I'm a midwife," Adele told him. "But what happened wasn't anyone's fault." She sat down, exhausted from remembering that night.

"It's your midwife status, your record of success—or failure—that interests me."

"You're not here to take Polly away?"

"I'm here for a midwife. Or, rather, for my sister, who needs one. She's alone, recently widowed, and we are all that's left of our family, the two of us and now her unborn child. I've insisted she move here from North Carolina, but she is still grieving the death of her husband. She wants to be sure she'll have proper care. She prefers a midwife, though I advised her there was a doctor here."

"Doc Pederson. Very good man."

"Caroline doesn't trust doctors. They didn't save her husband after his accident. They bled him, which she felt made him weaker. You don't do any bleeding, do you?"

"Certainly not." What a fool she'd made of herself rambling on about the worst midwife case she'd ever had, the worst and yet the one that had eventually given her the greatest joy. Adele's tongue often wagged when it should have waned. "We're not physicians but rather women trained to be with women in our God-given commission to bring life into being. I work with physicians," she assured him. "I can give you references."

Mr. Schmidt frowned, adjusted himself on the chair.

*He won't want my services now. And I'll have to face him when I need my next farm loan, too.* "I should have waited to see what you needed before burdening you with my personal concerns."

He cleared his throat, paused, and awkwardly moved his legs as he pitched forward on the slanted chair. "I asked around regarding competent midwives. Your name came up often. My sister is quite. . .high-strung. She's forty years old, and this will be her first child."

"When is the baby due?"

He paused. "I'm not sure if we should continue this conversation. If you have drama involved in your deliveries—"

"I don't. Polly's mother's death was a tragic loss. I was barely twenty. It's the only death I've faced in all my years as a midwife. I like to be involved at the very beginning, helping prepare the mother and encouraging her confidence in being able to bring the infant safely into the world."

"The woman who died, had you been involved from the beginning?"

Adele swallowed. "Yes. Serena was a good friend. I might have known of her pregnancy even before her husband did. I would have given my own life to save hers, but she. . .the doctor said it was the way of things." Adele took a deep breath. "I've delivered dozens since. Polly has been my helper these last three years. The baby is due when?"

"Winter," he said. He tugged at his watch fob, and Adele couldn't tell if he was anxious to leave because of another appointment or if her grandmother's chair was taking its toll.

"Whatever your sister wishes will be honored. It's a mother's choice, and when she knows she's in control, the delivery goes much more smoothly."

"Oh, Caroline will definitely be in control."

"There are things that experience teaches," Adele told him. "Hopefully your sister is willing to consider those occasions of imparted wisdom from others."

"What my sister is willing to consider is anyone's guess." He fidgeted then, and Adele was about to suggest he move to another chair when he stood, turned, and looked at where he'd been sitting. "I suspect you'll be able to handle my sister, if this chair is any indication." He grinned at her. "I assume it wasn't inadvertently cut off in front?"

Adele felt her face grow warm. "It was my grandmother's chair." She stood, too. "She found it. . .useful with certain visitors."

"I might confiscate the idea," he told her. "It would limit some of the bores who take up my time at the bank."

"I'm happy to have assisted your banking operations." She curtsied and smiled.

"Indeed," Mr. Schmidt said. He stared at her longer than necessary she thought, a small smile creeping onto his rather handsome face. He chewed that lip again. "I'll send you notice when my sister arrives, and you may come and meet her, see if you're willing to take her on."

They discussed her fee, and Adele ushered him out. She stood on the porch, her hand shading the afternoon sun as he mounted his horse. He tipped his hat and rode down the lane, sitting the horse quite well. Mr. Schmidt had taken her slanted chair well, too. It was a good sign that he could adapt and might even have a sense of humor. Well, why should she care about that? He was a client's brother; nothing more. But she did like the arch of his eyebrows and the curl of his mouth as he sat on that chair and realized why he was sliding toward her.

# Chapter 3

## Memory Pushing to Wisdom

Sixteen-year-old Polly Schultz dismounted the old mule, letting the reins drop where she stood, her bare feet pushing up dust, her bonnet dangling down her back, threatening to tangle with her now-loosened chocolate-brown braid. Polly reminded Adele of a deer: light on her feet, fine-boned, and well, beautiful. "Who was that?"

"A gentleman seeking a midwife for his sister."

"He's handsome."

"Not that you could see much of him as you rattled on past him." Adele motioned with her hand. "Pick up those reins, and put Beulah away before she runs off."

"She hasn't done that in months, Mamadele." Polly used the affectionate name Adele's husband had suggested when Polly first began to talk. It was different than what her friends would eventually call their mothers, yet somehow alike. Polly knew of her mother and her father and that tragic night.

"Mules, like people, can forget good habits if they're not reinforced. That speaks of midwifery, too, you know. There are good practices, consistently attended to, that make all the difference when the birthing comes."

"I thought you said each birth is unique," Polly countered. She picked up the reins and held them loosely while the mule ripped at grass.

"Each is. But it's the usual practices that make one able to honor that uniqueness while sticking to things that are likely to ensure a good delivery."

Maybe that was why there'd been that terrible night with Serena. Adele simply hadn't had the years of experience she needed to know what to do. Adele and John were newly married, with no children of their own. The doctor said it might have been a blood clotting problem or an aneurysm and that it wasn't Adele's fault. Still, forgiveness wisped away like morning fog on the pond, to return only when conditions were right.

"Mamadele?"

"What? I'm sorry. My mind went visiting. Your planting looks chirk. We should have peas and carrots and beets in no time."

"I'd rather do almost anything than plant seeds, Mamadele."

"How fortunate for you, then. You'll be weeding from now on."

Polly groaned.

"Pull that bonnet up. Your face will be as brown as a bean, and what will people say?" Adele shooed her toward the barn while the girl tugged on the calico bonnet.

"After you've put Beulah up, I'll tell you what I know about this new client. It will be a challenge, I think; one that'll take both our good heads to handle."

❧

The midwife would do, Jerome decided. He sat at his desk at the bank, the pale light of the lantern washing across his papers. He chuckled about the slanted chair. She was inventive. She'd need that to handle Caroline. His sister was a demanding woman who insisted on doing things her way. But he knew she suffered now or she wouldn't have agreed to come. He'd had his own losses and felt they'd help each other even if it inconvenienced him for a time.

Jerome finished notes made on a recent loan application. The owner of the flour mill along Mirror Pond wanted to buy a new grist stone. He was inclined to grant the loan with stipulations. A good banker always had stipulations. The village of Mondovi was growing. Still, he was reluctant to invest in the town himself, though he wasn't sure why. He'd left Milwaukee, unable to stay in the same city as the woman who had spurned him. She'd found a more "substantial man," she'd told him. The words still stung, echoing as they did the words of his father, charging he'd never amount to much.

Jerome took his timepiece from his vest pocket and looked it over. He ought to rid himself of it. A broken engagement should carry no baggage, especially not baggage associated with time. Maybe he hadn't given the relationship with Clarissa enough time before he proposed, but he'd so wanted a wife and family to share his future.

He stood. There was no sense in thinking about past agonies. His sister would be here within the month, and he'd be able to tell her he'd found a suitable midwife for her. His thoughts returned to Mrs. Marley and how she'd challenged him for not giving her ample time to prepare for a visit. Her blue eyes had sparkled with upset when she opened the door, her protectiveness for her daughter granting her substance. She bore wide shoulders and a high forehead; comely, too, she was, her hair the color of fading yellow roses, wisping around delicate ears.

He'd make another ride out to her farm within the month, he decided. She did have a loan with the bank, after all. A woman running her farm alone wasn't always the best risk. He needed to reassure himself about her abilities to manage his sister, too. Should he make it a surprise visit? No. He sat back down and wrote a note. He'd give her time. He could tell she was a woman who didn't like surprises, and if he'd learned one thing from his soured engagement with Clarissa, it was to figure out what a woman didn't like—and avoid it.

# Chapter 4

## CAROLINE'S COMMAND PERFORMANCE

Adele had forgotten her bonnet and the sun beat on her face. The banker's visit flummoxed her, despite the week of preparation he'd given. He said he visited as part of her loan relationship with the bank, and he clearly evaluated the work she and Polly did. "I hire others to help with plowing and harvest," she assured him. "Most of the loan goes for labor." Polly walked behind them as robins chirped and hopped in the fields.

"One has to be a good judge of character to hire well, you being a widow and having a young girl around."

"Are you questioning my judgment?" She turned to look at him.

"Just a comment on managing risk. I wonder if you've thought about buying more land to pasture more cows, expand your herd."

"I'd have to go into greater debt for that. I've been cautious."

"Yes, yes, caution is important. But so is venturing into something that might have greater return. One can't cross the continent to new adventures without leaving the security of home."

"I'm not the adventurous type," Adele said. Then, "Is there some problem with my loan?"

"Making periodic visits is something I thought the bank should do, not wait until the annual payoff. Head off any problems that way."

"So you're visiting all the people with whom the bank has loans."

"Eventually."

"Do you anticipate problems with mine?"

"It might be good if I continued to check. A good businessman—or -woman— needs a fine lawyer, a skilled bookkeeper, and a future-thinking banker to be successful."

"I do my own bookkeeping. I've never had need of a lawyer, and until now, I didn't think I'd see my banker more than once a year."

"Times change."

Adele tripped then, stumbling on a rock. He quickly reached for her elbow to keep her from falling, and the warmth of his hand spread through her arm, causing alarm. It had been a long time since she'd felt such warmth.

"Now see, you might have fallen if I hadn't been here." He continued to hold her elbow.

"I wouldn't be walking around the field if you weren't here. I'd be working in it. I'm just a little clumsy is all."

"Nonsense," he said. "You're as agile as a deer."

She thought of herself more like a bear, rounder than need be for someone not hibernating in winter. A deer was a lithe animal, and. . .beautiful, like Polly. John had never called her beautiful or agile or compared her to anyone but his mother, whom he adored. He'd called Adele "handsome," a word she associated with men.

Jerome smiled at her when he said the words, and she felt the heat of his fingers even after she'd regained her physical balance and he'd stepped appropriately away.

"I hope you won't mind my monitoring the bank's interests. It's my calling, after all, to assist orphans and widows with their needs. A woman alone doesn't make the best decisions, it's been my experience."

Adele bristled. "I've kept this farm going on my own for three years. And as a midwife, I've made dozens of decisions on behalf of a mother and child. That's *my* calling."

"What women do for each other. A natural thing. Hardly a calling."

"You're mistaken." She stopped, hands on her hips. "If you lack confidence in my skills, perhaps you should simply have Doc Pederson attend the birth."

"No, no. My sister wants a midwife, that's certain. Please. I've upset you, and I didn't intend that." He wasn't looking at her with a banker's eyes now.

Adele wished she'd worn that bonnet to hide the confused stirrings caused by a man who demeaned her work, yet looked at her with pleading eyes.

❧

Mrs. Waste attended the church service. She expected her fourth child in October. "I love those experienced mothers," Adele said as she and Polly walked home from the circuit rider's monthly visit at the nearby school. As they walked, Adele noted that summer was in full bloom. "They bring their own methods to the lying-in and aren't as frightened as new mothers. We midwives can learn from them."

"More for your journal." Polly tugged on her shawl then looked back, waving a final good-bye to someone.

They finished the evening milking together. Adele looked forward to winter, when most of the cows dried up and had to be fed but not milked, when she and Polly could curl a little deeper beneath the feather comforter and wait for the sun to come up before stepping out onto the cold floor, dressing then heading outside to place the harvests of summer in the barn mangers. In spring and summer, the work was twice as much, tending to new calves and getting their mothers back into the routine of milking once the weaning (and bawling of mothers and their calves) was accomplished; cutting and putting up grass hay for winter; planting the garden, harvesting, picking berries; pulling porcupine quills from a calf's nose; whatever it took to tend the farm consumed summer. In between there would be babies to deliver, giving them both challenge and exquisite joy. She still followed up with the Bentz family, whose baby, Luke, was now a year old. That delivery had been a long, hard one, but both child and mother were doing fine.

"Could we have more lilac scent when we make soap next?" Polly asked as she washed her face before bed.

412

"Of course." It was the first time the girl had asked for something related to her grooming. *Is she thinking about boys?*

"Did you see someone special at church today?" Adele finished a stitch as she let the hem down on one of Polly's dresses in the waning evening light.

"Sam." She was always direct, a quality Adele admired. "He's smart in his schoolwork and not afraid to show it like some of the boys. I want to marry a smart boy."

"You'll need a smart one to keep up with you."

Polly dried her face, undid her braid. Before long Adele would gift her with the pearl cluster hair clip that Serena had given Adele as a birthday present one year. Adele had never worn it after Serena died, saving it for Polly to have on the day she married.

"Do you think Mr. Schmidt is smart?" Polly asked.

Adele felt a tug at her heart with the mention of Jerome Schmidt's name. That wasn't good.

"I suppose. He's a lawyer and a banker. A very good one, I think. He follows up on his clients at least. What made you think of Mr. Schmidt?"

"Your face got red when he was here last, Mamadele."

"Did it? Just the sun."

"He must have flummoxed you."

"Anytime a banker wants to talk about money I get flustered. But it's nothing more than business." They put out the candlelight then went upstairs together. Polly brushed her hair one hundred times and so did Adele, who was always thoughtful after the circuit rider preached. He wasn't a fear-raising man as some she'd heard but rather spoke often of forgiveness. The subject made her think of Serena and Arthur. Polly made Adele's life complete, Polly and the farm, her clients, her faith. She didn't need the complication of someone making her feel giddy, even if he did think of her as being as lovely as a deer. She blew out the candle. She also didn't need to jump to conclusions. The man was just doing his job.

Adele reread the letter Caroline Bevel sent requesting her presence the very next day. She smiled to herself. The tone was very much like her brother's, setting the date and assuming Adele would show up when told.

Adele had planned to go to town that day. She considered posing an alternate time, to exert control over this possibly difficult woman. But it was her duty as a midwife to give the future mother as much control as possible. Uncertainty tended to increase worry in some women, who then became rigid in their demands of others and on themselves. Caroline was a first-time mother at the age of forty, a grieving widow who had just moved halfway across the continent, all facts that could complicate a birth. Adele would give her as much power as she could.

Caroline shared her brother's height but lacked similar warmth in her brown eyes. One eyebrow arched higher than the other. She was almost too slender, Adele thought, as she stood on the landing of the Schmidt home, wondering if the woman ate little or if she was one of those naturally thin souls who could eat their menfolk under the table and still not gain an ounce. This wasn't Adele's problem.

"Please. Do come in. My brother hasn't yet secured a maid and I did not bring my own, so I am forced to welcome you myself." The lilt to her words reminded Adele of singing. "But he says such informalities are part of the Western experience and I will come to appreciate them, something I truly doubt." Caroline sniffed the air, and Adele wondered if she'd stepped into cow manure without realizing it. "I believe my lilac-scented candle has burned out," Caroline said.

"I love lilacs."

"Do you? I prefer orchids or magnolia. But the candle was a leaving gift, and I burned it to rid the place of my brother's smelly socks, which I believe are making my stomach truly uncomfortable." She sighed. "Now then, follow me, and we'll find as pleasant a place to sit as possible."

The move to the parlor allowed Adele to glance at the ephemera in the cherrywood china cabinet—a collection of salt dishes with tiny spoons, small Indian baskets, a pitcher that looked like Dresden. The walls held framed paintings of likely ancestors bearing that same arched eyebrow. Flowers made of hair and silk splayed out from a Chinese vase. Adele wondered if the furnishings were Jerome's or his sister's.

"It's quite lovely."

The woman turned. "No, it's not. It is replete with my brother's pedestrian choices. When my things arrive, by wagon I suppose, since we're in this outpost so far from civilization, I fully intend to have a housecleaning." She swirled in her hoop dress, an attire few women in western Wisconsin considered for daily wear because of the hoop's impracticality when milking, gardening, or fixing meals in small kitchens. "Now, let's sit, shall we? I have questions to ask you."

Adele sat. Today she'd listen and learn. Later she'd help prepare and advise, even though she wasn't sure Caroline had the temperament for either.

❧

Adele had her fill of tea and of Caroline's opinions, which she freely gave on everything from dress shields to slavery. And they hadn't yet gotten to the issues of Caroline's pregnancy. The woman talked nonstop, and Adele wondered who Jerome would get to be Caroline's maid and how long she might stay. She'd have to strategize with Polly about how to approach this difficult woman who, while never being pregnant before, assumed a doctor's level of knowledge. "I am well read on this subject and am fully prepared to contest anything I deem as inappropriate."

"As is your right." Adele set her teacup down. "The most important thing for a mother-to-be is to feel secure in her own strength and in the abilities and intentions of those she permits to assist her."

"Indeed." Caroline looked over the tops of her glasses into Adele's eyes then wagged her finger. "My brother was duly impressed with you, but of course I've done my own checking. You've not been here long."

"Five years, but I assisted with many mothers back in Milwaukee and even before that was my grandmother's aide. She delivered hundreds of babies."

"You've had no complications?"

"Those can happen to any woman, anytime," Adele said. "But I have done my best to adapt as the circumstances needed."

"You've lost no child?"

"None, praise God."

Oddly, the woman didn't pursue the next logical question, to ask of the mothers' fates. But Adele knew that people sometimes intuitively don't ask a question when they fear the answer.

"I'll want to be certain you're able to manage any number of possibilities," Caroline summarized. "I'm an older mother."

Adele nodded. "When did your former midwife determine the birth time will be?"

"It's to be a Christmas baby." Her eyes watered then and Adele saw for the first time the woman's vulnerability, her tears cloaked inside that wagging finger of control. "My husband's birthday was December 24th." Caroline dabbed her eyes as she looked away. "I believe I've taken enough of your time. Thank you for coming." She stood and brushed at her breast. As she did, she cried out in pain and knocked loose a cameo pin, the clasp's sharp needle springing out as her hand brushed past the pin.

"Are you all right?" Adele asked. It looked like a nasty scratch.

Blood poured from the wound as Adele pressed her handkerchief into the woman's palm. "I'll get the doctor."

"It's so. . .debilitating," Caroline said, looking up into Adele's eyes, worry mixed with wonder. "Jerome did tell you, didn't he? I'm a bleeder. There's nothing to be done about it."

# Chapter 5

## GAINING KNOWLEDGE, SEEKING FAITH

Once, Adele remembered, Serena cut her hand gutting a deer, and she said it bled a long time, but it stopped eventually. Adele should have been wary and sought advice beyond her own skills during Serena's delivery. She did know that most women were advised not to get pregnant if they learned they had blood that didn't clot. As Polly slept, Adele pawed through her grandmother's journal, seeking notes on blood clotting. She'd done this before but did it again. The book wasn't organized by any subject, something Adele did in her half of the book she intended one day to hand down to Polly. Her grandmother's book was a hodgepodge of recipes, reminiscences, and rules such as *"Always wash your hands before adding oil to woman parts,"* or *"If the labor stalls, consider baking bread. The aroma of it will comfort the mother and allow the process to proceed."*

The doctors Adele worked with usually scoffed at such practices, but what woman wanted someone with dirt beneath their nails to be touching her, and who was to say that the familiar aroma of bread couldn't bring comfort enough to help a mother deliver her infant? Adele knew music sped a stalled delivery, too, and she often sang softly, learning the mother's favorite hymns as part of becoming familiar with each mother-to-be.

*"Spend ample time before the birth getting to know your patient,"* Adele read. *"She must trust that you will be there for her no matter your own circumstances. Your own family, too, must be advised that the calling of the midwife means another's needs will take precedence over theirs. Trust is essential."*

Adele turned to her own section of the book and wrote the word *"Trust."* What behaviors build such trust? She wrote: *"Be honest, always. Be an even, stable influence, never cheery one day and morose the next. Be reliable. Arrive when you say you will. Remember preferences in food or concerns and help address them. Finally, you must accept the mother no matter your personal judgments about her decisions. If she wants her other children in the room with her during the delivery, accept this. If she wants to squat or lie down, accept this. Accept her."*

Adele closed the book.

She could do all those things except the last. Caroline never should have gotten pregnant. Adele wasn't sure her judgment of this woman's behavior could be set aside, especially when it reminded her of Adele's greatest disaster. Accepting another's choices wasn't easy for Adele. She still blamed Arthur for abandoning Polly, even though Adele had gained so much from it.

She must decline this patient. Besides, Jerome Schmidt had said nothing of his sister's blood condition. He'd misled her. She had every reason to cancel their verbal contract. It made her sad, but it must be done. She would tell Jerome Schmidt in the morning.

✃

"I am so sorry." The midwife sat before him in his bank office, his desk cleared of papers as he leaned back in his banker's chair and gazed at her pleasant face. Her bonnet had a small brim, which he liked because he could see her eyes, though they were in slight shadow. Jerome had agreed to see her without an appointment, without even advance notice as she'd insisted he give her. The woman continued, "I have met your sister, and—"

"She's pleased with you." He'd been so grateful to come home from the bank to his sister's first smile since she'd arrived. "She said you were both accommodating and competent, in that order, which is important for Caroline. Now, what are you sorry about?"

"I. . . She told me she is a bleeder." The midwife swallowed. "I don't think I'm skilled enough to care for her should something go wrong. She's already met Doc Pederson, due to her cut."

"A bleeder. Yes, I should have remembered that. Surely there are others with this malady."

"I've spoken with other midwives in the past. I've conferred with the doctor. I'm not the one to assist her."

"But she likes you!" She jerked back, and he lowered his voice. Caroline could be such a trial, and if he could not find someone willing to help, he wasn't sure he could endure the next three months of her lying-in. He needed a midwife as much as Caroline did. "I mean, she has confidence in you. Women still become with child despite these maladies. There must be someone who knows how to assist a bleeder. Please, contact other midwives, see if there isn't something to build your confidence—"

"It's not my confidence I'm worried about." She twisted the strings of her reticule. "It's your sister's health and that of her child."

"All the more reason it should be you doing the delivery. You care about her, even after so short a visit. Please. Look for answers before deciding. Trust yourself."

"I'll look. But you need to look, too, for another midwife."

He wanted to frighten her, intimidate her, maybe even suggest that her loan renewal was dependent upon her helping his sister. But he wasn't that kind of man.

✃

Imagine his suggesting that she lacked confidence, Adele thought as she walked to the dry goods store to pick up supplies. Telling her to trust herself. Hadn't she just yesterday written of trust in her journal? But Adele would see what she could find out about helping a bleeder.

Back at the farm, she and Polly dug in the garden. Adele wielded the fork, and Polly bent to pick the carrots and brush the dirt from them. She rubbed a long carrot with her apron then bit it. "I love the taste of carrots," she said. "Even with dirt on them."

"A little carrot dirt never hurt anyone." The thought made Adele wonder if what the mother ate had something to do with blood clotting. Perhaps potions or elixirs helped. That evening, after Adele had prayed, she decided to discuss her decision not to assist Mr. Schmidt's sister. It would be good for Polly to understand the difficulties and how sometimes a midwife simply couldn't be there for her charge. Midwifery meant being honest with the mother and, even more, with oneself.

"It's something in their blood." Adele explained the bleeding problem as best she could. "No one seems to know what would make it better. It's. . .part of why your mother died, I believe. The blood refused to clot. You remember my telling you that."

Polly looked thoughtful. "But doesn't that mean even more that you should be there for Mr. Schmidt's sister? Who else will take on such a difficult case?"

"She'll have to accept a doctor's assistance," Adele said.

"But if what you were told is true, then even a doctor won't be able to help. You have to be her midwife, Mamadele. You'd never forgive yourself if something bad happened to her and you weren't there."

Could she walk away? Maybe she didn't trust herself. Maybe she'd never forgiven herself for not helping Serena. The child could be right.

"Someone at a college might know new things that would help." Polly took another bite of carrot, cleaned now and lying in the dry sink. "Sam's going to a medical college in Louisville next year. They might answer your questions."

"That's a grand idea, Polly. Let's write the letter together."

When they finished she wrote in her journal under the section she'd titled *Insights*:"

*Polly is such a comfort to me, and she is also a good partner in midwifery. She's not afraid to ask for help, something I must remember. Or perhaps I taught her that. I struggled today with whether to take on this difficult patient because of a fear that I am not wise enough. And yet, I feel called. I must remember the midwives of Exodus who together defied Pharaoh when he instructed them to kill the Hebrew babies. Together, they resisted. My pharaoh is fear. I must pray to let God be my guide, to trust that if this is a calling, then like the Exodus midwives, I will not be alone. A midwife must always be willing to learn more, for we are intricately and wonderfully made, with complexities wrapped inside worries that only knowledge and faith can relieve.*

# Chapter 6

## When Needed

Jerome sighed. What he wouldn't give for a good newspaper to read. Surely he could manage better than this local rag. It only came out when it wanted to, so it was useless as advertising and rarely printed notice of events such as the Fourth of July picnic or the Harvest Festival with enough lead time for someone to actually plan to attend. Word of mouth was still the best way to get information to the people of Mondovi—that and pinning posters up at Olson's store. If he ever made it to Oregon, he'd start a newspaper and commit to getting it out on a regular basis so people could count on it.

He tossed the two-page paper in the trash basket and checked his watch. It was time to gird himself to address his sister's needs. *"I need a fresh peach, Jerome."* Or *"I need these sheets ironed, and I haven't the strength."* He couldn't get her the fresh peach, but the ironing he could do. He'd had two girls hired, but they left after Caroline's constant criticism of their efforts. He didn't mind ironing, because Caroline left him alone in the heat of the kitchen. He did wonder how she'd ever manage her "needs" over those of the child once it arrived. Hopefully maternal instincts appeared with birth. Maybe that little midwife would prepare her.

He was growing fond of time with Adele. He'd admired her concern about being the best midwife for his sister, and when she'd come to him later saying she'd had a change of heart, he'd been delighted. She'd found new information, she told him, and was ready to assist if Caroline would agree to her requests. She also said she'd prayed for guidance and decided he'd been right to suggest she might lack confidence in her own abilities. He couldn't have been more touched by her disclosure and her decision. He'd never told his sister Adele's service was questionable, instead telling Caroline that Adele's farm demanded much attention from her, but he was certain she'd be more attentive as her time drew near.

The biggest changes were the foods his sister now consumed. He hadn't realized midwives dealt with such things. She'd convinced Caroline to consume mounds of sauerkraut. The house reeked of it, and she said if mustard greens were in season, Caroline would be green from eating them at every meal. Stuffed bullock's heart was a regular, served with Caroline's southern corn pone. Adele came by every week now to talk with Caroline about this and that, fixing bran coffee with molasses, enough to last a week or more. Somehow Adele had gotten his sister to listen, even agreeing to allow the big Swedish doctor to attend the birth—if needed.

He checked his watch again. Adele usually came by at midday. With the days shortening, and cold settling on dusk's shoulder, Adele liked to be home before dark, and her farm was three miles out. He donned his hat and locked his office door, telling Miss Piggins he'd be back by two. He set his own time here; he really didn't have much to do at all. He needed challenges. He wondered if Adele would mind some suggestions for her farm.

As he walked, he considered how to broach the subject of Adele's staying with them as Caroline's delivery approached. He didn't want Adele to say no, but he didn't have any suggestions for how she could tend to the farm while she was gone. He assumed that would be the primary reason she'd refuse. He'd also begun considering another question for this woman he'd grown fond of. When he saw her mule tied up at his home, he felt his steps quicken. When he walked around the village, he noticed women's things in the window of the dry goods store. Women things and baby things. If Caroline could have a child at forty, surely Adele wasn't too old to bear a child. He was certain she was younger than Caroline.

Caroline. Would she stay with him after the baby was born? If Adele might one day marry him—he knew that was thinking awfully far ahead—would she want to share a house with Caroline? If he proposed to Adele and she accepted, was he ready to leave the village and move to her farm, leaving his sister and her baby alone in the house? He'd have to hire a cook and housekeeper for Caroline. If he didn't marry and Caroline remained, there'd be a houseful of women surrounding his time, and the cries of an infant to wake to. He'd have to get a maid to help. Caroline would be relentless in her demands.

He watched squirrels chatter and sprint up an oak tree along the path to his house. What kind of mother would his sister be? It worried him, he realized. A successful birth was only the beginning. Only thinking of Adele's intervention gave him ease. He'd have to seek her advice about what would happen after the baby arrived. He didn't know when midwives finished their work, but he hoped it wasn't on the night of the delivery.

❧

"It's not time to push yet, Melinda," Adele told the laboring woman.

"My body is riding that familiar crest, and I'm not sure I can stay in the boat."

"Polly, why don't you massage Melinda's back."

"I haven't had one like this before," Melinda Waste panted. "All the others came before I was even ready. My water broke, and before my husband could find the towel, it seemed like I was—oh, oh, oh, oh."

"That's right. Breathe just like that."

"I ain't breathing 'like that' for a reason," Melinda snapped. "It's 'cuz it hurts!"

"I know it does. But in a short while, you'll be pressing that baby to your breast and be the proudest mama around." Adele checked the woman's intimate parts, counted between the rise of her body and breath, squatted. "I see the baby's head. Nice black hair."

"Let me sit up. No, let me walk. Oh, oh, oh, I have to push, Adele, I have to."

"Polly, take her hand." With oiled fingers, Adele soothed the skin that formed a stretching halo around the infant's head then broke into song. "Hark! the herald angels sing—"

"Glory to the newborn King," Polly chimed in, and then Adele heard Melinda singing, too, in gasping breaths that groaned out this new life inside of her. Adele stopped singing to concentrate fully on the little head, little shoulder, body, and soul, slippery as an eel, willing itself into life and this family.

"It's a boy! Bigger than a pork ham. I bet he weighs close to ten pounds."

"No wonder he took so much time." Melinda cried now, tears of joy. "Charley!" She called for her husband. "You've got your boy at last."

Her husband rushed into the room, three little girls with wide eyes behind him. Charley bent to look at his son. "I knew he was coming when I heard you start to sing."

Adele turned her attention to Melinda. "Everything is fine. You did amazing work." She wiped the woman's forehead of perspiration and her cheeks of tears. "Polly, get a cold rag and we'll ease that pain."

"What's that?" Charley pointed to a patch of wrinkly skin on his son's tiny wrist.

"A sucking blister. He's been practicing in the womb."

"Well, I'll be. . . ," Charley said.

The room was filled with the spirit of hopefulness, of joy, of the mystery of life, and the cycle of birthing repeating itself. Adele felt a part of a larger gathering, of all women who had brought a child into the world, who see the work of creation nurtured within their bodies then brought forth to hear the voices of angels.

"May we speak a prayer of thanksgiving for you all?" Adele asked them.

"Oh, please do," Melinda said, and the little girls bowed their heads as Adele expressed gratitude for this new life, a safe journey, and God's blessings on the family for the years ahead.

❧

*November 5, 1859. Young Harold Waste has left behind the gentle waters and peaceful floating tethered to the life raft of placenta. He's on his own now, but he has many hands to help him become the man God intends for him to be. A loving father and mother, sisters who will spoil him, a home of sturdy logs with wood piled to the rafters, a faith to sustain them. Polly hummed "Hark! the Herald Angels Sing" all the way home beneath a star-filled sky. Note to Polly when you read this: Always remember to ask the mother if you may pray for her at the beginning and at the end. It is like a psalm and a benediction, assuring all that God is the center of the circle of this new life.*

# Chapter 7

## PRESSING THE CASE

"May I court you?" Jerome Schmidt surprised her as she donned her shawl and bonnet. They'd had a midday meal, and even Doc Pederson had stayed for sauerkraut sandwiches, making Caroline laugh her tinkling tones. Adele and Jerome were alone in the foyer of his home.

"What? Why?"

"Because I enjoy your company," Jerome said. "And because you're kind, of sound mind, and beautiful."

Adele laughed. "I'm not so sure about the sound mind part. Or the beautiful part either."

Adele's husband—God rest his soul—had never called her beautiful. He often used words like "sturdy," "good boned," and once even "comely" to describe her form. His word of choice—"handsome"—caused her the most distress. It was a word meant to describe a horse or a finely apportioned man, but a handsome woman? Who would find attraction in that? Jerome was kind and gracious, but he always greeted her with either "Mrs. Marley" or "How's the little midwife today?" The latter with a jocular tone, as though he diminished the work she did. Little midwife, indeed. But now he wanted to court her? The words were not romantic, and she realized she wished they were.

She also knew she liked his company, and there was no reason not to agree to his request. And so they'd taken a number of walkabouts together, past Mirror Pond where geese gathered, flying south. He drove out to join her and Polly on Sunday afternoons to attend the evening services. Caroline was always invited, but she preferred to be "at home" as she called it, saying Southern women wouldn't be seen in public in her "condition." Adele tried to tell her that she didn't have an illness. Her pregnancy could be concealed beneath her hoops so no one even need know, and the exercise would be good for her. But Caroline declined.

After Christmas, there'd be no circuit rider until spring, and Adele realized she'd miss both the pastor's messages and Jerome's presence on Sundays. He had an easy banter about most subjects, but he had opinions, oh yes, he did. Adele could see his sister in his thoughts at times, that certainty and demand, and both could carry on quite fascinating arguments. Those times Adele left their house feeling grateful she didn't have to live with the two of them, both as certain as rocks are hard.

And yet when she rode her mule into her yard a few days before Thanksgiving and saw that he was there, reading a gazette on the porch, the paper expanded between gloved hands and just the top of his fur hat visible, she sat a little straighter on the mule.

"Is everything all right, Mamadele?" Polly said. The girl rode beside her on her own mule.

"What? Of course everything's fine. This corset just pokes a bit after a three-mile ride."

"Doesn't it do the same thing when we're in the wagon? You never jerk up straight then."

Adele looked at her and saw the tease in her eyes.

"Yes. No. Never mind," Adele said, annoyed at being flustered by the man's presence and having Polly catch her in it. "You take these mules to the barn. Soon as you're finished, come change and we'll get started milking. At least there's only one to milk now."

A soft snow fell as Polly led the mules away.

"Has Caroline gone into labor?" Adele motioned for them to go inside.

"No, nothing like that, but it seemed time to discuss yet another stage in Caroline's condition with you. Might you have one of your hard rolls with peach jam to ease a man's stomach as we talk?"

"Here I thought it was my sweet disposition that brought you out in the cold."

"Oh it is, it is," he said. "Hard rolls and peach jam are just added value."

"Spoken like a banker." She took the bread from the oven where she stored it, gave him a jug of jam. "I have cows to tend to, and then we'd be pleased if you stayed for supper."

"I'd be a fool to say no to that." He grinned. Adele hoped it wasn't just the food that made him look delighted. She headed up the stairs to change her clothes, aware of his presence on the first floor of her house. She wondered if he scanned the room, seeing what he could about who she was by what she surrounded herself with. She came back downstairs about the time that Polly entered. The girl said hello then climbed the stairs to change her clothes, too.

Adele tied her kerchief around her head and donned John's warm barn coat. She felt comforted in it. "We shouldn't be too long," she said as she sat to pull on rubber boots.

"May I help?"

Surprised, Adele looked up. "Well, yes, that could be arranged, but you're not dressed for the occasion. I could offer you a pair of my husband's pants, but they'd come high above your ankles." The thought made her smile. "And I'm not sure if his boots will fit you."

"I've brought my own change of clothes," he said. "I thought I might meet up with you about chore time. Of course, you're most always at work, aren't you? It's part of what I admire about you, that sense of purpose and determination. May I call you Adele?" He looked straight at her when he said it.

Adele blinked, stopped pulling on her rubber boots. Sometimes he seemed to read her mind about things she hadn't ever shared with him. He made her name sound melodious. And his compliment about her commitment to her work warmed her perhaps more than his use of her name.

"Why, yes. I mean, maybe; few do. I—"

"Perhaps Miss Adele would lend a little formality to the occasion."

"And what occasion would that be?" Adele stood.

"The first time you've let me milk one of your cows," he said, moving closer to her. She could feel her face grow warm, her mouth turn dry. He plucked an errant piece of hay stuck on her kerchief. "That is, the occasion when you actually allow me to participate in your work. I believe such work is your greatest love."

"Polly is my greatest love. Then midwifery."

He was so close to her now that she could see the follicles of his beard like tiny pinpricks against his chin. Her heart pounded in her ears—or was that his heart she could hear? "I do like the work I do. Don't you? I mean, work is—"

He bent down to kiss her, and the warmth of his lips spread like sweet honey against hers, swirling emotion down her arms, her legs, tingling her toes. He stepped back and placed his hands on her shoulders. "Miss Adele," he whispered, "how beautiful you are." He touched her cheeks with both hands, smooth hands. "So beautiful," he repeated.

She wanted to let herself unfold like a flower onto his chest, but she was aware of Polly upstairs and of the cows waiting to be milked and fed, how warm the room had become, and how astonished she was to have been called beautiful while her hair was mashed by a hay-streaked kerchief, and she stood in rubber boots beneath an old dress and John's tattered coat.

"Work is. . . What were you saying about my name?"

"I wondered if I might call you Adele."

She cleared her throat. She needed to regain control. "I think your calling me Miss Adele while we're in the company of others will be just fine. But. . ." She didn't know how to say what she felt. "But you can call me that. . .other, anytime we're alone."

"Which I'm hoping will be often," he told her.

They heard Polly clumping down the stairs, and Jerome excused himself to get his boots and coat. Polly joined them, and the three walked to the barn swinging buckets they picked up from the porch. Adele was certain Polly would ask why her face had turned crimson, but she didn't. The three went on about their work. Jerome was a good learner, Adele decided, and when they finished milking, he helped put the evening feed in the cows' mangers. It was nice to have a man to do some of the heavy lifting. She watched his arms, strong though lean in appearance. It took half the time to finish up and head into the house for supper. Adele smiled. She couldn't be more grateful, and Thanksgiving was just around the corner.

᙭ᙊ

"There is one more thing we need to discuss before I go, Miss Adele," Jerome said. He liked looking at her and would be as proper as Adele wished with what he called her. Polly sat at the table and sketched in the lamplight. She had talent, though Jerome suspected that needlework would be a more practical avenue for a girl to pursue.

"And what would that be?" Adele asked. She put away the dishes Polly had washed that sat drying by the sink.

"It's Caroline. Her time will be soon, and I think it valuable for you to consider staying with us at the house."

"Of course I'll stay," Adele told him. "Once she goes into labor, I'll be there day and night, as soon as you come to get me to let me know it's her time."

"Yes. Well, that's the problem. I think you should consider staying beginning in December. In case there are storms and I can't come to get you. Planning ahead," he said. "As you did by writing to that college to get information about certain foods that might help Caroline. It seems like planning to be there in advance of labor would be wise."

"I can't be away from the farm that long," Adele said. "I have other clients, too. Besides, I still have a cow that isn't dry so needs milking, and the others to feed."

"I could do it, Mamadele."

"I can't leave you alone here, Polly. I'll need you to help. No, we'll feed heavy, give them extra, and then we'll go when Mr. Schmidt comes to get us."

"Maybe I could stay here and tend to the cows," he offered, "or you could bring the milk cow along. We have a small barn behind the house."

"And the feed?"

"Yes. Well, it might be best if I came here and milked and fed."

"If you can come to milk them, then you can get through storms to reach me and let me know Caroline's in labor and take us back with you when it's time."

"The baby could come sooner than mid-December. Caroline's not good with dates or timing."

"What does Caroline say about my staying for a longer time?"

"She doesn't know what she wants." Jerome pulled at his vest, straightened in his chair. "So I've made the decision for her. A man often has to do that." He could hear the frustration in his own voice.

"Such decisions aren't always the wisest." Adele began skimming the milk for the cream and putting it into the butter churn. Soon the rhythm of the plunger filled the room. He wondered if he should offer some new argument, but he couldn't think of one. He just wanted Adele to come sooner and not only for Caroline. He looked forward to the time with Adele in his own home. It would give him time to ask her the question he'd been harboring for weeks now, without the distraction of Polly or the farm.

"I'll talk with Caroline." Adele wiped her hands on her apron. "A midwife always listens to the mother-to-be and not the uncle-to-be, no matter how well intentioned."

He should have remembered that being the proper midwife trumped even the farm. He was in competition with that part of her life, and he wasn't certain he could come out on top.

# Chapter 8

## CONCENTRATE ON MIDWIFERY

Caroline leaned in toward Adele and whispered, "I don't think Jerome does well in a crisis, and I'm not at all certain he will be up to doing what is necessary unless someone wise is here to tell him what to do. He hasn't kept a maid, so please, come and stay as soon as you can. The laundry is in piles."

Adele had enough of her own laundry to tend to without doing Caroline's and Jerome's, too. That wasn't the activity she'd hired on for. Cooking, yes, and keeping the lying-in area spotless, those were part of her duties, but Jerome would have to find someone else to wash sheets.

"My work is to be available for your delivery, to assure your success in bringing this infant into your family. Laundry isn't on the list of things a midwife does."

"Not even if it would make me feel more secure?" Caroline lay on a fainting couch covered in a rose brocade, the evidence of her pregnancy mounding up like a half-moon rising over the treetops.

"I want you to feel safe, Caroline, so if not having the laundry done becomes an issue, we'll discuss it. But I'll ask your brother to persist in finding you domestic help." Then she thought to ask, "Who does it now?"

"Jerome. He's quite handy that way, but of course it's unseemly for a man to be doing such woman's work."

Adele rather liked the idea that Jerome was willing to do woman's work when needed. It added a pleasant dimension to him.

"I think he avoids hiring another maid just to save money. But my husband left me well-off."

"Not a bad reason," Adele said, wondering why Caroline whispered. "Maybe he just doesn't want any more females gathering in his house."

"Oh, my brother loves the company of women," Caroline said. "He so enjoys your visits. A man needs a good filler at the end of his day, don't you think?"

Adele stepped over the affront and hoped this new baby would be a boy so Jerome would have a comrade-in-arms. Caroline had put on quite a bit of weight in her pregnancy, and the lower position of the baby suggested to Adele that it just might be a boy. Caroline didn't seem to have a preference. She just wanted a healthy baby she could "love forever."

"Have you made plans for what you'll do after the baby arrives?" Adele asked.

"I'll stay right here. Jerome is engaged, you know, to a woman from Milwaukee. He's quite smitten with her and she him. She gave him that timepiece he carries so proudly, and apparently she didn't resist too much when he moved to this little outpost of a village. I'm sure she'll be joining him in the spring. He doesn't say much of course. Men never do. But I think that's why he hasn't wanted to hire another domestic. He knows that in the spring his Clarissa will arrive, and then I'll have help and the baby will have a family. It'll be a lovely arrangement, don't you think?"

Adele felt like a cow had just swatted her face with its wet tail. Her eyes watered; her face stung. "I hope they'll be very happy."

"They would have married by now, but of course my brother's opening his home to me set their plans back several months. He's so thoughtful, and Clarissa must be as well to have postponed a wedding. Goodness. A woman who would do that must have a heart of kindness."

"A heart of kindness, yes."

"So you'll come next week with plans to stay?"

Adele controlled her voice, which threatened to falter, and prevented a rush of tears down her cheeks. "If that's what you want, Caroline. I'll speak with Polly, and we'll see what can be done. I need to go now. I'll—"

"But my brother so likes it when you're here when he gets home. He enjoys your company. Please stay."

"He'll have plenty of my company for the next few weeks then, won't he?"

"I'll ask Roy—I mean, the doctor—to come for supper on Tuesday next. We'll have a happy foursome or five with Polly. Six, should Clarissa arrive at last. Oh, this will be such a fun time for us all!"

❧

She'd been so foolish, thinking that kiss was something special, that Mr. Schmidt thought she was beautiful even. The mule slipped on the icy road but kept his feet beneath him as he carried Adele back to the farm. A cold wind bit her cheeks, freezing the tears. It was better to find this out now about Jerome's—Mr. Schmidt's—entanglements before she did something foolish while staying in his home to help his sister, like letting him steal another kiss or expressing care for him. She was there to assist Caroline, that was all. She'd gotten distracted. Her joy should have been wrapped in the mother's joy. She had Polly. She had her farm. She'd had love once, and that was more than many had in a lifetime. The one great joy that had eluded her was to bear a child herself, but God had blessed her with so many other babies whose lives she was a part of, so how could she complain?

Jerome Schmidt had caused her to dream again. But she was awake now and would stay that way.

❧

At the farm she discussed with Polly what might be done about her being with Caroline longer than intended.

"I'll be fine here, Mamadele. I'd love to help you, and if the weather holds, I can come in when Mr. Schmidt comes to tell me that Mrs. Bevel is in labor. We'll feed the cows heavy before we join you, and I can come back and milk, even if it is later in the evening."

"You're a good girl," Adele told her, patting her hand. Polly sketched at the table.

"I just hate to leave you alone with the responsibilities. There's wood to chop, butter to churn, the chickens cooped and fed. All the work the two of us do, you'll have to do alone. Just keeping the fireplace going will take time."

"It'll make me feel like a grown-up."

Adele brushed maple crystals from her daughter's cheeks. "You've been at the maple cone, I see."

"I love sweets."

"As do I. Unfortunately, sweets migrate from my stomach to my hips."

"You have nice hips, Mamadele." Polly grinned. "I think Mr. Schmidt likes them. I've seen him watch you when he's been here and you're at the dry sink peeling potatoes."

Adele stiffened. "What Mr. Schmidt does or doesn't like is no concern of mine."

"I'm. . .I'm sorry."

"I didn't mean to snap at you," Adele said. "It's just. . .men. John was such a dear, forthright and honest. I miss him so much."

"Isn't Mr. Schmidt forthright and honest? He's a banker."

"And I suspect a good one. He plays his cards quite close to his chest so his clients might never see it coming that he intends to foreclose. But charming has its shadows."

"We don't have to worry about a foreclosure, do we?" Polly looked alarmed.

"Not at all." Adele patted Polly's hand. "We have a good herd, and with our harvest I paid the previous note. Come spring I'll borrow for operating expenses again. No, we're fine."

"And you have the midwife fees."

"Yes, though the Wastes paid in bacon and hams. But that's nothing to complain about. We'll have one of those hams for Christmas dinner. Maybe invite the Bentzes and their little Luke. You could invite your friend Sam and his family."

"Mr. Schmidt and his sister, too?"

"Once the baby comes, our paths aren't likely to cross with theirs again."

❧

Adele checked her midwife satchel. Oil, forceps—which she hoped she wouldn't need— needles and thread, special candles she'd scented with mint, clean rags, other sundries. Caroline would provide the cues for this delivery, for her and her baby. At least by staying at Jerome's, Adele would be able to see that Caroline consumed good portions of sauerkraut and onions, steaming even the old tops for breakfast. Eggs were good, too, the doctor from the college had written. Adele reread the letter before putting it into the journal. "*It is good to remember that physicians often find that in delivery, clotting improves for a hemophiliac, perhaps as a natural protection for both mother and baby, even when bleeding is an issue prior to pregnancy. We are all fearfully and wonderfully made, are we not?*"

Adele wished that had been so with Serena. She stuffed the letter then halted. Maybe Serena had died of something else! A torn artery, perhaps, or any of a dozen things that could go wrong. She'd settled on Serena being a bleeder because of what the doctor had said and because there'd been so much blood. But maybe she was wrong. She'd make note of that in her journal, something to encourage Polly one day and remind her that what she thought was so might not always be the case and to trust beyond herself, trust in the intricacies of creation, of the human body and its desire to bring new life safely into the world.

Her confidence increased with the doctor's reminder that God manages details like having blood clot as it should when needed for safe birthing.

# Chapter 9

## THERE WHEN NEEDED

I'm leaving," Adele called upstairs to Polly. It was December 15th, and the wind swirled around the outside of the house, pushing late-falling leaves across the three inches of packed snow that covered the rolling hills, dusted the woods. Adele had baked and baked. She'd made hardtack, brought in a smoked ham Polly could slice off for a week or more. The two of them steeped chicken soup, and Polly was reminded to put leftovers on the porch high up so no marauding wolves or bears would come by and snatch them. The girl had plenty of powder for the musket and knew how to keep it dry. She'd picked up new paper for Polly to sketch with and told her if she ran out of books to read, she could open up one—just one—of the wrapped boxes they'd placed under the Christmas tree. Polly was the most important person in her life, and she'd done what she could to attend to her. Now her thoughts would go to Caroline.

And Jerome Schmidt.

Fortunately, she had not encountered him since the news of his impending marriage so blithely shared by his sister. Adele wondered when he planned to tell her—or if he ever did. But of course now that she'd be staying with them, she'd have to listen to his baritone voice, be required to serve him. Maybe that was why he'd wanted her to come earlier—so he wouldn't have to cook anymore or hire a girl. She hoped that when he told her of his marriage, she could look happy for him, the scoundrel.

God had placed Jerome Schmidt in her way to give her a pleasant summer, and God had taken him away. She put her knitted scarf over her head and stuffed the wool around her neck for more warmth. Her hair would look like a flatiron had pressed it, but she didn't care. She just prayed she'd make it safely, that the baby would come and all would go well, and that in the meantime Polly would feel grown-up without having a crisis.

She didn't want any crisis of her own, either, facing Mr. Schmidt.

☙

"Miss Adele." He couldn't believe how pleased he was to see her safely arrived. He'd missed her. "Here, let me take your bag." He bent toward her as though to kiss her cheek.

She swept by him like a wolf pup spurting out of its den. "Just tend to the mule, if you would, Mr. Schmidt. And it's Mrs. Marley to you."

"What?" The word bounced off her back.

He returned to the house and heard the women chattering in the small bedroom that had been his since Caroline's lying-in. He'd given her the largest bedroom. He'd already moved most of his things into the loft area so that Adele could be close to Caroline in the night.

"Adele's brought me a mint-scented candle." Caroline held it up. "See how thoughtful she is?"

"Indeed. May I help you get settled in any way?"

"I'll be preparing hot meals for us, so if you'll see to the filling of the wood box, I'd be grateful. I have bean soup with ham. That should be good for us all. Caroline, would you like a back rub?"

"I would, I would." Caroline pushed her burgeoning body so she lay on her side on the fainting couch. She was nearly too large for it.

"I believe we need privacy now." Adele's eyes told him to leave.

Jerome started to back out of the room when Adele reached across then handed him his timepiece, the gift from Clarissa. "I believe this belongs to you?"

"Won't you need it?"

"I have my own timepiece." Her words dismissed him.

He backed out of the room, stung by her words. His hands shook. What had he done to upset her? He hadn't even had an occasion to press his case with her, and from the frost of her words and her physical avoidance of him, he had to assume something happened to turn her against him. Could Caroline have upset her? His sister loved Adele as much as she seemed able to love anyone other than herself. What had he done wrong?

❦

The next week bumped along. Adele made certain she was never alone with Jerome, who fortunately was there only in the evening or at midday, and that there were no lengthy conversations around the table. Caroline chattered about herself so easily there was really no need to speak, except to say, "Really?" or "How interesting."

Once Jerome had looked at her with piercing eyes while his sister told a family story, something about her husband's buying her a horse. His eyes were troubled with such hurt, Adele looked away. And later she nearly succumbed when he reached his hand out to her as she passed behind him in the kitchen. But she did not. Usually direct, she realized she had nothing to confront him about. He hadn't promised her anything; she'd merely let him into her heart and assumed it was where he wanted to be. His wounded look was just a shade of his charm, a way of "filling time" with Adele while he waited for his Clarissa. Adele would work to forgive herself for having been so naive as to think that if a man calls you beautiful it means he's in love.

At night, Adele read alone in her room, but she could hear Jerome moving above her in his loft. Once she thought she heard soft snoring. When she turned her face into her pillow, she imagined she could smell his cologne there even though she'd washed the pillow slip herself. She had to expel him. "*I can do all things through Him who strengthens me,*" she wrote in her journal, this time for her own delivery from longing.

In the second week of her stay, Adele told Caroline she was going to go home

431

for a day to make sure all was well with Polly. Caroline worked herself into a frenzy about what she'd do if the baby started to come and Adele was back at the farm, caught in a snowstorm, eaten by wolves. "The possibilities of danger are endless," Caroline wailed.

"There aren't that many wolves around here. And the sky is clear and blue, no snow clouds in sight. And Doc Pederson makes his way here easily."

Caroline began a silent crying. Adele could see her shoulders shake. Maybe she wasn't being dramatic; maybe she really was frightened of what could go wrong if Adele wasn't there to tend the birth. *A midwife does what she must to comfort and give assurance to the mother.* Adele stroked Caroline's hair. "I'll stay." Her obedience to her calling proved providential, for on December 24th the sky darkened, folded like a deep blue blanket over the treetops and houses of the village, and buried the skyline, dropping snow so heavily and for so long that Adele could barely see the shed where her mule and Jerome's horse stayed. On Christmas morning, snow pushed up to the windows and stood two feet on top of the woodpile. And of course, Caroline went into labor.

❧

"Let's walk." Adele urged her to stand.

"I can't walk," Caroline whined. "I don't like to walk."

"It will be good for the baby. You ate cabbage you didn't like either, remember? But you did it for your child."

The labor had stalled well into Christmas night, and Adele had decided she needed to get Caroline to move, despite her bulk. But Adele was so short she didn't offer much assurance to an unsteady Caroline. She'd have to ask for help.

"Mr. Schmidt," Adele called. "Can you assist?"

He appeared as though he sat right outside the room, and maybe he did. If he'd been listening, he would have heard Adele ask if Caroline minded if she prayed for her and her baby before they began to walk; and he would have heard her asking God to bless this child and this mother and then Caroline telling her which song was her favorite. But all that was past and the labor hadn't started up.

"What—what can I do?" Jerome's arched eyebrow expressed his eagerness.

"Get on the other side of Caroline and help support her. We're going to walk."

"Is that wise? What if she falls?"

"There, you see? What if I fall?" Caroline's eyes grew large.

Adele glared at Jerome. To Caroline she said, "You have to trust me, Caroline. I wouldn't ask you to do a single thing that might hurt the baby. Walking helps. Mothers often walk, and if it's a spring birth where they can get outside, smell the apple blossoms, feel warm air on their arms, it speeds up the delivery. The baby wants to be here now. He broke the water. Your body is contracting as it should to help move him out."

"How do you know it's a him?"

"I don't. I'm just saying *him*, Caroline. Now he's a little tired, too, maybe, so let's help him or her arrive."

Caroline groaned, but Jerome said, "Sister, you can do this." The three walked then from the bedroom to the kitchen table to the horsehair couch with a log cabin quilt hung over the side and then walked back again. Once or twice Adele felt Jerome's hand brush hers as they steadied Caroline. A tingle of desire ran up her arm, and she wished it would linger. She urged Caroline to talk about her childhood, speak of pleasant memories. Jerome chimed in a time or two when Caroline gasped for breath. "Good memories are important," Adele told them. "You're telling your baby what family he—or she—is being born into. Tell me about your parents, Caroline. Tell me what you loved about growing up in Milwaukee. Tell me about meeting the baby's father, all of that."

Caroline stopped to take a deep breath. The lamplight flickered with the howl of the wind, and Adele looked out the window. Snow fell again, the kind of snow that drifted up against the barns and made feeding animals difficult. She hoped Polly was all right, that she had plenty of wood in the wood box. Would she remember to tie a rope to the porch railing if the snow got too deep or the wind blew so she could always find her way back to the house from the barn? Assuming she could make it to the barn. She hoped Polly wouldn't try to feed the animals if the snow drifted deep and wet. The cows would have to fend for themselves. She prayed that the girl would be safe.

Adele was keeping one ear to the sound of Caroline's breathing and the other to the chatter between the brother and sister when Caroline arched her back and cried out: "Oh, that was horribly, horribly painful. Just horribly! You didn't tell me it would hurt so much."

Adele didn't argue with her. "You can endure this. You're strong enough to do this hard work of birthing." Adele broke into "Jingle Bells" then "Ain't Got Time to Tarry," with Caroline saying she'd heard that in the slave quarters and hadn't realized how fitting it could be for a woman walking toward motherhood. She laughed. "I want to sing 'Can Can.'" Can you imagine me doing that dance?"

Adele looked at Jerome, and both grinned. "I do believe I am no longer of good use here," he said.

But Adele told him he was. "Keep her walking and singing and laughing. What better home for a child to come into?"

❦

Adele heard Doc Pederson arrive with Jerome late in the night, but before she could greet him, Caroline succumbed to Adele's encouragement that she squat, even though Caroline protested that only "Cherokee and slaves" gave birth that way. "I've put a hole in the wicker chair so you can sit and push against the arms, so it's not exactly the same." Within minutes of the position, Caroline cried out, and Adele was there to reach down and catch the baby. She held it while Caroline leaned back, sobbing, but this time with relief. "It's a girl." Adele watched for excess bleeding. She saw none.

Doc Pederson nodded. "Everything looks fine."

What the college doctor had written to Adele was true. This was nothing like Serena's birth, and there was no sign of blood refusing to clot.

The baby cried when Adele cleared her tiny mouth and rubbed her slippery limbs. Caroline shouted for Jerome to enter, and Adele looked up to see tears in his eyes as he bent for his niece. Adele asked if she could offer a prayer of thanksgiving and Caroline nodded, but it was Jerome who spoke the words. "Our gratitude is beyond words, dear Lord." He turned to Adele. "My gratitude to you is beyond words as well."

Adele placed the baby on Caroline's breast and stood. Jerome reached out to Adele and she allowed it, a warm squeeze of a hand between two people who had worked together to make another's life better and to bring a new life into the fold. Adele freed herself then bent to attend to Caroline and her baby while Doc Pederson and Jerome left for cigars, Adele imagined, though she'd never seen Jerome smoke. Jerome would make a good father one day. Adele hoped this Clarissa person knew what she was getting.

☙

Jerome's help and kindness at the delivery were a compress to Adele's hurt and disappointment over severed hopes. She could see that he was a good brother and he was a good banker. He was just a rotten fiancé. He should have told her he was engaged, and he never should have kissed her or called her beautiful.

Adele stayed two more days. The snow had stopped for a time at least, when she indicated she'd be leaving.

"I did find a girl to come in," Jerome told her. "She'll look after Caroline while I'm at work."

*Until your fiancée arrives.*

"I've asked her to come over today, as I know you're anxious to go. I want to go with you to make sure you're safely back at the farm."

"That's not necessary," Adele said. "I think we both know what wagon rolls ahead for each of us, and we are in separate carriages."

"I had hoped that—"

"Don't. I understand, I do. I have my responsibilities as well. I wish you well, Mr. Schmidt. I will see you at the bank in the spring. Until then, enjoy your new status as uncle. It's a very important role."

"But what's happened? We had such pleasant conversations together. I. . .wanted more of—"

"You must know that I am not the kind of woman who would interfere with a man's plans," she said. "I regret allowing myself to. . .care. So much. I have my duties. My Polly and my farm and my life delivering babies. For a short time I thought it might not be enough, but now I know it is. Thank you for allowing me to find that out. Good-bye."

"I have to go with you. I have to," he insisted. "The drifts—"

She left the porch and his words. She lifted herself onto the mule Jerome had saddled and brought to the front. Once outside of town, she would give the mule his lead and let his chest break the drifts as she trudged along behind, hanging on to his tail. She didn't want to need Jerome's presence. She could live well on her own.

The sky was as blue as her Willow plates, the sun so bright she pulled her hat to shade her eyes, to prevent burning. It took several hours to make the three-mile trek, but finally she saw the smoke rising from her chimney. When she stomped on the steps, Polly stepped out. "I knew you'd come home today," she said, her arms going around Adele.

"How did you guess?"

"I was just about to run out of sketching paper. I knew you wouldn't let me go very long without that or anything else I really needed."

"Like a good midwife."

"Like a good mother."

# Chapter 10

## Final Decisions

The winter of 1859–60 was harsh. Winds and cold kept Adele and Polly pushing hay from stacks while cows bawled and stood chest deep in snow. Narrow trails through the deep drifts marked the paths of deer and cows to the creek, and a smaller trail showed paths between house and barn that left both women exhausted from daily chores. By February, with only hours instead of days between light snowfall, Adele wondered out loud if they had hay enough to feed until green sprouts signaled spring.

"What will we do if we run out?" Polly wiped grease on her cheeks, so chapped and red. "No one else has hay to spare either."

"No, they don't. We'll trust the Lord; that's all we can do." Adele stitched on a quilt face by the fireplace while Polly tried her hand at knitting. Adele didn't get much rest of late, and when she did fall into a deep sleep, she dreamed of Jerome Schmidt, much to her annoyance, in one of the dreams seeing him at the bank again to negotiate her loan. She'd have to seek a higher loan if they ran out of hay or had to replace stock that died in this thieving cold. At least she had the land. She read in the gazette that a Homestead Act was working its way through Congress that would allow land in the West to be had for twenty-five cents an acre. They could buy quite a spread if she sold the farm here in Buffalo County. And she wouldn't have to worry about begging Mr. Schmidt for money or running into his new wife either. At least she guessed he had a new wife by now. She really didn't have any local news, since her last visit with Caroline occurred in late January when there'd been a slight break in the cold. Adele had donned snowshoes and made her way to town, sure to time it so she didn't see Jerome, and he wouldn't see her.

In late February, when the temperature dropped well below zero and stayed there, they broke ice from the creek for the cows to drink and one morning woke to discover four calves frozen to the cold earth, not able to survive their delivery during the cold night.

When March revealed a thaw, Polly's friend Sam trudged through the melting snow to give word of the preacher's plan to be at the schoolhouse later in the month. He brought other news as well, that the Bentzes were planning to head west along with several other families from the village. "Fed up with this cold," he told them, holding a cup of warm coffee in his hands. "Figure by the time they arrive in Oregon, Congress will have passed the Homestead Act, and they'll have cheap land to buy. A quarter an acre they say." Sam had thick dark hair and long slender fingers. *A surgeon's hands*, Adele thought.

"Is your family considering such a thing?" Adele asked. "Heading west?"

"Nope. We're staying put. My pa is hoping to buy up the farms of those taking leave of their senses, as he puts it. And I'm still heading east to Kentucky this fall, to start college. A man needs to be well educated in these times to take care of his family. That's what my Pa says." He smiled at Polly over his coffee cup. "I'm not sure how I'll do in school without Miss Polly here to help me with homework. I do fine with science and arithmetic, but my English, well, that's not so grand."

Polly blushed, and Adele wondered how her daughter would fare with this young man's company no longer a possibility on a summer afternoon.

"You'll have lots of girls willing to help you in Kentucky," Polly told him. "You really don't need my help. You never did." She looked directly at him, and Adele realized the girl was an encourager supporting a friend, not someone she wanted to give her heart to. "I hope you'll write now and again. I'd like to know how it is in college," she continued. "I want to go myself one day."

"Could you carry a message to a doctor there?" Adele refilled the boy's cup. "He was very helpful in giving us information about a difficult case I had as a midwife. That Polly and I had," she amended.

"I didn't even get to help with that one, Mamadele," Polly protested.

"You helped by suggesting we write to the college and by staying here to keep things going. I'd have been lost if you hadn't. That's part of being a midwife, too, that your family keeps up their part of the bargain and allows the midwife to do her work."

"We're a team."

"That we are."

Adele hoped they always would be.

☙

They celebrated Polly's birthday after the circuit rider's visit in March. She turned seventeen, and all the talk, aside from how lovely she looked, spun on Oregon. The Bentzes especially enthused about their plans to go west.

"You ought to come along." Idella held her toddler's hand as they sat on the ground at the schoolhouse, eating fried chicken. A spring wind caused Adele to pull her shawl tighter. "I know lots of women aren't excited about going, but I am. And Adele"—she leaned in to whisper—"I'm with child. You promised you'd be my midwife again."

"That was before I knew you wouldn't be a mile or two down the road."

Idella's voice got serious. "It is the only thing that worries me just a little. Gustaf says it'll take six months to cross, and that's after leaving from Council Bluffs in Iowa. We'll need a month to get there, and we have to be there no later than May 15th. I'm already three months along. That means I will deliver somewhere between here and Oregon."

"You can do it," Adele told her.

"Aren't you ready for a new adventure? What do you have holding you here?"

Adele wasn't sure anymore. Surviving the winter had drained her, made her wonder if she could farm for the rest of her life. She didn't relish asking Jerome for another loan.

"It would be exciting, wouldn't it, Mamadele?" Polly said later. "All the talk about

Oregon. And Idella does need help. A good midwife could be essential on a wagon train. You'd be well appreciated there."

"We can talk about it," Adele told her, wondering at the little stirring of interest that fidgeted in her breast. At least she'd never have to run into Jerome on a wagon train west, and she wouldn't ever have to worry about Polly's father catching up with them either.

*&*

Jerome Schmidt's winter had been full of meeting Caroline's needs. He'd secured a young girl to come in to help. He'd hired three, in fact, as Caroline's demands sent the girls scurrying, one after the other. The latest—a Norwegian girl—said she could be as stubborn as an ox when he described Caroline's. . .ways. The girl stood up to her, and Caroline backed down. He realized what a gem Adele had been in being able to deal so well with his sister. Doc Pederson seemed to enjoy his sister's company, and Jerome didn't want to ask why. He appreciated the respite whenever the doctor took Caroline's attention. Meanwhile, little Emily grew fat and happy, and his time holding her was the joy of his life. The only joy in his life. He missed Adele and couldn't understand why she'd frozen him out so suddenly, just when he'd begun to believe she might have feelings for him. He hoped she'd be in soon for her interview about the loan. It was already mid-April, and several other farmers had come in so they could purchase seed and get planting as soon as the fields dried up. Adele was conscientious and should be coming in any day now. At least he might have a business relationship with her, and maybe in time. . .

He sighed then mumbled about the newspaper.

"What were you saying, Jerome?" Caroline rocked little Emily, smiling at the baby. Maybe Caroline would be an adequate mother after all, finding someone besides herself to truly care about.

"This rag," he said, folding the paper and tearing it into strips he'd use to start the fire. "It's a waste of good paper. Never says anything of import that I haven't already heard from the *Milwaukee Gazette*. I should start my own."

"There's little to be done about the news, anyway, so what does it matter if it's a month late?"

"Local news would be nice to get."

"You get that at the bank, don't you? Or Olson's store? Did you hear that a wagon train is starting out from the village with several from here joining up?"

"Yes, I heard the rumors, but there's nothing in the paper about it. And how did you learn of it?"

"Why, Adele came by for a final checkup with me and little Emily yesterday. She approves of your new hire, by the way, and she asked when Clarissa was going to arrive. I told her I didn't know. Any day, I suppose, though you certainly haven't said anything about the wedding date, dear brother. Not that I've asked. I'm not a meddler, you know."

"Clarissa?" he said. "Why on earth would Miss Adele mention Clarissa?"

"She knows she's your fiancée. I told her myself."

"What? When did you tell her?"

"Why, about the time she stayed here to help with Emily's birth. Was it a secret?"

"No secret, Caroline. But it also isn't true. I'm not marrying Clarissa. She isn't joining me here in Mondovi. She's already married someone else by now."

"How was I to know? You never said, and you always look at your timepiece with such longing. You said Clarissa gave it to you, and you told me you were engaged. I just assumed—"

"Wrongly. Quite wrongly." He stood, looked at his timepiece, sat down, then stood again. He could be at Adele's farm in less than an hour.

❧

"Should we take the cast-iron spider with us?" Polly shouted to Adele, who bent over a barrel in the bedroom, folding quilts into the bottom.

"Just one skillet, that's all we'll need. And the Dutch oven. Gustaf says enough is as good as a feast, so just take enough." Adele walked back out into the main room where Polly sat like a frog on a lily pad surrounded by sifters, dishes, ladles, and pans. "We'll bury the Willow dishes in the cornmeal barrel." She lifted a plate. The dishes would remind her of John, who had bought them as a wedding gift, although the color would always make her think of Jerome's deep blue eyes. "Yes, just one skillet, but we'll try for the entire set of dishes."

Adele's heart fluttered at the speed with which she'd made this decision. Polly had danced with joy when they'd discussed going west well into the night. She'd already sold the farm to Sam's dad, cows included. Idella was almost as happy as Polly about their decision. "I'll have two midwives, just like last time."

"And I can look after Luke in the meantime," Polly said.

With the purchase money, Adele bought a wagon and hired a mule skinner to drive it, a cousin of Gustaf's. The two wagons would join three others rumbling out from Mondovi by week's end, the high water from the snowmelt having peaked. She felt excited, full of possibilities. She was thirty-seven years old but not too old to start a new adventure. She could farm in Oregon—or who knew what she might do there? The choices were endless.

"Will we be ready by Friday, Mamadele?"

"We'd better be."

Adele found herself nostalgic, running her hands across furniture they'd have to leave, memories flooding over her like rivers over rocks. "Are you all right, Mamadele?"

Adele wiped her eyes with her apron. "Just saying good-bye," she said. "It's the right thing to do, I know it is. But change is still hard, isn't it?"

"I guess," Polly said, and Adele envied the girl's youth and flexibility. She'd have to mine some of that from her own past. "Rider coming." Polly squinted, looking down the lane. "He sits a horse like Mr. Schmidt, all tall and lean in the saddle."

Adele stopped her reminiscing, looked out the window.

"What could he want? I paid the loan."

The man barely pulled up his horse before he dismounted. "Adele. Miss Adele." He looked at Polly, who had moved in behind Adele on the porch.

"Is Caroline all right?"

"Yes, yes. How good of you to think of her. She's fine. Wonderful. In fact, she told me something that I have to confirm with you—" He looked around at the barrels

439

and wooden boxes on the porch. "Confirm with you before you go? Are you going somewhere?"

"To Oregon. It's going to be wonderful. Mamadele and I are teaming up with the Bentzes. She's having a baby, and Mamadele and I are her midwives. She gets two."

"Oregon? But—"

"There was really nothing holding us here. And Polly was ready for a new adventure. So was I," Adele said. "I found I longed for. . .something more."

"Listen, please, before you go. Caroline told me—" He was gasping for breath. He swallowed and started again.

"Can I get you water?"

"Yes, please, Polly. Adele, Miss Adele, please stay."

"I'll get it." Polly disappeared to the pump with a ladle in hand.

"Caroline told me this morning that she told you about Clarissa."

"Such news should have come from you." Adele's shoulders were straight as a wagon tongue.

"Yes, but it wasn't any news at all. I was engaged to Clarissa—"

"Which you should have told me."

"But the engagement was broken long before I even came to Mondovi. Clarissa broke it off, and when I met you, I knew it was the best thing that ever happened to me. I love you, Adele."

It was what she'd longed to hear, but now?

"If there is even the slightest hope that you might find it possible to love me, too, I'll go to the ends of the earth to wait until you tell me yes."

"Yes to what?"

"To my proposal of marriage. Will you marry me, Adele Marley?"

"What have I missed?" Polly asked, returning.

"Mr. Schmidt, Jerome, has just asked me to marry him." She was laughing, the joy bubbling up inside of her like steam in a pot.

"Will you?"

"I—I don't know." She looked into his blue eyes the color of her Willow blue and said, "Yes. I will. Yes."

Jerome whooped and lifted her, spinning her around, and he kissed her right there in front of Polly.

"What. . .what does this mean for Oregon?" Polly said.

Adele stopped. "I don't know."

"The Bentzes are counting on us, Mamadele. And you've sold the farm."

"Yes, they are counting on us." She looked at Jerome.

"I'm not known for making quick decisions," he said. "But the wagon can probably use another man to help, and if my intended wife is heading west, then I'm going to be right there with her."

"What about Caroline?"

He paused, thoughtful then. "She has resources, and Doc Pederson to manage them, it seems."

"But what will you do there?"

"Maybe I'll farm." Adele frowned. "Or I'll. . .start a newspaper or work for one. Whatever it takes. We'll find a way."

"And you'll not object to my being 'the little midwife'?"

"Object? How can a man object to a woman's clear calling?"

Adele laughed, and then she cried in joy.

"I guess we'll have a wedding first," Polly said.

"I guess we will," Adele and Jerome said together, and he swung Adele one more time around the porch.

It was during that second swing that Jerome lost his balance and, still holding Adele, fell against the wobbly porch post, which gave way. The two of them landed just a short distance in the rocky dirt, but enough distance for Jerome to groan in pain when they hit the dust. The horse sidestepped out of their way. When Adele lifted herself from him and he rolled, she saw the rock that had broken their fall. And she saw his leg askew.

"I—I think it's broken."

"I think you're right."

# Chapter 11

## New Beginnings

A fter the doctor set the bone and Jerome lay resting, with Caroline hovering, Adele led Polly to the Schmidt porch. Adele sat with her arm around the girl, struggling with the greatest difficulty in her life.

"You can't leave him, Mamadele."

"I know. But I can't disappoint Idella either."

Polly took a deep breath. "You don't have to. Idella needs one of us, and that can be me."

"Oh Polly. I'm not sure—"

"You can send your journal with me so I'll have your wisdom and God's help. You'll still be a midwife for Idella, in spirit and through me. You know I'm responsible. And I really, really want to go west."

Adele swallowed. "We could all wait until next year and go maybe, when Jerome's leg is healed."

"A midwife keeps her commitments. Isn't that what you said?"

"Yes, it is." Adele ached as though she were ripped apart.

"I might never see you again." Polly's eyes pooled with tears. "But either both of us stay here to help him heal or we sacrifice being together for another family." Polly tugged at her braid, adding, "One day I'll marry, and we'd part then, too."

Adele's voice caught at the truth of that. "You'd sacrifice having your Mamadele by your side?"

"Not just my Mamadele," Polly said. "But my mama. That's what you are." Adele hugged the girl, unable to speak. "I can do this, Mama, because you've taught me. I'll be strong, and you and Mr. Schmidt can have a new life here and come after, maybe."

"You did manage for two weeks on your own. A girl who can do that can travel west without her mother and help bring a new baby safely into this world."

Polly wiped away Adele's tears, pushing back her braid.

"You just have one last duty to perform before you leave."

"What's that?"

"To be my witness at our wedding."

☙

The members of the wagon train stood ready to drive away from the schoolhouse as soon as the 6:00 a.m. vows were spoken and they'd feasted at the wedding breakfast.

Jerome sat with his braced leg straight out from the chair, resting on a cassock. Adele stood next to him in her best gingham dress. There'd been no time to make a new dress or even alter the one Caroline offered. This church dress would do. Polly waited behind Adele, and Caroline stood to the side as a witness for her brother, Doc Pederson holding Emily. The women held a few tulips as the circuit rider led them in prayer.

They could have waited to marry until Jerome could stand, but Adele wanted Polly to be a part of this important day and Polly was heading west. The girl wore the pearl hair clip that had been her mother's. Adele had given it to her with the story that accompanied it that morning as they'd dressed. "Your mother gave me this, and I know she would want you to have it."

"It's beautiful." Polly rubbed her fingers on the pearls. "Smooth as a baby's bottom."

Adele smiled. "Wear it knowing you have always been loved and always will be."

Jerome had surprised them both just before several men helped carry him out by insisting that Polly take his timepiece with her. "You might need it for that counting thing you midwives do."

Adele couldn't remember when she'd been so happy and so sad at the same time. It was a little like being a midwife—the joy of a birth and the sadness of leaving this new family to their own ways and routines. This second chance at love was the greatest gift Adele had ever been given—save her Polly—and yet waving good-bye to Polly because of it, would be the hardest thing she'd ever do.

But it is what she did after the ceremony, handing Polly the old journal and pulling her close. "You remember to say your prayers." Adele patted the girl's back. "Nothing is impossible with God."

"I know, Mamade—" Polly stopped. "I know, Mama. I'll do my best to make you proud."

"You already have."

"I have something for you, too." Polly rushed to the back of the Bentz wagon and opened one of the boxes. "It's a self-portrait." She handed Adele the sketch paper. "I worked on it looking in a mirror while you were delivering Mr. Schmidt's niece. I think it looks like me."

"It does, oh, it does indeed." She would frame it and hang it. . .somewhere in a house that she and Jerome would share.

Gustaf Bentz stood beside her then. "Is time to go."

"I know. I know. You take good care of my girl." Adele clung to Polly, one hand on the sketch.

"And she takes good care of my Idella."

Polly pulled her hand loose and, fighting back tears, walked to the front of the wagon. Sunlight glinted off the pearl clip as the party moved out, the women and children walking beside. Polly turned and blew a kiss, and then Adele was standing back beside Jerome.

"You write!" Adele shouted. Polly nodded then walked down the hill out of sight.

Jerome reached for her hand. "Mrs. Schmidt, you are beautiful, even when you're crying."

She squeezed his hand back, staring into the space Polly left. "Mothers do cry, you know. In sadness and in joy."

# Epilogue

## One year later

My dearest Polly,

I hope this letter finds you happy and well. I await details of your new life. We are fine here. The ink for Jerome's new paper arrived late for the latest edition, but the story did get out about the President's refusal to sign the 1860 Homestead Act. Perhaps there'll be another so the Bentzes will have their Oregon farm after all one day.

My time goes well, though it keeps us from joining you. In two more months you will have a brother or sister. I have found a midwife comfortable with assisting at the first birth of an older mother. I wish it was you being my midwife, but I know you will be here in spirit. We midwives belong to that circle that tends and befriends, "with woman," wherever women gather and are together, no matter the separation of time or distance. We defy the pharaohs of fear and uncertainty and replace them with hope and joy. Blessings on your days, dear Polly. Keep writing in that journal. I seal this with tears of joy.

Your beloved mother

Award-winning author **Jane Kirkpatrick** is well known for her authentically portrayed historical fiction. She is also an acclaimed speaker and teacher with a lively presentation style. She and her husband live in Oregon and, until recently, lived and worked on a remote homestead for over twenty-five years.

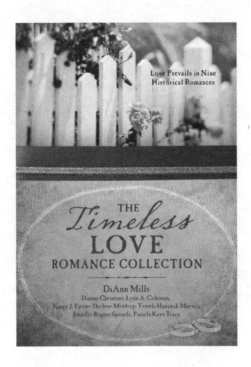